# THE RETURN OF

## THE HISTORY OF THE LORD OF THE RINGS, PART ONE

# THE HISTORY OF MIDDLE-EARTH

J.R.R. TOLKIEN

# THE RETURN OF
# THE SHADOW

*The History of*
*The Lord of the Rings*
*Part One*

Christopher Tolkien

HOUGHTON MIFFLIN COMPANY
Boston   New York

First Houghton Mifflin paperback edition 2000

For information about permission to reproduce selections from this book,
write to trade.permissions@hmhco.com or to Permissions, Houghton Mifflin Harcourt
Publishing Company, 3 Park Avenue, 19th Floor, New York, New York 10016.

Visit our Web site: www.hmhco.com

*Library of Congress Cataloging-in-Publication Data*
Tolkien, J.R.R. (John Ronald Reuel), 1892–1973. The
return of the shadow: the history of The lord of the
rings / J.R.R. Tolkien ; [edited by] Christopher
Tolkien. p. cm. — (The History of Middle-earth ; 6)
Includes index.
ISBN 0-395-49863-5
ISBN 0-618-08357-X (pbk.)
1. Tolkien, J.R.R. (John Ronald Reuel), 1892–1973. Lord of the
rings — Criticism, Textual. 2. Fantastic fiction, English — History
and criticism. 3. Middle Earth (Imaginary place) I. Tolkien,
Christopher. II. Title. III. Series: Tolkien, J.R.R. (John
Ronald Reul), 1892–1973. History of Middle Earth ; 6.
PR6039.032L6374 1988 88-22986
823.912—dc19 CIP

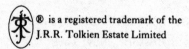
Printed in the United States of America

28 2021
4500841061

*To*
*RAYNER  UNWIN*

I met a lot of things on the way that astonished me. Tom Bombadil I knew already; but I had never been to Bree. Strider sitting in the corner at the inn was a shock, and I had no more idea who he was than had Frodo. The Mines of Moria had been a mere name; and of Lothlórien no word had reached my mortal ears till I came there. Far away I knew there were the Horse-lords on the confines of an ancient Kingdom of Men, but Fangorn Forest was an unforeseen adventure. I had never heard of the House of Eorl nor of the Stewards of Gondor. Most disquieting of all, Saruman had never been revealed to me, and I was as mystified as Frodo at Gandalf's failure to appear on September 22.

J. R. R. Tolkien, in a letter to
W. H. Auden, 7 June 1955

# CONTENTS

*page*

## THE STORY CONTINUED

## ILLUSTRATIONS

# FOREWORD

As is well known, the manuscripts and typescripts of *The Lord of the Rings* were sold by J. R. R. Tolkien to Marquette University, Milwaukee, a few years after its publication, together with those of *The Hobbit* and *Farmer Giles of Ham*, and also *Mr. Bliss*. A long time elapsed between the shipment of these latter papers, which reached Marquette in July 1957, and that of *The Lord of the Rings*, which did not arrive until the following year. The reason for this was that my father had undertaken to sort, annotate, and date the multifarious manuscripts of *The Lord of the Rings*, but found it impossible at that time to do the work required. It is clear that he never did so, and in the end let the papers go just as they were; it was noted when they reached Marquette that they were 'in no order'. Had he done so, he must have seen at that time that, very large though the manuscript collection was, it was nonetheless incomplete.

Seven years later, in 1965, when he was working on the revision of *The Lord of the Rings*, he wrote to the Director of Libraries at Marquette, asking if a certain scheme of dates and events in the narrative was to be found there, since he had 'never made out any full schedule or note of the papers transferred to you.' In this letter he explained that the transfer had taken place at a time when his papers were dispersed between his house in Headington (Oxford) and his rooms in Merton College; and he also said that he now found himself still in possession of 'written matter' that 'should belong to you': when he had finished the revision of *The Lord of the Rings* he would look into the question. But he did not do so.

These papers passed to me on his death eight years later; but though Humphrey Carpenter made reference to them in his *Biography* (1977) and cited from them some early notes, I neglected them for many years, being absorbed in the long work of tracing the evolution of the narratives of the Elder Days, the legends of Beleriand and Valinor. The publication of Volume III of 'The History of Middle-earth' was already approaching before I had any idea that the 'History' might extend to an account of the writing of *The Lord of the Rings*. During the last three years, however, I have been engaged at intervals in the decipherment and analysis of *The Lord of the Rings* manuscripts in my possession (a task still far from completed). It has emerged from this that the papers left behind in 1958 consist largely of the earliest phases of composition, although in some cases (and most notably in the first chapter, which was rewritten many times over) successive versions found among these papers bring the narrative to an advanced state. In general, however, it was only the initial notes and earliest drafts, with outlines for the further course of the story, that remained in England when the great bulk of the papers went to Marquette.

I do not of course know how it came about that these particular manuscripts came to be left out of the consignment to Marquette; but I think that an explanation in general terms can be found readily enough. Immensely prolific as my father was ('I found not being able to use a pen or pencil as defeating as the loss of her beak would be to a hen,' he wrote to Stanley Unwin in 1963, when suffering from an ailment in his right arm), constantly revising, re-using, beginning again, but never throwing any of his writing away, his papers became inextricably complex, disorganised, and dispersed. It does not seem likely that at the time of the transfer to Marquette he would have been greatly concerned with or have had any precise recollection of the early drafts, some of them supplanted and overtaken as much as twenty years before; and no doubt they had long since been set aside, forgotten, and buried.

However this may be, it is self-evidently desirable that the separated manuscripts should be joined together again, and the whole corpus preserved in one place. This must have been my father's intention at the time of the original sale; and accordingly the manuscripts at present in my keeping will be handed over to Marquette University.

The greater part of the material cited or described in this book is found in the papers that remained behind; but the third section of the book (called 'The Third Phase') constituted a difficult problem, because in this case the manuscripts were divided. Most of the chapters in this 'phase' of composition went to Marquette in 1958, but substantial parts of several of them did not. These parts had become separated because my father had rejected them, while using the remainder as constituent elements in new versions. The interpretation of this part of the history would have been altogether impossible without very full co-operation from Marquette, and this I have abundantly received. Above all, Mr Taum Santoski has engaged with great skill and care in a complex operation in which we have exchanged over many months annotated copies of the texts; and it has been possible in this way to determine the textual history, and to reconstruct the original manuscripts which my father himself dismembered nearly half a century ago. I record with pleasure and deep appreciation the generous assistance that I have received from him, and also from Mr Charles B. Elston, the Archivist of the Memorial Library at Marquette, from Mr John D. Rateliff, and from Miss Tracy Muench.

This attempt to give an account of the first stages in the writing of *The Lord of the Rings* has been beset by other difficulties than the fact of the manuscripts being widely sundered; difficulties primarily in the interpretation of the sequence of writing, but also in the presentation of the results in a printed book.

Briefly, the writing proceeded in a series of 'waves' or (as I have called them in this book) 'phases'. The first chapter was itself reconstituted three times before the hobbits ever left Hobbiton, but the story then went all the way to Rivendell before the impulse failed. My father then started again from the beginning (the 'second phase'), and then again (the 'third phase'); and as new narrative elements and new names and relations among the characters appeared they were written into previous drafts, at different times. Parts of a text were taken out and used elsewhere. Alternative versions were incorporated into the same manuscript, so that the story could be read in more than one way according to the directions given. To determine the sequence of these exceedingly complex movements with demonstrable correctness at all points is scarcely possible. One or two dates that my father wrote in are insufficient to give more than very limited assistance, and references to the progress of the work in his letters are unclear and hard to interpret. Differences of script can be very misleading. Thus the determination of the history of composition has to be based very largely on clues afforded by the evolution of names and motives in the narrative itself; but in this there is every possibility of going astray through mistaking the relative dates of additions and alterations. Exemplification of these problems will be found throughout the book. I do not suppose for one moment that I have succeeded in determining the history correctly at every point: indeed there remain several cases where the evidence appears to be contradictory and I can offer no solution. The nature of the manuscripts is such that they will probably always admit of differing interpretations. But the sequence of composition that I propose, after much experimentation with alternative theories, seems to me to fit the evidence very much the best.

The earliest plot-outlines and narrative drafts are often barely legible, and become more difficult as the work proceeded. Using any scrap of the wretched paper of the war years that came to hand – sometimes writing not merely on the backs of examination scripts but across the scripts themselves – my father would dash down elliptically his thoughts for the story to come, and his first formulations of narrative, at tearing speed. In the handwriting that he used for rapid drafts and sketches, not intended to endure long before he turned to them again and gave them a more workable form, letters are so loosely formed that a word which cannot be deduced or guessed at from the context or from later versions can prove perfectly opaque after long examination; and if, as he often did, he used a soft pencil much has now become blurred and faint. This must be borne in mind throughout: the earliest drafts were put urgently to paper just as the first words came to mind and before the thought dissolved, whereas the printed text (apart from a sprinkling of dots and queries in the face of illegibility) inevitably conveys an air of calm and ordered composition, the phrasing weighed and intended.

Turning to the way in which the material is presented in this book, the most intractable problem lies in the development of the story through successive drafts, always changing but always closely dependent on what preceded. In the rather extreme case of the opening chapter 'A Long-expected Party', there are in this book six main texts to be considered and a number of abandoned openings. A complete presentation of all the material for this one chapter would almost constitute a book in itself, not to speak of a mass of repetition or near-repetition. On the other hand, a succession of texts reduced to extracts and short citations (where the versions differ significantly from their predecessors) is not easy to follow, and if the development is traced at all closely this method also takes up much space. There is no really satisfactory solution to this. The editor must take responsibility for selecting and emphasizing those elements that he considers most interesting and most significant. In general I give the earliest narrative complete, or nearly complete, in each chapter, as the basis to which subsequent development can be referred. Different treatment of the manuscripts calls for different arrangement of the editorial element: where texts are given more or less in full much use is

made of numbered notes (which may constitute an important part
of the presentation of a complex text), but where they are not the
chapter proceeds rather as a discussion with citations.

My father bestowed immense pains on the creation of *The Lord
of the Rings*, and my intention has been that this record of his first
years of work on it should reflect those pains. The first part of the
story, before the Ring left Rivendell, took by far the most labour
to achieve (hence the length of this book in relation to the whole
story); and the doubts, indecisions, unpickings, restructurings,
and false starts have been described. The result is necessarily
extremely intricate; but whereas it would be possible to recount
the history in a greatly reduced and abbreviated form, I am
convinced that to omit difficult detail or to oversimplify problems
and explanations would rob the study of its essential interest.

My object has been to give an account of the *writing* of *The Lord
of the Rings*, to exhibit the subtle process of change that could
transform the significance of events and the identity of persons
while preserving those scenes and the words that were spoken
from the earliest drafts. I therefore (for example) pursue in detail
the history of the two hobbits who ultimately issued in Peregrin
Took and Fredegar Bolger, but only after the most extraordinary
permutations and coalescences of name, character, and rôle; on
the other hand I refrain from all discussion that is not directly
relevant to the evolution of the narrative.

In the nature of the book, I assume conversance with *The
Fellowship of the Ring*, and comparison is made throughout of
course with the published work. Page-references to *The Fellowship of the Ring* (abbreviated FR) are given to the three-volume
hardback edition of *The Lord of the Rings* (LR) published by
George Allen and Unwin (now Unwin Hyman) and Houghton
Mifflin Company, this being the edition common to both England
and America, but I think that it will be found in fact that almost
all such references can be readily traced in any edition, since the
precise point referred to in the final form of the story is nearly
always evident from the context.

In the 'first phase' of writing, which took the story to Rivendell,
most of the chapters were title-less, and subsequently there was
much shifting in the division of the story into chapters, with
variation in titles and numbers. I have thought it best therefore to
avoid confusion by giving many of my chapters simple descriptive
titles, such as 'From Hobbiton to the Woody End', indicating the
content rather than relating them to the chapter-titles in *The*

*Fellowship of the Ring.* As a title for the book it seemed suitable to take one of my father's own suggested but abandoned titles for the first volume of *The Lord of the Rings*. In a letter to Rayner Unwin of 8 August 1953 (*The Letters of J. R. R. Tolkien*, no. 139) he proposed *The Return of the Shadow*.

No account is given in this book of the history of the writing of *The Hobbit* up to its original publication in 1937, although, from the nature of its relationship to *The Lord of the Rings*, the published work is constantly referred to. That relationship is curious and complex. My father several times expressed his view of it, but most fully and (as I think) most accurately in the course of a long letter to Christopher Bretherton written in July 1964 (*Letters* no. 257).

I returned to Oxford in Jan. 1926, and by the time *The Hobbit* appeared (1937) this 'matter of the Elder Days' was in coherent form. *The Hobbit* was not intended to have anything to do with it. I had the habit while my children were still young of inventing and telling orally, sometimes of writing down, 'children's stories' for their private amusement . . . *The Hobbit* was intended to be one of them. It had no necessary connexion with the 'mythology', but naturally became attracted towards this dominant construction in my mind, causing the tale to become larger and more heroic as it proceeded. Even so it could really stand quite apart, except for the references (unnecessary, though they give an impression of historical depth) to the Fall of Gondolin, the branches of the Elfkin, and the quarrel of King Thingol, Lúthien's father, with the Dwarves. . . .

The magic ring was the one obvious thing in *The Hobbit* that could be connected with my mythology. To be the burden of a large story it had to be of supreme importance. I then linked it with the (originally) quite casual reference to the Necromancer, whose function was hardly more than to provide a reason for Gandalf going away and leaving Bilbo and the Dwarves to fend for themselves, which was necessary for the tale. From *The Hobbit* are also derived the matter of the Dwarves, Durin their prime ancestor, and Moria; and Elrond. The passage in Ch. iii relating him to the Half-elven of the mythology was a fortunate accident, due to the difficulty of constantly inventing good names for new characters. I gave him the name Elrond casually, but as this came from the mythology (Elros and Elrond the two sons of Eärendel) I made him half-elven. Only in *The Lord* was he identified with the son of Eärendel, and so the great-grandson of Lúthien and Beren, a great power and a Ringholder.

How my father saw *The Hobbit* – specifically in relation to 'The Silmarillion' – at the time of its publication is shown clearly in the letter that he wrote to G. E. Selby on 14 December 1937:

I don't much approve of *The Hobbit* myself, preferring my own mythology (which is just touched on) with its consistent no-menclature – Elrond, Gondolin, and Esgaroth have escaped out of it – and organized history, to this rabble of Eddaic-named dwarves out of Völuspá, newfangled hobbits and gollums (invented in an idle hour) and Anglo-Saxon runes.

The importance of *The Hobbit* in *the history of the evolution* of Middle-earth lies then, at this time, in the fact that it was published, and that a sequel to it was demanded. As a result, from the nature of *The Lord of the Rings* as it evolved, *The Hobbit* was *drawn into* Middle-earth – and transformed it; but as it stood in 1937 it was not a part of it. Its significance for Middle-earth lies in what it would do, not in what it was.

Later, *The Lord of the Rings* in turn reacted upon *The Hobbit* itself, in published and in (far more extensive) unpublished revisions of the text; but all that lies of course far in the future at the point which this History has reached.

In the manuscripts of *The Lord of the Rings* there is extreme inconsistency in such matters as the use of capital letters and hyphens, and the separation of elements in compound names. In my representation of the texts I have not imposed any standard-ization in this respect, though using consistent forms in my own discussions.

# THE FIRST PHASE

# I

# A LONG-EXPECTED PARTY

*The First Version*

The original written starting-point of *The Lord of the Rings* – its 'first germ', as my father scribbled on the text long after – has been preserved: a manuscript of five pages entitled *A long-expected party*. I think that it must have been to this (rather than to a second, unfinished, draft that soon followed it) that my father referred when on 19 December 1937 he wrote to Charles Furth at Allen and Unwin: 'I have written the first chapter of a new story about Hobbits – "A long expected party".' Only three days before he had written to Stanley Unwin:

> I think it is plain that . . . a sequel or successor to The Hobbit is called for. I promise to give this thought and attention. But I am sure you will sympathize when I say that the construction of elaborate and consistent mythology (and two languages) rather occupies the mind, and the Silmarils are in my heart. So that goodness knows what will happen. Mr Baggins began as a comic tale among conventional Grimm's fairy-tale dwarves, and got drawn into the edge of it – so that even Sauron the terrible peeped over the edge. And what more can hobbits do? They can be comic, but their comedy is suburban unless it is set against things more elemental.

From this it seems plain that on the 16th of December he had not only not begun writing, but in all probability had not even given thought to the substance of 'a new story about Hobbits'. Not long before he had parted with the manuscript of the third version of *The Silmarillion* to Allen and Unwin; it was unfinished, and he was still deeply immersed in it. In a postscript to this letter to Stanley Unwin he acknowledged, in fact, the return of *The Silmarillion* (and other things) later on that day. Nonetheless, he must have begun on the new story there and then.

When he first put pen to paper he wrote in large letters 'When M', but he stopped before completing the final stroke of the M and wrote instead 'When Bilbo . . .' The text begins in a handsome script, but the writing becomes progessively faster and deteriorates at the end into a rapid scrawl not at all points legible. There are a good many alterations to the manuscript. The text that follows represents the original form as I judge it to have been, granting that what is 'original' and what is not cannot be perfectly distinguished. Some changes can be seen to have been made at the moment of writing, and these are taken up into the text; but others

(first form)

A long-expected party —

When X

When Bilbo, son of Bungo of the family of Baggins, *prepared to* celebrated his seventieth *71st* birthday there was for a day or two some talk in the neighbourhood. He had once had a little fleeting fame among the people of Hobbiton and Bywater — he had disappeared after breakfast one April 30th and not reappeared until lunchtime on June 22nd in the following year. A very odd proceeding for which he had never given any good reason, and of which he wrote a nonsensical account. After that he returned to normal ways; and the shaken confidence of the district was gradually restored, especially as Bilbo seemed by some unexplained method to have become more than comfortably off — if not positively wealthy. Indeed it was the magnificence of the party rather than the fleeting fame that at first caused the talk — after all that other odd business had happened some twenty years before and was becoming decently forgotten. The magnificence of the prepar—

The original opening page of *The Lord of the Rings*

are characteristic anticipations of the following version, and these are
ignored. In any case it is highly probable that my father wrote the
versions of this opening chapter in quick succession. Notes to this
version follow immediately on the end of the text (p. 17).

## A long-expected party[1]

When Bilbo, son of Bungo of the family of Baggins, [had
celebrated >] prepared to celebrate his seventieth birthday there
was for a day or two some talk in the neighbourhood. He had once
had a little fleeting fame among the people of Hobbiton and
Bywater – he had disappeared after breakfast one April 30th and
not reappeared until lunchtime on June 22nd in the following
year. A very odd proceeding for which he had never given any
good reason, and of which he wrote a nonsensical account. After
that he returned to normal ways; and the shaken confidence of the
district was gradually restored, especially as Bilbo seemed by
some unexplained method to have become more than comfortably
off, if not positively wealthy. Indeed it was the magnificence of the
party rather than the fleeting fame that at first caused the talk –
after all that other odd business had happened some twenty years
before and was becoming decently forgotten. The magnificence of
the preparations for the party, I should say. The field to the south
of his front door was being covered with pavilions. Invitations
were being sent out to all the Bagginses and all the Tooks (his
relatives on his mother's side), and to the Grubbs (only remotely
connected); and to the Burroweses, the Boffinses, the Chubbses
and the Proudfeet: none of whom were connected at all within the
memory of the local historians – some of them lived on the other
side of the shire; but they were all, of course, hobbits. Even the
Sackville-Bagginses, his cousins on his father's side, were not
forgotten. There had been a feud between them and Mr Bilbo
Baggins, as some of you may remember. But so splendid was the
invitation-card, all written in gold, that they were induced to
accept; besides, their cousin had been specializing in good food
for a long time, and his tables had a high reputation even in that
time and country when food was still what it ought to be and
abundant enough for all folk to practise on.

Everyone expected a pleasant feast; though they rather dreaded
the after-dinner speech of their host. He was liable to drag in bits
of what he called poetry, and even to allude, after a glass or two, to
the absurd adventures he said he had had long ago during his

ridiculous vanishment. They had a *very* pleasant feast: indeed an engrossing entertainment. The purchase of provisions fell almost to zero throughout the whole shire during the ensuing week; but as Mr Baggins' catering had emptied all the stores, cellars and warehouses for miles around, that did not matter. Then came the speech. Most of the assembled hobbits were now in a tolerant mood, and their former fears were forgotten. They were prepared to listen to anything, and to cheer at every full stop. But they were not prepared to be startled. But they were – completely and unprecedentedly startled; some even had indigestion.

'My dear people,' began Mr Baggins. 'Hear, hear!' they replied in chorus. 'My dear Bagginses,' he went on, standing now on his chair, so that the light of the lanterns that illuminated the enormous pavilion flashed upon the gold buttons of his embroidered waistcoat for all to see. 'And my dear Tooks, and Grubbs, and Chubbs, and Burroweses, and Boffinses, and Proudfoots.'² 'Proudfeet' shouted an elderly hobbit from the back. His name of course was Proudfoot, and merited; his feet were large, exceptionally furry, and both were on the table. 'Also my dear Sackville-Bagginses that I welcome back at last to Bag-end,' Bilbo continued. 'Today is my seventieth birthday.' 'Hurray hurray and many happy returns!' they shouted. That was the sort of stuff they liked: short, obvious, uncontroversial.

'I hope you are all enjoying yourselves as much as I am.' Deafening cheers, cries of yes (and no), and noises of trumpets and whistles. There were a great many junior hobbits present, as hobbits were indulgent to their children, especially if there was a chance of an extra meal. Hundreds of musical crackers had been pulled. Most of them were labelled 'Made in Dale'. What that meant only Bilbo and a few of his Took-nephews knew; but they were very marvellous crackers. 'I have called you all together,' Bilbo went on when the last cheer died away, and something in his voice made a few of the Tooks prick up their ears. 'First of all to tell you that I am immensely fond of you, and that seventy years is too short a time to live among such excellent and charming hobbits' – 'hear hear!' 'I don't know half of you half as well as I should like, and less than half of you half as well as you deserve.' No cheers, a few claps – most of them were trying to work it out. 'Secondly to celebrate my birthday and the twentieth year of my return' – an uncomfortable rustle. 'Lastly to make an *Announcement*.' He said this very loud and everybody sat up who could. 'Goodbye! I am going away after dinner. Also I am going to get married.'

He sat down. The silence was flabbergastation. It was broken only by Mr Proudfoot, who kicked over the table; Mrs Proudfoot choked in the middle of a drink.

That's that. It merely serves to explain that Bilbo Baggins got married and had many children, because I am going to tell you a story about one of his descendants, and if you had only read his memoirs up to the date of Balin's visit – ten years at least before this birthday party – you might have been puzzled.[3]

As a matter of fact Bilbo Baggins disappeared silently and unnoticed – the ring was in his hand even while he made his speech – in the middle of the confused outburst of talk that followed the flabbergasted silence. He was never seen in Hobbiton again. When the carriages came for the guests there was no one to say good-bye to. The carriages rolled away, one after another, filled with full but oddly unsatisfied hobbits. Gardeners came (by appointment) and cleared away in wheelbarrows those that had inadvertently remained. Night settled down and passed. The sun rose. People came to clear away the pavilions and the tables and the chairs and the lanterns and the flowering trees in boxes, and the spoons and knives and plates and forks, and crumbs, and the uneaten food – a very small parcel. Lots of other people came too. Bagginses and Sackville-Bagginses and Tooks, and people with even less business. By the middle of the morning (when even the best-fed were out and about again) there was quite a crowd at Bag-end, uninvited but not unexpected. ENTER was painted on a large white board outside the great front-door. The door was open. On everything inside there was a label tied. 'For Mungo Took, with love from Bilbo'; 'For Semolina Baggins, with love from her nephew', on a waste-paper basket – she had written him a deal of letters (mostly of good advice). 'For Caramella Took, with kind remembrances from her uncle', on a clock in the hall. Though unpunctual she had been a niece he rather liked, until coming late one day to tea she had declared his clock was fast. Bilbo's clocks were never either slow or fast, and he did not forget it. 'For Obo Took-Took, from his great-nephew', on a feather bed; Obo was seldom awake before 12 noon or after tea, and snored. 'For Gorboduc Grubb with best wishes from B. Baggins' – on a gold fountain-pen; he never answered letters. 'For Angelica's use' on a mirror – she was a young Baggins and thought herself very comely.[4] 'For Inigo Grubb-Took', on a complete dinner-service – he was the greediest hobbit known to history. 'For

Amalda Sackville-Baggins *as a present'*, on a case of silver spoons. She was the wife of Bilbo's cousin, the one he had discovered years ago on his return measuring his dining-room (you may remember his suspicions about disappearing spoons: anyway neither he nor Amalda had forgotten).[5]

Of course there were a thousand and one things in Bilbo's house, and all had labels – most of them with some point (which sank in after a time). The whole house-furniture was disposed of, but not a penny piece of money, nor a brass ring of jewelry, was to be found. Amalda was the only Sackville-Baggins remembered with a label – but then there was a notice in the hall saying that Mr Bilbo Baggins made over the desirable property or dwelling-hole known as Bag-end Underhill together with all lands thereto belonging or annexed to Sago Sackville-Baggins and his wife Amalda for them to have hold possess occupy or otherwise dispose of at their pleasure and discretion as from September 22nd next. It was then September 21st (Bilbo's birthday being on the 20th of that pleasant month). So the Sackville-Bagginses did live in Bag-end after all – though they had had to wait some twenty years. And they had a great deal of difficulty too getting all the labelled stuff out – labels got torn and mixed, and people tried to do swaps in the hall, and some tried to make off with stuff that was [not] being carefully watched; and various prying folk began knocking holes in walls and burrowing in cellars before they could be ejected. They were still worrying about the money and the jewelry. How Bilbo would have laughed. Indeed he was – he had foreseen how it would all fall out, and was enjoying the joke quite privately.

There, I suppose it has become all too plain. The fact is, in spite of his after-dinner speech, he had grown suddenly very tired of them all. The Tookishness (not of course that all Tooks ever had much of this wayward quality) had quite suddenly and uncomfortably come to life again. Also another secret – after he had blowed his last fifty ducats on the party he had not got *any money or jewelry left*, except the ring, and the gold buttons on his waistcoat. He had spent it all in twenty years (even the proceeds of his beautiful . . . . which he had sold a few years back).[6]

Then how could he get married? He was not going to just then – he merely said 'I am going to get married'. I cannot quite say why. It came suddenly into his head. Also he thought it was an event that might occur in the future – if he travelled again amongst other folk, or found a more rare and more beautiful race of hobbits somewhere. Also it was a kind of explanation. Hobbits had a curious habit in their weddings. They kept it (always officially and very often actually) a dead secret for years who they were going to marry, even when they knew. Then they suddenly went and got married and went off without an address for a week or two (or even longer). When Bilbo had disappeared this is what at first his neighbours thought. 'He has gone and got married. Now who can it be? – no one else has disappeared, as far as we know.' Even after a year they would have been less surprised if he had come back with a wife. For a long while some folk thought he was keeping one in hiding, and quite a legend about the poor Mrs Bilbo who was too ugly to be seen grew up for a while.

So now Bilbo said before he disappeared: 'I am going to get married.' He thought that that – together with all the fuss about the house (or hole) and furniture – would keep them all busy and satisfied for a long while, so that no one would bother to hunt for him for a bit. And he was right – or nearly right. For no one ever bothered to hunt for him at all. They decided he had gone mad, and run off till he met a pool or a river or a steep fall, and there was one Baggins the less. Most of them, that is. He was deeply regretted by a few of his younger friends of course ( . . . Angelica and Sar . . . . . . ). But he had not said good-bye to all of them – O no. That is easily explained.

## NOTES

1  The title was written in subsequently, but no doubt before the chapter was finished, since my father referred to it by this title in his letter of 19 December 1937 (p. 11).

2  After 'Burroweses' followed 'and Ogdens', but this was struck out – almost certainly at the time of writing. 'Proudfoots' was first written 'Proudfeet', as earlier in the chapter, but as the next sentence shows it was changed in the act of writing.

3  The reference is to the conclusion of *The Hobbit*, when Gandalf and Balin called at Bag End 'some years afterwards'.

4  At this point a present to Inigo Baggins of a case of hairbrushes was mentioned, but struck out, evidently at the time of writing, since the present to another Inigo (Grubb-Took) immediately follows.

5  Various changes were made to the names and other details in this passage, not all of which were taken up in the third version (the second ends before this point). Mungo Took's gift (an umbrella) was specified; and Caramella Took was changed from niece to cousin. Gorboduc Grubb became Orlando Grubb. Pencilled proposals for the name of Mrs Sackville-Baggins, replacing Amalda, are Lonicera

(Honeysuckle) and Griselda, and her husband Sago (named in the next paragraph of the text) became Cosmo.

6  Cf. the end of *The Hobbit*: 'His gold and silver was mostly [*afterwards changed to* largely] spent in presents, both useful and extravagant'. The illegible word here might possibly be *arms*, but it does not look like it, and cf. the same passage in *The Hobbit*: 'His coat of mail was arranged on a stand in the hall (until he lent it to a Museum).'

★

Writing of this draft in his *Biography*, Humphrey Carpenter says (p. 185):

The reason for his disappearance, as given in this first draft, is that Bilbo 'had not got any money or jewels left' and was going off in search of more dragon-gold. At this point the first version of the opening chapter breaks off, unfinished.

But it may be argued that it was in fact finished: for the next completed draft of the chapter (the third – the second seems certainly unfinished, and breaks off at a much earlier point) ends only a very little further on in the narrative (p. 34), and shortly before the end has:

But not all of them had said good-bye to him. That is easily explained, and soon will be.

And the explanation is not given, but reserved for the next chapter. Nor is it made so explicit in the first draft that Bilbo was 'going off in search of more dragon-gold'. That lack of money was a reason for leaving his home is certainly the case, but a sudden Tookish disgust with hobbit dulness and conventionality is also emphasized; and in fact there is not so much as a hint of what Bilbo was planning to do. It may well be that on 19 December 1937 my father had no idea. The rapidly-written conclusion of the text strongly suggests uncertain direction (and indeed he had said earlier in the chapter that the story was going to be about one of Bilbo's descendants).

But while there is no sign of Gandalf, most of the essentials and many of the details of the actual party as it is described in *The Fellowship of the Ring* (FR) emerge right at the beginning, and even some phrases remained. The Chubbs (or Chubbses, p. 13), the Boffinses, and the Proudfoots now appear – the families named Burrowes (Burrows in FR) and Grubb had been mentioned at the end of *The Hobbit*, in the names of the auctioneers at the sale of Bag End; and the hobbits' land is for the first time called 'the shire' (see, however, p. 31). But the first names of the hobbits were only at the beginning of their protean variations – such names as Sago and Semolina would be rejected as unsuitable, others (Amalda, Inigo, Obo) would have no place in the final genealogies, and yet others (Mungo, Gorboduc) would be given to different persons; only the vain Angelica Baggins survived.

★

(ii)

*The Second Version*

The next manuscript, while closely based on the first, introduced much new material – most notably the arrival of Gandalf, and the fireworks. This version breaks off at the words 'Morning went on' (FR p. 45).

The manuscript was much emended, and it is very difficult to distinguish those changes made at the time of composition from those made subsequently: in any case the third version no doubt followed hard upon the second, superseding it before it was completed. I give this second text also in full, so far as it goes, but in this case I include virtually all the emendations made to it (in some cases the original reading is given in the notes which follow the text on p. 25).

## Chapter 1

### A long-expected party

When Bilbo, son of Bungo, of the respectable family of Baggins prepared to celebrate his seventy-first[1] birthday there was some little talk in the neighbourhood, and people polished up their memories.[2] Bilbo had once had some brief notoriety among the hobbits of Hobbiton and Bywater – he had disappeared after breakfast one April 30th and had not reappeared until lunch-time on June 22nd in the following year. A very odd proceeding, and one for which he had never accounted satisfactorily. He wrote a book about it, of course: but even those who had read it never took that seriously. It is no good talking to hobbits about dragons: they either disbelieve you, or feel uncomfortable; and in either case tend to avoid you afterwards. Mr Baggins, however, had soon returned to more or less normal ways; and though the shaken confidence of the countryside was never quite restored, in time the hobbits agreed to pardon the past, and Bilbo was on calling-terms again with all his relatives and neighbours, except of course the Sackville-Bagginses. For one thing Bilbo seemed by some unexplained method to have become more than comfortably off, in fact positively wealthy. Indeed it was the magnificence of the preparations for his birthday-party far more than his brief and distant fame that caused the talk. After all that other odd business had happened some twenty years ago and was all but forgotten; the party was going to happen that very month of September. The weather was fine, and there was talk of a display of fireworks such as had not been seen since the days of Old Took.

Time drew nearer. Odd-looking carts with odd-looking pack-ages began to toil up the Hill to Bag-end (the residence of Mr Bilbo Baggins). They arrived by night, and startled folk peered out of their doors to gape at them. Some were driven by outlandish folk singing strange songs, elves, or heavily hooded dwarves. There was one huge creaking wain with great lumbering tow-haired Men on it that caused quite a commotion. It bore a large B under a crown.[3] It could not get across the bridge by the mill, and the Men carried the goods on their backs up the hill – stumping on the hobbit road like elephants. All the beer at the inn vanished as if down a drain when they came downhill again. Later in the week a cart came trotting in in broad daylight. An old man was driving it all alone. He wore a tall pointed blue hat and a long grey cloak. Hobbit boys and girls ran after the cart all the way up the hill. It had a cargo of fireworks, that they could see when it began to unload: great bundles of them, labelled with a red G.

'G for grand,' they shouted; and that was as good a guess as they could make at its meaning. Not many of their elders guessed better: hobbits have rather short memories as a rule. As for the little old man,[4] he vanished inside Bilbo's front door and never reappeared.

There might have been some grumbling about 'dealing locally'; but suddenly orders began to pour out from Bag-end, and into every shop in the neighbourhood (even widely measured). Then people stopped being merely curious, and became enthusiastic. They began to tick off the days on the calendar till Bilbo's birthday, and they began to watch for the postman, hoping for invitations.

Then the invitations began pouring out, and the post-office of Hobbiton was blocked, and Bywater post-office was snowed under, and voluntary postmen were called for. There was a constant stream of them going up The Hill to Bag-end carrying letters containing hundreds of polite variations on 'thank-you, I shall certainly come.' During all this time, for days and days, indeed since September [10th >] 8th, Bilbo had not been seen out or about by anyone. He either did not answer the bell, or came to the door and cried 'Sorry – Busy!' round the edge of it. They thought he was only writing invitation cards, but they were not quite right.

Finally the field to the south of his front door – it was bordered by his kitchen garden on one side and the Hill road on the other –

began to be covered with tents and pavilions. The three hobbit-
families of Bagshot Row just below it were immensely excited.
There was one specially large pavilion, so large that the tree that
stood in the field was inside it, standing growing in the middle.[5] It
was hung all over with lanterns. Even more promising was the
erection of a huge kitchen in a corner of the field. A draught of
cooks arrived. Excitement rose to its height. Then the weather
clouded over. That was on Friday, the eve of the party. Anxiety
grew intense. Then Saturday September [20th >] 22nd[6] actually
dawned. The sun got up, the clouds vanished, flags were un-
furled, and the fun began.

Mr Baggins called it a party – but it was several rolled into one
and mixed up. Practically everybody near at hand was invited to
something or other – very few were forgotten (by accident), and as
they turned up anyhow it did not matter. Bilbo met the guests (and
additions) at the gate in person. He gave away presents to all and
sundry – the latter were those that went out again by the back way
and came in again by the front for a second helping. He began with
the youngest and smallest, and came back again quickly to the
smallest and youngest. Hobbits give presents to other people on
their birthdays: not very expensive ones, of course. But it was not
a bad system. Actually in Hobbiton and Bywater, since every day
in the year was somebody's birthday, it meant that every hobbit
got a present (and sometimes more) almost every day of his life.
But they did not get tired of them. On this occasion the hobbit-fry
were wildly excited – there were toys the like of which they had
never seen before. As you have guessed, they came from Dale.

When they got inside the grounds the guests had songs, dances,
games – and of course food and drink. There were three official
meals: lunch, tea, and dinner (or supper); but lunch and tea were
marked chiefly by the fact that at those times everybody was
sitting down and eating at the same time. Drinking never stopped.
Eating went on pretty continuously from elevenses to six o'clock,
when the fireworks started.

The fireworks of course (as you at any rate have guessed) were
by Gandalf, and brought by him in person, and let off by him – the
main ones: there was generous distribution of squibs, crackers,
sparklers, torches, dwarf-candles, elf-fountains, goblin-barkers
and thunderclaps. They were of course superb. The art of Gandalf
naturally got the older the better. There were rockets like a flight
of scintillating birds singing with sweet voices; there were green
trees with trunks of twisted smoke: their leaves opened like a

whole spring unfolding in a few minutes, and their shining branches dropped glowing flowers down upon the astonished hobbits – only to disappear in a sweet scent before they touched head hat or bonnet. There were fountains of butterflies that flew into the trees; there were pillars of coloured fires that turned into hovering eagles, or sailing ships, or a flight of swans; there were red thunderstorms and showers of yellow rain; there was a forest of silver spears that went suddenly up into the air with a yell like a charging army and came down into The Water with a hiss like a hundred hot snakes. And there was also one last thing in which Gandalf rather overdid it – after all, he knew a great deal about hobbits and their beliefs. The lights went out, a great smoke went up, it shaped itself like a mountain, it began to glow at the top, it burst into flames of scarlet and green, out flew a red-golden dragon (not life-size, of course, but terribly life-like): fire came out of its mouth, its eyes glared down, there was a roar and it whizzed three times round the crowd. Everyone ducked and some fell flat. The dragon passed like an express train and burst over Bywater with a deafening explosion.

'That means it is dinner-time,' said Gandalf. A fortunate re-mark, for the pain and alarm vanished like magic. Now really we must hurry on, for all this is not as important as it seemed. There was a supper for all the guests. But there was also a very special dinner-party in the great pavilion with the tree. To that party invitations had been limited to twelve dozen, or one gross (in addition to Gandalf and the host), made up of all the chief hobbits, and their elder children, to whom Bilbo was related or with whom he was connected, or by whom he had been well-treated at any time, or for whom he felt some special affection. Nearly all the living Baggins[es] had been invited; a quantity of Tooks (his relations on his mother's side); a number of Grubbs (connections of his grandfather's), dozens of Brandybucks (connections of his grandmother's), and various Chubbs and Burrowses and Boffins and Proudfeet – some of whom were not connected with Bilbo at all, within the memory of the local historians; some even lived right on the other side of the Shire; but they were all, of course, hobbits. Even the Sackville-Bagginses, his first cousins on his father's side, were not omitted. There had been some coolness between them and Mr Baggins, as you may remember, dating from some 20 years back. But so splendid was the invitation card, written all in gold, that they felt it was impossible to refuse. Besides, their cousin had been specializing in

food for a good many years, and his tables had a high reputation
even in that time and country, when food was still all that it ought
to be, and abundant enough for all folk to practise both discrimi-
nation and satisfaction.

All the 144 special guests expected a pleasant feast; though they
rather dreaded the after-dinner speech of their host. He was liable
to drag in bits of what he called 'poetry'; and sometimes, after a
glass or two, would allude to the absurd adventures he said he had
had long ago – during his ridiculous vanishment. Not one of the
144 were disappointed: they had a *very* pleasant feast, indeed
an engrossing entertainment: rich, abundant, varied, and prolonged. The purchase of provisions fell almost to zero throughout
the district during the ensuing week; but as Mr Baggins' catering
had depleted most of the stores, cellars, and warehouses for miles
around, that did not matter much.

After the feast (more or less) came the Speech. Most of the
assembled hobbits were now in a tolerant mood – at that delicious
stage which they called filling up the 'corners' (with sips of their
favourite drinks and nips of their favourite sweetmeats): their
former fears were forgotten. They were prepared to listen to
anything, and to cheer at every full stop. But they were not
prepared to be startled. Yet startled they certainly were: indeed,
completely blowed: some even got indigestion.

*My dear people*, began Mr Baggins, rising in his place.

'Hear, hear, hear!' they answered in chorus, and seemed reluctant to follow their own advice. Meanwhile Bilbo left his place and
went and stood on a chair under the illuminated tree. The lantern
light fell upon his beaming face; the gold buttons shone on his
flowered waistcoat. They could all see him. One hand was in his
pocket. He raised the other.

*My dear Bagginses!* he began again. *And my dear Tooks and
Brandybucks and Grubbs and Chubbs and Burroweses and
Bracegirdles and Boffinses and Proudfoots.*

'Proud*feet*!' shouted an elderly hobbit from the back. His
name, of course, was Proudfoot, and merited: his feet were large,
exceptionally furry, and both were on the table.

*Also my good Sackville-Bagginses that I welcome back at last to
Bag-end. Today is my seventy-first birthday!*

'Hurray, hurray! Many Happy Returns!' they shouted, and
they hammered joyously on the tables. Bilbo was doing splendidly.
That was the sort of stuff they liked: short, obvious, uncontroversial.

*I hope you are all enjoying yourselves as much as I am.*
Deafening cheers. Cries of Yes (and No). Noises of horns and
trumpets, pipes and flutes, and other musical instruments. There
were many junior hobbits present, for hobbits were easygoing
with their children in the matter of sitting up late – especially if
there was a chance of getting them an extra meal free (bringing up
young hobbits took a great deal of provender). Hundreds of
musical crackers had been pulled. Most of them bore the mark
*Dale* on them somewhere or other, inside or out. What that meant
only Bilbo and a few of his close friends knew (and you of course);
but they were very marvellous crackers. They contained instruments small but of perfect make and enchanting tone. Indeed in
one corner some of the younger Tooks and Brandybucks, sup-
posing Bilbo to have finished his speech (having said all that was
needed), now got up an impromptu orchestra, and began a merry
dance tune. Young Prospero Brandybuck[7] and Melba Took got on
a table and started to dance the flip-flap, a pretty thing if rather
vigorous. But Bilbo had *not* finished.

Seizing a horn from one of the children he blew three very loud
notes. The noise subsided. *I shall not keep you long*, he cried.
Cheering broke out again. *BUT I have called you all together for a
Purpose.*

Something in his voice made a few of the Tooks prick up their
ears. *Indeed for three Purposes. First of all, to tell you that I am
immensely fond of you all; and that seventy-one years is too short a
time to live among such excellent and admirable hobbits.*

Tremendous outburst of approval.

*I don't know half of you half as well as I would like, and less than
half of you half as well as you deserve.*

No cheers this time: it was a bit too difficult. There was some
scattered clapping; but not all of them had yet had time to work it
out and see if it came to a compliment in the end.

*Secondly, to celebrate my birthday, and the twentieth anniver-
sary of my return.* No cheers; there was some uncomfortable
rustling.

*Lastly, to make an Announcement.* He said this so loudly and
suddenly that everyone sat up who could. *I regret to announce
that – though, as I have said, 71 years is far too short a time among
you – this is the END. I am going. I am leaving after dinner. Goodbye!*

He stepped down. One hundred and forty-four flabbergasted
hobbits sat back speechless. Mr Proudfoot removed his feet from

the table. Mrs Proudfoot swallowed a large chocolate and choked. Then there was complete silence for quite forty winks, until suddenly every Baggins, Took, Brandybuck, Chubb, Grubb, Burrowes, Bracegirdle, Boffin and Proudfoot began to talk at once.

'The hobbit's mad. Always said so. Bad taste in jokes. Trying to pull the fur off our toes (a hobbit idiom). Spoiling a good dinner. Where's my handkerchief. Won't drink his health now. Shall drink my own. Where's that bottle. Is he going to get married? Not to anyone here tonight. Who would take him? Why good-bye? Where is there to *go* to? What is he leaving?' And so on. At last old Rory Brandybuck[8] (well-filled but still pretty bright) was heard to shout: 'Where is he now, anyway? Where's Bilbo?'

There was not a sign of their host anywhere.

As a matter of fact Bilbo Baggins had disappeared silently and unnoticed in the midst of all the talk. While he was speaking he had already been fingering a small ring[9] in his trouser-pocket. As he stepped down he had slipped it on – and he was never seen in Hobbiton again.

When the carriages came for the guests there was no one to say good-bye to. The carriages rolled away, one after another, filled with full but oddly unsatisfied hobbits. Gardeners came (by arrangement) and cleared away in wheelbarrows those that had inadvertently remained behind, asleep or immoveable. Night settled down and passed. The sun rose. The hobbits rose rather later. Morning went on.

## NOTES

1  *seventy-first* emended from *seventieth*; but *seventy-first* in the text of Bilbo's farewell speech as first written.

2  At this point my father wrote at first:

> Twice before this he had been a matter of local news: a rare achievement for a Baggins. The first time was when he was left an orphan, when barely forty years old, by the untimely death of his father and mother (in a boating accident). The second time was more remarkable.

Such a fate in store for Bungo Baggins and his wife seems most improbable in the light of the words of the first chapter of *The Hobbit*:

> Not that Belladonna Took ever had any adventures after she became Mrs Bungo Baggins. Bungo, that was Bilbo's father, built the most luxurious hobbit-hole for her . . . and there they remained to the end of their days.

They seem an unlikely couple to have gone 'fooling about with boats', in Gaffer Gamgee's phrase, and his recognition of this was no doubt the reason why my father immediately struck the passage out; but the boating accident was not forgotten, and it became the fate of (Rollo Bolger >) Drogo Baggins and his Brandybuck wife, Primula, for whom it was a less improbable end (see p. 37).

3　At this stage only 20 years separated Bilbo's adventure in *The Hobbit* and his farewell party, and my father clearly intended the B on the waggon to stand for Bard, King of Dale. Later, when the years had been greatly lengthened out, it would be Bain son of Bard who ruled in Dale at this time.

4　In the original *Hobbit* Gandalf at his first appearance was described as 'a little old man', but afterwards the word 'little' was removed. See p. 315.

5　The single tree in the field below Bag End was already in the illustration of Hobbiton that appeared as the frontispiece to *The Hobbit*, as also were Bilbo's kitchen-garden and the hobbit-holes of Bagshot Row (though that name first appears here).

6　September 20th was the date of Bilbo's birthday in the first version (p. 16).

7　Prospero Brandybuck was first written Orlando Brandybuck, the second bearer of the name: in the list of Bilbo's gifts in the first version (p. 17 note 5) Gorboduc Grubb had been changed to Orlando Grubb.

8　A very similar passage, indicating the outraged comments of the guests, was added to the manuscript of the original draft at this point, but it was Inigo Grubb-Took who shouted 'Where is he now, anyway?' It was the greedy Inigo Grubb-Took who received the dinner-service (p. 15), and in this respect he survived into the third version of the chapter.

9　*a small ring*: emended from *his famous ring*.

I have given this text in full, since taken together with the first it provides a basis of reference in describing those that follow, from which only extracts are given; but it will be seen that the Party – the preparations for it, the fireworks, the feast – had already reached the form it retains in FR (pp. 34–9), save in a few and quite minor features of the narrative (and here and there in tone). This is the more striking when we realize that at this stage my father still had very little idea of where he was going: it was a beginning without a destination (but see pp. 42–3).

Certain changes made to the manuscript towards its end have not been taken up in the text given above. In Bilbo's speech, his words 'Secondly, to celebrate my birthday, and the twentieth anniversary of my return' and the comment 'No cheers; there was some uncomfortable rustling' were removed, and the following expanded passage substituted:

> *Secondly, to celebrate OUR birthdays: mine and my honourable and gallant father's.* Uncomfortable and apprehensive silence. *I am only half the man that he is: I am 72, he is 144. Your numbers are chosen to do honour to each of his honourable years.* This was really dreadful – a regular braintwister, and some of them felt insulted, like leap-days shoved in to fill up a calendar.

This change gives every appearance of belonging closely with the writing of the manuscript: it is clearly written in ink, and seems distinct from various scattered scribbles in pencil. But the appearance is misleading. Why should Bilbo thus refer to old Bungo Baggins, underground these many years? Bungo was pure Baggins, 'solid and comfortable' (as he is described in *The Hobbit*), and surely died solidly in his bed at Bag End. To call him 'gallant' seems odd, and for Bilbo to say 'I am half the man that he *is*' and 'he *is* 144' rather tastelessly whimsical.

The explanation is in fact simple: it was not Bilbo who said it, but his son, Bingo Baggins, who enters in the third version of 'A Long-expected Party'. The textual point would not be worth mentioning here were it not so striking an example of my father's way of using one manuscript as the matrix of the next version, but not correcting it coherently throughout: so in this case, he made no structural alterations to the earlier part of the story, but pencilled in the name 'Bingo' against 'Bilbo' on the last pages of the manuscript, and (to the severe initial confusion of the editor) carefully rewrote a passage of Bilbo's speech to make it seem that Bilbo had taken leave of his senses. It is clear, I think, that it was the sudden emergence of this radical new idea that caused him to abandon this version.

Other hasty changes altered 'seventy-first' to 'seventy-second' and '71' to '72' at each occurrence, and these belong also with the new story that was emerging. In this text, Bilbo's age in the opening sentence was 70, as in the first version, but it was changed to 71 in the course of the chapter (note 1 above). The number of guests at the dinner-party was already 144 in the text as first written, but nothing is made of this figure; that it was chosen for a particular reason only appears from the expanded passage of the speech given above: 'I am 72, he is 144. Your numbers are chosen to do honour to each of his honourable years.' It seems clear that the change of 71 to 72 was made because 72 is half of 144. The number of guests came first, when the story was still told of Bilbo, and at first had no significance beyond its being a dozen dozens, a gross.

A few other points may be noticed. Gandalf was present at the dinner-party; Gaffer Gamgee had not yet emerged, but 'old Rory Brandybuck' makes his appearance (in place of Inigo Grubb-Took, note 8 above); and Bilbo does not disappear with a blinding flash. At each stage the number of hobbit clans named is increased: so here the Brandybucks emerge, and the Bracegirdles were pencilled in, to appear in the third version as written.

★

(iii)

## The Third Version

The third draft of 'A Long-expected Party' is complete, and is a good clear manuscript with relatively little later correction. In this section numbered notes again appear at the end (p. 34).

Discussion of the change made to Bilbo's speech in the second version has already indicated the central new feature of the third: the story is now told *not of Bilbo, but of his son*. On this substitution Humphrey Carpenter remarked (*Biography* p. 185):

> Tolkien had as yet no clear idea of what the new story was going to be about. At the end of *The Hobbit* he had stated that Bilbo 'remained very happy to the end of his days, and those were extraordinarily long.' So how could the hobbit have any new adventures worth the name without this being contradicted? And had he not explored most of the possibilities in Bilbo's character? He decided to introduce a new hobbit, Bilbo's son – and to give him the name of a family of toy koala bears owned by his children,[6] 'The Bingos'.[1] So he crossed out 'Bilbo' in the first draft and above it wrote 'Bingo'.[2]

This explanation is plausible. In the first draft, however, my father wrote that the story of the birthday party 'merely serves to explain that Bilbo Baggins got married and had many children, *because I am going to tell you a story about one of his descendants*' (in the second version we are given no indication at all of what was going to happen after the party – though there is possibly a suggestion of something similar in the words (p. 22) 'Now really we must hurry on, for all this is not as important as it seemed'). On the other hand, there are explicit statements in early notes (p. 41) that for a time it was indeed going to be Bilbo who had the new 'adventure'.

The first part of the third version is almost wholly different from the two preceding, and I give it here in full, with a few early changes incorporated.

## A long-expected party

When Bingo, son of Bilbo, of the well-known Baggins family, prepared to celebrate his [fifty-fifth >] seventy-second[3] birthday there was some talk in the neighbourhood, and people polished up their memories. The Bagginses were fairly numerous in those parts, and generally respected; but Bingo belonged to a branch of the family that was a bit peculiar, and there were some odd stories about them. Bingo's father, as some still remembered, had once made quite a stir in Hobbiton and Bywater – he had disappeared one April 30th after breakfast, and had not reappeared until lunch-time on June 22nd in the following year. A very odd proceeding, and one for which he had never accounted satisfactorily. He wrote a book about it, of course; but even those who had read it never took that seriously. It is no good telling hobbits about dragons: they either disbelieve you, or feel uncomfortable; and in either case tend to avoid you afterwards.

Bilbo Baggins, it is true, had soon returned to normal ways (more or less), and though his reputation was never quite restored, he became an accepted figure in the neighbourhood. He was never perhaps again regarded as a 'safe hobbit', but he was undoubtedly a 'warm' one. In some mysterious way he appeared to have become more than comfortably off, in fact positively wealthy; so naturally, he was on visiting terms with all his neighbours and relatives (except, of course, the Sackville-Bagginses). He did two more things that caused tongues to wag: he got married when seventy-one (a little but not too late for a hobbit), choosing a bride from the other side of the Shire, and giving a wedding-feast of memorable splendour; he disappeared (together with his wife) shortly before his hundred-and-eleventh birthday, and was never seen again. The folk of Hobbiton and Bywater were cheated of a funeral (not that they had expected his for many a year yet), so they had a good deal to say. His residence, his wealth, his position (and the dubious regard of the neighbourhood) were inherited by his son Bingo, just before his own birthday (which happened to be the same as his father's). Bingo was, of course, a mere youngster of 39, who had hardly cut his wisdom-teeth; but he at once began to carry on his father's reputation for oddity: he never went into mourning for his parents, and said he did not think they were dead. To the obvious question: 'Where are they then?' he merely winked. He lived alone, and was often away from home. He went about a lot with the least well-behaved members of the Took family (his grandmother's people and his father's friends), and he was also fond of some of the Brandybucks. They were his mother's relatives. She was Primula Brandybuck[4] of the Brandybucks of Buckland, across Brandywine River on the other side of the Shire and on the edge of the Old Forest – a dubious region.[5] Folk in Hobbiton did not know much about it, or about the Brandybucks either; though some had heard it said that they were rich, and would have been richer, but for a certain 'recklessness' – generosity, that is, if any came your way.

Anyway, Bingo had lived at Bag-end Underhill now for some [16 >] 33 years[6] without giving any scandal. His parties were sometimes a bit noisy, perhaps, but hobbits don't mind that kind of noise now and again. He spent his money freely and mostly locally. Now the neighbourhood understood that he was planning something quite unusual in the way of parties. Naturally their memories awoke and their tongues wagged, and Bingo's wealth was again guessed and re-calculated at every fireside. Indeed the magnificence of the preparations quite overshadowed the tales of the old folk about his father's vanishments.

'After all,' as old Gaffer Gamgee of Bagshot Row[7] remarked, 'them goings-on are old affairs and over; this here party is going to happen this very month as is.' It was early September and as fine as you could wish. Somebody started a rumour about fireworks. Very soon it was accepted that there were going to be fireworks such as had not been seen for over a century, not since the Old Took died.

It is interesting to see the figures 111 and 33 emerging, though afterwards they would be differently achieved: here, Bilbo was 111 when he left the Shire, and Bingo lived on at Bag End for 33 years before his farewell party; afterwards, 111 was Bilbo's age at the time of the party – when it had become his party again – and 33 Bingo's (Frodo's) age at the same time.

In this passage we also see the emergence of a very important piece of topography and toponymy: Buckland, the Brandywine, and the Old Forest. For the names first written here see note 5.

For the account in this version of the preparations for the Party, the Party itself, and its immediate aftermath, my father followed the emended second version (pp. 19–25) extremely closely, adding a detail here and there, but for the most part doing little more than copy it out (and of course changing 'Bilbo' to 'Bingo' where necessary). I give here a list of interesting – though mostly extremely minor – shifts in the new narrative. The page references are to those of the second version.

(20–1)   'B under a crown' on the waggon driven by Men becomes 'B painted in yellow', and 'B' was emended on the text to 'D' (i.e. 'Dale').

When the Men came down the Hill again, it is added that 'the elves and dwarves did not return'; and 'the draught of cooks' who arrived were 'to supplement the elves and dwarves (who seemed to be staying at Bag-end and doing a lot of mysterious work)'.

The notice refusing admittance on the door of Bag End now appears, and 'a special entrance was cut in the bank leading to the road; wide steps and a large white gate were built' (as in FR). Gaffer Gamgee comes in again: 'he stopped even pretending to garden.'

The day of the party was still a Saturday (September 22nd).

Many of the toys ('some obviously magical') that had come from Dale were 'genuinely dwarf-made'.

(22)  It is Bingo, not Gandalf, who at the end of the fireworks says 'That is the signal for supper!'; and though it was said at first, as in the second version, that the total of 144 guests did not include the host and Gandalf, this was struck out (see p. 106, note 12).

A new Hobbit family-name enters in the list of guests: 'and various Burroweses, Slocums, Bracegirdles, Boffinses and Proudfoots'; but 'Slocums' was then changed to 'Hornblowers', which was also added in to the text at subsequent points in the chapter. The Bolgers appear in pencilled additions, and are present from the start in the fourth version. In his letter to the *Observer* newspaper published on 20 February 1938 (*Letters* no. 25) my father said: 'The full list of their wealthier families is: Baggins, Boffin, Bolger, Bracegirdle, Brandybuck, Burrowes, Chubb, Grubb, Hornblower, Proudfoot, Sackville, and Took.' – The Grubbs, connexions of Bingo's grandfather, became by a pencilled change connexions of his grandmother; and the Chubbs, in a reverse change, were first said to be connexions of his grandmother and then of his grandfather.
     Where in the first and second versions it is said that some of the hobbits at the party came from 'the other side of the shire', it is now said that some of them 'did not even live in that county', changed to 'in that Shire'; and 'in that Shire' was retained in the fourth version. The use of 'that' rather than 'the' suggests that the later use (cf. the Prologue to LR, p. 14: 'The Hobbits named it the Shire, as the region of the authority of their Thain') was only in the process of emergence.

The coldness between the Bagginses of Bag End and the Sackville-Bagginses had now lasted, not 20 years as in the first two versions, but 'some seventy-five years and more': this figure depends on 111 (Bilbo's age when he finally disappeared) less 51 (he was 'about fifty years old or so' at the time of his great adventure, according to *The Hobbit*), plus the 16 years of Bingo's solitary residence at Bag End. 'Seventy-five' was emended to 'ninety' (a round figure), which belongs with the change of 16 to 33 (p. 30).

(23)    Bingo was liable to allude to 'the absurd adventures of his "gallant and famous" father'.

(24)    The two young hobbits who got on the table and danced are still Prospero Brandybuck and Melba Took, but Melba was changed in pencil first to Arabella and then to Amanda.

Bingo now said, as did Bilbo in FR (p. 38), '*I like* less than half of you half as well as you deserve.'

Bingo's 'second purpose' is expressed in exactly the words written into the second version (see p. 27): to celebrate OUR birthdays: mine and my honourable and gallant father's. I am only half the man he is: I am 72, and he is 144', &c.

Bingo's last words, 'I am leaving after dinner', were corrected on the manuscript to 'I am leaving now.'

(25)    The collected comments after Bingo's concluding remarks now begin: 'The hobbit's mad. Always said so. And his father. He's been dead 33 years, I know. 144, all rubbish.' And Rory Brandybuck shouts: 'Where is Bilbo – confound it, Bingo I mean. Where is he?'

After 'he was never seen in Hobbiton again' is added: 'The ring was his father's parting gift.'

From the point where the second version ends at the words 'Morning went on' the third goes back to the original draft (p. 15) and follows it closely until near the end, using pretty well the same phrases, and largely retaining the original list (as emended, p. 17 note 5) of names and labels for the recipients of presents from Bag End – these being now, of course, presents from Bilbo's son Bingo.

*Semolina Baggins* is called 'an aunt, or first cousin once removed';

*Caramella Took* (changed later to *Bolger*) 'had been favoured among [Bingo's] junior and remoter cousins';

*Obo Took-Took* who received a feather-bed remained as a great-uncle, but *Obo* was emended on the manuscript to *Rollo*;

*Gorboduc* (> *Orlando*) *Grubb* of the first draft, recipient of a gold fountain-pen, becomes *Orlando Burrowes*;

*Mungo Took, Inigo Grubb-Took,* and *Angelica Baggins* remain; and two new beneficiaries are named before Mrs Sackville-Baggins at the end of the list:

For the collection of Hugo Bracegirdle, from a contributor: on an (empty) bookcase. Hugo was a great borrower of books, but a small returner.

*For Cosimo Chubb, treat it as your own, Bingo:* on the barometer.
Cosimo used to bang it with a large fat finger whenever he came to call.
He was afraid of getting wet, and wore a scarf and macintosh all the
year round.

*For Grimalda* [> *Lobelia*] *Sackville-Baggins, as a present:* on a case
of silver spoons. It was believed by Bilbo Baggins that she had
acquired a good many of his spoons while he was away – ninety odd
years before. Bingo inherited the belief, and Grimalda [> Lobelia]
knew it.

It is also mentioned that 'Bingo had very carefully disposed of his
treasures: books, pictures, and a collection of toys. For his wines
he found a very good (if temporary) home. Most of them went to
Marmaduke Brandybuck' (predecessor of Meriadoc). The original draft
is closely followed in the absence of any money or jewelry, and in the legal
notice disposing of Bag End to the Sackville-Bagginses (but Bilbo's
cousin now becomes Otho, and their occupancy is to start from September 24th) – 'and they got Bag-end after all, though they had to wait 93
years longer for it than they had once expected': 111 less 51 plus 33, see
pp. 31–2.[8] Sancho Proudfoot appears, excavating in the pantry where he
thought there was an echo (as in FR, p. 48); physically attacked by Otho
Sackville-Baggins, he was only finally ejected by the lawyers, first called
'Grubbs and Burrowes', as in *The Hobbit*, then changed to 'Messrs. Iago
Grubb and Folco Burrowes (Bingo's lawyers)'.
The conclusion of the third version I give in full.

The fact is Bingo's money had become a legend, and everybody
was puzzled and anxious – though still hopeful. How he would
have laughed. Indeed he was as near laughing as he dared at that
very moment, for he was inside a large cupboard outside the
dining-room door, and heard most of the racket. He was inside, of
course, not for concealment, but to avoid being bumped into,
being totally invisible. He had to laugh rather privately and
silently, but all the same he was enjoying his joke: it was turning
out so much like his expectation.

I suppose it is now becoming all too plain to everyone but the
anxious and grabsome hobbits. The fact is that (in spite of certain
things in his after-dinner speech) Bingo had grown suddenly tired
of them all. A violent fit of Tookishness had come over him – not
of course that all Tooks had much of this wayward quality, their
mothers being Chubbs, Hornblowers, Bolgers, Bracegirdles,
Grubbs and what not; but Tooks were on the whole the most
jocular and unexpected of Hobbits. Also I can tell you something
more, in case you have not guessed: Bingo had no money or

jewelry left! Practically none, that is. Nothing worth digging up a nice hobbit-hole for. Money went a prodigious way in those days, and one could get quite a lot of things without it; but he had blown his last 500 ducats on the birthday party. That was Brandybuck-some of him. After that he had nothing left but the buttons on his waistcoat, a small bag-purse of silver, and his ring. In the course of 33 years he had contrived to spend all the rest – what was left, that is, by his father, who had done a bit of spending in fifty years[9] (and had required some travelling-expenses).

Well, there it is. All things come to an end. Evening came on. Bag-end was left empty and gloomy. People went away – haggling and arguing, most of them. You could hear their voices coming up the Hill in the dusk. Very few gave a thought to Bingo. They decided he had gone mad, and run off, and that was one Baggins the less, and that was that. They were annoyed about the legend-ary money, of course, but meanwhile there was tea waiting for them. There were some, of course, who regretted his sudden disappearance – a few of his younger friends were really dis-tressed. But not all of them had said good-bye to him. That is easily explained, and soon will be.

Bingo stepped out of the cupboard. It was getting dim. His watch said six. The door was open, as he had kept the key in his pocket. He went out, locked the door (leaving the key), and looked at the sky. Stars were coming out.

'It is going to be a fine night,' he said. 'What a lark! Well, I must not keep them waiting. Now we're off. Goodbye!' He trotted down the garden, jumped the fence, and took to the fields, and passed like an invisible rustle in the grasses.

## NOTES

1  I find it difficult to believe this, yet if it is not so the coincidence is strange. If Bingo Baggins did get his name from this source, I can only suppose that the demonic character (composed of monomaniac religious despotism and a lust for destruction through high explosive) of the chief Bingo (not to mention that of his appalling wife), by which my sister and I now remember them, developed somewhat later.

2  The substitution was not made in the first draft, but in pencilled corrections to the end of the second version (p. 27).

3  The change of 'fifty-fifth' to 'seventy-second' was made at the same time as the 16 years during which Bingo lived at Bag End after his

parents' departure were changed to 33 (note 6). These changes were made before the chapter was finished, since later in it, in Bingo's farewell speech, the revised figures are present from the first writing. When at the outset he wrote 'fifty-fifth birthday' and '16 years' my father was presumably intending to get rid of the idea, appearing in rewriting of the second version (see p. 27), that the number of 144 guests was chosen for an inner reason, since on Bingo's 55th birthday his father Bilbo would have been 127 (having left the Shire 16 years before at the age of 111, when Bingo was 39).

4   *Primula* was first written *Amalda*. In the first version (p. 16) Amalda was the name of Mrs Sackville-Baggins. In the fourth version of 'A long-expected party', when Bilbo had returned to his bachelor state, Primula Brandybuck, no longer his wife, remained Bingo's mother.

5   My father first wrote here: 'the Brandybucks of Wood Eaton on the other side of the shire, on the edge of Buckwood – a dubious region.' He first changed (certainly at the time of writing) the name of the Brandybuck stronghold from Wood Eaton (a village in the Cherwell valley near Oxford) to Bury Underwood (where 'Bury' is the very common English place-name element derived from Old English *byrig*, the dative of *burg* 'fortified place, town'); then he introduced the name of the river, replaced Bury Underwood by Buckland, and replaced Buckwood by the Old Forest.

6   This change was made at the same time as '55' to '72' for Bingo's years at the time of the birthday party; see note 3.

7   This is the first appearance of Gaffer Gamgee, living in Bagshot Row (first mentioned in the second version, p. 21).

8   As mentioned in note 3, the later figure of 72 for 55 as Bingo's age on this birthday, and 33 for 16 as the number of years in which he lived on alone at Bag End after Bilbo's departure, which appear as emendations in the early part of the text, are in the later part of the chapter present from the first writing.

9   One would expect 'sixty' (111 less 51): see pp. 31, 252.


## Note on Hobbit-names

It will be seen that delight in the names and relations of the hobbit-families of the Shire from which the ramifying genealogies would spring was present from the start. In no respect did my father chop and change more copiously. Already we have met, apart from Bilbo and Bungo Baggins and Belladonna Took who appeared in *The Hobbit*:

*Baggins:* Angelica; Inigo; Semolina
*Bolger:* Caramella (replacing Caramella Took)
*Bracegirdle:* Hugo
*Brandybuck:* Amalda > Primula; Marmaduke; Orlando > Prospero; Rory

*Burrowes:* Folco; Orlando (replacing Orlando Grubb)
*Chubb:* Cosimo
*Grubb:* Gorboduc > Orlando; Iago
*Grubb-Took:* Inigo
*Proudfoot:* Sancho
*Sackville-Baggins:* Amalda > Lonicera or Griselda > Grimalda >
    Lobelia; Sago > Cosmo > Otho
*Took:* Caramella; Melba > Arabella > Amanda; Mungo
*Took-Took:* Obo > Rollo

★

(iv)

## The Fourth Version

Two further changes, embodying an important shift, were made to the
manuscript of the third version. They were carefully made, in red ink,
but concomitant changes later in the text were not made. In the first
sentence of the chapter (p. 28) 'Bingo, son of Bilbo' was altered to 'Bingo
Bolger-Baggins'; and in the third sentence 'Bingo's father' was altered to
'Bingo's uncle (and guardian), Bilbo Baggins.'

We come now therefore to a further stage, where the 'long-expected
party' is still Bingo's, not Bilbo's, but Bingo is his nephew, not his son,
and Bilbo's marriage (as was inevitable, I think) has been rejected.

The fourth version is a typescript, made by my father. It was emended
very heavily later on, but these changes belong to the second phase of the
writing of *The Fellowship of the Ring,* and here I ignore them. The
alterations to the third version just referred to were now incorporated
into the text (which therefore now begins: 'When Bingo Bolger-Baggins
of the well-known Baggins family prepared to celebrate his seventy-
second birthday . . .'), but otherwise it proceeds as an exact copy of the
third version as far as 'he was on visiting terms with all his neighbours
and relatives (except, of course, the Sackville-Bagginses)' (p. 29). Here it
diverges.

But folk did not bother him much. He was frequently out. And if
he was in, you never knew who you would find with him: hobbits
of quite poor families, or folk from distant villages, dwarves, and
even sometimes elves.

He did two more things that caused tongues to wag. At the age
of ninety-nine he adopted his nephew – or to be accurate (Bilbo
scattered the titles nephew and niece about rather recklessly) his
first cousin once removed, Bingo Bolger, a lad of twenty-seven.
They had heard very little about him, and that not too good (they

said). As a matter of fact Bingo was the son of Primula Brandybuck (and Rollo Bolger, who was quite unimportant); and she was
the daughter of Mirabella Took (and Gorboduc Brandybuck, who
was rather important); and she was one of three remarkable
daughters of the Old Took, for long the head of the hobbits who
lived across The Water. And so the Tooks come in again – always a
disturbing element, especially when mixed with Brandybuck. For
Primula was a Brandybuck of Buckland, across the Brandywine
River, on the other side of the Shire and at the edge of the Old
Forest – a dubious region. Folk in Hobbiton did not know much
about it, or about the Brandybucks either; though some had heard
it said that they were rich, and would have been richer, if they had
not been reckless. What had happened to Primula and her husband was not known for certain in Hobbiton. There was rumour
of a boating accident on the Brandywine River – the sort of thing
that Brandybucks would go in for. Some said that Rollo Bolger
had died young of overeating; others said that it was his weight
that had sunk the boat.

Anyway, Bilbo Baggins adopted Master Bolger, announced
that he would make him his heir, changed his name to Bolger-
Baggins, and still further offended the Sackville-Bagginses. Then
shortly before his hundred-and-eleventh birthday Bilbo disappeared finally and was never seen in Hobbiton again. His relatives
and neighbours lost the chance of a funeral, and they had a good
deal to say. But it made no difference: Bilbo's residence, his
wealth, his position (and the dubious regard of the more influen-
tial hobbits), were inherited by Bingo Bolger-Baggins.

Bingo was a mere youngster of thirty-nine and had hardly cut
his wisdom-teeth; but he at once began to carry on his uncle's
reputation for oddity. He refused to go into mourning, and within
a week gave a birthday-party – for himself and his uncle (their
birthdays happened to be on the same day). At first people were
shocked, but he kept up the custom year after year, until they got
used to it. He said he did not think Bilbo Baggins was dead. When
they asked the obvious question: 'Where is he then?' he merely
winked. He lived alone, and was often away from home. He went
about a good deal with the least well-behaved members of the
Took family (his grandmother's people); and he was also fond of
the Brandybucks (his mother's relatives).

Anyway, Bingo Bolger-Baggins had been the master of Bag-end
Underhill now for thirty-three years without doing anything
outrageous. His parties were sometimes a bit noisy . . .

With Gorboduc Brandybuck and Mirabella Took (one of 'the three remarkable daughters of the Old Took' who had been mentioned in *The Hobbit*) the genealogy now becomes that of LR, except that Primula Brandybuck's husband (Bilbo in the third version) is Rollo Bolger, not Drogo Baggins; and the boating accident reappears (see p. 25, note 2).

From here to the end the typescript follows the third version (as emended) very closely, and there is little further to add. Bilbo becomes Bingo's 'uncle' throughout, of course; Bingo was liable to allude to 'the absurd adventures of his "gallant and famous" uncle' (see p. 32). But, with this change, Bingo's remarks in his speech on the ages of himself and his uncle and the number of guests at the party remain exactly the same, and 'The ring was his uncle's parting.gift' (*ibid.*).

Small changes of wording move the text towards the final form in FR; for example, where in the third version Rory Brandybuck is described as 'well-filled but still brighter than many', it is now said of him that his 'wits neither old age, nor surprise, nor an enormous dinner, had quite clouded'. But to set out even a portion of such developments in expression between closely related versions would obviously be quite impracticable. There are however a few minor narrative shifts which I collect in the following notes, with page-references indicating where the relevant passages in earlier versions are to be found.

(30)   Gaffer Gamgee had a little more to say:

'. . . A very nice well-spoken gentlehobbit is Mr Bolger-Baggins, as I've always said.' And that was perfectly true; for Bingo had always been very polite to Gaffer Gamgee, calling him Mr Gamgee, and discussing potatoes with him over the hedge.

(21, 31)   The day of the party now becomes Thursday (not Saturday) 22 September (a change made to the typescript, but carefully over an erasure and clearly belonging to the time of typing).

(31)   There is no further reference to Gandalf in the chapter, after the fireworks.

(24, 32)   The young hobbits who danced on the table are Prospero Took and Melissa Brandybuck.

(32–3)   Several names are changed among the recipients of gifts from Bag End, Caramella (Took >) Bolger becomes Caramella Chubb; the comatose Rollo Took-Took becomes Fosco Bolger (and is Bingo's uncle); Inigo Grubb-Took the glutton, who had survived from the first draft, is now Inigo Grubb; and Cosimo Chubb the barometer-tapper becomes Cosimo Hornblower.

(33)   It is now added that 'The poorer hobbits did very well, especially old Gaffer Gamgee, who got about half a ton of potatoes'; that Bingo had a collection of *magical* toys; and that he and his friends drank

nearly all the wine, the remainder still going to Marmaduke Brandybuck.

(16, 33)    The legal notice in the hall at Bag End is extended, and followed by a new passage:

> *Bingo Bolger-Baggins Esqre. departing hereby devises delivers and
> makes over by free gift the desirable property and messuage or
> dwelling-hole known as Bag-end Underhill with all lands thereto
> belonging and annexed to Otho Sackville-Baggins Esqre. and his
> wife Lobelia for them jointly to have hold possess occupy let on lease
> or otherwise dispose of at their pleasure as from September the
> twenty fourth in the seventy second year of the aforesaid Bingo
> Bolger-Baggins and the one hundred and forty fourth year of Bilbo
> Baggins who as former rightful owners hereby relinquish all claims to
> the abovesaid property as from the date aforesaid.*

The notice was signed *Bingo Bolger-Baggins for self and uncle*.
Bingo was not a lawyer, and he merely put things that way to please
Otho Sackville-Baggins, who was a lawyer. Otho certainly was
pleased, but whether by the language or the property is difficult to
say. Anyway, as soon as he had read the notice he shouted: 'Ours at
last!' So I suppose it was all right, at least according to the legal
notions of hobbits. And that is how the Sackville-Bagginses got Bag-
end in the end, though they had to wait ninety-three years longer for
it than they had once expected.

(33)    The lawyers who ejected Sancho Proudfoot do not appear.

An addition is made to the passage describing the character of the
Tooks: and since they had inherited both enormous wealth and no
little courage from the Old Took, they carried things off with a pretty
high hand at times.'

(34)    The reference to Bilbo's having 'done a bit of spending in fifty
years' was changed; the text now reads: '– what was left him by his
Uncle, that is; for Bilbo had done a bit of spending in his time.'

'A few were distressed at his sudden disappearance; one or two were
not distressed, because they were in the know – but they were not at
Bag-end.'

Thus it is never explained why Bingo (or Bilbo in the first version), for
whom money was now a severe problem (and one of the reasons for his
departure), simply handed over 'the desirable property known as Bag-
end' to the Sackville-Bagginses 'by free gift'.

There were further twists still to come in this amazingly sinuous
evolution before the final structure was reached, but this was how
the opening chapter stood for some time, and Bingo Bolger-Baggins,
'nephew' or more properly first cousin once removed of Bilbo Baggins,

is present throughout the original form of Book I of *The Fellowship of the Ring*. I set out briefly here the major shifts and stages encountered thus far.

### A Long-expected party

Version I    *Bilbo gives the party, aged* 70. ('I am going to tell you a story about one of his descendants')

Version II    *Bilbo gives the party, aged* 71.

Version III    Bilbo married, and disappeared from Hobbiton with his wife (Primula Brandybuck) when he was 111.
*His son Bingo Baggins gives the party, aged* 72.

Version IV    Bilbo, unmarried, adopted his young cousin Bingo Bolger (son of Primula Brandybuck), changed his name to Bingo Bolger-Baggins, and disappeared from Hobbiton when he was 111.
*His adopted cousin Bingo Bolger-Baggins gives the party, aged* 72.

### (v)

### 'The Tale that is Brewing'

It was to the fourth version (writing on the typescript shows that it went to Allen and Unwin) that my father referred in a letter to Charles Furth on 1 February 1938, six weeks after he began the new book:

> Would you ask Mr Unwin whether his son [Rayner Unwin, then twelve years old], a very reliable critic, would care to read the first chapter of the sequel to *The Hobbit*? I have typed it. I have no confidence in it, but if he thought it a promising beginning, could add to it the tale that is brewing.

What was 'the tale that is brewing'? The texts of 'A Long-expected Party' provide no clues, except that the end of the third version (p. 34) makes it clear that when Bingo left Bag End he was going to meet, and go off with, some of his younger friends – and this is hinted at already at the end of the first draft (p. 17); in the fourth version this is repeated, and 'one or two' of his friends were 'in the know' – and 'they were not at Bag-end' (p. 39). Of course it is clear, too, that Bilbo is not dead; and (with knowledge of what was in fact to come) we may count the references to Buckland and the Old Forest (pp. 29, 37) as further hints.

But there are some jottings from this time, written on two sides of a single sheet of paper, that do give some inkling of what was 'brewing'. The first of these reads:

Bilbo goes off with 3 Took nephews: Odo, Frodo, and Drogo [*changed to* Odo, Drogo, and Frodo]. He has only a small bag of money. They walk all night – East. Adventures: troll-like: witch-house on way to Rivendell. Elrond again [*added*: (by advice of Gandalf?)]. A tale in Elrond's house.

Where is G[andalf] asks Odo – said I was old and foolish enough now to take care of myself said B. But I dare say he will turn up, he is apt to.

There follows a note to the effect that while Odo believed no more than a quarter of 'B.'s stories', Drogo was less sceptical, and Frodo believed them 'almost completely'. The character of this last nephew was early established, though he was destined to disappear (see p. 70): he is *not* the forerunner of Frodo in LR. All this seems to have been written at one time. On the face of it, it must belong with the second (unfinished) version of 'A Long-expected Party', since it is Bilbo who 'goes off' (afterwards my father bracketed the words 'Bilbo goes off with 3 Took nephews' and wrote 'Bingo' above). The implication is presumably that when Bilbo set out with his nephews Gandalf was no longer present.

Then follows, in pencil: 'Make return of ring a motive.' This no doubt refers to the statement in the third version that 'The ring was his [Bingo's] father's parting gift' (p. 32).

After a note suggesting the coming of a dragon to Hobbiton and a more heroic rôle for hobbits, a suggestion rejected with a pencilled 'No', there follows, apparently all written at one time (but with a later pencilled heading 'Conversation of Bingo and Bilbo'):

'No one,' said B., 'can escape quite unscathed from dragons. The only thing is to shun them (if you can) like the Hobbitonians, though not nec[essarily] to disbelieve in them (or refuse to remember them) like the H[obbitonians]. Now I have spent all my money which seemed once to me too much and my own has gone after it [*sic*]. And I don't like being without after [?having] – in fact I am being lured. Well, well, twice one is not always two, as my father used to say. But at any rate I think I would rather wander as a poor man that sit and shiver. And Hobbiton rather grows on you in 20 years, don't you think; grows too heavy to bear, I mean. Anyway, we are off – and it's autumn. I enjoy autumn wandering.'

Asks Elrond what he can do to heal his money-wish and unsettlement. Elrond tells him of an island. Britain? Far west where the Elves still reign. Journey to perilous isle.

I want to look again on a live dragon.

This is certainly Bilbo, and the passage (though not of course the pencilled heading) precedes the third version, as the reference to '20 years' shows (see pp. 22, 31). – At the foot of the page are these faint pencilled scrawls:

Bingo goes to find his father.

You said you . . . . end your days in contentment – *so I hope to*

The illegible word might possibly be 'want'. – On the reverse of the page is the following coherent passage in ink:

> *The Ring:* whence its origin. Necromancer? Not very dangerous, when used for good purpose. But it exacts its penalty. You must either lose it, or *yourself.* Bilbo could not bring himself to lose it. He starts on a holiday [*struck out:* with his wife] handing over ring to Bingo. But he vanishes. Bingo worried. Resists desire to go and find him – though he does travel round a lot looking for news. Won't lose ring as he feels it will ultimately bring him to his father.
>
> At last he meets Gandalf. Gandalf's advice. You must stage a *disappearance*, and the ring may then be cheated into letting you follow a similar path. But you have got to *really disappear* and give up the past. Hence the 'party'.
>
> Bingo confides in his friends. Odo, Frodo, and Vigo (?) insist on coming too. Gandalf rather dubious. You will share the same fate as Bingo, he said, if you dare the ring. Look what happened to Primula.

A couple of pencilled changes were made to this: above 'Vigo(?)' my father wrote 'Marmaduke'; and he bracketed the last sentence. – Since Bingo is here Bilbo's son this note belongs with the third version. But the watery death of Primula Brandybuck (no longer Bilbo's wife, but still Bingo's mother) is first recorded in the fourth version (p. 37), and the Ring could not possibly be associated with that event; so that the reference to 'Primula' here must refer to something else of which there is no other trace.

Particularly noteworthy is the suggestion that the idea of the Party arose from Gandalf's advice to Bingo concerning the Ring. It is indeed remarkable that already at this stage, when my father was still working on the opening chapter, so much of the Ring's nature was already present in embryo. – The final two notes are in pencil. The first reads:

> Bilbo goes to Elrond to cure dragon-longing, and settles down in Rivendell. Hence Bingo's frequent absences from home. The dragon-longing comes on Bingo. Also ring-lure.

With Bingo's 'frequent absences from home' cf. 'he was often away from home' in the third version (p. 29), and 'Resists desire to go and find him – though he does travel round a lot looking for news' in the note on the Ring given above. And the last:

> Make dubious regions – Old Forest on way to Rivendell. South of River. They turn aside to call up Frodo Br[andybuck] [*written above:* Marmaduke], get lost and caught by Willowman and by Barrow-wights. T. Bombadil comes in.

'South' was changed from 'North', and 'East' is written in the margin.

On a separate page (in fact on the back of my father's earliest surviving map of the Shire) is a brief 'scheme' that is closely associated with these last notes; at the head of it my father afterwards wrote *Genesis of 'Lord of the Rings'*.

> B.B. sets out with 2 nephews. They turn S[outh]ward to collect Frodo Brandybuck. Get lost in Old Forest. Adventure with Willowman and Barrow-wights. T. Bombadil.
>
> Reach Rivendell and find Bilbo. Bilbo had had a sudden desire to visit the Wild again. But meets Gandalf at Rivendell. Learns about [*sic; here presumably the narrative idea changes*] Gandalf had turned up at Bag-end. Bilbo tells him of desire for Wild and gold. Dragon curse working. He goes to Rivendell between the worlds and settles down.
>
> Ring must eventually go back to Maker, or draw you towards it. Rather a dirty trick handing it on?

It is interesting to see the idea already present that Bingo and his companions would turn aside to 'collect' or 'call up' another hobbit, at first named Frodo Brandybuck, but changed to Marmaduke (Brandybuck). Frodo Brandybuck also appears in initial drafting for the second chapter (p. 45) as one of Bingo's three companions on his departure from Hobbiton. There are various ways of combining all these references to the three (or two) nephews, so as to present a series of successive formulations, but names and rôles were still entirely fluid and ephemeral and no certainty is possible. Only in the first full text of the second chapter does the story become clear (for a time): Bingo set out with two companions, Odo Took and Frodo Took.

It is to be noted that Tom Bombadil, the Willow-man, and the Barrow-wights were already in existence years before my father began *The Lord of the Rings*; see p. 115.

★

On 11 February 1938 Stanley Unwin reported to my father that his son Rayner had read the first chapter and was delighted with it. On 17 February my father wrote to Charles Furth at Allen and Unwin:

> They say it is the first step that costs the effort. I do not find it so. I am sure I could write unlimited 'first chapters'. I have indeed written many. The Hobbit sequel is still where it was, and I have only the vaguest notions of how to proceed. Not ever intending any sequel, I fear I squandered all my favourite 'motifs' and characters on the original 'Hobbit'.

And on the following day he replied to Stanley Unwin:

> I am most grateful to your son Rayner: and am encouraged. At the same time I find it only too easy to write opening chapters – and for the

moment the story is not unfolding. I have unfortunately very little time, made shorter by a rather disastrous Christmas vacation. I squandered so much on the original 'Hobbit' (which was not meant to have a sequel) that it is difficult to find anything new in that world.

But on 4 March 1938, in the course of a long letter to Stanley Unwin on another subject, he said:

The sequel to *The Hobbit* has now progressed as far as the end of the third chapter. But stories tend to get out of hand, and this has taken an unpremeditated turn. Mr Lewis and my youngest boy are reading it in bits as a serial. I hesitate to bother your son, though I should value his criticism. At any rate if he would like to read it in serial form he can.

The 'unpremeditated turn', beyond any doubt, was the appearance of the Black Riders.

# II
# FROM HOBBITON TO THE
# WOODY END

The original manuscript drafts for the second chapter of *The Lord of the Rings* do not constitute a completed narrative, however rough, but rather, disconnected parts of the narrative, in places in more than one version, as the story expanded and changed in the writing. The fact that my father had typed out the first chapter by 1 February 1938 (p. 40), but on 17 February wrote (p. 43) that while first chapters came easily to him 'the Hobbit sequel is still where it was,' suggests strongly that the original drafting of this second chapter followed the typing of the fourth version of 'A Long-expected Party'.

There followed a typescript text, with a title 'Three's Company and Four's More'; this will be given in full, but before doing so earlier stages of the story (one of them of the utmost interest) must be looked at.

The first rough manuscript begins with Odo and Frodo Took (but Frodo at once changed to Drogo) sitting on a gate at night and talking about the events at Bag End that afternoon, while 'Frodo Brandybuck was sitting on a pile of haversacks and packs and looking at the stars.' Frodo Brandybuck, it seems, was brought in here from the rôle prepared for him in the notes given on pp. 42–3, in one of which he was replaced by Marmaduke (Brandybuck). Bingo, coming up behind silently and invisibly, pushed Odo and Drogo off the gate; and after the ensuing raillery the draft continues:

'Have you three any idea where we are going to?' said Bingo.

'None whatever,' said Frodo, '– if you mean, where we are going to land finally. With such a captain it would be quite impossible to guess that. But we all know where we are making for first.'

'What we don't know,' put in Drogo, 'is how long it is going to take us on foot. Do you? You have usually taken a pony.'

'That is not much faster, though it is less tiring. Let me see – I have never done the journey in a hurry before, and have usually taken five and a half weeks (with plenty of rests). Actually I have *always* had some adventure, milder or less so, every time I have taken the road to Rivendell.'

'Very well,' said Frodo, 'let's put a bit of the way behind us tonight. It is jolly under the stars, and cool.'

'Better turn in soon and make an early start,' said Odo (who was fond of bed). 'We shall do more tomorrow if we begin fresh.'

'I back councillor Frodo,' said Bingo. So they started, shouldering packs, and gripping long sticks. They went very quietly over fields and along hedgerows and the fringes of small coppices until night fell, and in their dark [?green] cloaks they were quite invisible without any rings. And of course being Hobbits they could not be heard – not even by Hobbits. At last Hobbiton was far behind, and the lights in the windows of the last farmhouse were twinkling on a hilltop a long way away. Bingo turned and waved a hand in farewell.

At the bottom of a slight hill they struck the main road East – rolling away pale grey into the darkness, between high hedges and dark wind-stirred trees. Now they marched along two by two; talking a little, occasionally humming, often tramping in time for a mile or so without saying anything. The stars swung overhead, and the night got late.

Odo gave a big yawn and slowed down. 'I am so sleepy,' he said, 'that I shall fall down on the road. What about a place for the night?'

Here the original opening draft ends. Notably, the hobbits are setting out expressly for Rivendell, and Bingo has been there several times before; cf. the note given on p. 42: 'Bilbo . . . settles down in Rivendell. Hence Bingo's frequent absences from home.' But there is no indication, nor has there been any, why they should be in any particular hurry.

It is clear that when the hobbits struck the East Road they took to it and walked eastward along it. At this stage there is no suggestion of a side road to Buckland, nor indeed that Buckland played any part in their plans.

A revised beginning followed. Drogo Took was dropped, leaving Odo and Frodo as Bingo's companions (Frodo now in all probability a Took). The passage concerning Rivendell has gone, and instead the plan to go first 'to pick up Marmaduke' appears. The description of the walk from Hobbiton is now much fuller, and largely reaches the form in the typescript text (p. 50); it is interesting to observe here the point of emergence of the road to Buckland:

After a rest on a bank under some thinly clad birches they went on again, until they struck a narrow road. It went rolling away, pale grey in the dark, up and down – but all the time gently climbing southward. It was the road to Buckland, climbing away from the main East Road in the Water Valley, and winding away past the skirts of the Green Hills towards the south-east corner of the Shire, the Wood-end as the Hobbits called it. They marched along it, until it plunged between high hedges and dark trees rustling their dry leaves gently in the night airs.

Comparison of this with the description of the East Road in the first draft ('rolling away pale grey into the darkness, between high hedges and dark wind-stirred trees') shows that the one was derived from the other. Perhaps as a result, the crossing of the East Road is omitted; it is merely said that the Buckland road diverged from it (contrast FR p. 80).

After Odo's words (typescript text p. 50) 'Or are you fellows going to sleep on your legs?' there follows:

> *The Road goes ever on and on*
> *down from the Door where it began:*
> *before us far the Road has gone,*
> *and we come after it, who can;*
> *pursuing it with weary feet,*
> *until it joins some larger way,*
> *where many paths and errands meet,*
> *and whither then? – we cannot say.*

There is no indication, in the manuscript as written, who spoke the verse (for which there is also a good deal of rough working); in the typescript text (pp. 52–3) it is given to Frodo and displaced to a later point in the story.

The second draft then jumps to the following day, and takes up in the middle of a sentence:

. . . on the flat among tall trees growing in scattered fashion in the grasslands, when Frodo said: 'I can hear a horse coming along the road behind!'

They looked back, but the windings of the road hid the traveller.

'I think we had better get out of sight,' said Bingo; 'or you fellows at any rate. Of course it doesn't matter very much, but I would rather not be met by anyone we know.'

They [*written above at the same time:* Odo & F.] ran quickly to the left down into a little hollow beside the road, and lay flat. Bingo slipped on his ring and sat down a few yards from the track. The sound of hoofs drew nearer. Round a turn came a white horse, and on it sat a bundle – or that is what it looked like: a small man wrapped entirely in a great cloak and hood so that only his eyes peered out, and his boots in the stirrups below.

The horse stopped when it came level with Bingo. The figure uncovered its nose and sniffed; and then sat silent as if listening. Suddenly a laugh came from inside the hood.

'Bingo my boy!' said Gandalf, throwing aside his wrappings.

'You and your lads are somewhere about. Come along now and
show up, I want a word with you!' He turned his horse and rode
straight to the hollow where Odo and Frodo lay. 'Hullo! hullo!' he
said. 'Tired already? Aren't you going any further today?'

At that moment Bingo reappeared again. 'Well I'm blest,' said
he. 'What are you doing along this way, Gandalf? I thought you
had gone back with the elves and dwarves. And how did you know
where we were?'

'Easy,' said Gandalf. 'No magic. I saw you from the top of the
hill, and knew how far ahead you were. As soon as I turned the
corner and saw the straight piece in front was empty I knew you
had turned aside somewhere about here. And you have made a
track in the long grass that I can see, at any rate when I am looking
for it.'

Here this draft stops, at the foot of a page, and if my father continued
beyond this point the manuscript is lost; but I think it far more likely that
he abandoned it because he abandoned the idea that the rider was
Gandalf as soon as written. It is most curious to see how directly the
description of Gandalf led into that of the Black Rider – and that the
original sniff was Gandalf's! In fact the conversion of the one to the
other was first carried out by pencilled changes on the draft text, thus:

Round a turn came a white [> black] horse, and on it sat a bundle – or
that is what it looked like: a small [> short] man wrapped entirely in a
great [*added:* black] cloak and hood so that only his eyes peered out [>
so that his face was entirely shadowed] . . .

If the description of Gandalf in the draft is compared with that of the
Black Rider in the typescript text (p. 54) it will be seen that with further
refinement the one still remains very closely based on the other. The new
turn in the story was indeed 'unpremeditated' (p. 44).

Further rough drafting begins again with the workings for the song
*Upon the hearth the fire is red* and continues through the second
appearance of the Black Rider and the coming of the Elves to the end of
the chapter. This material was followed very closely indeed in the
typescript text and need not be further considered (one or two minor
points of interest in the development of the narrative are mentioned in
the Notes). There is however a separate section in manuscript which was
not taken up into the typescript, and this very interesting passage will be
given separately (see p. 73).

I give here the typescript text – which became an extremely complex
and now very battered document. It is clear that as soon as, or before, he
had finished it my father began revising it, in some cases retyping pages
(the rejected pages being retained), and also writing in many other
changes here and there, most of these being very minor alterations of

wording.[1] In the text that follows I take up all these revisions silently, but some earlier readings of interest are detailed in the Notes at the end of it (pp. 65 ff.).

## II

### *Three's Company and Four's More*[2]

Odo Took was sitting on a gate whistling softly. His cousin Frodo was lying on the ground beside a pile of packs and haversacks, looking up at the stars, and sniffing the cool air of the autumn twilight.

'I hope Bingo has not got locked up in the cupboard, or something,' said Odo. 'He's late: it's after six.'

'There's no need to worry,' said Frodo. 'He'll turn up when he thinks fit. He may have thought of some last irresistible joke, or something: he's very Brandybucksome. But he'll come all right; quite reliable in the long run is Uncle Bingo.'

There was a chuckle behind him. 'I'm glad to hear it,' said Bingo suddenly becoming visible; 'for this is going to be a very Long Run. Well, you fellows, are you quite ready to depart?'

'It's not fair sneaking up with that ring on,' said Odo. 'One day you will hear what *I* think of you, and you won't be so glad.'

'I know already,' said Bingo laughing, 'and yet I remain quite cheerful. Where's my pack and stick?'

'Here you are!' said Frodo jumping up. 'This is your little lot: pack, bag, cloak, stick.'

'I'm sure you have given me all the heaviest stuff,' puffed Bingo, struggling into the straps. He was a bit on the stout side.

'Now then!' said Odo. 'Don't start being Bolger-like. There's nothing there, except what you told us to pack. You'll feel the weight less, when you have walked off a bit of your own.'

'Be kind to a poor ruined hobbit!' laughed Bingo. 'I shall be thin as a willow-wand, I'm sure, before a week is out. But now what about it? Let's have a council! What shall we do first?'

'I thought that was settled,' said Odo. 'Surely we have got to pick up Marmaduke first of all?'

'O yes! I didn't mean that,' said Bingo. 'I meant: what about this evening? Shall we walk a little or a lot? All night or not at all?'

'We'd better find some snug corner in a haystack, or somewhere, and turn in soon,' said Odo. 'We shall do more tomorrow, if we start fresh.'

'Let's put a bit of the road behind us to-night,' said Frodo. 'I want to get away from Hobbiton. Beside it's jolly under the stars, and cool.'

'I vote for Frodo,' said Bingo. And so they started, shouldering their packs, and swinging their stout sticks. They went very quietly over fields and along hedgerows and the borders of coppices, until night fell. In their dark grey cloaks they were invisible without the help of any magic rings, and since they were all hobbits, they made no noise that even hobbits could hear (or indeed even wild creatures in the woods and fields).

After some time they crossed The Water, west of Hobbiton, where it was no more than a winding ribbon of black, lined with leaning alders. They were now in Tookland; and they began to climb into the Green Hill Country south of Hobbiton.[3] They could see the village twinkling away down in the gentle valley of The Water. Soon it disappeared in the folds of the darkened land, and was followed by Bywater beside its grey pool. When the light of the last farmhouse was far behind, peeping out of the trees, Bingo turned and waved a hand in farewell.

'Now we're really off,' he said. 'I wonder if we shall ever look down into that valley again.'

After they had walked for about two hours they rested. The night was clear, cool, and starry, but smoky wisps of mist were creeping up the hills from the streams and deep meadows. Thin-clad birches swaying in a cold breeze above their heads made a black net against the pale sky. They ate a very frugal supper (for hobbits), and then went on again. Odo was reluctant, but the rest of the council pointed out that this bare hillside was no place for passing the night. Soon they struck a narrow road. It went rolling up and down until it faded grey into the gathering dark. It was the road to Buckland, climbing away from the main East Road in the Water-valley, and winding over the skirts of the Green Hills towards the south-eastern corner of the Shire, the Woody End as the hobbits called it. Not many of them lived in that part.

Along this road they marched. Soon it plunged into a deeply cloven track between tall trees that rustled their dry leaves in the night. It was very dark. At first they talked, or hummed a tune softly together: then they marched on in silence, and Odo began to lag behind. At last he stopped, and gave a big yawn.

'I am so sleepy,' he said, 'that soon I shall fall down on the road. What about a place for the night? Or are you fellows going to sleep on your legs?'[4]

'When does Marmaduke expect us?' asked Frodo. 'Tomorrow
night?'

'No,' said Bingo. 'We should not get there by tomorrow night,
even with a forced march, unless we went on many more miles
now. And I must say I don't feel like it. It is getting on for
midnight already. But it is all right. I told Marmaduke to expect us
the night after tomorrow; so there is no hurry.'

'The wind's in the West,' said Odo. 'If we go down the other
side of this hill we are climbing, we ought to find a spot fairly dry
and sheltered.'

At the top of the hill over which the road ran they came upon a
patch of fir-wood, dry and resin-scented. Leaving the road they
went into the deep darkness of the wood, and gathered dead sticks
and cones to make a fire. Soon they had a merry crackle of flame at
the foot of a great fir, and sat round it for a while, until they began
to nod with sleep. Then each in an angle of the great tree's roots
they curled up in their cloaks and blankets, and were soon fast
asleep.

There was no danger: for they were still in the Shire. A few
creatures came and looked at them, when the fire had died away. A
fox passing through the wood on business of his own stopped
several minutes and sniffed. 'Hobbits!' he thought. 'Well, what
next? I have heard a good many tales of queer goings on in this
Shire; but I have never heard of a hobbit sleeping out of doors
under a tree! Three of them! There's something mighty queer
behind this.' He was quite right, but he never found out any more
about it.

The morning came rather pale and clammy. Bingo woke up
first, and found that a tree-root had made a hole in his back and
that his neck was stiff. It did not seem such a lark as it had the day
before. 'Why on earth did I give that beautiful feather-bed to that
old pudding Fosco?'[5] he thought. 'The tree-roots would have been
much better for him.' 'Wake up, hobbits!' he cried. 'It's a beautiful
morning!'

'What's beautiful about it?' said Odo, peering over the edge of
his blanket with one eye. 'Have you got the bath-water hot? Get
breakfast ready for half past nine.'

Bingo stripped the blanket off him, and rolled him over on top
of Frodo; and then he left them scuffling and walked to the edge of
the wood. Away eastward the sun was rising red out of the mists
that lay thick on the world. Touched with gold and red the
autumn trees in the distance seemed to be sailing rootless in a

shadowy sea. A little below him to the left the road plunged down
into a hollow between two slopes and vanished.

When he got back the other two had got a good fire going.
'Water!' they shouted. 'Where's the water?'

'I don't keep water in my pockets,' said Bingo.

'I thought you had gone to find some,' said Odo. 'You had better
go now.'

'Why?' asked Bingo. 'We had enough left for breakfast last
night; or I thought we had.'

'Well, you thought wrong,' said Frodo. 'Odo drank the last
drop, I saw him.'

'Then he can go and find some more, and not put it on Uncle
Bingo. There's a stream at the foot of the slope; the road crosses it
just below where we turned aside last night.'

In the end, of course, they all went with their water-bottles and
the small kettle they had brought with them. They filled them in
the stream where it fell a foot or two over a small outcrop of grey
stone in its path. The water was icy cold; and Odo spluttered as he
bathed his face and hands. Luckily hobbits grow no beards (and
would not shave if they did).

By the time their breakfast was over, and their packs all trussed
up again, it was ten o'clock at least, and beginning to turn into a
day even finer and hotter than the day of Bingo's birthday, that
already seemed quite a long while past. They went down the
slope, across the stream, and up the next slope, and by that time
their cloaks, blankets, water, food, spare clothes and other gear
already seemed a heavy load. The day's march was going to be
something quite different from a country walk.

After a time the road ceased to roll up and down: it climbed to
the top of a steep bank in a tired zigzagging sort of way, and then
prepared to go down for the last time. In front of them they saw
the lower lands dotted with small clumps of trees that melted away
in the distance to a hazy woodland brown. They were looking
across the Woody End towards the Brandywine River. The road
wound away before them like a piece of string.

'The road goes on for ever,' said Odo, 'but I can't without a rest.
It is high time for lunch.'

Frodo sat down on the bank at the side of the road and looked
away east into the haze, beyond which lay the River and the end of
the Shire in which he had spent all his life. Suddenly he spoke, as
if half to himself:

*The Road goes ever on and on*
*Down from the door where it began.*
*Now far ahead the Road has gone,*
*And we must follow if we can,*
*Pursuing it with weary feet,*
*Until it joins some larger way,*
*Where many paths and errands meet.*
*And whither then? We cannot say.*[6]

'That sounds like a bit of Old Bilbo's rhyming,' said Odo. 'Or is it one of Bingo's imitations? It does not sound altogether encouraging.'

'No, *I* made it up, or at any rate it came to me,' said Frodo.

'I've never heard it before, certainly,' said Bingo. 'But it reminds me very much of Bilbo in the last years, before he went away. He used often to say that there was only one Road in all the land; that it was like a great river: its springs were at every doorstep, and every path was its tributary. "It's a dangerous business, Bingo, going out of your door," he used to say. "You step into the Road, and if you don't keep your feet, there is no knowing where you might get swept off to. Do you realize that this is the very path that goes through Mirkwood, and that if you let it, it might take you to even farther and worse places than the Lonely Mountain?" He used to say that on the path outside the front-door at Bag-end, especially after he had been out for a walk.'

'Well, the Road won't sweep me anywhere for an hour at least,' said Odo, unslinging his pack. The others followed his example, putting their packs against the bank and their legs out into the road. After a rest they had lunch (a frugal one) and then more rest.

The sun was beginning to get lower and the light of afternoon was on the land as they went down the hill. So far they had not met a soul on the road. This way was not much used, and the ordinary way to Buckland was along the East Road to the meeting of the Water and the Brandywine River, where there was a bridge, and then south along the River. They had been jogging along again for an hour or more, when Frodo stopped a moment as if listening. They were now on level ground, and the road, after much winding, lay straight ahead through grassland sprinkled with tall trees, outliers of the approaching woods.

'I can hear a horse or a pony coming along the road behind,' said Frodo.

They looked back, but the turn of the road prevented them from seeing far.

'I think we had better get out of sight,' said Bingo; 'or you two at any rate. Of course, it does not matter much, but I have a feeling that I would rather not be seen by anyone just now.'

Odo and Frodo ran quickly to the left, down into a little hollow not far from the road, and lay flat. Bingo slipped on his ring and stepped behind a tree. The sound of hoofs drew nearer. Round the turn came a black horse, no hobbit-pony but a full-sized horse; and on it sat a bundle, or that is what it looked like: a broad squat man, completely wrapped in a great black cloak and hood, so that only his boots in the stirrups showed below: his face was shadowed and invisible.

When it came on a level with Bingo, the horse stopped. The riding figure sat quite still, as if listening. From inside the hood came a noise as of someone sniffing to catch an elusive scent; the head turned from side to side of the road. At last the horse moved on again, walking slowly at first, and then taking to a gentle trot.

Bingo slipped to the edge of the road and watched the rider, until he dwindled in the distance. He could not be quite sure, but it seemed to him that suddenly, before they passed out of sight, the horse and rider turned aside and rode into the trees.

'Well, I call that very queer, and even a little disturbing,' said Bingo to himself, as he walked back to his companions. They had remained flat in the grass, and had seen nothing; so Bingo described to them the rider and his strange behaviour. 'I can't say why, but I felt perfectly certain he was looking or *smelling* for me: and also I felt very clearly that I did not want him to discover me. I've never seen or felt anything quite like it in the Shire before.'

'But what has one of the Big People got to do with us?' said Odo. 'And what is he doing in this part of the world at all? Except for those Men from Dale the other day[7] I haven't seen one of that Kind in our Shire for years.'[8]

'I have though,' said Frodo, who had listened intently to Bingo's description of the black rider. 'It reminds me of something I had almost forgotten. I was walking away up in the North Moor – you know, right up on the northern borders of the Shire – early last spring, when a similar rider met me. He was riding south, and he stopped and spoke, though he did not seem able to speak our language very well; he asked me if I knew where a place called Hobbiton was, and if there were any folk called Baggins there. I thought it very queer at the time; and I had a queer uncomfortable feeling, too. I could not see any face under his hood. I never heard whether he turned up in Hobbiton or not. If I did not tell you, I meant to.'

'You didn't tell me, and I wish you had,' said Bingo. 'I should have asked Gandalf about it; and probably we should have taken more care on the road.'

'Then you know or guess something about the rider?' said Frodo. 'What is he?'

'I don't know, and I don't want to guess,' said Bingo. 'But somehow I don't believe either of these riders (if there are two) was really one of the Big People, not one of the kind like Dale-men, I mean. I wish Gandalf was here; but now it will be a long time before we find him. In a way I suppose I ought to be pleased; but I am not quite prepared for adventures yet, and I was not expecting any in our own Shire. Do you two wish to go on with the Journey?'

'Of course!' said Frodo. 'I am not going to turn back, not for an army of goblins.'

'I shall go where Uncle Bingo goes,' said Odo. 'But what is the next thing to do? Shall we go on at once, or stay here and have some food?[9] I should like a bite and a sip, but somehow I think we had better move on from here. Your talk of sniffing riders with invisible noses has made me feel quite uncomfortable.'

'I think we will move on now,' said Bingo; 'but not on the road, in case that rider comes back, or another one follows him. We ought to do a good step more today; Buckland is still miles away.'

The shadows of the trees were long and thin on the grass, as they started off again. They now kept a stone's throw to the left of the road, but their going was slow, for the grass was thick and tussocky and the ground uneven. The sun had gone down red behind the hills at their back, and evening was coming on, by the time they had come to the end of the straight stretch. There the road bent southward, and began to wind again as it entered a wood of ancient scattered oak trees.[10]

Close to the road they came on the huge hulk of an aged tree.[11] It was still alive and had leaves on small branches that it had put out round the broken stumps of its long fallen limbs; but it was hollow, and could be entered by a great crack on the far side. The hobbits went in and sat upon the floor of old leaves and decayed wood. There they rested and had a meal, talking quietly and listening in between.

They had just finished and were thinking of setting out again, when they heard quite clearly the sound of hoofs walking slow along the road outside. They did not move. The hoofs stopped, as far as they could judge, on the road beside their tree, but only for a moment. Soon they went on again and faded away – down the road, in the direction of Buckland. When Bingo at last stole out of the tree and peered up and down the road, there was nothing to be seen.

'Most peculiar!' he said, coming back to the others. 'I think we had better wait inside here for a bit.'

It grew almost dark inside the tree-trunk. 'I really think we shall have to go on now,' said Bingo. 'We have done very little to-day and we shan't get to Buckland tomorrow night at this rate.'

Twilight was about them, when they crept out. There was no living sound, not even a bird-call in the wood. The West wind was sighing in the branches. They stepped into the road and looked up and down again.

'We had better risk the road,' said Odo. 'The ground is much too rough off the track, especially in a fading light. We are probably making a fuss about nothing. It is very likely only a wandering stranger who has got lost; and if he met us, he would just ask us the way to Buckland or Brandywine Bridge, and ride on.'

'I hope you are right,' said Bingo. 'But anyway there is nothing for it but the open road. Luckily it winds a good deal.'

'What if he stops us and asks if we know where Mr Bolger-Baggins lives?' said Frodo.

'Give him the true answer: *Nowhere*,' said Bingo. 'Forward!'

They were now entering the Woody End, and the road began to fall gently but steadily, making south-east towards the lowlands of the Brandywine River. A star came out in the darkening East. They went abreast and in step, and their spirits rose; the uncomfortable feeling vanished, and they no longer listened for the sound of hoofs. After a mile or two they began to hum softly, as hobbits have a way of doing when twilight closes in and the stars come out. With most hobbits it is a bed-song or a supper-song; but these hobbits hummed a walking-song (though not, of course, without any mention of bed and supper). Bilbo Baggins had made the words (the tune was as old as the hills), and taught it to Bingo as they walked in the lanes of the Water-valley and talked about Adventure.

*Upon the hearth the fire is red,*
*Beneath the roof there is a bed;*
*But not yet weary are our feet,*
*Still round the corner we may meet*
*A sudden tree or standing stone*
*That none have seen, but we alone.*
*Tree and flower and leaf and grass,*
    *Let them pass! Let them pass!*
*Hill and water under sky,*
    *Pass them by! Pass them by!*

*Still round the corner there may wait*
*A new road or a secret gate,*
*And even if we pass them by,*
*We still shall know which way they lie,*
*And whether hidden pathways run*
*Towards the Moon or to the Sun.*
*Apple, thorn, and nut and sloe,*
    *Let them go! Let them go!*
*Sand and stone and pool and dell,*
    *Fare you well! Fare you well!*

*Home is behind, the world ahead,*
*And there are many paths to tread*
*Through shadow to the edge of night,*
*Until the stars are all alight.*
*Then world behind and home ahead,*
*We'll wander back to fire and bed.*
*Mist and twilight, cloud and shade,*
    *Away shall fade! Away shall fade!*
*Fire and lamp and meat and bread,*
    *And then to bed! And then to bed!*[12]

The song ended. 'And *now* to bed! And *now* to bed!' sang Odo
in a loud voice. 'Hush!' said Frodo. 'I think I hear hoofs again.'

They stopped suddenly, and stood as silent as tree-shadows,
listening. There was a sound of hoofs on the road some way
behind, but coming slow and clear in the stillness of the evening.
Quickly and quietly they slipped off the road and ran into the
deeper shade under the oak-trees.

'Don't let's go too far!' said Bingo. 'I don't want to be seen, but I
want to see what I can this time.'

'Very well!' said Odo; 'but don't forget the sniffing!'

The hoofs drew nearer. They had no time to find any hiding-place[13] better than the general darkness under the trees; so Odo and Frodo lay behind a large tree-trunk, while Bingo slipped on his ring and crept forward a few yards towards the road. It showed grey and pale, a line of fading light through the wood. Above it the stars were now coming out thick in the dim sky, but there was no moon.

The sound of hoofs ceased. As Bingo watched he saw something dark pass across the lighter space between two trees, and then halt. It looked like the black shade of a horse led by a smaller black shadow. The black shadow stood close to the point where they had left the road, and it swayed from side to side. Bingo thought he heard the sound of sniffing. The shadow bent to the ground, and then began to crawl towards him.

At that moment there came a sound like mingled song and laughter. Voices clear and fair rose and fell in the starlit air. The black shadow straightened and retreated.[14] It climbed on to the shadowy horse and seemed to vanish across the road into the darkness on the other side. Bingo breathed again.

'Elves!' said Frodo in an excited whisper behind him. 'Elves! How wonderful! I have always wished to hear elves singing under the stars; but I did not know any lived in the Shire.'

'Oh yes!' said Bingo. 'Old Bilbo knew there were some down in the Woody End. They don't really live here, though; but they often come across the river in spring and autumn. I am very glad they do!'

'Why?' said Odo.

'You didn't see, of course,' said Bingo; 'but that black rider (or another of the same sort) stopped just here and was actually crawling towards us, when the song started. As soon as he heard the voices he slipped away.'

'Did he sniff?' asked Odo.

'He did,' said Bingo. 'It is mysterious, uncomfortably mysterious.'

'Let's find the Elves, if we can,' said Frodo.

'Listen! They are coming this way,' said Bingo. 'We have only to wait by the road.'

The singing drew nearer. One clear voice rose above the others. It seemed to be singing in the secret elf-tongue, of which Bingo knew only a little, and the others knew nothing, yet the sound of the words blending with the tune seemed to turn into words in their own listening thought, which they only partly understood.

Frodo and Bingo afterwards agreed that the song went something
like this:

> Snow-white! Snow-white! O Lady clear!
>    O Queen beyond the Western Seas!
> O Light to us that wander here
>    Amid the world of woven trees!
>
> Gilthoniel! O Elbereth!
>    Clear are thy eyes and cold thy breath!
> Snow-white! Snow-white! We sing to thee
>    In a far land beyond the Sea.
>
> O Stars that in the Sunless Year
>    With shining hand by her were sown,
> In windy fields now bright and clear
>    We see your silver blossom blown!
>
> O Elbereth! Gilthoniel!
>    We still remember, we who dwell
> In this far land beneath the trees,
>    Thy starlight on the Western Seas.[15]

The hobbits sat in shadow by the roadside. Before long the
Elves came down the road towards the valley. They passed slowly
and the hobbits could see the starlight glimmering on their hair
and in their eyes.[16] They bore no lights, yet as they walked a
shimmer, like the light of the moon above the rim of the hills
before it rises, seemed to fall about their feet. They had stopped
singing, and as the last elf passed he turned and looked towards the
hobbits, and laughed.

'Hail Bingo!' he said. 'You are out late – or are you perhaps lost?'
Then he called aloud in the elf-tongue, and all the company
stopped and gathered round.

'Well! Isn't this wonderful!' they said. 'Three hobbits in a wood
at night! What is the meaning of this? We haven't seen anything
like it, since dear Bilbo went away.'

'The meaning of this, my good Elves,' said Bingo, 'is simply
that we seem to be going the same way as you are. I was brought up
by Bilbo, so I like walking, even under the stars. And I can put up
with Elves for lack of other company!'

'But we have no need of other company, and hobbits are so
dull,' they laughed. 'Come along now, tell us all about it! We see

you are simply swelling with secrets we should like to hear.
Though some we know, of course, and some we guess. Many
Happy Returns of yesterday – we have heard all about that, of
course, from the Rivendell people.'[17]

'Then who are you, and who is your lord?' said Bingo.

'I am Gildor,' said the Elf who had hailed him. 'Gildor Inglorion
of the house of Finrod. We are exiles, one of the few companies
that still remain east of the Sea, for our kindred went back to the
West long ago. We are Wise-elves, and the elves of Rivendell are
our kinsfolk.'[18]

'O Wise People,' said Frodo, 'tell us about the Black Rider!'

'The Black Rider!' they said in low voices. 'Why do you ask
about the Black Rider?'

'Because three Black Riders have overtaken us today, or one
three times,'[19] said Bingo; 'and only a few moments ago one
slipped away as you drew near.'

The Elves did not answer at once, but spoke together softly in
the elf-tongue. At last Gildor turned to the hobbits: 'We will not
speak more of this here,' he said. 'We think you had better come
with us. As you know, it is not our custom; but for Bilbo's sake we
will take you on our road, and you shall lodge with us to-night, if
you wish.'

'I thank you indeed, Gildor Inglorion,' said Bingo bowing. 'O
Fair Folk! This is a good fortune beyond my best hope,' said
Frodo. Odo also bowed, but said nothing aloud. 'Rather good
luck?' he whispered to Bingo. 'I suppose we shall get a really good
bed and supper?'

'You can reckon your luck in the morning,' said Gildor, as if he
had been spoken to. 'We shall do what we can, though we have
heard that hobbits are hard to satisfy.'

'I beg your pardon,' stammered Odo. Bingo laughed: 'You
must be careful of Elvish ears, Odo!' 'We count our luck already,'
he said to the Elves; 'and I think that you will find that we are very
easy to please (for hobbits).' He added in the elf-tongue a greeting
that Bilbo had taught him: 'The stars shine on the hour of our
meeting.'

'Be careful, friends!' cried Gildor laughing. 'Speak no secrets!
Here is a scholar in the elf-latin.[20] Bilbo was indeed a good
master! Hail! elf-friend,' he said, bowing to Bingo, 'come now and
join our company![21] You had best walk in the middle, so that you
will not stray. You may be weary before we halt.'

'Why? Where are you going?' asked Bingo.

'To the woods near Woodhall down in the valley. It is some miles; but it will shorten your journey to Buckland to-morrow.'

They marched along in silence, and passed like shadows and faint lights; for both Elves and hobbits could walk when they wished without a sound. They sang no more songs. Odo began to feel sleepy, and stumbled once or twice; but each time a tall elf by his side put out his arm and saved him from a fall.

The woods on either side became denser; the trees were younger and more thick, and as the road went lower there were many deep brakes of hazel. At last they turned right from the road: a green ride lay almost unseen through the thicket. This they followed until they came suddenly to a wide space of grass, grey under the night. The wood bordered it on three sides; but on the east the ground fell steeply, and the tops of the dark trees growing in the fold below were level with their feet. Beyond them the low land lay dim and flat under the stars. Nearer at hand there was a twinkle of lights: the village of Woodhall.

The Elves sat on the grass, and seemed to take no further notice of the hobbits. They spoke together in soft voices. The hobbits wrapped themselves in cloak and blankets, and drowsiness crept over them. The night drew on, and the lights in the valley went out. Odo fell asleep, pillowed on a smooth hillock.

Out of the mists away eastward a pale gold light went up. The yellow moon rose; springing swiftly out of the shadow, and then climbing round and slow into the sky. The Elves all burst into song. Suddenly under the trees to one side a fire sprang up with a red light.

'Come!' the Elves called to the hobbits. 'Come! Now is the time for speech and merriment.'

Odo sat up and rubbed his eyes. He shivered. 'Come, little Odo!' said an elf. 'There is a fire in the hall, and some food for hungry guests.'

On the south side of the green-sward the wood drew close. Here there was a space green-floored, but entirely overshadowed by tall trees. Their trunks ran like pillars down each side, and their interlaced branches made a roof above. In the middle there was a wood-fire blazing; upon the sides of the tree-pillars torches with lights of gold and silver were burning steadily without smoke. The Elves sat round the fire upon the grass or upon the sawn rings of old trunks. Some went to and fro bearing cups and pouring drink;

others brought food on heaped plates and dishes, and set them on the grass.

'This is poor fare,' they said to the hobbits; 'for we are lodging in the greenwood far from our halls. If ever you are our guests at home, we will treat you better.'

'It seems to me good enough for a birthday party,' said Bingo.

Actually it was Odo that ate the least after all. The drink in his cup seemed sweet and fragrant; he drained it, and felt all weariness slip away, and yet sleep came softly down upon him. He was already half wrapped in warm dreams as he ate; and afterwards he could remember nothing more than the taste of bread – yet a bread that was like the best hobbit-bread ever baked (and that was Bread indeed) eaten after a long fast, only this bread was better. Frodo afterwards recalled little of either food or drink, for his mind was filled with the light under the trees, the elf-faces, the sound of voices so various and so beautiful that he felt in a waking dream. But he remembered taking a draught that had the warmth of a golden autumn afternoon and the cool of a clear fountain; and he remembered too the taste of fruits, sweet as wild berries, richer than the tended fruits of hobbit-gardens (and those are fruits indeed).

Bingo sat and ate and drank and talked, and simply remembered having had something of all the foods he liked best; but his mind was chiefly on the talk. He knew something of the elf-tongue, and listened eagerly. Now and again he spoke to those that served him and thanked them in their own language. They smiled on him and said laughing: 'Here is a jewel among hobbits!'[22]

After a while Odo and Frodo fell fast asleep, and were lifted up and borne away to bowers under the trees; they were laid there upon soft beds and slept the night away. But Bingo remained talking with Gildor, the leader of the Elves.[23]

'Why did you choose this moment to set out?' asked Gildor.

'Well, really it chose itself,' answered Bingo. 'I had come to the end of my treasure. It had always held me back from the Journey which half of my heart wished for, ever since Bilbo went away; but now it was gone. So I said to my stay-at-home half: "There is nothing to keep you here. The Journey *might* bring you some more treasure, as it did for old Bilbo; and anyway on the road you will be able to live more easily without any. Of course if you like to stay in Hobbiton and earn your living as a gardener or a carpenter, you can." The stay-at-home half surrendered; it did not want to make other people's chairs or grow other people's potatoes. It was

soft and fat. I think the Journey will do it good. But of course the
other half is not really looking for treasure, but for Adventure –
later rather than sooner. At the moment it also is soft and fat, and
finding walking over the Shire quite enough.'

'Yes!' laughed Gildor. 'You still *look* just like an ordinary
hobbit!'

'I daresay,' said Bingo. 'But my birthday the day before yesterday[24] seems already a long way behind. Still a hobbit I am, and a
hobbit I shall always be.'

'I only said *look*,' replied the Elf. 'You seem to me a most
peculiar hobbit inside, quite as peculiar as Bilbo; and I think
strange things will happen to you and your friends. If you go
looking for Adventure, you usually find as much of it as you can
manage. And it often happens that when you think it is ahead, it
comes on you unexpectedly from behind.'

'So it seems,' said Bingo. 'But I did not expect it ahead or
behind so soon – not in our own Shire.'

'But it is not your Shire alone, nor for ever,' said Gildor. 'The
Wide World is all about it. You can fence yourselves in, but you
have no means of fencing it out.'

'All the same, it is disturbing,' said Bingo. 'I want to get to
Rivendell, if I can – though I hear the road has not grown easier of
late years. Can you tell me anything to guide me or help me?'

'I do not think you will find the road too hard. But if you are
thinking of what you call the Black Rider, that is another matter.
Have you told me all your reasons for leaving secretly? Did
Gandalf tell you nothing?'

'Not even a hint, at least none that I understood. I seldom saw
him after Bilbo went away, twice a year at most. I saw him last
spring, when he turned up unexpectedly one night; and I told him
then of the plan I was beginning to make for the Journey. He
seemed pleased, and told me not to put it off later than the
autumn. He came again to help me with the Party, but we were too
busy then to talk much, and he went off with the dwarves and the
Rivendell elves as soon as the fireworks were over. He did hint that
I might meet him again in Rivendell, and suggested that I should
make for that place first.'

'Not later than the autumn!' said Gildor. 'I wonder. He may all
the same not have known that they were in the Shire; yet he knows
more about them than we do. If he did not tell you any more, I do
not feel inclined to do so, for fear of frightening you from the
Journey. Because I think it is clear that your Journey started none

THE RETURN OF THE SHADOW

too soon; by what seems strange good luck you went just in time. You ought to go on, and not turn back, though you have met adventure, and danger, much sooner than you expected. You ought to go quickly; but you must be careful, and look not only ahead, but also behind, and even perhaps to both sides as well.'

'I wish you would say things plainer,' said Bingo. 'But I am glad to be told that I ought to go on; for that is what I want to do. Only I now rather wonder if I ought to take Odo and Frodo. The original plan was just a Journey, a sort of prolonged (and perhaps permanent) holiday from Hobbiton, and I am sure they did not expect any more adventures for a long time than getting wet and hungry. We had no idea we should be *pursued*.'

'O come! They must have known that if you intend to go wandering out of the Shire into the Wide World, you must be prepared for anything. I cannot see that it makes so much difference, if *something* has turned up rather soon. Are they not willing to go on?'

'Yes, they say so.'

'Then let them go on![25] They are lucky to be your companions: and you are lucky to have them. They are a great protection to you.

'What do you mean?'

'I think the Riders do not know that they are with you, and their presence has confused the scent, and puzzled them.'

'Dear me! It is all very mysterious. It is like solving riddles. But I have always heard that talking to Elves is like that.'

'It is,' laughed Gildor. 'And Elves seldom give advice; but when they do, it is good. I have advised you to go to Rivendell with speed and care. Nothing else that I could tell you would make that advice any better.[26] We have our own business and our own sorrows, and those have little to do with the ways of hobbits or of other creatures. Our paths cross those ways seldom, and mostly by accident. In our meeting there is perhaps something more than accident, yet I do not feel sure that I ought to interfere. But I will add a little more advice: if a Rider finds you or speaks to you, do not answer, and do not name yourself. Also do not again use the ring to escape from his search. I do not know,[27] but I guess that the use of the ring helps them more than you.'

'More and more mysterious!' said Bingo. 'I can't imagine what information would be more frightening than your hints; but I suppose you know best.'

'I do indeed,' said Gildor, 'and I will say no more.'

'Very well!' said Bingo. 'I am now all of a twitter; but I am much obliged to you.'

'Be of good heart!' said Gildor. 'Sleep now! In the morning we shall have gone; but we will send our messages through the land. The wandering Companies shall know of you and your Journey. I name you elf-friend, and wish you well. Seldom have we had such delight in strangers; and it is pleasant to hear words of our own tongue from the lips of other wanderers in the World.'

Bingo felt sleep coming upon him, even as Gildor finished speaking. 'I will sleep now, he said. Gildor led him to a bower beside Odo and Frodo, and he threw himself upon a bed, and fell at once into a dreamless slumber.

## NOTES

1 For emendation of the typescript at this stage my father used black ink. This was fortunate, for otherwise the historical unravelling of the text would be scarcely possible: in a later phase of the work he returned to it and covered it with corrections in blue and red inks, blue chalk and pencil. In one case, however, an addition in black ink belongs demonstrably to the later phase. It is possible therefore that some of the emendations which I have adopted into the text are really later; but none seem to me to be so, and in any case all changes of any narrative significance are detailed in the following notes.

2 The meaning of this title is not clear. The phrase 'Three's company, but four's more' is used however by Marmaduke Brandybuck during the conversation in Buckland, where he asserts that he will certainly be one of the party (p. 103). Conceivably, therefore, my father gave the original second chapter this title because he believed that it would extend as far as the arrival in Buckland. Subsequently he crossed out the words 'and Four's More', but it cannot be said when this was done.

3 In the second draft of the opening of the chapter, which had reached virtually the form of the typescript text in this passage, the crossing of the East Road was omitted, and the omission remains here (see p. 47).

4 In the draft text the verse *The Road goes ever on and on* is placed here (see p. 47).

5 Fosco Bolger, Bingo's uncle: see p. 38.

6 In FR (pp. 82–3) the verse has *I* for *we* in lines 4 and 8, but is otherwise the same; there, however, it is an echo from Bilbo's speaking it in Chapter 1 (FR p. 44). For the earliest form see p. 47; and see further p. 246 note 18.

7 *Men from Dale:* see pp. 20, 30.

8   The next portion of the narrative, from *'I have though,' said Frodo*
    and extending to the end of the song *Upon the hearth the fire is red*
    (p. 57), was early re-typed to replace two pages of the original
    typescript, and a substantial alteration and expansion of the story
    was introduced (see notes 9 and 11).

9   This first part of the re-typed section (see note 8) was not greatly
    changed from the earlier form. In the earlier, Frodo described his
    encounter with a Black Rider 'up in the North Moors' in the
    previous spring in almost exactly the same words; but Bingo's
    response was somewhat different:

    'That makes it even queerer,' said Bingo. 'I am glad I had the
    fancy not to be seen on the road. But, somehow, I don't believe
    either of these riders was one of the Big People, not of the Kind
    like the Dale-men, I mean. I wonder what they were? I rather
    wish Gandalf was here. But, of course, he went away immediately
    after the fireworks with the elves and dwarves, and it will be ages
    before we see him now.'

    'Shall we go on now, or stay here and have some food?' asked
    Odo . . .

    In the later versions of *A Long-expected Party* there is no reference
    to Gandalf after the fireworks (see pp. 31, 38; 63).

10  *There the road bent southward:* on the map of the Shire in FR the
    road does not bend southward 'at the end of the straight stretch'; it
    bends left or northward, while a side road goes on to Woodhall. But
    at this stage there was only one road, and at the place where the
    hobbits met the Elves it was falling steadily, 'making south-east
    towards the lowlands of the Brandywine River' (p. 56). Certainly by
    oversight, the present passage was preserved with little change in
    the original edition of FR (p. 86):

    The sun had gone down red behind the hills at their backs, and
    evening was coming on before they came to the end of the long
    level over which the road ran straight. At that point it bent
    somewhat southward, and began to wind again, as it entered a
    wood of ancient oak-trees.

    It was not until the second edition of 1966 that my father changed
    the text to agree with the map:

    At that point it bent *left* and went down into the lowlands of the
    Yale making for Stock; but *a lane branched right*, winding
    through a wood of ancient oak-trees on its way to Woodhall. 'That
    is the way for us,' said Frodo.

    Not far from *the road-meeting* they came on the huge hulk of a
    tree . . .

    This is also the reason for change in the second edition of 'road' to
    'lane' (also 'path', 'way') at almost all the many subsequent occur-
    rences in FR pp. 86–90: it was the 'lane' to Woodhall they were on,
    not the 'road' to Stock.

11   The entire passage from 'Close to the road they came on the huge
     hulk of an aged tree' is an expansion in the replacement typescript
     (see note 8) of a few sentences in the earlier:

> Inside the huge hollow trunk of an aged tree, broken and
> stumpy but still alive and in leaf, they rested and had a meal.
> Twilight was about them when they came out and prepared to go
> on again. 'I am going to risk the road now,' said Bingo, who had
> stubbed his toes several times against hidden roots and stones in
> the grass. 'We are probably making a fuss about nothing.'

     Though the enlarged description of the hollow tree was preserved in
     FR (p. 86), the second passage of a Black Rider was not, and the tree
     has again no importance beyond being the scene of the hobbits'
     meal. In the third chapter Bingo, talking to Marmaduke in Buck-
     land, refers to this story of a Rider heard while they sat inside the
     tree (p. 103); see also note 19 below.

12   The version of the song in the rejected typescript (see note 8) had
     the second and third verses thus:

> *Home is behind, the world ahead,*
> *And there are many paths to tread;*
> *And round the corner there may wait*
> *A new road or a secret gate,*
> *And hidden pathways there may run*
> *Towards the Moon or to the Sun.*
> *Apple, thorn, &c.*
>
> *Down hill, up hill walks the way*
> *From sunrise to the falling day,*
> *Through shadow to the edge of night,*
> *Until the stars are all alight; &c.*

13   In the initial drafting for this passage Bingo proposed that they stow
     their burdens in the hollow of an old broken oak and then climb it,
     but this was rejected as soon as written. This was no doubt where
     the 'hollow tree' motive first appeared.

14   In the original draft my father first wrote here: 'Suddenly there was
     a sound of laughter and a creak of wheels on the road. The shadow
     straightened up and retreated.' This was soon replaced, without the
     creak of wheels being explained; but it suggests that he had some
     intervention other than Elves in mind.

15   This was another portion that was re-typed. The passage immedi-
     ately preceding the Elves' song was different in the earlier form:

> It seemed to be singing in the secret elf-tongue, and yet as they
> listened the sounds, or the sounds and the tune together, seemed
> to turn into strange words in their own thought, which they only
> partly understood. Frodo afterwards said that he thought he
> heard words like these:

The song also had certain differences, including a second verse that was rejected.

> *O Elbereth! O Elbereth!*
> *O Queen beyond the Western Seas!*
> *O Light to him that wandereth*
> *Amid the world of woven trees!*
>
> *O Stars that in the Sunless Year*
> *Were kindled by her silver hand,*
> *That under Night the shade of Fear*
> *Should fly like shadow from the land!*
>
> *O Elbereth! Gilthonieth!*
> *Clear are thy eyes, and cold thy breath! &c.*

In the last verse the form is *Gilthoniel*. Extensive rough workings are also found, in which the first line of the song appears also as *O Elberil! O Elberil!* (and the third *O Light to us that wander still*); from these is also seen the meaning of *the Sunless Year*, since my father first wrote *the Flowering Years* (with reference to the Two Trees; see the *Quenta Silmarillion* §19, V.212). – It seems to have been here that the name *Elbereth* was first applied to Varda, having been previously that of one of the sons of Dior Thingol's Heir: see V.351.

16  In the original draft it was added here that the Elves 'were crowned with red and yellow leaves'; rejected, no doubt, because it was dark and they bore no lights.

17  At an earlier point in the chapter (p. 52) the typescript read 'a day even finer and hotter than the day before (Bingo's birthday, that already seemed quite a long while past).' It was of course on the evening of the day following the birthday party that Bingo and his companions set out, and my father realising this simply changed 'before' to 'of' and removed the brackets, as in the text printed. Here, however, he neglected to change 'yesterday' (see also note 24). These slips are odd, but do not seem to have any particular significance.

It is seen subsequently how these Elves could have 'heard all about that from the Rivendell people', for Bingo tells Gildor (p. 63) that Gandalf 'went off with the dwarves *and the Rivendell elves* as soon as the fireworks were over.' The meeting between them is in fact mentioned later (p. 101).

18  The typescript runs straight on from *we have heard all about that, of course, from the Rivendell people* to 'O Wise People,' said Frodo, and the passage beginning 'Then who are you, and who is your lord?' *said Bingo* is an addition. In the typescript as typed the leader of the Elves is not named until towards the end, where after they had eaten

'Bingo remained talking with Gildor, the leader of the Elves'
(p. 62); all references to *Gildor* before that are corrections in ink

19  As the text was typed, Bingo said: 'Because we have seen two Black
Riders, or one twice over, today.' The changed text accompanies the
story of the Rider who paused momentarily beside the hollow tree
(see note 11).

20  For the 'elf-latin' (*Qenya*) see the *Lhammas* §4, V.172.

21  This passage is an alteration of the text as typed, which read:
... we are very easy to please (for hobbits). For myself I can only
say that the delight of meeting you has already made this a day of
bright Adventure.'
'Bilbo was a good master,' said the Elf bowing. 'Come now, join
our company, and we will go. You had best walk in the middle ...'

22  This sentence replaced the following:
'Be careful, friends,' said one laughing. 'Speak no secrets! Here
is a scholar in the elf-latin and all the dialects. Bilbo was indeed a
good master.'
See note 21 and the altered passage referred to there.

23  This is the first occurrence of the name *Gildor* in the text as typed;
see note 18.

24  For *my birthday the day before yesterday* the text as typed had
*yesterday*; see note 17.

25  The conversation between Bingo and Gildor to this point, beginning at *You can fence yourselves in, but you have no means of
fencing it out* (p. 63), is the last of the replacement typescript pages.
The differences from the earlier form are in fact very slight, except
in these points. Bingo did not say that Gandalf had told him not to
put off his journey later than the autumn, but simply 'He helped me,
and seemed to think it a good idea'; and Gildor's reply therefore
begins differently: 'I wonder. He may not have known they were in
the Shire; yet he knows more about them than we do.' And Bingo
said that Odo and Frodo 'only know that I am on a Journey – on a
sort of prolonged (and possibly permanent) holiday from Hobbiton; and making for Rivendell to begin with.'

26  Struck from the typescript here: 'and it might prevent you from
taking it.'

27  Struck from the typescript here: '(for the matter is outside the
concern of such Elves as we are).'

★

It is characteristic that while the *dramatis personae* are not the same, and
the story possesses as yet none of the dimension, the gravity, and the
sense of vast danger, imparted by the second chapter of *The Fellowship of
the Ring*, a good part of 'Three is Company' was already in being; for

once the journey has started not only the structure of the final narrative
but much of the detail is present, though countless modifications in
expression were to come, and in several substantial passages the chapter
was scarcely changed afterwards.

While 'Bingo' is directly equatable with the later 'Frodo', the other
relations are more complex. It is true that, comparing the text as it was
at this stage with the final form in FR, it may be said simply that
'Odo' became 'Pippin' while Frodo Took disappeared: of the individual
speeches in this chapter which remained into FR almost every remark
made by Odo was afterwards given to Pippin. But the way in which this
came about was in fact strangely tortuous, and was by no means a simple
substitution of one name for another (see further pp. 323–4). Frodo
Took is seen as a less limited and more aware being than Odo, more
susceptible to the beauty and otherness of the Elves; it is he who speaks
*The Road goes ever on and on*, and it is to him that the recollection of the
words of the song to Elbereth is first attributed (note 15). Some element
of him might be said to be preserved in Sam Gamgee (who of course
imparts a new and entirely distinctive air to the developed form of the
chapter); it was Frodo Took who with bated breath whispered *Elves!*
when their voices were first heard coming down the road.

Most remarkable is the fact that when the story of the beginning of the
Journey, the coming of the Black Riders, and the meeting with Gildor
and his company, was written, and written so that its content would not
in essentials be changed afterwards, Bingo has no faintest inkling of what
the Riders want with him. Gandalf has told him nothing. He has no
reason to associate the Riders with his ring, and no reason to regard it as
more than a highly convenient magical device – he slips it on each time a
Rider passes, naturally.

Of course, the fact that Bingo is wholly ignorant of the nature of the
pursuing menace, utterly baffled by the black horsemen, does not imply
that my father was also. There are several suggestions that new ideas had
arisen in the background, not explicitly conveyed in the narrative, but
deliberately reduced to dark hints of danger in the words of Gildor (that
this was so will be seen more clearly at the beginning of the next chapter).
It may be that it was the 'unpremeditated' conversion of the cloaked and
muffled horseman who overtook them on the road from Gandalf to a
'black rider' (p. 48), combining with the idea already present that Bilbo's
ring was of dark origin and strange properties (pp. 42–3) that was the
impulse of the new conceptions.

From the early rewriting of the conversation between Gildor and
Bingo (see p. 63 and note 25) it emerges that Gandalf had warned
Bingo not to delay his departure beyond the autumn (though without,
apparently, giving him any reason for the warning), and in both forms of
the text Gildor evidently knows something about the Riders, says that
'by what seems strange good luck you went just in time', and associates
them with the Ring: warning Bingo against using it again to escape them,

and suggesting that the use of it 'helps them more than you.' (The Ring had not been mentioned in their conversation, but we can suppose that Bingo had previously told Gildor that he had used it when the Riders came by).

The idea of the Riders and the Ring was no doubt evolving as my father wrote. I think it very possible that when he first described the halts of the black horsemen beside the hiding hobbits he imagined them as drawn by scent alone (see p. 75); and it is not clear in any case in what way the use of the Ring would 'help them more than you.' As I have said, it is deeply characteristic that these scenes emerged at once in the clear and memorable form that was never changed, but that their bearing and significance would afterwards be enormously enlarged. The 'event' (one might say) was fixed, but its meaning capable of indefinite extension; and this is seen, over and over again, as a prime mark of my father's writing. In FR, from the intervening chapter *The Shadow of the Past*, we have some notion of what that other feeling was which struggled with Frodo's desire to hide, of why Gandalf had so urgently forbidden him to use the Ring, and of why he was driven irresistibly to put it on; and when we have read further we know what would have happened if he had. The scenes here are empty by comparison, yet they are the same scenes. Even such slight remarks as Bingo's 'I don't know, and I don't want to guess' (p. 55) – in the context, a mere expression of doubt and discomfort, if with a suggestion that Gandalf must have said *something*, or rather, that my father was beginning to think that Gandalf must have said something – survived to take on a much more menacing significance in FR (p. 85), where we have a very good idea of what Frodo chose not to guess about.

Frodo Took's story of his meeting with a Rider on the moors in the North of the Shire in the previous spring is the forerunner of Sam's sudden remembering that a Rider had come to Hobbiton and spoken with Gaffer Gamgee on the evening of their departure; but it seems strange that the beginning of the hunt for 'Baggins' should be set so long before (see p. 74 and note 4).

The striking out of Gildor's words 'for the matter is outside the concern of such Elves as we are' (note 27) is interesting. At first, I think, my father thought of these Elves as 'Dark-elves'; but he now decided that they (and also the Elves of Rivendell) were indeed 'High Elves of the West', and he added in Gildor's words to Bingo on p. 60 (see note 18): they were 'Wise-elves' (Noldor or Gnomes), 'one of the few companies that still remain east of the Sea', and he himself is Gildor Inglorion of the house of Finrod. With these words of Gildor's cf. the *Quenta Silmarillion* §28, in V.332:

Yet not all the Eldalië were willing to forsake the Hither Lands where they had long suffered and long dwelt; and some lingered many an age in the West and North ... But ever as the ages drew on and the Elf-folk faded upon earth, they would set sail at eve from the western shores of this world, as still they do, until now there linger few anywhere of their lonely companies.

At this time Finrod was the name of the third son of Finwë (first Lord of the Noldor). This was later changed to Finarfin, when Inglor Felagund his son took over the name Finrod (see I.44), but my father did not change 'of the house of Finrod' here (FR p. 89) to 'of the house of Finarfin' in the second edition of *The Lord of the Rings*. See further p. 188 (end of note 9).

The geography of the Shire was now taking more substantial shape. In this chapter there emerge the North Moor(s); the Green Hill Country lying to the south of Hobbiton; the Pool of Bywater (described in rough drafting for the passage as a 'little lake'); the East Road to the Brandywine Bridge, where the Water joined the Brandywine; the road branching off from it southward and leading in a direct line to Buckland; and the hamlet of Woodhall in the Woody End.

# III

# OF GOLLUM AND THE RING

I have suggested that by this stage my father knew a good deal more about the Riders and the Ring than Bingo did, or than he permitted Gildor to tell; and evidence for this is found in the manuscript draft referred to on p. 48. This begins, at any rate, as a draft for a part of the conversation between Bingo and Gildor, but the talk here moves into topics which my father excluded from the typescript version (pp. 62–5). Gildor is not yet named, in fact, and indeed it was apparently in this text that he emerged as an individual: at first the conversation is between Bingo and an undifferentiated plural 'they'.

The passage begins with an apparently disconnected sentence: 'Since he did not tell his companions what he discovered I think I shall not tell you.' (Does this refer to what Bingo discovered from the Elves?) Then follows:

'Of course,' they said, 'we know that you are in search of Adventure; but it often happens that when you think it is ahead, it comes up unexpectedly from behind. Why did you choose this moment to set out?'

'Well, the moment was really inevitable, you know,' said Bingo. 'I had come to the end of my treasure. And by wandering I thought I *might* find some more, like old Bilbo, and at least should be able more easily to live without any. I thought too it might be good for me. I was getting rather soft and fat.'

'Yes,' they laughed, 'you *look* just like an ordinary hobbit.'

'But though I can do a few things – like carpentry and gardening: I did not feel inclined somehow to make other people's chairs, or grow other people's vegetables for a living. I suppose some tiny touch of dragon-curse came to me. I am gold-lazy.'

'Then Gandalf did not tell you anything? You were not actually escaping.'

'What do you mean? What from?'

'Well, this black rider,' they said.

'I don't understand them at all.'

'Then Gandalf told you nothing?'

'Not about them. He warned Bilbo a long time ago about the Ring, of course.[1] "Don't use it too much!" he used to say. "And only use it for proper purposes. I mean, do not use it except for jest, or for escaping from danger and annoyance – don't use it for harm, or for finding out other people's secrets, and of course not for theft or worse things. Because it may get the better of you." I did not understand.

'I seldom saw Gandalf after Bilbo went away. But about a year ago he came one night, and I told him of the plan I was beginning to make for leaving Bag-end. "What about the Ring?" he asked. "Are you being careful? Do be careful: otherwise you will be overcome by it." I had as a matter of fact hardly ever used it – and I did not use it again after that talk until my birthday party.'

'Does anyone else know about it?'

'I cannot say; but I don't think so. Bilbo kept it very secret. He always told me that I was the only one who knew about it (in the Shire).[2] I never told anyone else except Odo and Frodo who are my best friends. I have tried to be to them what Bilbo was to me. But even to them I never spoke of the Ring until they agreed to come with me on this Journey a few months ago. They would not tell anyone – though we often speak of it among ourselves. – Well, what do you make of it all? I can see you are bursting with secrets, but I cannot guess any of them.'

'Well,' said Elf. 'I don't know much about this. You must find Gandalf as quick as you can – Rivendell I think is the place to go to. But it is my belief that the Lord of the Ring[3] is looking for you.'

'Is that bad or good?'

'Bad; but how bad I cannot say. Bad enough if he only wants the ring back (which is unlikely); worse, if he wants payment; very bad indeed if he wants you as well (which is quite likely). We fancy that he must at last after many years have found out that Bilbo had it. Hence the asking for Baggins.[4] But somehow the search for Baggins failed, and then something must have been discovered about you. But by strange luck you must have held your party and vanished just as they found out where you lived. You put off the scent; but they are hot on it now.'

'Who are they?'

'Servants of the Lord of the Ring – [?people] who have passed through the Ring.'

This ends a sheet, and the following sheet is not continuous with what precedes; but as found among my father's papers they were placed together, and on both of them he wrote (later) 'About Ring-wraiths'. The second passage is also part of a conversation, but there is no indication of who the speaker is (whoever it is, he is obviously speaking to Bingo). It was written at great speed and is extremely difficult to make out.

Yes, if the Ring overcomes you, you yourself become permanently invisible – and it is a horrible cold feeling. Everything becomes very faint like grey ghost pictures against the black background in which you live; but you can smell more clearly than you can hear or see.[5] You have no power however like a Ring of making other things invisible: you are a ringwraith. You can wear clothes. [> you are just a ringwraith; and your clothes are visible, unless the Lord lends you a ring.] But you are under the command of the Lord of the Rings.[6]

I expect that one (or more) of these Ringwraiths have been sent to get the ring away from hobbits.

In the very ancient days the Ring-lord made many of these Rings: and sent them out through the world to snare people. He sent them to all sorts of folk – the Elves had many, and there are now many elfwraiths in the world, but the Ring-lord cannot rule them; the goblins got many, and the invisible goblins are very evil and wholly under the Lord; dwarves I don't believe had any; some say the rings don't work on them: they are too solid. Men had few, but they were most quickly overcome and . . . . . The men-wraiths are also servants of the Lord. Other creatures got them. Do you remember Bilbo's story of Gollum?[7] We don't know where Gollum comes in – certainly not elf, nor goblin; he is probably not dwarf; we rather believe he really belongs to an ancient sort of hobbit. Because the ring seems to act just the same for him and you. Long ago [?he belonged] . . . . to a wise, cleverhanded and quietfooted little family. But he disappeared underground, and though he used the ring often the Lord evidently lost track of it. Until Bilbo brought it out to light again.

Of course Gollum himself may have heard news – all the mountains were full of it after the battle – and tried to get back the ring, or told the Lord.

At this point the manuscript stops. Here is a first glimpse of an earlier history of Gollum; a suggestion of how the hunt for the Ring originated; and a first sketching of the idea that the Dark Lord gave out Rings among the peoples of Middle-earth. The Rings conferred invisibility, and (it is at least implied) this invisibility was associated with the fate (or at least the peril) of the bearers of the Rings: that they become 'wraiths' and – in the case of goblins and men – servants of the Dark Lord.

Now at some very early stage my father wrote a chapter, without number or title, in which he made use of the passage just given; and this is the first drafting of (a part of) what ultimately became Chapter 2, 'The Shadow of the Past'. As I have noticed, in the second of these two passages marked 'About Ring-wraiths' it is not clear who is speaking. It may be Gildor, or it may be Gandalf, or (perhaps most likely) neither the one nor the other, but indeterminate; but in any case I think that my father decided when writing the draft text of the second chapter that he would not have Gildor discussing these matters with Bingo (as he certainly does in the first of these 'Ring-wraith' passages, p. 74), but would reserve them for Gandalf's instruction, and that this was the starting-point of the chapter which I now give, in which as I have said he made use of the second 'Ring-wraith' passage. Whether he wrote this text at once, before going on to the third chapter (IV in this book), seems impossible to say; but the fact that Marmaduke is mentioned shows that it preceded 'In the House of Tom Bombadil', where 'Meriadoc' and 'Merry' first appear. This, at any rate, is a convenient place to put it.

Subsequently my father referred to it as a 'foreword' (see p. 224), and it is clear that it was written as a possible new beginning for the book, in which Gandalf tells Bingo at Bag End, not long before the Party, something of the history and nature of his Ring, of his danger, and of the need for him to leave his home. It was composed very rapidly and is hard to read. I have introduced punctuation where needed, and occasionally put in silently necessary connective words. There are many pencilled alterations and additions which are here ignored, for they are anticipations of a later version of the chapter; but changes belonging to the time of composition are adopted into the text. There is no title.

One day long ago two people were sitting talking in a small room. One was a wizard and the other was a hobbit, and the room was the sitting-room of the comfortable and well-furnished hobbit-hole known as Bag-end, Underhill, on the outskirts of Hobbiton in the middle of the Shire. The wizard was of course Gandalf and he looked much the same as he had always done, though ninety years and more[8] had gone by since he last came into any story that is now remembered. The hobbit was Bingo Bolger-Baggins, the nephew (or really first cousin once removed) of old Bilbo Baggins, and his adopted heir. Bilbo had quietly disappeared many years before, but he was not forgotten in Hobbiton.

Bingo of course was always thinking about him; and when Gandalf paid him a visit their talk usually came back to Bilbo. Gandalf had not been to Hobbiton for some time: since Bilbo disappeared his visits had become fewer and more secret. The people of Hobbiton had not in fact seen or at any rate noticed him for many years: he used to come quietly up to the door of Bag-end in the twilight and step in without knocking, and only Bingo (and one or two of his closest friends) knew he had been in the Shire. This evening he had slipped in in his usual way, and Bingo was more than usually glad to see him. For he was worried, and wanted explanations and advice.[9] They were now talking of Bilbo, and his disappearance, and particularly about the Ring (which he had left behind with Bingo) – and about certain strange signs and portents of trouble brewing after a long time of peace and quiet.[10]

'It is all very peculiar – and most disturbing and in fact terrifying,' said Bingo. Gandalf was sitting smoking in a high chair, and Bingo near his feet was huddled on a stool warming his hands by a small wood-fire as if he felt chilly, though actually it was rather a warm evening for the time of the year [*written above:* at the end of August].[11] Gandalf grunted – the sound might have meant 'I quite agree, but it can't be helped,' or else possibly 'What a silly thing to say.' There was a long silence. 'How long have you known all this?' asked Bingo at length; 'and did you ever talk about it to Bilbo?'

'I guessed a good deal immediately,' answered Gandalf slowly, as if searching back in memory. Already to him the days of the journey and the Dragon and the Battle of Five Armies began to seem far off – in an almost legendary past. Perhaps even he was at last getting to feel his age a little; and in any case many dark and curious adventures had befallen him since then. 'I guessed much,' he said, 'but soon I learnt more, for I went, as Bilbo may have told you, to the land of the Necromancer.'[12] For a moment his voice faded to a whisper. 'But I knew that all was well with Bilbo,' he went on. 'Bilbo was safe, for that kind of power was powerless over him – or so I thought, and I was right in a way (if not quite right). I kept an eye on him and it, of course, but perhaps I was not careful enough.'

'I am sure you did your best,' said Bingo, meaning to console him. 'O dearest and best friend of our house, may your beard never grow less! But it must have been rather a blow when Bilbo disappeared.'

'Not at all,' said Gandalf, with a sudden return to his ordinary tones. He sent out a great jet of smoke with an indignant *poof* and it coiled round his head like a cloud on a mountain. 'That did not worry me. Bilbo is all right. It is you and all these other dear, silly, charming, idiotic, helpless hobbits that trouble me! It would be a mortal blow if the dark power should overcome the Shire, and all these jolly, greedy, stupid Bolgers, Bagginses, Brandybucks, Hornblowers, Proudfoots and whatnot became Wraiths.'

Bingo shuddered. 'But why should we?' he asked; 'and why should the Lord want such servants, and what has all this to do with me and the Ring?'

'It is the only Ring left,' said Gandalf. 'And hobbits are the only people of whom the Lord has not yet mastered any one.

'In[13] the ancient days the dark master made many Rings, and he dealt them out lavishly, so that they might be spread abroad to ensnare folk. The elves had many, and there are now many elf-wraiths in the world; the goblins had some and their wraiths are very evil and wholly under the command of the Lord. The dwarves it is said had seven, but nothing could make them invisible. In them it only kindled to flames the fire of greed, and the foundation of each of the seven hoards of the Dwarves of old was a golden ring. In this way the master controlled them. But these hoards are destroyed, and the dragons have devoured them, and the rings are melted, or so some say.[14] Men had three rings, and others they found in secret places cast away by the elf-wraiths: the men-wraiths are servants of the Lord, and they brought all their rings back to him; till at last he had gathered all into his hands again that had not been destroyed by fire – all save one.

'It fell from the hand of an elf as he swam across a river; and it betrayed him, for he was flying from pursuit in the old wars, and he became visible to his enemies, and the goblins slew him.[15] But a fish took the ring and was filled with madness, and swam upstream, leaping over rocks and up waterfalls until it cast itself on a bank and spat out the ring and died.

'There was long ago living by the bank of the stream a wise, cleverhanded and quietfooted little family.[16] I guess they were of hobbit-kind, or akin to the fathers of the fathers of the hobbits. The most inquisitive and curious-minded of that family was called Dígol. He was interested in roots and beginnings; he dived in deep pools, he burrowed under trees and growing plants, he tunnelled into green mounds, and he ceased to look up at flowers, and hill-tops, or the birds that are in the upper air: his head and eyes were downward. He found the ring in the mud of the river-bank under the roots of a thorn tree; and he put it on; and when he returned home none of his family saw him while he wore it. He was pleased with his discovery and concealed it, and he used it to discover secrets, and put his knowledge to malicious use, and became sharp-eyed and keen-eared for all that was unpleasant. It is not to be wondered at that he became very unpopular, and was shunned (when visible) by all his relatives. They kicked him, and he bit their feet. He took to muttering to himself and gurgling in his throat. So they called him Gollum, and cursed him, and told him to go far away. He wandered in loneliness up the stream and caught fish with his fingers in deep pools and ate them raw. One day it was very hot, and as he was bending over a pool he felt a burning on the back of his head, and a dazzling light from the water pained his eyes. He wondered, for he had almost forgotten about the sun; and for the last time he looked up and shook his fist at it; but as he lowered his eyes again he saw far ahead the tops of the Misty Mountains. And he thought suddenly: "It would be cool and shady under those mountains. The sun could never find me there. And the roots of those peaks must be roots indeed; there must be great secrets buried there which have not been discovered since the beginning." So he journeyed by night towards the mountains, and found a hole out of which a stream issued; and he wormed his way in like a maggot in the heart of the hills, and disappeared from all knowledge. And the ring went into the shadows with him, and even the Master lost it. But whenever he counted his rings, besides the seven rings that the Dwarves had held and lost, there was also one missing.'

'Gollum!' said Bingo. 'Do you mean that Gollum that Bilbo met? Is that his history? How very horrible and sad. I hate to think that he was connected with hobbits, however distantly.'

'But that surely was plain from Bilbo's own account,' said Gandalf. 'It is the only thing that explains the events – or partly explains them. There was a lot in the background of both their minds and memories that was very similar – they understood one another really (if you think of it) better than hobbits ever understood dwarves, elves, or goblins.'

'Still, Gollum must have been, or be, very much older than the oldest hobbit that ever lived in field or burrow,' said Bingo.

'That was the Ring,' said Gandalf. 'Of course it is a poor sort of long life that the Ring gives, a kind of stretched life rather than a continued growing – a sort of thinning and thinning. Frightfully wearisome, Bingo, in fact finally tormenting. Even Gollum came at last to feel it, to feel he could not bear it, and to understand dimly the cause of the torment. He had even made up his mind to get rid of it. But he was too full of malice. If you want to know, I believe he had begun to make a plan that he had not the courage

left to carry out. There was nothing new to find out; nothing left
but darkness, nothing to do but cold eating, and regretful remembering. He wanted to slip out and leave the mountains, and smell
the open air even if it killed him – as he thought it probably would.
But that would have meant leaving the Ring. And that is not easy
to do. The longer you have had one the harder it is. It was
especially hard for Gollum, as he had had a Ring for ages, and it
hurt him and he hated it, and he wanted, when he could no longer
bear to keep it, to hand it on to someone else to whom it would
become a burden – [?bind] itself as a blessing and turn to a curse.[17]
That is in fact the best way of getting rid of its power.'

'Why not give it to the goblins, then?' asked Bingo.

'I don't think Gollum would have found that amusing enough,'
said Gandalf. 'The goblins are already so beastly and miserable
that it was wasting malice on them. Also it would have been
difficult to escape from the hunters if there was an invisible goblin
to reckon with. But I suppose he might have put it in their path in
the end (if he had plucked up enough courage to do anything); but
for the unexpected arrival of Bilbo. You remember how surprised
he was. But as soon as the riddles started a plan formed in his mind
– or half-formed. I dare say his old bad habits would have beaten
his resolves and he would have eaten Bilbo if it had proved easy.
But there was the sword, you remember. In his heart, I fancy, he
never seriously expected to get a chance of eating Bilbo.'

'But he never gave Bilbo the ring,' said Bingo. 'Bilbo had got it
already!'

'I know,' said Gandalf. 'And that is why I said that Gollum's
ancestry only partly explained events. There was, of course,
something much more mysterious behind the whole thing –
something quite beyond the Lord of the Rings himself, peculiar to
Bilbo and his great Adventure. There was a queer fate over these
rings, and especially over [?this] one. They got lost occasionally,
and turned up in strange places. This one had already slipped
away from its owner treacherously once before. It had slipped
away from Gollum too. That is why I let Bilbo keep the ring so
long.[18] But for the moment I am trying to explain Gollum.'

'I see,' said Bingo doubtfully. 'But do you know what happened
afterwards?'

'Not very clearly,' said Gandalf. 'I have heard a little, and can
guess more. I think it certain that Gollum knew in the end that
Bilbo had somehow got the Ring. He may well have guessed it
soon. But in any case the news of the later events went all over

Wilderland and far beyond, East, West, and South and North.
The mountains were full of whispers and reports; and that would
give Gollum enough to think about.[19] Anyway, it is said that
Gollum left the mountains – for the goblins had become very few
there, and the deep places more than ever dark and lonely, and the
power of the ring had left him. He was probably feeling old, very
old, but less timid. But I do not think he became less wicked.
There is no news of what happened to him afterwards. Of course,
it is quite likely that wind and the mere shadow of sunlight killed
him pretty quickly. But it is possible that it did not. He was
cunning. He could hide from daylight or moonlight till he slowly
grew more used to things. I have in fact a horrible fancy that he
made his slow sneaking way bit by bit to the dark tower, to the
Necromancer, the Lord of the Rings. I think that Gollum is very
likely the beginning of our present trouble; and that through him
the Lord found out where to look for this last and most precious
and potent of his Rings.'

'What a pity Bilbo did not stab the beastly creature when he said
goodbye,' said Bingo . . . .

'What nonsense you do talk sometimes, Bingo,' said Gandalf.
'Pity! It was pity that prevented him. And he could not do so,
without doing wrong. It was against the rules. If he had done so he
would not have had the ring, the ring would have had him at once.
He might have been a wraith on the spot.'

'Of course, of course,' said Bingo. 'What a thing to say of Bilbo.
Dear old Bilbo! But why did *he* keep the thing, or why did you let
him? Didn't you warn him about it?'

'Yes,' said Gandalf. 'But even over Bilbo it had *some* power.
Sentiment . . . . . . . He liked to keep it as a memento. Let us be
frank – he continued to be proud of his Great Adventure, and to
look on the ring now and again warmed his memory, and made
him feel just a trifle heroic. But he could hardly have helped
himself anyway: if you think for a moment, it is not really very
easy to get rid of a Ring once you have got it.'

'Why not?' said Bingo, after thinking for a moment. 'You can
give it away, throw it away, or destroy it.'

'Yes,' said Gandalf – 'or you can surrender it: to the Master.
That is if you wish to serve him, and to fall into his power, and to
greatly increase his power.'

'But no one would wish to do that,' said Bingo, horrified.

'Nobody that you can imagine, perhaps,' answered Gandalf.
'Certainly not Bilbo. That is what made it difficult for him. He

dared not throw it away lest it get into evil hands, and be misused, and find its way back to the Master after doing much evil. He would not give it away to bad folk for the same reason; and he would not give it away to good folk or people he knew and trusted because he did not wish to burden them with it, any sooner than he was obliged. And he could not destroy it.'

'Why not?'

'Well, how would you destroy it? Have *you* ever tried?'

'No; but I suppose one could hammer it, or melt it, or do both.'

'Try them,' said Gandalf, 'and you will find out what Bilbo found out long ago.'

Bingo drew the Ring out of an inner pocket, and looked at it. It was plain and smooth without device, emblem, or rune; but it was of gold, and as he looked at it it seemed to Bingo that its colour was rich and beautiful, and its roundness perfect. It was very admirable and wholly precious. He had thought of throwing it into the hot embers of the fire. He found he could not do so without a struggle. He weighed the Ring in his hand, and then with an effort of will he made a movement as if to throw it in the fire; but he found he had put it back in his pocket.

Gandalf laughed. 'You see? You have always regarded it as a great treasure, and an heirloom from Bilbo. Now you cannot easily get rid of it. Though as a matter of fact, even if you took it to an anvil and summoned enough will to strike it with a heavy hammer, you would make no dint on it. Your little wood-fire, of course, even if you blew all night with a bellows would hardly melt any gold. But old Adam Hornblower the smith down the road could not melt it in his furnace. They say only dragonfire can melt them – but I wonder if that is not a legend, or at any rate if there are any dragons now left in which the old fire is hot enough. I fancy you would have to find one of the Cracks of Earth in the depths of the Fiery Mountain, and drop it down into the Secret Fire, if you really wanted to destroy it.'[20]

'After all your talk,' said Bingo, half solemnly and half in pretended annoyance, 'I really do want to destroy it. I cannot think how Bilbo put up with it for so long, if he knew as much – but he actually used it sometimes, and joked about it to me.'

'The only thing to do with such perilous treasures that Adventure has bestowed on you is to take them lightheartedly,' said Gandalf. 'Bilbo never used the ring for any serious purpose after he came back. He knew that it was too serious a matter. And I think he taught you well – after he had chosen you as his heir from among all the hobbits of his kindred.'

There was a long silence again, while Gandalf puffed at his pipe in apparent content, though under his lids his eyes were watching Bingo intently. Bingo gazed at the red embers, that began to glow as the light faded and the room grew slowly dark. He was thinking about the fabled Cracks of Earth and the terror of the Fiery Mountain.

'Well?' said Gandalf at last. 'What are you thinking about? Are you making any plans or getting any ideas?'

'No,' said Bingo coming back to himself, and finding to his surprise that he was in the dark. 'Or perhaps yes! As far as I can see I have got to leave Hobbiton, leave the Shire, leave everything and go away and draw the danger after me. I must save the Shire somehow, though there have been times when I thought it too stupid and dull for anything, and fancied a big explosion or an invasion of dragons might do it good! But I don't feel like that now. I feel that as long as the Shire lies behind safe and comfortable, I shall find wandering and adventures bearable. I shall feel there is some foothold somewhere, even if I can't ever stand on it myself again. But I suppose I must go alone. I feel rather minute, don't you know, and extremely uprooted, and, well, frightened, I suppose. Help me, Gandalf, best of friends.'

'Cheer up, Bingo, my lad,' said Gandalf, throwing two small logs of wood on the fire and puffing it with his mouth. Immediately the wood blazed up and filled the room with dancing light. 'No, I don't think you need or should go alone. Why not ask your three best friends to, beg them to, order them to (if you must) – I mean the three, the only three who you have (perhaps indiscreetly but perhaps with wise choice) told about your secret Ring: Odo, Frodo, and Marmaduke [*written above:* Meriadoc]. But you must go quickly – and make it a joke, Bingo, a joke, a huge joke, a resounding jest. Don't be mournful and serious. Jokes are really in your line. That's what Bilbo liked about you (among other things), if you care to know.'

'And where shall we go, and what shall we steer by, and what shall be our quest?' said Bingo, without a trace of a smile or the glimmer of a jest. 'When the huge joke is over, what then?'

'At present I have no idea,' said Gandalf, quite seriously and much to Bingo's surprise and dismay. 'But it will be just the opposite of Bilbo's adventure – to begin with, at any rate. You will set out on a journey without any known destination; and as far as

you have any object it will not be to win new treasure but to get rid
of a treasure that belongs (one might say) inevitably to you. But
you cannot even start without going East, West, South, or North;
and which shall we choose? Towards danger, and yet not too
rashly or too straight towards it. Go East. Yes, yes, I have it. Make
first for Rivendell, and then we shall see. Yes, we shall see then.
Indeed, I begin to see already!' Suddenly Gandalf began to
chuckle. He rubbed his long gnarled hands together and cracked
the finger-joints. He leant forward to Bingo. 'I have thought of a
joke,' he said. 'Just a rough plan – you can set your comic wits to
work on it.' And his beard wagged backwards and forwards as he
whispered long in Bingo's ear. The fire burned low again – but
suddenly in the darkness an unexpected sound rang out. Bingo
was rocking with laughter.

## NOTES

1  My father's own thought is surely transparent here. Bingo introduces
the subject of the Ring as if it had some connection with the Riders,
whereas he is obviously intended to appear as quite unable even to
guess at their significance; and there is no suggestion in the drafts
that the Ring had been mentioned before this point.

2  *(in the Shire):* my father first wrote 'except Gandalf'. The words *'(in
the Shire)'* probably mean no more than that: i.e., no one save Bilbo
and Bingo, and outside the Shire only Gandalf, and anyone else
whom Gandalf might possibly have told.

3  This is probably the first time that the expression *The Lord of the
Ring* was used; and *The Lord of the Rings* occurs below (note 6). (My
father gave *The Lord of the Ring* as the title of the new work in a letter
to Allen and Unwin of 31 August 1938).

4  *Hence the asking for Baggins:* this is not mentioned in the manuscript drafts, but see the typescript version, p. 54 and note 9. The
following sentence, 'But somehow the search for Baggins failed, and
then something must have been discovered about you' perhaps
explains the story that Frodo Took met a Black Rider on the North
Moor as early as the previous spring (see p. 71).

5  My father first wrote here that the clothing of one who has thus
become permanently invisible was invisible also, but rejected the
statement as soon as written.

6  This seems to be the first appearance of the expression *The Lord of
the Rings*; see note 3.

7  After this sentence my father wrote: 'Gollum I think some sort of
distant kinsman of the goblin sort.' Since this is contradicted in the

next sentence it was obviously rejected in the act of writing; he crossed it out later.

8  *ninety years and more:* see pp. 31–3.

9  At no point in this text is there any further mention of Bingo's 'worry'; and the advice that he asks is entirely based on what Gandalf now tells him and which is obviously entirely new to him. There is also no further reference to the 'strange signs and portents of trouble brewing' spoken of in the next sentence, nor any explanation of Gandalf's remark (p. 81) that 'Gollum is very likely the beginning of *our present trouble*.'

10  This ends the first page of the manuscript. At the head of the second page my father wrote in pencil: 'Gandalf and Bingo discuss Rings and Gollum', and 'Draft: Later used in Chapter II', and he numbered the pages (previously unnumbered) in Greek letters, beginning at this point. Thus the first page is left out. But these pencillings were clearly put in long after, and in my view they cast no doubt on the validity of the opening section as an integral part of the text. May be it had at one time become separated and mislaid; but as the papers were found it was placed with the rest.

11  Rumour of the Party – decided on between Gandalf and Bingo at the end of this text – began to circulate early in September (p. 30).

12  In *The Hobbit* (Chapter I) Gandalf told Thorin at Bag End that he found his father Thráin 'in the dungeons of the Necromancer'. In the Tale of Years in LR Appendix B this, Gandalf's second visit to Dol Guldur, took place in the year 2850, forty years before Bilbo's birth; it was then that he 'discovered that its master was indeed Sauron' (cf. FR p. 263). But here the meaning is clearly that Gandalf went to the land of the Necromancer *after* Bilbo's acquisition of the Ring. Later my father altered the text in pencil to read: 'for I went back once more to the land of the Necromancer.'

13  Here the earlier draft concerning the Rings is used: see p. 75.

14  See FR p. 60 and LR Appendix A pp. 357–8.

15  This is the first germ of the story of the death of Isildur.

16  This is also derived from the text referred to in note 13.

17  This sentence as first written ended: 'and he wanted to hand it on to someone else.' It is to this that the following sentence refers.

18  The passage beginning 'There was a queer fate' was an addition, and 'That is why I let Bilbo keep the ring so long' refers to the sentence ending '. . . peculiar to Bilbo and his great Adventure.'

19  Cf. the draft passage given on p. 75: 'Of course Gollum himself may have heard news – all the mountains were full of it after the battle – and tried to get back the ring.'

20  The first mention of the Fiery Mountain and the Cracks of Earth in its depths.

★

It will be seen that a part of the 'Gollum' element in 'The Shadow of the Past' (Chapter 2 in FR) was at once very largely achieved, even though Dígol\* (later Déagol) is Gollum himself, and not his friend whom he murdered, though Gandalf had never seen him (and so no explanation is given of how he knows his history, which of its nature could only be derived from Gollum's own words), and though it is only surmised that he went at last to the Dark Lord.

It is important to realise that when my father wrote this, he was working within the constraints of the story as originally told in *The Hobbit*. As *The Hobbit* first appeared, and until 1951, the story was that Gollum, encountering Bilbo at the edge of the subterranean lake, proposed the riddle game on these conditions: 'If precious asks, and it doesn't answer, we eats it, my preciousss. If it asks us, and we doesn't answer, we gives it a present, gollum!' When Bilbo won the contest, Gollum held to his promise, and went back in his boat to his island in the lake to find his treasure, the ring which was to be his present to Bilbo. He could not find it, for Bilbo had it in his pocket, and coming back to Bilbo he begged his pardon many times: 'He kept on saying: "We are ssorry: we didn't mean to cheat, we meant to give it our only present, if it won the competition".' '"Never mind!" he [Bilbo] said. "The ring would have been mine now, if you had found it; so you would have lost it anyway. And I will let you off on one condition." "Yes, what iss it? What does it wish us to do, my precious?" "Help me to get out of these places", said Bilbo.' And Gollum did so; and Bilbo 'said good-bye to the nasty miserable creature.' On the way up through the tunnels Bilbo slipped on the ring, and Gollum at once missed him, so that Bilbo perceived that the ring was as Gollum had told him – it made you invisible.

This is why, in the present text, Gandalf says 'I think it certain that Gollum knew in the end that Bilbo had got the ring'; and why my father had Gandalf develop a theory that Gollum was actually ready to give the ring away: 'he wanted . . . to hand it on to someone else . . . I suppose he might have put it in [the goblins'] path in the end . . . but for the unexpected arrival of Bilbo . . . as soon as the riddles started a plan formed in his mind.' This is all carefully conceived in relation to the text of *The Hobbit* as it then was, to meet the formidable difficulty: if the Ring were of such a nature as my father now conceived it, how *could* Gollum have. really intended to give it away to a stranger who won a riddle contest? – and the original text of *The Hobbit* left no doubt that that was indeed his serious intention. But it is interesting to observe that Gandalf's remarks about the affinity of mind between Gollum and Bilbo, which survived into FR (pp. 63–4), originally arose in this context, of explaining how it was that Gollum was willing to let his treasure go.

---

\*Old English *dígol*, *déagol*, etc. 'secret, hidden'; cf. LR Appendix F (p. 415).

Turning to what is told of the Rings in this text, the original idea (p. 75) that the Elves had many Rings, and that there were many 'Elf-wraiths' in the world, is still present, but the phrase 'the Ring-lord cannot rule them' is not. The Dwarves, on the other hand, at first said not to have had any, now had seven, each the foundation of one of 'the seven hoards of the Dwarves', and their distinctive response to the corruptive power of the Rings enters (though this was already foreshadowed in the first rough draft on the subject: 'some say the rings don't work on them: they are too solid.') Men, at first said to have had 'few', now had three – but 'others they found in secret places cast away by the elf-wraiths' (thus allowing for more than three Black Riders). But the central conception of the Ruling Ring is not yet present, though it was, so to say, waiting in the wings: for it is said that Gollum's Ring was not only the only one that had not returned to the Dark Lord (other than those lost by the Dwarves) – it was the *most precious and potent* of his Rings' (p. 81). But in what its peculiar potency lay we are not told; nor indeed do we learn more here of the relation between the invisibility conferred by the Rings, the tormenting longevity (which now first appears), and the decline of their bearers into 'wraiths'.

The element of moral will required in one possessed of a Ring to resist its power is strongly asserted. This is seen in Gandalf's advice to Bilbo in the original draft (p. 74): 'don't use it for harm, or for finding out other people's secrets, and of course not for theft or for worse things. *Because it may get the better of you*'; and still more expressly in his rebuke to Bingo, who said that it was a pity that Bilbo did not kill Gollum: 'He could not do so, without doing wrong. It was against the rules. If he had done so he would not have had the ring, *the ring would have had him at once*' (p. 81). This element remains in FR (pp. 68–9), but is more guardedly expressed: 'Be sure that he took so little hurt from the evil, and escaped in the end, because he began his ownership of the Ring so.'

The end of the chapter – with Gandalf actually himself proposing the Birthday Party and Bingo's 'resounding jest' – was to be quickly rejected, and is never heard of again.

# IV
# TO MAGGOT'S FARM AND BUCKLAND

The third of the original consecutive chapters exists in complete form only in a typescript, where it bears the number 'III' but has no title; there are also however incomplete and very rough manuscript drafts, which were filled out and improved in the typescript but in all essentials left unchanged. Near the end the typescript ceases (note 16), not at the foot of a page, and the remainder of the chapter is in manuscript; for this part also rough drafting exists.

I again give the text in full, since in this chapter the original narrative was far removed from what finally went into print. Subsequent emendation was here very slight. I take up into the text a few manuscript changes that seem to me to be in all probability contemporary with the making of the typescript.

The end of the chapter corresponds to FR Chapter 5 'A Conspiracy Unmasked'; at this stage there was no conspiracy.

## III

In the morning Bingo woke refreshed. He was lying in a bower made by a living tree with branches laced and drooping to the ground; his bed was of fern and grass, deep and soft and strangely fragrant. The sun was shining through the fluttering leaves, which were still green upon the tree. He jumped up and went out.

Odo and Frodo were sitting on the grass near the edge of the wood; there was no sign of any elves.

'They have left us fruit and drink, and bread,' said Odo. 'Come and have breakfast! The bread tastes almost as good as last night.'

Bingo sat down beside them. 'Well?' said Odo. 'Did you find anything out?'

'No, nothing,' said Bingo. 'Only hints and riddles. But as far as I could make them out, it seems to me that Gildor thinks there are several Riders; that they are after *me*; that they are now ahead and behind and on both sides of us; that it is no use going back (at least not for me); that we ought to make for Rivendell as quickly as possible, and if we find Gandalf there so much the better; and that we shall have an exciting and dangerous time getting there.'

'I call that a lot more than nothing,' said Odo. 'But what about the sniffing?'

'We did not discuss it,' said Bingo with his mouth full.

'You should have,' said Odo. 'I am sure it is very important.'

'In that case I am sure Gildor would have told me nothing about it. But he did say that he thought you might as well come with me. I gathered that the riders are not after you, and that you rather bother them.'

'Splendid! Odo and Frodo are to take care of Uncle Bingo. They won't let him be sniffed at.'

'All right!' said Bingo. 'That's settled. What about the method of advance?'

'What do you mean?' said Odo. 'Shall we hop, skip, run, crawl on our stomachs, or just walk singing along?'

'Exactly. And shall we follow the road, or risk a cross-country cut? There is no choice in the matter of time; we must go in daylight, because Marmaduke is expecting us to-night. In fact we must get off as soon as possible; we have slept late, and there are still quite eighteen miles to go.'

'*You* have slept late, you mean,' said Odo. 'We have been up a long time.'

So far Frodo had said nothing. He was looking out over the tree-tops eastward. He now turned towards them. 'I vote for striking across country,' he said. 'The land is not so wild between here and the River. It ought not to be difficult to mark our direction before we leave this hill, and to keep pretty well to it. Buckland is almost exactly south-east from Woodhall[1] down there in the trees. We should cut off quite a corner, because the road bears away to the left – you can see a bit of it over there – and then sweeps round south when it gets nearer to the River.[2] We could strike it above Buckland before it gets really dark.'

'Short cuts make long delays,' said Odo; 'and I don't see that a Rider is any worse on the road than in the woods.'

'Except that he probably won't be able to see so well, and may not be able to ride so fast,' said Bingo. 'I am also in favour of leaving the road.'

'All right!' said Odo. 'I will follow you into every bog and ditch. You two are as bad as Marmaduke. I suppose I shall be outvoted by three to one, instead of two to one, when we collect him, if we ever do.'

The sun was now hot again; but clouds were beginning to come

up from the West. It looked likely to turn to rain, if the wind fell.
The hobbits scrambled down a steep green bank and struck into
the trees below. Their line was taken to leave Woodhall on their
left, and there was some thickish wood immediately in front of
them, though after a mile or two it had looked from above as if the
land became more open. There was a good deal of undergrowth,
and they did not get on very fast. At the bottom of the slope they
found a stream running in a deeply dug bed with steep slippery
banks overhung with brambles. They could not jump across, and
they had the choice of going back and taking a new line, or of
turning aside to the left and following the stream until it became
easier to cross. Odo looked back. Through the trees they could see
the top of the bank which fell from the high green which they had
just left. 'Look!' he said, clutching Bingo by the arm. On the top of
the slope a black rider sat on a horse; he seemed to be swaying
from side to side, as if sweeping all the land eastward with his gaze.

The hobbits gave up any idea of going back, and plunged
quickly and silently into the thickest bushes by the stream. They
were cut off from the West wind down in the hollow, and very
soon they were hot and tired. Bushes, brambles, rough ground,
and their packs, all did what they could to hold them back.

'Whew!' said Bingo. 'Both parties were right! The short cut has
gone crooked; but we got under cover only just in time. Yours are
the sharpest ears, Frodo. Can you hear – can you hear *anything*
behind?'

They stopped and looked and listened; but there was no sign or
sound of pursuit. They went on again, until the banks of the
stream sank and its bed became broad and shallow. They waded
across and hurried into the wood on the other side, no longer quite
sure of the line they should take. There were no paths, but the
ground was fairly level and open. A tall growth of young oaks,
mixed with ash and elm, was all round them, so that they could not
see far. The leaves of the trees blew upwards in sudden gusts, and
spots of rain began to fall; then the wind died away, and the rain
came down steadily.

They trudged along fast through thick leaves, while all about
them the rain pattered and trickled; they did not talk, but kept
glancing from side to side, and sometimes behind. After about an
hour Frodo said: 'I suppose we have not struck too much to the
south, and are not walking longwise through this wood? From
above it looked like a narrow belt, and we ought to have crossed it
by now, I should have thought.'

'It is no good starting going in zigzags now,' said Bingo. 'Let's keep on. The clouds seem to be breaking, and we may get a helpful glimpse of the sun again before long.'

He was right. By the time they had gone another mile, the sun gleamed out of ragged clouds; and they saw that they were in fact heading too much to the south. They bore a little to their left; but before long they decided by their feelings as much as by the sun that it was time for a mid-day halt and some food.

The rain was still falling at intervals; so they sat under an elm-tree, whose leaves were still thick, though they were fast turning yellow. They found that the Elves had filled their water-bottles with some clear golden drink: it had the scent rather than the taste of honey made of many flowers, and was mightily refreshing. They made a merry meal, and soon were laughing and snapping their fingers at rain and black riders. The next few miles they felt would soon be put behind them. With his back to the tree-trunk Odo began to sing softly to himself:

> Ho! ho! ho! To my bottle I go
> To heal my heart and drown my woe.
> Rain may fall and wind may blow,
> And many miles be still to go,
> But under the elm-tree I will lie
> And let the clouds go sailing by!
>
> Ho! ho! ho! ———

It will never be known whether the next verse was any better than the first; for just at the moment there was a noise like a sneeze or a sniff. Odo never finished his song. The noise came again: sniff, sniff, sniff; it seemed to be quite close. They sprang to their feet, and looked quickly about; but there was nothing to be seen anywhere near their tree.[3]

Odo had no more thought of lying and watching the clouds go by. He was the first to be packed and ready to start. In a few minutes from the last sniff they were off again as fast as they could go. The wood soon came to an end; but they were not particularly pleased, for the land became soft and boggy, and hobbits (even on a Journey) don't like mud and clay on their feet. The sun was shining again, and they felt both too hot and too exposed to view away from the trees. Far back now behind them lay the high green where they had breakfasted; every time they looked back towards it they expected to see the distant figure of a horseman against the sky. But none appeared; and as they went on the land about them got steadily more tame. There were hedges and gates and dikes for drainage; everything looked quiet and peaceful, just an ordinary corner of the Shire.

'I think I recognize these fields,' said Frodo suddenly. 'They belong to old Farmer Maggot,[4] unless I am quite lost. There ought to be a lane somewhere near, that leads from his place into the road a mile or two above Buckland.'[5]

'Does he live in a hole or a house?' asked Odo, who did not know this part of the country.

It was a curious thing about the hobbits of those days that this was an important distinction. All hobbits had, of course, origin-ally lived in holes; but now only the best and the poorest hobbits did so, as a rule. Important hobbits lived in luxurious versions of the simple holes of olden times; but the sites for really good hobbit-holes were not to be found everywhere. Even in Hobbiton, one of the most important villages, there were houses. These were specially favoured by the farmers, millers, blacksmiths, carpen-ters, and people of that sort. The custom of building houses was supposed to have started among the hobbits of the woody river-side regions, where the land was heavy and wet and had no good hills or convenient banks. They began making artificial holes of mud (and later of brick), roofed with thatch in imitation of natural grass. That was a long time ago, and on the edge of history; but houses were still considered an innovation. The poorest hobbits still lived in holes of the most ancient sort – in fact just holes, with only one window, or even none.[6] But Odo was not thinking about hobbit-history. He merely wanted to know where to look for the farm. If Farmer Maggot had lived in a hole, there would have been rising ground somewhere near; but the land ahead looked per-fectly flat.

'He lives in a house,' answered Frodo. 'There are very few holes in these parts. They say houses were invented here. Of course the Brandybucks have that great burrow of theirs at Bucklebury in the high bank across the River; but most of their people live in houses. There are lots of those new-fashioned brick houses – not too bad, I suppose, in their way; though they look very naked, if you know what I mean: no decent turf-covering, all bare and bony.'

'Fancy climbing upstairs to bed!' said Odo. 'That seems to me most inconvenient. Hobbits aren't birds.'

'I don't know,' said Bingo. 'It isn't as bad as it sounds; though personally I never like looking out of upstairs windows, it makes me a bit giddy. There are some houses that have three stages, bedrooms above bedrooms. I slept in one once long ago on a holiday; the wind kept me awake all night.'

'What a nuisance, if you want a handkerchief or something when you are downstairs, and find it is upstairs,' said Odo.

'You could keep handkerchiefs downstairs, if you wished,' said Frodo.

'You could, but I don't believe anybody does.'

'That is not the houses' fault,' said Bingo; 'it is just the silliness of the hobbits that live in them. The old tales tell that the Wise Elves used to build tall towers; and only went up their long stairs when they wished to sing or look out of the windows at the sky, or even perhaps the sea. They kept everything downstairs, or in deep halls dug beneath the feet of the towers. I have always fancied that the idea of building came largely from the Elves, though we use it very differently. There used to be three elftowers standing in the land away west beyond the edge of the Shire. I saw them once. They shone white in the Moon. The tallest was furthest away, standing alone on a hill. It was told that you could see the sea from the top of that tower; but I don't believe any hobbit has ever climbed it.[7] If ever I live in a house, I shall keep everything I want downstairs, and only go up when I don't want anything; or perhaps I shall have a cold supper upstairs in the dark on a starry night.'

'And have to carry plates and things downstairs, if you don't fall all the way down,' laughed Odo.

'No!' said Bingo. 'I shall have wooden plates and bowls, and throw them out of the window. There will be thick grass all round my house.'

'But you would still have to carry your supper *up*stairs,' said Odo.

'O well then, perhaps I should not have supper upstairs,' said Bingo. 'It was only just an idea. I don't suppose I shall ever live in a house. As far as I can see, I am going to be just a wandering beggar.'

This very hobbit-like conversation went on for some time. It shows that the three were beginning to feel quite comfortable again, as they got back into tame and familiar country. But even invisible sniffs could not damp for long the spirits of these excellent and peculiarly adventurous hobbits, not in any kind of country.

While they talked they plodded steadily on. It was already late

afternoon when they saw the roof of a house peeping out of a
clump of trees ahead and to their left.

'There is Farmer Maggot's!' said Frodo.

'I think we will go round it,' said Bingo, 'and strike the lane on
the far side of the house. I am supposed to have vanished, and I
would rather not be seen sneaking off in the direction of Buckland,
even by good Farmer Maggot.'

They went on, leaving the farmhouse away on their left, hidden
in the trees several fields away. Suddenly a small dog came
through a gap in a hedge, and ran barking towards them.

'Here! Here! Gip! Gip!' said a voice. Bingo slipped on his ring.
There was no chance for the others to hide. Over the top of the low
hedge appeared a large round hobbit-face.

'Hullo! Hullo! And who may you be, and what may you be
doing?' he asked.

'Good evening, Farmer Maggot!' said Frodo. 'Just a couple of
Tooks, from away back yonder; and doing no harm, I hope.'

'Well now, let me see – you'll be Mr Frodo Took, Mr Folco
Took's son, if I'm not mistook (and I seldom am: I've a rare
memory for faces). You used to stay with young Mr Marmaduke.
Any friend of Mr Marmaduke Brandybuck is welcome. You'll
excuse my speaking sharp, before I recognized you. We get some
strange folk in these parts at times. Too near the river,' he said,
jerking back his head. 'There's been a very funny customer round
here only an hour back. That's why I'm out with the dog.'

'What kind of a customer?' asked Frodo.

'A funny customer and asking funny questions,' said Farmer
Maggot, shaking his head. 'Come along to my house and have a
drink and we'll pass the news more comfortably like, if you and
your friend are willing, Mr Took.'

It seemed plain that Farmer Maggot would only pass the news
in his own time and place, and they guessed that it might be
interesting; so Frodo and Odo went along with him. The dog
remained behind jumping and frisking round Bingo to his annoyance.

'What's come to the dog?' said the farmer, looking back. 'Here,
Gip! Heel!' he called. To Bingo's relief the dog obeyed, though it
turned back once and barked.

'What's the matter with you?' growled Farmer Maggot. 'There
seems to be something queer abroad this day. Gip went near off
his head when that stranger came along, and now you'd think he
could see or smell something that ain't there.'

They went into the farmer's kitchen and sat by the wide fireplace. Mrs Maggot brought them beer in large earthenware mugs. It was a good brew, and Odo found himself wishing that they were going to stay the night in the house.

'I hear there have been fine goings on up Hobbiton way,' said Farmer Maggot. 'Fireworks and all; and this Mr Bolger-Baggins disappearing, and giving everything away. Oddest thing I have heard tell of in my time. I suppose it all comes of living with that Mr Bilbo Baggins. My mother used to tell me queer tales of him, when I was a boy: not but what he seemed a very nice gentleman. I have seen him wandering down this way many a time when I was a lad, and that Mr Bingo with him. Now we take an interest in him in these parts, seeing as he belongs here, being half Brandybuck, as you might say. We never thought any good would come of his going away to Hobbiton, and folk are a bit queer back there, if you'll pardon me. I was forgetting you come from those parts.'

'O, folk are queer enough in Hobbiton – and Tookland,' said Frodo. 'We don't mind. But we know, I mean knew, Mr Bingo very well. I don't think any harm's come to him. It really was a very marvellous party, and I can't see that anyone has anything to complain of.' He gave the farmer a full and amusing account of the proceedings, which pleased him mightily. He stamped his feet and slapped his legs, and called for more beer; and made them tell his wife most of the tale over again, especially about the fireworks. Neither of the Maggots had ever seen fireworks.

'It must be a sight to do your eyes good,' said the farmer.

'No dragons for me!' said Mrs Maggot. 'But I would have liked to have been at that supper. Let's hope old Mr Rory Brandybuck will take the idea and give a party down in these parts for his next birthday. – And what did you say has become of Mr Bolger-Baggins?' she said, turning to Frodo.

'Well – er, well, he's vanished, don't you know,' said Frodo. He half thought he heard the ghost of a chuckle somewhere not far from his ear, but he was not sure.

'There now – that reminds me!' said Farmer Maggot. 'What do you think that funny customer said?'

'What?' said Odo and Frodo together.

'Well, he comes riding in at the gate and up to the door on a big black horse; all black he was himself too, and cloaked and hooded up as if he didn't want to be known. "Good Heavens!" I said to myself. "Here's one of the Big People! Now what in the Shire can he want?" We don't see many of the Big People down here, though they come over the River at times; but I've never heard tell of any like this black chap. "Good day to you," I says. "This lane don't go no further, and wherever you be going your quickest way will be back to the road." I did not like the look of him, and when Gip came out he took one sniff and let out a howl as if he had been bitten; he put down his tail and bolted howling all the way.

'"I come from over yonder," he answered stiff and slow like, pointing back West, over *my* fields, Woodhall-way. "Have you ever seen Mist-er Bolg-er Bagg-ins?" he asked in a queer voice and bent down towards me, but I could see no face, his hood fell so low. I had a sort of shiver down my back; but I didn't see why he should come riding so bold over my land. "Be off!" I said. "Mr Bolger-Baggins has vanished, disappeared, if you take my meaning: gone into the blue, and you can follow him!"

'He gave a sort of hiss, seeming angry and startled like, it seemed to me; and he spurred his great horse right at me. I was standing by the gate, but I jumped out of the way mighty quick, and he rode through it and down the lane like mad. What do you think of that?'

'I don't know what to think,' said Frodo.

'Well, I'll tell you what to think,' said the farmer. 'This Mr Bingo has got himself mixed up in some trouble, and disappeared *a purpose*. There are plainly some folk as are mighty eager to find him. Mark my words, it'll all be along of some of those doings of old Mr Bilbo's. He ought to have stuck at Bolger and not gone tacking on Baggins. They are queer folk up Hobbiton way, begging your pardon. It's the Baggins that has got him into trouble, mark my words!'

'That certainly is an idea,' said Frodo. 'Very interesting, what you tell us. I suppose you've never seen any of these – er – black chaps before?'

'Not that I remember,' said Farmer Maggot, 'and I don't want to see any again. Now I hope you and your friend will stay and have a bite and a sup with me and the wife.'

'Thank you very much!' said Odo regretfully, 'but I am afraid we ought to go on.'

'Yes,' said Frodo, 'we have some way to go before night, and really we have already rested too long. But it is very kind of you all the same.'

'Well! Here's your health and good luck!' said the farmer, reaching for his mug. But at that moment the mug left the table, rose, tilted in the air, and then returned empty to its place.

'Help and save us!' cried the farmer jumping up. 'Did you see that? This is a queer day and no mistake. First the dog and then me seeing things that ain't.'

'Oh, I saw the mug too,' said Odo, unable to hide a grin.

'You did, did you!' said the farmer. 'I don't see no cause to laugh.' He looked quickly and queerly at Odo and Frodo, and now seemed only too glad that they were going. They said good-bye politely but hurriedly, and ran down the steps and out of the gate. Farmer Maggot and his wife stood whispering at their door and watched them out of sight.

'What did you want to play that silly trick for?' said Odo when the farmhouse was well behind. 'The old man had done you a good turn with that Rider, or so it seemed to me.'

'I daresay,' said a voice behind him. 'But you did me a pretty poor turn, going inside and drinking and talking, and leaving me in the cold. As it was I only got half a mug. And now we are late. I shall make you trot after this.'

'Show us how to trot!' said Odo.

Bingo immediately reappeared and went off as fast as he could down the lane. The others hurried after him. 'Look!' said Frodo pointing to one side. Along the edge of the lane, in the mud made by the day's rain, there were deep hoofmarks.

'Never mind!' said Bingo. 'We knew from old Maggot's talk that he went this way. It can't be helped. Come along!'

They met nothing in the lane. The afternoon faded and the sun went down into low clouds behind them. The light was already failing when they reached the end of the lane and came at last back to the road.[8] It was growing chilly and thin strands of mist were crawling over the fields. The twilight was clammy.

'Not too bad,' said Frodo. 'It is four miles from here to the landing stage opposite Bucklebury. We shall make it before it is quite dark.'

They now turned right along the road, which here ran quite straight, drawing steadily nearer to the River. There was no sign of any other traveller upon the way. Soon they could see lights in the distance ahead and to their left, beyond the dim line of the shadowy willow-trees along the borders of the river, where the far bank rose almost into a low hill.

'There's Bucklebury!' said Frodo.

'Thank goodness!' said Odo. 'My feet are sore, sticky, and mud-tired. Also it is getting chilly.' He stumbled into a puddle and splashed up a fountain of dirty water. 'Drat it!' he said. 'I've nearly had enough of to-day's walk. Do you think there is any chance of a bath to-night?' Without waiting for an answer he suddenly began a hobbit bathroom song.

> *O Water warm and water hot!*
> *O Water boiled in pan and pot!*
> *O Water blue and water green,*
> *O Water silver-clear and clean,*
>     *Of bath I sing my song!*
> *O praise the steam expectant nose!*
> *O bless the tub my weary toes!*
> *O happy fingers come and play!*
> *O arms and legs, you here may stay,*
>     *And wallow warm and long!*
> *Put mire away! Forget the clay!*
> *Shut out the night! Wash off the day!*
> *In water lapping chin and knees,*
> *In water kind now lie at ease,*
>     *Until the dinner gong!*

'Really you might wait till you are *in* the bath!' said Frodo.

'I warn you,' added Bingo, 'that you will have yours last, or else you will not wallow very long.'

'Very well,' said Odo; 'only I warn *you* that if you go first you must not take all the hot water, or I shall drown you in your own bath. I want a hot bath and a clean one.'

'You may not get any,' said Bingo. 'I don't know what Marmaduke has arranged, or where we are sleeping. I didn't order baths, and if we get them they will be our last for some time, I expect.'

Their talk flagged. They were now getting really tired, and went along with their chins down and their eyes in front of their toes. They were quite startled when suddenly a voice behind them cried: 'Hi!' It then burst into a loud song:

> *As I was sitting by the way,*
>     *I saw three hobbits walking:*
> *One was dumb with naught to say,*
>     *The others were not talking.*
>
> *'Good night!' I said. 'Good night to you!'*
>     *They heeded not my greeting:*
> *One was deaf like the other two.*
>     *It was a merry meeting!*

'Marmaduke!' cried Bingo turning round. 'Where did you spring from?'

'You passed me sitting at the road-side,' said Marmaduke. 'Perhaps I ought to have lain down in the road; but then you would have just trodden on me and passed gaily on.'

'We are tired,' said Bingo.

'So it seems. I told you you would be – but you were so proud and stiff. "Ponies! Pooh!" you said. "Just a little leg-stretcher before the real business begins."'

'As it happens ponies would not have helped much,' said Bingo. 'We have been having *adventures*.' He stopped suddenly and looked up and down the dark road. 'We will tell you later.'

'Bless me!' said Marmaduke. 'But how mean of you! You shouldn't have adventures without me. And what are you peering about for? Are there some big bad rabbits loose?'

'Don't be so Marmadukish all at once! I can't bear it at the end of the day,' said Odo. 'Let's get off our legs and have some food, and then you shall hear a tale. Can I have a bath?'

'What?' said Marmaduke. 'A bath? That would put you right out of training again. A bath! I am surprised at such a question. Now lift up your chins and follow me!'

A few yards further on there was a turning to the left. They went down a path, neat and well-kept and edged with large white stones. It led them quickly to the river-bank. There there was a landing-stage big enough for several boats. Its white posts glimmered in the gloom. The mists were beginning to gather almost hedge-high in the fields, but the water before them was dark with only a few curling wisps of grey like steam among the reeds at the sides. The Brandywine River flowed slow and broad. On the other side two lamps twinkled upon another landing-stage with many steps going up the high bank beyond. Behind it the low hill loomed, and out of the hill through stray strands of mist shone many round hobbit-windows, red and yellow. They were the lights of Brandy Hall, the ancient home of the Brandybucks.

Long, long ago the Brandybucks had crossed the River (the original boundary of the Shire on this side), attracted by the high bank and the drier rolling ground behind. But their family (one of the oldest hobbit families) grew, and grew, until Brandy Hall occupied the whole of the low hill, and had three large front doors, several back doors, and at least fifty windows. The Brandybucks and their numerous dependants then began to burrow and later to

build all round about. That was the origin of the village of
Bucklebury-by-the-River. A great deal of the land on the west side
of the river still belonged to the family, almost as far as Woodhall,
but most of the actual Brandybucks lived in Buckland: a thickly
inhabited strip between the River and the Old Forest, a sort of
colony from the old Shire.

The people of the old Shire, of course, told strange tales of the
Bucklanders; but as a matter of fact the Bucklanders were hobbits,
and not really very different from other hobbits of the North,
South, or West – except in one point: they were fond of boats and
some of them could swim. Also they were unprotected from the
East except by a hedge, THE HEDGE. It had been planted ages ago.
It now ran all the way from Brandywine Bridge to Haysend in a
big loop, furthest from the River behind Bucklebury, something
like forty miles from end to end.[9] It was thick and tall, and was
constantly tended. But of course it was not a complete protection.
The Bucklanders kept their doors locked, and that also was not
usual in the Shire.

Marmaduke helped his friends into a small boat that lay at the
stage. He then cast off and taking a pair of oars pulled across the
river. Frodo and Bingo had often been to Buckland before.
Bingo's mother was a Brandybuck. Marmaduke was Frodo's
cousin, since his mother Yolanda was Folco Took's sister, and
Folco was Frodo's father. Marmaduke was thus Took plus
Brandybuck, and that was apt to be a lively blend.[10] But Odo had
never been so far East before. He had a queer feeling as they
crossed the slow silent river, as if he had now at last started, as if he
was crossing a boundary and leaving his old life on the other shore.

They stepped quietly out of the boat. Marmaduke was tying it
up, when Frodo said suddenly in a whisper: 'I say, look back! Do
you see anything?'

On the stage they had left they seemed to see a dark black
bundle sitting in the gloom; it seemed to be peering, or sniffing,
this way and that at the ground they had trodden.

'What in the Shire is that?' said Marmaduke.

'Our Adventure, that we have been and left behind on the other
side; or at least I hope so,' said Bingo. 'Can horses get across the
River?'

'What have horses got to do with it? They can get across, I
suppose, if they can swim; but I have never seen them do it here.
There are bridges. But what have horses to do with it?'

'A great deal!' said Bingo. 'But let's get away!' He took Marmaduke by the arm and hurried him up the steps on to the path above the landing. Frodo looked back, but the far shore was now shrouded in mist and nothing more could be seen.

'Where are you taking us for the night?' asked Odo. 'Not to Brandy Hall?'

'Indeed not!' said Marmaduke. 'It's crowded. And anyway I thought you wanted to be secret. I am taking you to a nice little house on the far side of Bucklebury. It's a mile more, I am afraid, but it is quite cosy and out of the way. I don't expect anyone will notice us. You wouldn't want to meet old Rory just now, Bingo! He is in a ramping mood still, about your behaviour. They treated him badly at the inn at Bywater on the party night (they were more full up than Brandy Hall); and then his carriage broke down on the way home, on the hill above Woodhall, and he blames you for these accidents as well.'

'I don't want to see him, and I don't much mind what he says or thinks,' said Bingo. 'I wanted to get out of the Shire unseen, just to complete the joke, but now I have other reasons for wanting to be secret. Let's hurry.'

They came at length to a little low one-storied house. It was an old-fashioned building, as much like a hobbit-hole as possible: it had a round door and round windows and a low rounded roof of turf. It was reached by a narrow green path, and surrounded by a circle of green lawn, round which close bushes grew. It showed no lights.

Marmaduke unlocked the door, and light streamed out in friendly fashion. They slipped quickly in, and shut the light and themselves inside. They were in a wide hall from which several doors opened. 'Here we are!' said Marmaduke. 'Not a bad little place. We often use it for guests, since Brandy Hall is so frightfully full of Brandybucks. I have got it quietly ready in the last day or two.'

'Splendid fellow!' said Bingo. 'I was dreadfully sorry you had to miss that supper.'

'So was I,' said Marmaduke. 'And after hearing the accounts of Rory and Melissa[11] (both entirely different, but I expect equally true), I am sorrier still. But I had a merry ride with Gandalf and the dwarves and Elves.[12] We met some more Elves on the way,[13] and there was some fine singing. I have never heard anything like it before.'

'Did Gandalf send me any message?' asked Bingo.

'No, nothing special. I asked him, when we got to Brandywine Bridge, if he wouldn't come along with me and wait for you, so as to be a guide and helping hand. But he said he was in a hurry. In fact, if you want to know, he said: "Bingo is now old enough and foolish enough to look after himself for a bit."'[14]

"I hope he is right,' said Bingo.

The hobbits hung up their cloaks and sticks, and piled their packs on the floor. Marmaduke went forward and flung open a closed door. Firelight came out and a puff of steam.

'Bath!' cried Odo. 'O blessed Marmaduke!'

'Which way shall we go: eldest first, or quickest first? You will be last either way, Odo,' said Frodo.

'Ha! ha!' said Marmaduke. 'What kind of an innkeeper do you think I am? In that room there are three tubs; and also a copper over a merry furnace that seems to be nearly on the boil. There are also towels, soap, mats, jugs, and what not. Get inside!'

The three rushed in and shut the door. Marmaduke went into the kitchen, and while he was busy there he heard snatches of competing songs mixed with the sound of splashing and wallowing. Over all the rest Odo's voice suddenly rose in a chant:

> *Bless the water O my feet and toes!*
> *Bless it O my ten fingers!*
> *Bless the water, O Odo!*
> *And praise the name of Marmaduke!*[15]

Marmaduke knocked on the door. 'All Bucklebury will know you have arrived before long,' he said. 'Also there is such a thing as supper. I cannot live on praise much longer.'

Bingo came out. 'Lawks!' said Marmaduke looking in. The stone floor was all in pools. Frodo was drying in front of the fire; Odo was still wallowing.

'Come on, Bingo!' said Marmaduke. 'Let's begin supper, and leave them!'

They had supper in the kitchen on a table near the open fire. The others soon arrived. Odo was the last, but he quickly made up for lost time. When they had finished Marmaduke pushed back the table, and drew chairs round the fire. 'We'll clear up later,' he said. 'Now tell me all about it!'[16]

Bingo stretched his legs and yawned. 'It's easy in here,' he said, 'and somehow our adventure seems rather absurd, and not so important as it did out there. But this is what happened. A Black Rider came up behind us yesterday afternoon (it seems a week ago), and I am sure he was looking for us, or me. After that he kept on reappearing (always behind). Let me see, yes, we saw him four times altogether, counting the figure on the landing-stage, and once we heard his horse,[17] and once we thought we heard just a -sniff.'

'What are you talking about?' said Marmaduke. 'What is a black rider?'

'A black figure on a horse,' said Bingo. 'But I will tell you all about it.' He gave a pretty good account of their journey, with occasional additions and interruptions by Frodo and Odo. Only Odo was still positive that the sniff they thought they heard was really part of the mystery.

'I should think you were making it all up, if I had not seen that queer shape this evening,' said Marmaduke. 'What is it all about, I wonder?'

'So do we!' said Frodo. 'Do you think anything of Farmer Maggot's guess, that it has something to do with Bilbo?'

'Well, it was only a guess anyway,' said Bingo. 'I am sure old Maggot does not know anything. I should have expected the Elves to tell me, if the Riders had anything to do with Bilbo's adventures.'

'Old Maggot is rather a shrewd fellow,' said Marmaduke. 'A good deal goes on behind his round face which does not come out in his talk. He used to go into the Old Forest at one time, and had the reputation of knowing a thing or two outside the Shire. Anyway I can guess no better. What are you going to do about it?'

'There is nothing to do,' said Bingo, 'except to go home. Which is difficult for me, as I haven't got one now. I shall just have to go on, as the Elves advised. But you need not come, of course.'

'Of course not,' said Marmaduke. 'I joined the party just for fun, and I am certainly not going to leave it now. Besides, you will need me. Three's company, but four's more. And if the hints of the Elves mean what you think, there are at least four Riders, not to mention an invisible sniff, and a black bundle on the landing-stage. My advice is: let us start off even earlier tomorrow than we planned, and see if we can't get a good start. I rather fancy Riders will have to go round by the bridges to get across the River.'

'But we shall have to go much the same way,' said Bingo. 'We shall have to strike the East Road near Brandywine Bridge.'

'That's not my idea,' said Marmaduke. 'I think we should avoid

the road at present. It's a waste of time. We should actually be
going back westward if we made for the road-meeting near the
Bridge. We must make a short cut north-east through the Old
Forest. I will guide you.'

'How can you?' asked Odo. 'Have you ever been there?'

'O yes,' said Marmaduke. 'All the Brandybucks go there
occasionally, when the fit takes them. I often go – only in daylight,
of course, when the woods are fairly quiet and sleepy. Still I know
my way about. If we start early and push along we ought to be
quite safe and clear of the Forest before tomorrow night. I have
got five good ponies waiting – sturdy little beasts: not speedy of
course, but good for a long day's work. They're stabled in a shed
out in the fields behind this house.'

'I don't like the idea at all,' said Odo. 'I would rather meet these
Riders (if we must meet them) on a road, where there is a chance
of meeting ordinary honest travellers as well. I don't like woods,
and I have heard queer tales of the Old Forest. I think Black
Riders will be very much more at home there than we shall.'

'But we shall probably be out of it again before they get in,' said
Marmaduke. 'It seems to me silly, anyway, when you are beginning an adventurous journey to start by going back and jogging
along a dull river-side road – in full view of all the numerous
hobbits of Buckland.[18] Perhaps you would like to call and take
leave of old Rory at the Hall. It would be polite and proper; and he
might lend you a carriage.'

'I knew you would propose something rash,' said Odo. 'But I
am not going to argue any more, if the others agree. Let's vote –
though I am sure I shall be the odd man out.'

He was – though Bingo and Frodo took some time to make up
their minds.

'There you are!' said Odo. 'What did I say this morning? Three
to one! Well, I only hope it comes off all right.'

'Now that's settled,' said Marmaduke, 'we had better get to bed.
But first we must clear up, and do all the packing we can. Come
on!'

It was some time before the hobbits finished putting things
away, tidying up, and packing what they needed in the way of
stores for their journey. At last they went to bed – and slept in
proper beds (but without sheets) for the last time for many a long
day.[19] Bingo could not go to sleep for some time: his legs ached.
He was glad he was riding in the morning. At last he fell asleep into
a vague dream, in which he seemed to be lying under a window

that looked out into a sea of tangled trees: outside there was a snuffling.

## NOTES

1　It is at first sight puzzling that Frodo should say that 'Buckland is almost exactly south-east from Woodhall', and again immediately below that they could strike the road again 'above Buckland', since later in this chapter (p. 100) Buckland is described as 'a thickly inhabited strip between the River and the Old Forest', defended by the Hedge some forty miles long – clearly too large an area to be described as 'almost exactly south-east from Woodhall'. The explanation must be, however, that my father changed the meaning of the name *Buckland* in the course of the chapter. At first *Buckland* was a place, a village, rather than a region (at its first occurrence it replaced *Bury Underwood*, which in turn replaced *Wood Eaton*, p. 35 note 5), and it still was so here; but further on in the chapter the village of Bucklebury-by-the-River emerged (p. 92), and Buckland then became the name of the Brandybucks' land beyond the River. See note 5, and the note on the Shire Map, p. 107.

2　See the note on the Shire Map, p. 107.

3　A hastily pencilled note on the typescript here reads: 'Sound of hoofs going by not far off.' See p. 287.

4　*Maggot* was later struck out in pencil and replaced by *Puddifoot*, but only in this one instance. On the earliest map of the Shire (see p. 107) the farm is marked, in ink, *Puddifoot*, changed in pencil to *Maggot*. The Puddifoots of Stock are mentioned in FR, p. 101.

5　Here again *Buckland* still signifies the village (see note 1); but *Bucklebury* appears shortly after (p. 92), the name being typed over an erasure.

6　The substance of this passage about hobbit-holes and hobbit-houses was afterwards placed in the Prologue. See further pp. 294, 312.

7　Towers built on the western coasts of Middle-earth by exiles of Númenor are mentioned in the second version of *The Fall of Númenor* (V.28, 30). – The substance of this passage .was also afterwards placed in the Prologue (see note 6), and there also the towers are called 'Elf-towers'. Cf. *Of the Rings of Power* in *The Silmarillion*, p. 292: 'It is said that the towers of Emyn Beraid were not built indeed by the exiles of Númenor, but were raised by Gil-galad for Elendil, his friend.'

8　*came at last back to the road:* this is of course the road they had been walking on originally, 'the road to Buckland'; at this time there was no causeway road running south from the Brandywine Bridge on the west bank of the river (and no village of Stock).

9　In FR (p. 109) the distance is 'well over twenty miles from end to end.' See p. 298.

10  This genealogy was afterwards wholly abandoned, of course, but the mother of Meriadoc (Marmaduke) remained a Took (Esmeralda, who married Saradoc Brandybuck, known as 'Scattergold').

11  Melissa Brandybuck appeared in the fourth version of 'A Long-expected Party', on which occasion she danced on a table with Prospero Took (p. 38).

12  Bingo told Gildor (p. 63) that Gandalf 'went off with the dwarves and the Rivendell elves as soon as the fireworks were over.' This is the first appearance of the story that Marmaduke/Meriadoc had been at Hobbiton but had left early.

13  *We met some more Elves on the way:* these were the Elves of Gildor's company, who thus already knew about the Party when Bingo, Frodo and Odo encountered them (p. 68, note 17).

14  Cf. the note cited on p. 41: 'Where is G[andalf] asks Odo – said I was old and foolish enough now to take care of myself said B.'

15  This 'chant' was emended on the typescript thus:

> *Bless the water, O my feet and toes!*
> *Praise the bath, O my ten fingers!*
> *Bless the water, O my knees and shoulders!*
> *Praise the bath, O my ribs, and rejoice!*
> *Let Odo praise the house of Brandybuck,*
> *And praise the name of Marmaduke for ever.*

This new version belongs to the time of the manuscript portion at the end of the chapter (note 16).

16  Here the typescript ends, and the remainder is in manuscript; see p. 109.

17  *and once we heard his horse:* this is a reference to the revised passage in the second chapter, where it is told that a Black Rider stopped his horse for a moment on the road beside the tree in which the hobbits were sitting (p. 55 and note 11).

18  This is a reference to the road within Buckland. Cf. p. 53: 'the ordinary way to Buckland was along the East Road to the meeting of the Water and the Brandywine River, where there was a bridge, *and then south along the River.*'

19  It is clear from this that my father had not yet foreseen the hobbits' visit to the house of Tom Bombadil.

### Note on the Shire Map

There are four extant maps of the Shire made by my father, and two which I made, but only one of them, I think, can contain an element or layer that goes back to the time when these chapters were written (the first months of 1938). This is however a convenient place to give some indications concerning all of them.

I   An extremely rough map (reproduced as the frontispiece), built up in stages, and done in pencil and red, blue, and black inks; extending from Hobbiton in the West to the Barrow-downs in the East. In its inception this was the first, or at least the first that survives. Some features were first marked in pencil and then inked over.

II   A map on a smaller scale in faint pencil and blue and red chalks, extending to the Far Downs in the West, but showing little more than the courses of roads and rivers.

III   A map of roads and rivers on a larger scale than II, extending from Michel Delving in the West to the Hedge of Buckland, but without any names (see on map V below).

IV   A small scale map extending from the Green Hill country to Bree, carefully drawn in ink and coloured chalks, but soon abandoned and marking only a few features.

V   An elaborate map in pencil and coloured chalks which I made in 1943 (see p. 200), for which III (showing only the courses of roads and rivers) was very clearly the basis and which I followed closely. No doubt III was made by my father for this purpose.

VI   The map which was published in *The Fellowship of the Ring*; this I made not long before its publication (that is to say, some ten years after map V).

In what follows I consider only certain features arising in the course of this chapter.

*Buckland is almost exactly south-east from Woodhall* (p. 89). *Buckland* was still here the name of the village (see note 1 above); *Bucklebury* first appears on p. 92. On map I Bucklebury does indeed lie south-east (or strictly east-south-east) from Woodhall, but on map II the Ferry is due east, and on III it is east-north-east, whence the representation on my maps V and VI. In the original edition of FR (p. 97) the text had here 'The Ferry is south-east from Woodhall', which was corrected to 'east' in the revised edition (second impression 1967) when my father observed the discrepancy with the published map. The shifting had clearly come about unintentionally. (It may be noticed incidentally that all the maps show Woodhall on a side road (the 'lane') going off from that to Buckland; see p. 66, note 10).

*The road bears away to the left ... and then sweeps round south when it gets nearer to the River* (p. 89). This southward sweep is strongly marked on map I (and repeated on map II), where the Buckland road joins the causeway road above the village of Stock (as Frodo says in FR, p. 97: 'It goes round the north of the Marish so as to strike the causeway from the Bridge above Stock'). At the time when this chapter was written there was no causeway road (note 8). This is another case where the text of FR accords with map I, but not with the published map (VI); in this case, however, my father did not correct the text. On map III the Buckland road does not 'sweep round south': but after bearing away to the left or north (before reaching Woodhall) it runs *in a straight line due east* to meet the road from the Bridge. This I followed on my map V; but the village of Stock was not marked on III, which only shows roads and rivers, and I placed the road-meeting actually in the village, not to the north of it. Although, as I clearly recollect, map V was made in his study and in conversation with him, my father cannot have noticed my error in this point. The published map simply follows V.

One other point may be noticed here. Marmaduke twice (pp. 100, 103) refers to 'bridges' over the Brandywine, but none of the maps shows any other bridge but that which carried the East Road, the Brandywine Bridge.

★

My father's letter to Stanley Unwin quoted on page 44 shows that he had finished this chapter by 4 March 1938. Three months later, on 4 June 1938, he wrote to Stanley Unwin saying:

I meant long ago to have thanked Rayner for bothering to read the tentative chapters, and for his excellent criticism. It agrees strikingly with Mr Lewis', which is therefore confirmed. I must plainly bow to my two chief (and most well-disposed) critics. The trouble is that 'hobbit talk'* amuses me privately (and to a certain degree also my boy Christopher) more than adventures; but I must curb this severely. Although longing to do so, I have not had a chance to touch any story-writing since the Christmas vacation.

And he added that he could not 'see any loophole left for months.' On 24 July he said in a letter to Charles Furth at Allen and Unwin:

The sequel to *the Hobbit* has remained where it stopped. It has lost my favour, and I have no idea what to do with it. For one thing the original *Hobbit* was never intended to have a sequel – Bilbo 'remained very happy to the end of his days and those were extraordinarily long': a sentence I find an almost insuperable obstacle to a satisfactory link. For another nearly all the 'motives' that I can use were packed into the original book, so that a sequel will appear either 'thinner' or merely repetitional. For a third: I am personally immensely amused by hobbits as such, and can contemplate them eating and making their rather fatuous jokes indefinitely; but I find that is not the case with even my most devoted 'fans' (such as Mr Lewis, and ?Rayner Unwin). Mr Lewis says hobbits are only amusing when in unhobbitlike situations. For a last: my mind on the 'story' side is really preoccupied with the 'pure' fairy stories or mythologies of the *Silmarillion*, into which even Mr Baggins got dragged against my original will, and I do not

---

*Rayner Unwin had said that the second and third chapters 'have I think a little too much conversation and "hobbit talk" which tends to make it lag a little.'

think I shall be able to move much outside it – unless it is finished (and perhaps published) – which has a releasing effect.

At the beginning of this extract my father was repeating what he had said in his letters of 17 and 18 February quoted on pp. 43–4, when he had written no more than 'A Long-expected Party'. But it is very hard to see why he said here that he found the sentence in *The Hobbit*, that Bilbo 'remained very happy to the end of his days and those were extraordinarily long', 'an almost insuperable obstacle to a satisfactory link'; since what he had written at this stage was not about Bilbo but about his 'nephew' Bingo, and in so far as Bilbo was mentioned nothing had been said to show that he did not remain happy till the end of his extraordinarily long days.

This then is where the narrative stopped, and stayed stopped through some six months or more. With abundant 'hobbit-talk' on the way, he had got Bingo, Frodo, and Odo to Buckland on the way to Rivendell, whither Gandalf had preceded them. They had encountered the Black Riders, Gildor and his company of Elves, and Farmer Maggot, where their visit ended in a much less satisfactory way than it would do later, through an outrageous practical joke on Bingo's part (the comic potential of which had by no means been exhausted); they had crossed the Brandywine, and arrived at the little house prepared for them by Marmaduke Brandybuck. In his letter to Charles Furth just cited he said that he had 'no idea what to do with it'; but Tom Bombadil, the Willowman and the Barrow-wights were already envisaged as possibilities (see pp. 42–3).

On 31 August 1938 he wrote again to Charles Furth, and now a great change had taken place:

In the last two or three days . . . I have begun again on the sequel to the 'Hobbit' – The Lord of the Ring. It is now flowing along, and getting quite out of hand. It has reached about Chapter VII and progresses towards quite unforeseen goals.

He said 'about Chapter VII' on account of uncertainty over chapter-divisions (see p. 132).

The passage in manuscript at the end of the present chapter (see note 16 above) was (I feel certain) added to the typescript at this time, and was the beginning of this new burst of narrative energy. My father had now decided that the hobbits' journey would take them into the Old Forest, that 'dubious region' which had appeared in the third version of 'A Long-expected Party' (p. 29), and where he had already suggested in early notes (p. 43) that the hobbits should become lost and caught by the Willow-man. And 'the sequel to *The Hobbit*' is given – for the first time, it seems – a title: *The Lord of the Ring* (see p. 74 and note 3).

# V

# THE OLD FOREST AND THE WITHYWINDLE

In the letter of 31 August 1938 quoted at the end of the last chapter my father said that 'in the last two or three days' he had turned again to the book, that it was 'flowing along, and getting quite out of hand', and that it had reached 'about Chapter VII'. It is clear that in those few days the hobbits had passed through the Old Forest by way of the Withywindle valley, stayed in the house of Tom Bombadil, escaped from the Barrow-wight, and reached Bree,

There is very little preliminary sketching of the original fourth chapter, and such as there is I give here. There is first a page dashed down in soft pencil and now very difficult to read; I introduce some necessary punctuation and small connective words that were omitted, and expand the initial letters that stand for names.

They got on to the ponies and rode off into the mist. After riding more than an hour they came to the Hedge. It was tall and netted over with silver cobwebs.

'How do we get through this?' said Odo.

'There is a way,' said Marmaduke. Following him along the Hedge they came to a small brick-lined tunnel. It went down a gully and dived right under the Hedge, coming out some twenty yards at the far side, where it was closed by a gate of close iron bars. Marmaduke unlocked this, let them out, and locked it again. As it snapped back they all felt a sudden pang.

'There,' said Marmaduke. 'You have now left the Shire – and are [?outside] and close to the edge of the Old Forest.'

'Are the stories about it true?' said Odo.

'I don't know what stories you mean – if you mean the old bogey stories our nurses used to tell us, about goblins and wolves and things of that sort, no. But it is queer. Everything in the Old Forest is very much more alive, more aware of what is going on, than in the Shire. And they don't like strangers. The trees watch you. But they don't do much in daylight. [?Occasionally] the most malicious ones may drop a branch or stick a root out or grasp at you with long trailers. But at night things can get most disturbing – I am told. I have only once been in the Old Forest, and then only near the edge, after dark. I thought the trees were all whispering to each other although there was no wind, and the branches waved about and groped. They do say the trees actually move and can surround strangers and hem them in. They used long ago to attack the Hedge, come and plant themselves right by it and lean over it. But we burn[t] the ground all along the east side for miles and they gave it up. There are also queer things living deep in the Forest and on the far side. But I have not heard that they are very fierce – at least not in daytime. But something makes paths and keeps them open. There is the beginning of a great and broad one that goes more or less in our direction. That is the one I am making for.'

The ground was rising steadily and as their ponies plodded along the trees became darker and thicker and taller. There was no sound, save an occasional drip; but they all got an uncomfortable feeling which steadily increased that they were being watched – with disapproval if not dislike. Marmaduke tried to sing, but his voice soon fell to a hum and then died away. A small branch fell from an old tree with a crack on the ground behind them. They stopped, startled, and looked round.

'The trees seem to object to my singing,' said Marmaduke cheerfully. 'All right, we'll wait till we get to a more open point.'

Clearing   hillock   view   sun up   mist goes   turns hot
Trees bar way.   They turn [?always . . . . . . side]
Willowman.   Meeting with Tombombadil.
[*Struck out:* Barrow-wights]
Camp on the downs

Whereas this piece begins as narrative and tails off into notes, another page is expressly a 'sketch' of the story to be written:

The path winds on and they get tired. They cannot get any view. At last they see a bare hillock (crowned by a few pines) ahead looking down onto the path. They reach this and find the mist gone, and the sun very hot and nearly above. 11 o'clock. They rest and eat. But they can see only forest all round, and cannot make out either Hedge or line of the road northward, but the bare downland East and South lies green-grey in the distance. Beyond the hillock the path turns *southwards*. They determine to leave it and strike N.E. by the sun. But trees bar the way. They are going downhill, and brambles and bushes, hazels and whatnot block them. Every . . . . . [?opening] leads them away to their right. Eventually when it is already afternoon they find themselves coming to a willow-bordered river – the Withywindle.[1] Marmaduke knows this flows through the forest from the downs to join the Brandywine at Haysend. There seems some sort of rough path going upstream. But a great sleepiness comes on them. Odo and Bingo cannot go on without a rest. They sit down with their backs to a great willow, while Frodo and Marmaduke attend to the ponies. Willowman traps Bingo and Odo. Suddenly a singing is heard in the distance. (Tom Bombadil not named). The Willow relaxes its hold.

They get through to end of forest as evening comes on, and climb on to the downs. It gets very cold – mist is followed by a chilly drizzle. They shelter under a big barrow. Barrow-wight takes them inside. They wake to find themselves buried alive. They shout. At last Marmaduke and Bingo begin a song. An answering song outside. Tom Bombadil opens the stone door and lets them out. They go to his house for the night – two Barrow-wights come [?galloping] after them, but stop every time Tom Bombadil turns and looks at them.

At this stage, then, their first encounter with Tom Bombadil was to be very brief, and they would not be his guests until after their escape from the barrow up on the downs; but no narrative of this form is found, and doubtless none was written.

It is of course possible that other preliminary drafting has been lost, but the earliest extant text of the original fourth chapter (numbered 'IV' but with no title) looks like composition *ab initio*, with many words and sentences and even whole pages rejected and replaced at the time of writing. For most of its length, however, this is an orderly and legible manuscript, though rapidly written, and increasingly so as it proceeds (see note 3). It is then remarkable that this text reaches at a stroke the narrative as published in FR (Chapter 6, 'The Old Forest'), with only the most minor differences – other than the different cast of characters (largely a matter of names) and different attribution of 'parts', and often and for substantial stretches with almost exactly the wording of the final form. My father might well say that *The Lord of the Ring* was 'now flowing along'.

There are a few particular points to notice. First, as regards the characters, the 'spoken parts' are variously distributed as between the first form and the final. Fredegar Bolger is of course not present to see them off at the entrance to the tunnel under the Hedge, and his question 'How are you going to get through this?' (FR p. 120) is given to Odo ('How do we get through this?', cf. p. 110). The verse *O! Wanderers in the shadowed land*,[2] Frodo's in FR (p. 123), is here Marmaduke's, but changed, probably immediately, to Frodo Took's. Pippin's objection to taking the path by the Withywindle (FR pp. 126–7) is Bingo's; and in the scene with Old Man Willow the parts are quite distinct. In the original version it is Bingo and Odo who are totally overcome by sleep and lay themselves against the willow-trunk, and it is Marmaduke who is more resistant and alarmed at the onset of drowsiness. Frodo Took ('more adventurous') goes down to the river-bank (as does Frodo Baggins in FR), and falling asleep at the Willow's feet is tipped into the water and held under by a root, while Marmaduke plays the later part of Sam in rounding up the ponies, rescuing Frodo (Took or Baggins) from the river, and discussing with him how to release the prisoners from the tree. Yet despite the later redistribution of parts in this scene, and the advent of Sam Gamgee, the old text is very close to the final form, as may be seen from this example (cf. FR p. 128).

Marmaduke gripped him [Frodo Took] by the back of his jacket, and dragged him from under the tree-root, and laid him on the bank. Almost at once he woke, and coughed and spluttered.

'Do you know,' he said, 'the beast *threw* me in! I felt it and saw it: the big root just twizzled round and threw me in.'

'You were dreaming,' said Marmaduke. 'I left you asleep, though I thought it rather a silly place to sit in.'

'What about the other two?' asked Frodo. 'I wonder what sort of dreams *they've* had?'

They went round to the landward side. Marmaduke then understood the click. Odo had vanished. The crack he lay in had closed to, so that not a chink could be seen. Bingo was trapped; for his crack had closed to about his waist . . .

There are also a few minor points of topography to mention. It is said in the outline (p. 111) that the hillock was crowned with pines, and this was retained: it had 'a knot of pine-trees at the top', under which the hobbits sat. In FR (p. 124) the hill is likened to a bald head, and the trees about it to 'thick hair that ended sharply in a circle round a shaven crown.' – When later they came to the end of the gully and looked out from the trees at the Withywindle, they were at the top of a cliff:

Suddenly the woodland trees came to an end, and the gully ended at the top of a bank that was almost a cliff. Over this the stream dived, and fell in a series of small waterfalls. Looking down they saw that below them was a wide space of grass and reeds . . .

Marmaduke scrambled down to the river, and disappeared into the long grass and low bushes. After a while he reappeared and called up to them from a patch of turf some thirty feet below. He reported that there was fairly solid ground between the bank and the river . . .

In FR (p. 126) it is clear that the hobbits, following the little stream down the gully, had reached the level of the Withywindle valley while still in the deep woodland:

Coming to the opening they found that they had made their way down through a cleft in a high steep bank, almost a cliff. At its feet was a wide space of grass and reeds . . .

[Merry] passed out into the sunshine and disappeared into the long grasses. After a while he reappeared, and reported . . .

Subsequently, in the original version, there is anxiety about the descent of the ponies from the cliff; they got down in fact without difficulty, but Frodo Took 'put too much weight on a grassy lump that stuck out like a step, and went down with his head over heels for the last fifteen feet or so; but he came to no great harm at the bottom, for the ground was soft.' In FR (p. 127) the hobbits merely 'filed out' from the trees.

The last part of the chapter, in which Tom Bombadil appears, and which ends with the same words as in FR ('a golden light was all about them'), is so close to the final form[3] that only one small matter need be mentioned. It is made just as clear here as in FR that the path which the hobbits followed beside the Withywindle lay on the north side of the river, the side from which they descended out of the forest, and it is therefore strange that the approach to Tom Bombadil's house should be described thus:

The grass under their feet was smooth and short, and seemed to be mown and shaven. The forest edge behind them was as clipped and trim as a hedge. The path was edged with white stones; and *turning sharp to the left went over a little bridge*. It then wound up onto the top of a round knoll . . .

But the path was already on the left side of the river as it went upstream. Later on, this text was very heavily corrected, and the FR version all but achieved; yet this detail was retained: 'The path was bordered with white stones; and turning sharp to the left it led them over a wooden bridge.' Later again, the word 'left' was changed to 'right', implying that Tom Bombadil's house lay on the south side of the Withywindle. In FR there is no mention of a bridge. My father's map of the Shire (see p. 107: map I) probably shows that he changed his mind on this point; for the underlying pencil shows 'TB', with a dark mark beside it, on the south side, whereas the ink overlay shows the house to the north of the stream. See further pp. 327–8.

## NOTES

1  The first occurrence of the name *Withywindle*.
2  The verse has *shadow-land* for *shadowed land* in the first line, but is otherwise as in FR. Rough working for a verse in this place is also found. My father first wrote: 'O wanderers in the land of trees / despair not for there is no wood', but this was broken off and the following suggested:

> *think not of hearth that lies behind*
> *but set your hearts on distant hills*

> *beyond the rising of the sun.*
> *The journey is but new begun,*
> *the road goes ever on before*
> *past many a house and many a door*
> *over water and under wood*

3   Towards the end of the chapter the manuscript becomes extremely confused. From the point where Marmaduke and Frodo Took discover that Bingo and Odo are trapped by the Willow-man my father changed from ink to pencil, and degenerating into a rapid scribble the chapter seems to have petered out in the course of their rescue by Tom Bombadil; but he subsequently erased most of the pencilled text, or overwrote it in ink, and continued on in ink to the end of the chapter. This concluding portion departs from the preliminary sketch given on p. 112, where the hobbits after their rescue went up on to the Downs and were captured by the Barrow-wight; here, as in FR, Tom invites them to come to his house, and goes on ahead up the path beside the Withywindle. The last part of the manuscript is probably, strictly speaking, a subsequent addition; but the matter is of slight importance, since all this writing obviously belongs to the same period of work, at the end of August 1938.

### Note on Tom Bombadil

Tom Bombadil, Goldberry, Old Man Willow, and the Barrow-wight had already existed for some time, appearing in print in the pages of *The Oxford Magazine* (Vol. LII, no. 13, 15 February 1934). In a letter of 1954 my father said:

> I don't think Tom needs philosophizing about, and is not improved by it. But many have found him an odd or indeed discordant ingredient. In historical fact I put him in because I had already 'invented' him independently (he first appeared in the Oxford Magazine) and wanted an 'adventure' on the way.*

On a small isolated piece of paper are found the following verses. At the top of the page my father wrote: 'Date unknown – germ of Tom Bombadil so evidently in mid 1930s'; and this note was written at the same time as the text, which is certainly quite late. There is no trace of the text from which it was copied.

> *(Said I)*
> *'Ho! Tom Bombadil*
> *Whither are you going*
> *With John Pompador*
> *Down the River rowing?'*

---

*\*The Letters of J. R. R. Tolkien*, no. 153. Some major observations on Tom Bombadil are found in this letter and in no. 144.

*(Said he)*
*'Through Long Congleby,*
*Stoke Canonicorum,†*
*Past King's Singleton*
*To Bumby Cocalorum –*

*To call Bill Willoughby*
*Whatever he be doing,*
*And ax Harry Larraby*
*What beer he is a-brewing.'*

*(And he sang)*
*'Go, boat! Row! The willows are a-bending,*
*reeds are leaning, wind is in the grasses.*
*Flow, stream, flow! The ripples are unending;*
*green they gleam, and shimmer as it passes.*

*Run, fair Sun, through heaven all the morning,*
*rolling golden! Merry is our singing!*
*Cool the pools, though summer be a-burning;*
*in shady glades let laughter run a-ringing!'*

The poem published in *The Oxford Magazine* in 1934 bore the title *The Adventures of Tom Bombadil* (in earlier forms it was *The History of Tom Bombadil*). Many years later (1962) my father made it the first poem in the collection to which it gave the title (and added also a new poem, *Bombadil Goes Boating*, in which he meets Farmer Maggot in the Marish). Various changes were made in this later version, and references to the Withywindle were introduced, but the old poem was very largely preserved. In it are to be found the origin of many things in this and the following chapters – the closing crack in the Great Willow (though in the poem it was Tom himself who was caught in it), the supper of 'yellow cream and honeycomb, and white bread, and butter', the 'nightly noises' that included the tapping of the branches of Old Man Willow on the window-pane, the words of the Barrow-wight (who in the poem was inside Tom's house) 'I am waiting for you', and much else.

†Mediaeval name of what is now Stoke Canon in Devonshire.

# VI
# TOM BOMBADIL

A very brief outline shows my father's first thoughts for the next stage of the hobbits' journey: their visit to the house of Tom Bombadil.

Tom Bombadil rescues them from Willow Man. He says it was lucky he came that way – he had gone to the water-lily pool for some white water-lilies for Goldberry (my wife).
He turns out to know Farmer Maggot. (Make Maggot not a hobbit, but some other kind of creature – not dwarf, but akin to Tom Bombadil). They rest at his house. He says *only* way out is along his path beside the Withywindle. Description of feast and (?willow] fire. *Many noises at night.*
Tom Bombadil wakes them singing *derry dol*, and opening all the windows (he lives in a little house under the down-side facing the forest edge and the [?east corner] of the wood). He tells them to go north but avoid the high Downs and barrows. *He warns them of barrow-wights*; tells them a song to sing if the barrow-wights frighten them or
A cold day. The mist thickens and they get lost.

This scheme was written at great speed in pencil. As will be seen shortly, at this stage the hobbits only spent the one night with Tom Bombadil, and left the following morning. Another set of notes, also obviously preceding the first actual narrative text, is also very difficult to read:

Water-lily motive – last lilies of summer for Goldberry.
Relation of Tom Bombadil to Farmer Maggot (Maggot not a hobbit?)
Tom Bombadil is an 'aborigine' – he knew the land before men, before hobbits, before barrow-wights, yes before the necromancer – before the elves came to this quarter of the world.
Goldberry says he is 'master of water, wood and hill'. Does all this land belong to him? No! The land and the things belong to themselves. He is not the possessor but the master, because he belongs to himself.
Description of Goldberry, with her hair as yellow as the flag-lilies, her green gown and light feet.

Barrow-wights related to Black-riders. Are Black-riders actually
horsed Barrow-wights?

The guests sleep – there is a noise as of wind surging in the edges
of the forest and . . . . . through the panes and gables and the
doors. Galloping of [?horses] round the house.

The first actual narrative (incomplete) of this chapter is a very rough
and difficult manuscript in ink, becoming very rough indeed before it
peters out on the first morning at Bombadil's house. It has no title, but is
rather oddly numbered 'V or VI'. Here, even more than in the last
chapter, the final form – until just at the end – is already present in all but
detail of expression.

Most interesting is the story of the hobbits' dreams during the night,
which is told thus:

In the dead night Bingo woke and heard noises: a sudden fear
came over him [?so that] he did not speak but lay listening
breathless. He heard a sound like a strong wind curling round the
house and shaking it, and down the wind came a galloping, a
galloping, a galloping: hooves seemed to come charging down the
hillside from the east, up to the walls and round and round, hooves
thudding and wind blowing, and then dying away back up the hill
and into the darkness.

'Black riders,' thought Bingo. 'Black riders, a black host of
riders,' and he wondered if he would ever again have the courage
even in the morning to leave the safety of these good stone walls.
He lay and listened for a while, but all had become quiet again,
and after a while he fell asleep. At his side Odo lay dreaming. He
turned and groaned, and woke to the darkness, and yet the dream
went on. Tap, tap, squeak: the noise was like branches fretting in
the wind, twigs like fingers scraping wall and window . . . [&c. as
in FR p. 138].

It was the sound of water the Frodo heard falling into his sleep
and slowly waking him. Water streaming gently down at first, and
then spreading all round the house, gurgling under the walls . . .
[&c. as in FR p. 139].

Meriadoc[1] slept on through the night in deep content.

As told here, there seems no reason not to understand that Black
Riders (or Barrow-wights) actually came and rode round Tom Bombadil's house during the night. It will be seen that it is said explicitly that
Bingo woke, and after a while fell asleep. In the initial sketch given on
p. 112 (where the hobbits only went to stay with Tom after their capture
by a Barrow-wight up on the Downs) 'Two Barrow-wights come

[?galloping] after them'; cf. also the note on p. 118: 'Barrow-wights related to Black-riders. Are Black-riders actually horsed Barrow-wights?' –
followed by 'Galloping of [?horses] round the house.' In any case, the
end of the present text (unhappily so eccentrically scribbled as to make
its interpretation extremely difficult) is explicit. Here, as in the later
story, Bingo waking looks out of the east window of their room on to the
kitchen-garden grey with dew.

He had expected to see turf right up to the walls, turf all pocked
with hoof-marks. Actually his view was screened by a tall line of
green beans on poles, but above and far beyond them the grey top
of the hill loomed up against the sunrise. It was a grey morning
with soft clouds, behind which were deeps of yellow and pale red.
The light was broadening quickly and the red flowers on the beans
began to shine against the wet green leaves.

Frodo looks from the western window, as does Pippin in FR, and sees
the Withywindle disappearing into the mist below, and the flower-
garden: 'there was no willow-tree to be seen.'

'Good morning, merry friends!' said Tom, opening the east
window wide. A cool air flowed in. 'The sun will [?heat] you when
the day is older. I have been walking far, leaping on the hill-tops,
since the grey twilight [?came] and the night foundered, wet grass
underfoot . . . . . . .'
When they were dressed [*struck out as written:* Tom took them
up the hillside] the sun was already risen over the hill, and the
clouds were melting away. In the forest valley trees were appearing like tall heads rising out of the curling sea of mist. They were
glad of breakfast – indeed they were glad to be awake and safe and
at the merry end of a day again. The thought of going was heavy on
them – and not only for fear of the road. Had it been a [?merry]
road and the road home they would still have wished to tarry
there.
But they knew that could not be. Bingo too found in his heart
that the noise of hoofs was not only dream. They must escape
quickly or else . . . [?pursued] here. So he made up his mind to get
such help and advice as [?old] Bombadil could or would give.
'Master,' he said, 'we cannot thank you for your kindness for it
has been beyond thanks. But we must go, against our wish and
quickly. For I heard horsemen in the night and fear we are
pursued.'
Tom looked at him. 'Horsemen,' he said. 'Dead men [?riding
the wind. 'Tis long since they came hence.] What ails the Barrow-

wights to leave their old mounds? You are strange folk to come out
of the Shire, [?even stranger than my news told me.] Now you had
best tell me all – and I will give you counsel.'

Here the text ends, but following it are these notes in pencil:

Make it sudden rainy day. They spend it at Tom's house, and
tell him the tale; and he of Willow-man and the . . . . . . .[2] He is
concerned about the riders; but says he will think of counsel. Next
day is fine. He takes them to the hilltop. They . . . . the barrows.

This is where the story of the wet second day spent in long talk with
Bombadil entered; before this the weather was to have become fine, and
the hobbits were to have left when they had told Tom their story and
received his advice. In this earliest narrative Bingo was so convinced of
the reality of what he had heard in the night that he raised the matter with
Tom, and Tom seems to take him seriously; and in this context the word
'Actually' (retained in FR) in 'Actually his view was screened by a tall line
of beans on poles' suggests that if it had not been for this he would indeed
have seen the turf 'all pocked with hoof-prints.'

A second narrative followed, obviously written immediately after the
first, and this is complete. Here the chapter is numbered 'V', still without
title. The first text was now refined and ordered in expression, the
morning bodes rain, and the new version becomes, to the point where the
first ended, scarcely distinguishable from that of FR, except in the
matter of the 'dreams'. These are still told in the same unambiguous
language as if they were real events in the night; but nothing more is said
of them afterwards than is said in FR. In the final story Frodo's dream is a
vision of Gandalf standing on the pinnacle of Orthanc and of the descent
of Gwaihir to bear him away, but that vision is still accompanied by the
sound of the Black Riders galloping out of the East; and it was that sound
that woke him. It is still said that he thought in the morning to find the
ground round the house marked by hoofs, but this is now no more than a
way of emphasising the vividness of his experience in the night.

The remainder of the second version of the chapter generally
approaches extraordinarily closely to the final form,[3] but there are not a
few interesting differences.

In Tom Bombadil's long talk with the hobbits on the second day, his
voice is described as 'always in a sing-song or actually singing' (cf. FR
p. 140: 'Often his voice would turn to song'). The passage concerning
Old Man Willow was first written thus:

Amongst his talk there was here and there much said of Old Man
Willow, and Merry learned enough to content him[4] (more than
enough, for it was not comfortable lore), though not enough for
him to understand how that grey thirsty earth-bound spirit had

become imprisoned in the greatest Willow of the Forest. The tree did not die, though its heart went rotten, while the malice of the Old Man drew power out of earth and water, and spread like a net, like fine root-threads in the ground, and invisible twig-fingers in the air, till it had infected or subjugated nearly all the trees on both sides of the valley.[5]

Bombadil's talk about the Barrow-wights of the Barrow-downs remained almost word for word into FR (pp. 141–2), with one difference: for FR 'A shadow came out of dark places far away' this text has 'A dark shadow came up out of the middle of the world'; in the underlying pencilled text (see note 3) can be read 'a dark shadow came up out of the South.' At the end of his talk, where FR has 'still on and back Tom went singing out into ancient starlight', the present version has 'and still further Tom went singing back before the Sun and before the Moon, out into the old starlight.'

A detail worth remarking is the sentence in the old version: 'Whether the morning and evening of one day or of many days had passed Bingo could not tell (nor did he ever discover for certain).' The bracketed words were soon to be removed, when the dating of the journey to Bree became precise; the hobbits stayed with Bombadil on the 26th and 27th of September, and left on the morning of the 28th (see p. 160).

Tom Bombadil's answer to Bingo's question 'Who are you, Master?' has some interesting differences from the final form (FR p. 142):

'Eh, what?' said Tom sitting up, and his eyes glinted in the gloom. 'I am an Aborigine, that's what I am, the Aborigine of this land. [*Struck out at once:* I have spoken a mort[6] of languages and called myself by many names.] Mark my words, my merry friends: Tom was here before the River or the Trees. Tom remembers the first acorn and the first rain-drop. He made paths before the Big People, and saw the Little People arriving. He was here before the kings and the graves and the [ghosts >] Barrow-wights. When the Elves passed westward Tom was here already – before the seas were bent. He saw the Sun rise in the West and the Moon following, before the new order of days was made. He knew the dark under the stars when it was fearless – before the Dark Lord came from Outside.'

In FR Tom Bombadil calls himself 'Eldest', not 'Aborigine' (cf. the notes given on p. 117: 'Tom Bombadil is an "aborigine"'); and the reference here to his having seen 'the Sun rise in the West and the Moon following' was dropped (though 'Tom remembers the first acorn and the first rain-drop', which was retained, says the same). These words are extremely surprising; for in the *Quenta Silmarillion* which my father had only set aside at the end of the previous year it is told that 'Rana [the Moon] was first wrought and made ready, and first rose into the region of the stars, and was the elder of the lights, as was Silpion of the Trees' (V.240); and the Moon first rose as Fingolfin set foot upon Middle-earth, but the Sun when he entered Mithrim (V.250).

Tom Bombadil was 'there' during the Ages of the Stars, before Morgoth came back to Middle-earth after the destruction of the Trees; is it to this event that he referred in his words (retained in FR) 'He knew the dark under the stars when it was fearless – *before the Dark Lord came from Outside*'? It must be said that it seems unlikely that Bombadil would refer to Valinor across the Great Sea as 'Outside', especially since this was long ages 'before the seas were bent', when Númenor was drowned; it would seem much more natural to interpret the word as meaning 'the Outer Dark', 'the Void' beyond the Walls of the World. But in the mythology as it was when my father began *The Lord of the Rings* Melkor entered 'the World' with the other Valar, and never left it until his final defeat. It was only with his return to *The Silmarillion* after *The Lord of the Rings* was completed that there entered the account found in the published work (pp. 35–7) of the First War, in which Melkor was defeated by Tulkas and driven into the Outer Dark, from which he returned in secret while the Valar were resting from their labours on the Isle of Almaren, and overthrew the Lamps, ending the Spring of Arda. It seems then that either Bombadil must in fact refer to Morgoth's return from Valinor to Middle-earth, in company with Ungoliant and bearing the Silmarils, or else that my father had already at this date developed a new conception of the earliest history of Melkor.

After the reference to Farmer Maggot, from whom Tom Bombadil got his knowledge of the Shire, and whom he 'seemed to regard as a person of more importance than they had fancied' (FR p. 143), this text adds: 'We are kinsfolk, he and I. In a way of speaking: distantly and far back, but near enough for friendship' (in the original draft: 'We are akin, he said, distantly, very distantly, but near enough to count'). Cf. the notes given on p. 117, concerning the possibility that Farmer Maggot was not a hobbit at all, but a being of a wholly different kind, and akin to Bombadil.[7] At the end of this passage, the reference in FR to Tom's dealings with Elves, and to his having had news of the flight of Frodo (Bingo) from Gildor, is absent from the present text. (Tom indeed said earlier, FR p. 137, that he and Goldberry had heard of their wandering, and 'guessed you'd come ere long down to the water', and this is found in both the original texts).

Of Tom's questioning of Bingo it is said here that Bingo 'found himself telling him more about Bilbo Baggins and his own history and about the business of his sudden flight than he told before even to his three friends'; in FR (p. 144) this became 'telling him more about Bilbo and his own hopes and fears than he had told before even to Gandalf.' It may be noted that in the old narrative thus far there has been no suggestion that Bingo's departure from Hobbiton was a 'sudden flight' – except perhaps in the 'foreword' given in Chapter III, where Gandalf said to him before the Party 'But you must go quickly' (p. 83).

The episode of Tom and the Ring is told in virtually the same words as in FR, the only and very slight difference being that when Bingo put on the Ring Tom cried: 'Hey, come Bingo there, where be you a-going? What be you a-grinning at? Are you tired of talking? Take off that Ring of yours and sit down a moment. We must talk a while more . . .' Against this my father wrote later: 'Make the seeing clearer', and substituted (after 'where be you a-going?'): 'Did you think I should not see when you had the Ring on? Ha, Tom Bombadil's not as blind as that yet. Take off your golden Ring, and sit down a moment.'

Lastly, at the very end of the chapter, the rhyme that Tom Bombadil taught the hobbits to sing if in need of him is different from that in FR:

> Ho! Tom Bombadil! Whither do you wander?
> Up, down, near or far? Here, there, or yonder?
> By hill that stands, wood that grows, and by the water falling,
> Here now we summon you! Can you hear us calling?

This rhyme was at first present in the next chapter, when Bingo sang it in the barrow; but it was replaced there at the time of writing by *Ho! Tom Bombadil, Tom Bombadillo!* etc., as in FR (p. 153). In the present passage my father wrote in the margin: 'Or substitute rhyme in chapter VI', and that was done (FR p. 145).

## NOTES

1   This is the first occurrence of *Meriadoc* for *Marmaduke* in a manuscript as originally written.

2   The word looks very much like *badgers*. If this is so, it must be a reference to the badgers who captured Tom Bombadil in the poem ('By the coat they caught him, pulled Tom inside the hole, down their tunnels brought him'); see *The Adventures of Tom Bombadil* (1962), pp. 12–13 (the verses describing Tom's encounter with the badgers were left virtually unchanged in the later version). In the next text of this chapter Tom was telling the hobbits 'an absurd story about badgers and their odd ways' when Bingo slipped on the Ring; and this was retained in FR.

3   The story of the wet second day at Bombadil's was written *ab initio* in pencil, then a part of the manuscript overwritten in ink; for the last part of the chapter, from supper on the second day, there is both pencilled draft and manuscript in ink. But it is clear that all this work was continuous and overlapping.

4   The question about Old Man Willow on the night before is asked by Merry (by Frodo in FR); i.e. by one who had not been imprisoned in the tree.

5   A passage very close to that in FR (from 'Tom's words laid bare the
    hearts of trees') was substituted, probably while the manuscript was
    in progress or very soon after.
6   *a mort:* a great many.
7   Conceivably, some pencilled emendations to the typescript of the
    third chapter were added at this time and in this connection. Frodo
    Took's words of Farmer Maggot, 'He lives in a house' (p. 92), were
    thus extended: 'He is not a hobbit – not a pure hobbit anyway. He is
    rather large and has hair under his chin. But his family has had these
    fields time out of mind.' And when Maggot appears (p. 94), 'a large
    round hobbit-face' was changed to 'a large round hair-framed face.'
    Afterwards, in the Prologue to LR, the hobbits of the Eastfarthing
    were decribed as being 'rather large and heavy-legged': 'they were
    well known to be Stoors in a large part of their blood, as indeed was
    shown by the down that many grew on their chins. No Harfoot or
    Fallohide had any trace of a beard.' See p. 294.
        There has already been a hint earlier that Farmer Maggot was not
    altogether what he appeared to be, in Merry's remark (p. 103): 'He
    used to go into the Old Forest at one time, and had the reputation of
    knowing a thing or two outside the Shire.' This was retained in FR
    (p. 113).

# VII

# THE BARROW-WIGHT

My father's earliest thoughts on the encounter with the Barrow-wight (written down while he was working on the story of the hobbits in the Old Forest) have been given on p. 112. When he came to write this chapter he began with a pencilled draft[1] that took the story as far as the hobbits' waking beside the standing stone in the hollow circle on the Downs, and leading their ponies down from it into the fog (FR p. 149). Like many of his preliminary drafts, this would be virtually illegible had he not followed it closely in the first full manuscript (in ink), for words that could be interpreted in a dozen ways without context can then be identified at once. In this case he did no more than improve the hasty wording of the draft, and add the passage describing the view northwards from the stone pillar, with the dark line in the distance that Merry took for trees bordering the East Road.

If the draft continued beyond this point it is lost now; but in fact the manuscript in ink could well be the primary composition. There is however a very rough pencilled plot-outline for the story from the point where 'Bingo comes to himself inside a barrow', and this outline continues the story to Rivendell. This is so rapidly written and now so faint that I cannot after much effort make it all out. The worst part, however, is at the beginning, extending from Bingo's finding himself in the barrow to Tom's waking Odo, Frodo, and Merry, and from what is legible it can be seen that while very concise and limited all the essentials of the narrative were present. I shall not therefore try to represent this part, but give the remainder of the outline in full in this place, since it is of great interest in showing my father's thoughts on the further course of the story at this juncture – i.e. before the 'Barrow-wight' chapter had been completed.

Tom sings a song over Odo Frodo Merry. Wake now my merry . . .!
. . . . . . . .[2] of the [?pillar] and how they became separated. Tom puts a blessing or a curse on the gold and lays it on the top of the mound. None of the hobbits will have any but Tom takes a brooch for Goldberry.

Tom says he will go with them, after chiding them for sleeping by the stone pillar. They soon find the Road and the way seems short. They turn along the Road. [?Gallops] come after them. Tom turns and holds up his hand. They fly back.[3] As dusk falls they see a . . . light. Tom says goodbye – for Goldberry will be waiting.

They sleep at the inn and hear news of Gandalf. Jolly landlord. Drinking song.

Pass rapidly over rest of journey to Rivendell. Any riders on the Road? Make them foolishly turn aside to visit Troll Stones. This delays them. One day at last they halted on a rise and looked forward to the Ford. Galloping behind. Seven (3? 4?) Black-riders hastening along the Road. They have gold rings and crowns. Flight over Ford. Bingo [*written above:* Gandalf?] flings a stone and imitates Tom Bombadil. Go back and ride away! The Riders halt as if astonished, and looking up at the hobbits on the bank the hobbits can see no faces in their hoods. Go back says Bingo, but he is not Tom Bombadil, and the riders ride into the ford. But just then a rumbling rush is heard and a great [?wall] of water bowling stones roars down the river from the mountains. *Elves arrive.*

The Riders draw back just in time in dismay. The hobbits ride as hard as they can to Rivendell.

At Rivendell    *sleeping Bilbo*    Gandalf. Some explanations. Ringmail of Bingo in barrow and the dark rocks – (the 3 hobbits had dashed *past* the rocks when suddenly they all became [?shut] off??) Gandalf had sent the water down with Elrond's permission.

Gandalf astonished to hear about Tom.

Consultation of hobbits with Elrond and Gandalf.

The Quest of the Fiery Mountain.

This projection ends here. While my father had already conceived the scene at the Ford, with the sudden rising of the Bruinen (and the cry of Bingo/Frodo to the Riders: Go back!), Strider (not at first called Strider) would only emerge with the greatly increased significance of the Inn (which here first appears) at Bree in the next chapter; and there is no hint of Weathertop. If the 'dark rocks' are the 'two huge standing stones' through which Bingo/Frodo passed in the fog on the Downs (FR p. 150) – they are called 'standing rocks' in the first version – it is odd that discussion of this was postponed till the hobbits reached Rivendell; but possibly the words 'some explanations' imply that Gandalf was able to throw light on what had happened.[4] On the 'Ring-mail of Bingo in barrow' see p. 223. The Cracks of Earth in the depths of the Fiery Mountain are named by Gandalf as the only heat great enough to destroy Bilbo's ring (p. 82); here for the first time the Fiery Mountain enters the story as the goal for which they will in the end be bound.

The first full manuscript of this chapter (simply headed 'VI' and as usual at this stage without title) is fully legible for most of its length, but as so frequently becomes quicker and rougher, ending in rapid pencil. This my father went over here and there in ink, partly to improve the expression, partly to clarify his own writing; this certainly belongs to the same period, but after he had started on the next chapter.

As with the previous two chapters, the final form of FR Chapter 8 ('Fog on the Barrow-downs') is very largely present: for most of its length only very minor alterations were made afterwards. In what follows I note points of difference that seem to me of interest, though most are very slight.

In the opening paragraph the song and vision 'in dreams or out of them' is told in the same words in the old text, but is ascribed not to Bingo (Frodo in FR) alone, but to all the hobbits.

When they looked back over the forest and saw the knoll on which they had rested before their descent to the Withywindle valley, 'the fir-trees growing there could be seen now small and dark in the West' (see p. 113).

When the hobbits became separated in the fog, and Bingo cried out miserably 'Where are you?' (FR p. 150), my father at first had a quite different story in mind:

'Here! Here!' came the voices suddenly plain and not far to the right. Plunging blindly towards them he bumped suddenly into the tail of a pony. An undoubted hobbit-voice (it was Odo's) gave a shriek of fright, and [he] fell over something on the ground. The something kicked him, and gave a yell. 'Help!' it cried in the undoubted voice of Odo.

'Thank goodness,' said Bingo, rolling on the ground in Odo's arms. 'Thank goodness I have found you!'

'Thank goodness indeed!' said Odo in a relieved voice; 'but need you really run away without warning and then jump down out of the sky on top of me?'

My father rejected this as soon as written, and wrote instead, as in FR: 'There was no reply. He stood listening', etc.

A first version of the Barrow-wight's incantation was rejected and replaced by the form that appears in FR (p. 152); but the changes made were very slight except in line 7, where for 'till the dark lord lifts his hand' the first version had 'till the king of the dark tower lifts his hand.'[5] In the rough workings for this verse my father wrote: 'The dark lord sits in the tower and looks over the dark seas and the dark world', and also 'his hand stretches over the cold sea and the dead world.'

The arm 'walking on its fingers' crept towards Frodo Took (Sam in FR); and where in FR 'Frodo fell forward over Merry, and Merry's face felt cold', in the old version Bingo fell forward over Frodo Took. There is

no evident pattern in the changed ascriptions when the 'cast of characters' was altered; so later in the chapter Odo says 'Where are my clothes?'
(Sam in FR), and when Tom Bombadil says 'You won't find your clothes
again' it is Frodo Took who asks 'What do you mean?' (Pippin in FR).
In general I do not further note such points unless they seem significant.

On the rejected form of the rhyme taught to the hobbits by Tom
Bombadil and sung by Bingo in the barrow see p. 123. The first two
lines of the rejected rhyme were used later in the chapter, when Tom
goes off after the ponies (FR p. 155).

When Merry said 'What in the name of wonder?' as he felt the gold
circlet that had slipped over one eye, the old version continues: 'Then he
stopped, and a shadow came over his face. "I begin to remember," he
said. "I thought I was dead – but don't let us speak of it."' There is no
mention of the Men of Carn Dûm (FR p. 154).

Tom Bombadil's names for the ponies go back to the beginning, with
the exception of 'Sharp-ears', who was first called 'Four-foot'! When he
bade the treasures lying in the sun on the top of the mound lie there 'free
to all finders, bird, beast, elves or men and all kind creatures', he added:
'For the makers and owners of these things are not here, and their day is
long past, and the makers cannot claim them again until the world is
mended." And when he took the brooch for Goldberry he said: 'Fair was
she who long ago wore this on her shoulder, and Goldberry shall wear it
now, and we shall not forget them, the vanished folk, the old kings, the
children and the maidens, and all those who walked the earth when the
world was younger.'

While in the outline given on p. 125 the hobbits refuse to take anything
from the treasure in the mound, in the first text the story is that Tom
chose for them 'bronze swords, short, leaf-shaped and keen', but nothing
further is said in description of them (cf. FR p. 157), though the
following was added in pencil and perhaps belongs to the time of the
writing of the manuscript: 'These, he said, were made many ages ago by
men out of the West. They were foes of the Ring-lord.' The manuscript
continues:

and they hung them from the leather belts beneath their jackets;
though they did not yet see the purpose of them. Fighting had not
occurred to any of them as among the possible adventures that
their flight might bring them to. As far as Bingo could remember
even the great and heroic Bilbo had somehow avoided using his
small sword even on goblins – and then he remembered the
spiders of Mirkwood and tightened his belt.

Of the hints in Tom's words in FR concerning the history of Angmar and
the coming of Aragorn there is of course no suggestion.

As already noted, the end of the chapter is roughly pencilled and here
and there overwritten in ink. The crossing of the dyke – boundary of an

old kingdom, about which 'Tom seemed to remember something unhappy and would not say much' – and their coming at last to the Road is
much as in FR (p. 158), but the remainder is best given in full, as
originally pencilled, so far as that can be made out.

Bingo rode down onto the track and looked both ways. There
was no one in sight. 'Well, here we are again at last!' he said. 'I
suppose we haven't lost more than a day by Merry's short cut. We
had better stick to the beaten way after this.'

'You had better,' said Tom, 'and ride fast.'

Bingo looked at him. Black riders came back into his thought.
He looked a little anxiously back towards the setting sun, but the
road was brown and empty. 'Do you think,' he asked hesitatingly,
'do you think we shall be – er, pursued tonight?'

'Not tonight,' said Tom. 'No, not tonight. Not perhaps the next
day. Not perhaps for days to come.

The next passage is very confused and little can be made out (of the first
pencilled text); as overwritten in ink it reads:

But I cannot say for certain. Tom is not master of the Riders that
come out of the Black Land far beyond his country.' All the same
the hobbits wished that Tom was coming with them. They felt
that he would know how to deal with them – if anyone did. They
were now at last going forward into lands wholly strange to them,
and beyond all but the most distant legends of the Shire, and they
began to feel really lonely, exiled, and rather helpless. But Tom
was now wishing them a final farewell, bidding them have good
heart, and ride till dark without halting.

The pencilled text continues:

But he encouraged them – a little – by telling them that he guessed
the Riders (or some of them) were seeking now among the
mounds. For he seemed to think that the Riders and Barrow-
wights had some kind of kinship or understanding. If that were so,
it might prove in the end well that they had been captured. They
learned from him that some miles away along the road was the old
village of Bree, on the west side of Bree-hill.[6] It had an inn that
could be trusted: the White Horse [*written above:* Prancing
Pony]. The keeper was a good man and not unknown to Tom.
'Just you mention my name and he will treat you fairly. There you
can sleep sound, and after that the morning will speed you well
upon your way. Go now with my blessing.' They begged him to
come as far as the inn and drink once more with them. But he

laughed and refused, saying: 'Tom has his house to mind, and
Goldberry is waiting.' Then he turned, tossed up his hat, leaped
on Lumpkin's back, and rode over the bank and away singing into
the gathering dusk.

This passage, as far as 'Go now with my blessing', was rejected, and
a new version written in ink on a separate sheet; this second text is the
same as Tom's farewell speech in FR p. 159 ('Tom will give you good
advice . . .'), but it is here written out in verse-lines, and with these
differences: the 'worthy keeper' is Barnabas Butterbur, not Barliman,
and the reference to him is followed by:

> He knows Tom Bombadil, and Tom's name will help you.
> Say 'Tom sent us here' and he will treat you kindly.
> There you can sleep sound, and afterwards the morning
> Will speed you upon your way. Go now with my blessing!
> Keep up your merry hearts, and ride to meet your fortune!

That these revisions are later than the first pencilled draft of the next
chapter is seen from the fact that throughout that draft the innkeeper's
name was Timothy Titus, not yet Barnabas Butterbur (p. 140 note 3).
    The end of this chapter is again overwritten in ink, but so far as I can
make out this was only to clarify the almost illegible pencilled text:

The hobbits stood and watched him out of sight. Then, feeling
heavy at heart (in spite of his encouragement), they mounted their
ponies, not without some glances back along the Road, and went
off slowly into the evening. They did not sing, or talk, or discuss
the events of the night before, but plodded silently along. Bingo
and Merry rode in front, Odo and Frodo, leading the spare pony,
were behind.
    It was quite dark before they saw lights twinkling some distance
ahead. Before them rose Bree Hill, barring the way, a dark slope
against the misty stars, and under it and on its western side nestled
the little village.

## NOTES

1  This draft is in fact continuous with that for the Bombadil chapter
   (p. 123 note 3), but my father soon after drew a line on the pencilled
   text between 'and led them with candles back to their bedroom' and
   'That night they heard no noises', entering the chapter-number 'VI?'.
2  The illegible word begins *Expl* but the remainder does not seem to be
   *(Expl)anation*.
3  Cf. the outline given on p. 112: 'two Barrow-wights come [?gallop-
   ing] after them, but stop every time Tom Bombadil turns and looks at
   them.'

4  In a very early form of the chapter 'Many Meetings' (a passage retained word for word in FR, pp. 231–2) Bingo says to Gandalf at Rivendell: 'You seem to know a great deal already. I have not spoken to the others about the Barrow. At first it was too horrible, and afterwards there were other things to think about. How did you know about it?' And Gandalf replies: 'You have talked long in your sleep, Bingo.' But I doubt that this is relevant.

5  The 'dark tower' of the Necromancer is referred to by Gandalf in the text given in Chapter III (p. 81), and indeed goes back to *The Hobbit*, where at the end of Chapter VI 'Queer Lodgings' Gandalf speaks of the 'dark tower' of the Necromancer, in the south of Mirkwood. But it is difficult to feel sure where at this stage my father imagined the Dark Tower to stand. Tom Bombadil says (p. 129) that he 'is not master of the Riders that come out of the Black Land far beyond his country', and the name *Mordor* had certainly arisen: cf. the second version of *The Fall of Númenor* (V.29, 31), 'And they came at last even to Mordor the Black Country, where Sauron, that is in the Gnomish tongue named Thû, has rebuilt his fortresses.' See further p. 218 note 17.

6  My father first put 'an old village which had an inn', but the change to 'the old village of Bree, on the west side of Bree-hill. It had an inn' was almost certainly made as he wrote (and 'Prancing Pony' above 'White Horse' likewise). This is where the name first appears, based on Brill in Buckinghamshire, a place which he knew well, for it sits on a hill in the Little Kingdom of Farmer Giles of Ham (see Carpenter, *Biography*, p. 160). The name *Brill* is derived from the old British word *bre* 'hill', to which the English added their own word *hyll*; cf. LR Appendix F (p. 414), and the *Guide to the Names in The Lord of the Rings* (in Lobdell, *A Tolkien Compass*, 1975), entry *Archet*.

# VIII
## ARRIVAL AT BREE

My father continued on into a description of the Breelanders without a break. Subsequently he wrote over the original pencilled text in ink, and in that form, necessarily, I give it here.[1]

Little in a sense – it had perhaps some 50 houses on the hillside, and a large inn because of the goings and comings on the Road (though those were now less than they had once been). But it was actually a village built by Big People – mainly (the nearest settled habitation of that large and mysterious race to the Shire). Not many lived as far West as that in those days, and the Bree-folk (together with the neighbouring villages of Staddle and Crick) were an odd and rather isolated community, belonging to nobody but themselves (and more accustomed to dealing with hobbits, dwarves, and the other odd inhabitants of the world than Big People were or are). They were brown-faced, dark-haired, broad, shortish, cheerful and independent. They nor any one else knew why or when they had settled where they were. The land thereabouts and for many miles eastward was pretty empty in those days. There were hobbits about, of course – some higher up on the slopes of Bree-hill itself, and many in the valley of Combe on the east side. For not all hobbits lived in the Shire by any means. But the Outsiders were a rustic, not to say (though in the Shire it was often said) uncivilized sort. Some were in fact no better than tramps and wanderers, ready to dig a hole in any bank, and to stay there just as long or short a time as it suited them. So the folk of Bree were, you see, familiar enough with hobbits, civilized or otherwise – for Brandywine Bridge was not so far off. But our hobbits were not familiar with Bree-folk, and the houses seemed strange, large and tall (almost hillocks), as they trotted in on their ponies.

My father then struck this out, and began again. He was still numbering the pages continuously from the beginning of Chapter VI (the story of the Barrow-wight), but when he reached Bingo's song at the inn he realised that he was well into a new chapter, and wrote in 'VII' at this point, i.e. at the beginning of this new account of the people of Bree. Once again there is no title.

The manuscript of this chapter is an exceedingly complicated document: pencil overlaid with ink (sometimes remaining partly legible, sometimes not at all), pencil not overlaid but struck through, pencil allowed to stand, and fresh composition in ink, together with riders on slips and complex directions for insertions. There is no reason to suppose that the 'layers' are significantly separated in time, but the story was evolving as my father wrote: and the only way to present a coherent text is to give the manuscript in its last form. The chapter is given almost in full, since although much was retained it can only be seen clearly from a complete text just what the story was; but for convenience I divide it into two chapters in this book, breaking the narrative at the point where FR Chapter 9 'At the Sign of *The Prancing Pony*' ends and 10 'Strider' begins.

The interrelations of chapter-structure in the following part of the story are inevitably complex, and can best be seen from a table:

|  | *Original text* | | *This Book* | |
|---|---|---|---|---|
| VII | Arrival at Bree, and Bingo's song | VIII | 9 | 'At the Sign of *The Prancing Pony*' |
| | Conversation with Trotter and Butterbur | IX | 10 | 'Strider' |
| | Attack on the inn | | 11 | 'A Knife in the Dark' |
| | Journey to Weathertop | | | |
| VIII | Attack on Weathertop | X | | |
| | Weathertop to Rivendell | XI | 12 | 'Flight to the Ford' |

It will be seen at the beginning of this text that the presence of Men at Bree had been temporarily abandoned, and the description of their appearance in the rejected passage just given is now applied to the hobbits of the Bree-land; the innkeeper is a hobbit, and *The Prancing Pony* has a round front door leading into the side of Bree-hill.

They were hobbit-folk of course that lived in Bree (and the neighbouring villages of Combe and Archet).[2] Not all the hobbits lived in the Shire by any means, but the Outsiders were a rustic, not to say (though in the Shire it was often said) uncivilized lot, and not held in much account. There were probably a good many more of them scattered about in the West of the world in those days than people in the Shire imagined, though many were indeed no better than tramps and wanderers, ready to dig a rough hole in any bank, and stay only as long as it suited them. The villagers of Bree, Combe, and Archet, however, were settled folk (in reality not more rustic than most of their distant relations in Hobbiton) –

but they were rather odd and independent, and belonged to
nobody but themselves. They were browner-skinned, darker-
haired, slightly stouter, a good deal broader (and perhaps a trifle
tougher) than the average hobbit of the Shire. Neither they nor
anyone else knew why or when they had settled just there; but
there they were, moderately prosperous and content. The land all
round about was very empty for leagues and leagues in those days,
and few folk (Big or Little) would be seen in a day's march. Owing
to the Road the inn at Bree was fairly large; but the comings and
goings, East or West, were less than they had been, and the inn
was now chiefly used as a meeting-place for the idle, talkative,
sociable or inquisitive inhabitants of the villages and the odd
inhabitants of the wilder country round about.

When our four hobbits at last rode into Bree they were very
glad. The inn door was open. It was a large round door leading
into the side of Bree-hill, at which the road turned, looping to the
right, and disappeared in the darkness. Light streamed into the
road from the door, over which there was a lamp swinging and
beneath that a sign – a fat white pony standing on his hind legs.
Over the door was painted in white letters: The Prancing Pony by
Barnabas Butterbur.[3] Someone was singing a song inside.

As the hobbits got off their ponies the song ended and there was
a burst of laughter. Bingo stepped inside, and nearly bumped into
the largest and fattest hobbit that he had ever set eyes on in all his
days in the well-fed Shire. It was obviously Mr Butterbur himself.
He had on a white apron and was scuttling out of one door and in
through another with a tray full of full mugs. 'Can we . . . ?' said
Bingo.

'Half a moment if you please,' the landlord shouted over his
shoulder, and vanished into a babel of voices and a cloud of smoke
beyond the door. In a moment he was out again wiping his hands
on his apron. 'Good evening, master,' he said. 'What may you be
wanting?'

'Beds for four and stabling for five ponies,' said Bingo, 'if that
can be managed. We have come far today. Are you Mr Butterbur,
perhaps?'

'That's right,' he answered, 'Barnabas is my name, Barnabas
Butterbur at your service – if it is possible. But the house is nearly
full, and so are the stables.'

'I was afraid it might be,' said Bingo. 'I hear it is an excellent
house. We were specially recommended to stop here by our friend
Tom Bombadil.'

'In that case *anything* can be managed!' said Mr Butterbur, slapping his thighs and beaming. 'Come right inside! And how is the old fellow? Mad and merry, but merrier than mad, I'll be bound! Why didn't he come along too, and then we should have had some fun! Hi! Nob![4] Come here! Where are you, you woolly-footed slow-coach? Take the guests' bags! Where's Bob? You don't know? Well, find out! Double sharp. I haven't got six legs, nor six arms, nor six eyes either. Tell Bob there's five ponies that have to be stabled. And well, mind you. Well, you must make room then, if they have to go in bedrooms![5] Come right inside, sirs, all of you. Pleased to meet you! What names did you say? Mr Hill, Mr Rivers, Mr Green, and Mr Brown.[6] Can't say I have heard those names before, but I am pleased to meet you and hear them now.' Bingo had made them up, of course, on the spur of the moment, suddenly feeling that it would not be at all wise to publish their real names in a hobbit-inn on the high road. Hill, Rivers, Green, Brown sounded much stranger as names to hobbits than they do to us, and Mr Butterbur had his own reasons for thinking them unlikely. However, he said nothing about that yet. 'But there,' he went on, 'I dare say there are lots of queer names and queer folk that we never hear of in these parts. We don't see so many Shire-folk in these days. Time was when the Tooks, now, often came along to have a crack with me or my old dad. Rare good people were the Tooks. They say they had Bree blood in 'em, and were not quite like other Shire-folk, but I don't know the rights of it. But there! I must be running off. But wait a minute now! Four riders and five ponies? Let me see, what does that remind me of? Never mind, it will come back. All in good time. One thing drives out another, as they say. I am a bit busy tonight. Lots of folk have dropped in, unexpected. Hi, Nob! Take these bags to the guests' rooms. That's right. Seven to ten down the west passage. Be quick now! And will you be wanting supper? You will. I thought so. Soon, I shouldn't wonder. Very well, masters, soon it shall be. This way now! Here's a room will suit you nicely, I hope. Excuse me, now. I must be trotting. 'Tis hard work for two legs, but I don't get thinner. I'll look in again later. If you want anything, ring the hand-bell, and Nob will come. If he don't, shout!'

Off he went, leaving them feeling a little breathless. He had not stopped talking to them (mixed with the giving of orders and instructions to other scuttling hobbits in the passages) from the time that he welcomed Bingo, until he ushered them into a small but cosy private parlour. There was a bit of bright fire burning;

there were some very comfortable chairs, and there was a round table, already spread with a white cloth. On it was a large hand-bell. But Nob, a small round curly-haired red-faced hobbit, came bustling back long before they thought of using it.

'Will you be wanting anything to drink, masters?' he asked. 'Or shall I show you your rooms, while supper is making?'

They were washed, and in the middle of a good deep mug of beer each, before Mr Butterbur came trotting in again, followed by Nob. A fine smell came with them. In a twinkling the table was laid. Hot soup, cold meats, new loaves, mounds of butter, cheese and fresh fruits, all the good solid plain food dear to hobbit-hearts, was set before them in plenty. They went at it with a will – not without a passing thought (in Bingo's mind especially) that it had to be paid for, and that they had no endless store of money. The time would come all too soon when they would have to pass good inns (even if they could find them).[7] Mr Butterbur hovered round for a bit, and then prepared to leave. 'I don't know whether you would care to join the company after supper,' he said, standing in the door. 'But perhaps you would rather find your beds. Still, the company would be pleased to welcome you, if you had a mind. We don't get travellers from the Shire – outsiders we call 'em, begging your pardon – too often in these days; and we like to hear the news, or any new song you may have in mind. But as you like, sirs. Ring the bell, if you wish for anything.'

There was nothing omitted that they could wish for, so they did not need to ring the bell. So refreshed and encouraged did they feel at the end of their supper (about 55 minutes steady going, not hindered by unnecessary talk) that they decided to join the company. At least Odo, Frodo, and Bingo did. Merry said he thought it would be too stuffy. 'I shall either sit here quietly by the fire, or else go out for a snuff of the air outside. Mind your Ps and Qs, and don't forget that you are supposed to be escaping in secret, and are Mr Hill, Mr Green, and Mr Brown.' 'All right,' they said. 'Mind yourself! Don't get lost, and don't forget that it is safest indoors.' Then they went and joined the company in the big meeting-room of the inn. The gathering was large, as they dis-covered as soon as their eyes became used to the light. This came chiefly from a large fire on a wide hearth, for the rather dim rays of three lamps hanging from the roof were clouded with smoke. Barnabas Butterbur was standing near the fire. He introduced them, so quickly that they did not catch half the names he mentioned, nor discover to whom the names they caught be-

longed. There seemed to be several Mugworts (an odd name to
their way of thinking), and also other rather botanical names like
Rushlight, Heathertoes, Ferny, and Appledore (not to mention
Butterbur);[8] there were also some (to hobbits) natural names like
Banks, Longholes, Brockhouse, Sandheaver, and Tunnelly,
which were not unknown among the more rustic inhabitants of the
Shire.

But they got on well enough without surnames (which were
very little used in that company). On the other side the company,
as soon as they discovered that the strangers were from the
Shire, were disposed to be friendly, and curious. Bingo had not
attempted to conceal where they came from, knowing that their
clothes and talk would give them away at once. But he gave out
that he was interested in history and geography, at which there
was much wagging of heads (although neither of these words were
familiar in Bree-dialect); and that he was writing a book (at which
there was silent astonishment); and that he and his friends were
going to try and find out something about the various scattered
eastern hobbits. At this a regular chorus of voices broke out, and if
Bingo had really been going to write such a book (and had had
many ears and sufficient patience) he would have learned a good
deal in a few minutes, and also obtained lots of advice on who to
apply to for more and profounder information.

But after a time, as Bingo did not show any sign of writing a
book on the spot, the company returned to more recent and
engaging topics, and Bingo sat in a corner, listening and looking
round. Odo and Frodo made themselves very quickly at home,
and were soon (rather to Bingo's disquiet) giving lively accounts of
recent events in the Shire. There was some laughter and wagging
of heads, and some questions. Suddenly Bingo noticed that a
queer-looking, brown-faced hobbit, sitting in the shadows behind
the others, was also listening intently. He had an enormous mug
(more like a jug) in front of him, and was smoking a broken-
stemmed pipe right under his rather long nose. He was dressed in
dark rough brown cloth, and had a hood on, in spite of the
warmth, – and, very remarkably, he had wooden shoes! Bingo
could see them sticking out under the table in front of him.

'Who is that over there?' said Bingo, when he got a chance
to whisper to Mr Butterbur. 'I don't think you introduced him.'

'Him?' said Barnabas, cocking an eye without turning his head.
'O! that is one of the wild folk – rangers we call 'em. He has been
coming in now and again (in autumn and winter mostly) the last

few years; but he seldom talks. Not but what he can tell some rare tales when he has a mind, you take my word. What his right name is I never heard, but he's known round here as Trotter. You can hear him coming along the road in those shoes: clitter-clap – when he walks on a path, which isn't often. Why does he wear 'em? Well, that I can't say. But there ain't no accounting for East or West, as we say here, meaning the Rangers and the Shire-folk, begging your pardon.' Mr Butterbur was called away at that moment, or he might have whispered on in that fashion indefinitely.

Bingo found Trotter looking at him, as if he had heard or guessed all that was said. Presently the Ranger, with a click and a jerk of his hand, invited Bingo to come over to him; and as Bingo sat down beside him he threw back his hood, showing a long shaggy head of hair, some of which hung over his forehead. But it did not hide a pair of keen dark eyes. 'I'm Trotter,' he said in a low voice. 'I am very pleased to meet you, Mr — Hill, if old Barnabas had your name right?'⁹ 'He had,' said Bingo, rather stiffly: he was feeling far from comfortable under the stare of those dark eyes.

'Well, Mr Hill,' said Trotter, 'if I were you, I should stop your young friends from talking too much. Drink, fire, and chance meetings are well enough, but – well, this is not the Shire. There are queer folk about – though I say it as shouldn't,' he added with a grin, seeing Bingo's look. 'And there have been queer travellers through Bree not long back,' he went on, peering at Bingo's face.

Bingo peered back, but Trotter made no further sign. He seemed suddenly to be listening to Odo. Odo was now giving a comic account of the Farewell Party, and was just reaching Bingo's disappearing act. There was a hush of expectation. Bingo felt seriously annoyed. What was the good of vanishing out of the Shire, if the ass went away and gave their names to a mixed crowd in an inn on the highway! Even now Odo had said enough to set shrewd wits (Trotter's for instance) guessing; and it would soon become obvious that 'Hill' was no other than Bolger-Baggins (of Bag-end Underhill). And Bingo somehow felt that it would be dangerous, even disastrous, if Odo mentioned the Ring.

'You had better do something quick!' said Trotter in his ear.

Bingo jumped on the table, and began to talk. The attention was shifted from Odo at once, and several of the hobbits laughed and clapped (thinking possibly that Mr Hill had been taking as much ale as was good for him). Bingo suddenly felt very nervous, and found himself, as was his habit when making a speech, fingering the things in his pocket. Vaguely he felt the chain and the Ring there, and jingled it against a few copper coins; but this did not help him much, and after a few suitable words, as they would have said in the Shire (such as 'We are all very much gratified by the kindness of your reception', and things of that sort), he stopped and coughed. 'A song! A song!' they shouted. 'Come on now, Master, sing us something.' In desperation Bingo began an absurd song, which Bilbo had been fond of (he probably wrote it).[10]

[Song][11]

There was loud applause. Bingo had a good voice, and the company was not over particular. 'Where's old Barney?' they cried. 'He ought to hear this. He ought to larn his cat the fiddle, and then we'd have a dance. Bring in some more ale, and let's have it again!' They made Bingo have another drink and then sing the song once more, while many of them joined in; for the tune was well-known and they were quick at picking up words.

Much encouraged Bingo capered about on the table; and when he came a second time to 'the cow jumped over the moon', he jumped in the air. Much too vigorously:[12] for he came down bang into a tray full of mugs, and then slipped and rolled off the table with a crash, clatter, and bump. But what interested the company far more and stopped their cheers and laughter dead was his vanishing. As Bingo rolled off the table he simply disappeared with a crash as if he had thudded through the floor without making a hole.

The local hobbits sprang to their feet and shouted for Barnabas. They drew away from Odo and Frodo, who found themselves left alone in a corner and eyed darkly and doubtfully from a distance, as if they were the companions of a travelling wizard of dubious origin and unknown powers and purpose. There was one swarthy-faced fellow who stood looking at them with a knowing sort of look that made them feel uncomfortable. Very soon he slipped out of the door followed by one of his friends: not a well-favoured pair.[13] Bingo in the meanwhile feeling a fool (quite rightly) and not knowing what else to do crawled away under the tables to the corner by Trotter, who was sitting still quite unconcerned. He then sat back against the wall, and took off the Ring. By bad luck he had been fingering it in his pocket just at the fatal moment, and had slipped it on in his sudden surprise at falling.

'Hullo!' said Trotter. 'What did you mean by that? Worse than anything your friends could have said. You've fair put your foot and finger in it, haven't you?'

'I don't know what you mean,' said Bingo (annoyed and alarmed).

'O yes you do,' said Trotter. 'But we had better wait till the uproar has died down. Then, if you don't mind, Mr Bolger-Baggins, I should like a quiet word with you.'

'What about?' said Bingo, pretending not to notice the sudden use of his proper name. 'O, wizards, and that sort of thing,' said Trotter with a grin. 'You'll hear something to your advantage.' 'Very well,' said Bingo. 'I'll see you later.'

In the meantime argument in a chorus of voices had been going on by the fireplace. Mr Butterbur had come trotting in, and was trying to listen to many conflicting accounts at the same time.

The next part of the text, as far as the end of Chapter 9 in FR, is almost word for word the same as in the final version, with only such differences as are to be expected: 'Mr Underhill' of FR is 'Mr Hill'; 'There's Mr Took, now: he's not vanished' is 'There's Mr Green and Mr Brown, now: they've not vanished'; and there is no mention of the Men of Bree, of the Dwarves, or of the strange Men – it is simply 'the company' that went off in a huff. But at the end, when Bingo said to the landlord: 'Will you see that our ponies are ready?', the old narrative differs:

'There now!' said the landlord, snapping his fingers. 'Half a moment. It's come back to me, as I said it would. Bless me! Four hobbits and five ponies!'

As already explained, though I end this chapter here the earliest version goes on into what was afterwards Chapter 10 'Strider' without a break; see the table on p. 133.

## NOTES

1   Bits of the underlying text can in fact be made out: enough to show that the conception of Bree as a village of Men, though with 'hobbits about', was present.

2   *Crick* (p. 132) has disappeared for good (but cf. 'Crickhollow'); *Staddle* also, but only temporarily.

3   *Barnabas Butterbur* is written in ink over the original name in pencil: *Timothy Titus*. Timothy Titus was the name of the innkeeper in the underlying pencilled text throughout the chapter. This was a name that survived from an old story of my father's, of

which only a couple of pages exist (no doubt all that was ever written down); but that Timothy Titus bore no resemblance whatsoever to Mr Butterbur.

4   Nob was at first called Lob; this survived into the inked manuscript stage and was then changed.

5   The original pencilled text went on from here:

> Come right inside. Pleased to meet you. Mr Took, did you say? Lor now, I remember that name. Time was when Tooks would think nothing of riding out here just to have a crack with my old dad or me. Mr Odo Took, Mr Frodo Took, Mr Merry Brandy-buck, Mr Bingo Baggins. Lemme see, what does that remind me of? Never mind, it will come back. One thing drives out another. Bit busy tonight. Lots of folk dropped in. Hi, Nob! Take these bags (etc.)

My father struck this out, noting 'hobbits must hide their names', and wrote these two passages on an added slip in pencil:

> Mr Frodo Walker, Mr Odo Walker – can't say I have met that name before. (Bingo had made it up on the spur of the moment, suddenly realizing that it would not be wise to publish their real names in a hobbit-inn on the high road).
>
> What name did you say – all Walkers, Mr Ben Walker and three nephews. Can't say I have met that name before, but I'm pleased to meet you.

These also were struck out, and the passage that follows in the text ('Come right inside, sirs, all of you . . .'), in pencil overwritten in ink, was adopted.

6   In the underlying pencilled text of this passage my father wrote *Ferny* but at once changed it to *Hill*; and in the text in ink he wrote *Fellowes* but changed it to *Green*. Later on, in rejected pencilled drafting, Mr Butterbur says: 'You don't say, Mr Mugwort. Well, as long as Mr Rivers and the two Mr Fellowes don't vanish too (without paying the bill) he is welcome' (i.e. to vanish into thin air, as Mugwort has asserted that he did: FR p. 173).

7   CF. Bingo's words to Gildor, p. 62: 'I had come to the end of my treasure.' The present passage was rejected and does not appear in FR: but cf. p. 172 note 3.

8   *Appledore*: 'apple-tree' (Old English *apuldor*). – In FR (p. 167) these 'botanical' names are primarily names of families of Men in Bree.

9   The underlying pencilled text still had here: 'I am very pleased to meet Mr Bingo Baggins'; and Trotter's next words began: 'Well, Mr Bingo . . .' See note 5.

10  Here follows: 'It went to a well-known tune, and the company joined in the chorus', referring to the song which was originally given to Bingo here (see note 11), where there is a chorus; the sentence was struck out when 'The Cat and the Fiddle' was chosen instead.

11   My father first wrote here 'Troll Song', and a rough and unfinished
     version of it is found in the manuscript at this point. He apparently
     decided almost at once to substitute 'The Cat and the Fiddle', and
     there are also two texts of that song included in the manuscript, each
     preceded by the words (as in FR p. 170):

     It was about an Inn, and I suppose that is what brought it to
     Bingo's mind. Here it is in full, though only a few words of it are
     now generally remembered.

     For the history and early forms of these songs see the *Note on the
     Songs at the Prancing Pony* that follows. – That there was to be a
     song at Bree is already foreseen in the primitive outline given on
     p. 126: 'They sleep at the inn and hear news of Gandalf. Jolly
     landlord. Drinking song.'

12   In the original text, where the song was to be the Troll Song, the
     comments of the audience on the cat and the fiddle are of course
     absent. Instead, after 'the company was not over particular', there
     followed:

     They made him have a drink and then sing it all over again. Much
     encouraged Bingo capered about on the table, and when he came
     a second time to 'his boot to bear where needed' he kicked in the
     air. Much too realistically: he overbalanced and fell . . .

     The line *His boot to bear where needed* is found in the version of the
     Troll Song written for this episode.

13   As the people of Bree were conceived at this stage, the ill-favoured
     pair would presumably be hobbits; and indeed in the next chapter
     Bill Ferny is explicitly so (p. 165). His companion here is the origin
     of the 'squint-eyed Southerner' who had come up the Greenway
     (FR p. 168); but there is no suggestion as yet of that element in what
     was still a very limited canvas.

### Note on the Songs at the Prancing Pony

### (i) The Troll Song

When my father came to the scene where Bingo sings a song in *The
Prancing Pony* he first used the 'Troll Song' (note 11 above). The
original version of this, called *The Root of the Boot*, goes back to his time
at the University of Leeds; it was privately printed in a booklet with the
title *Songs for the Philologists*, University College, London, 1936 (for
the history of this publication see pp. 144–5). My father was extremely
fond of this song, which went to the tune of *The fox went out on a winter's
night*, and my delight in the line *If bonfire there be, 'tis underneath* is
among my very early recollections. Two copies of this booklet came into
my father's possession later (in 1940–1), and at some time undetermin-
able he corrected the text, removing some minor errors that had crept in.
I give the text here as printed in *Songs for the Philologists*, with these
corrections.

## THE ROOT OF THE BOOT

*A troll sat alone on his seat of stone,*
*And munched and mumbled a bare old bone;*
*And long and long he had sat there lone*
*    And seen no man nor mortal –*
*        Ortal! Portal!*
*And long and long he had sat there lone*
*    And seen no man nor mortal.*

*Up came Tom with his big boots on;*
*'Hallo!' says he, 'pray what is yon?*
*It looks like the leg o' me nuncle John*
*    As should be a-lyin' in churchyard.*
*        Searchyard, Birchyard! etc.*

*'Young man,' says the troll, 'that bone I stole;*
*But what be bones, when mayhap the soul*
*In heaven on high hath an aureole*
*    As big and as bright as a bonfire?*
*        On fire, yon fire!'*

*Says Tom: 'Oddsteeth! 'tis my belief,*
*If bonfire there be, 'tis underneath;*
*For old man John was as proper a thief*
*    As ever wore black on a Sunday –*
*        Grundy, Monday!*

*But still I doan't see what is that to thee,*
*Wi' me kith and me kin a-makin' free:*
*So get to hell and ax leave o' he,*
*    Afore thou gnaws me nuncle!*
*        Uncle, Buncle!'*

*In the proper place upon the base*
*Tom boots him right – but, alas! that race*
*Hath a stonier seat than its stony face;*
*    So he rued that root on the rumpo,*
*        Lumpo, Bumpo!*

*Now Tom goes lame since home he came,*
*And his bootless foot is grievous game;*
*But troll's old seat is much the same,*
*    And the bone he boned\* from its owner!*
*        Donor, Boner!*

\**bone*: steal, make off with.

In addition to correcting errors in the text printed in *Songs for the Philologists* my father also changed the third line in verse 3 to *Hath a halo in heaven upon its poll.*

The original pencilled manuscript of the song is still extant. The title was *Pēro & Pōdex* ('Boot and Bottom'), and verse 6 as first written went:

> *In the proper place upon the base*
> *Tom boots him right – but, alas! that race*
> *Hath as stony a seat as it is in face,*
> *And Pero was punished by Podex.*
> *Odex! Codex!*

My father made a new version of the song for Bingo to sing in *The Prancing Pony*, suitable to the intended context, and as already mentioned this is found in the manuscript of the present chapter; but it is still in a rough state, and uncertain, and was abandoned when still incomplete. When he decided that he would not after all use it in this place he did not at once reintroduce it into *The Lord of the Rings*; it will be seen in Chapter XI that while the visit of the hobbits to the scene of Bilbo's encounter with the three Trolls was fully present from the first version, there was no song. It was only introduced here later; but the earlier drafts of Sam's 'Troll Song' proceed in series form the version intended for Bingo at Bree.

*Songs for the Philologists.*

The origin of the material in this little booklet goes back to Leeds University in the 1920s, when Professor E. V. Gordon (my father's colleague and close friend, who died most untimely in the summer of this same year, 1938) made typescripts for the use of students in the Department of English. 'His sources', in my father's words, 'were MSS of my own verses and his . . . with many additions of modern and traditional Icelandic songs taken mostly from Icelandic student songbooks.'

In 1935 or 1936 Dr. A. H. Smith of London University (formerly a student at Leeds) gave one of these typescripts (uncorrected) to a group of Honours students there for them to set up on the Elizabethan printing-press. The result was a booklet bearing the title

## SONGS FOR THE PHILOLOGISTS

### By J. R. R. Tolkien, E. V. Gordon & Others

Privately Printed in the Department of
English at University College, London
MCMXXXVI

In November 1940 Winifred Husbands of University College wrote to my father and explained that 'when the books were ready, Dr Smith realised that he had never asked your permission or that of Professor

Gordon, and he said that the books must not be distributed till that had been done – but, so far as I know, he has never written or spoken to you on the subject, though I spoke of it to him more than once. The sad result is that most of the copies printed, being left undistributed in our rooms in Gower Street, have perished like the press itself in the fire which destroyed that part of the College building.' My father was therefore asked to give his retrospective permission. At that time there were 13 copies known to her, but subsequently she found more, I do not know how many; my father received two (p. 142).

There are 30 *Songs for the Philologists*, in Gothic, Icelandic, Old, Middle and Modern English, and Latin, and some poems in a macaronic mixture of languages. My father was the author of 13 (6 in Modern English, 6 in Old English, 1 in Gothic), and E. V. Gordon of two. Three of my father's Old English poems, and the one in Gothic, are printed with translations as an appendix to Professor T. A. Shippey's *The Road to Middle-earth* (1982).*

### (ii) The Cat and the Fiddle

'The Cat and the Fiddle', which became Bingo's song at *The Prancing Pony*, was published in 1923 in *Yorkshire Poetry*, Vol. II no. 19 (Leeds, the Swan Press). I give here the text as it is found in the original manuscript, written on Leeds University paper.

THE CAT AND THE FIDDLE,
or
A Nursery Rhyme Undone and its Scandalous Secret
Unlocked

> *They say there's a little crooked inn*
> *Behind an old grey hill,*
> *Where they brew a beer so very brown*
> *The man in the moon himself comes down,*
> *And sometimes drinks his fill.*

*This is a convenient place to cite my father's explanation of the significance of the Birch-tree that appears in two of the poems given by Professor Shippey (see his book pp. 206–7); cf. also 'Birchyard' in the chorus to verse 2 of *The Root of the Boot*. In a note on one of his copies of *Songs for the Philologists* my father wrote: 'ᛒ, B, Bee and (because of the runic name of ᛒ) Birch all symbolize mediaeval and philological studies (including Icelandic); while A, and Āc (oak = ᚫ) denote 'modern literature'. This more pleasing heraldry (and friendly rivalry and raillery) grew out of the grim assertion in the Syllabus that studies should be "divided into two Schemes, Scheme A and Scheme B". A was mainly modern and B mainly mediaeval and philological. Songs, festivities and other gaieties were however mainly confined to ᛒ.'

*And there the ostler has a cat*
    *That plays a five-stringed fiddle;*
*Mine host a little dog so clever*
*He laughs at any joke whatever,*
    *And sometimes in the middle.*

*They also keep a hornéd cow,*
    *'Tis said, with golden hooves –*
*But music turns her head like ale,*
*And makes her wave her tufted tail,*
    *And dance upon the rooves.*

*But O! the rows of silver dishes*
    *And the store of silver spoons:*
*For Sunday there's a special pair,*
*And these they polish up with care*
    *On Saturday afternoons.*

★

*The man in the moon had drunk too deep,*
    *The ostler's cat was totty,\**
*A dish made love to a Sunday spoon,*
*The little dog saw all the jokes too soon,*
    *And the cow was dancing-dotty.*

*The man in the moon had another mug*
    *And fell beneath his chair,*
*And there he called for still more ale,*
*Though the stars were fading thin and pale,*
    *And the dawn was on the stair.*

*Then the ostler said to his tipsy cat:*
    *'The white horses of the Moon,*
*They neigh and champ their silver bits,*
*For their master's been and drowned his wits,*
    *And the Sun'll be rising soon –*

*Come play on your fiddle a hey-diddle-diddle,*
    *A jig to wake the dead.'*
*So the cat played a terrible drunken tune,*
*While the landlord shook the man in the moon:*
    *''Tis after three,' he said.*

*They rolled him slowly up the hill*
    *And bundled him in the moon,*
*And his horses galloped up in rear,*
*And the cow came capering like a deer,*
    *And the dish embraced the spoon.*

\**totty*: tottery, shaky, dizzy.

*The cat then suddenly changed the tune,*
*    The dog began to roar,*
*The horses stood upon their heads,*
*The guests all bounded from their beds,*
*    And danced upon the floor.*

*The cat broke all his fiddle-strings,*
*    The cow jumped over the moon,*
*The little dog howled to see such fun,*
*In the middle the Saturday dish did run*
*    Away with the Sunday spoon.*

*The round moon rolled off down the hill,*
*    But only just in time,*
*For the Sun looked up with fiery head,*
*And ordered everyone back to bed,*
*    And the ending of the rhyme.*

The two versions found in the manuscript of the present chapter move progressively towards the final form, and with emendations made to the second of them it is virtually attained (FR pp. 170–2).

# IX
# TROTTER AND THE JOURNEY TO
# WEATHERTOP

The original titleless chapter VII continues without a break through
what became in FR Chapter 10 'Strider', ending part way through FR
Chapter 11 'A Knife in the Dark'; but the first part of the narrative to be
given now exists in two structurally quite distinct forms (both written
legibly in ink). These my father marked 'Short' and 'Alternative', but for
the purposes of this chapter I shall call them A ('Alternative') and B
('Short'). The relation between the two is a textual conundrum, though I
think it can be explained;[1] the question is however of no great importance for the history of the narrative, since the two versions obviously
belong to the same time. I give first the alternative A (on which my father
subsequently wrote 'Use this version').

'There now!' said the landlord, snapping his fingers. 'Half a
moment. It's come back to me, as I said it would. Bless me! Four
hobbits and five ponies! There's been some enquiries for a party of
your description in the last few days; and perhaps I might have a
word with you.'

'Yes, certainly!' said Bingo with a sinking feeling. 'But not here.
Won't you come to our room?'

'As you wish,' said the landlord. 'I'll be coming along to bid you
good night and see that Nob has brought all you need, as soon as
I've seen to a thing or two: we may have a word then.'

Bingo, Odo, and Frodo made their way back to their parlour.[2]
There was no light. Merry was not there, and the fire had burned
low. It was not until they had puffed up the embers into a blaze
and put on a faggot that they discovered Trotter had come with
them. There he was calmly sitting in a chair in the corner.

'Hullo!' said Odo. 'What do you want?'

'This is Trotter,' said Bingo hastily. 'I believe he wants a word
with me too.'

'I do and I don't,' said Trotter. 'That is: I have my price.'

'What do you mean?' asked Bingo, puzzled and alarmed.

'Don't be frightened. I mean just this: I will tell you what I
know, and give you what I've got, and what's more I'll keep your
secret under my hood (which is closer than you or your friends
keep it) – but I shall want my reward.'

'And what will that be, pray?' said Bingo, angrily; he not unnaturally suspected that they had met a rascal, and he thought uncomfortably of his small remaining purse of money.[3] All of it would hardly satisfy a rascal, and he could not spare any of it.

'Not much,' answered Trotter with an amused grin. 'Just this: you must take me along with you, until I want to leave you!'

'Oh, indeed!' replied Bingo, surprised but not much relieved. 'But even if I was likely to say yes, I would not promise any such thing until I knew a lot more about you, and your news, Mr Trotter.'

'Excellent!' said Trotter, crossing his legs. 'You seem to be coming to your senses again; and that is all to the good. You have not been half suspicious enough so far. Very well then: I will tell you what I know, and leave the rest to you. That's fair enough.'

'Go on then!' said Bingo. 'What do you know?'

'Well, it's like this,' said Trotter, dropping his voice; he got up and went to the door, opened it quickly, looked out, and then shut it quietly and sat down again. 'I have quick ears, and though I can't disappear into thin air, I can take care no one sees me, when I don't wish them to. I was behind a hedge when a party of travellers was halted by the Road not far west from here. There was a cart and horses and ponies; a whole pack of dwarves, one or two elves, and – a wizard. Gandalf, of course; there's no mistaking him, you'll agree. They were talking about a certain Mr Bingo Bolger-Baggins and his three friends, that were supposed to be riding on the Road behind. A bit incautious of Gandalf, I must say; but then, he was speaking low and I have quick ears, and was lying pretty close.

'I followed him and his party here to this inn. There was a fine commotion for a Sunday morning, I can tell you, and old Barnabas was running round in rings; but they kept themselves to themselves and did not talk outside closed doors. That would be five days ago.[4] They went away next morning. Now up comes a hobbit and three friends out of the Shire, and though he gives out the name of Hill, he and his friends seem to know a lot of the doings of Gandalf and of Mr Bolger-Baggins of Underhill. I can put two and two together. But that need not trouble you: for I am going to keep the answer under my hood, as I said. Maybe Mr Bolger-Baggins has his own good reasons for leaving his name behind. But if so, I should advise him to remember that there are more folk than Trotter that can add two and two together; and not all are to be trusted.'

'I am obliged to you,' said Bingo, feeling relieved, for Trotter did not seem to know anything very serious. 'I *have* my reasons for leaving my name behind, as you put it; but I can't quite see how any one else would guess my real name from what has occurred, unless he had your skill in eavesdropping, in – er – collecting information. Nor what use my real name would be to anybody in Bree.'

'Can't you?' said Trotter rather grimly; 'but eavesdropping, as you put it, is not unknown in Bree, and besides, I have not told you all yet.'

But at that moment he was interrupted by a knock on the door. Mr Barnabas Butterbur was there, with a tray of candles, and Nob behind him with jugs of hot water. 'Thinking you might wish to give some orders before you went to bed,' said the landlord, putting the candles on the table, 'I've come to wish you a good night. Nob! Take the water to the rooms.' He came in and shut the door.

'It's like this, Mr – er – Hill,' he said. 'I've been asked more than once to look out for a party of four hobbits from the Shire, four hobbits with five ponies. Hullo, Trotter, you here!'

'It's all right,' said Bingo. 'Say what you want. Trotter has my leave to stay.' Trotter grinned.

'Well,' began Mr Butterbur again, 'it's like this. Five days ago (yes, that's right, it would be Sunday morning, when all was quiet and peaceful) up rode a whole pack of travellers. Queer folk, dwarves and what not, with a cart and horses. And old Mr Gandalf was with them. Now says I to myself, there's been some doings in the Shire; and they'll be returning from the Party.'

'From the Party?' said Bingo. 'What Party?'

'Lor bless you, yes, sir! From the party your Mr Green was telling of. Mr Bolger-Baggins' party. A rare lot of traffic went westward through here earlier in the month. Some Men there were too. Great Big Folk. There hasn't been anything like it in my time. Those that would say anything gave out that they were going or taking stuff to a Mr Bolger-Baggins' birthday party. It seems he was a relation of that Mr Bilbo Baggins there was once strange tales about. Indeed they are still told in Bree, sir; though I daresay they are forgotten in the Shire. But we are slower-moving in Bree, so to speak, and like to hear old tales again. Not that I believe all these stories, mind you. Legends, I call 'em. They may be true, and then again mayhap they ain't. Now, where was I? Yes. Last Sunday morning in came old Mr Gandalf and his dwarves and all.

"Good morning," said I. "And where may you be going to, and where may you be coming from?" says I pleasant like. But he winks at me, and says nothing, and neither did any of his folk. But later on he drew me aside, and he said: "Butterbur," said he, "I have some friends behind that will be passing your way before long. They should be here by Tuesday,[5] if they can follow a plain road. They are hobbits: one is a round-bellied little chap (begging your pardon, sir) with red cheeks, and the others just young hobbits. They'll be riding on ponies. Just tell them to push along, will you? I'll go on slow from here, and they had best catch me up, if they can. Now don't go telling anybody else, and don't encourage them to stop here for a holiday. Your beer's good; but they must take what they can quick, and move on. See?"

'Thankyou,' said Bingo, thinking Mr Butterbur had finished; and relieved again to find that there seemed nothing very serious behind the mystery.

'Ah, but wait a minute,' said Barnabas Butterbur, dropping his voice. 'That wasn't the end of it. There was others that enquired after four hobbits; and that's what is puzzling me. On Monday evening there came riding in a big fellow on a great black horse. All hooded and cloaked he was. I was standing by my door, and he spoke to me. Very strange I thought his voice, and could hardly make out his talk at first. I did not like the looks of him at all. But sure enough he was asking for news of four hobbits with five ponies[6] that were riding out of the Shire. There's something funny here, thought I; but remembering what old Mr Gandalf said, I gave him no satisfaction. "I haven't seen any such party," I said. "What may you be wanting with them, or with me?" At that he whipped up his horse without another word, and rode off eastward. The dogs were all yammering, and the geese a-screaming, as he went through the village. I was not sorry to see him go, I can tell you. But I heard tell later that three were seen going along the road towards Combe behind the hill, though where the other two sprang from no one could say.

'But will you believe me, they came back, or some others as like 'em as night and dark followed after them. On Tuesday evening, there was a bang at the door, and my dog in the yard set up a yelping and a howling. "It's another of they black Men,' said Nob coming to fetch me with his hair all on end. Sure enough it was, when I went to the door: not one though, but four of 'em; and one was sitting there in the twilight with his horse nigh on my doorstep. He stooped down at me, and spoke in a sort of whisper.

It made me go queer down me back, if you understand me, as if someone had poured cold water behind me collar.[7] It was the same story: he wanted news of four hobbits with five ponies. But he seemed more pressing and eager like. Indeed to tell you the truth he offered me a tidy bit of gold and silver if I would tell him which way they had gone, or promise to watch out for them.

'"There's lots of hobbits and ponies round here and on the Road," said I (thinking things mighty curious, and not liking the sound of his voice). "But I haven't seen any party of that sort. If you give me a name, maybe I could give a message, if they happen to call at my house." At that he sat silent for a moment. And then, sir, he says: "The name is Baggins, Bolger-Baggins," and he hissed out the end of it like a snake. "Any message?" says I, all of a twitter. "Nay, just tell him that we are seeking him in haste," he hissed; "you may see us again, perhaps," and with that he and his fellows rode away, and disappeared quick in the darkness, being all wrapped up in black, like.

'Now what do you make of that, Mr Hill? I must say that it comes in my mind to wonder if that is your right name, begging your pardon. But I hope I have done right: for it seems to me that those black fellows mean no good by Mr Bolger-Baggins, if that is who you are.'

'Yes! He is Mr Bolger-Baggins all right,' said Trotter suddenly. 'And he ought to be grateful to you. He has only himself and his friends to thank, if all the village knows his name by now.'

'I *am* grateful,' said Bingo. 'I am sorry I cannot tell you the whole story, Mr Butterbur. I am very tired, and rather worried. But to put it briefly, these – er – black riders are just what I'm trying to escape. I should be very grateful (and so also will Gandalf be, and I expect old Tom Bombadil as well) if you would forget that anyone but Mr Hill passed this way; though I hope these abominable riders won't bother you any more.'

'I hope not indeed!' said Barnabas.

'Well, now good night!' said Bingo. 'Thankyou again for your kindness.'

'Good night, Mr Hill. Good night, Trotter!' said Barnabas. 'Good night, Mr Brown, sir, and Mr Green. Bless me now, where's Mr Rivers?'

'I don't know,' said Bingo; 'but I expect he is outside. He said something about going out for a breath of air. He'll be in before long.'

'Very well. I'll not go locking him out,' said the landlord. 'Good

night to you all!' With that he went out, and his feet died away
down the passage.

'There now!' said Trotter, before Bingo could speak. 'Old
Barnabas has told you a good deal of what I still had to say. I saw
the Riders myself. There are seven at least. That rather alters
things, doesn't it?'

'Yes,' said Bingo, hiding his alarm as well as he could. 'But we
knew already that they were after us; and they did not find out
anything new, it seems. How lucky that they came *before* we
arrived!'

'I should not be sure,' said Trotter. 'I've still some more to add.
[*Added in pencil:* I first saw the Riders last Saturday away west
of Bree, before I ran across Gandalf. I am not at all sure they
were not following *his* trail, too. I also saw those that called on
Barnabas. And] on Tuesday night I was lying on a bank under the
hedge of Bill Ferny's garden; and I heard Bill Ferny talking. He is
a queer fellow, and his friends are like him. You may have noticed
him among the company: a swarthy fellow with a scowl. He
slipped out just after the song and the 'accident'. I wouldn't trust
him. He would sell *anything* to *anybody*. Do you take my meaning? I did not see who Ferny was talking to, nor did I hear what
was said: the voices were hisses and whispers. That is the end of
my news. You must do what you like about my 'reward'. But as for
my coming with you, I will say just this: I know all the lands
between the Shire and the Mountains, for I've wandered over
most of them in the course of my life; and I'm older now than I
look. I might prove useful. For I fancy you'll have to leave the
open Road after tonight's accident. I don't think somehow that
you will be wanting to meet any of these Black-riders, if you can
help it. They give me the creeps.' He shuddered, and they saw
with surprise that he had drawn his hood over his face which was
buried in his hands. The room seemed very still and quiet and the
lights dim.

'There! It has passed!' he said after a moment, throwing back
his hood and pushing his hair from his face. 'Perhaps I know or
guess more about these Riders then even you do. You do not fear
them enough – yet. But it seems likely enough to me that news of
you will reach them before the night is old. Tomorrow you will
have to go swiftly and secretly (if possible). But Trotter can take
you by ways that are little trod. Will you have him?'

Bingo made no answer. He looked at Trotter: grim and wild

and rough-clad. It was hard to know what to do. He did not doubt that most of his tale was true (borne out as it was by the landlord's account); but it was less easy to feel sure of his good intent. He had a dark look – and yet there was something in it, and in his speech which often strayed from the rustic manner of the rangers and Bree-folk, that seemed friendly, and even familiar. The silence grew, and still Bingo could not make up his mind.

'Well, I'm for Trotter, if you want any help in deciding,' said Frodo at last. 'In any case I daresay he could follow us wherever we went, even if we refused.'

'Thankyou!' said Trotter, smiling at Frodo. 'I could, and I should, for I should feel it my duty. But here is a letter which I have for you – I daresay it will help you to make up your mind.'

To Bingo's amazement he took from a pocket a small sealed letter and handed it over. On the outside it was inscribed: 'B from G ⚭'

'Read it,' said Trotter.⁸

Bingo looked carefully at the seal before he broke it. It seemed undoubtedly to be Gandalf's, as was the writing and the Rune ⚭. Inside was the following message. Bingo read it aloud.

*Monday morning Sept. 26. Dear B. Don't stop long in Bree – not for the night, if you can help it. Have learned some news on the way. Pursuit is getting close: there are 7 at least, perhaps more. On no account use It again, not even for a joke. Don't move in dark or mist. Push along by day! Try and catch me up. I cannot wait here for you; but I shall go slow for a day or two. Look out for our camp on Weathertop Hill.⁹ I shall wait there as long as I dare. I am giving this to a ranger (wild hobbit) known as Trotter: he is dark, long-haired, has wooden shoes! You can trust him. He is an old friend of mine and knows a great deal. He will guide you to Weathertop and further if necessary. Push along! Yours* ᚷᚪᚾᛞᚪᛚᚠ *Gandalf* ⚭ ¹⁰

Bingo looked at the trailing handwriting – it seemed as plainly genuine as the seal. 'Well, Trotter!' he said, 'if you had told me right away that you had this letter, it would have smoothed things out a lot, and saved a lot of talk. But why did you invent all that about eavesdropping?'

'I did not,' laughed Trotter. 'I gave old Gandalf quite a start when I popped up from behind the hedge. I told him he was lucky that it was an old friend. We had a long talk, about various things – Bilbo and Bingo and the [*added in pencil:* Riders and the] Ring, if you want to know. He was very pleased to see me, as he was in a hurry and yet anxious to get in touch with you.'

'Well, I must admit I am glad to have a word from him,' said Bingo. 'And if you are a friend of Gandalf's then we are lucky to meet you. I am sorry if I was unnecessarily suspicious.'

'You weren't,' said Trotter. 'You weren't half suspicious enough. If you had had previous experience of your present enemy, you would not trust your own hands without a good look, once you knew that he was on your track. Now I *am* suspicious: and I had to make quite sure that *you* were genuine first, before handing over any letter. I've heard of shadow-parties picking up messages that were not meant for them – it has been done by enemies before now. Also, if you want to know, it amused me to see if I could induce you to take me on – just by my gifts of persuasion. It would have been nice (though quite wrong) if you had accepted me for my manners without testimonial! But there, I suppose my looks are against me!'

'They are!' said Odo laughing. 'But handsome is as handsome does, we say in the Shire, and anyway I daresay we shall all look much the same before long, after lying in hedges and ditches.'

'It will take more than a few days (or weeks or years) wandering in the world to make you look like Trotter,' he answered, and Odo subsided. 'You would die first, unless you are made of tougher stuff than you look to be.'

'What are we to do?' said Bingo. 'I don't altogether understand his letter. Gandalf said "don't stay in Bree." Is Barnabas Butterbur all right?'

'Perfectly!' said Trotter. 'As sound a hobbit as you would find between the West Towers and Rivendell. Faithful, kind, shrewd enough in his plain business; but not overcurious about anything but the daily events among the simple Bree-folk. If anything strange happens he just invents an explanation or else forgets it. 'Queer,' he says, and scratches his head, and goes back to his larder, or his brewhouse. That is just as well for you! I expect he has now convinced himself that there was "some mistake", and that the light was tricky, and that all the hobbits in the room merely imagined that "Mr Hill" disappeared. The black riders will become ordinary travellers looking for a friend, in a week or two – if they don't come back.'

'Well, is it safe then to stay the night here?' said Bingo, with a look at the comfortable fire and the candle-light. 'I mean, Gandalf said: "push along"; but also: "don't move in the dark".'

It is here that the alternative version B (see p. 148 and note 1) joins or merges with version A just given (though before this point, as will be seen, there are substantial passages in common). The beginning of the narrative is here quite different:

'There now!' said the landlord, snapping his fingers. 'Half a moment. It's come back to me, as I said it would. Bless me! Four hobbits and five ponies! I think I have a letter for your party.'

'A letter!' said Bingo, holding out his hand.

'Well,' said he, hesitating; 'he did say that I must be careful to deliver it to the right hands. So perhaps, if you don't mind, you would be so good as to tell me, who you might expect a message from.'

'Gandalf?' said Bingo. 'An old – er– man' (he thought perhaps *wizard* was an inadvisable word) 'with a tall hat and a long beard?'

'Gandalf it was,' said Butterbur; 'and old he is, but there is no call to describe him. All folk know *him*. A wizard they say he is; but that's as may be. But what may your first name be, if you will excuse my asking, sir?'

'Bingo.'

'Ah!' said Barnabas.[11] 'Well, that seems all right; though he did say that you should be here by Tuesday, not Thursday, as it is.[12] Here is the letter.' From his pocket he drew a small sealed envelope, on which was written: *To Bingo from G.* ⚒ *by the hand of Mr B. Butterbur, landlord of the Prancing Pony, Bree.*

'Thankyou very much, Mr Butterbur,' said Bingo, pocketing the letter. 'Now, if you will excuse me, I will say good night. I am very tired.'

'Good night, Mr Hill! I'll be sending water and candles to your room as soon as may be.' He trotted off; and Bingo, Frodo, and Odo made their way back to their parlour.

Version B now agrees with version A virtually word for word from here (p. 148) to Trotter's words 'but eavesdropping, as you put it, is not unknown in Bree, and besides, I have not told you all yet' (p. 150), at which point in A he was interrupted by the arrival of Mr Butterbur; thus in B also, Trotter tells them of his overhearing Gandalf talking about Bingo with the Dwarves and Elves on the Road west of Bree. B now diverges again:

. . . Besides, I have not yet told you the most important part. There were *other* folk enquiring after four hobbits.'

Bingo's heart sank: he guessed what was coming. 'Go on,' he said quietly.

'On Monday evening at the west end of the village I nearly ran into a horse and rider going fast in the dusk: all hooded and cloaked in black he was, and his horse was tall and black. I hailed him with a curse, not liking the looks of him; and he halted and spoke. He had a strange voice, and I could hardly make out his talk at first. Sure enough, he was asking for news of four hobbits with five ponies that were riding out of the Shire. I stood still and did not answer; and he brought his horse step by step nearer to me. When he was quite close he stooped and sniffed. Then he hissed, and rode off through the village, eastward. I heard the dogs yammering, and geese screaming. From the talk in the inn that night I gathered that *three* riders had been seen in the dusk going along the Road towards Combe behind the hill; though I don't know where the other two sprang from.

'On Tuesday I was on the look-out all day. Sure enough, as evening drew in, I saw the same riders again, or others as like them as night is to darkness – coming down the Road from the West again. Four this time, though, not three. I hailed them from behind a hedge as they passed; and they all halted suddenly, and turned towards my voice. One of them – he seemed larger and mounted on a taller horse – came forward in my direction. "Where are you going, and what is your business?" I said. The rider leaned forward as if he was peering – or smelling; and then riding to the hedge he spoke in a sort of whisper. I felt cold shivers run down my back. It was the same story: he wanted news of four hobbits and five ponies. But he seemed more pressing and eager. Indeed (and it is that that is worrying me at the moment) he offered a deal of silver and gold, if I could tell him which way they had gone, or promise to watch out for them. "I have seen no such party," I said, "and I am a wanderer myself, and maybe shall be far West or East by tomorrow. But if you give me a name, maybe I could give a message, if I happen to meet such folk in my way." At that he sat silent for a while; and then he said suddenly: "The name is Baggins, Bolger-Baggins," and he hissed out the end of it like a snake. "What message?" I asked all trembling. "Just tell him that we are seeking him in haste," he hissed; and with that he rode away with his companions, and their black robes were quickly swallowed up in the dark. What do you think of that? It rather alters things, doesn't it?'

'Yes,' said Bingo, hiding his alarm as well as he could. 'But we knew already that they were after us; and they do not seem to have found out anything new.'

'If you can trust me!' said Trotter, with a look at Bingo. 'But even so, I should not be too sure. I've a little more to tell. On Tuesday night I was lying on a bank under the hedge of Bill Ferny's garden . . .

Here version B returns again to the other (p. 153), and is almost word for word the same as far as 'The silence grew, and still Bingo could not make up his mind' (p. 154), the only difference being that after 'Bingo did not doubt that most of his tale was true' the words '(borne out as it was by the landlord's account)' are necessarily absent, since in this version Mr Butterbur has not encountered the Riders. Now follows in B:

'I should take a look at that letter of Gandalf's, if I were you,' said Trotter quietly. 'It might help you to make up your mind.'

Bingo took the letter, which he had almost forgotten, out of his pocket. He looked at the seal carefully before he broke it. It seemed certainly to be Gandalf's, as was the writing, and the runic ⊗. He opened it, and read it aloud.

The letter is the same as in version A, except at the end, since in this story Gandalf gave the letter not to Trotter but to the landlord:[13]

 . . . *If you meet a ranger (wild hobbit: dark, long-haired, has wooden shoes!) known as Trotter, stick to him. You can trust him. Old friend of mine: I have seen him, and told him to look out for you. He knows a lot. He will guide you to Weathertop and further if necessary. Push along! Yours*
✗ ᚠ ᛉ ᛗ ᚠ ᚱ ᚤ *Gandalf* ⊗·

Bingo looked at the trailing handwriting. It seemed as plainly genuine as the seal. 'Well, Trotter,' he said, 'if you had told me right away that you had seen Gandalf to speak to, and that he had written this letter, it would have smoothed things out a lot, and saved a lot of talk.'

'As for the letter,' said Trotter, 'I knew nothing about it, till old Barnabas brought it out. Gandalf put two strings to his bow. I expect he was afraid I might miss you.'

'But why did you invent all that tale about eavesdropping?'

'I did not invent it,' laughed Trotter. 'It was true. I gave old Gandalf quite a start when I popped up from behind the hedge.

The two texts coincide again from this point (p. 154) – except of course that Trotter does not say here 'I had to make quite sure that *you* were genuine first, before handing over any letter', but simply 'I had to make sure that *you* were genuine.' But when Bingo says 'I don't altogether understand this letter. He says "don't stop in Bree"' (p. 155), in version B he gets no further, for:

At that moment there came a knock on the door. Mr Butterbur was there again, with a tray of candles, and Nob behind him with jugs of hot water. 'Here's your water and lights, if you be wishing for your beds,' said he. 'But your Mr Rivers has not come in yet. I hope he will not be long, for I've a mind for bed myself, but I won't leave the locking-up to anyone else tonight; not with these pestering black foreigners about.'

'Where can Merry have got to?' said Frodo. 'I hope he's all right.'

'Give him a few more minutes, Mr Butterbur,' said Bingo. 'I am sorry to bother you.' Very good,' he said, putting the candles on the table. 'Nob, take the water to the rooms! Good night, sirs.' He shut the door.

'What I was going to say,' Bingo went on quietly after a moment, 'was: why not stop in Bree? Is Butterbur all right? Of course, Tom Bombadil said so; but I'm learning to be suspicious.'

'Old Barnabas!' said Trotter. 'He's perfectly all right. As sound a hobbit as there is between the West Towers and Rivendell. Gandalf was only afraid you might be too comfortable here! Barney is faithful, kind, shrewd in plain business – and not overcurious about anything but the daily events among his Bree-folk. If anything strange happens, he just invents an explanation, or puts it out of his mind as soon as possible. "Queer," he says, and scratches his head, and then goes back to his larder or his brewhouse.'

'Well, is it safe to stay the night here?' said Bingo, with a look at the comfortable fire and the candles. 'At any rate Gandalf said "Don't move in the dark".'

At this point the two versions finally merge. It will be seen that the essential differences of B from A are these. In B, Butterbur has Gandalf's letter and gives it to Bingo at the outset (though Bingo does not read it there and then). Trotter not only, as in A, 'eavesdrops' on Gandalf and his companions on the Road west of Bree, but he, not Butterbur, has the encounter with the Riders, and not of course at the inn door but on the road. The 'material' of the two accounts is closely similar, allowing for the Butterburian quality of the one, and the difference of place.

In version A Trotter, to help him make up his mind, gives Bingo the letter when Mr Butterbur has gone; in B, he reminds Bingo about it (as in FR p. 181). And in B, Butterbur only now comes into the parlour, so that the realisation that Merry has not come back is postponed.

A characteristic combination of, or selection from, these divergent accounts is found in the relation between the final story in FR and the two original variants; for A is followed in making Mr Butterbur enter in the middle of the conversation between the hobbits and Trotter/Strider – but B in making it Butterbur who has Gandalf's letter. It is extremely characteristic, again, that Trotter's 'eavesdropping' on Gandalf and his companions behind the hedge on the Road west of Bree survives in FR (p. 176), but becomes the eavesdropping of Strider on the hobbits themselves – for, of course in FR Gandalf had been in Bree and left the letter long before, at the end of June, and at the time of the Birthday Party was far away. But while the relative chronology, as between Gandalf's movements and those of the hobbits, would be entirely reconstructed, that of the latter was never changed.

| | | | |
|---|---|---|---|
| Thurs. | Sept. 22 | Birthday Party | Gandalf and Merry, with Dwarves and Elves, left Hobbiton (after the fireworks) |
| Fri. | Sept. 23 | Bingo, Frodo, and Odo left Hobbiton and slept out | |
| Sat. | Sept. 24 | The hobbits passed the night with Gildor and the Elves | |
| Sun. | Sept. 25 | The hobbits reached Buckland at night | Gandalf and his companions arrived at Bree in the morning |
| Mon. | Sept. 26 | The hobbits in the Old Forest; first night with Tom Bombadil | Gandalf and his companions left Bree, Gandalf leaving letter for Bingo. Black Rider comes to the inn (or encounters Trotter on the Road) |
| Tues. | Sept. 27 | Second night with Tom Bombadil | Four Riders come to the inn (or Trotter encounters them on the Road) |
| Wed. | Sept. 28 | Hobbits captured by Barrowight | |
| Thurs. | Sept. 29 | | Hobbits arrive at Bree |

The same dates for the hobbits' movements appear in The Tale of Years in LR Appendix B (p. 372). That the 22nd of September, the day of the Birthday Party, was a Thursday first appears in the fourth version of 'A Long-expected Party' (FR p. 34); originally it was a Saturday (see pp. 21, 38).

For the significance of the additions in pencil on pp. 153–4, whereby Trotter is made to have seen the Riders 'away west of Bree' already on the Saturday, before Gandalf arrived there, and to have spoken with Gandalf about them when they met, see p. 217, note 11.

From the point where the two versions join, the text (in ink over pencil) proceeds thus. I give it in full, since though much was retained in FR there are a very great many differences in detail.

'You mustn't,' said Trotter; 'and so you can't help staying here tonight. What has been done can't be helped; and we must hope that all will be well. I don't think anything will get inside this inn, once it is locked. But, of course, we must get off as early as may be in the morning. I shall be up and about sooner than the Sun and I'll see all is ready. You are two or three days behind – somehow. Perhaps you will tell me as we go along what you have been up to. Unless you start early, and go fast, I doubt if you'll find any camp on Weathertop.'

'In that case let's get to bed now!' said Odo yawning. 'Where's that silly fellow Merry? It would be too much, if we had to go out now and look for him.'

At that very moment they heard a door slam, and feet running in the passage. Merry came in with a rush, shut the door hastily, and leaned against it. He was out of breath. They stared at him in alarm for a moment; then he gasped: 'I've seen one, Bingo. I've seen one!'

'What?' they cried all together.

'A Black Rider!'

'Where?' said Bingo.

'Here. In the village,' he answered. 'I had come back from a stroll, and was standing just outside the light from the door, looking at the stars: it is a fine night, but dark. I felt something coming towards, if you know what I mean: there was a sort of dark shadow; and then I saw him for a second,[14] just as he passed through the beam of light from the door. He was leading his horse along the grass-edge on the other side of the Road, and hardly made a sound.'

'Which way did he go?' asked Trotter.

Merry started, noticing the stranger for the first time. 'Go on,' said Bingo. 'This is a messenger from Gandalf. He will help us.'

'I followed him,' said Merry. 'He went through the village, right to the east end, where the Road turns round the foot of the hill.

Suddenly he stopped under a dark hedge; and I thought I heard him speaking, or whispering, to someone on the other side. I wasn't sure, though I crept as near as I dared. But I'm afraid I came over all queer and trembling suddenly, and bolted back.'

'What's to be done?' said Bingo, turning to Trotter.

'Don't go to your rooms!' said Trotter at once. 'That must have been Bill Ferny – for his hole is at the east end of Bree; and it is more than likely that he will have found out which rooms you have got. They have small windows looking back west and the outside walls are not very thick. We'll all stay in here, bar the door and window, and take turns to watch.[15] But first we had better fetch your baggage – and arrange the beds!'

At this point my father interrupted his original pencilled draft text to set down a sketch of the story to come, and since he did not overwrite this part of the manuscript in ink it can be read – or could be, if it were not written in a scribble at the very limit of legibility and beyond.

That was done. Pillows put in beds. Nothing happens that night – but in the morning windows open, pillows on floor. The ponies have all vanished. Timothy [i.e. Timothy Titus the landlord] in a great state. They . . . . . [?a bill]. He pays for ponies [?but there are] no more to be had. Shortage in the village. They go on with Trotter on foot. Trotter takes them to a wild hobbit hole, and [?gets his friend] to run on ahead and send a message to Weathertop by pony? Trotter [?guides them by quiet paths off the . . . .] road and going through the woods. Once far in distance on a hill which looked down on to a piece of the road they thought they saw a Black Rider sitting on his horse [?scanning] the road [?and the country round].

. . . . . Weathertop [?about] 50 [written beside: 100] miles from Bree.

Commanding view all round.

Gandalf had gone, but left a pile of stones – message. Waited two days. Must go on. Push on for ford. Help will be easy from Rivendell, if I get there.

They come to Troll Stones . . . . . of Road. Here owing to River ahead they [?are obliged] to go back to Road. Black Riders evidently expect them to visit Troll-wood [> Trollshaw] and are waiting on road where path joined it.

At this stage, then, my father did not at all foresee the attack on the hobbits at Weathertop, just as in the earlier sketch given on p. 126 he did not foresee the attack on the inn. The visit to the Troll Stones had already been envisaged in that sketch (there described as 'foolish'), and there as here the Riders would only finally come upon them at the Ford.

This is the first occurrence of the name *Trollshaw*, which appears on the LR map (*Trollshaws*) but nowhere in the text.

The text in ink continues:

Trotter was now accepted as a member of the party, indeed as their guide. They at once did as he suggested; and creeping to their bedrooms they disordered the clothes, and put a pillow longwise in each bed. Odo added a brown fur mat, a more realistic substitute for his head. When they were all gathered in the sitting-room again, they piled their things on the floor, pushed a low chair against the door, and shut the window. Peeping out Bingo saw it was still a clear night: he then closed and barred the heavy inside shutters, drew the curtains, and blew out the candles. The hobbits lay on their blankets with their feet towards the fire. Trotter lay in the chair against the door. They did not talk much, but fell asleep one by one.[16] Nothing happened in the night to disturb them. Both Merry and Bingo woke up once in the early and still dark hours, fancying they had heard or felt something moving; but soon they fell asleep again. They noticed that Trotter seemed to be sitting awake in his chair with his eyes open. It was also Trotter that drew the curtains and opened the shutters and let in the early light. He seemed to be able to do with next to no sleep. As soon as he had roused them they tiptoed along the passage to their bedrooms.

There they found how good Trotter's advice had been. The windows were open and swinging, and the curtains were flapping. The beds were tossed about, and the pillows flung on the floor – ripped open. Odo's mat was torn to pieces.

Trotter promptly went in search of Mr Butterbur, and roused him out of bed. What exactly he said to him he did not tell Bingo; but the landlord appeared very quickly, and he seemed very frightened, and very apologetic.

'Never has such a thing happened in my time, or my dad's,' said he, raising his hands in horror. 'Guests unable to sleep in their beds, and all. What are we coming to? But this has been a queer week, and no mistake.' He did not seem surprised that they were anxious to leave as soon as possible, before folk were up and about; and bustled off to get them some breakfast at once, and have their ponies got ready.

But before long he came back in dismay. The ponies had vanished! The stabledoors had been broken open in the night, and they were gone, and all the other ponies in the place as well. This was crushing news. They were already probably too late to overtake Gandalf. On foot there was no hope of it – they could not reach Weathertop for days, nor Rivendell for weeks.

'What *can* we do, Mr Butterbur?' asked Bingo desperately. 'Can we borrow any more ponies in the village, or the neighbourhood? Or hire them?' he added rather doubtfully.

'I doubt it,' said Mr Butterbur. 'I doubt if there be four riding-ponies left in all Bree; and I don't suppose one of them is for sale or hire. Bill Ferny has one, a poor overworked creature; but he won't part with that for less than thrice its worth, not if I know him. But I'll do what I can. I'll rout out Bob and send him round right away.'

In the end, after an hour and more's delay, it turned out that only *one* pony could be got – and that had to be bought for six silver pennies (a high price for those parts). But Mr Barnabas Butterbur was an honest hobbit, and a generous one (not but what he could afford to be both); and he insisted on paying Mr Rivers (that is Merry) for the lost five animals, 20 silver pennies,[17] less the cost of their food and lodging. That made a very valuable addition to their travelling funds, since silver pennies were very valuable in those days; but it was not at the moment much comfort for their loss and delay. It must have been rather a serious blow for poor old Barnabas, even though he was comfortably off.*

Of course all this bother about the ponies not only took time, but brought the hobbits and their affairs very much into public notice. There was no chance of keeping their departure secret any longer – much to their dismay, and to Trotter's. Indeed they did not get off until after nine o'clock, and by that time all the Bree-folk were out to watch them go. After saying farewell to Nob and Rob,[18] and taking leave of Mr Butterbur, they tramped off,

---

*Footnote. Still, I believe he came out on the right side in the end; for it turned out that the ponies, wild with terror, had escaped, and having a great deal of sense eventually made their way to find old Fatty Lumpkin. And that proved useful. For Tom Bombadil saw them, and was afraid that disaster had befallen the hobbits. So he went off to Bree to find out what he could; and there he learned all that Barnabas could tell him (and a bit more). Also he bought the ponies off Barnabas (as they belonged to him now). That was very much to the delight of Fatty Lumpkin, who now had friends to whom he could tell tales, and (as they were his juniors) on to whom he could shift most of the little work there was to do.

anxious and downhearted. Trotter walked in front leading their only pony, which was laden with the greater part of their luggage. Trotter was chewing an apple: he seemed to have a pocketful of them. Apples and tobacco, he said, were the things he most missed when he could not get them. They took no notice of the many inquisitive heads poking out of doors or popping over fences as they passed through the village; but as they drew near to the east end, Bingo saw a squat sullen-faced hobbit (rather goblinish, he thought to himself): he was looking over a hedge. He had black eyes, a large mouth, and an unpleasant leer, and was smoking a blackened pipe. He took the pipe out of his mouth, and spat back over his shoulder as they went by.

'Morning, Trotter!' he said. 'Found some new friends?' Trotter nodded, but did not answer.

'Morning, gentles!' he said to the hobbits. 'I suppose you know who you are going with? That's dirty Trotter, that is; or so he calls himself – though I have heard other names not so pretty. But maybe a ranger is good enough for you.'

Trotter turned round quickly. 'Bill Ferny!' he said. 'You put your ugly face out of sight, or you'll get it broken. Not that that'll do it much harm.' With a sudden flick, quick as lightning, half an apple left his hand and hit Bill square on the nose. He ducked and vanished with a yowk;[19] and they did not listen to the curses that came from behind the hedge.

After leaving the village they went along the Road for some miles. It wound to the right, round the south side of Bree hill, and then began to run downwards into wooded country.[20] Away north of the Road they could see first Archet on some higher ground like an island in the trees; and then down in a deep hollow, to the east of Archet, wisps of rising smoke that showed where Combe lay. After the Road had run down some way and left Bree hill behind, they came on a narrow track that ran northward away from the Road. 'This is where we leave the open, and take to cover!' said Trotter. '*Not* a short cut, I hope,' said Bingo. 'It was a short cut through woods that made us two days late before.' 'Ah, but you had not got me with you,' said Trotter. 'My cuts, short or long, don't go wrong.' His plan, as far as they could gather, not knowing the country, was to pass near Combe[21] and keep under cover of the woods while the Road was still near, and then to steer as straight as they could over the wild country to Weathertop Hill. They would in that way (if all went well) cut off a great loop of the Road, which further on bent away south to avoid the Flymarshes [*written above:* Midgewater]. Trotter also had a notion that if he came across any of his friends among the wild hobbits, one that he could trust, they might send him on ahead on the pony to Weathertop. But the others did not think well of his plan, as it would mean carrying heavy packs, and thought the Flymarshes [*written above:* Midgewater] would prove bad enough (from Trotter's description) without that. [22] However, in the meantime walking was not unpleasant. Indeed, if it had not been for the disturbing events of the night before, they would have enjoyed this part of the journey better than any up to that time. The sun was shining, clear but not hot. The woods were still leafy and full of colour, and seemed peaceful, clean, and wholesome. Trotter guided them confidently among the many crossing ways, although very soon they themselves lost all sense of direction; but as he explained to them, they were not yet going in a straight line, but making a zig-zag course, to put off any pursuit.

'Bill Ferny will have watched where we left the Road, for certain,' he said; 'but I don't think he will follow us far himself, though he knows the land round here well enough. It's what he tells other – people that matters. If they think we have made for Combe, so much the better.' Whether because of Trotter's skill or for some other reason, they saw no sign, and heard no sound, of any other living thing all that day, and all the next day: neither two-footed (save birds), nor four-footed (except foxes and rabbits). On the third day out from Bree they came out of the woodlands. Their way had trended downwards all the time, and now they came to flatter and more difficult country.

They were on the borders of the Midgewater Marshes. The ground became damper, in places boggy, and here and there there were pools, and wide stretches of reeds and rushes, full of hidden warbling birds. They had to pick their way carefully to keep both dry-footed and on their line. At first they made fair progress: in fact they were probably going quite as quickly on foot as they could have done mounted. But as they went on their way became slower and more dangerous. The marshes were wide and treach-erous, and across them there was only a winding ranger-trail, which it taxed Trotter's skill to find. The flies became a torment: particularly the clouds of tiny midges that crept up their sleeves and breeches and under their hair.

'I'm being eaten alive!' said Odo. 'Midgewater! There are more midges than water. What do they live on, when they can't get hobbits?'

They were two miserable days in this lonely and unpleasant country. Their camping places were damp and cold, for there was no good fuel. Armfuls of dry reeds and rush and grass blazed away all too soon. And of course the biting things would not let them sleep. There were also some abominable over-grown cousins of the cricket that squeaked all round, and nearly drove Bingo wild. He hated crickets, even when he was not kept awake by bites to listen to them. But these crickets were shriller than any cricket he had met, and even more persistent. They were more than glad, when early on the fifth day from Bree they saw the land before them slowly rising again, sloping up until in the distance it became a line of low hills.[23]

To the right of the line there was a tall conical hill with a slightly flattened top. 'That is Weathertop,' said Trotter. 'The old Road, which we have left far away on our right, runs to the south of it, and passes not far from its foot. We might reach it by noon tomorrow; and I suppose we had better make for it.'

'What do you mean?' asked Bingo.

'I mean: when we do get there, it is not certain what we shall find. It is close to the Road.'

'But was not Gandalf going to camp there?'

'Yes – but what with one thing and another, you are already three or even four days behind the time when he expected you to get there. You will be four or five days late by the time we reach the top. I wonder very much if we shall find *him* there. On the other hand, if certain persons were warned that you went east out of Bree, and have failed to find us in the wilderness, they may not unlikely make for Weathertop themselves. It commands a wide view of the lands all round. Indeed there are many birds and beasts in this country that could see us as we stand here from that hill-top. There are even some of the rangers that on a clear day could spy us from there, if we moved. And not all the rangers are to be trusted, nor all the birds and beasts.'

The hobbits looked anxiously at the distant hill. Odo looked up in the pale sky, as if he feared to see hawks or eagles hovering over them. 'You make me feel most uncomfortable,' said Bingo; 'but I suppose it is all for our good. We ought to realize what danger we are in. What do you advise us to do?'

'I think,' answered Trotter slowly and as if he was for the first time not quite sure of his plans, 'I think the best thing is to go straight forward, or as straight as we can, from this point, and make for the line of hills. There we can strike certain paths that I know, and in fact will bring us to Weathertop from the North, and less openly. Then we shall see what we shall see.'

There seemed nothing else to do. In any case they could not stop in that comfortless land, and the line of march that Trotter proposed was more or less in the direction that they must take, if ever they were to get to Rivendell. All that day they plodded along, until the cold and early evening came down. The land became drier and more barren; but mists and vapours lay behind them on the wide marshes. A few melancholy birds were piping, until the round red sun sank slowly into the western shadows. They thought how its soft light would be glancing through the cheerful windows looking on to the garden at Bag-end far away. They came upon a stream that wandered down from the hills to lose itself in the stagnant marshland, and this they followed while the light lasted. It was already nearly dark when they camped under some stunted alder-trees on the stony banks of the stream; now dark before them loomed the bare side of the nearest hill, bleak and barren. They set a watch that night, but those that were not watching slept uneasily. The moon was waxing, and in the early night hours a grey cold light lay on the land.

Next morning they set out again soon after sunrise. There was a frost in the air, and the sky was a pale clear blue. They felt refreshed, as if they had had a night of good sleep, and were glad to have left the damp heavy air of the marshes. Already they were getting used to much walking, and to short commons (or shorter at any rate than they would have thought possible to walk on in the Shire). Odo declared that Bingo was looking twice the hobbit that he was.

'Very odd,' said Bingo, tightening his belt, 'considering that there is actually a great deal less of me. I hope the thinning-process won't go on indefinitely, or I shall become a wraith.'

'Don't speak of such things!' said Trotter quickly, and with surprising earnestness.

Before long they reached the feet of the hills; and there they found, for the first time since they left the Road, a track plain to see. This they took, turning and following it south-west.[24] It led them up and down, following a line of country that contrived to keep them hidden as often and as long as possible from view, either from the hill-tops above, or from the flats to the West. It dived into dells, and hugged steep banks, and found crossings over the streams, and ways round the bogs that these made in hollow places. Where it crossed a flatter and more open space it often had lines of large boulders on either side, screening the marchers almost like a hedge.

'I wonder who made this path, and what for?' said Frodo, as they passed along one of these avenues, where the stones were unusually large and closely set. 'I am not sure I quite like it – it has a, well, rather barrow-wightish look? Is there any barrow on Weathertop?'

'No!' said Trotter. 'There is no barrow on Weathertop nor on any of these hills. The Men of the West did not live here. I do not know who made this path, nor how long ago, but it was made to provide a way to Weathertop that could be defended. It is told by some that Gilgalad and Valandil [*later* > Elendil] made a fort and strong place here in the Ancient Days, when they marched East.'

'Who was Gilgalad?' asked Frodo; but Trotter did not answer, and seemed to be lost in thought.[25]

It was already mid-day when they came towards the south-eastern end of the line of hills, and saw before them, in the pale clear light of the October sun, a green-grey ridge leading up like a sagging bridge on to the northward side of the tall conical hill. They decided to make for the top at once, while the day was broad. Concealment was no longer possible, and they could only hope for the best. Nothing could be seen moving on the hill.

After an hour's slow plodding climb, Trotter reached the crown of the hill. Bingo and Merry followed, tired and breathless. The last slope had been steep and stony. Odo and Frodo were left below with the baggage and the pony, in a sheltered hollow under the western flank of the hill. On the top they found only a pile of stones – a cairn of long forgotten meaning. There was no sign of Gandalf, or of any living thing. All about and below them was a wide view, for the most part of a land empty, deserted, and featureless – except for patches of woodland away to the south, where they caught also the occasional glint of distant water. Beneath them, on the southward side, ran the ribbon of the Old Road, coming out of the West and winding up and down until it faded behind a ridge of dark land in the East. It too was empty. Nothing was moving on it. Following its line eastward they beheld the Mountains – now plain to see, the nearer foothills brown and brooding, with taller greyer shapes behind, and behind them again the high white peaks glimmering out of clouds.

'Well, here we are!' said Merry. 'And very cheerless and uninviting it all looks. There is no water, and no shelter. I don't blame Gandalf for not waiting here! He would have to leave the waggon, and horses, and most of his companions, too, I expect, down near the Road.'

'I wonder,' said Trotter thoughtfully. 'He must certainly have come here, since he said he would. It is not like him to leave no sign. I hope nothing has happened to him – though it is not easy to imagine *him* coming to grief.' He pushed the pile of stones with his foot, and the topmost stones fell down with a clatter. Something white, set free, began to flutter in the wind. It was a piece of paper. Trotter seized it eagerly, and read out the message scrawled on it:

*Waited three days. Must go. What has happened to you. Push on for the Ford beyond Troll-shaw, as fast as you can. Help will come there from Rivendell, as soon as I can manage it. Be watchful. G.* ⨂

'Three days!' said Trotter. 'Then he must have left while we were still in the marshes. I suppose we were too far away for any glimpse of our miserable fires.'

'How far is the Ford, and Rivendell?' said Bingo wearily. The world looked wild and wide from the hill-top.

'Let me think!' said Trotter. 'I don't know if the Road has ever been measured beyond the Forsaken Inn – a day's journey east of Bree. But the stages, in days taken by waggon, pony, or horse, or on foot, are pretty well known, of course. I should reckon it is about 120 long-miles from Bree to Weathertop – by the Road, which loops south and north. We have come a shorter but not quicker way: between 80 and 90 miles in the last six days. It is nearer 40 than 30 miles from Brandywine Bridge to Bree. I don't know, but I should make the count of miles from your Bridge to the Ford under the Misty Mountains a deal over 300 miles. So it must be close on 200 from Weathertop to the Ford. I have heard it said that from Bridge to Ford can be done in a fortnight going hard with fair weather; but I have never met any that had made the journey in that time. Most take nigh on a month, and poor hobbit-folk on foot take more.

This passage, from 'But the stages, in days taken by waggon, pony, or horse, or on foot', was enclosed within square brackets; and against it my father wrote: '? Cut out – as this though it can be kept as a narrative time guide is too cut and dried and spoils the feeling. ?' He then wrote the following replacement on a slip (cf. FR p. 200):

Some say it is so far, and some say otherwise. It is a queer Road. And folk are glad to reach their journey's end, be the time longer or shorter. But I know how long it would take me, with fair weather and no illfortune, just a poor ranger on his own feet: between three weeks and a month going hard from Brandywine Bridge to the Ford under the Misty Mountains. More than two days from the Bridge to Bree, a week from Bree to Weathertop. We have made it in that time, but we have come by a shorter way, for the Road bends south and north. Say ten days. Then we have a fortnight before us, maybe less, but more likely more.'

'A fortnight!' said Bingo. 'A lot may happen in that time.' They all fell silent. Bingo felt for the first time in that lonely place the full realization of his danger and exile. He wished that his fortune had left him in the quiet and beloved Shire. He stared at the hateful Road – leading back westward – to his old home. Suddenly he was aware that two black specks were moving along the ribbon, going westward, and looking closer he saw now that several more were crawling slowly eastward to meet them. He gave a cry and clutched Trotter's arm. 'Look!' he said, pointing.

'Get down!' cried Trotter, pulling Bingo flat on the ground beside him. Merry flung himself alongside. 'What is it?' he whispered. 'I don't know, but I fear,' said Trotter. They wormed their way to the edge of the flat hilltop and peered out from behind a stony outcrop. The light was not bright, for the clear morning had faded, and clouds crawled slowly out of the East and had now caught the sun, as it began to go west. They could see the black specks, but neither Bingo nor Merry could make out their shape for certain. Yet something told them that there below were Black Riders assembling on the Road, beyond the hill's foot. 'Yes,' said Trotter, whose keener sight left him in no doubt. 'The enemy is here.'

Hastily they crawled away, and slipped down the north side of the hill to find Odo and Frodo.

Here the original Chapter VII, which I have divided into two, ends.

## NOTES

1   Of the original pencilled draft, overwritten by version B, little can now be read; it was dashed down in faint pencil, and except here and there the text in ink effectively obliterates it. Enough can be seen, however, to show that the story was that of version B (in which

Gandalf's letter was given to the landlord of the inn, not to Trotter); and though this is less certain, I suspect that at this stage there was no mention of Black Riders having come to Bree before Bingo, Merry, Frodo, and Odo arrived. On the other hand, it is perfectly clear that when my father wrote out version B on top of the original draft he had version A in front of him.

The explanation of this odd situation can be seen, I think, in the fact that version B is much longer than the pencilled draft and not at all closely associated with it; some of it is on slips added in. I think that my father wrote out version A *first*, on the basis of the pencilled draft, but changed the story as he did so (by giving Gandalf's letter to Trotter, and introducing Butterbur's story of the Riders who came to the inn); he *then* returned to the pencilled draft and wrote version B on top of it, going back to the story that the letter had been entrusted to Butterbur, and again introducing the story of the Black Riders at Bree but ascribing it now to Trotter, who encountered them on the Road. For this text he used version A and followed it very closely so far as the changed story allowed. Thus the textual history was:

(1)   Original pencilled draft: Gandalf's letter left with Butterbur; (probably) no story as yet of Black Riders having already come to Bree.

(2)   Version A: the story changed: Gandalf's letter left with Trotter; Butterbur tells of the coming of the Riders to the inn.

(3)   Version B, written over the original draft, but using much of the wording of A: Gandalf's letter left with Butterbur; Trotter tells of his encounters with the Riders on the Road.

Finally, some new phrases in B were written back into A.

2   It is with this sentence that Chapter 10 'Strider' begins in FR, but I include the preceding passage here since it forms part of the narrative which is treated in alternative ways (see p. 156).

3   Cf. p. 141 note 7. But even though the old idea that Bingo 'had come to the end of his treasure' (and that a vague object of his 'Journey' was that it might bring him some more, p. 62) disappeared, it remained in FR (p. 175) that 'he had brought only a little money with him.'

4   *That would be five days ago:* see the chronology given on p. 160. Gandalf and his companions arrived at the inn on Sunday morning, and it was now Thursday night.

5   *They should be here by Tuesday:* Gandalf had assumed that they would follow the Road from the Brandywine Bridge to Bree, and take two days over it. Cf. Trotter's calculations (pp. 170–1): 'It is nearer 40 than 30 miles from Brandywine Bridge to Bree', and 'More than two days from the Bridge to Bree' (on foot).

6   How did the Black Riders know this? See p. 350, note 7.

7   Here my father wrote: 'Now he described your party very exactly, sir, more exactly than Mr Gandalf did: colour of your ponies, look of your faces,' but struck it out as soon as written, probably because it was not consistent with his conception of the Black Riders: he had already said (p. 75) that for Ring-wraiths 'Everything becomes very faint like grey ghost pictures against the black background in which you live; but you can smell better than you can hear or see.' It seems very likely that the idea of the 'wraith-world', into which in some sense the bearer of a Ring entered if he put it on his finger, and in which he then became fully visible to the denizens of that world, had already arisen; a hint of this appears in Gildor's words (p. 64) 'I guess that the use of the ring helps them more than you', and in Gandalf's letter in the present chapter he is urgent that Bingo should never wear the Ring for any purpose – now that he has learned that the Riders are in pursuit.

8  These words are at the bottom of a manuscript page. At the bottom my father scribbled in pencil:

> Nov. 19 Motive *trailing Gandalf*. Gandalf drawing them off. *No camp at Weathertop* or again Gandalf leads them off.

With this cf. the pencilled addition on p. 153: 'I first saw the Riders last Saturday away west of Bree, before I ran across Gandalf. I am not at all sure they were not following *his* trail too.'

'Nov. 19' presumably refers to the date of the note, i.e. 19 November 1938; by then my father had got well beyond this point in the narrative, judging by what he said in a letter to Stanley Unwin of 13 October 1938: 'I have worked very hard for a month . . . on a sequel to *The Hobbit*. It has reached Chapter XI (though in rather an illegible state) . . .'

9   The first mention of Weathertop Hill; the actual first occurrence of the name must be in the original pencilled draft of Gandalf's letter, which can be partly made out (note 13).

10  The runes are the Old English runes, as in *The Hobbit*. Gandalf uses the English (Common Germanic) rune ╳ for G in writing his name, but uses also as a sign for himself a rune ⬡. In the *Angerthas* (LR Appendix E pp. 401–4) this rune meant (in the usage of the Dwarves of Moria) [ng].

11  Oddly, the manuscript in ink has here *Timothy*, not *Barnabas*; but it can only be a slip, returning momentarily to the landlord's original name (p. 140 note 3).

12  *Tuesday, not Thursday:* see note 5.

13  The ending of the letter can be read in the pencilled draft:

> *Don't be out after dark or in mist. Push along. Am so anxious that I shall wait [?two] days for you . . . . . Weathertop Hill. If you meet a ranger (wild hobbit) called Trotter, stick to him. I have told him to look out. He will guide you to Weathertop and further if necessary. Push along.*

14    The text as first written here (in ink: the pencilled text beneath is
      illegible) had: 'I felt something moving behind me, and when I
      turned I saw one going along the Road.' – For 'coming towards' in
      the revised sentence perhaps read 'coming towards me'.

15    *bar the door and window* was written in above *and take turns to
      watch*, which was not struck out. See note 16.

16    The underlying pencilled text can be read here:
      They did not talk much but fell asleep one by one. Trotter
      watched for three hours; he said he could do with very little sleep.
      Next came Merry. Nothing happened . . .
      A first version in ink reads:
      He could do with very little (he said): 'give me three hours, and
      then wake me, and I will watch for the rest of the time.' Bingo
      took the first watch; the others talked for a while and then fell
      asleep.
      At this point FR Chapter 10 'Strider' ends, and Chapter 11 'A Knife
      in the Dark' begins – where that chapter takes up the story at Bree
      again: of the attack by the Black Riders on the house at Crickhollow
      with which it begins there is as yet no trace.

17    *20* (silver pennies) was later changed to *25*.

18    *Rob:* at previous occurrences (pp. 135, 164) the name of the ostler at
      *The Prancing Pony* is certainly *Bob*, as in FR.

19    *a yowk:* the verb *yowk* 'howl, bawl, yelp' is given in Joseph Wright,
      *The English Dialect Dictionary*.

20    A tiny pencilled sketch in the body of the manuscript, belonging
      with the underlying draft, shows the Road, after it has curved down
      round the south side of Bree-hill, bending up north again and
      continuing the same line east of Bree as it had to the west of the
      village.

21    *Combe* changed in pencil to *Archet* (as in FR, p. 193).

22    These two sentences, from *Trotter also had a notion*, were enclosed
      in square brackets, probably at the time of writing. Cf. the outline
      (p. 162): 'Trotter takes them to a wild hobbit hole, and gets his
      friend to run on ahead and send a message to Weathertop by pony?'.

23    The pencilled text beneath the ink can be read sufficiently to show
      that the passage of the marshes (unnamed) was described in a couple
      of sentences.

24    Since at the end of the next sentence my father wrote 'from the flats
      to the East', which is an obvious slip and which he later corrected to
      'West', it seems likely that the 'south-west' course of the track along
      the feet of the hills is also a slip for 'south-east'; a little later it is said
      that 'they came towards the south-eastern end of the line of hills.'

25    For the story of Gil-galad and Elendil and the Last Alliance as it was
      at this time see the second version of *The Fall of Númenor* §14
      (V.28-9) and pp. 215-16. Though Elendil is present in *The Fall of
      Númenor* my father does not seem to have been entirely satisfied

with the name: here he wrote *Valandil* first, and in the original draft of the next chapter he changed *Elendil* temporarily to *Orendil* (p. 197 note 3). In *The Lost Road* Valandil was the name of Elendil's father (V.60, 69), and in a later version of *The Fall of Númenor* Valandil is Elendil's brother (V.33).

★

In the latter part of this chapter, from the point where the variant versions join (pp. 159, 161), all the essential structure of the immediate narrative in FR (pp. 185–201) is in place, though the larger bearings and the glimpses of ancient history are conspicuously absent. The narrative runs in a narrower dimension in any case, from the fact that there are no Men in the story: Butterbur is a hobbit, the wild 'rangers', of whom Trotter is one, are hobbits, Bill Ferny is a hobbit (p. 165) – though it is true that the range of hobbit character is greatly extended by these 'Outsiders' who live beyond the Shire's borders.

A few specific points of difference may be briefly mentioned. The pony bought in Bree is not in fact said to be Ferny's (p. 164), though it seems to be implied; and the subsequent history of the five ponies from Buckland, recorded in the footnote to the text (p. 164), was afterwards largely changed (FR p. 191). The encounter of Merry with the Black Rider outside the inn at Bree does not end with his being attacked; and it is Trotter who plays the later part of Sam in having a pocketful of apples and discomfiting Bill Ferny with one on the nose.

The journey from Bree to Weathertop has the same structure as that in FR (pp. 194–7), except at the end. The chronology is:

| Days out of Bree | Date | Place |
|---|---|---|
| 1 | Fri. Sept. 30 | In the woods (Chetwood) |
| 2 | Sat. Oct. 1 | In the woods |
| 3 | Sun. Oct. 2 | First day and camp in the marshes |
| 4 | Mon. Oct. 3 | Second day and camp in the marshes |
| 5 | Tues. Oct. 4 | Camp by the stream under alders |

But in FR the hobbits made another night camp at the feet of the western slopes of the Weather Hills – and that was 'the night of the fifth day of October, and they were six days out from Bree' (p. 197); this camp is not in the original version, and thus they reached Weathertop on Wednesday October 5. Trotter on Weathertop says that they have covered between 80 and 90 miles 'in the last six days': he was including that day also, for it was already after noon.

In the old story Gandalf stayed on Weathertop for three days, and he left there a note in a pile of stones, written on paper. This message ('Help will come there [i.e. to the Ford] from Rivendell, as soon as I can manage it') gives the first clear indication in the story of what Gandalf's intentions were; and with this can be taken the words scribbled on the manuscript that are given in note 8. Gandalf was trying to lure the Riders after *him*.

Looking back over the whole of the original Chapter VII, the story from the hobbits' arrival in Bree to the sight of the Black Riders on the Road far below the summit of Weathertop, there appears again and in the most striking form the characteristic of my father's writing that elements emerge suddenly and clearly conceived, but with their 'meaning' and context still to undergo huge further development, or even complete transformation, in the later narrative (cf. p. 71). A small example here is the face that Bingo thought 'goblinish' as they walked out of Bree (p. 165) – which is here the face of Bill Ferny (a hobbit): in FR (p. 193) it will be that of 'the squint-eyed southerner' whom Frodo glimpsed through the window of Ferny's house, and thought that he looked 'more than half like a goblin.' In a 'chrysalis' state are the 'Rangers', wanderers in the wildnerness, and Trotter is a Ranger, grim and weatherworn, deeply learned in the lore of the wild, and in many other matters; but they are hobbits, and of any further or larger significance that they might have in the history of Middle-earth there is no hint. Trotter is at once so fully realized that his tone in this part of the narrative (indeed not a few of his actual words) was never changed afterwards; yet such little as is glimpsed of his history at this stage bears no relation whatsoever to that of Aragorn son of Arathorn. He is a hobbit, marked out by wearing wooden shoes (whence his name Trotter); there seems to be something in his history that gives him a special knowledge of, and horror of, the Ring-wraiths (p. 153); and Bingo finds something about him that distinguishes him from other 'Rangers', and is in a way familiar (p. 154). These things will be explained later, before they are finally swept away.

# X
# THE ATTACK ON WEATHERTOP

This chapter, numbered VIII, and titleless as usual (though later my father pencilled in 'A Knife in the Dark'), begins on the same manuscript page as the end of the last; it was obviously continuous work, and the manuscript proceeds as before, in ink, rapid but always legible, over pencilled drafts of which only words or phrases here and there are visible (see p. 188). The text goes on through FR Chapter 12 'Flight to the Ford' without any sort of break, but as with the original Chapter VII I divide it into two (see the table on p. 133).

There was a hollow dell beneath the north-west shoulder of Weathertop, right under the long ridge that joined it to the hills behind. There Odo and Frodo had been left to wait for them. They had found the signs of a recent camp and fire, and, a great (and most unexpected) boon, behind a large rock was piled a small store of fire-wood. Better still, under the fuel they found a wooden case with some food in it. It was mostly cram-cakes, but there was some bacon, and some dried fruits. There was also some tobacco!

*Cram* was, as you may remember, a word in the language of the men of Dale and the Long-lake – to describe a special food they made for long journeys. It kept good indefinitely and was very sustaining, but not entertaining, as it took a lot of chewing and had no particular taste. Bilbo Baggins brought back the recipe – he used *cram* after he got home on some of his long and mysterious walks. Gandalf also took to using it on his perpetual journeys. He said he liked it softened in water (but that is hard to believe). But *cram* was not to be despised in the wilderness, and the hobbits were extremely grateful for Gandalf's thoughtfulness. They were still more grateful when the three others came down with their alarming news, and they all realized that they had a long journey still ahead, before they could expect to get help. They immediately held a council, and found it hard to decide what to do. It was the presence of the fire-wood (of which they could not have carried much away) that finally decided them to go no further that day, and to camp for that night in the dell.[1] It seemed unsafe, not to say desperate, to go on at once, or until they found out whether their arrival at the hill was known or expected. For, unless they were to make a long detour back north-west along the hills, and abandon the direction of Rivendell altogether for a while, it would not be easy to find any cover or concealment. The Road itself was impossible; but they must at least cross it, if they were to get into the more broken land, full of bushy thickets, immediately to the south of it. To the north of the Road, beyond the hills, the land was bare and flat for many miles.

'Can the – er – enemy *see*?' asked Merry. 'I mean, they seem usually to have *smelt* rather than seen, at least in the daytime. But you made us lie down flat.'

'I don't know,' said Trotter, 'how they perceive what they seek; but I fear them. And their horses can see.'[2]

It was now already late afternoon. They had had no food since breakfast. In spite of their fear and uncertainty they were very hungry. So down in the dell where all was still and quiet they made a meal – as good a meal as they dared take, after they had examined their stores. But for Gandalf's present they would not have dared to have more than a bite. They had left behind the countries where inns or villages could be found. There were Big People (so Trotter said) away to the South of them. But North and East the neighbouring lands were empty of all save birds and beasts, unfriendly places deserted by all the races of the world: Elves, Men, Dwarves, or Hobbits, and even by goblins. The more adventurous Rangers journeyed occasionally into those regions, but they passed and did not stay. Other wanderers were rare, and of no good sort: Trolls might stray at times down out of the further hills and Mountains. Only on the Road would travellers be found, Big People rarely in those days, Elves perhaps sometimes, most often Dwarves hurrying along on business, and with no help and few words to spare for strangers.

So now – since Gandalf had gone – they had to depend on what they carried with them – probably until they found their way at last to Rivendell. For water they were obliged to trust to chance. For food they could perhaps just have managed to go ten or eleven days; and now with Gandalf's additions they could with economy probably hold out for more than a fortnight. It might have been worse. But starving was not their only fear.

It became very cold as evening fell. There was some mist again over the distant marshes; but the sky above cleared again, and the clouds were blown away by a chill east wind. Looking out from the lip of the dale [*read* dell] they could see nothing but a grey land

quickly vanishing in shadows, under an open sky filling slowly
with twinkling stars.

They lit a small fire down at the lowest point in the hollow, and
sat round it clothed and wrapped in every garment and blanket
they possessed: at least Bingo and his companions did so. Trotter
seemed content with a single blanket, and sat some little way from
the fire puffing his short pipe. They took it in turns to sit on guard
on the edge of the dell, at a point where the steep sides of
Weathertop Hill, and the gentler slope down from the ridge, could
be seen – as far as anything could be seen in the gathering dusk.

As the evening deepened Trotter began to tell them tales to keep
their minds from fear. He knew much lore concerning wild
animals, and claimed to speak some of their languages; and he had
strange stories to tell of their lives and little known adventures. He
knew also many histories and legends of the ancient days, of
hobbits when the Shire was still wild, and of things beyond the
mists of memory out of which the hobbits came. They wondered
where he had learned all his lore.

'Tell us of Gil-galad!' said Frodo – 'you spoke that name not
long ago,[3] and it is still ringing in my ears. Who was he?'

'Don't you know!' said Trotter. 'Gil-galad was the last of the
great Elf-kings: Gil-galad is Starlight in their tongue. He overthrew the Enemy, but he himself perished. But I will not tell that
tale now; though you will hear it, I think, in Rivendell, when we
get there. Elrond should tell it, for he knows it well. But I will tell
you the tale of Tinúviel – in brief, for in full it is a long tale of
which the end is not known, and there is no one that remembers it
in full as it was told of old, unless it be Elrond. But even in brief it
is a fair tale – the fairest that has come out of the oldest days.' He
fell silent for a moment, and then he began not to speak, but to
chant softly:

Put in *Light on Linden Tree* [*sic*] emended. Or the alliterative
lines. Follow with brief Tinúviel story.

My father then went straight on in the manuscript to the beginning of a
prose résumé of the story of Beren and Lúthien. He had not gone far with
this, however, when he abandoned it, and returning to Trotter's words
about the story changed the end of them to: 'It is a fair tale, though it is
sad as are the tales of Middle-earth, and yet it may lift up the hearts of the
enemies of the Enemy.' He then wrote:

*Lo Beren Gamlost the boldhearted*[4]

but struck this out also. He had suggested just above that 'the alliterative lines' might be used. He was referring to the passage of alliterative verse that preceded *Light as Leaf on Lindentree* as published in *The Gryphon* (Leeds University) in 1925,[5] a passage itself closely related to lines in the second version of the alliterative *Lay of the Children of Húrin*, 355 ff., where Halog, one of Túrin's guides on the journey to Doriath, sang this song 'for hearts' uplifting' as they wandered in the forest. But he now decided against the alliterative lines for this place, and wrote in the manuscript a new version of *Light as Leaf on Lindentree*. This text of the poem moves it far towards the final version in FR pp. 204–5, but has elements surviving from the old poem that were afterwards lost, and elements common to neither. There are many later emendations to the text, and many alternative readings (mostly taken up into the final version) written at the time of composition; but here I give the primary text without variants or later corrections.

> The leaves were long, the grass was thin,
>     The fall of many years lay thick,
> The tree-roots twisted out and in,
>     The rising moon was glimmering.
> Her feet went lilting light and quick
>     To the silver flute of Ilverin:[6]
> Beneath the hemlock-umbels thick
>     Tinúviel was shimmering.
>
> The noiseless moths their wings did fold,
>     The light was lost among the leaves,
> As Beren there from mountains cold
>     Came wandering and sorrowing.
> He peered between the hemlock leaves
>     And saw in wonder flowers of gold
> Upon her mantle and her sleeves,
>     And her hair like shadow following.
>
> Enchantment took his weary feet,
>     That over stone were doomed to roam,
> And forth he hastened, strong and fleet,
>     And grasped at moonbeams glistening.
> Through woven woods of Elvenhome
>     They fled on swiftly dancing feet,
> And left him lonely still to roam,
>     In the silent forest listening.
>
> He heard at times the flying sound
>     Of feet as light as linden leaves,
> Or music welling underground

*In the hidden halls of Doriath.*
*But withered were the hemlock sheaves,*
*And one by one with sighing sound*
*Whispering fell the beechen leaves*
*In the wintry woods of Doriath.*

*He sought her ever, wandering far*
*Where leaves of years were thickly strewn,*
*By light of moon and ray of star*
*In frosty heavens shivering.*
*Her mantle glistened in the moon,*
*As on a hill-top high and far*
*She danced, and at her feet was strewn*
*A mist of silver quivering.*

*When winter passed she came again,*
*And her song released the sudden spring,*
*Like rising lark, and falling rain,*
*And melting water bubbling.*
*There high and clear he heard her sing,*
*And from him fell the winter's chain;*
*No more he feared by her to spring*
*Upon the grass untroubling.*

*Again she fled, but clear he called:*
*Tinúviel, Tinúviel.*
*She halted by his voice enthralled*
*And stood before him shimmering.*
*Her doom at last there on her fell,*
*As in the hills the echoes called;*
*Tinúviel, Tinúviel,*
*In the arms of Beren glimmering.*

*As Beren looked into her eyes*
*Within the shadows of her hair*
*The trembling starlight of the skies*
*He saw there mirrored shimmering.*
*Tinúviel! O elven-fair!*
*Immortal maiden elven-wise,*
*About him cast her shadowy hair*
*And white her arms were glimmering.*

*Long was the way that fate them bore*
*O'er stony mountains cold and grey,*

*Through halls of iron and darkling door*
*And woods of night-shade morrowless.*
*The Sundering Seas between them lay*
*And yet at last they met once more,*
*And long ago they passed away*
*In the forest singing sorrowless.*

He paused before he spoke again. 'That is a song,' he said, 'that tells of the meeting of Beren the mortal and Lúthien Tinúviel, which is but the beginning of the tale.

'Lúthien was the daughter of the elven-king Thingol of Doriath in the West of the Middle-world, when the earth was young. Her mother was Melian, who was not of the Elf-race but came out of the Far West from the land of the Gods and the Blessed Realm of Valinor. It is said that the daughter of Thingol and Melian was the most fair maiden that ever was or shall be among all the children of the world. No limbs so fair shall again run upon the green earth, no face so beautiful shall look upon the sky, till all things are changed.

The passage in praise of Lúthien that follows is almost word for word the same as that in the *Quenta Silmarillion* (1937), largely retained in the published work (p. 165, 'Blue was her raiment . . .').

'But Beren was son of Barahir the Bold. In those days the fathers of the fathers of Men came out of the East; and some there were that journeyed even to the West of Middle-earth, and there they met the Elves, and were taught by them, and became wise, but they were mortal and shortlived, for such is their fate. Yet many of them aided the Elves in their wars. For in that time the Elves besieged the Enemy in his dreadful fortress in the North. Angband it was called, the Halls of Iron beneath the thunderous towers of the black mountain Thangorodrim.

'But he broke the siege, and drove Elves and Men ever south-ward; and Barahir was slain. Ruin came upon the West-lands, but Doriath long endured because of the power and enchantment of Melian the Queen that fenced it about so that no evil could come within. In the song it is told[7] how Beren flying southward through many perils came at last into the hidden kingdom and beheld Lúthien. Tinúviel he called her, which is Nightingale, for he did not yet know her name.

'But Thingol the Elven-king was wroth, despising him as a mortal, and a fugitive; and he sent Beren upon a hopeless quest ere

he could win Lúthien. For he commanded him to bring him one of
the three jewels from the crown of the King of Angband, out of the
deeps of the Iron Halls. These were the Silmarils renowned in
song, filled with power and a holy light, for they had been made by
the Elves in the Blessed Realm, but the Enemy had stolen them,
and guarded them with all his strength. Yet Beren achieved that
Quest, for Lúthien fled from her father's realm and followed after
him; and with the aid of Húan hound of the Gods, who came
out of Valinor, she found him once again; and together thereafter
they passed through peril and darkness; and they came even to
Angband and beguiled the Enemy, and overthrew him, and took a
Silmaril and fled.

'But the wolf-warden of the dark gate of Angband bit off the
hand of Beren that held the Silmaril, and he came near to death.
Yet it is told that at length Lúthien and Beren escaped and
returned to Doriath, and the king and all his people marvelled.
But Thingol reminded Beren that he had vowed not to return save
with a Silmaril in his hand.

'"It is in my hand even now," he answered.

'"Show it to me!" said the king.

'"That I cannot do," said Beren, "for my hand is not here," and
he held up his maimed arm. And from that hour he was named
Beren Erhamion the Onehanded.

'Then the tale of the Quest was told in the king's hall and his
mood was softened, and Lúthien laid her hand in Beren's before
the throne of her father.

'But soon fear came upon Doriath. For the dread wolf-warden
of Angband, being maddened by the fire of the Silmaril that
consumed his evil flesh within, roamed through the world, wild
and terrible. And by fate and the power of the jewel he passed the
guarded borders and came ravening even into Doriath; and all
things fled before him. Thus befell the Wolf-hunt of Doriath, and
to that hunt went King Thingol, and Beren Erhamion, and Beleg
the Bowman and Mablung the heavy-handed, and Húan the
hound.

'And the great wolf leaped upon Beren and felled him and
grievously wounded him; and Húan slew the wolf but himself was
slain. And Mablung cut the Silmaril from the belly of the wolf,
and gave it to Beren, and Beren gave it to Thingol. Then they bore
Beren back with Húan at his side to the king's hall. And Lúthien
bade him farewell before the gates, bidding him await her beyond
the Great Seas; and he died in her arms.

'But the spirit of Lúthien fell down into darkness, for such was the doom upon the elven-maid for her love of a mortal man; and she faded slowly, as the Elves do under the burden of a grief unbearable. Her fair body lay like a flower that is suddenly cut off and lies for a while unwithered on the grass;[8] but her spirit journeyed over the Great Seas. And it is said that she sang before the Gods, and her song was made of the sorrows of the two kindreds, of Elves and Men. So fair was she and so moving was her song that they were moved to pity. But they had not the power long to withhold within the confines of the world the spirits of mortal men that died; nor to change the sundered fate of the two kindreds.

'Therefore they gave this choice to Lúthien. Because of her sorrow and of the Silmaril that was regained from the Enemy, and because her mother Melian came from Valinor, she should be released from the Halls of Waiting, and return not to the woes of Middle-earth, but go to the Blessed Realm and dwell with the Gods until the world's end, forgetting all sadness that her life had known. Thither Beren could not come. The other choice was this. She might return to earth, and take with her Beren for a while, there to dwell with him again, but without certitude of life or joy. Then she would become mortal even as he; and ere long she should leave the world for ever, and her beauty become only a memory of song, until that too faded. This doom she chose, forsaking the Blessed Realm, and thus they met again, Beren and Tinúviel, beyond the Great Seas, as she had said; and their paths led together, and passed long ago beyond the confines of the world. So it was that Lúthien alone of all the Elven-kin has died indeed. But by her choice the Two Kindreds were joined, and she is the fore-mother of many in whom the Elves see yet, though the world changeth, the likeness of Lúthien the beloved whom they have lost.'[9]

As Trotter was speaking, the darkness closed in; night fell on the world. They could see his queer eager face dimly lit in the glow of the red wood-fire. Above him was a black starry sky. Suddenly a pale light appeared behind the crown of Weathertop behind him. The moon, now nearly half-full, was climbing slowly above the hill that overshadowed them. The stars above its top grew pale.

The story ended. The hobbits moved and stretched. 'Look!' said Merry. 'The moon is rising. It must be getting late.' The others looked up. Even as they did so they saw something small and dark on the hill-top against the glimmer of the moonlight. It was perhaps only a large stone or jutting rock shown up by the pale light.

At that moment Odo, who had been on guard (being less reluctant than the others to miss Trotter's tale-telling) came hurrying down to the fire. 'I don't know what it is,' he said, 'but I *feel* that something is creeping up the hill. And I *thought* (I couldn't be sure) that away there, westwards, where the moonlight is falling, there were two or three black shapes. They seemed to be moving this way.'

'Keep close beside the fire, with your faces outwards!' said Trotter. 'Get some of these pine-wood sticks ready in your hands!'

For a long while they sat there silent and alert with their backs turned to the little fire, which was thus almost entirely screened. Nothing happened. There was no sound or movement. Bingo was just about to whisper a question to Trotter, who sat next to him, when Frodo gasped: 'What's that?' '*Sh,*' said Trotter.

It was just as Odo had said: over the lip of the hollow, on the side away from the hill, they *felt* a shadow rise, one shadow or more than one. They strained their eyes, and the shadows seemed to grow. Soon there could be no doubt: three or four tall black figures were standing there, on the slope above them. Bingo fancied that he heard faintly a sound like breath being drawn in with a hiss. Then the shapes advanced slowly.

Terror seized Odo and Frodo, and they threw themselves flat on the ground. Merry shrank to Bingo's side. Bingo was no less afraid; he was quaking as if he was bitter cold. But his fear was swallowed up in a sudden temptation to put on the Ring. It seized him, and he could think of nothing else. He did not forget the Barrow, nor the message of Gandalf, but he felt a desperate desire to disregard all warnings. Something seemed to be compelling him; he longed to yield. Not with the hope of escaping, or of doing anything, good or bad. He simply felt that he must take the Ring, and put it on his finger. He could not speak. He struggled for a while, but resistance became unbearable; and at last he slowly drew out the chain, unfastened the Ring, and put it on the forefinger of his left hand.

Immediately – though everything else remained as before, dim and dark – the shapes became terribly clear. He seemed able to see beneath their black wrapping. There were three tall figures: in their white faces burned keen and merciless eyes; under their black mantles were long grey robes, upon their grey hair were helms of silver;[10] in their haggard hands were swords of steel.

Their eyes fell upon him and pierced him, as they rushed towards him. Desperate, he drew his own sword; and it seemed to him that it flickered redly as if it was a fire-brand. Two of the figures halted. But the third was taller than the others. His hair was long and gleaming, and on it was a crown. The hand that held the long sword glowed with a pale light. He sprang forward and bore down upon Bingo.

At that moment Bingo threw himself forward onto the ground, and he heard himself crying aloud (though he did not know why): *Elbereth! Gilthoniel! Gurth i Morthu.*[11] At the same time he struck at the feet of his enemy. A shrill cry rang out in the night; and he felt a pain like a dart of poisoned ice touch his [*added:* left] shoulder. Even as he swooned Bingo caught a glimpse of Trotter leaping out of the darkness with a flaming fire-brand in each hand. With a last effort he slipped the Ring from his finger, and closed his hand on it.

## NOTES

1   This passage, from 'Better still, under the fuel they found a wooden case', is an insertion on a slip, certainly written at the same time as the main text, replacing the (ink) text as first written:

> Gandalf, it would seem, had taken thought for them. It was the presence of fuel that decided them to go no further that day, and to make their camp in the dell.

With the passage here about *cram*, not found in FR, cf. *The Hobbit*, Chapter XIII 'Not at Home':

> If you want to know what *cram* is, I can only say that I don't know the recipe, but it is biscuitish, keeps good indefinitely, is supposed to be sustaining, and is certainly not entertaining, being in fact very uninteresting except as a chewing exercise. It was made by the Lake-men for long journeys.

In the *Etymologies* (V.365) *cram*, defined as 'cake of compressed flour or meal (often containing honey and milk) used on long journeys', appears as a Noldorin word (stem KRAB- 'press'). – In FR the fire-wood, alone of the stores found on Weathertop, survived, but it had been left by Rangers, not by Gandalf.

2   Strider gives a much more elaborate and informed account of the perceptions of the Ring-wraiths in FR (p. 202). See p. 173, note 7.

3   See p. 169 and note 25.

4   Beren's name *Camlost* or *Gamlost* ('Empty-handed') occurs in the *Quenta Silmarillion* (interrupted at the end of 1937); for the variation in the initial consonant see V.298, 301.

5   For the text and textual history of *Light as Leaf on Lindentree* see
    III.108–10, 120–3.

6   *To the silver flute of Ilverin:* in *Light as Leaf on Lindentree* (III.108)
    Dairon is named here. The name Ilverin occurs in *The Book of Lost
    Tales* as one of the many names of Littleheart, the 'Gong-warden' of
    Mar Vanwa Tyaliéva (I.46, 255), but there seems no basis to seek
    any kind of connection. In the margin my father at some point
    pencilled other names: *Neldorín, Elberin, Diarin*. See note 9, at
    end.

7   Trotter has mentioned no song, but it is of course the *Lay of
    Leithian* that is meant.

8   Struck out at the time of writing:
       But her spirit came to the Halls of Waiting, where are the places
       appointed for the Elven-kin beyond the Blessed Realms in the
       West, on the confines of the world. And she knelt before the Lord
       [of the Halls of Waiting]

9   This concluding paragraph of Trotter's tale is very close to the
    account of the Choices of Lúthien that my father had written while
    the *Quenta Silmarillion* was with the publishers at the end of 1937,
    and which appears in the published *Silmarillion* on p. 187; see
    V.293, 303–4.
       There are other very roughly written texts giving a résumé of a
    part of 'The Silmarillion' found among the papers at this point.
    They attempt to condense a much greater part of the history of the
    Elder Days than that strictly concerned with the story of Beren and
    Lúthien, and have interesting features which must be mentioned,
    though their discussion scarcely falls within the history of the
    writing of *The Lord of the Rings*. Most notable is the following
    passage:
       For as it is told the Blessed Realms of the West were illumined by
       the Two Trees, Galathilion the Silver Cherry, and Galagloriel
       that is Golden Rain. But Morgoth, the greatest of the Powers,
       made war upon the Gods, and he destroyed the Trees, and fled.
       And he took with him the immortal gems, the Silmarils, that were
       made by the Elves of the light of the Trees, and in which alone
       now the ancient radiance of the days of bliss remained. In the
       north of the Middle-earth he set up his throne Angband, the Halls
       of Iron under Thangorodrim the Mountain of Thunder; and he
       grew in strength and darkness; and he brought forth the Orcs and
       goblins, and the Balrogs, demons of fire. But the High Elves of
       the West forsook the land of the Gods and returned to the earth,
       and made war upon him to regain the jewels.
    The names *Galathilion* and *Galadlóriel* first appear in the *Quenta
    Silmarillion* (V.209–10) as the Gnomish names for Silpion and
    Laurelin. 'Silver Cherry' and 'Golden Rain' are not the actual
    meanings of the names (as seems to be implied here): see the

*Etymologies* in Vol. V, stems GALAD- (where the form *Galagloriel* is also given), LAWAR-, THIL-. That the blossom of Silpion was like that of a cherry-tree, and the flowers of Laurelin like those of the laburnum ('Golden Rain') was however often said (see e.g. V.209).

On Morgoth 'the greatest of the Powers' see V.157 and note 4. Very curious is the statement here that when Morgoth returned to Middle-earth after the destruction of the Trees 'he brought forth the Orcs and goblins, *and the Balrogs, demons of fire.*' It was certainly my father's view at this period that the Orcs were then first engendered (see V.233, §62 and commentary), but the Balrogs were far older in their beginning (V.212, §18), and indeed came to rescue Morgoth from Ungoliantë at the time of his return: 'to his aid there came the Balrogs that lived yet in the deepest places of his ancient fortress.'

The term 'High Elves' is here used to mean the Elves of Valinor, not, as in the *Quenta Silmarillion*, the First Kindred (*Lindar*, *Vanyar*): see V. 214, §25 and commentary.

A very surprising point is the mention, a little later in this text, of *Finrod Inglor the fair* (see p. 72). In the first edition of LR (Appendices) *Finrod* was still the name of third son of Finwë, as in the *Quenta Silmarillion*, and his son was *Felagund* (in QS also named *Inglor*); it was not till the second edition of 1966 that Finrod son of Finwë became Finarfin, and his son Inglor Felagund became *Finrod Felagund*.

In another of these drafts the minstrel of Doriath is named *Iverin*, not Dairon; see note 6.

10  My father first wrote here: 'upon their long grey hair were crowns and helms of pale gold'. This was no doubt changed at once, with the emergence immediately below of the tall king, a crown on his long hair. See p. 198 note 6.

11  For *Morthu* see V.393, stem THUS-.

★

My father's practice at this time of overwriting his first pencilled drafts largely denies the possibility of seeing the earliest forms of the narrative. In this chapter the underlying text can only be made out here and there and with great difficulty; but at least it can be seen that the opening passage quickly declined into an abbreviated outline for the story. Trotter's tales were only to be concerned with animals of the wild; and then follows at once: 'Fight in dell', with a sketch in a few lines, scribbled down at great speed, of which however something can be disinterred:

Bingo is tempted to put on ring. He does so. The riders [?come] at him. He sees them plain – fell white faces . . . . . He draws his sword and it shines like fire. They draw back but one Rider with long silver hair and a [?red hand] leaps forward. Bingo . . . . . hears himself shouting *Elbereth Gilthoniel* . . . . . struck at the leg of the Rider. He felt . . . . . cold [?pain] in the shoulder. There was a flash . . . . .

The attack on the dell entered before the idea that Trotter should chant to them, and tell them a tale of ancient days; and the material of his tale remains in this manuscript in a very rough state, the primary stage of composition, obviously demanding the compression that it afterwards received.

More developed pencilled drafting takes up again from the point where Trotter comes to an end, and from what can be read it seems that the final story of the attack by the Ring-wraiths was now fully present. Then, apart from a few details (as that there are three Ring-wraiths, not five), the text written in ink on top of the draft achieved the finished story: no element in the potent scene, the fearful suspense on the cold hillside in the moonlight, the dark shapes looking down on the hobbits huddled round the fire, the irresistible demand on the Ringbearer to reveal himself, and the final revelation of what lay beneath the black cloaks of the Riders, is absent – and all is told virtually in the very words of *The Fellowship of the Ring*. The significance of the Ring, in its power to reveal and to be revealed, its operation as a bridge between two worlds, two modes of being, has been attained, once and for all.

The completeness, and the resonance, of this scene on Weathertop Hill is the more remarkable, when we consider that (in relation to *The Lord of the Rings* as it was ultimately achieved) all was still extremely restricted in scope. If the nature of the Ring in its effect on the bearer was now fully conceived, there is as yet no suggestion that the fate of Middle-earth lay within its tiny circle. It is indeed far from certain that the idea of the Ruling Ring had yet arisen. Of the great lands and histories east and south of the Misty Mountains – of Lothlórien, Fangorn, Isengard, Rohan, the Númenórean kingdoms – there is no shadow of a hint. I very much doubt that when the Ring-wraiths rose up over the lip of the dell beneath Weathertop my father foresaw any more of the Journey than that the Ring must pass over the Mountains and find its end in the depths of the Fiery Mountain (p. 126). In October 1938 he could still say to Stanley Unwin (see p. 173) that he had hopes of being able to submit the new story early in the following year.

# XI
# FROM WEATHERTOP TO THE FORD

The manuscript of the original Chapter VIII continues, without any break, in the same form, ink over pencil. While in the earlier part of this chapter I have given the full original text even in the concluding passage, where there is scarcely any material difference from FR (since the attack of the Ring-wraiths is a scene of exceptional importance), in this part I do not do so throughout. The narrative is very close to that of FR Chapter 12, 'Flight to the Ford' (with a fair number of minor differences and some less minor), and for much of its length the wording almost the same. In those parts where the original text is not given, however, it can be understood that all differences of any significance are remarked.

After it is told that the hobbits (Sam in FR) heard Bingo's voice crying out strange words, it is further said that they 'had seen a red flash; and Trotter came dashing up with flaming wood.' So also in the fragmentary outline given on pp. 188–9 'There was a flash'; but this is absent in FR. Perhaps the reference is to Bingo's sword that 'flickered redly as if it was a firebrand' (p. 186), a detail preserved in FR p. 208. Trotter's first return to the dell is slightly differently told, but this is chiefly because Sam's distrust of Strider is of course absent, and there is nothing in the old version corresponding to Strider's words to Sam apart (FR pp. 209–10). When Trotter lifted the black cloak from the ground he said only: 'That was the stroke of your sword. What harm it did to the Rider I do not know. Fire is better.'

*Athelas* is not said to have been brought by Men of the West to Middle-earth: 'it is a healing plant, known only to Elves, and to some of those who walk in the wild: *athelas* they name it.'[1] A curious detail is that when *athelas* was applied to Bingo's wound he 'felt the pain and the sense of frozen cold lessen in his right side'; and again later in the chapter 'his right arm was lifeless' (FR p. 215). Similarly, when Bingo drew his sword and faced the Riders at the Ford, my father first wrote: 'His sword he had hung at his right side; with his left hand he gripped the hilt and drew it', though this he struck out. He evidently decided that it was Bingo's left shoulder that was stabbed, and therefore wrote in the word 'left' in the description of the actual wounding (p. 186); but he did not correct the occurrences of 'right' just mentioned.

When they left the dell beneath Weathertop they took Gandalf's firewood with them ('For Trotter said that from now onwards fire-wood must always be a part of their stores, when they were away from trees').

Nothing is said of the rejuvenation of Bill Ferny's pony (if indeed it was Bill Ferny's, p. 175). The distant cries of Black Riders which they heard as they crossed the Road in FR (p. 211) are absent from the old version.

The description of the eastward journey from Weathertop is at first fairly close to that in FR, though the timing is slightly different; but the geography was to be significantly altered. I give the passage following the words 'Even Trotter seemed tired and dejected' (FR p. 212) in full.

Before the first day's march was over Bingo's pain began to grow again, but for a long time he did not speak of it. In this way three or four days passed without the ground or the scene changing much, except that behind them Weathertop slowly sank, and before them the distant mountains loomed a little nearer. The weather remained dry, but was grey with cloud; and they were oppressed with the fear of pursuit. But of this there was no sign by day; and though they kept watch by night nothing happened. They dreaded to see black shapes stalking in the dim grey night under the waxing moon veiled by thin cloud; but they saw nothing, and heard nothing, but the sigh of withering leaves and grass. It seemed that, as they had hardly dared to hope, their swift crossing of the Road had not been marked, and their enemy had for the moment lost their trail.

At the end of the fourth day the ground began once more to rise slowly out of the wide shallow valley into which they had come. Trotter now bent their course again towards the north-east; and before long, as they reached the top of a slow-climbing slope, they saw ahead a huddle of wooded hills. Late on the fifth day they came to a ridge on which a few gaunt fir-trees stood. A little below them the Road could be seen curving away towards a small river that gleamed pale in a thin ray of sunshine, far away on their right. Next day, early in the morning, they again crossed the Road. Looking anxiously along it, westward and eastward, they hurried quickly across, and went towards the wooded hills.

Trotter was still leading them in as straight a line as the country allowed towards the distant Ford. In the hills their path would be more uncertain, but they could no longer keep to the south side of the Road, because the land became bare and stony and ahead lay the river. 'That river,' he said, 'comes down out of the Mountains, and flows through Rivendell.[2] It is not wide, but it is deep and strong, being fed by the many small torrents that come out of the wooded hills. Over these the Road goes by little fords or bridges; but there is no ford or bridge over the river until we come to the Ford under the Mountains.' The hobbits looked at the dark hills ahead, and though they were glad to leave the cheerless lands behind them, the land ahead seemed threatening and unfriendly.

In the developed geography, the Road traverses two rivers between Weathertop and Rivendell: the Hoarwell or Mitheithel that flowed down out of the Ettenmoors, crossed by the Last Bridge, and the Loudwater or Bruinen, crossed by the Ford of Rivendell; these rivers joined a long way to the south, becoming the Greyflood. In the original story, on the other hand, there is only one river, not named, flowing down through Rivendell and crossed at the Ford.

In FR the travellers came down, early in the morning on the seventh day out from Weathertop, to the Road (i.e. approaching it from the south), and went along it for a mile or two to the Last Bridge, where Strider found the elf-stone lying in the mud; they crossed the bridge, and after a further mile turned off the Road to the left and went up into the hills. In the original story, they came to the Road early on the sixth day and crossed it, going up into the hills; there is no river (Hoarwell) and no bridge. Some sort of explanation is given why they had to cross the Road here and stay no longer to the south of it: 'the land became bare and stony and ahead lay the river.' But the fact of there being no ford or bridge over the river except that below Rivendell only meant that that is where they would have to cross; it does in itself explain why they could not stay south of the Road until they got there. Thus it is only the 'bare and stony' nature of the land south of the Road that really offers an explanation: Trotter sought to pass through country that provided more concealment? The 'real' explanation, it might be said, why they crossed the Road and went up into the wooded hills is quite other: my father had already suggested, when sketching out the story from the Barrow-downs to Rivendell (p. 126), that the hobbits should 'foolishly turn aside to visit Troll Stones'. On the other hand, Trotter was taking the straightest line to the Ford that he could (p. 191), and the sketches on p. 201 show clearly that the great southward loop of the Road (already mentioned in the original text, p. 199) must force him to cross it and go up into the hills to the north. – On the different chronology in the two versions see the Note on Chronology, p. 219.

When they came into the hills, the conversation with Trotter arising from their sight of the ruined towers is somewhat different from that with Strider in FR (pp. 213–14):

'Who lives in this land?' he [Bingo] asked; 'and who built these towers? Is this troll-country?'

'No,' said Trotter; 'trolls do not build. No one lives in this land. Men once dwelt here, ages ago. But none now remain. They were an evil people, as far as tales and legends tell; for they came under the sway of the Dark Lord. It is said that they were overthrown by Elendil, as King of Western Men, who aided Gilgalad, when they made war on the Dark Lord.[3] But that was so long ago that the hills have forgotten them, though a shadow still lies on the land.'

'Where did you learn such tales?' asked Frodo, 'if all the land is empty and forgetful? The birds and beasts do not tell tales of that sort.'

'Many things are remembered in Rivendell,' said Trotter.

'Have you often been to Rivendell?' said Bingo.

'I have,' said Trotter; 'many a time; and I wonder now that I was ever so foolish as to leave it. But it is not my fate to sit quiet, even in the fair house of Elrond.'

The journey in the hills north of the Road had lasted for three days when the weather turned to rain, but two in FR (p. 214); thus the shorter journey from Weathertop till the return to the Road is made up, though there is still a difference of one day, since they had reached Weathertop a day earlier in the original story (p. 175): as I understand it, the first morning after the rain (FR p. 215) was in the old version that of October 16, but in FR that of October 17. When the rain stopped, on the eleventh day from Weathertop, and Trotter climbed up to see the lie of the land, he said when he came back:

'We have got too far to the North; and we *must* find some way to turn southwards, or at least sharp to the East. If we keep on as we are going, we shall get into impassable country among the skirts of the Mountains. Somehow or other we must strike the Road again before it reaches the Ford. But even if we manage that fairly quickly, we still cannot hope to get to Rivendell for some days yet, four or even five I fear.'

In the night spent up on the ridge (FR pp. 215–16) Sam's questioning of Strider concerning Frodo's wound is given to Merry; and Frodo's dream that 'endless dark wings were sweeping over him, and that on the wings rode pursuers seeking for him in all the hollows of the hills' is present. It is not said in the original text that 'the trees about him seemed shadowy and dim', nor on the following day that 'a mist seemed to obscure his sight' (FR pp. 215, 217); but later, when Glorfindel searched Bingo's wound with his finger (FR p. 223), 'he saw his friends' faces more clearly, though all day he had been troubled by the feeling that a shadow or a mist was coming between him and them.'

When they came to the old trolls turned to stone, 'Trotter walked forward unconcernedly. "Hullo, William!" he said, and slapped the stooping troll soundly.' And he said: '"In any case you might have noticed that Bert has got a bird's nest behind his ear."' In FR the trolls' names from *The Hobbit* were excluded.

After 'They rested in the clearing for a while, and had their midday

meal right under the shadow of the trolls' large legs' the original narrative
goes straight on with 'In the afternoon they went on down through the
woods'; there is no suggestion that the Troll Song would be introduced
here (see p. 144). Their return to the Road is thus described:

Eventually they came out upon the top of a high bank above the
Road. This was now beginning to bend rather away from the
river, and clung to the feet of the hills, some way up the side of the
narrow valley at the bottom of which the river ran. Not far from
the borders of the Road Trotter pointed out a stone in the grass;
on it roughly cut and much weathered could still be seen two runic
letters G · B in a circle: ⊗ꟼ

'That,' he said, 'is the stone that once marked the place where
Gandalf and Bilbo hid the trolls' gold.' Bingo looked at it – rather
sadly: Bilbo and he himself had long ago spent all that gold.

The Road, bending now northward, lay quiet under the
shadows of early evening. There was no sign of any other travellers to be seen.

Only minor differences (except in one matter) are to be recorded in the
encounter with Glorfindel: the whole scene was present, and in very
much the same words, from the beginning. The sentence in FR (p. 221)
'To Frodo it appeared that a white light was shining through the form
and raiment of the rider, as if through a thin veil' is absent.[4] To Trotter
Glorfindel cried out: *Ai Padathir, Padathir! Mai govannen!*[5] But it is
not said subsequently that he spoke to Trotter 'in the elf-tongue' (FR
p. 224); rather he spoke 'in a low tone.' The drink that Glorfindel gave
them instantly reminded the hobbits of the drink in Bombadil's house,
'for the drink they took was refreshing like spring-water, but filled them
also with a sense of warm vigour.' 'Cram-cake' is mentioned together
with the stale bread and dried fruit which is all they had to eat.

The conversation with Glorfindel on the road is different from that in
FR (p. 222), for the number of the Black Riders was not known to
anybody at this stage (not even to my father), and in FR Gandalf had not
yet reached Rivendell when Glorfindel and others were sent out by
Elrond nine days before – Elrond having heard news from the Elves led
by Gildor whom the hobbits encountered in the Shire. The element of
Glorfindel's leaving the jewel on the Last Bridge is also of course absent
(p. 192).

'This is Glorfindel, one of those that dwell in Rivendell,' said
Trotter. 'He has news for us.'

'Hail and well met at last!' said Glorfindel to Bingo. 'I was sent
from Rivendell to look on the Road for your coming. Gandalf was
anxious and afraid, for unless something evil had befallen you,
you should have come there days ago.'

'We have not been on the Road for many, many days until this day,' said Bingo.

'Well, now you must return to it, and go with all speed,' said Glorfindel. 'A day's swift riding back westward there is a company of evil horsemen, and they are travelling this way with all the haste that frequent search of the land upon either side of the Road allows them. You must not halt here, nor anywhere tonight, but must journey on as long and far as you are able. For when they find your trail, where it rejoined the Road, they will search no longer but ride after you like the wind. I do not think they will miss your footsteps where the path runs down from Trolls-wood; for they have a dreadful skill in hunting by scent, and darkness helps and does not hinder them.'

'Then why must we go on now by night, against the warning of Gandalf?' asked Merry.

'Do not fear Gandalf's warning now,' answered Glorfindel. 'Speed is your chief hope; and now I will go with you. And I do not think that there is any peril ahead; but the pursuit is hard behind.'

'But Bingo is wounded and sick and weary,' said Merry. 'He should not ride any more without rest!'

Glorfindel shook his head and looked grave, when he heard the account of the attack upon the dell under Weathertop, and the hurt to Bingo's arm. He looked at the knife-hilt that Trotter had kept, and now drew out to show him. He shuddered.

'There are evil things written on that hilt,' he said, 'though maybe they are not for your eyes to see. Keep it till we get to Rivendell, Padathir, but be wary, and handle it as little as you may.'

The chief structural difference in the narrative of this chapter from that in FR appears in Glorfindel's words 'I do not think that there is any peril ahead'; contrast FR (p. 222): 'There are five behind us . . . Where the other four may be, I do not know. I fear that we may find the Ford is already held against us.'

Only three Riders (at first) came out of the tree-hung cutting through which the Road passed before the flat mile to the Ford, not five as in FR (p. 225). The story is the same that Bingo halted, feeling the command of the Riders upon him to wait, but filled with sudden hatred drew his sword; and that Glorfindel cried to his horse, so that it sped away towards the Ford. But all the Riders were behind; there was no ambush by four of them lying in wait at the Ford. The conclusion of the chapter I give in full.

'Ride on! Ride on!' cried Glorfindel and Trotter; and then
Glorfindel spoke a word in the elf-tongue: *nora-lim, nora-lim*. At
once the white horse sprang away and sped along the last lap of the
Road. At the same moment the black horses of the Riders leaped
down in pursuit; and others following came flying out of the
wood. Bingo looking back over his shoulder thought he could
count [as many as twelve >] at least seven. They seemed to run
like the wind, and to grow swiftly larger and darker as they
overtook him stride by stride. He could no longer see his friends.
Through them and over them the Riders must now be hurtling.
Bingo turned and lay forward, encouraging with urgent words.
The Ford still seemed far ahead. Once more he looked back. It
seemed to him that the Riders had cast aside their hoods and black
cloaks; they appeared now to be robed in white and grey. Swords
were in their pale hands, helm and crown were on their heads;[6]
their cold eyes glittered from afar.

Fear now swallowed up Bingo's mind. He thought no longer of
his sword. No cry came from him. He shut his eyes and clung to
the mane of the horse. The wind whistled in his ears, and wildly
the bells rang, clear and shrill. It seemed bitter cold.

Suddenly he heard the splash of water. It foamed about his feet.
He felt the stumbling scramble of the horse as it struggled up the
stony path, climbing the steep further bank of the river. He was
across the Ford! But the Riders were now hard behind.

At the top of the bank the horse halted snorting. Bingo turned
about and opened his eyes. [*Struck out as soon as written:*
Forgetting that the horse belonged to the folk of Rivendell and
knew all that land, he determined to face his enemies, thinking it
useless to] He felt that it was useless to try to escape over the long
uncertain path from the Ford to the lip of Rivendell – if once the
Riders crossed. Though they had all thought of the Ford as the
goal of their flight and the end of peril, it came to him now that he
knew of nothing that would prevent the dread Riders from
crossing as easily as he. In any case he felt now commanded
urgently to halt, and though again hatred stirred in him he had no
longer the strength to refuse. He saw the horse of the foremost
Rider check at the water, and rear up. With a great effort he stood
in his stirrups and brandished his sword.

'Go back!' he cried. 'Go back to the Dark Lord and follow me no
more.'[7] His voice sounded shrill in his ears. The Riders halted,
but Bingo had not the power of Tom Bombadil.[8] They laughed – a
harsh chilling laughter. 'Come back! Come back!' they called. 'To

Mordor we will take you.'[9] 'Go back,' he whispered. 'The Ring, the Ring,' they cried with deadly voices, and immediately their leader rode forward into the water, closely followed by two others.

'By Elbereth and Lúthien the fair,'[10] said Bingo with a last effort, lifting up his sword, 'you shall have neither me nor it.' Then the leader, who was now half across the river, stood up menacing in his stirrup and raised up his hand. Bingo grew dumb; he felt his tongue cleave to his mouth, and his eyes grow misty. His sword broke and fell out of his shaking hand. The horse under him reared and snorted, as the foremost of the black horses came near the shore.

Even at that moment there came a roaring and a rushing: a noise of loud waters rolling many stones. Dimly he saw the river rise, and come galloping down along its course in a plumed cavalry of waves. The three Riders that were still upon the Ford disappeared, overwhelmed and buried under angry foam. Those that were behind drew back in dismay.

With his last failing sense Bingo heard cries, and it seemed to him that behind the Riders there appeared suddenly one shining white figure followed by other smaller and more shadowy figures waving flames. Redly they flamed in the white mist that was over all. Two of the Riders turned and rode wildly away to the left down the bank of the river; the others borne by their plunging horses were driven into the flood, and carried away. Then Bingo heard a roaring in his ears and felt himself falling, as if the flood had reached up to the high bank, and engulfed him with his enemies. He heard and saw no more.

## NOTES

1    In the *Lay of Lethian* my father wrote *athelas* against the passage where

> Huan came and bore a leaf,
> of all the herbs of healing chief,
> that evergreen in woodland glade
> there grew with broad and hoary blade

for the allaying of Beren's wound (III.266, 269).

2    *That river . . . flows through Rivendell:* see the note on Rivendell, pp. 204–5.

3    In the underlying pencilled text, which is here visible for a stretch, Trotter's words about the 'Big People' who used to live in those regions are much the same, but he says that they were overthrown by *Elendil Orendil* and Gil-galad; apparently *Orendil* was substi-

tuted for *Elendil* in the act of writing. Both names were struck out, and then *Elendil* again written in. See p. 174 note 25.

4   The 'bit and bridle' of Glorfindel's horse flickered and flashed, as in the First Edition, where the Second Edition has 'headstall'. Cf. *Letters* no. 211, p. 279 (14 October 1958):

> . . . *bridle* was casually and carelessly used for what I suppose should have been called a *headstall*. Or rather, since *bit* was added (I.221) long ago (Chapter I 12 was written very early) I had not considered the natural ways of elves with animals. Glorfindel's horse would have an ornamental *headstall*, carrying a plume, and with the straps studded with jewels and small bells; but Glorfindel would certainly not use a *bit*. I will change *bridle and bit* to *headstall*.

5   The pencilled text, after various forms struck out, had *Ai Rimbedir*; this was then changed to *Ai Padathir*, etc., with a translation 'Hail Trotter, Trotter, well met.'

6   *helm and crown were on their heads:* in the story of the attack on Weathertop my father first wrote that all three Ringwraiths were crowned, but changed the text to say that only the leader ('the pale king' as Bingo called him) wore a crown (pp. 185–6 and note 10). Cf. the citation in note 8 below.

7   The pencilled draft has: 'Ride back to the Dark Tower of your lord.' For early references to the Dark Tower see p. 131 note 5.

8   It is interesting to look back to the earliest sketch for the flight over the Ford (p. 126):

> One day at last they halted on a rise and looked forward to the Ford. Galloping behind. Seven (3? 4?) Black-riders hastening along the Road. They have gold rings and crowns. Flight over Ford. Bingo flings a stone *and imitates Tom Bombadil*. Go back and ride away! The Riders halt as if astonished, and looking up at the hobbits on the bank the hobbits can see no faces in their hoods. Go back says Bingo, *but he is not Tom Bombadil*, and the riders ride into the ford.

At that stage my father envisaged the hobbits crossing the Ford together; and the rising of the river does not destroy the Riders: they 'draw back just in time in dismay.'

The words in the present text, retained in FR, 'Bingo (Frodo) had not the power of Tom Bombadil', must now refer to Bombadil's rout of the Barrow-wight; but behind them surely lies the unused idea of his power to arrest the onset of the evil beings by raising his hand in authority: cf. the outline given on p. 112, 'two Barrow-wights come galloping after them, but stop every time Tom Bombadil turns and looks at them', and the earlier part of the outline just cited (p. 125), where when they reach the Road west of Bree 'Tom turns and holds up his hand. They fly back.'

9    This is the first occurrence of the name *Mordor* in *The Lord of the Rings*; see p. 131 note 5.

10   In the pencilled text visible beneath the ink, Bingo took the names of Gil-galad and Elendil, together with that of Lúthien.

★

In this chapter it is made plain that the commands of the Ring-wraiths are communicated wordlessly to the bearer of the Ring, and that they have great power over his will. Moreover the idea has now entered that the wound of the Ring-wraith's knife produces, or begins to produce, a similar effect to that brought about by putting on the Ring: the world becomes shadowy and dim to Bingo, and at the end of the chapter he can see the Riders plain, beneath the black wrappings that to others cloak their invisibility.

### Note on the course of the Road between Weathertop and Rivendell

This was an element in the geography to which my father made various alterations in the Revised Edition of *The Lord of the Rings* (1966). I set out first three passages from the chapter 'Flight to the Ford' for comparison.

(1)    Page 212.
  *Original text:*
  (the original text has no passage corresponding)
  *First Edition:* 'That is Loudwater, the Bruinen of Rivendell,' answered Strider. 'The Road runs along it for many leagues to the Ford.'
  *Second Edition:* 'That is Loudwater, the Bruinen of Rivendell,' answered Strider. 'The Road runs along the edge of the hills for many miles from the Bridge to the Ford of Bruinen.'

(2)    Page 214.
  *Original text:* The hills now shut them in. The Road looped away southward, towards the river; but both were now lost to view.
  *First Edition:* The hills now began to shut them in. The Road bent back again southward towards the River, but both were now hidden from view.
  *Second Edition:* The hills now began to shut them in. The Road behind held on its way to the River Bruinen, but both were now hidden from view.

(3)    Page 220.
  *Original text (p. 194):* Eventually they came out upon the top of a high bank above the Road. This was now beginning to bend rather away from the river, and clung to the feet of the hills,

some way up the side of the narrow valley at the bottom of which the river ran.

*First Edition:* After a few miles they came out on the top of a high bank above the Road. At this point the Road had turned away from the river down in its narrow valley, and now clung close to the feet of the hills, rolling and winding northward among woods and heather-covered slopes towards the Ford and the Mountains.

*Second Edition:* After a few miles they came out on the top of a high bank above the Road. At this point the Road had left the Hoarwell far behind in its narrow valley, and now clung close to the feet of the hills, rolling and winding eastward among woods (etc.)

Taking first citation (2), from small-scale and large-scale maps made by my father there is no question that the Road after passing south of Weathertop made first a great swing or loop to the North-east: cf. FR p. 211 – when they left Weathertop it was Strider's plan 'to shorten their journey by cutting across another great loop of the Road: east beyond Weathertop it changed its course and took a wide bend northwards.' This goes back to the original text. The Road then made a great bend southwards, round the feet of the Trollshaws, as stated in the original text and in the First Edition in citation (2). All my father's maps show the same course for the Road in respect of these two great curves. The two sketches on p. 201 are redrawn from very rough large-scale maps which he made (the second in particular is extremely hard to interpret owing to the multiplicity of lines made as he pondered different configurations).

In 1943 I made an elaborate map in pencil and coloured chalks for *The Lord of the Rings*, and a similar map of the Shire (see p. 107, item V). These maps are referred to in *Letters* nos. 74 and 98 (pp. 86, 112). On my LR map the course of the Road from Weathertop to the Ford is shown exactly as on my father's maps, with the great northward and southward swings. On the map that I made in 1954 (published in the first two volumes of *The Lord of the Rings*), however, the Road has only a feeble northward curve between Weathertop and the Hoarwell Bridge, and then runs in a straight line to the Ford. This was obviously simply carelessness due to haste on my part. My father doubtless observed it at the time but felt that on so small a scale the error was not very grievous: in any case the map was made, and it had been a matter of urgency. But I think that this error was the reason for the change in the Second Edition given in citation (2), from 'the Road bent back again southward towards the River' to 'the Road behind held on its way to the River Bruinen': my father was making the discrepancy with the map less obvious. A similar instance has been seen already in the change that he made in the Second Edition in respect of the direction of Bucklebury Ferry from Woodhall, p. 107. In his letter to Austin Olney of Houghton Mifflin, 28 July 1965

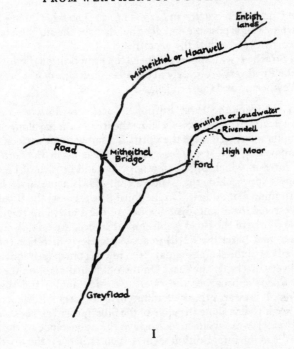

I

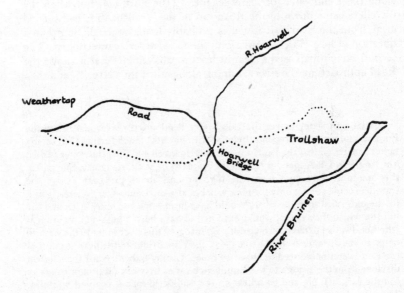

II

(an extract from which is given in *Letters* no. 274) he said: 'I have finally decided, where this is possible and does not damage the story, to take the *maps* as "correct" and adjust the narrative.'

Barbara Strachey (who apparently used the First Edition) deduced the course of the Road very accurately in her atlas, *Journeys of Frodo* (1981), map 13 'Weathertop and the Trollshaws'.

Citation (1) from the First Edition is perfectly illustrated in the sketches on p. 201, which precisely show the Road running alongside the Loudwater 'for many leagues to the Ford.' My father made various small-scale maps covering a greater or lesser part of the lands in *The Lord of the Rings*, on three of which this region appears; and on two of these the Road is shown approaching the Loudwater at a fairly acute angle, but by no means running alongside it. On the third (the earliest) the Road runs close to the river for a long distance before the Ford; and this is less because the course of the Road is different than because on this map the river flows at first (after the Ford) in a more westerly direction towards the Hoarwell (as in the sketch-maps).* On my 1943 map (see above) this is also and very markedly the case. On the published map, on the other hand, the Road, approaches the river at a wide angle; and this was another error. It is clear, I think, that the changed Second Edition text in citation (1), with 'runs along the edge of the hills' instead of 'runs along it [the Loudwater]', was again made to save the appearance of the map.

Citation (3) in the First Edition seems to contradict (1): the Road runs along the Loudwater for many leagues to the Ford (1), but when the travellers came down to the Road out of the Trollshaws it had turned away from the river (3). But it is probably less a contradiction than a question of how closely 'runs along the Loudwater' is interpreted. The second sketch-map seems clear at least to this extent, that it shows the Road approaching the river, running alongside it for a stretch, and then

---

*Barbara Strachey makes the Loudwater bend sharply west just below the Ford and flow in this direction (before turning south) much further than on my father's maps, so that the land between the Hoarwell and the Loudwater (called 'the Angle' in LR Appendix A, p. 320) ceases to be at all triangular. She makes this assumption because from the high ground above the Last Bridge the travellers could see not only the Hoarwell but also the Loudwater, whereas going by the published map the rivers 'would have been some 100 miles apart and the hill [on which they stood] would have had to have been a high mountain for it [the Loudwater] to have been visible.' By bringing this river so far to the west on her map the distance from the hill above the Last Bridge to the nearest point of the Loudwater is reduced to about 27 miles. On my father's maps the shortest distance from the Bridge to the Loudwater varies between (approximately) 45 (on the earliest), 60, and 62 miles; on the published map it is about 75 miles. Thus the objection that the Loudwater was too far away to be seen is real; but it cannot be resolved in this way.

bending somewhat away and 'clinging to the feet of the hills' before returning to it at the Ford.

The changed reading of the Second Edition in (3) – made so as not to alter the amount of text – makes the words 'narrow valley' refer to the Hoarwell, and there is no longer any statement at this point about the course of the Road in relation to the Loudwater. This was clearly another accommodation to the published map (and is not an entirely happy solution), as also was 'northward' (cf. Sketch II) to 'eastward'.

### Note on the River Hoarwell

The absence of the River Hoarwell (p. 192), which had still not emerged in the next version of this part of the story (p. 360), is interesting. In the original story in Chapter II of *The Hobbit*, when Bilbo, Gandalf, and the Dwarves were approaching the hills crowned with old castles on an evening of heavy rain, they came to a river:

> . . . it began to get dark. Wind got up, and the willows along the river-bank [*no river has been mentioned*] bent and sighed. I don't know what river it was, a rushing red one, swollen with the rains of the last few days, that came down from the hills and mountains in front of them.
>
> Soon it was nearly dark. The winds broke up the grey clouds . . .

The river here ran *alongside* the road (described as 'a very muddy track'); they only crossed it finally by a ford, beyond which was the great slope up into the Mountains (beginning of Chapter III, 'A Short Rest'). In the third edition (1966) the passage quoted was changed:

> . . . it began to get dark as they went down into a deep valley with a river at the bottom. Wind got up, and willows along its banks bent and sighed. Fortunately the road went over an ancient stone bridge, for the river, swollen with the rains, came rushing down from the hills and mountains in the north.
>
> It was nearly night when they had crossed over. The wind broke up the grey clouds . . .

The river now becomes the Hoarwell, over which the road passed by the Last Bridge (and the river which they forded before climbing up towards Rivendell becomes distinct (the Loudwater), by changing 'they forded the river' to 'they forded a river'.) But my father did nothing to change what follows in the original story. There, the company stopped for the night where they did because that is where they were when it got dark, and it was beside a river. From that spot the light of the Trolls' fire became visible. By the introduction of the Last Bridge at this point into the old narrative, while everything else is left untouched, the company stops for the night as soon as they have crossed it – near enough to the river for one of the ponies to break loose and dash into the water, so that most of the food was lost – and the Trolls' fire is therefore visible from the Bridge, or very near it. And at the end of the chapter the pots of gold from the Trolls' lair are still buried 'not far from the track by the river' – a phrase unchanged from the original story, when the river flowed alongside the track.

Karen Fonstad puts the matter clearly (*The Atlas of Middle-earth*, 1981, p. 97), noting the inconsistency between *The Hobbit* (as it is now) and *The Lord of the Rings* as to the distance between the river and the Trolls' clearing:

The Trolls' fire was so close to the river that it could be seen 'some way off', and it probably took the Dwarves no more than an hour to reach; whereas Strider led the Hobbits north of the road [turning off a mile beyond the Bridge], where they lost their way and spent six days reaching the clearing where they found the Stone-trolls. Lost or not, it seems almost impossible that the time-pressed Ranger would have spent six days reaching a point the Dwarves found in an hour.

Earlier, apparently in 1960, in an elaborate rewriting of *The Hobbit* Chapter II which was never used,* my father had introduced the Last Bridge at the same point in the narrative; but there the passage of the river took place in the morning, and the camp from which the Trolls' fire was seen was made at the end of the day and many miles further east. The present text of *The Hobbit*, deriving from corrections made in 1965 and first published in 1966, here introduces an element from *The Lord of the Rings* but fails to harmonise the two geographies. This highly uncharacteristic lapse is no doubt to be attributed simply to the haste with which my father worked under the extreme pressure imposed on him in 1965.

### Note on the river of Rivendell

Trotter says expressly that the river which the Road crosses at the Ford flows through Rivendell (p. 191). In the corresponding passage in FR (p. 212) Strider names the river: 'That is Loudwater, the Bruinen of Rivendell.' Later, in 'Many Meetings' (FR p. 250), it is said that Bilbo's room 'opened on to the gardens and looked south across the ravine of the Bruinen'; and at the beginning of 'The Council of Elrond' (FR p. 252) Frodo 'walked along the terraces above the loud-flowing Bruinen.' This is quite unambiguous; the maps, however, are not in this point perfectly clear.

In the map of Wilderland in *The Hobbit* (endpaper), the unnamed river receives, some way north of the Ford, a tributary stream, and Elrond's house is placed between them, near the confluence, and nearer

---

*My father was greatly concerned to harmonise Bilbo's journey with the geography of *The Lord of the Rings*, especially in respect of the distance and time taken: in terms of *The Lord of the Rings* Gandalf, Bilbo, and the Dwarves took far too long, seeing that they were mounted (see Karen Fonstad's discussion in *The Atlas of Middle-earth*, p. 97). But he never brought this work to a definitive solution.

the tributary – exactly as in Sketch I on p. 201.* On one of his copies of *The Hobbit* my father pencilled in a few later names on the map of Wilderland, and these included *Bruinen or Loudwater* against the river north of the house (again as in Sketch I), and *Merrill* against the tributary flowing just to the south of it.† When therefore in *The Hobbit* (Chapter III) the elf said to Gandalf:

> You are a little out of your way: that is, if you are making for the only path across the water and to the house beyond. We will set you right, but you had best get on foot, until you are over the bridge

it would seem to be the Merrill that must be crossed by the bridge. Barbara Strachey (*Journeys of Frodo*, maps 15–16) shows very unambiguously the ravine of Rivendell as the ravine of the tributary stream, Elrond's house being some mile and a half from its confluence with the Loudwater; while Karen Fonstad (*The Atlas of Middle-earth*, pp. 80, 101, etc.) likewise places Rivendell on the southerly stream – calling it (p. 127) the Bruinen.

The lines of rivers and Road in Sketch I were first drawn in ink, and subsequently coloured over in blue and red chalk. When my father did this he changed the course of the 'tributary stream' south of Elrond's house by bending it up northwards and joining it to the Bruinen some way to the east; thus the house at Rivendell is at the western end of land enclosed between two streams coming down from the Mountains, parting, and then joining again. It might therefore be supposed that both were called 'Bruinen' (discounting the name 'Merrill' written on the Wilderland map in *The Hobbit*). But I do not think that detailed conclusions can be drawn from this sketch-map.

## Note on the Entish Lands

The name *Entish Lands* on Sketch I needs a word of explanation. Originally the region in which the Hoarwell rose was called *Dimrill-dale(s)* (p. 360), but when that name was displaced it was briefly called *Hoardale* (p. 432 note 3), and then *Entish Dales*, *Entish Lands*. *Entish* here was used in the Old English sense of *ent*, 'giant'; the *Entish Lands* were the 'troll-lands' (cf. the later names *Ettendales* and *Ettenmoors* of this region in FR, containing Old English *eoten* 'giant'), and are in no way associated with the *Ents* of *The Lord of the Rings*.

*In two of my father's small-scale maps the tributary stream is not marked, and Rivendell is a point on or beside the Bruinen; the third is too rubbed and faint to be sure of, but probably shows the tributary, and Rivendell between the two streams, as in the *Hobbit* map, and as my 1943 map certainly does (and that published in *The Lord of the Rings*).

†This name, which I have found nowhere else, is unfortunately not quite clear, though *Me-* and *-ll* are certain, and it is hard to read it in any other way. – Another name added to the Wilderland map was *Rhimdath* 'Rushdown', the river flowing from the Misty Mountains into Anduin north of the Carrock (see the Index to Vol. V, p. 446).

# XII

# AT RIVENDELL

Some preliminary ideas for this chapter (which in FR is Book II, Chapter 1, 'Many Meetings') have been given on p. 126. The original narrative draft is extant in a very rough manuscript, first in ink, then in pencil and petering out. It was variously emended and added to, but I give it here as my father seems to have set it down – granting that there is often no clear distinction between changes made at once and changes made after (and probably no significant distinction in time, in any case). This and the two following drafts all bear the number 'IX' without title.

He awoke to find himself lying in bed; and also feeling a great deal better. 'Where am I and what's the time?' he said aloud to the ceiling. Its dark carved beams were touched by sunlight. Distantly he heard the sound of a waterfall.

'In Elrond's house, and it is ten o'clock in the morning: the morning of October 24th to be exact,'[1] said a voice.

'Gandalf!' said Bingo sitting up. There was the wizard sitting in a chair by the open window.

'Yes,' said the wizard. 'I'm here all right – and you're lucky to be here too, after all the absurd things you have done since you left home.'

Bingo felt too peaceful and comfortable to argue – and in any case he did not imagine he would get the best of the argument: the memory came back to him of the disastrous short cut through the Old Forest, of his own stupidity in the inn, and of his nearly fatal madness in putting on the ring on Weathertop Hill.

There was a long silence broken only by the soft puffs of Gandalf's pipe as he blew smoke-rings out of the window.

'What happened at the Ford?' asked Bingo at last. 'It all seemed so dim somehow, and it still does.'

'Yes!' answered Gandalf. 'You were beginning to fade. They would have made a wraith of you before long – certainly if you had put on the Ring[2] again. How does the arm and side feel now?'

'I don't know,' said Bingo. 'It does not feel at all, which is better than aching, but' – he made an effort – 'I can move it a little again: yes: it feels as if it were coming back to life. It is not cold now,' he added, touching his right hand with his left.[3]

'Good!' said Gandalf. 'Elrond bathed and doctored it for hours last night after you were brought in. He has great power and skill, but I was very anxious, for the craft and malice of the Enemy is very great.'

'Brought in?' said Bingo. 'Of course: the last I remember was the rush of water. What happened? Where are the others? Do tell me, Gandalf!'

'What happened – as far as I can make out from Glorfindel and Trotter (who both have some wits in their different ways) – was this: the pursuers made straight for you (as Glorfindel expected they would). The others might have been trampled down, but Glorfindel made them leap out of the way off the road. Nothing could save you if the white elf-horse could not; so they followed cautiously behind on foot, keeping out of sight as much as they could behind bushes and rocks. When they had got as near to the Ford as they dared go, they made a fire hastily, and rushed out on the Riders with flaming brands, just at the moment when the flood came down. Between the fire and water these pursuers were destroyed – if they can be wholly destroyed by such means – all but two that vanished into the wild.

'The rest of your party and the elf then crossed the ford, with some difficulty as it is too deep for hobbits and deep even for a horse. But Glorfindel crossed on your pony and regained his horse. They found you lying on your face in the grass at the top of the slope: pale and cold. At first they feared you were dead. They carried you towards Rivendell: a slow business, and I don't know when they would have arrived, if Elrond had not sent some Elves out to help you, at the same time as the water was released.'

'Did Elrond make the flood then?' asked Bingo.

'No, I did,'[4] said Gandalf. 'It is not very difficult magic, in a stream that comes down from the mountains. The sun has been fairly hot today. But I was surprised to find how well the river responded. The roar and rush was tremendous.'

'It was,' said Bingo. 'Did you also send Glorfindel?'

'Yes,' said Gandalf, '– or rather, I asked Elrond to lend him to me. He is a wise and noble elf. Bilbo is – was – very fond of him. I also sent Rimbedir[5] (as they call him here) – that Trotter fellow. From what Merry tells me I gather he has been useful.'

'I should think he has,' said Bingo. 'I was very suspicious of him at first – but we should never have got here without him. I have grown very fond of him. I wish indeed that he was going to go on wandering with me as long as I must wander. It is an odd thing, you know, but I keep on feeling that I have seen him somewhere before.'

'I daresay you do,' said Gandalf. 'I often have that feeling when I look at a hobbit – they all seem to remind me of one another, don't you know. Really they are extraordinarily alike!'

'Nonsense,' said Bingo. 'Trotter is most peculiar. However I feel extremely hobbit-like myself, and I could wish that I was not doomed to wander. I have now had more than a month of it, and that is about 28 days too much for me.' He fell silent again, and began to doze. 'What did those dreadful pursuers do to me in Weathertop dell?' he said half to himself, on the edge of a shadowy dream.

'They attempted to pierce you with the sword of the Necromancer,' said Gandalf. 'But by some grace of fortune, or by your own courage (I have heard an account of the fight) and by the confusion caused by the elf-name which you cried, only your shoulder was grazed. But that was dangerous enough – especially with the ring on. For while the ring was on, you yourself were in the wraith-world, and subject to their weapons.[6] They could see you, and you them.'

'Why can we see their horses?'

'Because they are real horses. Just as the black robes they wear to give shape to their nothingness are real robes.'

'Then why, when all other animals – dogs, horses, ponies – are filled with terror of them, do these horses endure them on their backs?'

'Because they are born and bred under the power of the evil Lord in the dark kingdom. Not all his servants and chattels are wraiths!'

'It is all very threatening and confusing,' said Bingo sleepily.

'Well, you are quite safe for the present,' said Gandalf, 'and are mending rapidly. I should not worry about anything now, if I were you.'

'All right,' said Bingo, and fell fast asleep.[7]

Bingo was now as you know in the Last Homely House west of the Mountains, on the edge of the wild, the house of Elrond: that house was (as Bilbo Baggins had long ago reported) 'a perfect house, whether you like food or sleep or work or story-telling or singing, or just sitting and thinking, best, or a pleasant mixture of them all.' Merely to be there was a cure for weariness and sadness. As evening drew on Bingo woke up and found that he no longer felt like sleep but had a mind for food and drink, story-telling and singing. So he got up, and found his arm already nearly as useful as ever it had been. As soon as he was dressed he went in search of his friends. They were sitting in the porch of the house that faced west: shadows were fallen in the valley, but the light was still upon high eastern faces of the hills far above, and the air was warm. It was seldom cold in the fair valley of Rivendell. The sound of the waterfalls was loud in the stillness. There was a scent of trees and flowers [?in harmony].

'Hullo,' said Merry, 'here is our noble uncle. Three cheers for Bingo Lord of the Ring!'

'Hush!' said Gandalf. 'Evil things do not come into this valley, but nonetheless we should not name them. The Lord of the Ring is not Bingo, but the Lord of the Dark Tower of Mordor,[3] whose power is growing again, and we are here sitting only in a fortress of peace. Outside it is getting dark.'

'Gandalf has been saying lots of cheerful things like that,' said Odo. 'Just to keep us in order: but it seems impossible somehow to feel gloomy or depressed in Elrond's house. I feel I could sing – if I knew how: only I never was any good at making up words or tunes.'

'You never were,' said Bingo, 'but I daresay even that could be cured in time, if you stayed here long enough. I feel much the same myself. Though at the moment I feel more hungry than anything else.'

His hunger was soon cured. For before long they were summoned to the evening meal. The hall was filled with many folk: elves for the most part, though there were a few guests and travellers of various sort. Elrond sat in the high seat, and next to him sat Gandalf. Bingo did not see Trotter or Glorfindel: they were probably at one of the other halls among their friends, but to his surprise he found sitting next to him a dwarf of venerable appearance and rich dress – his beard was white, nearly as white as the snow-white cloth of his garments; he wore a belt of silver and a chain of silver and diamonds.

'Welcome and well met,' said the dwarf, rising and bowing. 'Glóin at your service!' and he bowed again.

'Bingo Bolger-Baggins at your service and your family's,' replied Bingo. 'Am I right in imagining that you are *the* Glóin, one of the twelve companions of the great Thorin?'

'You are,' said he. 'And I need not ask, since I have already been told that you are the friend and adopted son of our dear friend

Bilbo Baggins. I wonder much what brings *four* hobbits so far from their homes. Nothing like it has occurred since Bilbo left Hobbiton. But perhaps I should not ask this; since Elrond and Gandalf do not seem disposed to tell?'

'I think we will not speak of such things, at any rate yet,' said Bingo politely – he wanted to forget about his troubles for the moment. 'Though I am equally curious to know what brings so important a dwarf so far from the Mountain.'

Glóin looked at him and laughed – indeed he actually winked. 'I am no spoil-sport,' he said. 'So I will not tell you – yet. But there are many other things to tell.'

Throughout the meal they talked together. Bingo told news of the Shire, but he listened more than he talked, for Glóin had much to tell of the Dwarf-kingdom under the Mountain, and of Dale. There Dáin was still king of the dwarfs,[9] and was now ancient (some 200 years old), venerable, and fabulously rich. Of the ten companions that had survived the battle, seven were still with him: Dwalin, Dori, Nori, Bifur and Bofur and Bombur.[10] But the last was now so fat that he could not move himself from his couch to his chair, and it took four young dwarves to lift him. In Dale the grandson of Bard, Brand son of Bain, was lord.

My father stopped here, and scribbled down a few notes before at once beginning the chapter anew. The notes at the end of the first draft include the following:

What of Balin etc. They went to colonize (Ring needed to found colony?) Bilbo must be seen. Who is Trotter?

The second text is a clear manuscript, but it had proceeded no farther than Gandalf's account of the flood in the Bruinen when my father again stopped and started again. This is an intermediate text much nearer to the third than to the first, and need not be considered more closely.

The third text, the last in this phase of the work, but again abandoned before its conclusion (going in fact scarcely any farther than the first draft), is very close to 'Many Meetings' in FR, but there are many minor differences (quite apart, of course, from those that are constant at this stage, as Trotter/Strider-Aragorn and the absence of Sam). The opening is now almost identical to that in FR, but the date is October 26, and Gandalf adds, after 'You were beginning to fade', 'Trotter noticed it, to his great alarm – though of course he said nothing.' But after Gandalf's 'It is no small feat . . .' (FR p. 232) the old narrative goes on:

'. . . But I am delighted to have you all here safe. I am really rather to blame. I knew there were some risks – but if I had known more before I left the Shire I should have arranged matters differently.

But things are moving fast,' he added in a lower voice as if to himself, 'even faster than I feared. I *had* to get here quickly. But if I had known the Riders were already out!'

'Did not you know that?' asked Bingo.

'No I did not – not until we came to Bree. It was Trotter that told me.[11] And if I had not known Trotter and trusted him, I should have waited for you there. And as it has turned out, he saved you and brought you through in the end.'

'We should never have got here without him,' said Bingo. 'I was very suspicious of him at first, but I have grown very fond of him. Though he is rather queer. I wish that he was going to go on wandering with me – as long as I must wander. It is an odd thing, you know, but I keep on feeling that I have seen him somewhere before – that, that I ought to be able to put a name to him, a name different to Trotter.'

'I dare say you do,' laughed Gandalf. 'I often have that feeling when I look at a hobbit: they all seem to remind me of one another, if you know what I mean. They are wonderfully alike!'

'Nonsense!' said Bingo, sitting up again in protest. 'Trotter is most peculiar. And he has shoes! However, I am feeling a very ordinary hobbit myself at the moment. I wish now that I need not go any further. I have had more than a month of exile and adventures, and that is about four weeks more than enough for me.'[12]

The text now becomes very close to that of FR pp. 233–4, but there are several differences. As in FR, Bingo cannot understand how he can be out in his reckoning of the date, but in this version Gandalf has told him that it is the 26th of October (not as in FR the 24th), and he calculates that they must have reached the Ford on the 23rd (the 20th in FR). On this question see the Note on Chronology on p. 219. In contrast to the first draft, where Gandalf says that Bingo was brought in to Rivendell 'last night', he has been unconscious for a long time, and the mortal danger of his wound is emphasized. Gandalf calls the weapon that was used 'a deadly blade, the knife of the Necromancer which remains in the wound', not 'a Morgul-knife', and he explains to Bingo that 'You would have become a Ring-wraith (the only hobbit Ring-wraith) and you would have been under the dominion of the Dark Lord. Also they would have got possession of the Ring. And the Dark Lord would have found some way of tormenting you for trying to keep it from him, and of striking at all your friends and kinsfolk through you, if he could.' He says that the Riders wear black robes 'to give shape to their nothingness in our world'; and he includes among the servants of the Dark Lord 'orcs and goblins' and 'kings, warriors, and wizards.'

Gandalf's reply to Bingo's question 'Is Rivendell safe?' is similar to that in FR (pp. 234–5), but has some notable features:

'Yes, I hope so. He has seldom overcome any of the Elves in the past; and all Elves now are his enemies. The Elves of Rivendell are indeed descendants of his chief foes: the Gnomes, the Elven-wise ones, that came out of the Far West, and whom Elbereth Gilthoniel still protects.[13] They fear no Ring-wraiths, for they live at once in both worlds, and each world has only half power over them, while they have double power over both. But such places as Rivendell (or the Shire in its own way) will soon become besieged islands, if things go on as they are going. The Dark Lord is moving again. Dreadful is the power of the Necromancer. Still,' he said, standing suddenly up and sticking out his chin while his beard stuck out like bristling wire, 'the Wise say that he is doomed in the end. We will keep up our courage. You are mending rapidly, and you need not worry about anything at the moment.'

The passage in which Gandalf looked closely at Frodo, and then spoke to himself, is lacking; but his story of the events at the Ford is in all essentials the same as in FR, with a few features still retained from the first draft – most important, Gandalf still says that two of the Riders escaped into the wild. The difficult passage of the deep ford is still described, as in the first draft, and Gandalf still says 'I was surprised to find how well the river responded to a little simple magic.' But Elrond's power over the river, and Gandalf's waves like white horses with white riders, now enter. The end of Bingo's talk with Gandalf, however, has differences:

'. . . I thought I was drowning – and all my friends and enemies together. It is wonderful that Elrond and Glorfindel and such great people should take all this trouble over me – not to mention Trotter.'

'Well – there are many reasons for that. I am one good reason. You may discover others.[14] For one thing they are – were – very fond of Bilbo Baggins.'

'What do you mean – "are fond of Bilbo"?' said Bingo sleepily.

'Did I say that? Just a slip of the tongue,' answered Gandalf. 'I thought I said "were".'

'I wish old Bilbo could have been here and heard all about this,' murmured Bingo. 'I could have made him laugh. The cow jumped over the moon. Hullo William!' he said. 'Poor old troll!' and then he fell asleep.

The next section of the narrative follows the first draft (p. 208) pretty

closely, but Bingo's discovery of green garments laid out for him now
enters the story, with a further addition that only survived in part in FR:

He put on his own best waistcoat with the gold buttons (which he
had brought in his luggage as his only remaining treasure). But it
seemed very loose. Looking in a little mirror he was startled to see
a very much thinner reflection of Bingo than he had seen for a long
while. It looked remarkably like the young nephew of Bilbo that
used to go tramping with his uncle in the Shire, though it was a bit
pale in the face. 'And I feel like it,' he said, slapping his chest and
tightening his waistcoat strap. Then he went in search of his
friends.

There is nothing corresponding to Sam's entering Frodo's room.

The feast in Elrond's house moves far to the final text. The descrip-
tions of Elrond, Gandalf, and Glorfindel now appear (they were written
on an inserted slip, but it seems to belong to the same time) and in almost
the same words as in FR (p. 239) – but there is mention of Elrond's smile,
'like the summer sun', and his laughter. There is no mention of Arwen.
Bingo 'could not see Trotter, nor his nephews. They had been led to
other tables.'

The conversation with Glóin proceeds as in the first draft, with some
touches and phrases that move it to the final text (FR p. 240). Glóin is
now described as 'a dwarf of solemn dignity and rich dress', but he still
winks (as he does not in FR).

At the point where the first draft ends (p. 210) my father only added a
further couple of lines before again stopping:

In Dale the grandson of Bard the Bowman ruled, Brand son of
Bain son of Bard, and he was become a strong king whose realm
included Esgaroth, and much land to the south of the great falls.[15]

On the reverse of the sheet the conversation continues in a different
script and a different ink: Glóin gives an account of Balin's history (his
return to Moria) – but it is Frodo, not Bingo, that he is speaking with,
and this side of the page belongs to a later phase in the writing of the book
(see pp. 369, 391).

A passage on a detached slip, forming part of Gandalf's conversation
with Bingo, seems to belong to the time of the third draft of this chapter.
There is no direction for its insertion into the text, and there is no echo of
it in FR.

Things work out oddly. But for that 'short cut' you would not have
met old Bombadil, nor had the one kind of sword the Riders fear.[16]
Why did not I think of Bombadil before! If only he was not so far
away, I would go straight back now and consult him. We have

never had much to do with one another up till now. I don't think he quite approves of me somehow. He belongs to a much older generation, and my ways are not his. He keeps himself to himself and does not believe in travel. But I fancy somehow that we shall all need his help in the end – and that he may have to take an interest in things outside his own country.

Among my father's earliest ideas for this part of the story (p. 126) appears: 'Gandalf astonished to hear about Tom.' – Another brief passage on the same slip of paper was struck out at the time of writing:

Not to mention courage – and also swords and a strange and ancient name. Later on I must be told about that curious sword of yours, and how you knew the name of Elbereth.'
    'I thought you knew everything.'
    'No,' said Gandalf. 'You

Some notes that were scribbled down at Sidmouth in Devon in the late summer of 1938 (see Carpenter, *Biography*, p. 187) on a page of doodles evidently represent my father's thoughts for the next stages of the story at this time:

Consultation. Over M[isty] M[ountains]. Down Great River to Mordor. Dark Tower. Beyond (?) which is the Fiery Hill.
    Story of Gilgalald told by Elrond? Who is Trotter? Glorfindel tells of his ancestry in Gondolin.

'The Quest of the Fiery Mountain' (preceded by 'Consultation of hobbits with Elrond and Gandalf') was mentioned in the outline given on p. 126, but here is the first hint of the journey that was to be undertaken from Rivendell, and the first mention of the Great River in the context of *The Lord of the Rings*.
    My father had already asked the question 'Who is Trotter?' and he would ask it again. A hint of one solution, in the end rejected, has been met already in Bingo's words to Gandalf in this chapter: 'I keep on feeling that I have seen him somewhere before – that, that I ought to be able to put a name to him, a name different to Trotter'; and indeed earlier, in the inn at Bree (p. 154): 'He had a dark look – and yet there was something in it . . . that seemed friendly, and even familiar.'
    Also very notable is 'Glorfindel tells of his ancestry in Gondolin.' Years later, long after the publication of *The Lord of the Rings*, my father gave a great deal of thought to the matter of Glorfindel, and at that time he wrote: '[The use of *Glorfindel*] in *The Lord of the Rings* is one of the cases of the somewhat random use of the names found in the older legends, now referred to as *The Silmarillion*, which escaped reconsideration in the final published form of *The Lord of the Rings*.' He came to the conclusion that Glorfindel of Gondolin, who fell to his death in combat

with a Balrog after the sack of the city (II.192–4, IV.145), and Glorfindel of Rivendell were one and the same: he was released from Mandos and returned to Middle-earth in the Second Age.

A single loose page, which has nothing to connect it with any other writing, is perhaps the 'story of Gilgalad told by Elrond' mentioned in these notes, and I give it here. Other than the first, the changes noted were made subsequently, in pencil on the manuscript written in ink.

'Now in the dark days Sauron the Magician [*first written* Necromancer, *then* Necromancer *written again above* Magician] had been very powerful in the Great Lands, and nearly all living things had served him out of fear. And he pursued the Elves that lived on this side of the Sundering Sea with especial hatred, for they did not serve him, although they were afraid. And there were some Men that were friends of the Elves, though not many in the darkest of days.'

'And how,' said Bingo, 'did his overthrow come about [> was his power made less]?'

'It was in this way,' said Elrond. 'The lands and islands in the North-west of the Great Lands of the Old World were called long ago Beleriand. Here the Elves of the West had dwelt for a long while until [> during] the wars with the Power of darkness, in which the Power was defeated but the land destroyed. Sauron alone of his chief servants escaped. But still after the Elves had mostly departed [> Although most of the Elves returned] again into the West, there were many Elves and Elf-friends that dwelt [> still dwelt in after days] in that region. And thither came many of the Great Men of old out of the Far West Island which was called by the Elves Númenor (but by some Avallon) [> out of the land of Westernesse (that they called Númenor)]; for Sauron had destroyed their island [> land], and they were exiles and hated him. There was a king in Beleriand of Númenórean race and he was called Elendil, that is Elf-friend. And he made an alliance with the Elf-king of those lands, whose name is Gilgalad (Starlight), a descendant of Fëanor the renowned. I remember well their council – for it reminded me of the great days of the ancient war, so many fair princes and captains were there, yet not so many or so fair as once had been.'

'You remember?' said Bingo, looking astonished at Elrond. 'But I thought this tale was of days very long ago.'

'So it is,' said Elrond laughing. 'But my memory reaches back a long way [> to long ago]. My father was Eärendel who was born in Gondolin seven years before it fell, and my mother was Elwing

daughter of Lúthien daughter of King Thingol of Doriath, and I
have seen many ages in the West of the world. I was at the council I
speak of, for I was the minstrel and counsellor of Gilgalad. The
armies of Elves and Men were joined once more, and we marched
eastward, and crossed the Misty Mountains, and passed into the
inner lands far from the memory of the Sea. And we became
weary, and sickness was heavy on us, made by the spells of Sauron
– for we had come at last to Mordor, the Black Country, where
Sauron had rebuilt his fortress. It is on part of that dreary land
that the Forest of Mirkwood now stands,[17] and it derives its
darkness and dread from the ancient evil [added: of the soil].
Sauron could not drive us away, for the power of the Elves was in
those days still very great, though waning; and we besieged his
stronghold for 7 [> 10] years. And at last Sauron came out in
person, and wrestled with Gilgalad, and Elendil came to his
rescue, and both were mortally wounded; but Sauron was thrown
down, and his bodily shape was destroyed. His servants were
dispelled and the host of Beleriand broke his stronghold and razed
it to the ground. Gilgalad and Elendil died. But Sauron's evil
spirit fled away and was hidden for a long while in waste places.
Yet after an age he took shape again, and has long troubled the
northern world [added: but his power is less than of old].

If this extremely interesting piece is compared with the end of the
second version of *The Fall of Númenor* ('FN II') in V.28–9 it will be
seen that while an important new element has entered the two texts are
closely related and have closely similar phrases: citing the form in FN II,
'in Beleriand there arose a king, who was of Númenórean race, and he
was named Elendil, that is Elf-friend'; the hosts of the Alliance 'passed
the mountains and came into inner lands far from the Sea'; 'they came at
last even to Mordor the Black Country, where Sauron . . . had rebuilt his
fortresses'; 'Thû was thrown down, and his bodily shape destroyed, and
his servants were dispelled, and the host of Beleriand destroyed his
dwelling'; 'Thû's spirit fled far away, and was hidden in waste places.'
Moreover in both texts Gil-galad is descended from Fëanor. The new
element is the appearance of Elrond as the minstrel and counsellor of Gil-
galad (in FN II §2 Elrond was the first King of Númenor, and a mortal; a
conception now of course abandoned, with the emergence of Elros his
brother, V.332, §28). There is no suggestion here that any sort of
'Council' was in progress: it seems rather that Elrond was recounting the
tale to Bingo, as Trotter had said on Weathertop (p. 179): 'you will hear
it, I think, in Rivendell, when we get there. Elrond should tell it, for he
knows it well.' But an element survived into FR (II) Chapter 2, 'The
Council of Elrond': Bingo's amazement at the vast age of Elrond, and

Elrond's reply, naming his lineage and recollecting the hosts of the Last Alliance.[18]

## NOTES

1   On this puzzling date see the Note on Chronology, p. 219.

2   *the Ring:* changed from *that ring*.

3   *touching his right hand with his left:* on the wound having been originally in Bingo's right shoulder see p. 190.

4   *'No, I did'* changed from *'Yes'*. Cf. the original sketch of the story (p. 126): 'Gandalf had sent the water down with Elrond's permission.'

5   *Rimbedir* as the Elvish name for Trotter appears in the pencilled draft of the last chapter, p. 198 note 5 (*Padathir* in the overwritten text in ink). This shows that the present text was written before my father had rewritten the last chapter, or at least before he had completed it. Later he replaced *Rimbedir* by *Padathir* in the present passage. – By 'I also sent Rimbedir' Gandalf must mean that he sent Trotter to them at *The Prancing Pony*.

6   This passage was changed in the following text to the form in FR (p. 234), i.e. 'you yourself were *half* in the wraith-world, and they might have seized you', with the words 'and subject to their weapons' removed.

7   From this point the manuscript was continued in rapid pencil.

8   *the Dark Tower of Mordor:* see note 17.

9   On the plural form *dwarfs* see V.277.

10   Glóin is missed out (so also in the third text, where his name was inserted subsequently). The companions of Thorin not named are (as in FR) Balin, Ori, and Óin.

11   *It was Trotter that told me:* Gandalf left a letter for Bingo at Bree before he left on Monday 26 September, and in this he said that he had *'learned some news on the way'* (from Hobbiton): 'Pursuit is getting close: there are 7 at least, perhaps more' (p. 154). When my father wrote this he cannot have had in mind Trotter's meeting with Gandalf on the Road on the Sunday morning (pp. 149, 154), because the first Black Rider did not come to Bree until the Monday evening (pp. 151, 157). It was no doubt when he decided that Gandalf learnt about the Black Riders from Trotter that he added the passages on p. 153, where Trotter says 'I first saw the Riders last Saturday away west of Bree, before I ran across Gandalf', and on p. 154, where he says that their conversation also included the Black Riders.

12   *more than a month* (as in the first draft) replaced *30 odd days* at the time of writing. See the Note on Chronology on p. 219.

13   *The Elves of Rivendell are indeed the descendants of his chief foes: the Gnomes, the Elvenwise ones:* see p. 71.

14  My father added in pencil at the foot of the page, but it is impossible
to say when: 'The Ring is another, and is becoming more and more
important.'

15  Cf. *The Hobbit*, Chapter X 'A Warm Welcome':
At the southern end [of the Long Lake] the doubled waters [of
the Running River and the Forest River] poured out again over
high waterfalls and ran away hurriedly to unknown lands. In the
still evening air the noise of the falls could be heard like a distant
roar.

16  An isolated note says: 'What of the sword of the Barrow-wights?
Why did the Black Riders fear it? – because it belonged to Western
Men.' Cf. *The Two Towers* III. 1, p. 17.

17  Elrond's statement here that Mirkwood is itself in Mordor, 'the
Black Country', and that the forest 'derives its darkness from the
ancient evil' of the time when Sauron had his fortress in that region
is interesting. Both here and in the very similar passage in the
second version of *The Fall of Númenor* (V.29) Sauron is said to have
'rebuilt' his fortress(es) in Mordor, and I take this to mean that
it was in Mordor that he established himself after the downfall
of Morgoth and the destruction of Angband. That fortress was
destroyed by the hosts of the Last Alliance; and in the first version of
*The Fall of Númenor* (V.18) when Thû was defeated and his
dwelling destroyed 'he fled to a dark forest, and hid himself.' In *The
Hobbit* the 'dark tower' of the Necromancer was in southern Mirkwood. At the end of *The Hobbit* it is told that the white wizards 'had
at last driven the Necromancer from his dark hold in the south of
Mirkwood', but it is not said that it was destroyed. If 'it is on part of
that dreary land [Mordor] that the Forest of Mirkwood now stands',
it might be argued that (at this stage of the development of the story)
Sauron had returned there, to 'the Dark Tower of Mordor' – in the
south of Mirkwood. (There seems no positive evidence that the
geography of Middle-earth had yet been extended south and east of
the map of Wilderland in *The Hobbit*, beyond the conception of the
Fiery Mountain, whose actual placing seems to be entirely vague;
and it certainly cannot be assumed that my father yet conceived of
the mountain-defended land of Mordor far away in the South-east.)
   But I do not think this at all probable. Not long after the point
we have reached, my father wrote in the chapter 'Ancient History'
(p. 253) that the Necromancer 'had flown from Mirkwood [i.e. after
his expulsion by the white wizards] *only to reoccupy his ancient
stronghold in the South*, near the midst of the world of those days, in
the Land of Mordor; and it was rumoured that the Black Tower had
been raised anew.' 'His ancient stronghold' was of course the
fortress destroyed in the War of the Last Alliance.

18  For previous references to the story of Gil-galad and Elendil in the
texts thus far see pp. 169, 179, 192.

## Note on the Chronology

In the first draft of this chapter Gandalf tells Bingo when he wakes up in Elrond's house that it is the morning of October 24; but this seems to be at variance with all the indications of date that have been given. (October 24 is the date in FR, p. 231, but this was differently achieved.)

At Weathertop there is one day's difference between the original chronology and that of FR: they reached it on October 5 in the old version, but on October 6 in FR (see p. 175). The hobbits came back to the Road again from the lands to the south, and crossed it, on the sixth day from Weathertop (p. 192), i.e. October 11, whereas in FR they took an extra day (contrast 'At the end of the fourth day the ground began once more to rise' in the old version, p. 191, with FR p. 212, 'At the end of the fifth day'): thus there is now a lag of two days between the two accounts, and in FR they came back to the Road and crossed the Last Bridge on October 13. In the hills to the north of the Road, on the other hand, they took a day longer in the old version (see p. 193), and thus came down out of the hills, and met Glorfindel, on the evening of the 17th (the 18th in FR). There are no further differences in respect of chronology in this chapter, and therefore in the original story they reached the Ford on October 19 (October 20 in FR). How then can it be the 24th of October when Bingo wakes in Rivendell, if, as Gandalf says, he was 'brought in last night'?

In the second and third versions of the opening of this chapter the date on which Bingo woke up in Elrond's house becomes October 26, and he says that it ought to be the 24th: 'unless I lost count somewhere, we must have reached the Ford on the 23rd.' Gandalf tells him that Elrond tended him for 'three nights and two days, to be exact. The Elves brought you to Rivendell at night on the 23rd, and that is where you lost your count'; and he refers to Bingo's having borne the splinter of the blade for 'fifteen days or more' (seventeen in FR). This does not help at all with the chronological puzzle, for in all the drafts for the opening of Chapter IX my father was assuming that the hobbits reached the Ford on October 23, and not, as the actual narrative seems clearly to show, on October 19. It is equally odd that Gandalf should say that Bingo had borne the splinter of the blade for 'fifteen days or more', if the crossing of the Ford actually was on the 23rd and Elrond finally removed the shard 'last night' (October 25): the total should be 20 (October 6 to 25); in FR the number is seventeen days (October 7 to 23).

# XIII
## 'QUERIES AND ALTERATIONS'

In this chapter I give a series of notes which my father headed *Queries and Alterations*. I think that it can be shown clearly that they come from the time we have now reached.

He had abandoned his third draft for Chapter IX (later to be called 'Many Meetings') at the point where Glóin was telling Bingo about King Brand of Dale; this is at the bottom of a page that bears the number IX.8. I have already noticed (p. 213) that on the reverse of this page, numbered IX.9, the conversation continues – but it is obviously discontinuous with what precedes, being written in different ink and a different script, and Glóin is now talking to 'Frodo', not 'Bingo'; and in fact, after this point in the narrative of *The Lord of the Rings* 'Bingo' never appears again.

Now the first of these *Queries and Alterations* is concerned precisely with the conversation of Bingo and Glóin, and actually refers to the last page of the 'Bingo' part of the chapter, IX.8 (perhaps it had just been written). In another of these notes my father was for the first time considering the substitution of 'Frodo' for 'Bingo'; but he here decided against it – and when he came to write a new version of 'A Long-expected Party' (a question discussed in these same notes) Bilbo's heir was still 'Bingo', not 'Frodo'.

I conclude, therefore, that it was just at the time when he abandoned Chapter IX that he wrote *Queries and Alterations*; that when he abandoned it he returned again to the beginning of the book; and that it was some considerable time – during which 'Bingo' became 'Frodo' – before he took up again the conversation with Glóin at Rivendell.

There are two pages of these notes, mostly set out in ink in an orderly and legible way; but there are also many hasty pencilled additions, and these may or may not, in particular cases, belong to the same time (granting that the intervals of time are not likely to be great: but in attempting to trace this history it is 'layers' and 'phases' that are significant rather than weeks or months). Some of the suggestions embodied in these notes had no future, but others are of the utmost interest in showing the actual emergence of new ideas.

I set them out in what seems to be the order in which they were written down, taking in the additions as convenient and relevant, and adding one or two other notes that belong to this time.

(1)   Dale Men and Dwarfs at Party – is this good? Rather spoils meet-
      ing of Bingo and Glóin (IX.8). Also unwise to bring Big People to
      Hobbiton. Simply make Gandalf and dwarfs bring things from
      Dale.

For the 'great lumbering tow-haired Men' who went 'stumping on the
hobbit road like elephants' and drank all the beer in the inn at Hobbiton
see p. 20 (the account of them had survived without change into the
fourth version of 'A Long-expected Party'). By 'Dale Men and Dwarfs at
Party' my father meant 'in Hobbiton at that time', not of course that they
were present at the Party. The Men would be abandoned in the next
version of 'A Long-expected Party', but the Dwarves remained into FR
(p. 33). Perhaps my father felt that whereas the Men would certainly
have told Bingo the news from Dale, the Dwarves need have no
particular connection with the Lonely Mountain.

(2)   *Too many hobbits.* Also Bingo Bolger-Baggins a bad name. Let
      Bingo = Frodo, a son of Primula Brandybuck but of father Drogo
      Baggins (Bilbo's first cousin). So Frodo (= Bingo) is Bilbo's first
      cousin once removed both on Took side and on Baggins. Also he
      has as proper name *Baggins*.
      [Frodo *struck out*] No – I am now too used to Bingo.
      Frodo [*i.e.* Took] and Odo are in the know and see Bingo off at
      gate after the Party. Would it not be well to cancel *sale*, and have
      Odo as heir and in charge? – though many things could be given
      away. The Sackville-Bagginses could quarrel with Odo?
      Frodo (and possibly Odo) go on the first stage of road (because
      Frodo's news about Black Riders is necessary) [see pp. 54–5].
      But Frodo says goodbye at Bucklebury. Only Merry and Bingo
      ride on into exile – because *Merry insists*. Bingo originally in-
      tended to go alone.
      Probably best would be to have only Frodo Took – who sees
      Bingo to Bucklebury; and then Merry. *Cut out Odo.* Even better
      to have Frodo and *Merry* at the gate: Frodo says goodbye then,
      and is left in charge of the Shire [i.e. 'in the Shire', at Bag End].
      *Merry* see Black Riders in North.

All of this, from 'No – I am now too used to Bingo', was struck out in
pencil, and at the same time my father wrote 'Sam Gamgee' in the
margin, and to 'Bingo originally intended to go alone' he added 'with
Sam'. It may be that this is where he first set down Sam Gamgee's name.
   There is a first hint here, in 'Frodo says goodbye at Bucklebury', of the
hobbit who would remain behind at Crickhollow when the others
entered the Old Forest; while 'Too many hobbits' and 'Cut out Odo' are
the first signs of what before long would become a major problem and an
almost impenetrable confusion.
   The genealogy as it now stood in the fourth version of 'A Long-

expected Party' is found on p. 37. Bingo was already Bilbo's first cousin once removed on the Took side, but his father was Rollo Bolger (and when Bilbo adopted him he changed his name from Bolger to Bolger-Baggins). With the appearance of Drogo Baggins, Bingo would become Bilbo's first cousin once removed on the Baggins side also: we must suppose that Drogo's father was to be brother of Bilbo's father Bungo Baggins. In the later genealogy Drogo became Bilbo's second cousin, as Gaffer Gamgee explained to his audience at *The Ivy Bush*: 'so Mr. Frodo is [Mr. Bilbo's] first *and* second cousin, once removed either way, as the saying is, if you follow me' (FR p. 31).

An abandoned genealogy on one of these pages shows my father evolving the Baggins pedigree. This little table begins with Inigo Baggins (for a previous holder of this name see p. 17), whose son was Mungo Baggins, father of Bungo: Mungo, first appearing here, survived into the final family tree. Bungo has a sister Rosa, who married 'Young Took'; Rosa also survived, but not as Bilbo's aunt – she became Bungo's first cousin, still with a Took husband (Hildigrim). In this table Drogo is Bungo's brother, but it was at this point that the table was abandoned.

The reference in this note to the 'sale' is on the face of it very puzzling. 'A Long-expected Party' was still in its fourth version – when the Party was given by Bingo Bolger-Baggins, and the major revision whereby it reverted to Bilbo had not yet been undertaken. Then what 'sale' is referred to? There has been no sale of Bag End: Bingo 'devised delivered and made over by free gift the desirable property' to the Sackville-Bagginses (p. 39). The sale of Bag End to the Sackville-Bagginses only arose with the changed story. There is however another reference to the *sale*, in a scribbled list of the days of the hobbits' journey from Hobbiton found on the manuscript of the Troll Song which Bingo was to sing at Bree (p. 142 note 11): this list begins 'Party *Thursday, Friday* "Sale" and departure of Odo, Frodo, and Bingo,' etc. The fact that the word is here enclosed in inverted commas may suggest that my father merely had in mind the auction of Bag End to which Bilbo returned at the end of *The Hobbit*: the earlier clear-out of Bilbo's home, which was a sale, made the word a convenient if misleading shorthand for the clear-out in the new story, which was not a sale.

At the foot of the page the following note was hastily jotted in pencil, and then struck out:

(3)  Gandalf is against Bingo's telling *anyone* where he is off to. Bingo is to take *Merry*. Bingo is reluctant to give pain to Odo and Frodo. He tells them – suddenly saying goodbye, and Frodo (Odo) meets what looks like a *hobbit* on the way up hill. He asks after Bingo – and Frodo or Odo tells him he is off to Bucklebury. So Black Riders know and ride after Bingo.

This is the embryo of the final story, that a Rider came and spoke to Gaffer Gamgee, who sent him on to Bucklebury (FR p. 85).

**(4)** *Sting.* Did Bilbo take this? What of the armour? Various possibilities: (a) Bingo has armour, but loses it in Barrow; (b) Gandalf urges him to take armour, but it is heavy and he leaves it at Bucklebury; (c) he likes it, and it saves him in the Barrow, but is *stolen* at Bree.

The point is, of course, that he cannot be wearing armour on Weathertop. With this note compare the mention in the original 'scheme' for Chapter IX (p. 126) of 'Ring-mail of Bingo in barrow' – this was apparently to be an element in 'some explanations' when the hobbits reached Rivendell.

Another note, on another page, is almost the same as this, but asserts that Bilbo did take Sting, and says that if Bingo's armour was stolen at Bree 'discovery of the burgled rooms is before night.' The meaning of this is presumably that according to the existing story (pp. 162–3) the hobbits had taken all their belongings out of the bedrooms into their parlour before the attack, and that this would have to be changed.

In FR (pp. 290–1) Bilbo gave Sting to Frodo at Rivendell, together with the coat of mithril.

**(5)** Bree-folk are *not* to be hobbits. Bring in bit about the *upstairs windows*. As a result of the hobbits not liking it, landlord gives them rooms on side of the house where second floor is level with ground owing to hill-slope.

The 'bit about the upstairs windows' is presumably the passage in the original Chapter III (pp. 92–3) where the hobbits, approaching Farmer Maggot's, discuss the inconveniences of living on more than one floor. – In fact, in the original beginning of the *Prancing Pony* chapter (p. 132) the people of Bree were primarily Men (with 'hobbits about', 'some higher up on the slopes of Bree-hill itself, and many in the valley of Combe on the east side'); so that this new idea was, to some extent, a reversion. But a pencilled note on the same page, added in afterthought, asks: 'What is to happen at Bree now? What kind of talk can give away Mr Hill?' – and I take the implication of this to be that the Bree-folk were now to be exclusively Men (for they would be less curious and less informed about the Shire). See p. 236.

**(6)** Rangers are best *not* as hobbits, perhaps. But either Trotter (as a ranger) must be *not* a hobbit, or someone very well known: e.g. Bilbo. But the latter is awkward in view of 'happily ever after'. I thought of making Trotter into Fosco Took (Bilbo's first cousin) who vanished when a lad, owing to Gandalf. Who is Trotter? He must have had some bitter acquaintance with Ring-wraiths &c.

This note on Trotter is to be taken with Bingo's feeling that he had met Trotter before, and should be able to think of his true name (see p. 214). Bilbo's first cousin Fosco Took has not been mentioned before; possibly he was to be the son of Bilbo's aunt Rosa Baggins, who married a Took, according to the little genealogical table described above (p. 222). The ascription of Fosco Took's vanishing to Gandalf looks back to the beginning of *The Hobbit*, where Bilbo says to him: 'Not the Gandalf who was responsible for so many quiet lads and lasses going off into the Blue for mad adventures?'

There is here the first suggestion that my father, in his pondering of the mystery of Trotter, saw the possibility of his not being a hobbit. But this note, like several of the others, is elliptically expressed. The meaning is, I think: If rangers are not hobbits, then Trotter is not; but if nonetheless he *is* both, he must be a hobbit very well known.

(7)  Bingo must NOT put on his Ring when Black Riders go by – in view of later developments. He must *think* of doing so but somehow be prevented. Each time the temptation must grow stronger.

This refers to the original second chapter, pp. 54, 58. For the ways in which in the later story Frodo was prevented from putting on the Ring see FR pp. 84, 88. 'Later developments' refers of course to the evolution of the concept of the Ring that had by now supervened: the Riders could see the Ringbearer, as he could see them, when he put it on his finger. The temptation to do so arose from the Ring-wraiths' power to communicate their command to the Ringbearer and make it appear to him that it was his own urgent desire (see p. 199); but Bingo must not be allowed to surrender to the temptation until the disaster in the dell under Weathertop.

(8)  Some reason for Gandalf's uneasiness and the flight of Bingo which does not include Black Riders must be found. Gandalf knew of their existence (of course), but had no idea they were out yet. But Gandalf might give some kind of warning against use of Ring (after he leaves Shire?). Perhaps the idea of suddenly using Ring at party as a final joke should be a Bingoism, and contrary to Gandalf (not approved, as in my foreword).

The 'foreword' referred to here is the text given on pp. 76 ff., earliest form of FR Chapter 2 'The Shadow of the Past', – where indeed Gandalf does not merely 'approve' the idea, but actually suggests it (p. 84).

As regards the first sentence of this note, in the 'foreword' there is a reference to 'certain strange signs and portents of trouble brewing after a long time of peace and quiet', but there is no indication of what they were (p. 85 note 9). In the same text Gandalf says that 'Gollum is very likely the beginning of our present trouble'; but if 'our present trouble' was the fact that the Dark Lord was known to Gandalf to be seeking the only missing Ring in the direction of the Shire, it is in no way explained how he knew this. This was a very serious problem in the narrative structure: Gandalf cannot know of the coming of the Ring-wraiths, for if he had he would never have allowed Bingo and his companions to set off alone. The solution would require complex restructuring of parts of the opening narrative as it now stood, in respect of Gandalf's movements in the summer of that year (these in turn involved with the changed story of the Birthday Party); and would ultimately lead to Isengrad.

(9)  Why was Gandalf hurrying? Because Dark Lord knew of *him* and hated him. He had to get quick to Rivendell, and thought he was drawing pursuit off Bingo. Also he knew there was a council called at Rivendell for mid-September (Glóin &c. coming to see Bilbo?). It was postponed when the news of the Black Riders reached Rivendell and was not held till Bingo arrived.

For the idea that Gandalf was attempting to draw off the pursuit of the Black Riders see p. 173 note 7; cf. also his words to Bingo at Rivendell (p. 211): 'But things are moving fast, even faster than I feared. I *had* to get here quickly. But if I had known the Riders were already out!'
   This is probably the point at which the idea of the Council of Elrond arose, though there have been previous mentions of a 'consultation' with Elrond when the hobbits reached Rivendell (pp. 126, 214).

(10)  Should the Elves have Necromancer-rings? See note about their 'being in both worlds'. But perhaps only the High Elves of the West? Also perhaps Elves – if corrupted – would use rings differently: normally they were *visible in both worlds* all the time and equally with a ring they could appear *only in one* if they chose.

In the earliest statement about Elves and the Rings (p. 75) it is said that 'the Elves had many, and there are now many elfwraiths in the world, but the Ring-lord cannot rule them'; this was repeated exactly in the 'foreword' (p. 78), but without the words 'but the Ring-lord cannot rule them.' I have found no 'note' about the Elves 'being in both worlds', but my father may have been referring to Gandalf's words in the last chapter (p. 212): '[The Elves of Rivendell] fear no Ring-wraiths, for they live at once in both worlds, and each world has only half power over them, while they have double power over both.' With his remark here 'But perhaps only the High Elves of the West [are in both worlds]?' cf. the final form of this same passage in FR (p. 235): 'They do not fear the Ringwraiths, for *those who have dwelt in the Blessed Realm live at once in both worlds*, and against both the Seen and the Unseen they have great power.'

(11)  At Rivendell Bilbo must be seen by Bingo &c.
      Sleeping – in retirement?
      Shadows gathering in the South. Lord of Dale is suspected of being secretly corrupted. Strange men are seen in Dale?

What happened to Balin, Ori, and Óin? They went out to colonize – being told of rich hills in the South. But after a time no word was heard of them. Dáin feared the Dark Lord – rumour of his movements reached him. (One idea was that dwarves need *a Ring* as foundation of their hoard, and either Balin or Dáin sent to Bilbo to discover what had become of it. The dwarves might have received threatening messages from Mordor – for the Lord suspected that the One Ring was in their hoards.)

The thought that Trotter was really Bilbo is obviously not present here; and cf. the early outline given on p. 126: 'At Rivendell *sleeping Bilbo*'.

An isolated note elsewhere\* says: 'Glóin has come to see Bilbo. News of the world. Loss of the colony of Balin &c.' But the 'rich hills in the South' in note (11) are probably the first appearance of the idea of Moria, deriving from *The Hobbit* – though the absence of the name here might suggest that the identification had not yet been made. Cf. also the notes at the end of the abandoned first draft of the last chapter (p. 210): 'What of Balin etc. They went to colonize (Ring needed to found colony?)' In the earliest account of the Rings (p. 75) it was said that the Dwarves probably had none ('some say the rings don't work on them: they are too solid'); but in the 'foreword' (p. 78) Gandalf tells Bingo that the Dwarves were said to have had seven, 'but nothing could make them invisible. In them it only kindled to flames the fire of greed, and the foundation of each of the seven hoards of the Dwarves of old was a golden ring.'

Above the words *One Ring* at the end of note (11) my father wrote *missing*. He may therefore have meant only 'the one missing Ring', but the fact that he used capital letters suggests its great importance – and in the 'foreword' the missing Ring is the 'most precious and potent of his Rings' (pp. 81, 87).

(12)   Bilbo's ring proved to be the *one missing Ring* – all others had come back to Mordor: but this one had been lost.
       Make it taken from the Lord himself when Gilgalad wrestled with him, and taken by a flying Elf. It was more powerful than all the other rings. Why did the Dark Lord desire it so?

That Bilbo's Ring was the one missing Ring, and that it was the most potent of them all, is (as just noted) stated in the 'foreword' – the first sentence of note (12) is the restatement of an existing idea. What is new is the linking up of its earlier history to Gil-galad's wrestling with the Necromancer (see p. 216); in the 'foreword' (p. 78) Gollum's Ring had fallen 'from the hand of an elf as he swam across a river; and it betrayed him, for he was flying from pursuit in the old wars, and he became visible

---

\*This note was in fact written in ink across the faint pencilled outline for the story of the Barrow-wight (p. 125), and is presumably a thought that came to my father while he was thinking about the story of the arrival in Rivendell which comes at the end of this outline (p. 126).

to his enemies, and the goblins slew him.' This is where the story of Isildur began; but now the Elf (later to become Isildur the Númenórean) has it from Gil-galad, who took it from the Dark Lord. And the question is asked: 'Why did the Dark Lord desire it so?' Which means, since it is already conceived to be the most potent of the Rings and therefore self-evidently a chief object of the Dark Lord's desire, 'In what did its potency consist?'*

Subsequently my father pencilled rapid additions to the note. He marked the words 'all others had come back to Mordor' for rejection; and to the words 'It was more powerful than all the other rings' he added:

> though its power depended on the user – and its danger: the simpler the user and the less he used it. To Gollum it just helped him to hunt (but made him wretched). To Bilbo it was useful, but drove him wandering again. To Bingo as Bilbo. Gandalf could have trebled his power – but he dare not use it (not after he found out all about it). An Elf would have grown nearly as mighty as the Lord, but would have become dark.

At this time also he underlined the words 'Why did the Dark Lord desire it so?', put an exclamation mark against them, and wrote:

> Because if he had it he could see where all the others were, and would be master of their masters – control all the dwarf-hoards, and the dragons, and know the secrets of the Elf-kings, and the secret [?plans] of evil men.

Here the central idea of the Ruling Ring is clearly present at last, and it may be that it was here that it first emerged. But the note in ink and the pencilled addition (a faint scribble now only just legible) were obviously written at different times.

On the reverse of the second page of these notes is the following in pencil:

(13) Simpler Story.
    Bilbo disappears on his 100th [*written above:* 111] Birthday

---

*Humphrey Carpenter (*Biography*, p. 188) cites this note, but interprets it to be the moment at which the idea of the Ruling Ring emerged:
> There was also the problem of why the Ring seemed so important to everyone – this had not yet been established clearly. Suddenly an idea occurred to him, and he wrote: 'Bilbo's ring proved to be the *one ruling Ring* – all others had come back to Mordor: but this one had been lost.' The one ruling ring that controlled all the others . . .

But the note in question most certainly says 'Bilbo's ring proved to be the *one missing Ring*' (as the following words show in any case), not 'the *one ruling Ring*'. There would be no need to ask 'Why did the Dark Lord desire it so?' if the conception of the Ruling Ring emerged here.

party. Bingo is his heir – much to the annoyance of the Sackville-Bagginses.

['If you want to know what lay behind these mysterious events we must go back a month or two.' Then have a conversation of Bilbo and Gandalf.]

The talk dies down; and Gandalf is seldom seen again in Hobbiton.

Next chapter begins with Bingo's life. Gandalf's furtive visits. Conversation. Bingo is bored by Shire (ring-restlessness?): and makes up his mind to go and look for Bilbo. Also he has been rather reckless and the money is running out. So he sells Bag-end to the Sackville-Bagginses who thus get it 90 years too late, pockets the money, and goes off when 72 (144) – same tendency to longevity as Bilbo had had. Gandalf encourages him for reasons of his own. But warns him not to use the Ring outside the Shire – if he can help it [cf. note (8)]. Bilbo used it for a last big jest, but you had better not. (Bingo does not tell Gandalf that looking for Bilbo was his motive).

All this was subsequently struck through; and the passage which is here enclosed in square brackets was struck out separately, perhaps at the time of writing.

The narrative structure in its principal relations is now that of the final story:

Bilbo disappears (putting on the Ring) at his 111th birthday party, and leaves Bingo as his heir.

Years after, Gandalf talks to Bingo at Bag End; Bingo is anxious to leave for his own reasons, and Gandalf encourages him to go (but apparently without telling him much, though he warns him against using the Ring).

Although the Party now reverts to Bilbo, and is held on his 111th birthday – his age when he departed out of the Shire in the existing version of 'A Long-expected Party' (p. 40), Bingo still leaves at the age of 72 – his age when it was he who gave the Party. The bracketed figure 144 is presumably Bilbo's age at the time, as in the existing version, from which it follows that at the time of Bilbo's Farewell Party Bingo was 39; the total of their two ages was 150. But what my father had in mind on this point cannot be said, for he never wrote the story in this form.

The bracketed passage suggests that some account would be given, in a conversation between Bilbo and Gandalf a month or two *before* the party, of what had led up to Bilbo's decision to leave the Shire in this way; and this account would *follow* the opening chapter describing the festivity. What this conversation would be about is suggested by another note, doubtless written at the same time:

Place 'Gollum' chapter after 'Long-expected party': with a heading: 'If

you want to know what lay behind these mysterious events, we must go
back a month or two.'
This presumably means that my father was thinking of making the
conversation between Bilbo and Gandalf before the Party (but standing
in the narrative after it) cover the story of Gollum and the Ring. The
'Gollum chapter' would thus be in its final place, though the context here
suggested for it would be entirely changed.

Lastly, a scribbled note reads:

(14)   Bilbo carries off 'memoirs' to Rivendell.

# THE SECOND PHASE

# XIV
# RETURN TO HOBBITON

My father now settled at last for the 'simpler story' which he had roughed out in the *Queries and Alterations* (note 13); and so the Birthday Party at Bag End returns again to Bilbo, with whom it had begun (pp. 13, 19, 40). The following rough outline no doubt immediately preceded the rewriting of the opening chapter: the fifth version, and an exceedingly complicated document.

*Bilbo* disappears on his 111th birthday. 'Long-expected Party' chapter[1] suitably altered up to point where Gandalf disappears into Bag-End. Then a short conversation between Gandalf and Bilbo inside.

Bilbo says it is becoming wearisome – stretched feeling. He must get rid of it. Also he is tired of Hobbiton, he feels a great desire to go away. Dragon gold curse? or Ring. Where are you going? I don't know. Take care! I don't care. He gets Gandalf to promise to hand on Ring to his heir Bingo. He leaves it to him – but I don't want him to worry or to try and follow: not yet. So he does not even tell Bingo of the joke. At end of chapter make Bilbo say goodbye to Gandalf at gate, hand him a package (with Ring) for Bingo, and disappear.

Chapter II is then Bingo. Furtive visits of Gandalf. Gandalf urges him to go off – for reasons of his own. Bingo on his side never tells Gandalf that looking for Bilbo is his great desire. Gandalf does not [?tell ?talk] of the Ring. The Gollum business must come in later (at Rivendell) – after Bingo has met Bilbo; and Gandalf has now found out much more. It will probably be necessary to run this Chapter II on to head of present II 'Two's company – and three's more'.[2]

The fourth version of 'A Long-expected Party' had in fact reached quite an advanced stage in most respects – in some respects virtually the final form; but the Party was Bingo's on his 72nd birthday, Bilbo having quietly disappeared out of the Shire for good thirty-three years before, when he was 111 and Bingo was 39, and apart from providing the fireworks Gandalf played no part in the chapter at all.

The outline just given says that the chapter must be 'suitably altered up to the point where Gandalf disappears into Bag-End', and the story now begins: 'When Bilbo Baggins of the well-known Hobbiton family prepared to celebrate his one-hundred-and-eleventh (or eleventy-first) birthday, there was some talk in the neighbourhood,' etc. (see pp. 28, 36). The fourth version is then followed[3] as far as 'And if he was in, you never knew who you would find with him: hobbits of quite poor families, or folk from distant villages, dwarves, and even sometimes elves' (p. 36); here a new passage concerning Gandalf and Bilbo was introduced.

Gandalf the wizard, too, was sometimes seen going up the hill. People said Gandalf 'encouraged' him, and accused him in turn of 'encouraging' some of his more lively nephews (and removed cousins), especially on the Took side; but what exactly they meant was not clear. They may have been referring to the mysterious absences from home, and to the strange habit Bilbo and his encouraged young friends had of walking all over the Shire in untidy clothes.

As time wore on the prolonged vigour, not to say youthfulness, of Mr Bilbo Baggins also became the subject of comment. At ninety he seemed much the same as ever he had been. At 99 they began to call him 'well-preserved'; but 'unchanged' would have been nearer the mark. Nevertheless he surprised them all that year by making a considerable change in his habits: he adopted as his heir his favourite and most completely 'encouraged' nephew, Bingo. Bingo Baggins was then a mere lad of 27,[4] and was strictly speaking not Bilbo's nephew (a title he used rather loosely), but both his first and his second cousin, once removed in each case,[5] but he happened to have the same birthday, September 22, as Bilbo, which seemed an additional link between them.[6] He was the son of poor Primula Brandybuck and [> who married late and as last resort] Drogo Baggins (Bilbo's second cousin but otherwise quite unimportant).

In *Queries and Alterations*, note 2, my father had said that he was 'too used to Bingo' to change his name to Frodo, but he was now following up the suggestions in that note that *Bolger-Baggins* ('a bad name') should be got rid of, and that Bingo should be a Baggins in his own right. Later in this passage Drogo takes over the rumoured boating accident on the Brandywine from Rollo Bolger (see p. 37): 'some said that Drogo Baggins had died of over-eating while staying with the old gormandizer Gorboduc; others said that it was his weight that had sunk the boat.' It is now told that Bingo was twelve years old at the time, and that he

afterwards lived mostly with his grandfather [Gorboduc Brandybuck, p. 37] and his mother's hundred and one relatives in the Great Hole of Bucklebury,[7] the ancestral and very overcrowded residence of the gregarious Brandybucks. But his visits to 'Uncle' Bilbo became more and more frequent, until at last, as has been said, Bilbo adopted him, when he was a lad of 27.

But all that was old history. People had become in the last 12 years used to having Bingo about. Neither Bilbo nor Bingo did anything outrageous. Their parties were sometimes a bit noisy (and not too select), perhaps; but hobbits don't mind that kind of noise now and again. Bilbo – now in his turn 'encouraged' by Bingo – spent his money freely, and his wealth became a local legend. It was popularly believed that most of the Hill was full of tunnels stuffed with gold and silver. Now it was suddenly given out that Bilbo, perhaps struck with the curiosity of the number 111, was planning to give something quite unusual in the way of birthday-parties. 111 was a respectable age even for hobbits.[8] Naturally tongues wagged, and old memories were stirred, and new expectations aroused. Bilbo's wealth was guessed afresh . . . (*etc. as before, see p. 30*).

In the account of the comings and goings at Bag End there are a few slight changes. The Men and the waggon painted with a D (pp. 20, 30) have been removed, as proposed in *Queries and Alterations* (note 1), but Elves as well as Dwarves are still mentioned. The bundles of fireworks were labelled not only with a big red G but also with ⚜ – 'That was Gandalf's mark' (the same rune appears in his letter at Bree and in his note left on Weathertop). The disappointed children given pennies but no fireworks are introduced (FR p. 33); and now at last appears the 'short conversation between Gandalf and Bilbo inside Bag-End' sketched in the outline on p. 233.

Inside Bag-End Bilbo and Gandalf were sitting at the open window of the sitting-room looking west onto the garden. The late afternoon was bright and peaceful; the flowers were red and golden; snapdragons, and sunflowers, and nasturtians trailing all over the turf walls and peeping in at the windows.

'How bright your garden is!' said Gandalf.

'Yes,' said Bilbo. 'I am very fond indeed of it, and of all the dear old Shire; but I think the time has come.'

'You mean to go on with your plan then?' asked Gandalf.

'Yes, I do,' Bilbo answered. 'I have made up my mind at last. I really must get rid of It.[9] "Well-preserved" indeed!' he snorted. 'Why, I feel all thin – sort of stretched, if you know what I mean: like a string that won't quite go round the parcel, or – or – butter that is scraped over too much bread. And that can't be right.'

'No!' said Gandalf thoughtfully. 'No. I daresay your plan is the best, at any rate for you. At least at present I know nothing against it, and can think of nothing better.'

'Yes, I suppose it may seem a bit hard on Bingo,' said Bilbo. 'But what can I do? I can't destroy it, and after what you have told me I am not going to throw it away; but I don't want it, in fact I can't abide it any more. But you did promise me, didn't you, to keep an eye on him, and help him if he needs it later on? Otherwise, of course, I should have to.'

'I will do what I can for him,' said Gandalf. 'But I hope you will take care of yourself.'

'Take care! I don't care!' said Bilbo, and then going suddenly into verse (as was becoming his habit more and more) he went on in a low voice looking out of the window with a far-away look in his eyes:

The Road etc. as II.5

(This is a reference to the typescript of 'Three's Company', p. 53). All of this new passage, from the words 'I really must get rid of It', was struck out in pencil and marked 'Later' (see pp. 237 and 239–40).

The text continues: 'More carts rolled up the Hill next day, and still more carts. There might have been some grumbling about "dealing locally",' etc. (p. 20). From this point in the fourth version (essentially the same as the third and second, pp. 31, 38, and as FR) the fifth of course very largely follows the old drafts, 'Bingo' being changed to 'Bilbo' where necessary. To the guests at the select dinner party are now added members of the families of Gawkroger[10] (Goodbody in FR) and Brockhouse: the latter 'did not live in the Shire at all, but in Combe-under-Bree, a village on the Eastern Road beyond Brandywine. They were supposed to be remotely connected with the Tooks, but were also friends Bilbo had made in the course of his travels.' On this see *Queries and Alterations* note 5, and my comment on it; cf. also the original Chapter VII (p. 137), of the hobbits at *The Prancing Pony*: 'there were also some (to hobbits) natural names like Banks, Longholes, Brockhouse ... which were not unknown among the more rustic inhabitants of the Shire.'

A curious point is that at this stage there were 'eight score or one hundred and sixty' guests at the dinner party in the pavilion under the tree, not 144; and in his speech Bilbo said: 'For it is of course also the birthday of my heir and nephew, Bingo. Together we score one hundred and sixty. Your numbers were chosen to fit this remarkable total.' Emendations to the preceding part of the chapter relate to this: Bingo's age at his adoption was changed from 27 to 37, so that when Bilbo was 111 (twelve years later) Bingo was 49 – totalling 160. My father had of course decided – the party being Bilbo's, and both he and Bingo being present – that the significance of the number of guests must now relate, not as previously to the elder hobbit's years, but to the total of their combined ages; but why he did not stick to 144 and reduce Bingo's age accordingly to 144 minus 111 I cannot say.

Bilbo now refers to its being the anniversary of his arrival by barrel at Lake-town; but there is still no flash when he stepped down and vanished.

This part of the text was soon revised – indeed before the story had gone much further,[11] and in a rewritten version of Bilbo's speech the number of guests reverts to 144, Bingo becomes 33 (which is the year of his 'coming of age'), and there is a blinding flash of light when he vanishes. Emendation to the earlier part of the text now changed Bingo's age at adoption once more, and finally, to 21.

In the hubbub that followed Bilbo's disappearance

there was one person harder hit than all the rest: and that was Bingo. He sat for some time quite silent in his seat beside the empty chair of his uncle, ignoring all remarks and questions; and then abandoning the party to look after itself he slipped out of the pavilion unnoticed.[12]

'What do we do now?' This question became more and more popular, and louder and louder. Suddenly old Rory Brandybuck, whose wits neither old age, nor surprise, nor an enormous dinner, had quite clouded was heard to shout: 'I never saw him go. Where is he now, anyway? Where is Bilbo – and Bingo, too, confound him?' There was no sign of their hosts, anywhere.

As a matter of fact, Bilbo Baggins, even while he was making his speech, had been fingering a small ring in his pocket: his magic ring, that he had kept secret for so many years. As he stepped down he slipped it on – and was never seen in Hobbiton again.

There now enters a wholly new element in the narrative, and it was clearly at this time that the passage of conversation between Gandalf and Bilbo inside Bag End before the party was largely struck out and marked 'Later' (pp. 235–6); at this time also that that conversation was re-extended from the point where Bilbo says 'Yes, I do. I have made up my mind at last', as follows (cf. FR pp. 33–4):

'Very well,' said Gandalf. 'I can see you mean to have your own way. I hope it will turn out all right – for all of us.'

'I hope so,' said Bilbo. 'Anyway I mean to enjoy myself on Thursday, and have my little joke in my own way.'

'Well, I hope you will still be laughing this time next year,' said Gandalf.

'And I hope you will, too,' retorted Bilbo.

The new version continues (from 'and he was never seen in Hobbiton again'):

He walked briskly back to his hole, and stood listening with a smile for a moment to the sounds of merrymaking going on in various parts of the field. Then he went in. He took off his party clothes, folded up and wrapped in tissue paper his embroidered waistcoat with the silk [> gold] buttons and put it away. Then he put on some old and untidy garments,[13] and from a locked bottom drawer (reeking of mothballs) he got out an old cloak and an old hood that seemed to have been laid up as carefully as if they were very precious, though they were so weatherstained and mended that their original colour (probably dark green) could hardly be guessed. They were rather too big for him. He put a large bulky envelope on the mantelpiece, on which was written BINGO.

He chose his favourite thick stick from the hall stand, and then whistled. Several dwarves appeared from various rooms where they had been busy.

'Is everything ready?' Bilbo asked. 'Everything packed up [added: and labelled]?'

'Everything,' they said.

'Well, let's start then. Lofar, you are stopping behind, of course [added: for Gandalf]: please make sure that Bingo gets the letter on the dining room mantelpiece as soon as he comes in. Nar, Anar, Hannar, are you ready?[14] Right. Off we go.'

He stepped out of the front door. It was a fine clear night, and the black sky was full of stars. He looked up, sniffing the air. 'What fun!' he said. 'What fun to be off again – on the Road with dwarves: this is what I have really been longing for for years.' He waved his hand to the door: 'Goodbye,' he said. He turned away from the lights and voices in the field and the tents, and followed by his three companions went round to the garden on the west side of Bag-End, and trotted down the long sloping path. They jumped the low place in the hedge at the bottom and took to the meadows, passing like a rustle in the grasses.

At the bottom of the Hill they came to a gate opening on to a narrow lane. As they climbed over, a dark figure in a tall hat rose up from under the hedge.

'Hullo, Gandalf!' cried Bilbo. 'I wondered if you would turn up.'

'And I wondered if you would,' replied the wizard; 'or if you would think better of it.[15] I suppose you feel that everything has gone off splendidly, and just as you intended?'

'Yes,' said Bilbo. 'Though that flash was surprising: it quite startled *me*, let alone the others. A little addition of yours, I suppose?'

'It was,' answered Gandalf. 'You have wisely kept that Ring secret all these years; and it seemed to me necessary to give them all some reason to explain their not noticing your sudden vanishment [> to give them all something they would think explained your sudden vanishment].'

'You are an interfering old busybody,' laughed Bilbo; 'but I expect you know best, as usual.'

'I do,' said Gandalf, 'when I know anything. But I do not feel too sure about the whole affair. Still, it has now come to the final point. You have had your joke, and successfully alarmed or offended all your friends and relations, and given the whole Shire something to talk about for nine days (or ninety-nine more likely). Are you going to go any further?'

'Yes, I am,' answered Bilbo.[16] 'I really must get rid of It, Gandalf. *Well-preserved*, indeed,' he snorted. 'Why, I feel all thin – sort of stretched, if you know what I mean: like string that won't quite go round a parcel, or, or, butter that is scraped over too much bread. And that can't be right.'

'No,' said Gandalf thoughtfully. 'No. I was afraid it might come to that. I dare say your plan is the best, at any rate for you. At least at present I do not feel I know enough to say anything definite against it.'

'What else can I do? I can't destroy the thing, and after what you have told me I am not going to throw it away. Oddly enough I find that impossible to make up my mind to do – I simply put it back in my pocket. I find it very hard even to leave behind! And yet I don't want it, indeed I can't abide it any more. But you did promise to keep an eye on Bingo, didn't you, and to help him if he needs it, later on? Otherwise, of course, I should hardly be able to go. I should have to stop and put up with it.'

'I will do what I can for him,' said Gandalf. 'What have you done with it meanwhile?'

'It is in the envelope with my will and other papers. Lofar is giving it to Bingo as soon as he comes in.'

'My dear Bilbo! And with Otho Sackville-Baggins about the place, and that Lobelia wife of his! Really you *are* getting reckless. And I suppose you left the door unlocked as usual?'

'Yes, I am afraid I did. I rather fancy Bingo will be creeping off home before anyone else.'

'Fancy is not safe enough! But you may be right. He knows about it, of course?'

'He knows that I have, or had, the Ring: he has read my private memoirs,[17] for one thing; and he also has some idea [> he may have an inkling] that it has some other – er – effects than just making you invisible on occasion. But he doesn't, or didn't, know quite what I was beginning to feel about it. But after all, as it cannot be destroyed, and can only be handed on – it had best be handed on to him: I chose him as the best in all the Shire: and he is my heir. He knows that I am leaving that to him with all the rest. I don't suppose he would ask to be excused this responsibility, and take only the money.'

'He will miss you pretty badly, you know?'

'Yes, I found it very hard to make up my mind. It is hard on him – but not too hard, I think. The time has come for him to be his own master. After all, if things had been more – er – normal, he would have been losing me soon anyway, if he had not already done so. I am sorry to cheat all my dear people of a grand funeral – how they all did enjoy Old Took's – but there it is.'

'Does he know where you are going?'

'No! I am not sure myself, really. And I think that is just as well for everybody. He might want to *follow* me.'

'So might I. I hope you will take care of yourself!'

'Take care! I don't care. And don't be unhappy about me: I am as happy as ever I have been, and that is saying a lot. But the time has come. I am being swept off my feet,' he added mysteriously, and then in a low voice as if to himself he sang softly in the darkness.

> *The Road goes ever on and on*
>   *Down from the Door where it began.*
> *Now far ahead the Road has gone,*
>   *And I must follow if I can,*
> *Pursuing it with weary feet,*
>   *Until it joins some larger way,*
> *Where many paths and errands meet.*
>   *And whither then? I cannot say.*[18]

He stopped silent a moment. Then 'Goodbye, Gandalf!' he cried, and made off into the night. Nar, Anar, and Hannar followed him.[19] Gandalf remained by the gate for a little, and then sprang over it and made his way up the Hill.[20]

It will be seen that in this passage, far different from that which occupies the same narrative place in FR pp. 40–4, my father was thinking about the effect of the Ring on its possessor on very much the same lines as in the chapter on Gollum (the 'foreword'), pp. 79–80. Moreover in FR the conversation – and quarrel – between Bilbo and Gandalf takes place in Bag End, so that the elements in the present version of Gandalf's anxiety about the Ring, left unguarded in an envelope at Bag End, and his going up the Hill to find Bingo, do not arise; Gandalf was sitting there waiting for him when he came in.

The clearing up of the party follows the earlier version, of course (FR p. 45); but the end of the chapter exists in two variant forms, marked as such. One of the variants, very much longer than the other and preceding it, is itself heavily modified. To look at this first: the list of presents remains the same, with some further changes in the names.[21] With 'Of course, this was only a selection of the presents' the new text advances very close to the form in FR (pp. 46–7), with the reflections on the cluttered nature of hobbit-holes (on which Bingo had remarked: 'We soon shan't be able to sit down for stools or tell the time for clocks in Bag-End'), and the gifts to Gaffer Gamgee (but Bilbo's collection of magical toys, pp. 33, 38, still remains); the dozen bottles of Old Winyards go to Rory Brandybuck, and are said to come from 'the south Shire', not yet the Southfarthing.

From 'not a penny piece or a brass farthing was given away' there is a rejected text and a replacement, differing from each other chiefly in the arrangement of the elements. As written first, the Sackville-Bagginses are introduced immediately, demanding to see the will – which is given at length;[22] then follows the rumour that the entire contents of Bag End were being distributed, and 'in the middle of the commotion' Bingo finds Lobelia investigating, ejects the three young hobbits, and has a fight with Sancho Proudfoot;[23] and the passage concludes with 'The fact is that Bilbo's money had become a legend . . .' (FR p. 48).

In the replacement text the structure in FR (pp.47-8) is reached, with the sole important difference that Merry's rôle is taken by the dwarf Lofar, who had stayed behind after Bilbo's departure (p. 238); and the only minor differences from FR are that Otho Sackville-Baggins is still a lawyer, the date of Bingo's entry into his inheritance is stated (midnight on 22 September), the witnessing of the will was by three hobbits of more than 33 years old, according to the custom, and the Sackville-Bagginses 'more than hinted that he or the wizard (or the pair of them together) were at the bottom of the whole business.' The exchange between Frodo and Merry on the subject of Lobelia's calling Frodo a Brandybuck is of course not present – Bingo merely 'shut the door behind her with a grimace.'

The short variant is very short, and was not adopted. The large crowd who arrived at Bag End on the morning after the party does no more than go away again when they see a notice on the gate saying: 'Mr Bilbo

Baggins has gone away. There is no further news. Unless your business is
urgent, please do not knock or ring. Bingo Baggins.' The Sackville-
Bagginses 'thought that their business was urgent. They knocked and
rang several times.' Admitted by Lofar the Dwarf, the remainder of the
passage is the same as in the (revised) long variant and FR – the interview
between Bingo and the Sackville-Bagginses in the study, ending with
Bingo's telling Lofar not to open the front door even against battering-
rams (and omitting the mopping-up operations against the three young
hobbits and Sancho Proudfoot). Thus the entire 'business' of the presents, and the invasion of Bag End, was in this variant removed. For my
father's intention here see p.276.

The reappearance of Gandalf at Bag End now enters the story, and
begins pretty well exactly as in FR (p.48), but soon significant differences enter the conversation, from the point where Gandalf says to Bingo
'What do you know already?' (FR p.49):

'Only Bilbo's tale of how he got it,[24] from that Gollum creature,
and how he used it afterwards, on his journey I mean. I don't think
he used it much after he came home; though he used to disappear
(or not be findable) rather mysteriously sometimes, if things were
a bit inconvenient. We saw the Sackville-Bagginses coming when
we were out walking one day, and he disappeared, and came out
from behind a hedge after they had gone by.[25] Being invisible has
its advantages.'

'But it also has its disadvantages. It does not do much harm as a
joke, nor even to avoid "inconveniences" – but even these things
have to be paid for. Also making you invisible, when you wish, is
not the only property of the Ring.'

'I know what you mean,' said Bingo; 'Bilbo did not seem to
change much. They called him well-preserved. But I must say
that also seems to me to have its advantages. I cannot make out
why the dear old thing left the Ring behind.'

'No, I expect you cannot yet. But you may find out the
disadvantages of that as well, in time. For instance, Bilbo seemed
a bit restless of late years, didn't he?'

'Yes, for quite a long time,'

'Well, I think that was a symptom too. I don't want to alarm
you, but I want you to be careful. Take care of the Ring, and take
care of yourself, and watch yourself. Don't use the Ring,[26] or let it
get any more, er, *power* over you than you can help. Keep it *secret*,
and let me know, if you hear, see, or feel anything at all odd.'

'All right. But what is all this about?'

'I am not quite sure. I begin to guess, and I don't like the
guesses. But I am now going off to find out as much as I can.

Before I have done so, I am not going to say any more, except to warn you, and to promise you what help I can give.'

'But you say you are going off?'

'Yes, for a bit. But you'll be safe for a year or two, in any case. Don't worry. I shall come and see you again as soon as I can – quietly, you know. I don't think I shall be visiting the Shire openly again very much. I find I have become rather unpopular: they say I am a nuisance and a disturber of the peace; and some people are accusing me of spiriting Bilbo away. It is supposed to be a little plot between me and you (if you want to know).'

'That sounds like Otho and Lobelia.[27] How outrageous! I only wish I knew why and where old Bilbo has gone. Do you? Do you think I could catch him up or find him if I went off at once? I would give Bag-end and everything in it to the Sackville-Bagginses if I could do that.'

'I don't think I should try. Let poor Bilbo get rid of the Ring – which he could only do (reluctantly) by handing it on to you, for a bit.[28] Do what he wished and hoped you would.'

'What is that?'

'Live on here; keep up Bag-end; guard the Ring – and wait.'

'All right – I will try; but I should prefer to go after Bilbo.[29] I don't know if that is a symptom, as you call it – though I have only had the Ring a day or less?'

'No, not yet. It merely means you were fond of Bilbo. He knew it was hard on you. He hated leaving you. But there it is. We may all understand this better before the end. I must say goodbye now. Look out for me – at any time, especially unlikely ones. If you really need me send a message to the nearest dwarves: I shall try and give them some knowledge of where I am.[30] Goodbye!'

Bingo saw him off. The dwarf Lofar went with him carrying a large bag. They walked away down the path to the gate at a surprising pace,[31] but Bingo thought the wizard looked rather bent, almost as if bowed under a heavy burden. The evening was closing in, and he soon vanished into the twilight. Bingo did not see him again for a long time.

About this time my father wrote a new experimental opening to the chapter, in which the facts and assertions about the family history were communicated through the talk of Gaffer Gamgee, Old Noakes, and Sandyman the miller in *The Ivy Bush*. The mention of Sam Gamgee as the Bag End gardener shows that it was in fact written after the second chapter, 'Ancient History', which now follows; for if this text had been already in existence my father would not have given an explanation of

who Sam Gamgee was when he appears in 'Ancient History' (p. 253).
But it is convenient to notice it here.

This version of the conversation had still a good way to go before it
reached the form in FR (pp. 30–2). The opening of the chapter was now
to be greatly compressed:

When Mr Bilbo Baggins of Bag-end, Under-hill, announced
that he would shortly be celebrating his eleventy-first birthday
with a party of special magnificence, there was much talk and
excitement in Hobbiton. Before long rumour of the event travelled all over the Shire, and the history and character of Mr Baggins
became once again the most popular topic of conversation. The
older folk who remembered something of the strange happenings
sixty years before found their reminiscences suddenly in demand,
and rose to the gratifying occasion with entertaining invention
when mere facts failed them.

No one had a more attentive audience than old Ham Gamgee,
commonly known as the Gaffer. He held forth at the *Ivy Bush*,[32] a
small inn on the Bywater Road; and he spoke with some authority,
for he had tended the garden at Bag-end for half a century, and
had helped his father in the same job before that. Now that he was
grown old and creaky in the joints he had passed the job on to one
of his own sons, Sam Gamgee.

The subject of Bingo is treated thus:

'And what about this Mr Bingo Baggins that lives with him?'
asked old Noakes of Bywater.[33] 'I hear he is coming of age on the
same day.'

'That's right,' said the Gaffer. 'He has the same birthday as Mr
Bilbo, September the twenty-second. It is a sort of link between
them, as you might say. Not but what they get on remarkably well,
and have done all the last twelve years, since Mr Bingo came to
Bag-end. Very much alike in every way, they are, being closely
related. Though Mr Bingo is half a Brandybuck by rights, and
that's a queer breed, as I've heard tell. They fool about with boats
and water, and that isn't natural. Small wonder that trouble came
of it, I say.'

For the rest, Mr Twofoot of Bagshot Row does not appear; Gorboduc
Brandybuck is called by the Gaffer 'the head of the family, and mighty
important down in Buckland, I'm told'; the miller does not suggest that
there was anything more sinister in the drowning of Drogo Baggins and
his wife than Drogo's weight; the hobbit who introduces the topic of the
tunnels packed with treasure inside the Hill is not 'a visitor from Michel

Delving' but 'one of the Bywater hobbits'; and there are many differences of phrasing.

## NOTES

1   My father actually wrote '"Unex[pected]P[arty]" chapter' – thinking of the first chapter of *The Hobbit*. Cf. my suggestion about his use of the word 'sale' in *Queries and Alterations*, note 2.

2   The actual title of Chapter II was 'Three's Company and Four's More' (p. 49). – A pencilled note on the same page says: 'Should Bingo spend all his money? Is it not better he should be sacrificing something? Though he must give out that he has spent it.'

3   The passage about Bilbo's book and the reception accorded to it, which had survived unchanged from the second version (p. 19), was at first repeated here, but subsequently replaced by the following:
    He told many tales of his adventures, of course, to those who would listen. But most of the hobbits soon got tired of them, and only one or two of his younger friends ever took them seriously. It is no good telling ordinary hobbits about dragons: they either disbelieve you or want to disbelieve you, and in either case stop listening. As he grew older Bilbo wrote his adventures in a private book of memoirs, in which he recounted some things that he had never spoken about (such as the magic ring); but that book was never published in the Shire, and he never showed it to anyone, except his favourite 'nephew' Bingo.

4   This was Bingo's age at the time of his adoption in the fourth version (p. 36), but it was changed in the course of the writing of the present text (see p. 236).

5   In *Queries and Alterations* (note 2) the suggestion was that Drogo Baggins should be Bilbo's first cousin.

6   This remark about Bilbo and Bingo having the same birthday was a pencilled addition, but the idea goes back to the third version (p. 29), when Bingo was Bilbo's son.

7   *The Great Hole of Bucklebury*: Brandy Hall has been named and described in the original version of 'A Short Cut to Mushrooms' (p. 99).

8   Added in pencil:
    and the Old Took himself had only reached the age of 125 (though the title Old was bestowed on him, it is true, not so much for his age as for his oddity, and because of the enormous number of the young, younger, and youngest Tooks).

9   This was to be the first, intentionally obscure, reference to the Ring in the story. With the shortening and alteration of this initial converation between Gandalf and Bilbo before the Party (p. 237) this reference was removed, and it is then first spoken of only after Bilbo's vanishment.

10   *Gawkroger* is an English (Yorkshire) surname, meaning 'clumsy Roger'.

11   The textual situation is in fact of fearful complexity in this part, the manuscript being constituted from two 'layers', and the earlier of the two being constituted partly from new manuscript and partly from the typescript of the fourth version. With the actual texts in front of one it can be worked out how my father was proceeding, but to present the detail in a printed book is neither possible nor necessary. It is demonstrable that the second 'layer', with revised dating of Bingo's life and the flash which accompanied Bilbo's vanishing, entered in the course of the composition of the chapter.

12   This perhaps suggests that Bingo had not been told of Bilbo's 'joke'; cf. the outline on p. 233: 'So he does not even tell Bingo of the joke.' A pencilled correction and addition changed the passage towards that in FR (p. 39).

    The only one who said nothing was Bingo, the most concerned. His feelings were mixed. On the one hand he appreciated the joke (if no one else did). It was quite after his own heart: he would have liked to laugh and dance with mirth; and was grateful that he had been allowed to get the full and delicious suspense, for on the other hand he would have liked to weep. He was immensely fond of Bilbo, and the blow was crushing. Was he really never to see him again – not even to take another farewell? He sat for some time quite silent in his seat . . .

13   Added later:

    and fastened on a leather belt round his waist. On it hung a short sword in an old black leather scabbard.

    Cf. *Queries and Alterations*, note 4, on the subject of Sting.

14   My father took all these four Dwarf-names from the same source in the Old Norse *Elder Edda* as those in *The Hobbit*.

15   Added later:

    But I want just a final word with you. Now, my good dwarves, just walk on down the lane a bit. I shan't keep you long!' He turned back to Bilbo. 'Well,' he said in a lowered voice.

16   From this point the earlier, rejected conversation between Bilbo and Gandalf before the Party (pp. 235–6, there marked 'Later') is taken up again, though not in the same form, and much extended.

17   A pencilled addition here probably says: '(the only one who has)'; see note 3.

18   This verse came into existence in the original form of the chapter 'Three is Company' (pp. 47, 53), where it will now become a recollection of Bilbo's verse from years before. The two versions are the same, except that in lines 4 and 8 Bilbo's form here has *I* for *we*. In FR (pp. 44, 82) both versions have *I*, not *we*; but Bilbo's has *eager* in the 5th line where Frodo's has *weary*. In the present text

*eager* is written above *weary*, and with this change the final form is reached in this instance (see p. 284 note 10).

19 This sentence was struck out when the addition given in note 15 was made.

20 The remainder of this part of the text is in very rough pencilled form, with alteration of the last passage in ink preceding it:

'Goodbye, Gandalf!' he cried, and made off into the night. Gandalf remained by the gate for a moment, staring into the dark after him. '*Adieu*, my dear Bilbo,' he said, '— or *au revoir*.' [This was marked with an X: Gandalf would not use French, however useful the distinction.] And then he jumped over the low gate and made his way quickly up the Hill. 'If I find Lobelia sneaking round,' he muttered, 'I'll turn her into a weasel!'

But he need not have worried. At Bag-End he found Bingo sitting on a chair in the hall with the envelope in his hand. He refused to have any more to do with the party.

21 The umbrella now goes, not to Mungo Took, but to Uffo Took (Adelard Took in FR). Semolina Baggins becomes Drogo's sister, aged 92 (in FR she is Dora Baggins, aged 99). The feather-bed goes now not to Fosco Bolger (who had been Bingo's uncle when he was still a Bolger), but to Rollo Bolger (an equally suitable recipient), 'from his friend'; Rollo Bolger has survived his displacement from Primula Brandybuck's husband and death by drowning in the Brandywine. The 'rather florid' dinner-service goes to Primo (not Inigo) Grubb; and the Hornblower who received the barometer now changes from Cosimo (by way of Carambo) to Colombo. Caramella Chubb, Orlando Burrows (so spelt), Angelica Baggins, Hugo Bracegirdle, and of course Lobelia Sackville-Baggins, remain, and their gifts. For the earlier lists see pp. 15, 32–3, 38.

22 'This is how the will ran:

*Bilbo (son of Bungo son of Mungo son of Inigo) Baggins hereinafter called the testator, now departing being the rightful owner of all properties and goods hereinafter named hereby devises, makes over, and bequeathes the property and messuage or dwelling-hole known as Bag-End Underhill near Hobbiton with all lands thereto belonging and annexed to his cousin and adopted heir Bingo (son of Drogo son of Togo son of Bingo son of Inigo Baggins hereinafter called the heir, for him to have hold possess occupy let on lease sell or otherwise dispose of at his pleasure as from midnight of the twenty-second day of September in the one hundred and eleventh or eleventy-first year of the aforesaid Bilbo Baggins. Moreover the aforesaid testator devises and bequeathes to the aforesaid heir all monies in gold silver copper brass or tin and all trinkets, armours, weapons, uncoined metals, gems, jewels, or precious stones and all furniture appurtenances goods perishable or imperishable and chattels movable and immovable belonging to the testator and*

*after his departure found housed kept stored or secreted in any
part of the said hole and residence of Bag-end or of the lands
thereto annexed, save only such goods or movable chattels as are
contained in the subjoined schedule which are selected and
directed as parting gifts to the friends of the testator and which the
heir shall dispatch deliver or hand over according to his convenience. The testator hereby relinquishes all rights or claims to all
these properties lands monies goods or chattels and wishes all his
friends farewell. Signed Bilbo Baggins.*

Otho, who was a lawyer, read this document carefully, and snorted.
It was apparently correct and incontestable, according to the legal
notions of hobbits. "Foiled again!" he said to his wife . . .' (etc. as in
FR p. 47).

23   'Old Proudfoot's son' (in FR 'old Odo Proudfoot's grandson', p. 48).

24   This sentence was extended in pencil as follows:

'Just what Bilbo's parting letter said: "Here's the Ring. Please
accept it. Take care of it, and yourself. Ask Gandalf, if you want
to know more." And of course I have read and heard Bilbo's tale of
how he got it . . .'

25   This mention of Bilbo's disappearance when he saw the Sackville-
Bagginses approaching was struck out in pencil, with the note 'Put
in later'. See p. 300.

26   'Don't use the Ring' was struck out in pencil, with 'If you take my
advice you will not use the Ring' substituted; and before the words
'Keep it *secret*' in the next sentence was added 'But have it by you
always.'

27   In this version, Otho and Lobelia have as good as said this to Bingo
(p. 241) – a passage not in FR.

28   This was rewritten in pencil: 'I don't think I should try. I don't
think it would please or help Bilbo. Let him get rid of the Ring –
which he can only do, if you will accept it, for a bit.'

29   This was rewritten in pencil: 'All right – I will try. But I want to
follow Bilbo. I think I shall in the end, anyway, if it is not then too
late ever to find him again.'

30   This sentence ('If you really need me . . .') was bracketed (in ink) for
probable exclusion.

31   This was rewritten in pencil:

Bingo saw Gandalf to the door. There the dwarf Lofar was
waiting. He popped up when the door was opened, and picked up
a large bag that was standing in the porch. 'Goodbye, Bingo,' he
said, bowing low. 'I am going with Gandalf.' 'Goodbye,' said
Bingo. Gandalf gave a final wave of his hand, and with the dwarf
at his side walked off down the path at a surprising pace . . .

At the end of the chapter my father wrote: 'Perhaps alter this –
Gandalf *has ring*. Meeting at gate prearranged: ring handed over
there. Gandalf's last visit is to give it to Bingo?' He struck this out

and wrote 'No' against it. This had in fact been his idea when he wrote the outline given on p. 233, where Bilbo is to 'say goodbye to Gandalf at gate, hand him a package (with Ring) for Bingo, and disappear.'

32 *Ivy Bush:* changed at the time of writing from *Green Dragon*. See note 33.

33 *old Noakes of Bywater:* changed at the time of writing from *Ted Sandyman, the miller's son*. This is a further indication that this version of the opening of 'A Long-expected Party' followed 'Ancient History', where the miller's son was named Tom until the very end of it (p. 269, note 9). The conversation between Sam Gamgee and Ted Sandyman in 'Ancient History' was in *The Green Dragon* at Bywater, and my father probably changed the rendezvous of Gaffer Gamgee's cronies to *The Ivy Bush* (note 32) for the same reason as he replaced the miller's son by Old Noakes.

★

I give here as much of the genealogy of Bilbo and Bingo as is established from the text at this time. The Baggins ancestry is derived from Bilbo's will (note 22); the names in brackets are those that differ in LR Appendix C, *Baggins of Hobbiton*.

The Old Took was evidently already known to have had many children beside his 'three remarkable daughters' (see note 8).

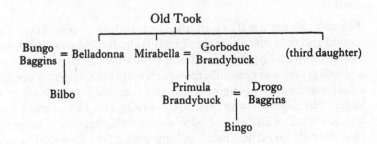

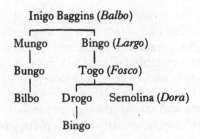

# XV
# ANCIENT HISTORY

A chapter titled 'II: Ancient History', precursor of 'The Shadow of the Past' in FR, was now introduced to follow 'A Long-expected Party'. It is of central importance in the evolution of *The Lord of the Rings*: for it was here that there emerged in the actual narrative the concept of the Ruling Ring, and Sam Gamgee as the companion of Bingo (Frodo) on his great journey. There is no trace of earlier drafting, save for a few notes so scrappy and disjointed that they can scarcely be reproduced. In these my father scribbled down salient features of Bingo's life after Bilbo's disappearance, and first devised the story of Bingo's own departure 17 years later, celebrated by a dinner party for Merry, Frodo, and Odo (here apparently said to have been given on the proceeds of the sale of Bag End). Against these notes my father wrote: 'Sam Gamgee to replace Odo' (cf. *Queries and Alterations*, p. 221).

The manuscript is rough, and in places very rough indeed, but legible virtually throughout. There is some emendation from a later phase, here ignored, and a good deal of pencilled change that can in some cases be seen to have been made while the chapter was in progress. These latter I adopt into the text, but in some cases refer in the notes to the text as first written.

The talk did not die down in nine or even ninety-nine days. The second and final disappearance of Mr Bilbo Baggins was discussed in Hobbiton and Bywater, and indeed all over the Shire, for a year and a day, and was remembered much longer than that. It became a fireside story for young hobbits; and eventually (a century or so later) Mad Baggins, who used to disappear with a bang and a flash and reappear with bags of gold and jewels, became a favourite character of legend and lived on long after all the true events were forgotten.

But in the meantime sober grown-ups gradually settled to the opinion that Bilbo had at last (after long showing symptoms of its coming on) gone suddenly mad, and had run off into the blue; where he had inevitably fallen into a pit or a pool, and come to a tragic but hardly untimely end. There was one Baggins the less and that was that.[1] In face of the evidence that this disappearance had been timed and arranged by Bilbo himself, Bingo was eventually relieved of suspicion. It was also plain that the departure of

Bilbo was a grief to him – more than to any other even of Bilbo's closest friends. But Gandalf was held finally responsible for inciting and encouraging 'poor old Mr Bilbo', for dark and unknown ends of his own.

'If only that wizard will leave young Bingo alone, perhaps he will settle down and grow some hobbit-sense,' they said. And to all appearances the wizard did leave Bingo alone, and he did settle down, though the growth of hobbit-sense was not so noticeable. Indeed Bingo at once carried on his uncle's reputation for oddity. He refused to go into mourning; and the next year he gave a party in honour of Bilbo's 112th birthday, which he called the Hundredweight Party; although only a few friends were invited and they hardly ate a hundredweight between them. People were rather pained; but he kept up the custom of giving 'Bilbo's birthday party' year after year, until they got used to it. He said he did not think Bilbo was dead. When they asked: 'Where is he, then?' he shrugged his shoulders.[2] He lived alone, but he went about a lot with certain younger hobbits that Bilbo had been fond of, and continued to 'encourage' them. The chief of these were Meriadoc Brandybuck (usually called Merry), Frodo Took, and Odo Bolger.[3] Merry was the son of Caradoc Brandybuck (Bingo's cousin) and Yolanda Took, and so the cousin of Frodo, son of Folco (whose sister was Yolanda). Frodo, or Frodo the Second, was the great-great-grandson of Frodo the First (otherwise known as the Old Took), and the heir and rather desperate hope of the Hole of Took, as the clan was called. Odo also had a Took mother and was a third cousin of the other two.[4] With these Bingo went about (often in untidy clothes) and walked all over the Shire. He was often away from home. But he continued to spend his money lavishly, indeed more lavishly than Bilbo had. And there still seemed to be plenty of it, so naturally his oddities were overlooked, as far as possible. As time went on it is true that they began to notice that Bingo also showed signs of good 'preservation': outwardly he retained the appearance of a strong and rather large and well-built hobbit just out of his 'tweens'. 'Some people have all the luck,' they said, meaning this enviable combination of cash and preservation; but they did not attach any particular significance to it, not even when Bingo began to approach the more sober age of 50.

Bingo himself, after the first shock of loss and change, rather enjoyed being his own master, and *the* Mr Baggins of Bag-end.

For a while, indeed several years, he was very happy, and did not think much about the future. He knew, of course, if no one else did, that the money was not unlimited, and was fast disappearing. Money went a prodigious long way in those days, and one could also get many things without it; but Bilbo had made great inroads on his inheritance and his acquired treasures in the course of sixty years, and had blown at least 500 pieces of gold on that last Party.[5] So an end would come sooner or later. But Bingo did not worry: down inside though suppressed there still remained his desire to follow Bilbo, or at all events to leave the Shire and go off into the Blue, or wherever chance took him.

One day, he thought, he would do it. As he approached 50 – a number he somehow felt was significant (or ominous), it was at any rate at that age that adventure had first come upon Bilbo – he began to think more seriously of it. He felt restless. He used to look at maps and wonder what it was like beyond the edges: hobbit maps made in the Shire did not extend very far east or west of its borders. And he began to feel, sometimes, a sort of thin feeling, as if he was being stretched out over a lot of days, and weeks, and months, but was not fully there, somehow. He could not explain any better than that to Gandalf, though he tried to. Gandalf nodded thoughtfully.

Gandalf had taken to slipping in to see him again – quietly and secretly, and usually when no one was about. He would tap an agreed signal on the window or door, and be let in: it was usually dark when he arrived, and while he was there he did not go out. He went off again, often without warning, either at night or in the very early morning before sunrise. The only people besides Bingo who knew of these visits were Frodo and Merry; though no doubt folk out in the country caught sight of him going along the road or over the fields, and scratched their heads either trying to remember who he was, or wondering what he was doing.

Gandalf turned up again first about three years after Bilbo's departure, took a look at Bingo, listened to the small news of the Shire, and went off again soon, seeing that Bingo was still quite settled. But he returned once or twice every year (except for one other long gap of nearly two years) until the fourteenth year. Bingo was then 47. After that he came frequently and stayed longer.[6] He began to be worried about Bingo; and also odd things were happening. Rumour of them had begun to reach the ears of even the deafest and most parochial hobbits. Bingo had heard a good deal more than any other hobbit of the Shire, for of course he continued Bilbo's habit of welcoming dwarves and odd strangers, and even occasionally of visiting elves. It was believed by his close friends Merry and Frodo at any rate that elves were friendly to him [*bracketed at the time of writing:* and that he knew some of their few haunts. This was in fact quite true. Bilbo had taught Bingo all that he knew, and had even instructed him in what he had learned of the two elf-languages used in those times and places (by the elves among themselves). There were very few elves actually in the Shire, and they were very seldom seen by anyone but Bilbo, and Bingo. *This was replaced at the time of writing by:*] and that he knew something of their secret languages – learned probably from Bilbo. And they were quite right.

Both elves and dwarves were troubled, especially those that occasionally arrived or passed by coming from a distance, from East or South. They would seldom, however, say anything very definite. But they constantly mentioned the Necromancer, or the [Dark Lord >] Enemy; and sometimes referred to the Land of Mor-dor and the Black Tower. It seemed that the Necromancer was moving again, and that Gandalf's confidence that the North would be freed from him for many an age had not been justified.[7] He had flown from Mirkwood only to reoccupy his ancient stronghold in the South, near the midst of the world in those days, in the Land of Mordor; and it was rumoured that the Black Tower had been raised anew. Already his power was creeping out over the lands again and the mountains and woods were darkened. Men were restless and moving North and West, and many seemed now to be partly or wholly under the dominion of the Dark Lord. There were wars, and there was much burning and ruin. The dwarves were growing afraid. Goblins were multiplying again and reappearing. Trolls of a new and most malevolent kind were abroad; giants were spoken of, a Big Folk only far bigger and stronger than Men the [?ordinary] Big Folk, and no stupider, indeed often full of cunning and wizardry. And there were vague hints of things or creatures more terrible than goblins, trolls, or giants. Elves were vanishing, or wandering steadily westward.

In Hobbiton there began to be some talk about the odd folk that were abroad, and often strayed over the borders. The following report of a conversation in the *Green Dragon* at Bywater one evening [about this time >] in the spring of Bingo's 49th? 50th? [*sic*] year[8] will give some idea of the feeling in the air.

Sam Gamgee (old Gaffer Gamgee's [eldest >] youngest and a good jobbing gardener) was sitting in one corner by the fire, and opposite him was Ted Sandyman[9] the miller's son from Hobbiton; and there were various other rustic hobbits listening.

'Queer things you do hear these days, to be sure, Ted,' said Sam.

There follows in the manuscript the original draft, written very roughly and rapidly, of the conversation at *The Green Dragon* found in FR, pp. 53–5; and it was scarcely altered afterwards save in little details of phrasing. The hobbit who saw the Tree-man beyond the North Moors (in FR Sam's cousin Halfast Gamgee, who worked for Mr Boffin at Overhill) is here 'Jo Button, him that works for the Gawkrogers [see p. 236] and goes up North for the hunting.' Sam's reference to 'queer folk' being turned back by the Bounders on the Shire-borders is absent; he speaks of the Elves journeying to the harbours 'out away West, away beyond the Towers',[10] but the reference to the Grey Havens is lacking.

Most interesting is the reference to the Tree-men. As my father first wrote Sam's words, he said: 'But what about these what do you call 'em – giants? They do say as one nigh as big as a tower or leastways a tree was seen up away beyond the North Moors not long back.' This was changed at the time of writing to: 'But what about these Tree-Men, these here – giants? They do say one nigh as big as a tower was seen,' etc. (Was this passage (preserved in FR, p. 53) the first premonition of the Ents? But long before my father had referred to 'Tree-men' in connection with the voyages of Eärendel: II.254, 261).

Sam's words about the Bagginses at the end of the conversation are different (and explain why the egregious Ted Sandyman used the word 'cracked' in FR):

'Well, I dunno. But that Mr Baggins of Bag-End, he thinks it is true; he told me and my dad so; and both he and old Mr Bilbo know a bit about Elves, or so my dad says and he ought to know. He's known the Bag-End folk since he was a lad, and he worked in their gardens till his joints cracked too much for bending, and I took on.'

'And they're both cracked ...'

After Ted Sandyman's last words,

Sam sat silent and said no more. He was due for a job of work in Bingo's garden next day, and was thinking he might have a chance of a word with Bingo, to whom he had transferred the reverence of his dad for old Bilbo. It was April and the sky was high and clear after much rain. The sun was gone, and a cool pallid sky was fading slowly. He went home through Hobbiton and up the hill whistling softly and thoughtfully.

About the same time Gandalf was quietly slipping in through the half-open front door of Bag-End.

Next morning after breakfast two people, Gandalf and Bingo, were sitting near the open window. A bright fire was on the hearth; but the sun was warm, and the wind was southerly: everything looked fresh, and the new green of Spring was shimmering in the fields and on the tips of the trees' fingers. Gandalf was thinking of a spring nearly 80 years before, when Bilbo had run out of Bag-end without a handkerchief. Gandalf's hair was perhaps whiter than it had been then, and his beard and eyebrows were perhaps longer and face wiser; but his eyes were no less bright and powerful, and he smoked and blew smoke-rings with as great vigour and delight as ever. He was smoking now in silence, for they had been talking about Bilbo (as they often did), and [other things >] the Necromancer and the Ring.

'It is all most disturbing, and in fact terrifying,' said Bingo. Gandalf grunted: the sound apparently meant 'I quite agree, but your remark is not helpful.' There was another silence. The sound of Sam Gamgee giving the lawn its first cut came from the garden.

'How long have you known all this?' asked Bingo at length. 'And did you tell Bilbo?'

'I guessed a good deal immediately,' answered Gandalf slowly . . .

My father had now returned to the text given on pp. 76 ff, the 'foreword' as he called it (see p. 224), which I have discussed on pp. 86-7, and in which of course the story was present that Bingo gave the Party: the conversation with Gandalf took place a few weeks before it, and it was indeed Gandalf's own idea. But my father followed parts of the old text closely, while extending it in certain very important ways.

In Gandalf's reply to Bingo's question (original text p. 77) he says:

'I guessed much, but at first I said little. I thought that all was well with Bilbo, and that he was safe enough, for that kind of power was powerless over him. So I thought, and I was right in a way; but not quite right. I kept an eye on him, of course, but perhaps I was not careful enough. I did not then know which of the many Rings this one was. Had I known I might have done differently – but perhaps not. But I know now.' His voice faded to a whisper. 'For I went back to the land of the Necromancer – twice.'[11]

'I am sure you have done everything you could,' said Bingo . . .

Gandalf says rather more about Bilbo: 'I was not greatly worried about Bilbo – his education was nearly complete, and I no longer felt respon-

sible for him. He had to follow his own mind, when he had made it up.'
And he speaks of the hobbits of the Shire being 'enslaved' (as in FR,
p. 58), not 'becoming Wraiths.'

But with Gandalf's reply to Bingo's 'I do not quite understand what all
this has got to do with me and Bilbo and the Ring' my father departed
altogether from the original text.

'To tell you the truth,' answered Gandalf, 'I believe he has
hitherto, *hitherto* mind you, entirely overlooked the existence of
hobbits – as Smaug the dragon had. For which you may be
thankful. And I don't think even now that he particularly wants
them: they would be obedient (perhaps), but not terribly useful
servants. But there is such a thing as malice and revenge. Miserable hobbits would please him more than happy ones. As for what
it has to do with you and the Ring: I think I can explain that –
partly at any rate. I do not yet know quite all. Give me the Ring a
minute.'

Bingo took it from his trouser pocket where it was clasped on a
chain that went round him like a belt. 'Good,' said Gandalf. 'I see
you keep it always on you. Go on doing so.' Bingo unclasped it and
handed it to Gandalf. It felt heavy, as if either it, or Bingo, were in
some curious way reluctant for Gandalf to touch it. It looked to be
made of pure and solid gold, thick, flattened, and unjointed.[12]
Gandalf held it up.

'Can you see any markings on it?' he said. 'No!' said Bingo. 'It is
quite plain, and does not even show any scratches or signs of
wear.'

'Well then, look,' said Gandalf, and to Bingo's astonishment
and distress the wizard threw it into the middle of a hot patch in
the fire. Bingo gave a cry and groped for the poker; but Gandalf
held him back. 'Wait!' he said in commanding tones, giving Bingo
a quick look from under his eyebrows.

No apparent change came over the Ring. After a while Gandalf
got up, closed the shutters outside the round window, and drew
the curtain. The room became dark and silent. The clack of Sam's
shears, now nearer the hole, could be heard outside. Gandalf
stood for a moment looking at the fire; then he stopped and
removed the Ring with the tongs, and at once picked it up. Bingo
gasped.

'It is quite cold,' said Gandalf. 'Take it!'

Bingo received it on his shrinking palm: it seemed colder and
even heavier than before. 'Hold it up!' said Gandalf, 'and look
inside.' As Bingo did so he saw fine lines, more fine than the finest

The original description of the writing on the Ring

pen strokes, running along the inside of the Ring – lines of fire that seemed to form the letters of a strange alphabet. They shone bright, piercingly bright, and yet it seemed remotely, as if out of a great depth.

'I cannot read the fiery letters,' said Bingo in a quavering voice. 'No,' said Gandalf; 'but I can – now. The writing says:

> *One Ring to rule them all, One Ring to find them,*
> *One Ring to bring them all, and in the darkness bind them.* [13]

This is part of a verse that I know now in full.

> *Three rings for the Elven-kings under the sky,*
> *Seven for the Dwarf-lords in their halls of stone,*
> *Nine for Mortal Men doomed to die,*
> *One for the Dark Lord on his dark throne*
> *In the Land of Mor-dor where the shadows lie.*
> *One Ring to rule them all, One Ring to find them,*
> *One Ring to bring them all, and in the darkness bind them,*
> *In the land of Mor-dor where the shadows lie.* [14]

'This,' said Gandalf, 'is the Master-ring: the One Ring to Rule them all! This is the One Ring that he lost many ages ago – to the great weakening of his power; and that he still so greatly desires. [15] But he must *not* get it!'

Bingo sat silent and motionless. Fear seemed to stretch out a vast hand like a dark cloud, rising out of the East and looming up to engulf him. 'This Ring?' he stammered. 'How on earth did it come to me?'

'I can tell you the part of the story that I know,' answered Gandalf. 'In ancient days the Necromancer, the Dark Lord Sauron, [16] made many magic rings of various properties that gave various powers to their possessors. He dealt them out lavishly and sowed them abroad to ensnare all peoples, but specially Elves and Men. For those that used the rings, according to their strength and will and hearts, fell quicker or slower under the power of the rings, and the dominion of their maker. [17] Three, Seven, Nine and One he made of special potency: [18] for their possessors became not only invisible to all in this world, if they wished, but could see both the world under the sun and the other side in which invisible things move. [19] And they had (what is called) good luck, and (what seemed) endless life. Though, as I say, what power the Rings conferred on each possessor depended on what use they made of them – on what they were themselves, and what they desired.

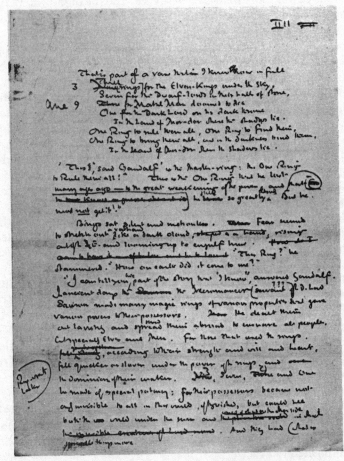

The Ring-verse, and the emergence of the Ruling Ring in the narrative

'But the Rings were under the command of the maker and were always drawing the possessors back to him. For he retained the ruling Ring, which, when *he* wore it, enabled him to see all the others, and to see even the thoughts of those that possessed them.[20] But he lost this Ring, and consequently lost control of all the others. Slowly through the years he has been gathering them and seeking them out – hoping to find the lost One. But the Elves resist his power more than all other races; and the high-elves of the West, of whom some still remain in the middle-world, perceive and dwell at once both [in] this world and the other side without the aid of rings.[21] And they having suffered and fought long against Sauron are not easily drawn into his net, or deluded by him. What has become of the Three Rings of earth, air, and sky I do not know.[22] Some say they have been carried far over the sea. Others say that hidden Elf-kings still keep them. The dwarves too proved tough and intractable: for they do not lightly endure any obedience or domination (even of their own kind). Nor are they easily made into shadows. With the dwarves the chief power of the Rings was to kindle in their hearts the fire of greed (whence evil has come that has aided Sauron). It is said that the foundation of each of the Seven Great Hoards of the dwarves of old was a golden Ring. But it is said that those hoards are plundered and the dragons have devoured them, and the Rings have perished molten in their fire; yet it is also said that not all the hoards have been broken, and that still some of the Seven Rings are guarded.

'But all the Nine Rings of Men have gone back to Sauron, and borne with them their possessors, kings, warriors, and wizards of old,[23] who became Ring-wraiths and served the maker, and were his most terrible servants. Men indeed have most often been under his dominion, and are now again throughout the middle-earth[24] falling under his power, especially in the East and South of the world, where the Elves are few.'

'Ring-wraiths!' exclaimed Bingo. 'What are they?'

'We will not speak of them now,' said Gandalf. 'Let us not speak of horrible things without need. They belong to the ancient days, and let us hope that they will never again arise. At least Gilgalad accomplished that.'[25]

'Who was Gilgalad?' asked Bingo.

'The one who bereft the Dark Lord of the One Ring,' answered Gandalf. 'He was the last in middle-earth of the great Elf-kings of the high western race, and he made alliance with Orendil[26] King of the Island who came back to the middle-world in those days. But I will not tell all that tale now. One day perhaps you may hear it from one who knows it truly. It is enough to say that they marched against Sauron and besieged him in his tower; and he came forth and wrestled with Gilgalad and Orendil, and was overthrown. But he forsook his bodily shape and fled like a ghost to waste places until he rested in Mirkwood and took shape again in the darkness. Gilgalad and Orendil were both mortally hurt and perished in the land of Mordor; but Isildor son of Orendil cut the One Ring from the finger of Sauron and took it for his own.[27]

'But when he marched back from Mordor, Isildor's host was overwhelmed by Goblins that swarmed down out of the mountains. And it is told that Isildor put on the Ring and vanished from their sight, but they trailed him by slot and scent, until he came to the banks of a wide river. Then Isildor plunged in and swam across, but the Ring betrayed him,[28] and slipped from his hand, and he became visible to his enemies; and they killed him with their arrows.[29] But a fish took the Ring and was filled with a madness, and swam up stream leaping over rocks and up waterfalls until it cast itself upon a bank, and spat out the Ring and died.' Gandalf paused. 'And there,' he said, 'the Ring passed out of knowledge and legend; and even so much of the story is now known and remembered by few. Yet I can now add to it, I think.

'Long after, but still very long ago, there lived by the bank of a stream on the edge of Wilderland a wise clever-handed and quiet-footed little family. . . .

For Gollum's earlier history my father followed the original text (pp. 78–9) very closely indeed, only introducing a slight change of wording here and there: thus Dígol is still Gollum himself, and not his friend. At the end of the passage the words 'and even the Master lost it' become 'and even the maker, when his power had grown again, could learn nothing of it', and the following sentence, about the Necromancer counting his rings and always finding one missing, is of course removed.

Gandalf's discussion of Gollum's mind and motives at the time of Bilbo's encounter with him (still of course based on the original story in *The Hobbit*, see p. 86) also remains very close to the old version (pp. 79–80). There are indeed many small improvements in the phrasing; but only two changes need be noticed. Gandalf's words about the longevity afforded to the possessor of the Ring (p. 79) are thus interestingly extended:

. . . Frightfully wearisome, Bingo, in fact finally tormenting (even if you do not become a Wraith). Only Elves can stand it, and even they fade.

And when Gandalf speaks of 'the unexpected arrival of Bilbo' (p. 80) he now goes on:

. . . You remember how surprised he was, and how soon he began talking of a present, though he gave himself a chance of keeping it if luck went that way. Even so I dare say his old habits might have beaten him in the end, and he might have tried to eat Bilbo, if it had been easy. But I am not sure: I guess he was using the Riddle Game (at which even a Gollum dare hardly cheat, as it is sacred and of immense antiquity) as a kind of toss-up to decide for him. And anyway Bilbo had the sword Sting, if you remember, so it was not easy.

But from the point where Bingo objects that Gollum never gave Bilbo the Ring, for Bilbo had it already, Gandalf's story takes a great step forward, with his announcement that he himself had found Gollum (in the original text there is no explanation of how he knew Gollum's history). I give the next part of the chapter, much of which is in a very rough state, in full.

'I know,' said Gandalf. 'And that is why I said that Gollum's ancestry only partly explained events. There was, of course, something much more mysterious behind the whole affair — something probably quite beyond the design of the Lord of the Rings himself, peculiar to Bilbo and his private Adventure. I can put it no clearer than by saying that *Bilbo was 'meant' to have the Ring*, and that he perhaps got involved in the Quest of the treasure mainly for that reason. In which case you were meant to have it. Which may (or may not) be a comforting thought. And there has also always been a queer fate over the Rings on their own account. They get lost, and turn up in strange places. The One had already slipped once from its owner and betrayed him to death. It had now slipped away from Gollum. But the evil they work according to their maker's design turns often to good that he did not intend, and even to his loss and defeat.[30] And that too may be a comforting thought, or not.'

'I don't find either of your thoughts very encouraging,' said Bingo; 'though I don't really understand what you mean. But how do you come to know or guess so much about Gollum?'

'As for the guessing, or the putting of one and one and one together, much of that has not been very difficult,' said Gandalf. 'The Ring that you had of Bilbo, and Bilbo had of Gollum, is shown by the fire-writing to be the One Ring. And concerning that the tale of Gilgalad and Isildor is known — to the wise. The filling in of the tale of Gollum and fitting it into the gap presents no special difficulty: to one who knows much about the history and the minds and ways of the creatures of middle-earth that he does not tell you. What was the first riddle Gollum asked: do you remember?'

'Yes,' said Bingo, thinking.

> *What has roots that nobody sees,*
> *Is higher than trees,*
> *Up, up it goes,*
> *And yet never grows?*

'More or less right!' said Gandalf. 'Roots and mountains! But as a matter of fact, I have not had to do much guessing from hints of that kind.[31] I know. I know because I found Gollum.'

'You found Gollum!' said Bingo astonished.

'The obvious thing to try to do, surely,' said Gandalf.

'Then what happened after Bilbo left? Do you know that?'

'Not so clearly. What I have told you Gollum was willing to tell; though not of course in the way I have reported it – he thought he was misunderstood and ill-treated, and he was full of tears for himself, and hatred of all other things. But after the Riddle Game he was unwilling to say anything, except in dark hints. One gathered that somehow or other Gollum was going to get his own back, and that people would see if he could be kicked and despised and stuck in a hole, and starved and *robbed*. They might get worse coming their way; for Gollum now had friends, powerful friends. You can imagine the spiteful stuff. He had found out eventually that Bilbo had in some way got "his" Ring, and what his name was.'

'How?' asked Bingo.

'I asked him, but he only leered and chuckled, and said "Gollum issn't deaf iss he, no Gollum, and he hass eyes, hassn't he, yes my preciouss, yes Gollum." But [32] one can imagine various ways in which that might happen. He could, for instance, have overheard the goblins talking about the escape of Bilbo from the gate. And the news of the later events went all over Wilderland, and would give Gollum plenty to think about. Anyway, after having been "robbed and cheated", as he put it, he left the Mountains: the goblins there became few and wary after the Battle; hunting was poor, and the deep places were more than ever dark and lonely. Also the power of the Ring had left him: he was no longer bound by it. He was feeling old, very old, but less timid, though he did not become less malicious.

'One might have expected wind and even the mere shadow of sunlight to kill him pretty quickly. But he was cunning. He could hide from daylight or moonlight, and travel softly and swiftly by night with his long pale eyes – and catch small frightened and unwary things. Indeed he grew for a while stronger with new food and new air. He crept into Mirkwood, which is not surprising.'

'Did you find him there?'

'Yes – I followed him there: he had left a trail of horrible stories behind him, among the beasts and birds and even the Woodmen of Wilderland. He had developed a skill in climbing trees to find nests, and creeping into houses to find cradles. He boasted of it to me.

'But his trail also ran away south, far south of where I actually came upon him – with the help finally of the Wood-elves. He would not explain that. He just grinned and leered, and said *Gollum*, rubbing his horrible hands together gleefully. But I have a suspicion – it is now much more than a suspicion – that he made his slow sneaking way bit by bit long ago down to the land of – *Mordor*,' said Gandalf almost in a whisper. 'Such creatures go naturally that way; and in that land he would soon learn much, and soon himself be discovered, and examined. I think indeed that Gollum is the beginning of our present troubles;[33] for if I guess right, through him the Necromancer discovered what became of the One Ring he had lost. He has even, one may fear, at last heard of the existence of hobbits, and may now be seeking the Shire, if he has not already found out where it is. Indeed I fear that he may even have heard[34] of the humble and long unnoticeable name of – Baggins.'

'But this is terrible!' cried Bingo. 'Far worse than I feared! O Gandalf, what am I to do, for now I am really afraid? What a pity that Bilbo didn't stab the beastly creature, when he said goodbye!'

'What nonsense you do talk sometimes, Bingo!' said Gandalf. 'Pity! It was pity that prevented him. And he could not do so, without doing wrong. It was against the Rules. If he had done so, he would not have had the Ring – the Ring would have had him at once. He would have been enslaved under the Necromancer.'

'Of course, of course,' said Bingo. 'What a thing to say of Bilbo! Dear old Bilbo! But I am frightened – and I cannot feel any pity for that vile Gollum. Do you mean to say that you, and the Elves, let him live on, after all those horrible stories? Now at any rate he is worse than a goblin, and just an enemy.'

'Yes, he deserved to die,' said Gandalf; 'but we did not kill him.

He is very old, and very wretched. The Wood-elves have him in prison, and treat [him] with such kindness as they can find in their wise hearts. They feed him on clean food. But I do not think much can be done to cure him: yet even Gollum might prove useful for good before the end.'[35]

'Well anyway,' said Bingo. 'if Gollum could not be killed, I wish you had not let Bilbo keep the Ring. Why did he? Why did you let him? Did you tell him all this?'

'Yes, I let him,' said Gandalf. 'But at first of course I did not even imagine that it was [one] of the nineteen[36] Rings of Power: I thought he had got nothing more dangerous than one of the lesser magic rings that were once more common – and were used (as their maker intended) chiefly by minor rogues and villains, for mean wickednesses. I was not frightened of Bilbo being affected by *their* power. But when I began to suspect that the matter was more serious than that, I told him as much as my suspicions warranted. He knew that it came in the long run from the Necromancer. But you must remember there was the Ring itself to reckon with. Even Bilbo could not wholly escape the power of the Ruling Ring. He developed – a sentiment. He would keep it as a memento. Frankly – he became rather proud of his Great Adventure, and used to look at the Ring now and again (and oftener as time went on) to warm his memory: it made him feel rather heroic, though he never lost his power of laughing at the feeling.

'But in the end it got a hold of him in that way. He knew eventually that it was giving him "long life", and thinning him. He grew weary of it – "I can't abide it any longer", he said – but to get rid of it was not so easy. He found it hard to bring himself to it. If you think for a moment: it is not really very easy to get rid of the Ring once you have got it.'[37]

From this point the text again follows the old (pp. 81–2) very closely. Bingo now of course draws the Ring out of his pocket 'again', and means to throw it 'back again' into the fire; and Gandalf says (as in FR, p. 70) that 'This Ring at any rate has already passed through your fire and come out unscathed, and even unheated.' Adam Hornblower the Hobbiton smith remains. Gandalf says here that 'you would have to find one of the Cracks of Earth in the depth of the Fiery Mountain, and drop it in there, if you really did wish to destroy it – or to place it out of all reach until the End.' Against 'Cracks of Earth' (the name in the original text, p. 82) my father wrote in the margin, at the same time, '? Cracks of Doom'; at the second occurrence of the name he wrote 'Cracks of Doom', but put 'Earth' above 'Doom'.

The original text is developed and extended from the point where Bingo says 'I really do wish to destroy it' (p. 82):

. . . I cannot think how Bilbo put up with it for so long. And also, I must say, I cannot help wondering why he passed it on to me. I knew, of course, that he had it – though I was the only one who did or does know; but he spoke of it jokingly, and on the only two or three occasions when I ever caught him using it he used it more or less as a joke – especially the last time.'

'Bilbo would: and when your fate has bestowed on you such perilous treasures it is not a bad way to take them – as long as you can do so. But as for passing it on to you: he did so only because he thought you were safe: safe not to misuse it; safe not to let it get into evil hands; safe from its power, for a while; and safe, as an unknown and unimportant hobbit in the heart of the quiet and easily overlooked little Shire, from the – enemy. I promised him, too, to help and advise you, if any difficulty arose. Also, I may say that I did not discover the letters of fire, or guess that this ring was the One Ring, until he had already decided to go away and leave it.[38] And I did not tell him, for then he would not have burdened you, or gone away. But for his own sake, I knew he ought to go. He had had that Ring for 60 years, and it was telling on him, Bingo. You have tried before now to describe to me your own feeling – the stretched feeling.[39] His was much stronger. The Ring would have worn him down in the end. Yet the only sure way of ridding him of it was to let someone else take on the burden, for a while. He is free. But you are his heir. And now that I have (since that time) discovered much more, I know that you have a heavy inheritance. I wish it could be otherwise. But do not blame Bilbo – or me, if you can help it. Let us bear what is laid upon us (if we can). But we must do something soon. The enemy is moving.'

There was a long silence. Gandalf puffed at his pipe in apparent content . . .

The new version then develops the old text (p. 83) almost to the form in FR (pp. 71–2), with Bingo's saying that he had often thought of going off, but imagined it as a kind of holiday, and his sudden strong desire, not communicated to Gandalf, to follow Bilbo and perhaps to find him, and to run out of Bag End there and then. The new text continues:

'My dear Bingo!' said Gandalf. 'Bilbo made no mistake in choosing you as his heir. Yes, I think you will have to go – before long, though not at once or without a little thought and care. And I am not sure you need go alone: not if you know of anyone you could trust, and who would be willing to go by your side – and who you would be willing to take into unknown dangers. But be careful in choosing, and in what you say even to your closest friends. The enemy has many spies, and many ways of hearing.' Suddenly he stopped as if listening.

The remainder of the chapter (the surprising of Sam outside the window, and Gandalf's decision that he should be Bingo's companion – cf. *Queries and Alterations* note 2, p. 221) is almost word for word the final form (FR pp. 72–3), which was reached almost at a stroke[40] and never changed.

## NOTES

1 This passage goes back to the original version of 'A Long-expected Party' (p. 17).

2 This passage goes back to the fourth version of 'A Long-expected Party' (p. 37), and indeed in part to the third (p. 29), when Bilbo was Bingo's father.

3 *Odo Bolger:* hitherto Odo has been Odo Took – or, at least, he was still Odo Took when his surname was last mentioned, which was in the original text of the 'Bree' chapter (p. 141, note 5). At the beginning, Odo Took could tell Bingo not to be 'Bolger-like' (p. 49); but perhaps my father felt that Odo had developed strong Bolger traits as the story proceeded. He retains, however, a Took mother.

4 This passage, from 'Merry was the son of Caradoc Brandybuck', was placed within square brackets, apparently at the time of writing. The genealogy (part of which has appeared before, p. 100) is of course very different from the final form, but when it is seen that Frodo Took occupies the place in the 'tree' afterwards taken by Peregrin Took (Pippin) it becomes at once much closer. In the following table the names in LR (Appendix C, *Took of Great Smials*) are given in brackets.

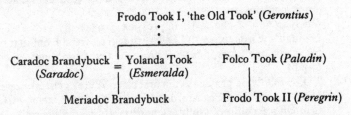

Frodo Took I, 'the Old Took' (*Gerontius*)

Caradoc Brandybuck = Yolanda Took   Folco Took (*Paladin*)
(*Saradoc*)            (*Esmeralda*)

Meriadoc Brandybuck              Frodo Took II (*Peregrin*)

Since Caradoc Brandybuck, Merry's father, is here said to be Bingo's cousin, it can be presumed that the genealogy given in the family tree of the Brandybucks in LR was already present, i.e. Caradoc was the son of Old Rory, the brother of Bingo's mother Primula. That Rory Brandybuck was Bingo's uncle is never actually said in LR, though of course it appears in the family tree, but it does appear in rejected versions of the Farmer Maggot episode (pp. 289, 296), and again later (pp. 385–6).

Merry Brandybuck and Frodo Took are the great-great-grandsons of the Old Took, as are Merry and Pippin in LR.

5   This passage goes back to the third version of 'A Long-expected Party' (p. 34). '500 pieces of gold' was later changed to '500 double-dragons (gold pieces of the highest value in the Shire)'; but this was not taken up into the next version of 'Ancient History', which returns to '500 gold pieces'. *sixty years:* 111 less 51 (see p. 31).

6   *Gandalf's visits to Hobbiton.* In *The Tale of Years* (LR Appendix B) Bilbo's Farewell Party took place in 3001; Gandalf visited Frodo in the years 3004–8, the last visit being in the autumn of 3008; and returned finally in April 3018 (after 9 and a half years): Frodo's 50th birthday was in September of that year, when he left Bag End. Cf. FR p. 55.

In the present text there was likewise a gap of three years after the Party before Gandalf came again; but then he came once or twice every year, with one gap of two years, till the 14th year after the Party, when Bingo was 47, and after that 'frequently'. The passage was subsequently rewritten to read:

    . . . seeing that Bingo was still quite settled. After that he returned several times, until he suddenly disappeared. Bingo heard no news of him between the 7th and 14th years after Bilbo's departure, when Gandalf suddenly reappeared one winter's night. After that the wizard came frequently and stayed longer.

For the year in which the conversation in 'Ancient History' took place (it was in the month of April, p. 254) see note 8.

7   This is a reference to *The Hobbit*, Chapter XIX 'The Last Stage':
    . . . they had at last driven the Necromancer from his dark hold in the south of Mirkwood.

    'Ere long now,' Gandalf was saying, 'the Forest will grow somewhat more wholesome. The North is freed from that horror for many an age.

On his copy of the sixth impression (1954) my father changed Gandalf's words to read: The North *will be* freed from that horror for many *long years, I hope.* This is the text from the third edition (1966).

The following passage is the first clear, if very general, statement of where the Land of Mordor lay; see p. 218, note 17. Cf. also Gandalf's account of Gollum's journey (p. 264): 'his trail also ran away south, far south of where I actually came upon him' (which was in Mirkwood).

8   *in the spring of Bingo's 49th? 50th? year.* At the beginning of the next chapter in this 'phase' it is said that Bingo decided to leave Bag End on September 22nd 'in this (his 50th) year.'

9 My father first made the miller's son Tom Tunnelly, changing it as he wrote to Tom Sandyman; *Tom* was changed to *Ted* in pencil, before the chapter was finished, for *Ted* appears, as first written, at the end of it. See p. 249, note 33.

10 It is a very old conception that appears here; see II.323 and note 44. – Bingo describes the Elf-towers to his companions on the walk to Farmer Maggot's: he says that he saw them once, shining white in the light of the Moon (p. 93). Trotter at Bree calls them the West Towers (pp. 155, 159).

11 On Gandalf's visits to the land of the Necromancer see p. 85, note 12.

12 Here my father wrote: 'Bingo had never seen it on any finger but his own forefinger', but at once struck it out.

13 My father first wrote 'One ring to bind them', changing it in pencil to 'and in the darkness bind them', which is the form as written from the first in the whole verse that immediately follows.

14 *The text of the verse of the Rings.* My father's original workings for this verse are extant. The first complete form reads:

> *Nine for the Elven-kings under moon and star,*
> *Seven for the Dwarf-lords in their halls of stone,*
> *Three for Mortal Men that wander far,*
> *One for the Dark Lord on his dark throne*
> *In the Land of Mor-dor where the shadows are.*
> *One Ring to rule them all, One Ring to find them,*
> *One Ring to bring them all and in the darkness bind them*
> *In the Land of Mor-dor where the shadows are.*

He was at this time still uncertain as to the disposition of the Rings among the different peoples. The verse in the text of the present chapter as first written also had 'Nine rings for the Elven-kings' and 'Three for Mortal Men' (in the original text, p. 78, 'the Elves had many', and 'Men had three rings', but 'others they found in secret places cast away by the elf-wraiths'). But he wrote in the margin (in ink and at the same time as the verse itself) '3' against 'Nine' and '9' against 'Three', subsequently changing the words in the verse itself: see note 22.

Another preliminary version of the verse has:

> *Twelve for Mortal Men doomed to die,*
> *Nine for the Dwarf-lords in their halls of stone,*
> *Three for the Elven-kings of earth, sea, and sky,*
> *One for the Dark Lord on his dark throne.*

'Twelve' and 'Nine' were then changed to 'Nine' and 'Seven'. On there being at one time twelve Black Riders see p. 196. In the text of the chapter (p. 260) the Three Rings are called the Rings 'of earth, air, and sky'.

15   The text as first written here was 'and now that he knows or guesses where it is he desires so greatly.'

16   My father wrote here: 'In ancient days the Necromancer [servant of ???] the Dark Lord Sauron.' The brackets and queries were put in at the time of writing or very soon after. I can only explain this on the assumption that he was momentarily thinking of Morgoth as the Dark Lord, before he wrote the name Sauron; but it is odd that he did not simply strike out the words 'servant of'.

17   Against this passage my father wrote in the margin: 'Ring-wraiths later' (see p. 260). In the original text (p. 78, and cf. the draft on which that was based, p. 75) the Wraiths are mentioned at this point.

18   My father wrote 'Nine, Seven, Three, and One', reversing 'Nine' and 'Three' in pencil. – Here appears explicitly for the first time the distinction between the lesser Rings and the Rings of Power.

19   The text as written, but probably changed immediately, was: 'but could see both the world under the sun and the phantom world [> the world of shadow] in which the invisible creatures of the Lord moved.'

20   With this account of the relation of the power of the Rings to the innate qualities of those who bore them, and of the potency of the One Ring in the hand of its maker, compare *Queries and Alterations*, note 12 (p. 227), where the idea of the Ruling Ring first explicitly appears.

21   Cf. p. 212, and *Queries and Alterations*, note 10 (p. 225).

22   Here the *Three* Rings of the Elves appear in the text as first written (and the *Nine* Rings of Men in the next paragraph): see note 14. In the draft of the Ring-verse given at the end of note 14 the Three Rings are 'of earth, sea, and sky', whereas here they are 'of earth, air, and sky.'

23   *wizards:* cf. p. 211, where Gandalf at Rivendell likewise includes 'wizards' among the servants of the Dark Lord.

24   *the middle-earth* was changed from *the middle-world*, which is used earlier in this passage and again subsequently.

25   The meaning appears to be that after the loss of the Ruling Ring to the Necromancer, the Ring-wraiths could no longer function as his servants; they were not definitively destroyed, but they had no effective existence. Gandalf was soon to be proved wrong in this opinion, of course; and it may be that my father introduced it here to explain Gandalf's failure to take them into account. In FR he is less confident: 'It is many a year since the Nine walked abroad. Yet who knows? As the Shadow grows once more, they too may walk again.'

26   The name of the King of Men was first written *Valandil*; above this my father wrote *E* and *Orendil*. The next part of Gandalf's story was constantly changed in the act of composition, and at subsequent occurrences the name of the King varies between *Valandil* >

*Orendil/Elendil, Elendil > Orendil*, and then *Orendil* unchanged; I read *Orendil* throughout. For previous hesitation over the name see p. 174 note 25 and p. 197 note 3.

27 Here my father first wrote: 'but ere he fell Gilgalad cut the One Ring from the hand finger of Sauron, and gave it to Ithildor that stood by, but Ithildor took it for his own.' This was changed at the time of writing to the text given. *hand finger* was left thus; I read *finger* because that is the word used in the next text of this chapter. – *Ithildor* was changed to *Isildor* at each occurrence until the last in this passage, where *Isildor* was the form first written. See note 29.

28 The original reading here was: 'but the Ring [or >] and his fate betrayed him'.

29 The story of the One Ring now moves further. In the original text (p. 78) it was simply that the Ring 'fell from the hand of an elf as he swam across a river; and it betrayed him, for he was flying from pursuit in the old wars, and he became visible to his enemies, and the goblins slew him.' In *Queries and Alterations* note 12 (p. 226) a new element was proposed: that the Ring was 'taken from the Lord himself when Gilgalad wrestled with him, and taken by a flying Elf'; the implication clearly being that Gilgalad took it (as said at first in the present text, see note 27). Now the Elf becomes Isildor son of Orendil (Elendil: note 26).

30 This passage, from 'And there has also always been a queer fate', was enclosed in brackets with a query; and the last sentence, 'But the evil they work . . .', additionally enclosed in double brackets with a double query. The sentences immediately following (Gandalf's 'And that too may be a comforting thought, or not', and the first part of Bingo's reply) are a pencilled addition. But it is not clear to me why Bingo should be discouraged by the suggestion that the evil wrought by the Rings could turn to good and against the design of their maker.

31 Bingo's version has slight deviations from the text in *The Hobbit*. – It is not very evident what Gandalf had deduced from Gollum's first riddle.

32 In place of this passage, from 'He had found out eventually', the text as first written had (much as in the original version, p. 80): 'I think it is certain that Gollum knew after a time that Bilbo had in some way got "his" Ring. One can imagine . . .'
With the pencilled extension Gandalf's explanation of how Gollum knew that the hobbit had got the Ring is extended to cover the fact that Gollum also found out what his name was. But this is odd, since in the original story in *The Hobbit* as in the revised version Bilbo told Gollum his name: '"What iss he, my precious?" whisperered Gollum. "I am Mr Bilbo Baggins . . ."' See further note 34 (and cf. FR p. 66).

33 This phrase of Gandalf's, 'I think indeed that Gollum is the

beginning of our present troubles', is repeated from the original text (p. 81), and here as there seems to refer to the fact that the Dark Lord was known to Gandalf to be seeking the Ring in the direction of the Shire. But it is still not really explained what kind of searching could lead Gandalf to describe it as 'our present trouble', since he knew nothing of the Black Riders (see *Queries and Alterations*, p. 224). He can hardly be referring to those things mentioned earlier in the chapter (p. 253): Men moving North and West, goblins multiplying, new kinds of trolls; for these were surely large manifestations of the growing power of the Dark Lord, rather than of the search for the Ring.

34   Here follows: '(for his ears are keen and his spies legion)', marked in pencil for deletion. This change perhaps goes with the puzzling addition referred to in note 32, where Gandalf suggests that Gollum had eventually found out Bilbo's name; for in that case, if Gollum had indeed been to Mordor, he himself could have told the Necromancer that 'Baggins' had taken the Ring.

35   From this point the text is written in faint pencil.

36   Above 'nineteen' is pencilled '20'. This is the first occurrence of the terms 'Rings of Power'.

37   From this point the text is again in ink, a good clear manuscript to the end of the chapter.

38   The meaning must surely be that Gandalf *had* 'discovered the letters of fire' on the Ring before Bilbo left Hobbiton; which is curious, since Gandalf also says that he did not tell Bilbo, and it is hard to imagine him conducting the test without Bilbo knowing of it. In FR (p. 65), when Frodo asked him when he discovered the fire-writing, he replied: 'Just now in this room, of course. But I expected to find it. I have come back from dark journeys and long search to make that final test.' Gandalf's words on p. 256 could be taken to mean that he did not know for certain until now: 'I do not yet know quite all. Give me the Ring a minute.' But they cannot mean this; and he refers (p. 262) to the fire-writing on the Ring as if it had been one of the main pieces of evidence in his deduction of the story which he now told to Bingo.

My father later pencilled an 'X' in the margin of the text here, and scribbled 'did not know until recently'.

39   See p. 252.

40   The original drafting for the episode is extant, scribbled faintly at the end of the manuscript of the original version of the chapter, and is naturally less finished; but already in this draft the final text is fully present except in details of expression.

# XVI
# DELAYS ARE DANGEROUS

From 'Ancient History' my father proceeded to the revision of the original second chapter, which had been given the title 'Three's Company and Four's More' (p. 49); this new version becomes Chapter III, but was given no title. Later, he scribbled in at the head of the text 'Delays are Dangerous' (which is the title *ab initio* of the following version of the chapter), and it is convenient to adopt this here.

Some exceedingly rough and fluid notes – the continuation of those mentioned at the beginning of the last chapter, p. 250 – are all that exist by way of preparatory writing for this revision. I have already noticed (p. 250) that the story of Bingo's dinner-party for Merry, Frodo Took, and Odo Bolger on the eve of departure was devised here, and that against this my father wrote 'Sam Gamgee to replace Odo' (these notes preceded the writing of 'Ancient History', where Sam Gamgee first emerged). But Odo could not be got rid of so easily. The notes continue:

Gandalf was *supposed to come to party* but did *not* turn up. Bingo waits till Friday [September 23] but foolishly did not wait any longer, as Sackville-Bagginses threaten to turn him out: but sets off on Friday night. Gives out he is going to stay with Merry and return to his Brandybuck relations.

A rejected suggestion that Odo remained at Hobbiton 'to give news to Gandalf' shows my father already pondering this question, which after a long history of change would ultimately lead to Fredegar Bolger remaining at Crickhollow (FR p. 118). In these notes a Brandybuck with the Arthurian name of Lanorac (changed from Bercilak), a cousin of Merry's, 'has been ordered to have all ready' in Buckland; and there is a suggestion for the story after they leave Buckland and enter the Old Forest: 'Frodo wants to come but is told *no*: to give news to Gandalf. Merry says nothing – but *does* come: locks door and throws key over hedge.' With this cf. *Queries and Alterations*, note 2 (p. 221): 'Frodo says goodbye at Bucklebury. Only Merry and Bingo ride on into exile – because *Merry insists*. Bingo originally intended to go alone' (this was written before Sam Gamgee entered).

The text of the new version of this chapter is the most complicated document yet encountered. It begins as manuscript, in which part of the narrative is in two variant forms, and then turns back to the original typescript (given in full on pp. 49–65), which was heavily corrected in two forms (with different inks to cover different versions): some of the more extensive changes are on inserted slips. At the end my father

abandoned the old typescript and concluded the chapter in a new
manuscript – the first part of it in three versions. To present the whole
complex in this book is obviously impossible, and is in any case in no way
necessary for the understanding of the development of the narrative.

The initial portion in manuscript extends as far as the beginning of the
hobbits' walk on the first night ('They went very quietly over fields and
along hedgerows and the borders of coppices, until night fell', p. 50), and
the opening of the chapter presents an entirely new narrative. Leaving
aside for the moment the passage existing in variant forms, the new text
while very rough reaches in all essentials the final form in FR, pp. 74–80.
There are many differences still in wording, and the chapter begins with
the local gossip about the sale of Bag End and then proceeds to Bingo's
discussion with Gandalf about his departure, rather than the other way
about;[1] but differences of substance are few and mostly slight. More
emphasis is placed on the fact that the 22nd of September was in that year
again a Thursday (as it was in FR, p. 77): 'that seemed to [Bingo's] fancy
to mark the date as the proper one for setting out to follow Bilbo.'
Gandalf's tone to Bingo is a bit grimmer, and has more asperity; and he
does not refer to the possibility that it may, or may not, be Bingo's task to
find the Cracks of Doom. His parting words to him are significantly
different from what he says in FR; and Bingo's state of mind on the eve of
his own departure is given a different emphasis. I give here a portion of
the text, taking it up from the point where Gandalf says that the direction
which Bingo takes when he leaves Hobbiton should not be known (FR
p. 74, at bottom).

'Well now,' said Bingo, 'do you know I have mostly thought just
about going, and have never decided on the direction! For where
shall I go, and by what shall I steer, and what is to be my quest?
This will indeed be the opposite of Bilbo's adventure: setting out
without any known destination, and to get rid of a treasure, not to
find one.'

'And to go *there* but not come *back again*, likely enough,' added
Gandalf grimly.

'That I know,' said Bingo, pretending not to be impressed. 'But
seriously, in what direction shall I start?'

'Towards danger, but not too rashly, nor too straight towards
it,' answered Gandalf. 'Make first for Rivendell, if you will at least
take that much advice. After that we shall see – if you ever get
there: the Road is not as easy as it was.'

'Rivendell!' said Bingo. 'Very good. That will please Sam.' He
did not add that it pleased him too; and that though he had not
decided, he had often thought of making for the house of Elrond;
if only because he thought that perhaps Bilbo, after he had become
free again, had chosen that way too.

The decision to go Eastwards directed Bingo's later plans. It was for this reason that he gave out that he was removing to Buckland, and actually did ask his Brandybuck cousins, Merry and Lanorac and the rest, to look out for a little place for him to live in.[2] In the meantime he went on much as usual, and the summer passed. Gandalf had gone off again. But he was invited to the farewell party, and had promised to arrive on the day before, or at latest on the 22nd itself. 'Don't go till you see me, Bingo,' he said, as he took his leave one wet dark evening in May. 'I may have news, and useful information about the Road. And I may want to come with you.'[3]

The autumn came on. No news came from Gandalf. There began to be signs of activity at Bag-End. Two covered carts went off laden. They were understood to be conveying such furniture as Mr Baggins had not sold to the Sackville-Bagginses to his new house in Buckland by way of the Brandywine Bridge. Odo Bolger, Merry Brandybuck, and Frodo Took were staying there with Bingo. The four of them seemed to be busy packing and the hole was all upside-down. On Wednesday September 21 Bingo began to look out anxiously for Gandalf, but there was no sign of him. His birthday morning September 22 dawned, as fair and clear as it had for Bilbo's party long ago (as it now seemed to Bingo). But still Gandalf did not appear. In the evening Bingo gave his farewell party. The absence of Gandalf rather worried Bingo and a little damped his spirits, which had been steadily rising – as every cool and misty autumn morning brought him closer to the day of his going. The only wrench now was parting from his young friends. The danger did not seem so threatening. He wanted to be off – at once. Everyone had been told that he was leaving for Bucklebury as soon as possible after his birthday. The Sackville-Bagginses got possession after midnight on the 23rd. All the same, he wanted to see Gandalf first. But his three friends were in high spirits . . .

From the end of Bingo's birthday dinner to the beginning of the hobbits' night walk the new text is almost the same as that in FR (pp. 77–80), apart from the different hobbits present (and still leaving aside the part existing in variant forms). The third cart, bearing 'the remaining and more valuable things', went off as in FR on the morning of the 23rd; at first Odo Bolger was said to be in charge of this, but he was changed, apparently at once, to Merry Brandybuck. (In FR Merry was accompanied by Fredegar Bolger, and my father queried in the margin here: 'Merry and Odo?'). Now enters the story of Bingo's overhearing Gaffer Gamgee talking (in almost the same words as in FR) to a stranger at the end of Bagshot Row: the first germ of this has been seen in *Queries and Alterations*, note 3 (p. 222). The only real difference is that the old discussion among the hobbits (p. 49) whether to walk far or not is still present, Odo disagreeing with Frodo and Bingo; but there are now four of them, and Bingo asks Sam for his opinion:

'Well, sir,' he answered, taking off his hat and looking up at the sky, 'I do guess that it may be pretty warm tomorrow. And walking in the sun, even at this time o' year, with a load on your back, can be wearisome, like. I votes with Mr Frodo, if you ask me.'

The variant section was written continuously with the preceding narrative – that is to say, it is the story as my father first intended to tell it, and the other version was written subsequently, at first as an alternative. The divergence begins after Merry's departure for Buckland on Friday September 23, Bingo's last day at Bag End.

After lunch people began to arrive – some by invitation, others brought by rumour and curiosity. They found the door open, and Bingo on the mat in the hall waiting to greet them. Inside the hall was piled an assortment of packages, bric-a-brac and small articles of furniture. On every package and item there was a label tied. . . .

On the manuscript my father wrote later that 'this variant depending on shortening in Chapter I and the transference of parting gifts etc. to III' was now rejected. The shortening of Chapter I proposed is in fact the short variant of the story of the aftermath of Bilbo's party which has been described on pp. 241–2: as I noted there, 'the entire "business" of the presents, and the invasion of Bag End, was in this variant removed', for it was now to be transferred to *Bingo's* departure – or at least, was under the option of being so transferred. Thus a further twist is given to the serpentine history of this element in *The Lord of the Rings*: for what is involved is not of course a simple reversion to the story as it was at the end of the 'first phase' of 'A Long-expected Party', where also the gifts were Bingo's, not Bilbo's. The new idea was that the gifts,[4] the invasion of Bag End, the ejection of the hobbits excavating in the pantry, and the fight with Sancho Proudfoot (his adversary here being Cosimo Sackville-Baggins,[5] supported by his mother, who broke her umbrella on Sancho's head) – that all this took place not after the great Birthday Party (which was now Bilbo's), but after *Bingo's* own discreet birthday party before *his* departure.

It is possible and even probable that my father's intention in this was to reduce the element of Hobbiton comedy that confronts the reader at the outset, and introduce sooner, in 'Ancient History', the very much weightier matters that had come into being since 'A Long-expected Party' was first written.

In this version the story of Bingo's walking a little way from Bag End, and so hearing Gaffer Gamgee talking to the Black Rider, was not yet present; and when he has sent Sam off with the key to his father, he leaves by himself. There is no mention of Odo Bolger and Frodo Took before the variant text ends, with Bilbo going down the garden path, jumping the fence at the bottom, and passing into the twilight. I cannot say for certain whether this is significant or not. It seems unlikely to be a mere casual oversight; but if it is not, it means presumably that my father was contemplating a wholly new course for the story: Bingo and Sam journeying through the Shire alone. He had certainly contemplated something of the sort earlier. However this may be, nothing came of it; and he passed on at once to the second version of this part of the narrative (the form in FR), where Bingo after listening to Gaffer Gamgee talking to the stranger returns to Bag End and finds Odo and Frodo (Pippin in FR) sitting on their packs in the porch.

Effectively, then, the third chapter of FR, as far as the departure of Bingo (Frodo) from Bag End, was now achieved. My father here, as I have said, turned back to the original typescript, and used it as the physical basis for his new text until near the end of the chapter. He emended it in different inks, and added this note on the typescript: *Corrections in black are for any version. Those in red are for the revised version (with Bilbo as party-giver and including Sam).*[6] In the new material, corrections and additions, he distinguished very carefully between the two types of change: in one case he wrote 'red emendation' against the first part of a new passage, and 'black emendation' against the next part, continuous with the first (the passage is given in note 11, and the reason for the distinction is very clear). It is hard to see why he should have gone to all this trouble, unless at this stage he was still (remarkably enough) uncertain about the new story, with 'Bilbo as party-giver and including Sam', and saw the possibility of returning to the old.

As I have said, the presentation of the results of this procedure here is impossible,[7] and unnecessary even if possible. The effect of all the emendations is to bring the original version very close indeed to the form in FR (pp. 80 ff.). In places the new version is a halfway house between the two, and in the latter part the corrections are less thoroughgoing, but only here and there is there anything of narrative importance to note; and in what follows it can be assumed unless the contrary is said that the FR text was already present in all particulars other than the choice of phrasing. But the hobbits are now four: Bingo, Frodo Took, Odo Bolger, and Sam Gamgee, so that there is in this respect also an intervening stage here between the original story (where there are three, Bingo, Frodo Took, and Odo Took) and FR (where there are again only three, but a different three, Frodo Baggins, Peregrin Took, and Sam

Gamgee), and some variation between the versions in the attribution of remarks to different characters (on this matter see p. 70). But things said by Sam in FR are said by him in this text also.[8]

At the beginning of this part of the chapter, where the old text (p. 50) had: 'They were now in Tookland; and they began to climb into the Green Hill Country south of Hobbiton', the new reads: 'They were now in Tookland and going southwards; but a mile or two further on they crossed the main road from Much Hemlock (in the Hornblower country) to Bywater and Brandywine Bridge. Then they struck eastward and began to climb . . .'[9] Beside this my father wrote: '?Michel Delving (the chief town of the Shire back west on the White Downs).' This is the first appearance of Michel Delving, and of the White Downs (see p. 295). 'Much Hemlock' echoes the name Much Wenlock in Shropshire (*Much* 'Great', as *Michel*).

The Woody End is not called 'a wild corner of the Eastfarthing' – the 'Farthings' had not yet been devised – but it is added that 'Not many of them [hobbits] lived in that part.'

The verse *The Road goes ever on and on*, now ascribed to Bingo and not to Frodo Took, is still as in the original version (p. 53).[10]

A slight difference from FR is present at the first appearance of the Black Rider on the road (old version p. 54):

Odo and Frodo ran quickly to the left, and down into a little hollow not far from the road. There they lay flat. Bingo hesitated for a second: curiosity or some other impulse was struggling with his desire to hide. Sam waited for his master to move. The sound of hoofs drew nearer. 'Get down, Sam!' said Bingo, just in time. They threw themselves flat in a patch of long grass behind a tree that overshadowed the road.[11]

In the discussion that followed the departure of the first Black Rider my father retained at this time the old version (p. 54), in which Frodo Took told of his encounter with a Black Rider in the north of the Shire:

. . . I haven't seen one of that Kind in our Shire for years.'

'There are Men about, all the same,' said Bingo; 'and I have heard many reports of strange folk on our borders, and within them, of late. Down in the south Shire they have had some trouble with Big People, I am told. But I have heard of nothing like this rider.'

'I have though,' said Frodo, who had listened intently to Bingo's description of the Black Rider. 'I remember now something I had quite forgotten. I was walking away up in the North Moor – you know, right up on the northern borders of the Shire –

this very summer, when a tall black-cloaked rider met me. He was riding south, and he stopped and spoke, though he did not seem able to speak our language very well; he asked me if I knew whether there were any folk called Baggins in those parts. I thought it very queer at the time; and I had a queer uncomfortable feeling, too. I could not see any face under his hood. I said *no*, not liking the look of him. As far as I heard, he never found his way to Hobbiton and the Baggins country.'

'Begging your pardon,' put in Sam suddenly, 'but he found his way to Hobbiton all right, him or another like him. Anyway it's from Hobbiton as this here Black Rider comes – and I know where he's going to.'

'What do you mean?' said Bingo, turning sharply. 'Why didn't you speak up before?'

Sam's report of the Gaffer's account to him of the Rider who came to Hobbiton is exactly as in FR, p. 85. Then follows:

'Your father can't be blamed anyway,' said Bingo. 'But I should have taken more care on the road, if you had told me this before. I wish I had waited for Gandalf,' he muttered; 'but perhaps that would have only made matters worse.'

'Then you know or guess something about the rider?' said Frodo, who had caught the muttered words. 'What is he?'

'I don't know, and I would rather not guess,' said Bingo. 'But I don't believe either this rider (or yours, or Sam's – if they are all different) was really one of the Big People, not an ordinary Man, I mean. I wish Gandalf was here; but now the most we can hope is that he will come quick to Bucklebury. Whoever would have expected a quiet walk from Hobbiton to Buckland to turn out so queer. I had no idea that I was letting you folk in for anything dangerous.'

'Dangerous?' said Frodo. 'So you think it is dangerous, do you? You are rather close, aren't you, Uncle Bingo? Never mind – we shall get your secret out of you some time. But if it is dangerous, then I am glad we are with you.'

'Hear, hear!' said Odo. 'But what is the next thing to do? Shall we go on at once, or stay here and have some food? . . .

My father still retained the development (see pp. 55–6 and note 11) that a Black Rider came past, and briefly stopped beside, the great hollow tree in which the hobbits sat, and only changed this story at its end:

. . . We are probably making a fuss about nothing [said Odo]. This second rider, at any rate, was very likely only a wandering stranger who has got lost; and if he met us, he would just ask us the way to Buckland or Brandywine Bridge, and ride on.'

'What if he stops us and asks if we know where Mr Baggins of Bag-end is?' said Frodo.

'Give him a true answer,' said Bingo. 'Either say: *Back in Hobbiton*, where there are hundreds; or say *Nowhere*. For Mr Bingo Baggins has left Bag-end, and not yet found any other home. Indeed I think he has vanished; here and now I become Mr Hill of Faraway.'

An alternative version is provided:

'What if he stops us and asks if we know where Mr Baggins of Bag-end is?' said Frodo.

'Tell him that he has vanished!' said Odo. 'After all one Baggins of Bag-end has vanished, and how should we know that it is not old Bilbo that he wants to pay a belated call on? Bilbo made some queer friends in his travels, by his own account.'

Bingo looked quickly at Odo. 'That is an idea,' he said. 'But I hope we shall not be asked that question; and if we are, I have a feeling the silence will be the best answer. Now let us get on. I am glad the road is winding.'

This entire element was removed in FR (p. 86).

When the singing of the Elves is heard (old version p. 58) Bingo still attributes to Bilbo his knowledge that there were sometimes Elves in the Woody End (cf. the passage in 'Ancient History', p. 253), and he says that they wander into the Shire in spring and autumn 'out of their own lands far beyond the river'; in FR (p. 88) Frodo knows independently of Bilbo that Elves may be met with in the Woody End, and says that they come 'out of their own lands away beyond the Tower Hills.' The conception of Elvish lands west of the Shire was of course fully present at this time: cf. Sam's words about Elves 'going to the harbours, out away West, away beyond the Towers' (p. 254). The hymn to Elbereth has the last emendation needed to bring it to the final form (see p. 59): *cold* to *bright* in the second line of the second verse. It is still said to be sung 'in the secret elf-tongue'. At its end, Bingo speaks of the High Elves as Frodo does in FR (p. 89), though without saying 'They spoke the name of Elbereth!' – thus it is not explained how he knows they are High Elves.[12]

Odo's unfortunate remark ('I suppose we shall get a really good bed and supper?') is retained, and Bingo's greeting that Bilbo had taught him, 'The stars shine on the hour of our meeting', remains only in translation. Gildor in his reply refers to Bingo's being 'a scholar in the elf-tongue', changed from 'the elf-latin' (p. 60), where FR has 'the Ancient

Tongue'. It is still the Moon, and not the autumn stars, that is seen in the sky; and the different recollections by the hobbits of the meal eaten with the Elves are retained from the old text, with the addition of the passage about Sam (FR p. 92).

From this point my father abandoned the old typescript, and though returning to it just at the end continued the text in manuscript. The beginning of Bingo's conversation with Gildor is extant in three forms. All three begin as in FR, p. 92 ('They spoke of many things, old and new'), but in the first Gildor goes on from 'The secret will not reach the Enemy from us' with 'But why did you not go before?' – the first thing that he says to Bingo in the original version ('Why did you choose this moment to set out?', p. 62). Bingo replies with a very brief reference to his divided mind about leaving the Shire, and then Gildor explains him to himself:

'That I can understand,' said Gildor. 'Half your heart wished to go, but the other half held you back; for its home was in the Shire, and its delight in bed and board and the voices of friends, and in the changing of the gentle seasons among the fields and trees. But since you are a hobbit that half is the stronger, as it was even in Bilbo. What has made it surrender?'

'Yes, I am an ordinary hobbit, and so I always shall be, I imagine,' said Bingo. 'But a most un-hobbitlike fate has been laid upon me.'

'Then you are not an ordinary hobbit,' said Gildor, 'for otherwise that could not be so. But the half that is plain hobbit will suffer much I fear from being forced to follow the other half which is worthy of the strange fate, until it too becomes worthy (and yet remains hobbit). For that must be the purpose of your fate, or the purpose of that part of your fate which concerns you yourself. The hobbit half that loves the Shire is not to be despised but it has to be trained, and to rediscover the changing seasons and voices of friends when they have been lost.'

Here the text ends. The second of these abandoned versions is nearer to FR, but has Gildor speak severely about Bingo's lateness on the road:

'Has Gandalf told you nothing?'

'Nothing about such creatures.'

'Is it not by his advice, then, that you have left your home? Did he not even urge you to make haste?'

'Yes. He wished me to go sooner in the year. He said that delay might prove dangerous; and I begin to fear that it has.'

'Why did you not go before?'

Bingo then speaks about his two 'halves', though without comment, moves into an explanation of why he lingered till autumn, and speaks of his dismay at the danger that is already threatening.

The third text is very close to and quite largely word for word the same as the final form until near the end of the conversation, where the matter though essentially the same is somewhat differently arranged. Gildor's advice about taking companions is more explicit than in FR ('Take such friends as are trusty and willing', p. 94): here he says 'If there are any whom you can wholly trust, and who are willing to share your peril, take them with you.' He is referring to Bingo's present companions; for he goes on (much as in the old version, p. 64): 'They will protect you. I think it likely that your three companions have already helped you to escape: the Riders did not know that they were with you, and their presence has for the time being confused the scent.' But at the very end there occurs this passage:

. . . In this meeting there may be more than chance; but the purpose is not clear to me, and I fear to say too much. But' – and he paused and looked intently at Bingo – 'have you perhaps Bilbo's ring with you?'

'Yes, I have,' said Bingo, taken aback.

'Then I will add this last word. If a Rider approaches or pursues you hard – do not use the ring to escape from his search. I guess that the ring will help him more than you.'

'More mysteries!' said Bingo. 'How can a ring that makes me invisible help a Black Rider to find me?'

'I will answer only this,' said Gildor: 'the ring came in the beginning from the Enemy, and was not made to delude his servants.'

'But Bilbo used his ring to escape from goblins, and evil creatures,' said Bingo.

'Black Riders are not goblins,' said the Elf. 'Ask no more of me. But my heart forebodes that ere all is ended you Bingo son of Drogo will know more of these fell things than Gildor Inglorion. May Elbereth protect you!'

'You are far worse than Gandalf,' cried Bingo; 'and I am now more completely terrified than I have ever been in my life. But I am deeply grateful to you.'

The end of the chapter is virtually the same in the old version, the present text, and FR; but now Gildor adds the salutation: 'and may the stars shine upon the end of your road.'

# NOTES

1   The different arrangement of the opening of the chapter introduces Bingo's intention to go and live in Buckland *before* it actually arose as a result of his conversation with Gandalf. It may be that my father afterwards reversed the order of these narrative elements in order to avoid this.

2   This passage, from 'and actually did ask his Brandybuck cousins', was struck out in pencil and replaced by the following:

> With the help of his Brandybuck cousin Merry he chose and bought a little house [*added subsequently:* at Crickhollow] in the country behind Bucklebury, and began to make preparations for a removal.

3   Gandalf's words were changed in pencil thus:

> 'I shall want to see you before you set out, Bingo,' he said, as he took his leave one wet dark evening in May. 'I may have news, and useful information about the Road.' Bingo was not clear whether Gandalf intended to go with him to Rivendell or not.

4   There is no new list of presents in this variant: my father contented himself with a reference to the latest version of 'A Long-expected party', which was to be 'suitably emended' (p. 247, note 21).

5   The Sackville-Bagginses' son now first appears. It is said in both variants that Lobelia 'and her pimply son Cosimo (and his over-shadowed wife Miranda) lived at Bag-end for a long while after-wards / for many a year after.' Lobelia was in both versions 92 years old at this time, and had had to wait seventy-seven years (as in FR) for Bag-end, which makes her a grasping fifteen year old when Bilbo came back at the end of *The Hobbit* to find her measuring his rooms; in FR she was a hundred years old, and in the second of these variant versions '92' is changed to '102'. In FR her son is 'sandy-haired Lotho', and no wife is named.

6   The corrections are in fact in blue, black, and red inks. I have said earlier (p. 48 and note 1) that those in black ink belong to a very early stage of revision. Those in blue and red were made at the present stage; but in his note on the subject my father no doubt meant by 'corrections in black' to include all those that were not in red.

7   I give an example, however, to show the nature of the procedure (original version p. 51):

> 'The wind's in the West,' said Odo. 'If we go down the other side of this hill we are climbing, we ought to find a spot fairly dry and sheltered.'

The red ink corrections are given here in italics; other changes from the original text are in black (actually blue, see note 6) ink.

> 'The wind's in the West,' said *Sam*. 'If we go down the other side of this hill we are climbing, we shall find a spot that is sheltered and snug enough, *sir*. There is a dry fir-wood just

ahead, if I remember rightly.' *Sam knew the land well within about twenty miles of Hobbiton, but that was the limit of his geography.*
See also note 11.

8   The text is actually rendered still more complicated by a layer of later emendation arising from my father's intention to get rid of Odo altogether, leaving Bingo, Frodo Took, and Sam, but this is here ignored.

9   In the original texts the crossing of the East Road had been omitted (see pp. 46–7, 50). – With 'Michel Delving' for 'Much Hemlock (in the Hornblower country)' and 'south-east' for 'eastward', this is the reading of FR – in the first edition of LR. In the second edition (1966) the text was changed to read:

A mile or two further south they hastily crossed the great road from the Brandywine Bridge; they were now in the Tookland and bending south-eastwards they made for the Green Hill Country. As they began to climb its first slopes they looked back and saw the lamps in Hobbiton far off twinkling . . .

Robert Foster, in *The Complete Guide to Middle-earth*, entry *Hornblower*, says that 'all or most' of the Hornblowers 'dwelt in the Southfarthing'; this seems to be based only on the statement in the Prologue to LR that Tobold Hornblower, first grower of pipeweed, lived at Longbottom in the Southfarthing, but may well be a legitimate deduction. A few hobbit 'family territories' are marked on my father's map of the Shire (p. 107, item I), but the Hornblowers are not among them. (The Bracegirdles are placed west of Girdley Island in the Brandywine; the Bolgers south of the East Road and north of the Woody End; the Boffins north of Hobbiton Hill – cf. Mr Boffin of Overhill, FR p. 53; and the Tooks in Tookland, south of Hobbiton.) See p. 304, note 1.

10  See p. 246, note 18. The verse is now a repetition, for Bilbo had sung it before he left Bag End (p. 240); but whereas in FR (pp. 82–3) the only difference between the two recitations is that Bilbo says 'eager feet' in the 5th line and Frodo 'weary feet', here Bingo has also 'we' for 'I' in the 4th and 8th lines (retained from the original text, p. 53).

11  This passage interestingly exemplifies the 'two-tier' system of emendation which my father employed in this text (see p. 277). The new passage in which Bingo wonders if it is Gandalf coming after them and proposes to surprise him, though feeling certain that it is not him – exactly as in FR pp. 83–4 – is a 'red' emendation: because according to the new story Gandalf might well be expected to have just missed them at Hobbiton and be following on their heels, whereas according to the old story – in which the Birthday Party was Bingo's – Gandalf left immediately after the fireworks and went east (see p. 101 and note 12).

The remainder of the new passage (cited in the text), describing Bingo's conflicting desires to hide and not to hide, is a 'black' emendation (i.e. covering both 'old' and 'new' stories) – as is the addition almost immediately following, in which Bingo feels an urgent desire to put on the Ring, but does not: because, whatever version is followed, the nature of the Ring demands these changes (cf. *Queries and Alterations*, note 7 (p. 224): 'Bingo must NOT put on his Ring when Black Riders go by – in view of later developments. He must *think* of doing so but somehow be prevented.')

12  The text of FR here, 'I did not know that any of that fairest folk were ever seen in the Shire', was emended in the second edition to 'Few of that fairest folk are ever seen in the Shire.' – For previous references to the High Elves (which means now the Elves of Valinor) see pp. 187, 225, 260.

# XVII
# A SHORT CUT TO MUSHROOMS

The third of the original chapters (pp. 88 ff.) was now rewritten, numbered 'IV', and given a title, 'A Short Cut to Mushrooms'. This is a readily legible but much altered manuscript, with a great deal of variant and rejected material. The final result, however, as achieved already at this time (if a long variant version of the Farmer Maggot interlude, not at once rejected, is ignored for the moment), is virtually Chapter 5 in *The Fellowship of the Ring*, to a very great extent word for word, and there is not much that needs to be said about it.

The chief difference from FR lies of course in the fact that there were still Frodo Took and Odo Bolger and not simply Pippin. Pippin's part and all the things he says in FR are present in almost exactly the same form; but where in FR it is Pippin who is familiar with the region and who knows Farmer Maggot, in the present text (as also in the original version) this is Frodo Took's part, and once they have got down into the flat country Odo is in the background.

A good deal of new geography enters with the discussion whether to take a short cut or not (FR p. 97). While the wet low-lying land is described in the original story (pp. 91–2), it is now called the Marish, and the northward curve of the road (p. 89) is explained: 'to get round the north of the Marish.' The way south from Brandywine Bridge now appears – first called 'the raised road', then 'the banked road', then 'the causeway': 'the causeway that runs from the Bridge through Stock and past the Ferry down along the River to Deephallow.' Here the village of Stock is first named (and its inn the *Golden Perch*, where according to Odo there used to be the best beer in 'the East Shire'), and also Deephallow, which though marked on my father's map of the Shire and on the map in FR is never mentioned in the text of *The Lord of the Rings*. (In the original version of this chapter there is no suggestion of the causeway road, and the hobbits leaving Maggot's lane came out on to the road they had left, shortly before it reached the Ferry: see p. 97 and note 8. Stock had not then been devised. Later in the old version Marmaduke, arguing for going through the Old Forest, says that it would be silly of them to start their journey by 'jogging along a dull river-side road – in full view of all the numerous hobbits of Buckland', but he is speaking of the road within Buckland, on the east side of the Brandywine: p. 106, note 18).

The argument about which way to go is mainly between Odo and Frodo, and is somewhat different from the final form. Odo, not knowing the country, argued that there would be 'all kinds of obstacles' when they got down into the Marish, to which Frodo replied that he did know it, and that the Marish was now 'all tamed and drained' (in FR Pippin, who takes Frodo Took's part in that he does know the country, but Odo's in that he has his eye on the *Golden Perch*, argues with Frodo (Baggins) that in the Marish 'there are bogs and all kinds of difficulties').[1]

The stream that barred their passage is now identified as the Stockbrook. The only other feature to mention before coming to Farmer Maggot is a rejected passage that was to take the place of the mysterious sniffing that interrupted Odo's song in praise of the bottle in the original version (p. 91). There, a pencilled note on the manuscript (p. 105, note 3) said: 'Sound of hoofs going by not far off.'

*Ho! ho! ho!* they began again louder. 'Hush!' said Sam. 'I think I can hear something.' They stopped short. Bingo sat up. Listening he caught or thought he caught the sound of hoofs, some way off, going at a trot. They sat silent for some while after the sound had died away; but at last Frodo spoke. 'That's very odd,' he said. 'There is not any road that I know of anywhere near, yet the hoofs were not going on turf or leaves – if they were hoofs.' 'But if they were, it does not follow that it was the sound of a Black Rider,' said Odo. 'The land is not quite uninhabited round here: there are farms and villages.'

This was replaced by the terrible signal cries, exactly as in FR (pp. 99–100). From a rejected page a little later, when they came into the 'tame and well-ordered lands', it is clear that the hoof-beats they heard were not in fact so mysterious: 'They were just beginning to think that they had imagined the sound of hoofs, when they came to a gate: beyond it a rutted lane wound away towards a distant clump of trees' (i.e. Farmer Maggot's) The horseman they heard was the Black Rider who came to Maggot's door.

When my father came in this version to Farmer Maggot, he followed the old story in this: Bingo put on the Ring in the lane outside the farm, then entered the house invisibly, and drank Farmer Maggot's beer, so that the departure of the others was highly embarrassing and unhappy. Considering all that had now been said concerning the Ring this is remarkable; but I think that my father was reluctant to lose this interlude (see also note 13), and although at this time he also wrote the story of the visit to Maggot's in exactly the form it has in FR, he retained this first, entirely different account of what happened in Maggot's house and marked it as a variant.

In it, Maggot becomes a violent and intransigeant character, with a black hatred of all Bagginses – a development clearly arising, as I think, from the need to explain the intensity of Bingo's alarm when he learns who is the owner of the farm, an alarm great enough (coupled with the ferocious dogs) to explain in turn how he could put the Ring on in the face of all counsel. In the original version Bingo put on the Ring as a matter of course, as he put it on when the Black Riders came by. Moreover, as the story stood then Frodo and Odo were perfectly familiar with his possession of a magic ring that conferred invisibility, and after they left Farmer Maggot's Odo addressed Bingo while he was still invisible, calling his behaviour 'a silly trick' (p. 97). But now they were not (cf. p. 245, note 3: 'Bilbo wrote his adventures in a private book of memoirs, in which he recounted some things that he had never spoken about (such as the magic ring); but that book was never published in the Shire, and he never showed it to anyone, except his favourite "nephew" Bingo.') The great problem now with this story, my father noted in the margin of the manuscript, was that it would necessitate making Odo, Frodo, and Sam all aware of Bingo's ring – 'which is a pity'; or else, he added, 'making the others equally astonished with Farmer Maggot – which is difficult.' He was even prepared, however, as he noted in the same place, to consider altering the structure to the extent of getting rid of Odo and Frodo from this episode by making them the advance party to Buckland, while Bingo's walk from Hobbiton would be with Merry and Sam – which seems to imply that Merry had been let into the secret of the Ring. Sam might be supposed to have known of it from his eavesdropping under the window of Bag End at the end of the chapter 'Ancient History'; and my father also revised the text here and there in pencil in order to 'allow this version to stand if Bingo's ring is *unknown* to any but Sam.' A point he did not make here is the distinction between the others knowing about the Ring and Bingo's knowing that they knew; and when he reached the conversation in the house in Buckland (not much later, for the text of the two chapters is continuous in the manuscript) he had decided that they did know, but had kept the knowledge to themselves (as in FR, p. 114).

I give now the greater part of this first variant version.

They came to a gate, beyond which a rutted lane ran between low hedges towards a distant clump of trees. Frodo stopped. 'I know these fields!' he said. 'They are part of old Farmer Maggot's land.[2] That must be his farm away there in the trees.'

'One trouble after another!' said Bingo, looking nearly as much alarmed as if Frodo had declared the lane to be the slot leading to a dragon's lair. The others looked at him in astonishment.

'What's wrong with old Maggot?' asked Frodo.[3]

'I don't like him, and he doesn't like me,' said Bingo. 'If I had thought my short cut would bring me near his farm today, I would have gone by the long road. I haven't been near it for years and years.'

'Why ever not?' said Frodo. 'He's all right, if you get on the right side of him. I thought he was friendly to all the Brandybuck clan. Though he is a terror to trespassers, and he does keep some ferocious-looking dogs. But after all we are near the borders here and folk have to be more on their guard.'

'That's just it,' said Bingo. 'I used to trespass on his land when I was a youngster at Bucklebury. His fields used to grow the best mushrooms.[4] I killed one of his dogs once. I broke its head with a heavy stone. A lucky shot, for I was terrified, and I believe it would have mauled me. He beat me, and told me he would kill me next time I put a foot over his boundaries. "I'd kill you now," he said, "if you were not Mr Rory's nephew,[5] more's the pity and shame to the Brandybucks."'

'But that's long ago,' said Frodo. 'He won't kill Mr Bingo Baggins, late of Bag-end, because of his misdeeds when he was one of the many young rascals of Brandy Hall. Even if he remembers about it.'

'I don't fancy Maggot is a good forgetter,' said Bingo, 'especially not where his dogs are concerned. They used to say he loved his dogs more than his children. And Bilbo told me (only a year or two before he left the Shire) that he was once down this way and called at the farm to get a bite and drink. When he gave his name old Maggot ordered him off. "I'll have no Baggins over my doorstep. A lot of thievish murderous rascals. You get back where you belong," he said, and threatened him with a stick. He's shaken his fist at me, if we passed on the road, many a time since.'[6]

'Well I'm blest,' said Odo. 'So now I suppose we shall all get beaten or bitten, if we are seen with the marauding Bingo.'

'Nonsense!' said Frodo. 'Get into the lane, and then you won't be trespassing. Maggot used to be quite friendly with Merry and me. I'll talk to him.'

They went along the lane, until they saw the thatched roofs of a large house and farm-buildings peeping out among the trees ahead. The Maggots and the Puddifoots of Stock and most of the folk of the Marish were house-dwellers . . .

At this point a long digression was introduced (following that in the original version, p. 92) on the subject of hobbits living in houses; see pp. 294-5.

. . . and this farm was stoutly built of brick and had a high wall all round it. There was a strong wooden gate in the wall opening on to the lane. Bingo lagged behind. Suddenly as they drew nearer a terrific baying and barking broke out, and a loud voice was heard shouting: 'Grip! Fang! Wolf! Go on, lads! Go on!'

This was too much for Bingo. He slipped on the Ring, and vanished. 'It can't do any harm this once,' he thought. 'I am sure Bilbo would have done the same.'

He was only just in time. The gate opened and three huge dogs came pelting out into the lane, and dashed towards the travellers. Odo and Sam shrank against the wall, while two large grey wolvish-looking dogs sniffed at them. The third dog halted near Bingo sniffing and growling with the hair rising on its neck, and a puzzled look in its eyes. Frodo walked on a few paces unmolested.

Through the gate came a broad thickset hobbit with a round red face[7] and a soft high-crowned hat. 'Hullo! hullo! And who may you be, and what may you be doing?' he asked.

'Good afternoon, Farmer Maggot!' said Frodo.

The farmer looked at him closely. 'Well now,' he said. 'Let me see – you'll be Mr Frodo Took, Mr Folco's son, if I am not mistook. I seldom am, I've a rare memory for faces. It's some time since I saw you round here, with Mr Merry Brandybuck . . .

The opening encounter with Maggot is then exactly as in the other variant of the episode, which is to say exactly as in FR p. 102, as far as 'to the great relief of Odo and Sam the dogs let them go free.' Then follows:

Odo and Frodo at once went through the gate, but Sam hesitated. So did the third dog. He remained standing growling and bristling.

This was altered in pencil to read:

Odo joined Frodo at the gate, but Sam hesitated in the lane. Frodo looked back to beckon Bingo, and wondered how to introduce him, whether to give his name, or hope that Maggot's memory was less good than he boasted, and say nothing; but there was no sign of Bingo to be seen. Sam was watching one of the dogs. It was still standing growling and bristling. It all seemed rather queer.

This was one of the changes made 'to allow this version to stand if Bingo's ring is unknown to any but Sam' (p. 288).

'Here, Wolf!' cried Farmer Maggot, looking back. 'Dang it, what's come to the dog. Heel, Wolf!'

The dog obeyed reluctantly, and at the gate turned back and barked.

'What's the matter with you?' said the farmer. 'This is a queer day, and no mistake. Wolf went near off his head when that fellow came riding up, and now you'd think he could see or smell something that ain't there.'

They went into the farmer's kitchen, and sat by the wide fireplace. The dogs were shut up, as neither Odo nor Sam concealed their uneasiness while they were about. 'They won't harm you,' said the farmer, 'not unless I tell them to.' Mrs Maggot brought out beer and filled four large earthenware mugs. It was a good brew, and Odo found himself fully compensated for missing the *Golden Perch*. Sam would have enjoyed it better, if he had not been anxious about his master.

'And where might you be coming from and going to, Mr Frodo?' asked Farmer Maggot with a shrewd look. 'Were you coming to visit me? For if so you had gone past my gate without my seeing you.'

'Well, no,' said Frodo. 'To tell you the truth (since you guess it already) we had been on your fields. But it was quite by accident. We lost our way back near Woodhall trying to take a short cut to the causeway near the Ferry. We are in rather a hurry to get over into Buckland.'

'Then the road would have served you better,' said the farmer. 'But you and Mr Merry have my leave to walk on my land, as long as you do no damage. Not like those thievish folk from way back West – begging your pardon, I was forgetting you were a Took by name, and only half a Brandybuck as you might say.⁸ But you aren't a Baggins or you'd not be inside here. That Mr Bingo Baggins he killed one of my dogs once, he did. It's more than 30 years ago, but I haven't forgotten it, and I'll remind him of it sharp too if ever he dares to come round here. I hear tell that he is coming back to live in Buckland. More's the pity. I can't think why the Brandybucks allow it.'

'But Mr Bingo's half a Brandybuck too,' said Odo (trying to keep from smiling). 'He's quite a nice fellow when you get on the right side of him; though he will go walking across country and he is fond of mushrooms.'

There seemed to be a breath, the ghost of an exclamation, not far from Odo's ear, though he could not be quite sure.⁹

'That's just it,' said the farmer. 'He used to take mine though I beat him for it. And I'll beat him again, if I catch him at it. But that reminds me: what do you think that funny customer asked me?'

Farmer Maggot then turns to his account of the funny customer, and his report, though briefer, goes pretty well as in the other variant version and in FR,[10] with this difference:

'. . . I had a sort of shiver down my back. But that question was too much for me. "Be off," I said. "There are no Bagginses here, and won't be while I am on my legs. If you are a friend of theirs you are not welcome. I give you one minute before I call my dogs."'

From '"I don't know what to think," said Frodo' the story in this version moves in the direction of farce.

'Then I'll tell you what to think,' said Maggot. 'This Mr Bingo Baggins has got into some trouble. I hear tell that he has lost or wasted most of the money he got from old Bilbo Baggins. And *that* was got in some queer fashion, in foreign parts, too, they say. Mark my words, this all comes of some of those doings of old Mr Bilbo's. Maybe there is some that want to know what has become of the gold and what not that he left behind. Mark my words.'

'I certainly will,' said Frodo, rather taken aback by old Maggot's guessing.[11]

'And if you'll take my advice, too,' said the farmer, 'you'll steer clear of Mr Bingo, or you'll be getting into more trouble yourself than you bargain for.'

There was no mistaking the breath and the suppressed gasp by Frodo's ear on this occasion.[12]

'I'll remember the advice,' said Frodo. 'But now we must be getting to Bucklebury. Mr Merry Brandybuck is expecting us this evening.'

'Now that's a pity,' said the farmer. 'I was going to ask if you and your friends would stay and have a bite and sup with me and my wife.'

'It is very kind of you,' said Frodo; 'but I am afraid we must be off now – we want to get to the Ferry before dark.'

'Well then, one more drink!' said the farmer, and his wife poured out some beer. 'Here's your health and good luck!' he said, reaching for his mug. But at that moment the mug left the table, rose, tilted in the air, and then returned empty to its place.

'Help us and save us!' cried the farmer jumping up and gaping. 'This day is bewitched. First the dog and then me: seeing things that ain't.'

'But I saw the mug get up too,' said Odo indiscreetly, and not fully hiding a grin.

This last sentence was struck out in pencil, as being unwanted 'if Bingo's ring is unknown to any but Sam.' The remainder of this version was written on that basis.

Odo and Frodo sat and stared. Sam looked anxious and worried. 'You did not ask me to have a bite or a sup,' said a voice coming apparently from the middle of the room. Farmer Maggot backed towards the fire-place; his wife screamed. 'And that's a pity,' went on the voice, which Frodo to his bewilderment now recognized as Bingo's, 'because I like your beer. But don't boast again that no Baggins will ever come inside your house. There's one inside now. A thievish Baggins. A very angry Baggins.' There was a pause. 'In fact BINGO!' the voice suddenly yelled just by the farmer's ear. At the same time something gave him a push in the waistcoat, and he fell over with a crash among the fire-irons. He sat up again just in time to see his own hat leave the settle where he had thrown it down, and sail out of the door, which opened to let it pass.

'Hi! here!' yelled the farmer, leaping to his feet. 'Hey, Grip, Fang, Wolf!' At that the hat went off at a great speed towards the gate; but as the farmer ran after it, it came sailing back through the air and fell at his feet. He picked it up gingerly, and looked at it in astonishment. The dogs released by Mrs Maggot came bounding up; but the farmer gave them no command. He stood still scratching his head and turning his hat over and over, as if he expected to find it had grown wings.[13]

Odo and Frodo followed by Sam came out of the house.

'Well, if that ain't the queerest thing that ever happened in my house!' said the farmer. 'Talk about ghosts! I suppose you haven't been playing any tricks on me, have you?' he said suddenly, looking hard at them in turn.

'We?' said Frodo. 'Why, we were as startled as you were. I can't make mugs drain themselves, or hats walk out of the house.'

'Well, it is mighty queer,' said the farmer, not seeming quite satisfied. 'First this rider asks for Mr Baggins. Then you folk come along; and while you are in the house Mr Baggins' voice starts playing tricks. And you are friends of his, seemingly. "Quite a nice fellow," you said. If there ain't some connexion between all these bewitchments, I'll eat this very hat. You can tell him from me to keep his voice at home, or I'll come and gag him, if I have to swim the River and hunt him all through Bucklebury. And now you'd best be going back to your friends, and leave me in peace. Good day to you.'

He watched them with a thoughtful scowl on his face until they turned a corner of the lane and passed out of his sight.

'What do you make of that?' asked Odo as they went along. 'And where on earth is Bingo?'

'What I make of it,' answered Frodo, 'is that Uncle Bingo has taken leave of his senses; and I fancy we shall run into him in this lane before long.'

'You won't run into me because I'm just behind,' said Bingo. There he was by Sam Gamgee's side.

This version of the episode ends here, with the note: 'This variant would proceed much as in older typed Chapter III' – i.e. in respect of the hobbits getting from Farmer Maggot's to the Ferry, if they are not driven there in Maggot's cart (see pp. 97–9).

Apart from any other considerations (which there may well have been), I think that it was primarily the difficulty with the Ring that killed this version. In the next chapter it turns out that the other hobbits had known about the Ring, but that Bingo had not known that they knew. So the ferocious Farmer Maggot, prone to ill-will, had already disappeared, and with him the last (more or less) light-hearted use of the Ring.[14] The second version of the Maggot episode in this manuscript evidently followed quite closely on the first, and this, as I have said, is (names apart) identical save for a word here and there with the story in FR.

There remains to notice the passage about hobbit architecture mentioned above (p. 289). Against it my father wrote 'Put in Foreword',[15] and in the second version of the Maggot story it is not included. It was somewhat developed from that in the original form of the chapter (p. 92), but has less detail than that in the Prologue to FR (pp. 15–16, in the first edition 16–17). The division of hobbits into Harfoots, Fallohides, and Stoors had not yet arisen, and the fact that some of the people in the Marish were 'rather large, and heavy-legged, and a few actually had a little down under their chins' is ascribed to their not being of pure hobbit-breed. In this account the art of house-building still originated, or was thought to have originated, among the hobbits themselves, down in the riverside regions (in the Prologue it is suggested that it was derived from the Dúnedain, or even from the Elves); but it 'had long been altered (and perhaps improved) by taking wrinkles from dwarves and elves and even Big Folk, and other people outside the Shire.'

The passage in the Prologue concerning the presence of houses in many hobbit villages is present, and here Tuckborough first appears. As this passage was first drafted it read:

Even in Hobbiton and Bywater, and in Tuckborough away in Tookland, and on the chalky Indowns in the centre of the Shire where there was a large population

My father then struck out *Indowns*, presumably meaning to include *on the chalky* as well, and substituted [*Much >*] *Micheldelving*, before abandoning the sentence and starting again. Michel Delving on the White Downs has appeared in the last chapter (p. 278), replacing 'Much Hemlock (in the Hornblower country)'. He was probably going to write 'Much Hemlock' here too. It seems that up till now he had not decided that the chief town was in the west of the Shire, if indeed there were any chief town; but he at once rewrote the passage, and it was very probably at this point that Michel Delving on the White Downs came into existence (and was then written into 'Delays are Dangerous'). As finally written, the sentence reads:

> In Hobbiton, in Tuckborough away in Tookland, and even in the most populous [village >] town of the Shire, Micheldelving, on the White Downs in the West, there were many houses of stone and wood and brick.

The name *Indowns* does not occur again; cf. the *Inlands* (*Mittalmar*), the central region of Númenor, *Unfinished Tales* p. 166.

The text of this chapter, following the arrangement of the original version, continues straight on without break from 'Suddenly Bingo laughed: from the covered basket he held the scent of mushrooms was rising', which ends Chapter 4 in FR, to '"Now we'd better get home ourselves," said Merry', which in FR begins Chapter 5; but not long after my father broke the text at this point, inserting the number 'V' and the title 'A Conspiracy is Unmasked', and I follow this arrangement here.

## NOTES

1  This passage of discussion was much rewritten. In rejected versions Odo proposes that they split up: 'Why all go the same way? Those who vote for short cuts, cut. Those who don't, go round – and they (mark you) will reach the *Golden Perch* at Stock before sundown'; and Frodo argues for going across country by saying 'Merry won't worry if we are late.' In another, Odo says: 'Then I must fall in behind, or go alone. Well, I don't think Black Riders will do anything to me. It's you, Bingo, they are sniffing for. If they ask after you, I shall say: I have quarrelled with Mr Baggins and left him. He lodged with the Elves last night – ask them.'
   A minute point in connection with the geography may be mentioned here. In 'the woods that clustered along the eastern side of the hill', FR p. 98 line 5, 'hill' should be 'hills', as it is in the present text.

2  At this first mention of the farmer in this text, he is called *Farmer Puddifoot*, but this was changed at once to *Maggot*, and *Maggot* is his name subsequently throughout. At the same place in the original

typescript, and only at that place, *Maggot* was changed to *Puddifoot* (p. 105, note 4).

3  Frodo continued: 'Of course these people down in the Marish are a bit queer and unfriendly, but the Brandybucks get on all right with them', but this was struck out as soon as written.

4  This is where the mushrooms entered the story: there is no mention of mushrooms in the original version.

5  On Bingo's being the nephew of Rory Brandybuck (Merry's grandfather) see p. 267, note 4.

6  Another version of Bingo's account makes it Bilbo and Bingo who had the encounter with Maggot, and the farmer a real ogre:

'That's just it,' said Bingo. 'I got on the wrong side of him, and of his hedge. We were trespassing, as he called it. We had been in the Shirebourn valley, and were making a cross-country line towards Stock – rather like today – when we got on to his land. It was getting dark, and a white fog came on, and we got lost. We climbed through a hedge and found ourselves in a garden; and Maggot found us. He set a great dog on us, more like a wolf. I fell down with the dog over me, and Bilbo broke its head with that thick stick of his. Maggot was violent. He is a strong fellow, and while Bilbo ws trying to explain who we were and how we came there he picked him up and flung him over the hedge into a ditch. Then he picked me up and had a good look at me. He recognized me as one of the Brandybuck clan, though I had not been to his farm since I was a youngster. "I was going to break your neck," he said, "and I will yet, whether you be Mr Rory's nephew or not, if I catch you round here again. Get out before I do you an injury!" He dropped me over the hedge on top of Bilbo.

'Bilbo got up and said: "I shall come around next time with something sharper than a stick. Neither you nor your dogs would be any loss to the countryside." Maggot laughed. "I have a weapon or two myself," he said; 'and next time you kill one of my dogs, I'll kill you. Be off now, or I'll kill you tonight." That'll be 20 years ago. But I don't imagine Maggot is a good forgetter. Ours would not be a friendly meeting.'

Frodo Took's reception of this story was strangely mild. 'How very unfortunate!' [he said.] 'Nobody seems to have been much to blame. After all, Bingo, you must remember that this is near the Borders, and people round here are a deal more suspicious than up in the Baggins country.'

Like Deephallow (p. 286), the Shirebourn, mentioned in this passage, is never named in LR, though marked both on my father's map of the Shire and on that published in FR (both are mentioned in *The Adventures of Tom Bombadil*, p. 9).

7  Farmer Maggot is again unambiguously a hobbit: see p. 122 and note 7.

8   There has in fact been no indication that Frodo Took's mother was a
    Brandybuck, as is seen to be the case from Maggot's remark here,
    supported also by Frodo's knowledge of the Marish and Maggot's
    familiarity with him as a companion of Merry Brandybuck. In LR
    the mother of Peregrin (who is related to Meriadoc as Frodo Took is
    at this stage, see p. 267, note 4) was Eglantine Banks.

9   This sentence is marked in pencil for deletion.

10  In this version the Black Rider does not say anything beyond 'Have
    you seen Mist-er Bagg-ins?' In the second version his words are
    almost as in FR, though he still calls him 'Mister Baggins'.

11  In the second version, as in FR (p. 104) 'the shrewd guesses of the
    farmer were rather disconcerting' to Bingo (Frodo); but here
    Maggot's guesses disconcert Frodo Took, which would suggest
    that he knew what the Black Riders were after.

12  This sentence is marked in pencil for deletion; cf. note 9.

13  Pencilled changes in this passage substitute the beer jug for Farmer
    Maggot's hat: 'He sat up again just in time to see the jug (still
    holding some beer) leave the table where he had lain it down, and
    sail out of the door . . . At that the jug went off at a great speed
    towards the gate, spilling beer in the yard; but as the farmer ran
    after it, it suddenly stopped and came to rest on the gatepost . . .
    He stood still scratching his head and turning the jug round and
    round . . .' (and 'jug' for 'hat' subsequently).

    In the margin of the manuscript my father wrote: 'Christopher
    queries – why was not *hat* invisible if Bingo's clothes were?' The
    story must have been that Bingo was actually wearing Maggot's hat,
    for otherwise the objection seems easily answered (the hat was an
    object external to the wearer of the Ring just as much as the beer-
    jug, or as anything else would be, whatever its purpose). Clearly, a
    subtle question arises if the Ring is put to such uses, a question my
    father sidestepped by substituting the jug. – I was greatly delighted
    by the story of Bingo's turning the tables on Farmer Maggot, and
    while I retain now only a dim half-memory I believe I was much
    opposed to its loss: which may perhaps explain my father's retaining
    it after it had become apparent that it introduced serious difficulties.

14  Unless the episode in Tom Bombadil's house (FR p. 144) can be so
    described.

15  The passage in the 'Foreword' is given on pp. 312–13.

# XVIII
# AGAIN FROM BUCKLAND TO
# THE WITHYWINDLE

## (i)

### *A Conspiracy is Unmasked*

The text of 'A Short Cut to Mushrooms', as I have said, continues
without break, but my father added in (not much later, see p. 302) a new
chapter number 'V' and the title 'A Conspiracy is Unmasked'. The text
now becomes very close indeed to FR Chapter 5 (apart of course from the
number of and names of the hobbits), and there are only a few particular
points to notice in it. For the earliest form see pp. 99 ff.

The history of the Brandybucks does not yet know Gorhendad
Oldbuck as the founder (FR p. 108). As the manuscript was first written,
the village was called Bucklebury-beyond-the-River, and (developing
the original text, p. 100) 'the authority of the head of the Brandybucks
was still acknowledged by the farmers as far west as Woodhall (which was
reckoned to be in the Boffin-country)';[1] this was changed to 'still acknowledged by the farmers between Stock and Rushey,' as in FR. Rushey here
first appears.[2]

It was in this passage that the Four Farthings of the Shire were first
devised, as the wording shows: 'They were not very different from the
other hobbits of the Four Farthings (North, West, South, and East), as
the quarters of the Shire were called.' Here too occur for the first time the
names Buck Hill and the High Hay – but Haysend goes back to the
original version, p. 100. The great hedge is still 'something over forty
miles from end to end.'[3] In answer to Bingo's question 'Can horses cross
the river?' Merry answers: 'They can go fifteen miles to Brandywine
Bridge', with '20?' pencilled over 'fifteen'. In FR the High Hay is 'well
over *twenty* miles from end to end', yet Merry still says: 'They can go
*twenty* miles north to Brandywine Bridge.' Barbara Strachey (*Journeys
of Frodo*, Map 6) points out this difficulty, and assumes that Merry
'meant 20 miles in all – 10 miles north to the Bridge and 10 miles south on
the other side'; but this is to strain the language: Merry did not mean
that. It is in fact an error which my father never observed: when the
length of Buckland from north to south was reduced, Merry's estimate of
the distance from the Bridge to the Ferry should have been changed
commensurately.[4]

The main road within Buckland is described (on a rejected page only)
as running 'from the Bridge to Standelf and Haysend.' Standelf is never

mentioned in the text of LR, though marked on my father's map of the Shire and on both of mine; on all three the road stops there and does not continue to Haysend, which is not shown as a village or any sort of habitation.[5]

At the first two occurrences of Crickhollow in this chapter the name was first *Ringhay*, changed to *Crickhollow* (in the passage cited in note 2 on p. 283 the name is a later addition to the text). At the third occurrence here *Crickhollow* was the name first written. *Ringhay* refers to the 'wide circle of lawn surrounded by a belt of trees inside the outer hedge.'[6]

The most important development in this chapter is that after the words 'the far shore seemed to be shrouded in mist and nothing could be seen' (FR p. 109) my father interrupted the narrative with the following note before proceeding:

From here onwards Odo is presumed to have gone with Merry ahead. The preliminary journey was Frodo, Bingo and Sam only. Frodo has a character a little more like Odo once had. Odo is now rather silent (and greedy).

Against this my father wrote: 'Christopher wants Odo kept.' Unhappily I have now only a very shadowy recollection of those conversations of half a century ago; and it is not clear to me what the issue really was. On the face of it, my 'wanting Odo kept' should mean that I wanted him kept as a member of the party that walked from Hobbiton, since my father had not proposed that Odo be dropped absolutely; on the other hand, since he had in mind the blending of 'Odo' elements into the character of Frodo Took, it may very well be that he was planning to cut him out of the expedition after the hobbits left Crickhollow. Perhaps the idea that Odo should remain on at Crickhollow was already present as a possibility, and 'Christopher wants Odo kept' was a plea for his survival in the larger narrative, as a member of the major expedition. This is no more than guesswork, but if there is anything in it, it seems that my objection temporarily won the day, since at the end of the chapter Odo is fully re-established, and prepared to go with the others into the Old Forest – as indeed he does, in the revision of that chapter in this 'phase'.

The situation in the text that follows this note on Odo is in any case extraordinarily difficult to interpret. As first written, Merry says that he will ride on and tell *Olo* that they are coming; when Bingo knocked on the door of (Ringhay) Crickhollow it was opened by Olo Bolger, and Merry refers to 'Olo and I' having got to Crickhollow with the last cartload on the day before; Merry and Olo prepared the supper in the kitchen. 'Olo' here plays the part of Fatty (Fredegar) Bolger in FR (pp. 110–11), but after these mentions he disappears from the text (and never appears again). In red ink my father noted: 'If Odo is kept alter in red,' and for a short distance some red ink alterations were made, changing 'You'll be last either way, Frodo' (concerning the order of entry into the bath) to

'Odo', changing 'three tubs' to 'four tubs', and cutting out the references to 'Olo'.[7]

The best explanation seems to be that when Odo was to be removed from the walking party and attached to Merry his name was to be changed also. Some alterations were made to preserve the option of retaining the received story. But from the moment when they sat down to supper Odo reappears in the text as first written, not merely as being present (which would only show that *Olo* had been rejected and *Odo* restored) but as having walked from Hobbiton (though in this case his name was bracketed). But Frodo Took now makes 'Odo-Pippin' remarks (as 'Oh! That was poetry!' FR p. 116 – he would hardly have said such a thing previously). See further pp. 323–4.

The bath-song (here sung by Frodo in his new Odoesque character) is all but identical to that which Pippin sings in FR; but in a red ink addition to the text (one of the optional additions made to bring Odo back in his original rôle) specimens of the 'competing songs' (FR p. 111) sung by Bingo and Odo are given: the first verse of the bath-song which Odo sang as they walked from Farmer Maggot's to the Ferry in the original version (p. 98) and which is thus no longer used, and the first two lines of the bath-chant sung by Odo when they reached their destination (p. 102), these last being struck out.

The revelation of the conspiracy is almost exactly as in FR, the burden of its exposition being taken here as there by Merry (Pippin's intervention 'You do not understand! . . .' being given here to Frodo Took). As in FR, Merry recounts the story of how he discovered the existence of Bilbo's ring, which was previously set in a quite different context (see p. 242 and note 25), and tells that he had had a rapid glance at Bilbo's 'memoirs' ('secret book' in FR).[8]

The report of what Gildor had said, here referred to by Merry rather than by Sam himself, on the subject of Bingo's taking companions reflects the text of that episode at this time (see p. 282): 'I know you have been advised to take us. Gildor told you to, and you can't deny it!'

The song that Merry and Pippin sang in FR (p. 116) is here sung by Merry, Frodo Took, and Odo,[9] and is very different:

> *Farewell! farewell, now hearth and hall!*
> *Though wind may blow and rain may fall,*
> *We must away ere break of day*
> *Far over wood and mountain tall.*

> *The hunt is up! Across the land*
> *The Shadow stretches forth its hand.*
> *We must away ere break of day*
> *To where the Towers of Darkness stand.*

*With foes behind and foes ahead,*
*Beneath the sky shall be our bed,*
*Until at last the Ring is cast*
*In Fire beneath the Mountain Red.*

*We must away, we must away,*
*We ride before the break of day.*

In a rejected version of his answer to Bingo's question whether it would be safe to wait one day at Crickhollow for Gandalf (FR p. 117), a passage rewritten several times, Merry refers to the gate-guards getting a message through to 'my father the Master of the Hall.' Merry's father was Caradoc Brandybuck (Saradoc 'Scattergold' in LR); see p. 251 and note 4.

When Bingo raises the question of going through the Old Forest, it is Odo who, filled with horror at the thought, voices the objections given in FR to Fatty Bolger (who is going to stay behind).

The end of the chapter is different from that in FR, and belongs rather with the original version (p. 104). (Merry does not mention, incidentally, that Bingo had ever been into the Forest).

'... I have often been in – only in the daylight, of course, when the trees are fairly quiet and sleepy. Still, I have some some knowledge of it, and I will try and guide you.'

Odo was not convinced, and was plainly far less frightened of meeting a troop of Riders on the open road than of venturing into the dubious Forest. Even Frodo was against the plan.

'I hate the idea,' said Odo. 'I would rather risk pursuers on the Road, where there is a chance of meeting ordinary honest travellers as well. I don't like woods, and the stories about the Old Forest have always terrified me. I am sure Black Riders will be very much more at home in that gloomy place than we shall.' Even Frodo on this occasion sided with Odo.

'But we shall probably be out of it again before they ever find out or guess that we have gone in,' said Bingo. 'In any case, if you wish to come with me, it is no good taking fright at the first danger: there are almost certainly far worse things than the Old Forest ahead of you. Do you follow Captain Bingo, or do you stay at home?'

'We follow Captain Bingo,' they said at once.

'Well, that's settled!' said Merry. 'Now we must tidy up and put the finishing touches to the packing. And then to bed. I shall call you all well before the break of day.'

When at last he got to bed Bingo could not sleep for some time.

His legs ached. He was glad that he was riding in the morning. At last he fell into a vague dream: in which he seemed to be looking out of a window over a dark sea of tangled trees. Down below among the roots there was a sound of something crawling and snuffling.

A note on the manuscript earlier says 'Pencillings = Odo stays behind.' These pencillings are in fact confined to the section just given. 'Even Frodo on this occasion sided with Odo' is bracketed and replaced by further words of Odo's: 'Also I feel certain it is wrong not to wait for Gandalf.' And after '"We follow Captain Bingo," they said at once' is inserted:

'I will follow Captain Bingo,' said Merry, and Frodo, and Sam. Odo was silent. 'Look here!' he said, after a pause. 'I don't mind admitting I am frightened of the Forest, but I also think you ought to try and get in touch with Gandalf. I will stay behind here and keep off inquisitive folk. When Gandalf comes as he is sure to I will tell him what you have done, and I will come on after you with him, if he will bring me.' Merry and Frodo agreed that that was a good plan.

This would be an important development, though ultimately rejected. These alterations derive, however, from a somewhat later stage.

(ii)

*The Old Forest*

Having completed 'A Conspiracy is Unmasked', my father continued his revision into the next chapter, afterwards called 'The Old Forest'. In this case he did not make a new manuscript, but merely made corrections to the original text (described on pp. 112–14), which as I have said had reached with only the most minor differences the form of the published narrative. The chapter was at this time renumbered, from IV to VI, showing that Chapter V 'A Conspiracy is Unmasked' had been separated off from 'A Short Cut to Mushrooms'. Extensive emendations, made in red ink to the original manuscript, bring the text still closer in detail of wording to that of FR (but the topographical differences noticed on pp. 113–14 remain). The parts played in the Willow-man episode are changed by the presence of Sam Gamgee in the party. Bingo and Odo are still the two who are caught in the cracks of the tree, and Frodo Took is still the one pushed into the river; but whereas in the original story it was Marmaduke (i.e. Merry) who rounded up the ponies and rescued Frodo Took from the water, Sam now takes over this part (as in FR), while Merry 'lay like a log.'

(iii)

## Tom Bombadil

The manuscript of the Tom Bombadil chapter, the number changed from V to VII but still title-less, underwent (with one important exception) minimal revision at this stage (there were indeed few changes ever made to it): scarcely more than a mention of Sam sleeping, with Merry, like a log, and the changing of the number of hobbits from four to five. The points of difference noticed on pp. 120–3 were nearly all left as they were; but Bombadil's remark about Farmer Maggot ('We are kinsfolk, he and I . . .') was marked with an X, probably at this time.

The one substantial change made is of great interest. On the manuscript my father marked 'Insert' before the passage concerning the hobbits' dreams on the first night in Tom Bombadil's house; and that the insertion belongs to this phase is made clear by the fact that Crickhollow was *empty* (i.e. Odo had gone with the others into the Old Forest).

As they slept there in the house of Tom Bombadil, darkness lay on Buckland. Mist strayed in the hollow places. The house at Crickhollow stood silent and lonely: deserted so soon after being made ready for a new master.

The gate in the hedge opened, and up the path, quietly but in haste, a grey man came, wrapped in a great cloak. He halted looking at the dark house. He knocked softly on the door, and waited; and then passed from window to window, and finally disappeared round the corner of the house-end. There was silence again. After a long time a sound of hoofs was heard in the lane approaching swiftly. Horses were coming. Outside the gate they stopped; and then swiftly up the path there came three more figures, hooded, swathed in black, and stooping low towards the ground. One went to the door, one to the corners of the house-end at either side; and there they stood silent as the shadows of black yew-trees, while time went slowly on, and the house and the trees about it seemed to be waiting breathlessly.

Suddenly there was a movement. It was dark, and hardly a star was shining, but the blade that was drawn gleamed suddenly, as if it brought with it a chill light, keen and menacing. There was a blow, soft but heavy, and the door shuddered. 'Open to the servants of the Lord!' said a voice, thin, cold, and clear. At a second blow the door yielded and fell back, its lock broken.

At that moment there rang out behind the house a horn. It rent the night like fire on a hill-top. Loud and brazen it shouted, echoing over field and hill: *Awake, awake, fear, fire, foe! Awake!*

Round the corner of the house came the grey man. His cloak

and hat were cast aside. His beard streamed wide. In one hand was
a horn, in the other a wand. A splendour of light flashed out before
him. There was a wail and cry as of fell hunting beasts that are
smitten suddenly, and turn to fly in wrath and anguish.

In the lane the sound of hoofs broke out, and gathering rapidly
to a gallop raced madly into the darkness. Far away answering
horns were heard. Distant sounds of waking and alarm rose up.
Along the roads folk were riding and running northward. But
before them all there galloped a white horse. On it sat an old man
with long silver hair and flowing beard. His horn sounded over hill
and dale. In his hand his wand flared and flickered like a sheaf of
lightning. Gandalf was riding to the North Gate with the speed of
thunder.

Against the end of this inserted text my father wrote in pencil: 'This
will require altering if Odo is left behind'; see the pencilled passage
added at the end of the last chapter (p. 302). And at the end of the text,
after the words 'a sheaf of lightning', he added in: 'Behind clung a small
figure with flying cloak', and the name 'Odo'. The significance of this will
become clear later.

## NOTES

1   On my father's map of the Shire the Boffins are placed north of
    Hobbiton, and the Bolgers north of the Woody End (p. 284, note 9),
    but this was an alteration of what he first wrote: the underlying names
    can be seen to be in the reverse positions.
2   The spelling *Rushy* on the published map of the Shire is an error,
    made first on my elaborate early map (p. 107, item V) through
    misreading of my father's. The second element is Old English *ey*
    'island'.
3   On my father's original map it can be roughly calculated (since Bingo
    estimated that they had eighteen miles to go in a straight line from the
    place where they passed the night with the Elves to Bucklebury
    Ferry) that the High Hay was about 43 miles measured in a straight
    line from its northern to its southern end.
4   On my father's later maps (see p. 107) measurement can only be very
    approximate, but on the same basis as the calculation in note 3 the
    High Hay cannot in these be much more than 20 miles (in a straight
    line between its ends).
5   *Standelf* means 'stone-quarry' (Old English *stān-(ge)delf*, surviving
    in the place-name *Stonydelph* in Warwickshire).
6   Just as in FR, the hobbits leaving the Ferry passed Buck Hill and
    Brandy Hall on their left, struck the main road of Buckland, turned

north along it for half a mile, and then took the lane to Crickhollow. On my original map of the Shire, made in 1943 (p. 107), the text – which was never changed here – was already wrongly represented, since the main road is shown as passing between the River and Brandy Hall (and the lane to Crickhollow leaves the road south of the hall, so that the hobbits would in fact, according to this map, still pass it on their left). This must have been a simple misinterpretation of the text which my father did not notice (cf. p. 108); and it reappeared on my map published in the first edition of FR. My father referred to the error in his letter to Austin Olney of Houghton Mifflin, 28 July 1965 (*Letters* no. 274); and it was corrected, after a fashion, on the map as published in the second edition. Karen Fonstad (*The Atlas of Middle-earth*, p. 121) and Barbara Strachey (*Journeys of Frodo*, Map 7) show the correct topography clearly.

7  These alterations to bring Odo back were made at the same time as the notes on the retention of the story that Bingo entered Farmer Maggot's house invisibly (p. 288); cf. p. 297, note 13.

8  In this text Merry says 'I was only in my tweens', whereas in FR he says 'teens'. In LR (Appendix C) Merry was born in (1382 =) 2982, and so in the year before the Farewell Party he was 18. Here, Merry is conceived to be somewhat older. – To Merry's question about Bilbo's book ('Have you got it, Bingo?') Bingo replies: 'No! He took it away, or so it seems.' Cf. the last note in *Queries and Alterations* (p. 229): 'Bilbo carries off "memoirs" to Rivendell.'

9  Changed from 'Merry and Frodo'.

# THE THIRD PHASE

# XIX

# THE THIRD PHASE (1):
# THE JOURNEY TO BREE

It seems to me extremely probable that the 'second phase' of writing, beginning with the fifth version of 'A Long-expected Party' (Chapter XIV in this book) now petered out, and once again a new start was made on the whole work. This 'third phase' is constituted by a long series of homogeneous manuscripts carrying the story from a sixth version of 'A Long-expected Party' right through to Rivendell. Though subsequently overwritten, interleaved, struck through, or 'cannibalised' to form parts of later texts, these manuscripts were at first clear and neat, and their rather distinctive, regular script makes it possible to reconstitute the series quite precisely despite the punishment they received later, and despite the fact that some parts remained in England when others went to Marquette University. They were indeed fair copies of the now chaotic existing texts, and few important narrative changes were made. But in these new texts 'Bingo' is finally supplanted by 'Frodo', and 'Frodo Took' becomes in turn 'Folco Took', taking over what had been his father's name (see pp. 251, 290). In describing these third phase versions I restrict myself here almost exclusively to the form they had when first written, and ignore the fearsome complexities of their later treatment.

There are three pieces of evidence available for the determination of the 'external' date. One is my father's letter of 13 October 1938, in which he said that the book 'has reached Chapter XI (though in rather an illegible state)' (*Letters* no. 34). Another is his letter of 2 February 1939, in which he recorded that although he had not been able to touch it since the previous December, it had by then 'reached Chapter 12 (and had been re-written several times), running to over 300 MS pages of the same size as this paper and written generally as closely.' The third is a set of notes, plot-outlines and brief narrative drafts all bearing the date 'August 1939': from these, as will be seen later, it is apparent that the third phase was already in being.

My guess – it can hardly be more – is that in October 1938 the third phase had not been begun, or had not proceeded far, since the book was 'in rather an illegible state'; while when my father wrote of having had to set the work aside in December 1938 it was to the third phase that he was referring: hence he said that it had been 're-written several times' (moreover 'Chapter XII' of this phase is the arrival at Rivendell, and it is here – as I think – that the new version was interrupted).

The third phase can be described quite rapidly, as far as the end of 'Fog on the Barrow-downs'; but first there is an interesting new text to be given. This my father called a *Foreword* (precursor of the *Prologue* in the published work). There is no preparatory material for it extant, but for a section of it he took up the passage concerning hobbit architecture from the second version of 'A Short Cut to Mushrooms', against which he had directed 'Put in Foreword' (see pp. 294–5). This was scarcely changed for its place in the *Foreword*, but there was now added a reference to the 'Elf-towers', which goes back to the earliest form of the 'architecture' passage in the original version of the chapter (pp. 92–3), where Bingo says that he had once seen the towers himself.

A number of changes were made to the manuscript of the *Foreword*, but apart from those that seem clearly to belong to the time of writing I ignore them here and print the text as it was first written.

### FOREWORD

## Concerning Hobbits

This book is largely concerned with hobbits, and it is possible to find out from it what they are (or were), and whether they are worth hearing about or not. But finding out things as you trudge along a road or plod through a story is rather tiring, even when it is (as occasionally happens) interesting or exciting. Those who wish to have things clear from the beginning will find some useful information in the brief account of Mr Bilbo Baggins' great Adventure, which led to the even more difficult and dangerous adventures recorded in this book. This account was called *The Hobbit* or *There and Back again*, because it was chiefly concerned with the most famous of all the old legendary hobbits, Bilbo; and because he went to the Lonely Mountain and came back again to his own home. But one story may well be all that readers have time or taste for. So I will put down some items of useful information here.

Hobbits are a very ancient people, once upon a time more numerous, alas! than they are to-day, when (or so I hear it sadly rumoured) they are vanishing rapidly; for they are fond of peace and quiet, and good tilled earth: a well-ordered and well-farmed countryside is their natural haunt. They are quite useless with machines more complicated than a bellows or a water-mill; though they are fairly handy with tools. They were always rather shy of the Big People (as they call us), and now they are positively scared of us.

And yet plainly they must be relatives of ours: nearer to us than elves are, or even dwarves. For one thing, they spoke a very similar language (or languages), and liked or disliked much the same things as we used to. What exactly the relationship is would be difficult to say. To answer that question one would have to re-discover a great deal of the now wholly lost history and legends of the Earliest Days;[1] and that is not likely to happen, for only the Elves preserve any traditions about the Earliest Days, and their traditions are mostly about themselves – not unnaturally: the Elves were much the most important people of those times. But even their traditions are incomplete: Men only come in to them occasionally, and Hobbits are not mentioned. Elves, Dwarves, Men, and other creatures only became aware of Hobbits after they had actually existed, jogging along in their uneventful fashion, for many ages. And they continued, as a rule, to jog along, keeping to themselves and keeping out of stories. In the days of Bilbo (and Frodo his heir) they became for a time very important, by what is called accident, and the great persons of the world, even the Necromancer, were obliged to take them into account, as these stories show. Though Hobbits had then already had a long history (of a quiet kind), those days are now very long ago, and geography (and many other things) were then very different. But the lands in which they lived, changed though they now are, must have been more or less in the same place as the lands in which they still linger: the North-west of the old world.

They are (or were) a small people, smaller than dwarves: less stout and stocky, that is, even when they were not in fact much shorter. Their height was, like the height of us Big People, rather variable, ranging between two and four feet (of our length): three feet was more or less an average. Very few hobbits, outside their own more fantastic legends, touched three foot six. Only Bandobras Took, son of Isengrim the First, known usually as the Bullroarer, of all the hobbits of history exceeded four feet. He was four foot five and rode a horse.[2]

There is, and always has been, very little magic about hobbits. Of course they possess the power which we sometimes confuse with real magic – it is really only a kind of professional skill, that has become uncanny through long practice, aided by close friend-ship with the earth and all things that grow on it: the power of disappearing quietly and quickly when large stupid folk like us come blundering along, making noises like elephants, which they can hear a mile off. Even long ago their great desire was to avoid trouble; and they were quick in hearing, and sharpsighted. And they were neat and deft in their movements, though they were inclined to be fat in the stomach, and did not hurry unnecessarily.

They dressed in bright colours, being particularly fond of green and yellow; but they wore no shoes, because their feet grew natural leathery soles and thick warm brown hair, curly like the brown hair of their heads. The only trade unknown among them was consequently shoemaking; but they had long clever brown fingers and could make many other useful things. They had good-natured faces, being as a rule good-natured; and they laughed long and deeply, being fond of simple jests at all times, but especially after dinner (which they had twice a day, when they could get it). They were fond of presents, and gave them away freely, and accepted them readily.

All hobbits had originally lived in holes in the ground, or so they believed; although actually already in Bilbo's time it was as a rule only the richest and the poorest hobbits that still did so. The poorest hobbits went on living in holes of the most antiquated kind – in fact just holes, with only one window, or even none. The most important families continued to live (when they could) in luxurious versions of the simple excavations of olden times. But suitable sites for these large and ramifying tunnels were not to be found everywhere. In Hobbiton, in Tuckborough in Tookland, and even in the one really populous town of their Shire, Michel-Delving on the White Downs, there were many houses of stone and wood and brick. These were specially favoured by the millers, blacksmiths, wheelwrights, and people of that sort: for even when they had holes to live in hobbits used to put up sheds and barns for workshops and storehouses.

The custom of building farms and dwelling-houses was believed to have begun among the inhabitants of the river-side regions (especially the Marish down by the Brandywine), where the land was flat and wet; and where perhaps the hobbit-breed was not quite pure. Some of the hobbits of the Marish in the East-farthing at any rate were rather large and heavy-legged; a few actually had a little down under their chins (no pure-bred hobbit had a beard); and one or two even wore boots in muddy weather.

It is possible that the idea of building, as of so many other things, came originally from the Elves. There were still in Bilbo's time three Elf-towers just beyond the western borders of the Shire. They shone in the moonlight. The tallest was furthest away, standing alone on a hill. The hobbits of the Westfarthing said that you could see the Sea from the top of that tower: but no hobbit had ever been known to climb it. But even if the notion of building came originally from the Elves, the hobbits used it in their own fashion. They did not go in much for towers. Their houses were usually long and low, and comfortable. The oldest kind were really artificial holes of mud (and later of brick), thatched with dry grass or straw, or roofed with turf; and the walls were slightly bulged. But, of course, that stage belonged to very ancient history. Hobbit-building had long been altered (and perhaps improved) by the taking of wrinkles from dwarves and even Big People, and other folk outside the Shire. A preference for round windows, and also (but to a less extent) for round doors, was the chief remaining characteristic of hobbit-architecture.

Both the houses and the holes of hobbits were usually large and inhabited by large families. (Bilbo and Frodo Baggins were in this point, as in many others, rather exceptional.) Sometimes, as in the case of the Brandybucks of Brandy Hall, many generations of relations lived in (comparative) peace together in one ancestral and ramifying mansion. All hobbits were, in any case, clannish, and reckoned up their relationships with great care. They drew long and elaborate family-trees with many branches. In dealing with hobbits it is most important to remember who is related to whom, and how, and why.

It would be impossible to set out in this book a family-tree that included even the more important members of the more important families of the Shire at the time we speak of. It would take a whole book, and everyone but hobbits would find it dull. (Hobbits would love it, if it was accurate: they like to have books full of things they already know set out fair and square with no contradictions.) The Shire was their own name for the very pleasant little corner of the world in which the most numerous, thoroughbred, and representative kind of hobbits lived in Bilbo's time. It was the only part of the world, indeed, at that time in which the two-legged inhabitants were all Hobbits, and in which Dwarves, Big People (and even Elves) were merely strangers and occasional visitors. The Shire was divided into four quarters, called the Four Farthings, the North, South, East and West Farthings; and also into a number of folklands, which bore the names of the important families, although by this time these names were no longer found only in their proper folklands. Nearly all Tooks still lived in Tookland, but that was not so true of other families, like the Bagginses or the Boffins. A map of the Shire will be found in this book, in the hope that it will be useful (and be approved as reasonably correct by those hobbits that go in for hobbit-history).

To complete the information some (abridged) family-trees are also given, which will show in what way the hobbit-persons mentioned are related to one another, and what their various ages were at the time when the story opens. This will at any rate make clear the connexions between Bilbo and Frodo, and between Folco Took and Meriadoc Brandybuck (usually called Merry) and the other chief characters.[3]

Frodo Baggins became Bilbo's heir by adoption: heir not only to what was left of Bilbo's considerable wealth, but also to his most mysterious treasure: a magic ring. This ring came from a cave in the Misty Mountains, far away in the East. It had belonged to a sad and rather loathsome creature called Gollum, of whom more will be heard in this story, though I hope some will find time to read the account of his riddle-competition with Bilbo in *The Hobbit*. It is important to this tale, as the wizard Gandalf tried to explain to Frodo. The ring had the power of making its wearer invisible. It had also other powers, which Bilbo did not discover until long after he had come back and settled down at home again. Consequently they are not spoken of in the story of his journey. But this later story is concerned chiefly with the ring, and so no more need be said about them here.

Bilbo it is told 'remained very happy to the end of his days and those were extraordinarily long.' They were. How extraordinarily long you may now discover, and you may also learn that remaining happy did not mean continuing to live for ever at Bag-end. Bilbo returned home on June 22nd in his fifty-second year, and nothing very notable occurred in the Shire for another sixty years, when Bilbo began to make preparations for the celebration of his hundred and eleventh birthday. At which point the present tale of the Ring begins.

### Chapter I: 'A Long-expected Party'

At the beginning of this sixth embodiment of the opening chapter the revised passage about Bilbo's book (p. 245, note 3) was now removed, and replaced by: 'He was supposed to be writing a book, containing a full account of his year's mysterious adventures, which no one was allowed to see.'

The conversation at *The Ivy Bush* is taken up from the preliminary version described on pp. 244–5, and now reaches virtually the form it has in FR; but at this stage the Gaffer's instruction on the subject of Bilbo and Frodo and their antecedents was still recounted in advance by the narrator also.[4]

The 'odd-looking waggons laden with odd-looking packages', driven by 'elves or heavily hooded dwarves,' which had survived from the second version of the chapter (p. 20), were now reduced to a single waggon, driven by dwarves, and no elves appear (see p. 235); but Gandalf's mark on the fireworks, here called 'runic', still remains, and he is still 'a little old man'. The guests still included the Gaukrogers (so spelt), but the remark that the Brockhouses had come in from Combe-under-Bree (p. 236) is dropped. The young Took who danced on the table changes his name from Prospero to Everard (as in FR), but his partner remains Melissa Brandybuck (Melilot in FR).

The pencilled addition to the fifth version (p. 246, note 12), showing that Bingo/Frodo was fully aware of what Bilbo intended to do, was taken up (but as in FR Frodo stays on long enough at the dinner-table to satisfy Rory Brandybuck's thirst: 'Hey, Frodo, just send that decanter round again!'); as also was the passage about Bilbo's taking Sting with him (p. 246, note 13). Bilbo now (as in FR) takes a leather-bound manuscript from a strong-box (though not the 'bundle wrapped in old cloths'), but gives the bulky envelope, which he addresses to Frodo and into which he puts the Ring, to the dwarf Lofar, asking him to put it in Frodo's room.

Gandalf still meets Bilbo at the bottom of the Hill after he has left Bag End with the Dwarves (still named Nar, Anar, and Hannar), and their conversation remains as it was (pp. 238–40): in answer to Gandalf's question 'He [Frodo] knows about it, of course?' Bilbo replies: 'He knows that I have a Ring. He has read my private memoirs (the only one I have ever allowed to read them).' Gandalf's return to Bag End after saying good-bye to Bilbo is incorporated from the very rough form in the fifth version (p. 247, note 20), the only difference being that Frodo is now actually reading Bilbo's letter as he sits in the hall.

The list of Bilbo's parting presents (p. 247, note 21) is now further changed by the loss of Caramella Chubb and her clock and Primo Grubb and his dinner-service (survivors from the original draft, p. 15, when they were Caramella Took and Inigo Grubb-Took); Colombo Hornblower and the barometer also disappear. Lofar still plays the rôle of Merry Brandybuck on the day following the Party, and Gandalf's conversation with Frodo on that day remains the same, with various later additions and omissions made to the fifth version (p. 248, notes 24–6, 28–30) incorporated: thus Bingo's reference to Bilbo's use of the Ring to escape from the Sackville-Bagginses is of course removed, in view of its use in 'A Conspiracy is Unmasked' (p. 300), as is Gandalf's suggestion that Bingo might be able to get in touch with him if necessary through 'the nearest dwarves'.

## Genealogy of the Tooks

On the reverse of one of the pages of this manuscript of 'A Long-expected Party' is the most substantial genealogy of the Tooks that has yet appeared.

The figures attached to the names are at first glance very puzzling: they are obviously neither dates according to an independent calendar, nor ages at death. The key is provided by 'Bilbo Baggins 111', and by the statement in the *Foreword* (p. 314) that the family-trees (of which this is the only one that survives, or was made at this time) would show 'what their various ages were at the time when the story opens.' The basis is the year of the Party, which is zero; and the figures are the ages of the persons *relative to the Party*. As between any two figures, the relative ages of the persons are given. Thus 311 against Ferumbras and 266 against Fortinbras means that Ferumbras was born 45 years before his son; Isengrim the First was born 374 years before Meriadoc Brandybuck eight generations later; Drogo Baggins was 23 years younger than Bilbo, and if he had not been drowned in the Brandywine and had been able to come to the Party would have been 88; and so on. The daggers of course show persons who were dead at the time of the Party.

A few of the figures were changed on the manuscript, the earlier ones being: Isengrim II 172, Isambard 160, Flambard 167, Rosa Baggins 151, Bungo Baggins 155, Yolanda 60, Folco Took 23, Meriadoc 25, Odo 24.

It will be seen that while there is no external chronological structure, the internal or relative structure is not so very different from that of the family tree of *Took of Great Smials* in LR Appendix C. In LR Meriadoc was born 362 years after Isengrim II (= Isengrim I in the old tree) and eight generations later.

Bandobras the Bullroarer (see p. 311 and note 2) is here the son of Isengrim, first of the Took line in the tree; and in the *Prologue* to LR (p. 11) he is likewise the son of that Isengrim (the Second). This was overlooked when the final Took tree was made, for Bandobras is there moved down by a generation, becoming the son (not the brother) of Isengrim's son Isumbras (III).[5]

The Old Took now acquires the name Gerontius, as in LR (earlier he was 'Frodo the First', p. 251). Four sons are named here; in LR he had nine. Rosa Baggins, wife of one of them (Flambard), has appeared in the little genealogy found in *Queries and Alterations* (p. 222): there she is the sister of Bungo Baggins, and she married 'Young Took'. The tree given on p. 267 is maintained here in respect of Merry's parents; Frodo Took has become Folco Took, and his father Folcard (see p. 309). Odo, here with a double-barrelled name Took-Bolger, was said earlier (p. 251) to have a Took mother and to be a third cousin of Merry and Frodo (Folco), as is shown in this tree.

Donnamira Took, second of the Old Took's daughters, is now named,

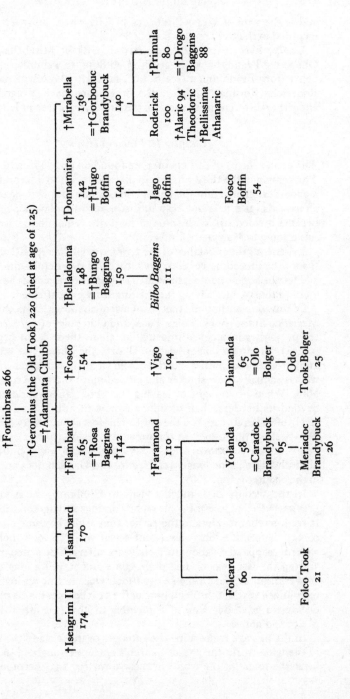

and is the wife of Hugo Boffin, as in LR, where however no issue is recorded in the tree: on this see p. 386.

Lastly, five further children (six in LR) of Mirabella Took and Gorboduc Brandybuck are given in addition to Primula, one of them being Rory Brandybuck (see p. 267, note 4), whose true name is here Roderick (Rorimac in LR); the other sons have Visigothic names altogether different from those in the Brandybuck tree in LR.

## Chapter II: 'Ancient History'

The earlier forms of this chapter are found on pp. 76 ff. and pp. 250 ff. The version in the third phase is in places difficult to interpret, for it was a good deal changed in the act of composition and very heavily altered afterwards, and it is not easy to distinguish the 'layers'; moreover, it became divided up, with some of its pages remaining in England and some going to Marquette University.

In general, the substance of the narrative remains remarkably close to that of the preceding version; my father had that before him, of course, and he was largely content merely to alter the expression as he went along – ubiquitously, but leaving the existing story little affected.

Of the younger hobbits that Frodo went about with, the chief are now Meriadoc Brandybuck, Folco Took, and Odo Bolger (on *Folco* for *Frodo* see p. 309); genealogical information about them is not provided (cf. p. 251). Frodo no longer 'walked all over the Shire,' nor was he 'often away from home'; rather, 'he did not go far afield, and after Bilbo left his walks gradually grew shorter and circled more and more round his own hole.' When he thought of leaving the Shire, and wondered what lay beyond its borders, 'half of him was now unwilling, and began to be afraid of walks abroad, lest the mud on his feet should carry him off.' The 'thin feeling' mentioned in the previous version (p. 252), 'as if he was being stretched out over a lot of days, and weeks, and months, but was not fully there', is no longer referred to, and Gandalf does not do so later in the chapter (cf. p. 266).

In the account of Gandalf's visits to Hobbiton, the passage in the previous version describing his secret comings and taps on the window is moved, so that it refers to the earlier time when he came often (cf. FR p. 55), before his long absence of seven years (p. 268, note 6). The wizard reappeared 'about fifteen years after Bilbo's departure', and 'during the last year he had often come and stayed a long time.' The conversation at *The Green Dragon* took place in 'the spring of Frodo's forty-ninth year' (at the beginning of the next chapter in this phase Frodo decides to leave Bag End in September of 'this (his fiftieth) year': see p. 253 and note 8).

In the passage concerning the rumours of trouble and the migrations in the wide world the site of Sauron's ancient stronghold in the South 'near the midst of the world in those days' (p. 253) becomes 'near the middle of the Great Land', but this was at once struck out; and the passage concerning giants becomes: 'Trolls and giants were abroad, of a new and more malevolent kind, no longer dull-witted but full of cunning and wizardry.' In the talk at the inn, the passage about the Grey Havens now appears, and the whole conversation moves almost to the form in FR (p. 54); but it is still Jo Button who saw the 'Tree-men' beyond the North Moors, though he works now for 'Mr Fosco Boffin' – with 'of Northope' added later, and then changed to 'at Overhill'. Fosco Boffin, Bilbo's first cousin once removed, appears in the Took genealogy given on p. 317; see p. 386.

The opening of the conversation between Gandalf and Frodo at Bag End was changed, probably at or very soon after the time of composition, from a form very close to that of the preceding version (p. 255) and still including Gandalf's mention of his two visits to the land of the Necromancer. The new form reads:

'You say the ring is dangerous, far more dangerous than I guess,' said Frodo at length. 'How long have you known that? And did Bilbo know? I wish you would tell me more now.'

'At first I knew very little,' answered Gandalf slowly, as if searching back in memory. Already the days of the journey and the Dragon and the Battle of Five Armies began to seem dim and far-off. Perhaps even he was at last beginning to feel his age; and in any case many dark and strange adventures had befallen him since. 'Then after I came back from the South and the White Council, I began to wonder what kind of magic ring he possessed; but I said nothing to Bilbo. All seemed well with him, and I thought that that kind of power was powerless over him. So I thought; and I was right in a way; but not quite right. I ought perhaps to have found out more, sooner than I did, and then I should have warned him earlier. But before he left I told him what I could – by that time I had begun to suspect the truth, but I knew very little for certain.'

'I am sure you did all you could,' said Frodo. 'You have been a good friend, and a wise counsellor to us. But it must have been a great blow to you when Bilbo disappeared.'

In Gandalf's account of the Rings (p. 260) he now says: 'Slowly through the years he has been seeking for them, hoping to recall their power into his own hands, and hoping always to find the One'; and his words concerning the Three Rings were early changed from their form in the second version (p. 260, but with 'earth, sea, and sky' for 'earth, air, and sky'):

What use they made of the Three Rings of Earth, Sea, and Sky, I do not know; nor do I know what has now become of them. Some say that hidden Elf-kings still keep them in fast places of the Middle-earth; but I believe they have long been carried far over the Great Sea.

Gandalf, again by early or immediate change, now concludes his remarks about the Seven Rings of the Dwarves, which some say have perished in the fire of the dragons, with the words: 'Yet that account, maybe, is not wholly true'; he does not now refer to the belief that some of the Seven Rings are preserved, though no doubt he implies it (cf. the first draft for the Council of Elrond, p. 398).

As my father first wrote here the passage about Gil-galad, he began by following the former text almost exactly, with 'Valandil, King of the Island' (see p. 260 and note 26), but he changed it in the act of writing to: 'and he made an alliance with Valandil, King of the men of Númenor, who came back over the sea from Westernesse into Middle-earth in those days.' *Valandil* was then changed to *Elendil*, probably almost immediately, and also at the subsequent occurrences of the name in this passage. *Isildor* of the second text is now written *Isildur*. Isildur's host was overwhelmed by 'Orcs', not 'Goblins' (see p. 437, note 35).

To Gandalf's story of Gollum nothing is added or altered from the preceding version (see p. 261), save that 'his grandmother who ruled all the family turned him out of her hole.'

The purport of Gandalf's discussion of Gollum's character and motives in respect of the Ring remains unchanged from the second version, though of course with continual slight development in expression, and in some passages with considerable expansion. The words 'Only Elves can stand it, and even they fade' (p. 261) are now omitted. Gandalf's meaning in his reply to Frodo's objection that Gollum never gave Bilbo the Ring is now made clearer:

'But he never gave Bilbo the Ring,' said Frodo. 'Bilbo had already found it lying on the floor.'

'I know, answered Gandalf, 'and I have always thought that that was one of the strangest things about Bilbo's adventure. That is why I said that Gollum's ancestry only partly explained what happened . . .'

It is still Gandalf himself who found Gollum, though Frodo's exclamation 'You found Gollum!' (p. 263) was subsequently changed to 'You have seen Gollum!', and Gandalf's reply to Frodo's question 'Did you find him there [in Mirkwood]?' (p. 264) was changed to 'I saw him there, but it was friends of mine who actually tracked him down, with the help of the Wood-elves.' Cf. the first version of the Council of Elrond, p. 401 and note 20. – Gandalf's account of Gollum's own story is expanded thus:

What I have told you, Gollum was willing to tell – though not, of course, in the way I have reported it. Gollum is a liar, and you have to sift his words. For instance, you may remember that he told Bilbo he had the Ring as a birthday-present. Very unlikely on the face of it: incredible when one suspects what kind of ring it really was. It was said merely to make Bilbo willing to accept it as a harmless kind of toy – one of Gollum's hobbit-like thoughts. He repeated this nonsense to me, but I laughed at him. He then told me the truer story, with a lot of snivelling and snarling. He thought he was misunderstood and ill-treated . . .

Gandalf still says, oddly, that Gollum 'had found out eventually, of course, that Bilbo had in some way got his Ring, and what his name was, and where he came from' (see p. 263 and note 32); indeed the point is now made more emphatically: 'And the news of later events went all over Wilderland, and *Bilbo's name was spoken* far and wide.'

When Gandalf pauses after saying 'he made his slow sneaking way bit by bit, years ago, down to the Land of Mordor' the heavy silence mentioned in FR p. 68 falls, and 'there was now no sound of Sam's shears.' The phrase 'I think indeed that Gollum is the beginning of our present troubles' is retained: see p. 271, note 33.

From '"Well anyway," said Frodo, "if Gollum could not be killed"' my father at first followed the earlier text (p. 265) very closely, but then rewrote it in a changed form.

'Well anyway,' said Frodo, 'if Gollum could not be killed, I wish Bilbo had not kept the Ring. Why did he?'

'Is not that clear from what you have now heard?' answered Gandalf. 'I remember you saying, when it first came to you, that it had its advantages, and that you wondered why Bilbo went off without it [see p. 242]. He had possessed it a long while before we knew that it was specially important. After that it was too late: there was the Ring itself to reckon with. It has a power and purpose of its own that clouds wise counsel. Even Bilbo could not altogether escape its influence. He developed a sentiment. Even when he knew that it came ultimately from the Necromancer he wished to keep it as a memento . . .'

Lastly, the passage beginning 'I really do wish to destroy it!' (p. 266) was changed and amplified:

'I really do wish to destroy it!' cried Frodo. 'But I wish more that the Ring need never have come to me. Why was I chosen?'

'Bilbo passed it on to you to save himself from destruction; and because he could find no one else. He did so reluctantly, but believing that, when you knew more, you would accept the burden for a while out of love for him. He thought you were safe: safe not to misuse it or to let it get into evil hands; safe from its power for a time; and safe in the quiet Shire of the hobbits from the knowledge of its maker. And I promised him to help you. He relied on that. Indeed for your sake and for his I have taken many perilous journeys.

'Also I may say that I did not discover the letters of fire or their meaning or know for certain that this was the Ruling Ring until he had already decided to go. I did not tell him, for then he would not have burdened you. I let him go. He had had the Ring for sixty years, and it was telling on him, Frodo. It would have worn him down in the end, and I dare not guess what might then have happened.

'But now, alas! I know more. I have seen Gollum. I have journeyed even to the Land of Mordor. I fear that the Enemy is searching. You are in a far graver peril than ever Bilbo dreamed of. So do not blame him.'

'But I am not strong enough!' said Frodo. 'You are wise and powerful. Will you not take the Ring?'

'No!' said Gandalf springing to his feet. 'With that Ring I should have power too great and terrible. And over me it would gain a power still greater and more deadly.' His eyes flashed and his face was lit as by a fire within. 'Do not tempt me! For I do not wish to become like the Dark Lord himself. Yet the way of the Ring to my heart is by pity for weakness and the desire of strength to do good. Do not tempt me!'

He went to the window and drew aside the curtain and shutters. Sunlight streamed back again into the room. Sam passed along the path outside, whistling. 'In any case,' said the wizard, turning back to Frodo, 'it is now too late. You would hate me and call me a thief; and our friendship would cease. Such is the power of the Ring. But together we will shoulder the burden that is laid on us.' He came and laid his hand on Frodo's shoulder. 'But we must do something soon,' he said. 'The Enemy is moving.'

The same curious idea is still present here that Gandalf discovered the letters of fire on Bilbo's ring, and knew that it was the Ruling Ring, *before* Bilbo left but *without* telling him (i.e. without Bilbo's knowledge that this test had been made): see p. 266 and note 38. – Gandalf's remark (p. 321) 'I think indeed that Gollum is the beginning of our present troubles', retained from the second version, now perhaps becomes less obscure (see p. 271, note 33): 'I have been to the Land of Mordor. I fear that the Enemy is searching.'

### Chapter III: 'Delays are Dangerous'

The new text of the third chapter, now given this title (which had been scribbled in on the second version), was another fine clear manuscript, replacing its appallingly difficult predecessor (pp. 273 ff.).

The chapter still begins with the gossip in *The Ivy Bush* and *The Green Dragon* (p. 274 and note 1) before turning to the conversation between Gandalf and Frodo. In that conversation Gandalf does now refer, as in FR, to the possibility that it may be Frodo's task to find the Cracks of Doom – indeed he goes further:

'And to go *there* but not come *back again*,' added Gandalf grimly. 'For in the end I think you must come to the Fiery Mountain, though you are not yet ready to make that your goal.'

That with Merry's help[6] Frodo had chosen a little house at Crickhollow (see p. 299) is now taken up from the pencilled change to the previous version (p. 283, note 2). Gandalf still leaves Hobbiton 'one wet dark evening in May'.

But a major change enters the story with the departure of Odo Bolger (not Took-Bolger, as in the family tree, p. 317) with Merry Brandybuck in the third cart from Hobbiton. My father had proposed this earlier (p. 299): 'From here onwards [i.e. after the arrival in Buckland] Odo is presumed to have gone with Merry ahead. The preliminary journey was Frodo [Took], Bingo and Sam only. Frodo has a character a little more like Odo once had. Odo is now rather silent (and greedy).' But the text that followed this direction was obscure and contradictory, apparently on account of my opposition to the proposal (see p. 299). Now the deed was done properly.

In the earlier versions of the chapter the young hobbits Frodo and Odo had distinct characters (see p. 70). The removal of Odo from the expedition does not mean, however, that Odo's character was removed; because my father always worked on the basis of preceding drafts, and a great deal of the original material of this chapter survived. Though Frodo Took, now renamed Folco Took (since Bingo had become Frodo), was the one who remained in the new narrative, he had to become the speaker of the things that the absent Odo had said – unless my father was to rewrite what he had written in a far more drastic way than he wished to. Despite the early note 'Sam Gamgee to replace Odo' (p. 250), Sam was too particularly conceived from the outset to be at all suitable to take up Odo's nonchalance. Moreover, in this version of the chapter the original contribution of Folco (Frodo) Took was in any case further reduced. The verse *The Road goes ever on and on* had already been given to Bingo in the second version (p. 278); now his account of meeting a Black Rider up on the North Moors was dropped, and his exclamation of delight when the singing of the Elves was heard ('Elves! How wonderful! I have always wished to hear elves singing under stars') was cut out apparently in the act of writing and replaced by Sam's hoarse whisper: 'Elves!' So Folco Took, with a diminished part of 'his own', and acquiring much of 'Odo's', becomes 'Odo' more completely than my father apparently foresaw when he said 'Frodo [Took] has a character a little more like Odo once had.'[7]

Yet Folco's *genealogical* place remains; for Odo himself (once surnamed Took but now a Bolger with a Took mother) has gone on ahead to Buckland, where a separate and distinct adventure (already glimpsed in advance, pp. 302, 304) will overtake him, while into Folco's place in the family tree of the Tooks, as first cousin of Merry Brandybuck (pp. 267, 317), will later step Peregrin Took (Pippin).

Cosimo Sackville-Baggins' 'overshadowed wife Miranda' disappears again, together with the remark that he and his mother Lobelia lived at Bag End 'for many a year after' (p. 283, note 5). – *The Road goes ever on and on* now attains the final form (p. 284, note 10). – At the first appearance of the Black Rider on the road, in the passage cited on p. 278, 'Odo and Frodo' become 'Folco and Sam', and the text of FR (p. 84) is reached.

As already noticed, Frodo Took's account of his meeting with a Black Rider on the North Moors of the Shire (p. 278) is now dropped, and the conversation between Bingo and Frodo Took on the subject of the Black Riders (p. 279) that follows Sam's revelation moves on to precisely the form in FR (p. 85), with of course Folco for Pippin. The brief halt of the Rider by the decayed tree in which the hobbits ate their supper is however retained in this version, and in the ensuing conversation Frodo still says, as did Bingo, that he will take the name of Mr Hill of Faraway.

When the singing of the Elves is heard Frodo says, as in FR p. 88: 'One can meet them sometimes in the Woody End', but he still says as in the preceding version (p. 280) that they come in spring and autumn 'out of their own lands far beyond the River'. As in FR, the hymn to Elbereth is now said to be sung 'in the fair Elven-tongue', and at the end of it Frodo says: 'These are High-elves! They speak the name of Elbereth!'

Odo's indiscreet remark about their good luck in landing unexpectedly good food and lodging disappears and is not handed on to Folco. Frodo's 'The stars shine on the hour of our meeting' was at first given as before (p. 280) only in translation, but my father changed this, clearly in the act of writing the manuscript, by the introduction of the Elvish words as well, *Eleni silir lúmesse omentiemman*, and then again to *Elen silë* . . . , 'A star shines . . .' At this Gildor says, as in FR, 'Here is a scholar in the Ancient Tongue.'

It is still the Moon that rouses the Elves to song; but the old wording ('The yellow moon rose; springing swiftly out of the shadow, and then climbing round and slow into the sky') surviving from the original version of the chapter (p. 61), was changed, apparently at or very near the time of writing, to: 'Above the mists away in the East the thin silver rind of the New Moon appeared, and rising swift and clear out of the shadow it swung gleaming in the sky.' My father no doubt made this change on account of what he had said elsewhere about the Moon; for there was a waxing moon as the hobbits approached Weathertop, and it was 'nearly half-full' on the night of the attack (pp. 168, 184): the attack was on 5 October (p. 175), and there could not be a full or nearly full Moon on 24 September, the night passed with the Elves in the Woody End (see p. 160). On that night it must have been almost New Moon. The dates of the phases of the Moon in the autumn and early winter of that year cited on p. 434, note 19, in fact give New Moon on 25 September, the First Quarter (half-full) on 2 October, and Full Moon on 10 October. But it is an odd and uncharacteristic aberration that my father envisaged a New Moon rising late at night in the East.[8] In FR, of course, there is no mention of the Moon in this passage: it was 'the Swordsman of the Sky, Menelvagor with his shining belt' that caused the Elves to burst into song.

In the passage describing the memories of the meal eaten with the Elves the text of FR is reached, with Folco retaining those of Frodo Took together with Odo's recollection of the bread.

Gildor's advice to Bingo (Frodo) that he should take trusty companions, and his opinion that his present companions have already confused the Riders, is retained (see p. 282); but at the end there is now no mention of the Ring, and their talk ends as in FR (p. 94).

*Chapter IV: 'A Short Cut to Mushrooms'*

In this new version of the chapter there is only to notice the curious result of the exclusion of Odo Bolger: with Folco Took adding Odo's part to that which he retained from Frodo Took's in the former narrative. In the previous version Odo argued against taking a short cut to the Ferry, because, while he did not know the country, he did know *The Golden Perch* at Stock, and Frodo Took argued for it – because he did know the country.[9] Now, the Frodo-element in Folco, retaining a knowledge of the country, uses it to support the desire of the Odo-element in him for the beer at Stock, and his opponent in the argument is Frodo (Baggins); thus Folco is here, and throughout the chapter, Pippin in all but name (see pp. 286–7).

Deephallow now disappears from the text (see p. 286).

*Chapter V: 'A Conspiracy Unmasked'*

This chapter had already reached in the second version (pp. 298 ff.) a form very close to that in FR, but there remained the confusion over whether Odo had been on the walk from Hobbiton or whether he had gone on ahead to Buckland with Merry (see pp. 299, 323). Following the new version of Chapter III, this is now resolved, of course: Odo is at Crickhollow, opens the door when they arrive, and cooks the supper with Merry – in fact, until the end of the chapter, he has become Fredegar (Fatty) Bolger. The text now reaches, until the end of the chapter, the form in FR, down to the smallest particulars of expression, with these differences only: the passage about Gorhendad Oldbuck is still not present (p. 298); the Hedge is still forty miles from end to end (*ibid.*); and the 'dwarf-song' *Farewell! farewell, now hearth and hall!* still retains the form in the previous version (pp. 300–1).[10]

The end of the chapter still differs altogether from that in FR, however. The form in the second version was preserved, with the pencilled additions incorporated (p. 302). Odo says 'But *we shan't* have any luck in the Old Forest' (whereas in FR Fredegar says 'But *you won't* have any luck'), because he is still potentially a member of the further expedition, even though my father had in fact decided that he would stay at Crickhollow till Gandalf came. I give the text from 'Do you follow Captain Frodo, or do you stay at home?'

'We follow Captain Frodo,' said Merry and Folco (and of course Sam). Odo was silent. 'Look here!' he said after a pause. 'I don't mind admitting that I am more terrified of the Forest than of anything I know about. I dislike woods of any kind, but the stories about the Old Forest are a nightmare. But I also think that you ought to try and keep in touch with Gandalf, who I guess knows more about the Black Riders than you do. I will stay behind here and keep off inquisitive folk. When Gandalf comes, as I think he is sure to, I will tell him what you have done, and I will come on after you with him, if he will bring me.'

The others agreed that this seemed on the whole an excellent plan; and Frodo at once wrote a brief letter to Gandalf, and gave it to Odo.

'Well, that's settled,' said Merry.

The rest of the chapter is as in the previous version.

A curious trace of this stage survives in the published text. Since Odo's staying behind had not formed part of the 'conspiracy', Merry had prepared six ponies, five for the five hobbits and one for the baggage. When the story changed, and Fredegar Bolger's task 'according to the original plans of the conspirators' (FR p. 118) was expressly to stay

THE JOURNEY TO BREE 327

behind, this detail was overlooked, and the six ponies remained at this point (FR p. 117).

### Chapter VI: 'The Old Forest'

The chapter now at last receives its title. Odo now said farewell to the others at the entrance to the tunnel under the Hedge in these words:

'I wish you were not going into the Forest. I don't believe you will get safely through; and I think it is very necessary that someone should warn Gandalf that you have gone in. I'm sure you will need rescuing before to-day is out. Still I wish you luck and I hope, perhaps, I shall catch you up again one day.'

The hill rising out of the forest was still crowned with a knot of trees (p. 113), but this was changed to the 'bald head' of FR in the act of writing this manuscript. The gully which the hobbits were forced to follow downwards because they could not climb out of it still ends as before (*ibid.*):

Suddenly the woodland trees came to an end, and the gully became deep and sheer-sided; its bottom was almost wholly filled by the noisy hurrying water. It ran down finally to a narrow shelf at the top of a rocky bank, over which the stream dived and fell in a series of small waterfalls. Looking down they saw that below them was a wide space of grass and reeds . . .

The old story of the descent down the thirty-foot bank is thus still present, with Folco falling the last fifteen feet.

In the original form of the story of the encounter with Old Man Willow (p. 113) Bingo and Odo were trapped in the tree, and Merry (then called Marmaduke) was the one who rounded up the ponies and rescued Frodo Took from the river. In the next stage (p. 302) this was changed to the extent that Sam took over Merry's part, and Merry simply 'lay like a log'. Now, with Frodo Took and Odo 'reduced' to Folco Took, it is still Frodo Baggins and Folco who are imprisoned in the tree, but Merry steps into Frodo Took's rôle as the one pushed into the river.

In the oldest version the path beside the Withywindle puzzlingly turned sharply to the left below Tom Bombadil's house and went over a little bridge; and in later revision this was retained, with, later again, the word 'left' changed to 'right', implying that Bombadil's house was on the south side of the Withywindle (see p. 114). The present text read at first here:

[The path] turned sharply to the right, and took them over a wooden bridge that crossed another smaller stream that came chattering down.

This retains the turn in the path and the bridge, but the bridge being over a tributary stream Bombadil's house is on the north side of the Withy-windle. My father struck the passage out, however, apparently as he wrote.

### Chapter VII: 'In the House of Tom Bombadil'

Like the last, this chapter now receives its title. The episode of the attack on Crickhollow (pp. 303–4) is now a part of the text, and was repeated from the earlier form with scarcely any significant change and almost word for word. The 'grey man' came up the path leading a white horse, but that Gandalf had a white horse appears later in the first version. More important, my father at first repeated the words 'Suddenly there was a movement', but struck them out and substituted: 'A curtain in one of the windows stirred. Then suddenly the figure by the door moved swiftly' (this change clearly belongs with the writing of the manuscript). Odo was in the house, of course. To the words pencilled at the end of the first version of the episode, 'Behind clung a small figure with flying cloak', and 'Odo', there is nothing corresponding in the next, and I think that they had not, in fact, yet been written in on the former; at this stage, it seems, my father had no further plans for Odo. But there is a pencilled addition to the second text of which, though it was erased, Mr Taum Santoski has been able to make out the following: 'Behind him ran Odo . . . and . . . wind. Cf. IX.22.' On this question see p. 336.

*The dreams.* The content of Frodo's dream remains the same, almost word for word, as Bingo's in the original version (p. 118), except that after the words 'hoofs thudding and wind blowing' there follows 'and faint and far the echo of a horn': this obviously echoes Gandalf's blowing of the horn at Crickhollow, which in this text immediately precedes Frodo's dream. But whereas in the story as told in the first phase 'Bingo woke' and then 'fell asleep again' (on the reality of the sounds he heard see p. 119), in this version Frodo 'lay in a dream without light': this is as in FR, but nothing is said here to suggest that he woke (contrast FR: '"Black Riders!" thought Frodo as he wakened.') On the other hand the passage in the present text ends as in FR: 'at last he turned and fell asleep again or wandered into some other unremembered dream.' Folco dreams what was originally Odo's dream, and like Pippin in FR 'woke, or thought he had waked', and then 'went to sleep again.' Merry takes over Frodo Took's dream of water, with the words 'falling into his quiet sleep and slowly waking him' retained from the old version, though struck out, probably at once; this passage ends, as in FR, 'He breathed deep and fell asleep again.' Sam 'slept through the night in deep content, if logs are contented.'

In Tom's talk with the hobbits on the second day, the old phrase 'A dark shadow came up out of the middle of the world' is retained (see p. 121); and Tom's reply to Frodo's question 'Who are you, Master?' is almost exactly as in the old version (p. 121): he says 'I am Ab-Origine, that's what I am,' and the words 'He saw the Sun rise in the West and the Moon following, before the new order of days was made' are retained (see my discussion of this passage, pp. 121–2).

In all the other minor differences mentioned on pp. 122–3 the present text reaches the final form.

### Chapter VIII: 'Fog on the Barrow-downs'

There is little that need be said about this chapter, which followed on the original text (pp. 127–30), and which now received its title. The 'arm walking on its fingers' in the barrow crept towards Folco, and Frodo fell forward upon him (p. 127). Merry's words when he woke remain unchanged (p. 128); and nothing more is said of the bronze swords that Tom Bombadil chose for the hobbits from the treasures of the mound than the words added to the original text: Tom said that 'they were made many ages ago by men out of the West: they were foes of the dark Lord.'

The conclusion of the chapter moves some way to the final form, but features of the original version are retained (pp. 129–30). Thus Frodo, riding down onto the Road, still says: 'I hope we shall be able to stick to the beaten track after this,' to which Bombadil replies: 'That's what you ought to do, as long as you are able: hold to the beaten way, but ride fast and wary.' In his parting advice he still says: 'Barnabas Butterbur is the worthy keeper: he knows Tom Bombadil, and Tom's name will help you. Say "Tom sent us here", and he will treat you kindly.' After he has gone there is no conversation among the hobbits recorded, and the chapter ends much as in the original text. Sam rode with Frodo in front, Merry and Folco behind, leading the spare pony; and Bree is still 'a little village'.

### NOTES

1  *Earliest Days*, occurring twice in this passage, was changed later to *Elder Days*. The latter expression occurs once in the *Quenta Silmarillion*, where it is not capitalised (V.259); cf. also *Elder Years* (V.90), *eldest years* (V.245).

2  Bandobras the Bullroarer reappears from *The Hobbit* (Chapter I); see further pp. 316–17.

3  Only one such tree is known to me, perhaps the only one made by my father at this time; see pp. 316–18.

4  Thus whereas in the preliminary version of the talk in *The Ivy Bush* (p. 244) the narrator's opening was to be reduced to a brief paragraph, my father was now both retaining the account of past history from earlier versions of the chapter and also adding Gaffer Gamgee's

own characteristic mode of retailing it. In FR the Gaffer becomes the sole source.

5   In *The Hobbit* Bandobras is called Bilbo's great-grand-uncle, but Bilbo himself calls him his great-great-great-grand-uncle – as he is in the present tree.

6   His cousin Lanorac Brandybuck (p. 275) has disappeared.

7   The discussion whether to walk far or not on the first night was still present (see p. 276), but Folco does not take on Odo's reluctance; the result is that all three of them agree, and the discussion being now rather pointless my father struck it out and replaced it with the words of FR (p. 80): 'Well, we all like walking in the dark, so let's put some miles behind us before bed.'

8   It is indeed so extraordinary, in view of his deep and constant awareness of all such modes and appearances, that one seeks for an explanation: can he have intended 'the Old Moon' but have written 'the New Moon' because he was thinking of the crescent form (characteristically 'the New Moon') rather than the phase? This seems unlikely; and in any case an 'old Moon' as a 'thin silver rind' is not seen till near dawn, for the Moon to have this appearance must be very near to the Sun.

9   In the earlier, abandoned variant of the Farmer Maggot episode in the previous version of the chapter Maggot says that Frodo Took is 'half a Brandybuck' (p. 291). This was already omitted in the second variant; but he was Merry Brandybuck's first cousin, and he tells Bingo that Maggot 'is a friend of Merry's, and I used to come here with him a good deal at one time' – just as Pippin tells Frodo in FR, p. 101.

10  My father first wrote that it was sung by Merry, Folco, and Odo, but Odo's name was no doubt due to its presence in the previous version (p. 300), and he struck it out at once.

## XX

## THE THIRD PHASE (2):
## AT THE SIGN OF THE
## PRANCING PONY

With Chapter IX, now given the title 'At the Sign of the Prancing Pony',
the narrative of this phase underwent a much more substantial development, but not at all in the direction of the final story in FR. Before
coming to this, however, there is a curious feature in the opening of the
chapter to be considered.

The opening now advanced far from the early forms given on
pp. 132–4: an initial account in which Bree was a village of Men, but
where 'there were hobbits about', changed to the story that there were
only hobbits in Bree, and Mr Butterbur was himself a hobbit. A later
note (p. 223) said however that 'Bree-folk are *not* to be hobbits.' Now my
father resolved the question by returning, more or less, to the original
idea: Men and Hobbits lived together in Bree. But he found it difficult to
achieve a form of the opening with which he could be satisfied, and there
is version after version soon tailing off, to be replaced by the next. All
these drafts are very similar, differing in the ordering of the material and
in the admission or omission of detail; all obviously belong to the same
time; and there is no need to look at them closely, except in one
particular. All the drafts contain the passage in FR (p. 161) concerning
the origin of the Men of Bree – one of them adding that they were
'descendants of the sons of Bëor' – and the return of the Kings of Men
over the Great Seas.[1] The passage that follows, as in FR, concerns the
Rangers, and is almost the same in all the draft forms of it:

No other Men lived now so far West, nor so near the Shire by a
hundred leagues and more. No settled people, that is: for there
were the Rangers, mysterious wanderers that the Men of Bree
regarded with deep respect (and a little fear), since they were said
to be the last remnant of the kingly people from beyond the Seas.
But the Rangers were few and seldom seen, and roamed at will in
the wild lands eastward, even as far as the Misty Mountains.

The curious thing is that in the form of the chapter-opening that was
allowed to stand the account of the Rangers is quite different, and does
not follow on from the words 'No other Men lived at that time so far
West, nor so near by a hundred leagues to the Shire', but is placed

further on (after 'There was Bree-blood in the Brandybuck family by all accounts', FR p. 162). This version reads:

In the wild lands east of Bree there roamed a few unsettled folk (men and hobbits). These the people of the Bree-land called Rangers. Some of them were well-known in Bree, which they visited fairly frequently, and were welcome as bringers of news and tellers of strange tales.

Later in the chapter, Butterbur answers Frodo's question about Trotter thus:

I don't rightly know. He is one of the wandering folk – Rangers, we call them. Not that he really is a Ranger, if you understand me, though he behaves like one. He seems to be a hobbit of some kind. He has been coming in pretty often during the past twelve months, especially since last spring; but he seldom talks.

In the original version at this place (p. 137) Butterbur says: 'O! that is one of the wild folk – rangers we call 'em.' And Gandalf in his letter to Frodo still refers in the third phase text, as in the old version, to Trotter as 'a ranger . . . dark rather lean hobbit, wears wooden shoes' (p. 352).

With these extracts compare the note in *Queries and Alterations* (p. 223): 'Rangers are best *not* as hobbits, perhaps.'

It is difficult to interpret this. In the third phase we find the statement (in draft versions) that Rangers are 'the last remnant of the kingly people from beyond the Seas'; and also the statements that Rangers are both men and hobbits, that one particular hobbit is a Ranger (so Gandalf), and that this same hobbit is 'not really a Ranger, though he behaves like one' (so Butterbur). The simplest explanation is to suppose that the Númenórean origin of the Rangers was an idea that my father was considering in the drafts, but which he set aside when he wrote the text of the chapter and the subsequent narrative (see further p. 393). Whatever the explanation, it is clear that the finished conception of the Rangers had a difficult emergence; and it is characteristic that even when the idea of the Rangers as the last descendants of the Númenórean exiles had arisen, and a place thus prepared, as it were, for Trotter, he did not at once move into that place.

The village of Staddle now reappears (see p. 132), on the other side of the hill; and Combe is set 'in a deep valley a little further eastward', Archet 'on the edge of Chetwood' – all as in FR p. 161. That Bree stood at an old meeting of the ways, the East Road and the Greenway running north and south, now appears. In the only one of the draft versions of the opening to reach the actual narrative, the hobbits

passed one or two detached houses before they came to the inn, and Sam and Folco stared at these in wonder. Sam was filled with deep suspicion, and doubted the wisdom of seeking any lodging in such an outlandish place. 'Fancy having to climb up a ladder to bed!' he said. 'What do they do it for? They aren't birds.'

'It's airier,' said Frodo, 'and safer too in wilder country. There is no fence around Bree that I can see.'

Here my father stopped; probably at that moment he decided that this was improbable. In the completed text of the chapter dike, hedge, and gate appear.

Frodo and his companions came at last to the Greenway-crossing and drew near the village. They found that it was surrounded by a deep ditch with a hedge and fence on the inner side. Over this the Road ran, but it was closed (as was the custom after nightfall) by a great gate of loose bars laid across strong posts on either side.

A little sketch-map, reproduced on p. 335, very likely belongs to just this time. Written beside the line marking the outer circuit of Bree is 'ditch & f', i.e. 'fence'. (For an earlier, very simple sketch-plan of Bree see p. 174, note 20).

The text continues:

There was a house just beyond the barrier, and a man was sitting at the door. He jumped up and fetched a lantern, and looked down over the gate at them in surprise.

'We are making for the inn here,' said Frodo in answer to his questions. 'We are journeying east, and cannot go further tonight.'

'Hobbits!' said the man. 'And what's more, Shire-hobbits from the sound of your talk! Well, if that is not a wonder: Shire-folk riding by night and journeying east!'

He removed the bars slowly and let them ride through. 'And what makes it stranger,' he went on: 'there's been more than one traveller in the last few days going the same way, and enquiring after a party of four hobbits on ponies. But I laughed at them and said there had been no such party and was never likely to be. And here you are! But if you go on to old Butterbur's I don't doubt you'll find a welcome, and more news of your friends, maybe.'

They wished him goodnight; but Frodo made no comment on his talk, though he could see in the lantern-light that the man was eyeing them curiously. He was glad to hear the bars dropped in their places behind them as they rode forward. One Black Rider at least was now ahead of them, or so he guessed from the man's words, but it was likely enough that others were still behind. And what about Gandalf? Had he, too, passed through, trying to catch them up while they were delayed in the Forest and Downs?

The hobbits rode on up a gentle slope, passing a few detached houses, and drew up outside the inn. . . .

The account of Sam's dismay at the sight of the tall houses, of the structure of the inn, and of their arrival, is almost word for word as in FR p. 164; and Barnabas Butterbur is now a man, not a hobbit. But the passage in the original version in which Bingo (Frodo) refers to Tom Bombadil's recommendation of *The Prancing Pony* and is then made welcome by the landlord (pp. 134–5) is retained. Frodo now introduces them by their correct names, except that he calls himself 'Mr Hill of Faraway' (see pp. 280, 324). Butterbur replies much as in the old version (p. 135), but his remarks there about the Tooks are now applied to the Brandybucks, and not merely in the general context of the Shire-folk but because Merry has been introduced as Mr Brandybuck; and he now mentions the strangers who had come up the Greenway the night before. The passage about their supply of money (see p. 136 and note 7) is retained, though the urgency is made less ('Frodo had brought some money with him, of course, as much as was safe or convenient; but it would not cover the expenses of good inns indefinitely.')

From 'The landlord hovered round for a little, and then prepared[2] to leave them' the new chapter reaches the final form for a long stretch with only minor differences and for the most part in the same words. The people in the common-room of the inn (including the strangers from the South, who 'stared curiously') are as in FR (and the botanical names of the Men of Bree, see p. 137 and note 8); but 'among the company [Frodo] noticed the gate-keeper, and wondered vaguely if it was his night off duty.' The 'squint-eyed ill-favoured fellow' who in FR foretold that many more people would be coming north in the near future is here simply 'one of the travellers' who had come up the Greenway. Folco Took is now of course 'the ridiculous young Took'; but he does not yet tell the tale of the collapse of the roof of the Town Hole in Michel Delving. Frodo 'heard someone ask what part the Hills lived in and where Faraway was; and he hoped Sam and Folco would be careful.'

As already noticed, Trotter remains a hobbit;[3] and the description of him in fact follows the original version (p. 137) closely, including the wooden shoes; his pipe was changed from 'broken' to 'short-stemmed' in the act of writing, and he had 'an enormous mug (large even for a man)' in front of him. In Frodo's first conversation with Trotter, and in all that follows to the end of Chapter 9 in FR, the present text moves almost to the final form (which has in any case been virtually attained, in the latter part, already in the original version, see p. 140). Frodo's feeling that the suggestion that he put on the Ring came to him 'from outside, from someone or something in the room' is present. At first my father wrote simply that the 'swarthy-faced fellow' (Bill Ferney)[4] 'slipped out of the

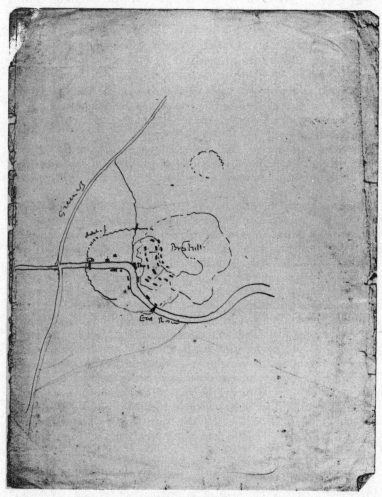

Plan of Bree

door, followed by one of the southerners: not a well-favoured pair'; but by a change that seems little later than the writing of the manuscript this became:

> Very soon he slipped out of the door, followed by Harry the gate-keeper, and by one of the southerners: the three had been whispering together in a corner most of the evening. For a moment he wondered if the Ring itself had not played him a trick – or perhaps obeyed orders other than his own. He did not like the looks of the three men that had gone out, especially not the [dark-eyed >] squint-eyed southerner.

In this text it has already been mentioned that the gate-keeper was present at the inn; this is not in FR, though it is said that he went out just behind the other two. – The text of *The Cat and the Fiddle* is now exactly in the final form.

In the original version I divided the text for convenience at the point where Chapter 9 ends in FR, though there is no break in the manuscript. The present version also continues without a break, and in this case it is more convenient to treat the old chapter as a whole.

The next part of the story follows the original form (pp. 148–9) very closely to the point where Trotter tells Bingo about his 'eavesdropping' on the Road. There, Trotter had overheard Gandalf and the Dwarves and Elves (returning from Hobbiton after Bingo Bolger-Baggins' 'long-expected party' and disappearance) talking about Bingo and his companions who were supposed to be on the Road behind them: the date was Sunday morning, September 25th (p. 160). The present version here introduces a major alteration into the narrative structure, but by no means to the story in FR, where Strider overhears the hobbits talking to Bombadil when he left them on the East Road (and hears Frodo say that he must be known as Underhill, not Baggins).

It seems likely that the new story, in which the further adventures of Odo Bolger first appear in formed narrative, arose when my father came to this chapter in his writing of the third phase manuscripts, and that it was at this stage that he pencilled in the notes about Odo leaving Crickhollow with Gandalf[5] after the rout of the Black Riders (see p. 328): that is why, in the note to the second text of the attack on Crickhollow, he gave the reference 'IX.22'. IX.22 is the manuscript page in which Trotter's story of his eavesdropping on Gandalf *and Odo* on the East Road appears in the present chapter.

It will be seen that version 'A' of the original story is used: see pp. 148 and 171 note 1.

The opening of this section of the story is duplicated, both versions appearing to belong to the same time of writing, and neither being struck out; but the second form given here was preferred. The one reads:

... I was behind a hedge, when a man on a horse halted on the Road not far [west of Bree > *(at time of writing)*] east of Bree. To my surprise there was a hobbit riding behind him on the same horse! They got off to take a meal, and started talking. Now, oddly enough, they were discussing a certain Frodo Baggins and his three companions. I gathered that these four strange folk were hobbits that had bolted out of the Shire (by a back-door, as you might say) last Monday, and ought to be on the Road somewhere. The travellers were very worried about Mr Baggins, and wondered whether he was on the Road or off it, in front of them or behind. They wanted to find him and *warn* him.

'A bit incautious, I must say, of Gandalf – there now! Gandalf it was, of course: there's no mistaking him, you'll agree – to go talking like that by the Road-side. But actually he was speaking low, and I happened to be lying very close. That would be yesterday noon: Wednesday.

The other reads:

... I was hiding under a hedge, by the Road some way west of Bree, trying to shelter from the rain, when a man on horseback halted close by. To my surprise there was a hobbit riding behind him on the same horse! They got off to rest, and take a little food, and they started talking. If you want to know, they were discussing a certain Frodo Baggins and his three companions. I gathered that these were four hobbits that had left the Shire in a great hurry the previous day. The horseman was trying to catch them up, but he was not sure if they were on the Road or off it, in front or behind. He seemed very worried, but hoped to find them at Bree. I thought it very strange, for it is not often that Gandalf's plans go wrong.'

Frodo stirred suddenly at the mention of the name, and Trotter smiled. 'Yes, Gandalf!' he said. 'I know what he looks like, and once seen never forgotten, you'll agree. He was speaking very low, but he had no idea that old Trotter was so close. That was on Tuesday evening, just as the light was failing.

The hobbits left Crickhollow early in the morning of Monday 26 September, and arrived in Bree at nightfall on Thursday 29 September (p. 160). The first of these variants makes Trotter see Gandalf and Odo on the road east of Bree on the Wednesday, i.e. after passing through the village; the second places the encounter a day earlier, on the Tuesday evening, before they reached Bree. Therefore Frodo calculates, in the passage that now follows, that Gandalf had reached Crickhollow 'on the

Monday, after they had left,' since Bree was a day's riding from the Brandywine Bridge. The rain on the Tuesday from which Trotter was sheltering was the rain that fell during the hobbits' second day in the house of Tom Bombadil. The text continues:

Now up comes a hobbit and three friends out of the Shire, and though he gives out the name of Hill, his friends call him Frodo, and they all seem to know a good deal about the doings of Gandalf and the Bagginses of Hobbiton. I can put two and two together, when it is as easy as that. But don't let it trouble you: I shall keep the answer to myself. Maybe, Mr Baggins has a good honest reason for leaving his name behind. But if so, I should advise him to remember that there are others besides Trotter that can do such easy sums – and not all are to be trusted.'

'I am obliged to you,' said Frodo, greatly relieved. Here at any rate was news of Gandalf; and of Odo too, apparently. Gandalf must have turned up at Crickhollow on the Monday, after they had left. But Frodo was still suspicious of Trotter, and was determined to pretend that the affair was of no special importance. 'I have not left my name behind, as you put it,' he said stiffly. 'I called myself Hill at this inn merely to avoid idle questions. Mr Butterbur has quite enough to say as it is. I don't quite see how anyone would guess my real name from what has occurred, unless he had your skill in eavesdropping. And I don't see, either, what special interest my name has for anybody in Bree, or for you, for that matter.'

Trotter laughed at him. 'Don't you?' he said grimly. 'But eavesdropping, as you put it, is not unknown in Bree. And besides, I have not told you all about myself yet.'

At that moment he was interrupted by a knock on the door. Mr Butterbur was there with a tray of candles, and Nob behind him with cans of hot water. 'I've come to wish you a good night,' said the landlord, putting the candles on the table. 'Nob! Take the water to the rooms.' He came in and shut the door. 'It's like this, Mr Hill,' he began: 'I've been asked more than once to look out for a party of four hobbits and five ponies. Hullo, Trotter! You here?'

'It's all right,' said Frodo. 'Say what you wish! Trotter has my leave to stay.' Trotter grinned.

'Well,' began Mr Butterbur again, 'it's like this: a couple of days ago, yes, it would be late on Tuesday night, just as I was going to lock up, there came a ring at the bell in the yard. Who should be standing at the door but old Gandalf, if you know who I mean! All wet through he was: it had been raining heavens hard all day.

There was a hobbit with him, and a white horse – very tired the poor beast was; for it had carried both of them a long way, it seemed. "Bless me, Gandalf!" says I. " What are you doing out in this weather at this time of night? And who's your little friend?" But he winked at me, and didn't answer my questions. "Hot drinks and warm beds!" he croaked, and stumbled up the steps.

'Later on he sent for me. "Butterbur," says he. "I'm looking for some friends: four hobbits. One is a round-bellied little fellow with red cheeks" – begging your pardon – "and the others just young hobbits. They should have five ponies and a good deal of baggage. Have you seen them? They ought to have passed through Bree some time today,[6] unless they have stopped here."

'He seemed very put out, when I said no such party was at *The Pony*, and none had passed through, to my certain knowledge. "That's bad news!" he said, tugging at his beard. "Will you do two things for me? If this party turns up, give them a message: *Hurry on! Gandalf is ahead.* Just that. Don't forget, because it's important! And if anyone – anyone, mind you, however strange – enquires after a hobbit called Baggins, tell them Baggins has gone east with Gandalf. Don't forget that either, and I shall be grateful to you."' The landlord paused, looking hard at Frodo.

'Thankyou very much!' said Frodo, thinking Mr Butterbur had finished, and relieved to find that his story was much the same as Trotter's, and no more alarming. All the same he was extremely puzzled by Gandalf's mysterious words about *Baggins*. He wondered if Butterbur had got it all wrong.

'Ah! But wait a minute!' said the landlord, lowering his voice. 'That wasn't the end of it. And that's what is puzzling me. On Monday a big black fellow went through Bree on a great black horse, and all the folk were talking about it. The dogs were all yammering and the geese screaming as he rode through the village. I heard later that three of these riders were seen on the Road by Combe; though where the other two had sprung from I couldn't say.

'Gandalf and his little friend Baggins went off yesterday, after sleeping late, about the middle of the morning. In the evening, just before the road-gate was shut, in rode the black fellows again, or others as like them as night and dark. "There's the Black Man at the door!" shouted Nob, running to fetch me with his hair all on end. Sure enough, it was: not one nor three, though, but four of them! One was sitting there in the twilight with his big black horse almost on my door-step. All hooded and cloaked he was. He bent down and spoke to me, and very cold I thought his voice sounded. And what do you think? He was asking for news of *four hobbits* riding east out of the Shire![7]

'I didn't like the sound or the looks of him, and I answered him short. "I haven't seen any such party," I said, "and I'm not likely to, either. What may you be wanting with them, or with me?'

'At that he sent out a breath that set me shivering. "We want news of them. We are seeking *Baggins*," he said, hissing out the name like a snake. "Baggins is with them. If he comes, you will tell us, and we will repay you with gold. If you do not tell us, we will repay you – otherwise."

'"Baggins!" said I. "He ain't with them. If you are looking for a hobbit of that name, he went off east this morning with Gandalf."

'At that name he drew in his breath and sat up. Then he stooped at me again. "Is that truth?" he said, very hard and quiet. "Do not lie to us!"

'I was all of a twitter, I can tell you, but I answered up as bold as I could: "Of course it's the truth! I know Gandalf, and he and his friend were here last night, I tell you." At that the four of them turned their horses and rode off into the darkness without another word.

'Now, Mr Hill, what do you make of all that? I hope I've done right. If it hadn't been for Gandalf's orders, I'd never have given them news of Baggins, nor of anyone else. For these Black Men mean no good to anyone, I'll be bound.'

'You've done quite right, as far as I can see,' said Frodo. 'From what I know of Gandalf, it is usually best to do what he asks.'

'Yes,' said the landlord, 'but I am puzzled all the same. How came these Black Men to think Baggins was one of *your* party? And I must say, from what I've heard and seen tonight, I wonder if maybe they aren't right. But Baggins or no, you are welcome to any help I can give to a friend of old Tom, and of Gandalf.'

'I'm very grateful,' said Frodo. 'I am sorry I can't tell you the whole story, Mr Butterbur. I am very tired, and very worried. But if you want to know, I *am* Frodo Baggins. I have no idea what Gandalf meant by saying that Baggins had gone east with him; for I think the hobbit's name was Bolger. But these – er – Black Riders are hunting us, and we are in danger. I am very grateful for your help; but I hope you won't get into any trouble yourself on our account. I hope these abominable Riders won't come here again.'

'I hope not indeed!' said Butterbur with a shiver.

'If they do, you must not risk their anger for my sake. They are dangerous. Once we have got clear away, you can do us little harm, if you tell them that a party of four hobbits *has* passed through Bree. Good night, Mr Butterbur! Thankyou again for your kindness. One day perhaps Gandalf will tell you what it is all about.'

'Good night, Mr Baggins – Mr Hill, I should say! Good night, Mr Took! Bless me! Where's Mr Brandybuck?'

'I don't know,' said Folco; 'but I expect he's outside. He said something about going out for a breath of air. He ought to be in before long.'

'Very good!' said Mr Butterbur. 'I'll see that he is not locked out. Good night to you all!' With a puzzled look at Trotter, and a shake of his head, he went out and his footsteps died away in the passage.

'There you go again!' said Trotter before Frodo could speak. 'Too trusting still! Why tell old Barnabas all that about being hunted; and why tell him the other hobbit was a Bolger?'

'Isn't he safe?' asked Frodo. 'Tom Bombadil said he was, and Gandalf seems to have trusted him.'

'Is he safe?' cried Trotter, throwing up his hands. 'Yes, he's safe, safer than houses. But why give him any more to puzzle about than is necessary? And why interfere with Gandalf's plan? You're not very quick, or it would have been plain at once to you that Gandalf wanted it *believed* that the hobbit with him was Baggins – precisely so that you would have a better chance, if you were still behind. And what about me? Am I safe? You're not sure (I know that), and yet you talk to Butterbur in front of me! However, I know now all that he had to say; and at least it will cut short what I still had to tell you – which was mostly about those Black Riders, as you call them. I saw them myself. I should say that seven all told have passed through Bree since Monday. You won't pretend any longer that you can't imagine what interest your real name might have. There is a reward offered for anyone who can report that four hobbits are here, and that one of them is probably a Baggins after all.'

'Yes, yes,' said Frodo. 'I see all that. But I knew already that They were after me; and so far at any rate they seem to have been sent off on a false scent.'

'I should not be too sure that they have all gone right away,' said Trotter; 'or that they are all ahead of you, and chasing after

Gandalf. They are cunning, and they divide their forces. I can still tell you a few things you have not heard from Butterbur. I first saw a Rider on Monday night, east of Bree as I was coming in out of the wilds. I nearly ran into him, going fast along the Road in the dark. I hailed him with a curse, for he had almost run over me; and he pulled up and came back. I stood still and made no sound, but he brought his horse step by step towards me. When he was quite close he stooped and sniffed. Then he hissed, and turned his horse and rode off.[8] Yesterday I saw the four that called at this inn. Last night I was on the look-out. I was lying on a bank under the hedge of Bill Ferney's garden; and I heard Bill Ferney talking. He is a surly fellow, and has a bad name in the Bree-land, and queer folk are known to call at his house sometimes. You must have noticed him among the company: a swarthy man with a scowl. He was very close tonight with Harry Goatleaf, the west-gate keeper (a mean old curmudgeon); and with one of the southern strangers. They slipped out together just after your song and accident. I don't trust Ferney. He would sell *anything* to *anybody*, if you understand me.'

'I don't understand you,' said Frodo.

'Well, I'm not going to say it plainer,' said Trotter. 'I just wonder whether this unusual arrival of strange travellers up the Greenway, and the appearance of the hunting horsemen come together by mere chance. Both might be looking for the same thing – or person. Anyway, I heard Bill Ferney talking last night. I know his voice, though I could not catch what was said. The other voice was whispering, or hissing. And that's all I have to tell you. You must do as you like about my reward. But as for my coming with you, I will say this: I know all the lands between the Shire and the Misty Mountains, for I've wandered over them many times in the course of my life – and I'm older now than I look. I might prove useful. You'll have to leave the open Road after tonight; for if you ask me, I should say that these Riders are patrolling it – and still looking for your party. I don't fancy that you wish to meet them. I don't! They give me the creeps!' he ended suddenly with a shudder.

The others looked at him and saw with surprise that his face was buried in his hands, and his hood was drawn right down. The room was very quiet and still and the lights seemed to have grown dim.

'There!' he cried after a moment, throwing back his hood and pushing the hair from his face. 'Perhaps I know more about these

pursuers than you do. You do not fear them enough – yet. It seems
to me only too likely that news of you will reach them before this
night is over. Tomorrow you will have to go swiftly, and secretly –
if you can. But Trotter can take you by paths that are seldom
trodden. Will you have him?'

Frodo made no answer. He looked at Trotter: grim and wild
and rough-clad. It was hard to know what to do. He did not doubt
that most of his tale was true; but it was less easy to feel sure of his
good will. Why was he so interested? He had a dark look – and yet
there was something in it that seemed friendly and even curiously
attractive. And his speech had changed as he talked, from the
unfamiliar tones of the Outsiders to something more familiar,
something that seemed to remind Frodo of somebody.[9] The
silence grew, and still he could not make up his mind.

'Well, I'm for Trotter, if you want any help in deciding,' said
Folco suddenly. 'In any case, I daresay he could follow us
wherever we went, even if we refused.'

'Thankyou!' said Trotter smiling at Folco. 'I could and I
should; for I should feel it was my duty. But here is a letter which I
have for you – that ought to make up your mind for you.' To
Frodo's amazement he took from his pocket a small sealed letter
and handed it over. On the outside was written: *F. from G.* ✖
'Read it!' said Trotter.

Here the chapter ends. It will be seen that in this narrative, despite the
radical differences in what Trotter and Butterbur communicated, the
original form of the story (in the 'A' version, but see note 8) was still
closely followed.

The manuscript of this chapter subsequently underwent immensely
intricate alteration, with long insertions and deletions, for my father used
the original text for two distinct developments, both involving major
structural change. The one he called the 'red' version, marked out and
paginated in red, the other the 'blue'; thus a rider on an inserted slip
bears the number 'rider to IX.3(g) = red IX.9 = blue IX.4'! The
relations can in fact be worked out perfectly satisfactorily. The 'blue'
version is the later, and peters out towards the end; this represents a later
plot, in which all references to the visit of Gandalf and Odo to *The
Prancing Pony* is cut out. The 'red' version, on the other hand, may well
be contemporary or nearly contemporary with the primary text; it is
carefully written (the alterations constituting the 'blue' version being
much rougher), and it tells the same story of Gandalf and Odo – but tells
it quite differently. It takes up from the end of the description of Bree,
and begins with Gandalf's arrival there with Odo, now told directly and
not in Butterburian narrative.

The Tuesday had been a day of heavy rain. Night had fallen some hours ago, and it was still pouring down. It was so dark that nothing could be heard but the seething noise of the rain, and the ripple of flood-rivers running down the hill – and the sound of hoofs splashing on the Road. A horse was slowly climbing up the long slope towards the village of Bree.

Suddenly a great gate loomed up: it stretched right across the Road from one strong post to another, and it was shut. There was a small house beyond it, dark and grey. The horse halted with its nose over the top bar of the gate, and the rider, an old man, dismounted stiffly, and lifted down a small figure that had been riding on a pillion behind him. The old man beat on the gate, and was just beginning to climb over it, when the door of the house opened and a man came out with a lantern, muttering and grumbling.

'A fine night to come hammering on the gate and getting a man out of his bed!' he said.

'And a fine night to be out in, wet through and cold, and on the wrong side of a gate!' replied the rider. 'Come on now, Harry! Get it open quick!'

'Bless me!' cried the gate-keeper, holding up the lantern. 'Gandalf it is – and I might have guessed it. There's never no knowing when you'll turn up next.' He opened the gate slowly, peering in surprise at the small bedraggled figure at Gandalf's side.

'Thank you!' said Gandalf, leading his horse forward. 'This is a friend of mine, a hobbit out of the Shire. Have you seen any more on the Road? There ought to be four of them ahead, a party on ponies.'

'There hasn't been any such party through, while I've been about,' said Harry. 'There *might* have been up to mid-day, for I was away in Staddle, and my brother was here. But I've heard no talk of it. Not that we watch the Road much between sunrise and nightfall, while the gate's open. But we shall have to be more heedful, I'm thinking.'

'Why?' asked Gandalf. 'Have any strange folk been about?'

'I should say so! Mighty queer folk. Black men on horses; and a lot of foreigners out of the South came up the Greenway at dusk. But if you're going to *The Pony*, I should get on before they lock up. You'll hear all the news there. I'll be getting back to my bed, and wish you good night.' He shut the gate and went in.

'Good night!' said Gandalf, and walked on into the village, leading his horse. The hobbit stumbled along beside him.

There was a lamp still shining over the entrance to the inn, but the door was closed. Gandalf rang the bell in the yard, and after a little delay a large fat man, in his shirt sleeves and with slippers on his feet, opened the door a crack and peered out.

'Good evening, Butterbur!' said the wizard. 'Any room for an old friend?'

'Heavens above, if they aren't all washed away!' cried the landlord. 'Gandalf! And what are you doing out in this weather and at this time of night? And who's your little friend?'

Gandalf winked at him. 'Hot drinks and warm beds – that's what we want, and not too many questions,' he said, and stumped up the steps.

'What about the horse?' asked the landlord.

'Give him the best you've got!' answered Gandalf. 'And if Bob grumbles at being got up again at this hour, tell him the beast deserves it: Narothal[10] has carried us both, fast and far today. I'll repay Bob in the morning according as my horse reports of him!'

A little later the wizard and his companion were sitting before the hot embers of a fire in Mr Butterbur's own room, warming and drying themselves and drinking mulled ale. The landlord came in to say that a room was ready for them.

'Don't you hurry yourselves!' said he, 'but when you're ready, I'll be going to my own bed. There's been an unusual lot of travellers in here today, more than I remember for years, and I'm tired.'

'Any hobbits among them?' asked Gandalf. 'I'm looking for four of them – a friend of mine out of the Shire and three companions.' He described Frodo carefully, but did not give his name. 'They should have five ponies and a fair amoung of baggage; and they ought to have reached Bree today. Harry hasn't seen them; but I hoped they might have come in without his noticing them.'

'Nay,' said the landlord, 'a party like that would have been heard of even by Harry, dull old grumbler though he be. We don't get many Outsiders from the Shire to Bree these days. There's no such party at *The Pony*, and there's been none along the Road to my certain knowledge.'

'That's bad news!' said Gandalf, tugging at his beard. 'I wonder where they have got to!'[11] He was silent for a moment. 'Look here, Butterbur!' he went on. 'You and I are old friends. You have eyes and ears in your head, and though you say a lot, you know what to

leave unsaid. I want to be private while I'm here, and if I see no
one but you and Bob I'll be pleased. Don't tell everyone that I've
asked after this party! But keep your eyes open, and if they turn up
after I've gone, give them this message: *Hurry on! Gandalf's
ahead.* Just that. Don't forget, because it's important. And if
anyone – anyone, mind you, however strange – enquires after a
hobbit called *Baggins*, tell them Baggins has gone east with
Gandalf. Don't forget that, either, and I shall be grateful to
you!'

'Right you are!' said Mr Butterbur. 'I hope I'll not forget,
though one thing drives out another, when I'm busy with guests in
the house. Baggins, you say? Let me see – I remember that name.
Wasn't there a Bilbo Baggins that they told some strange tales
about over in the Shire? My dad told me that he had stayed in this
house more than once. But your friend won't be him – he
disappeared in some funny way nigh on twenty years back:
vanished with a bang while he was talking, or so I've heard. Not
that I believe all the tales that come out of the West.'

'No need to,' said Gandalf, laughing. 'Anyway my young friend
here is not old Bilbo Baggins. Just a relation.'

'That's right!' said the hobbit. 'Just a relation – a cousin in fact.'

'I see,' said the landlord. 'Well, it does you credit. Bilbo was a
fine little fellow, and rich as a king into the bargain, if half I've
heard is true. I'll give your messages, if the chance comes,
Gandalf; and I'll ask no questions, strange though it all seems to
me. But you know your own business best, and you've done me
many a good turn.'

'Thankyou Barnabas!' said Gandalf. 'And now I'll do you
another – let you go to your bed at once.' He drained his mug and
stood up. The landlord put out the lights, and holding a candle in
each hand led them to their room.

In the morning Gandalf and his friend got up late. They
breakfasted in a private room, and spoke to no one but Mr
Barnabas Butterbur. It was close on eleven before Gandalf called
for his reckoning, and for his horse.

'Tell Bob to take him up the lane and wait for me near the
Greenway,' he said. 'I'm not going along the Road to be gaped at
this morning.'

He took his leave of the landlord at a side-door. 'Goodbye, my
friend,' he said. 'Don't forget the messages! One day, perhaps, I'll
tell you the whole story, and repay you, too, with something better

even than good news – that is, I will, if the whole story does not come to a bad end. Goodbye!'

He walked off with the hobbit up a narrow lane that ran north from the inn over the ditch round the village and on towards the Greenway.[12] Bob the ostler was waiting outside the village boundary. The white horse was glossy and well-groomed, and seemed thoroughly rested and eager for another day's journey. Gandalf called to him by name, and Narothal[13] whinnied, tossing up his head, and trotting back to his master, and nuzzling against his face.

'A good report, Bob!' said Gandalf, giving the ostler a silver piece. He mounted; and Bob helped the hobbit up on to a cushion behind the wizard, then he stood back with his cap in his hand, grinning broadly.

'That's right, my lad!' laughed Gandalf. 'We look a funny pair, I daresay. But we're not as funny as we look. When we've gone, remember that we've gone east, but forget that we set out along this lane. See? Goodbye!' He rode off and left Bob scratching his head.

'Curry me! if these aren't queer days!' he said to himself. 'Black men riding out of nowhere, and folk on the Greenway, and old Gandalf with a hobbit on a pillion and all! Things are beginning to move in Bree! But you watch yourself, Bob my lad – old Gandalf can hand out something hotter than silver.'

The fair morning that had followed the rain gave way later to cloud and mist. Nothing more happened in Bree that day until dusk was falling. Then out of the fog four horsemen rode though the gate. Harry peered through a window, and then hurriedly withdrew. He had been thinking of going out and shutting the gate, but he changed his mind. The horsemen were all clad and muffled in black, and rode high black horses. Some of the same sort had been seen in Bree two days before and wild stories were going about. Some said they were not human, and even the dogs were afeared of them. Harry locked the door and stood quaking behind it.

But the riders halted, and one dismounted and came and smote on the door. 'What do you want?' called Harry from inside.

'We want news!' hissed a cold voice through the keyhole.

'What of?' he answered, shaking in his boots.

'News of four hobbits,[14] riding on ponies out of the Shire. Have they passed?'

Harry wished they had, for it might have satisfied these riders, if he could have said *yes*. There was a threat and urgency in the cold voice: but he dared not risk a *yes* that was not true. 'No sir!' he said in a quavering voice. 'There's been no hobbits on ponies through Bree, and there isn't likely to be any. But there was a hobbit riding behind an old man on a white horse, last night. They went to *The Pony*.'

'Do you know their names?' said the voice.

'The old man was Gandalf,' said Harry.

A hiss came through the keyhole, and Harry started back, feeling as if something icy cold had touched him. 'You have our thanks', said the voice. 'You will keep watch for four hobbits, if you still wish to please us. We will return.'

Harry heard the sound of hoofs going off towards the village. He unlocked the door stealthily, and then crept out, and peered up the road. It was too foggy and already too dark to see much. But he heard the hoofs halt at the bend of the Road by the inn. He waited a while, and then quietly shut and locked the gate. He was just returning to his house, when in the misty air he heard the sound of hoofs again, starting up by the inn and dying away round the corner and down the Road eastward. It was turning very cold, he thought. He shivered and hurried indoors, bolting and barring the door.

The next morning, Thursday, was clear again, with a warm sun and the wind turning towards the South. Towards evening a dozen dwarves came walking out of the East into Bree with heavy packs on their backs. They were sullen and had few words for anybody. But no traveller came past the western gate all day. Night fell and Harry shut the gate, but he kept on going to his door. He was afraid of the threat in the cold voice, if he missed any strange hobbits.

It was dark and white stars were shining when Frodo and his companions came at last to the Greenway-crossing and drew near the village. They found that it was surrounded by a deep ditch with a hedge and fence on the inner side. Over and through this the Road ran, but it was now barred by the great gate. They saw a house on the other side, and a man sitting at the door. He jumped up and fetched a lantern, and looked down over the gate at them in surprise.

'What do you want and where do you come from?' he asked gruffly.

'We are making for the inn here,' answered Frodo. 'We are journeying east and cannot go further tonight.'

'Hobbits! Four hobbits! And what's more, out of the Shire from the sound of their talk,' said the gate-keeper, quietly and almost as if he was speaking to himself. He stared at them darkly for a moment, and then slowly opened the gate and let them ride through.

'We don't often see Shire-folk riding on the Road by night,' he went on, as they halted for a moment by his door. 'You'll pardon me wondering what business takes you away east of Bree.'

'I do,' said Frodo, 'though it does not seem very wonderful to us. But this does not seem a good place to talk of our business.'

'Ah well, your business is your own, no doubt,' said the gate-keeper. 'But you'll find maybe that there are more folk than old Harry at the gate that will ask questions. Are you expecting to meet any friends here?'

'What do you mean?' asked Frodo in surprise. 'Why should we?'

'And why not? Many folk meet at Bree even in these days. If you go on to *The Pony*, you may find you are not the only guests.'

Frodo wished him good night and made no further answer, though he could see in the lantern-light that the man was still eyeing them curiously. He was glad to hear the gate clang to behind them, as they rode forward. He wondered what the man had meant by 'meeting friends'. Could anyone have been asking for news of four hobbits? Gandalf, perhaps? He might have passed through, while they were delayed in the Forest and the Downs. But a Black Rider was more likely. There was something in the look and tone of the gate-keeper that filled him with suspicion.

Harry stared after them for a moment, and then he went to his door. 'Ned!' he called. 'I've business up at *The Pony*, and it may keep me a while. You must be on the gate, till I come back.'

From this point the 'red version' is only different from the first text in that Butterbur's story of Gandalf's visit is of course very greatly reduced from the form given on pp. 338–9.

## NOTES

1   The drafts have 'Few had survived the turmoils of the Earliest Days', an expression used in the *Foreword* (p. 329, note 1), where FR has 'Elder Days'; the earliest form of the passage has: 'Few had

survived the turmoils of those old and forgotten days, and the wars of the Elves and Goblins'.

2   *prepared:* FR has *'proposed* to leave them', but this is an error that arose at the typescript stage.

3   My father wrote 'a queer-looking brown-faced hobbit', struck out 'hobbit', and then wrote 'hobbit' again.

4   In this phase *Ferney* is spelt thus; *Ferny* in the original version and in FR.

5   The word *ran* in the erased note to the second text of the attack on Crickhollow ('Behind him ran Odo . . .', p. 328) is rather surprising, since it seems pointless: if Odo was to accompany Gandalf there seems no reason why he should not ride pillion from the first – and in any case he would have been quickly left far behind.

6   It is perhaps surprising that Gandalf should expect Frodo and his companions to have passed through Bree on the Tuesday, since he knew from Odo that they left the house at Crickhollow on the Monday morning and had gone into the Old Forest. When they would get to Bree was presumably now far more uncertain than if they had taken the Road (hostile interventions apart). Possibly this survives from the old form of the story – 'They should be here by Tuesday, if they can follow a plain road', p. 151 – when Gandalf had no reason to think that they had not simply ridden the East Road from the Brandywine Bridge. See note 11.

7   How did the Riders know that there were *four* hobbits? (In the old variant versions, pp. 152, 157, they knew even that the four hobbits had five ponies). Presumably they surmised it: they knew that three had come to Bucklebury Ferry and been met there by another. Beyond that they had no knowledge (on the Wednesday night when they came to the inn) of Frodo and his companions. – At some point my father struck out the word *four*; see note 14.

8   This episode derives from the old 'B' version, p. 157; but there the Rider questioned Trotter, who did not answer. The relations between the versions here are:

Old version 'A' (p. 151):
  (Monday) One Rider questions Butterbur at the inn-door
  (Tuesday) Four Riders come to the inn-door, and one questions Butterbur

Old version 'B' (p. 157):
  (Monday) One Rider questions Trotter on the Road
  (Tuesday) Four riders meet Trotter on the Road, and one questions him

The present version:
  (Monday) One Rider goes through Bree (p. 339), and meets Trotter on the Road east of Bree without speech (p. 342)
  (Wednesday) Four Riders come to the inn-door, and one questions Butterbur (pp. 339–40); they are seen by Trotter (p. 342)

9 The change in Trotter's speech remarked by Frodo, deriving from the original form of the story (p. 154), survived in FR (p. 178), though the significance is there quite different: 'I think you are not really as you choose to look. You began to talk to me like the Bree-folk, but your voice has changed.'

10 *Narothal* ('Firefoot'), the first name given to Gandalf's white horse, was replaced later in pencil by the suggestions: 'Fairfax, Snowfax', and pencilled in the margin is 'Firefoot Arod? Aragorn', but these latter were struck out. *Arod* became in LR the name of a horse of Rohan.

11 A pencilled note on the manuscript says: 'Since he has been to Crickhollow he must know of Old Forest' – i.e. Gandalf must know from Odo that the other hobbits went into the Old Forest. At the same time my father pencilled into the text at this point: 'I trusted Tom Bombadil to keep them out of trouble.'

12 This lane is marked on the sketch-map of Bree given on p. 335.

13 'Narothal' changed in pencil to 'Fairfax'; see note 10.

14 *four hobbits:* see note 7. Subsequently my father struck out *four*, and wrote instead: *hobbits, three or more*.

# XXI
# THE THIRD PHASE (3):
# TO WEATHERTOP AND RIVENDELL

The next chapter, numbered X and with the title 'Wild Ways to Weathertop', belongs with the base-form of 'At the Sign of the Prancing Pony'
and is continuous with it; but it begins by repeating almost exactly the
end of that chapter, from 'Frodo made no answer' to '"Read it!" said
Trotter' (p. 343). Then follows:

Frodo looked carefully at the seal before he broke it. It seemed
certainly to be Gandalf's, as did the writing also, and the runic G
⊗. Inside was the following message. Frodo read it and then
repeated it aloud for the benefit of Folco and Sam.

*The Prancing Pony, Wednesday, Sept. 28. Dear F. Where on
earth are you? Not still in the Forest, I hope! Could not help being
late, but explanations must wait. If you ever get this letter, I
shall be ahead of you. Hurry on, and don't stop anywhere!
Things are worse than I thought and pursuit is close. Look out for*
horsemen in black, *and avoid them. They are perilous: your
worst enemies. Don't use* It *again, not on any account. Don't
move in the dark. Try and catch me up. I dare not wait here, but
I shall halt at a place known to the bearer, and look out for you
there. I am giving this to a ranger known as Trotter: dark rather
lean hobbit, wears wooden shoes. He is an old friend of mine,
and knows a great deal. You can trust him. He will guide you to
appointed place through wild country. N.B. Odo* Baggins *is with
me. Hurry on! Yours* ᚷᚨᚾᛞᚨᛚᚠ · ⊗ ·

Frodo looked at the trailing handwriting: it seemed as plainly
genuine as the seal. 'It is dated Wednesday and from this house,'
he said. 'How did you come by it?'

'I met Gandalf by appointment near Archet,' answered Trotter.
'He did not leave Bree by the Road, but went up a side lane and
round the hill the other way.'

'Well, Trotter,' said Frodo after a pause, 'it would have made
things easier and saved a lot of time and talk, if you had produced

this letter at once. Why did you invent all that tale about eaves-dropping?'

'I didn't invent it,' laughed Trotter. 'I gave old Gandalf quite a shock when I popped up from behind the hedge. But he was very glad when he saw who I was. He said it was the first bit of luck he had had for some while. It was then that we arranged that I was to wait about here in case you were behind, while he pushed on and tried to draw the Riders after him. I know all about your troubles – including the Ring, I may say.'

'Then there's nothing more for me to say,' said Frodo, 'except that I am glad we have found you. I am sorry if I have been unnecessarily suspicious.'

The conversation proceeds very much as in the original story (p. 155), as far as the 'subsidence' of Folco (Odo) beneath Trotter's opinion of him.[1] Then follows:

'We shall all perish, tough or not, unless we have strange good luck, as far as I can see,' said Frodo. 'I cannot understand why you want to be mixed up in our troubles, Trotter.'

'One reason is that Gandalf asked me to help you,' he replied quietly.

'What do you advise then?' asked Frodo. 'I don't quite understand this letter: *don't stop anywhere* it says, and yet *don't move in the dark*. Is it safe to stop here till morning?' Frodo looked at the comfortable fire and the soft candlelight in the room, and sighed.

'No, it probably isn't safe – but it would be far more dangerous to start off by night. So we must wait for daylight and hope for the best. But we had better start early – it is a long way to Weathertop.'

'Weathertop?' said Folco. 'Where and what is that?'

'The *appointed place* mentioned in the letter,' Trotter replied. 'It is a hill, just north of the Road, somewhere about halfway to Rivendell from here.[2] It commands a very wide view all round. But you will start nearly two days behind Gandalf, and you'll have to go fast or you won't find him there.'

'In that case let's get to bed now, while there is still some night left!' said Folco yawning. 'Where's that silly fellow Merry? It would be too much, if we had to go out now and look for him.'

Merry's story of the Black Rider whom he saw outside the inn and followed differs in this, that whereas in the original version (pp. 161–2) the Rider went through the village from west to east and stopped at Bill Ferny's house (hole), here

'He was coming *from* the east,' Merry went on. 'I followed him down the Road almost to the gate. He stopped there at the keeper's house, and I thought I heard him talking to someone. I tried to creep near, but I did not dare to get very close. In fact, I am afraid I suddenly began to shiver and shake, and bolted back here.'

'What's to be done?' said Frodo, turning to Trotter.

'Don't go to your rooms!' he answered at once. 'I don't like this at all. Harry Goatleaf was here tonight and went off with Bill Ferney. It's quite likely that they have found out which rooms you have got.

While in the remainder of the chapter there are advances in detail to the text of FR (from p. 186, the end of Chapter 10 'Strider', to p. 201, in the course of Chapter 11 'A Knife in the Dark'), the narrative of this third phase version follows the original (pp. 162–71) closely in almost all points where that differed from FR, and ends at the same point.

It is now Trotter who imitated Frodo's head in the bed with a mat. The pony is expressly said to be Bill Ferney's, and is described as 'a bony, underfed, and rather dispirited animal.' There were two men looking over the hedge round Ferney's house: Ferney himself, and 'a southerner with a sallow face, and a sly and almost goblinish look in his slanting eyes.' This latter is not identified with the 'squint-eyed southerner' who left the inn the night before with Ferney and the gate-keeper (p. 336). In the old story (p. 165) it was Bill Ferny standing there alone, whom Bingo thought 'goblinish'. It is still Trotter who has the apples, and who hits Ferney on the nose with one. Archet, Combe, and Staddle are referred to as in FR (p. 193), in keeping with what is said of them in the description of the Bree-land at the opening of Chapter IX (p. 332), and Trotter's plan is now to make for Archet and pass it on the east (cf. p. 165 and note 21).

The lights in the eastern sky seen by the travellers from the Midgewater Marshes do not appear until the whole story of Gandalf's movements at this time had been changed. Trotter replies to Frodo's question 'But surely we were hoping to find Gandalf there?' (FR p. 195, original version p. 167) thus:

'Yes – but my hope is rather faint. It is four days since we left Bree, and if Gandalf has managed to get to Weathertop himself without being too hotly pursued, he must have arrived at least two days ago. I doubt if he has dared to wait so long, on the mere chance of your following him: he does not know for certain that you are behind or have got his messages . . .'

He still says: 'There are even some of the Rangers that on a clear day could spy us from there, if we moved. And not all the Rangers are to be trusted . . .'

The chronology is thus (cf. p. 175):

Wed.  Sept. 28  Gandalf and Odo left Bree

Thurs. Sept. 29  Frodo and companions reached Bree

Fri.  Sept. 30  Trotter, Frodo and companions left Bree; night in Chetwood

Sat.  Oct.  1  Night in Chetwood

Sun.  Oct.  2  First day and camp in marshes

Mon.  Oct.  3  Second day and camp in marshes

Tues. Oct.  4  Leaving the marshes. Camp by stream under alders.

On this day Trotter calculated that Gandalf, if he reached Weathertop, must have arrived there 'at least two days ago', i.e. on Sunday 2 October, which allows as much as four days and nights for the journey from Bree on horseback.

In the original version they reached Weathertop on 5 October, whereas in FR they camped at the feet of the hills that night (see p. 175). In the present text my father retained the former story, but then changed it to that of FR:

By night they had reached the feet of the hills, and there they camped. It was the night of October the fifth, and they were six days out from Bree. In the morning they found, for the first time since they left the Bree-land [> Chetwood], a track plain to see.

It will be seen shortly that this change was made before the chapter was finished.

The passage following Folco's question 'Is there any barrow on Weathertop?' (FR p. 197) remains exactly as in the original text (p. 169), with *Elendil* for *Valandil*; and when they reach the summit all remains as before, with only the necessary change of Merry's 'I don't blame Gandalf for not waiting here! He would have to leave the waggon, and horses, and most of his companions, too, I expect, down near the Road' to 'I don't blame Gandalf for not waiting long – if he ever came here.' But the paper that flutters from the cairn bears a different message (see p. 170):

*Wednesday Oct. 5. Bad news. We arrived late Monday. Odo vanished last night. I must go at once to Rivendell. Make for Ford beyond Trollshaw with all speed, but look out. Enemies may attempt to guard it.* G⚔³

'Odo!' cried Merry. 'Does that mean that the Riders have got him? How horrible!'

'Our missing Gandalf has turned out disastrous,' said Frodo. 'Poor Odo! I expect this is the result of pretending to be Baggins. If only we could all have been together!'

'Monday!' said Trotter. 'Then they arrived when we were in the marshes, and Gandalf did not leave till we were already close to the hills. They cannot have caught any glimpse of our miserable little fires on Monday, or on Tuesday. I wonder what happened here that night. Still it is no good guessing: there is nothing we can do but make for Rivendell as best we may.'[4]

'How far is Rivendell?' asked Frodo, looking round wearily. The world looked wild and wide from Weathertop.

From here the text follows the old version (pp. 170–1) almost exactly – with the revised form of Trotter's answer concerning the distance to Rivendell, p. 171 – to the end of the chapter, with Trotter, Frodo, and Merry slipping down from the summit of Weathertop to find Sam and Folco in the dell (where the original Chapter VII also ended).

Since Gandalf and Odo left Bree on the morning of Wednesday 28 September but did not reach Weathertop till late on Monday 3 October, they took longer even than Trotter had calculated (p. 355): nearly six days on horseback, whereas Trotter says (in this text as in the old, p. 171) that it would take 'a ranger on his own feet' about a week from Bree to Weathertop (in the rejected passage of the old text, p. 170, Trotter said that he reckoned it was 'about 120 long-miles' by the Road). Trotter's words 'I wonder what happened here that night', referring to the night on which Odo vanished (Tuesday 4 October), show that the night camp at the foot of the hills on 5 October had entered the narrative, and that it was now Thursday 6 October, for he would not say 'that night' if he meant 'last night'. The chronology given on p. 355 can therefore be completed for this stage of the development of the narrative thus:

Mon.   Oct. 3   Second day and camp in the marshes
                 Gandalf and Odo reach Weathertop late

Tues.   Oct. 4   Leaving the marshes. Camp by stream under alders
                 Odo disappears from Weathertop at night

Wed.   Oct. 5   Camp at feet of hills
                 Gandalf leaves Weathertop

Thurs.  Oct. 6   Trotter, Frodo and companions reach Weathertop

★

The next chapter, numbered XI but without title,[5] begins with an account of what Sam and Folco had been doing (FR p. 201), which is where the corresponding chapter VIII in the original version began (p. 177).

Sam and Folco had not been idle. They had explored the small dell and the surrounding valley. Not far away they had found a spring of clear water, and near it footprints not more than a day or two old. In the dell itself they had found recent traces of a fire and other signs of a small camp. But the most unexpected and most welcome discovery was made by Sam. There were some large fallen rocks at the edge of the dell nearest to the hill-side. Behind them Sam came upon a small store of fire-wood neatly stacked; and under the food was a bag containing food. It was mostly cakes of *cram*[6] packed in two small wooden boxes, but there was also a little bacon, and some dried fruits.

'Old Gandalf has been here, then,' said Sam to Folco. 'These packets of *cram* show that. I never heard tell of anyone but the two Bagginses and the wizard using that stuff. Better than dying of hunger, they say, but not much better.'

'I wonder if it was left for us, or if Gandalf is still about somewhere near,' said Folco. 'I wish Frodo and the other two would come back.'

Sam was more grateful for the *cram* when the others did return, hurrying back to the dell with their alarming news. There was a long journey ahead of them before they could expect to get help; and it seemed plain that Gandalf had left what food he could spare in case their own supplies were short.

'It is probably some that he did not need after poor Odo's disappearance,' said Frodo. 'But what about the wood?'

'I think they must have collected it on the Tuesday,' said Trotter, 'and were preparing to wait here in camp for some time. They would have to go some distance for it, as there are no trees close at hand.'

It was already late afternoon, and the sun was sinking. They debated for some while what they ought to do. It was the store of fuel that finally decided them to go no further that day, and to camp for the night in the dell.

The text now follows the old version (pp. 177-9) fairly closely. To Merry's question 'Can the enemies *see*?' Trotter now replies: 'Their horses can see. They do not themselves see the world of light as we do; but they are not blind, and in the dark they are most to be feared.' Trotter no longer says that there were Men dwelling in the lands away to the South of them; nor is it told that they took it in turns to sit on guard at the

edge of the dell. The passage describing Trotter's tales is a characteristic
blending of the old version (p. 179) with new elements that would
survive into FR (p. 203):

As night fell and the light of the fire began to shine out brightly,
Trotter began to tell them tales to keep their minds from fear. He
knew much lore concerning wild animals, and understood something of their languages; and he had strange tales to tell of their
hidden lives and little known adventures. He knew also many
histories and legends of the ancient days, of hobbits when the
Shire was still unexplored, and of things beyond the mists of
memory out of which the hobbits came. They wondered how old
he was, and where he had learned all this lore.

'Tell us of Gilgalad,' said Merry suddenly, when he paused at
the end of a story of the Elf-kingdoms. 'You spoke that name not
long ago, and it is still ringing in my ears. I seem to remember
hearing it before, but I cannot remember anything else about it.'

'You should ask the possessor of the Ring about that name,'
answered Trotter in a low voice. Merry and Folco looked at
Frodo, who was staring into the fire.

From this point the manuscript is defective, two sheets being missing;
but a rejected page carries the story a little further before tailing off:

'I know only the little that Gandalf told me,' he said. 'Gilgalad
was the last of the great elf-kings. Gilgalad is *Starlight* in their
tongue. With the aid of King Elendil, the Elf-friend, he overthrew
the Enemy, but they both perished. And I would gladly hear more
if Trotter will tell us. It was the son of Elendil that carried off the
Ring. But I cannot tell that tale. Tell us more, Trotter, if you will.'

'No,' said Trotter. 'I will not tell that tale now, in this time and
place with the servants of the Enemy at hand. Perhaps in the house
of Elrond you will hear it. For Elrond knows it in full.'

'Then tell us some other tale of old,' said Merry . . .

Trotter's song, and his story of Beren and Lúthien, are thus missing
here; and the manuscript takes up again at 'As Trotter was speaking they
watched his strange eager face . . .' From this point the text of FR, as far
as the end of Chapter 11 'A Knife in the Dark' was achieved, with
scarcely any difference even of wording, except for these points: Folco
stands for Pippin; there were still three Riders, not five, in the attack on
the dell; and Frodo as he threw himself on the ground cried out *Elbereth!
Elbereth!*

At this point Chapter 12 'Flight to the Ford' begins in FR, but as in the
original text (p. 190) the present version continues without break to the

Ford of Rivendell. The relations of chapter-structure between the present phase and FR can be shown thus (and cf. the table on p. 133):

| The present 'phase' | FR |
|---|---|
| IX *At the Sign of the Prancing Pony.* Ends with Trotter giving Frodo the letter from Gandalf. | 9 *At the Sign of the Prancing Pony.* Ends with Frodo, Pippin and Sam returning to their room at the inn. |
| X *Wild Ways to Weathertop.* Conclusion of conversation with Trotter. Attack on the inn, departure from Bree; ends with sight of the Riders below Weathertop. | 10 *Strider.* Conversations with Strider and Butterbur.<br>11 *A Knife in the Dark.* Attack on the inn, departure from Bree; ends with the attack on Weathertop. |
| XI *No title.* Attack on Weathertop. Journey from Weathertop to the Ford. | 12 *Flight to the Ford.* |

As is characteristic of these third phase chapters, the present text advances largely towards the form in FR in detail of wording and description, but retains many features of the original version; thus the 'red flash' seen at the moment of the attack on Weathertop survives, of the slash in the black robe Trotter still says only 'What harm it did to the Black Rider I do not know', and the distant cries of the Riders as they crossed the Road are not heard, while on the other hand the firewood left by Gandalf is no longer said to have been taken with them, and the rejuvenation of Bill Ferney's pony is described (for these elements in the narrative see pp. 190–1). Trotter now speaks aside to Sam, but what he says is different:

'I think I understand things better now,' he said in a low voice. 'Our enemies knew the Ring was here; perhaps because they have captured Odo, and certainly because they can feel its presence. They are no longer pursuing Gandalf. But they have now drawn off from us for the time, because we are many and more bold than they expected, but especially because they think they have slain or mortally wounded your master – so that the Ring will inevitably come soon into their power.'

The rest of his words to Sam are as in FR (p. 210). – In the discussion of what it were best to do now (FR p. 211) the present version reads:

The others were discussing this very question. They decided to leave Weathertop as soon as possible. It was already Friday morning, and the two days that Gandalf's message had asked for would soon be up. In any case it was no good remaining in so bare and indefensible a place, now that their enemies had discovered them, and knew also that Frodo had the Ring. As soon as the daylight was full they had some hurried food and packed.

For 'the two days that Gandalf's message had asked for' see notes 3 and 4.

The chronology of the journey remains as in the original text (see pp. 192–3, 219): they still recrossed the Road on the morning of the sixth day from Weathertop (the seventh in FR), and spent three days in the hills before the weather turned to rain (two in FR). But the lag of one day that remained between the original text and FR (owing to their earlier arrival on Weathertop), so that they reached the Ford of Rivendell on 19 October, is no longer present (see p. 356).

The rain that Trotter judged had fallen some two days before at the place where they crossed the Road again (FR p. 213) is now mentioned, but the River Hoarwell (Mitheithel) and the Last Bridge have still not emerged. The river which they could see in the distance, unnamed in the first version (p. 191), is now given a name: 'the Riven River, that came down out of the Mountains and flowed through Rivendell' (later in the chapter it is called 'the Rivendell River').

The conversation between Trotter, Folco and Frodo arising from the ruined towers in the hills remains as in the first version (pp. 192–3; FR p. 214).

When the rain stopped, and Trotter climbed up to see the lie of the land, he observed in the first version (p. 193) that 'if we keep on as we are going, we shall get into impassable country among the skirts of the Mountains.' This now becomes: 'we shall get up into the [Dimrill-lands >] Dimrill-dales far north of Rivendell.'[7] He continues, approaching Strider's words in FR:

'It is a troll-country, I have heard, though I have not been there. We could perhaps find our way through and come round to Rivendell from the north; but it would take long, and our food would not last. Anyway we ought to follow Gandalf's last message and make for the Rivendell Ford. So somehow or other we must strike the Road again.'

The encounter with the Stone Trolls follows the first version: Trotter slapped the stooping troll, called him William, and pointed out the bird's nest behind Bert's ear. There is still no suggestion of Sam's *Troll Song*; and when Frodo saw the memorial stone he 'wished that Bilbo had brought home no treasure more perilous than stolen money rescued from trolls.' The description of the Road here is nearly that of the First Edition of FR (see p. 200): 'At this point the Road had turned away from the river, leaving it at the bottom of a narrow valley, and clung close to the feet of the hills, rolling and winding northward among woods and heather-covered slopes towards the Ford and the Mountains.'

Glorfindel now calls Trotter not *Padathir* (p. 194) but *Du-finnion*, calling out *Ai, Du-finnion! Mai govannen!* The passage beginning with Trotter's signalling to Frodo and the others to come down to the road is found in two forms, the second to all appearance immediately replacing the first. The first runs:

'Hail and well met at last!' said Glorfindel to Frodo. 'I was sent from Rivendell to look for your coming. Gandalf feared that you might follow the Road.'

'Gandalf has arrived at Rivendell then?' cried Merry. 'Has he found Odo?'

'Certainly there is a hobbit of that name with him,' said Glorfindel; 'but I did not hear that he had been lost. He rode behind Gandalf from the north out of Dimrildale.'

'Out of Dimrildale?' exclaimed Frodo.

'Yes,' said the elf; 'and we thought that you also might go that way to avoid the peril of the Road. Some have been sent to seek for you in that country. But come! There is no time now for news or debate, until we halt. We must go on with all speed, and save our breath. Hardly a day's ride back westward there are horsemen, searching for your trail along the Road and in the lands on either side . . .

Glorfindel continues as in the first version (p. 195). The replacement passage differs mostly in small points: Glorfindel does not say of Odo 'but I did not hear that he had been lost'; *Dimrilldale* is so spelt (cf. p. 360), in place of *Dimrildale* in the rejected text; and the interjections of Merry and Frodo are reversed. The important difference lies in Glorfindel's words:

'There are horsemen back westward searching for your trail along the Road, and when they find the place where you came down from the hills, they will ride after us like the wind. But they are not all: there are others, who may be before us now, or upon either hand. Unless we go with all speed and good fortune, we shall find the Ford guarded against us by the enemy.'

From Frodo's faintness and Sam's objection to Glorfindel's urging the text of FR to the end of the chapter is achieved almost to the last word.[8] Yet there remain certain differences. Only three Riders came out of the tree-hung cutting behind the fugitives; and 'out from the trees and rocks away on the left other Riders came flying. Three rode towards Frodo; three galloped madly towards the Ford to cut off his escape.' And at the very end 'Three of the Riders turned and rode wildly away to the left down the bank of the River; the others, borne by their terrified and

plunging horses, were driven into the flood and carried away.' This is
derived from the first version (p. 197), where however there were only
two Riders that escaped the flood. The manuscript was changed to the
reading of the final paragraph of the chapter in FR, where no Riders
escaped, and this was done before or in the course of the writing of the
next chapter (see p. 364).

★

The first part of the next chapter, numbered XII, is the direct
development of the original title-less chapter IX, extant in three texts,
none of which goes further than the conversation between Bingo and
Glóin at the feast in Rivendell (pp. 206 ff., 210 ff.). The new version is
given the title 'The Council of Elrond'; see pp. 399–400. Here, for
reasons that will appear presently, I describe only that portion of the
chapter which derives from Chapter IX of the 'first phase'. In this, the
text of FR Book II, Chapter 1, 'Many Meetings' is achieved for long
stretches with only the most minor differences of wording, if any; on the
other hand there is still much preserved from the original text. In what
follows it can be understood that where no comment is made the FR text
was present at this time either exactly or in a close approximation.

The date of Frodo's awakening in the house of Elrond is now October
24th, and all the details of date are precisely as in FR (see pp. 219, 360).
The references to Sam in the FR text are none of them present in this
version as written until the feast itself, but were added in to the
manuscript probably after no very long interval.

Gandalf now adds, after 'You were beginning to fade' (p. 210, FR
p. 231), 'Glorfindel noticed it, though he did not speak of it to anyone but
Trotter'; and he still says (see p. 206) 'You would have become a wraith
before long – certainly, if you had put on the Ring again after you were
wounded.' Following his words 'It is no small feat to have come so far and
through such dangers, still bearing the Ring' (FR p. 232) the conversation is developed from the earlier text (p. 210) in a very interesting
way, naturally still far from the form in FR:

'. . . You ought never to have left the Shire without me.'

'I know – but you never came to my party, as was arranged; and
I did not know what to do.'

'I was delayed,' said Gandalf, 'and that nearly proved our ruin –
as was intended. Still after all it has turned out better than any
plan I should have dared to make, and we have defeated the black
horsemen.'

'I wish you would tell me what happened!'

'All in good time! You are not supposed to talk or worry about
anything today, by Elrond's orders.'

'But talking would stop me thinking and wondering, which are quite as tiring,' said Frodo. 'I am wide awake now, and remember so many things that want explaining. Why were you delayed? You ought to tell me that, at least.'

'You will soon hear all you wish to know,' said Gandalf. 'We shall have a Council, as soon as you are well enough. At the moment I will only say that I was held captive.'

'You!' cried Frodo.

'Yes!' laughed Gandalf. 'There are many powers greater than mine, for good and evil, in the world. I was caught in Fangorn and spent many weary days as a prisoner of the Giant Treebeard. It was a desperately anxious time, for I was hurrying back to the Shire to help you. I had just learned that the horsemen had been sent out.'

'Then you did not know of the Black Riders before.'

'Yes, I knew of them. I spoke of them once to you: for what you call the Black Riders are the Ring-wraiths, the Nine Servants of the Lord of the Ring. But I did not know that they had arisen again, and were let loose on the world once more – until I saw them. I have tried to find you ever since – but if I had not met Trotter, I don't suppose I ever should have done so. He has saved us all.'

'We should never have got here without him,' said Frodo. 'I was suspicious of him at first, but now I am very fond of him, though he is rather mysterious. It is an odd thing, you know, but I keep on feeling that I have seen him somewhere before; that – that I ought to be able to put a name to him, a name different to Trotter.'

'I daresay you do,' laughed Gandalf. 'I often have that feeling myself, when I look at a hobbit: they all remind me of one another, if you know that I mean.'

'Nonsense!' said Frodo, sitting up again in protest. 'Trotter is most peculiar. And he wears shoes! But I see you are in one of your tiresome moods.' He lay down again. 'I shall have to be patient. And it is rather pleasant resting, after all. To be perfectly honest I wish I need go no further than Rivendell. I have had a month of exile and adventures, and that is nearly four weeks more than enough for me.'

He fell silent and shut his eyes.

For the remainder of Frodo's conversation with Gandalf this text is mostly very close indeed to FR, and only a few differences need be noticed.

The 'Morgul-knife' (FR p. 234) is still the 'knife of the Necromancer'

(p. 211), and Gandalf says here: 'You would have become a wraith, and under the dominion of the Dark Lord. But you would have had no ring of your own, as the Nine have; for your Ring is the Ruling Ring, and the Necromancer would have taken that, and would have tormented you for trying to keep it – if any torment greater than being robbed of it was possible.'

Among the servants of the Dark Lord Gandalf still includes, as in the previous version, 'orcs and goblins' and 'kings, warriors, and wizards' (p. 211).

Gandalf's reply to Frodo's question 'Is Rivendell safe?' derives from the former text, but moves also towards that of FR:

'Yes, I hope so. He has less power over Elves than over any other creature: they have suffered too much in the past to be deceived or cowed by him now. And the Elves of Rivendell are descendants of his chief foes: the Gnomes, the Elvenwise, that came out of the West; and the Queen Elbereth Gilthoniel, Lady of the Stars, still protects them. They fear no Ring-wraiths, for those that have dwelt in the Blessed Realm beyond the Seas live at once in both worlds; and each world has only half power over them, while they have double power over both.'[9]

'I thought I saw a white figure that shone and did not grow dim like the others. Was that Glorfindel then?'

'Yes, you saw him for a moment as he is upon the other side: one of the mighty of the Elder Race. He is an elf-lord of a house of princes.'

'Then there are still some powers left that can withstand the Lord of Mordor,' said Frodo.

'Yes, there is power in Rivendell,' answered Gandalf, 'and there is a power, too, of another kind in the Shire. . . .

At the end of this passage Gandalf still says: 'the Wise say that he is doomed in the End, though that is far away' (see p. 212).

In Gandalf's story of what happened at the Ford he says, as in FR, 'Three were carried off by the first assault of the flood; the others were now hurled into the water by their horses and overwhelmed.' It thus appears that the rewriting of the end of the preceding chapter (p. 362) had already been carried out.

At the end of his conversation with Gandalf the story of Odo reappears:

'Yes, it all comes back to me now,' said Frodo: 'the tremendous roaring. I thought I was drowning, together with my friends and enemies. But now we are all safe! And Odo, too. At least, Glorfindel said so. How did you find him again?'

Gandalf looked [oddly >] quickly at Frodo, but he had shut his eyes. 'Yes, Odo is safe,' the wizard said. 'You will see him soon, and hear his account. There will be feasting and merrymaking to celebrate the victory of the Ford, and you will all be there in places of honour.'

Gandalf's 'odd' or 'quick' look at Frodo can only relate to his question about Odo, but since the story of Odo's vanishing from Weathertop and his subsequent reappearance (rescue?) was never told it is impossible to know what lay behind it. There is a suggestion that there was something odd about the story of his disappearance. Gandalf's tone, when taken with his 'look' at Frodo, seems to have a slightly quizzical air. Glorfindel says (p. 361): 'Certainly there is a hobbit of that name with him; but I did not hear that he had been lost': yet surely the capture of a hobbit by the Black Riders and his subsequent recovery was a matter of the utmost interest to those concerned with the Ring-wraiths? But whatever the story was, it seems to be something that will never be known. – It is curious that the wizard's sudden quick look at Frodo was preserved in FR (p. 236), when the Odo-story had of course disappeared, and Frodo's words that gave rise to the look were 'But now we are safe!'

Gandalf's slip of the tongue ('The people of Rivendell are very fond of Bilbo') and Frodo's noticing it are retained from the first version (p. 212), as is Frodo's recollection of Trotter's words to the troll as he fell asleep.

When Frodo goes down to find his friends in a porch of the house[10] the conversation is retained almost exactly from the original form (p. 209). Odo takes over from Merry 'Three cheers for Frodo, lord of the Ring!' and further says, as does Pippin in FR, 'You have shown your usual cunning in getting up just in time for a meal'; but despite Odo's increased prominence in Frodo's reception (in FR given to Pippin) there is no reference to his adventures. Frodo might surely be expected to make some remark about Odo's extremely perilous and altogether unlooked-for experiences since he had last seen him at the entrance into the Old Forest, especially since Gandalf had refrained from telling him what had happened on Weathertop and after.

The description of Elrond, Gandalf, and Glorfindel at the banquet had already appeared in almost the final form in the earlier text. The mention of Elrond's smile and laughter (p. 213) was at this time still retained; and there is of course still no hint of Arwen. In the description of the seating, the statement in the former version (*ibid.*) that Bingo 'could not see Trotter, nor his nephews. They had been led to other tables' was retained; but when Frodo 'began to look about him' he did see them, though not Trotter (the latter passage surviving into FR):

The feast was merry and all that his hunger could desire. He could not see Trotter, or the other hobbits, and supposed they were at one of the side tables. It was some time before he began to look about him. Sam had begged to be allowed to wait on his master, but was told that he was for this night a guest of honour. Frodo could see him sitting with Odo, Folco and Merry at the upper end of one of the side tables, close to the dais. He could not see Trotter.

Frodo's conversation with Glóin proceeds exactly as in FR as far as 'But I am equally curious to know what brings so important a dwarf so far from the Lonely Mountain.' In the original texts Glóin said that he wondered much what could have brought *four* hobbits on so long a journey (Bingo, Frodo Took, Odo, Merry; Trotter being excluded – presumably as being so altogether distinct, and not a hobbit of the Shire). The number is four in FR (Frodo, Sam, Pippin, Merry); but four is also found in the present text, where the hobbits (excluding Trotter) were now five: Frodo, Sam, Folco, Odo, Merry. Either 'four' was a slip, or Glóin excluded Odo since he knew that Odo had not arrived at Rivendell with the others. Glóin's reply to Frodo's question remains less grave than in FR:

Glóin looked at him, and laughed, indeed he winked. 'You'll soon find out,' he said; 'but I am not allowed to tell you – yet. So we will not speak of that either! But there are many other things to hear and tell.'

The conversation (so far as it goes in the portion of the manuscript dealt with here) remains almost exactly as it was, with the short extension at the end of the third of the early texts (p. 213), the only difference of any substance being that Dáin had now, as in FR, 'passed his two-hundred-and-fiftieth-year'.

It will be seen that from the series of once fine manuscripts that constitute the 'third phase' of the writing of *The Lord of the Rings* a wholly coherent story emerges. The following are essential points in that story in respect of the intricate later evolution:

- Gandalf did not return to Hobbiton in time for Frodo's small final party.
- Merry and Odo Bolger went off to Buckland in advance.
- Frodo, Sam, and Folco Took walked from Hobbiton to Buckland.
- At Buckland, Odo decided not to go with the others into the Old Forest, but to stay behind at Crickhollow and wait for Gandalf to come.
- Gandalf came to Crickhollow at night on the day that Frodo and his companions left (Monday 26 September), drove off the Riders, and rode after them with Odo on his horse.
- Gandalf and Odo (whose name was given out to be Odo Baggins)

spent the night of Tuesday 27 September at Bree. Near Bree they encountered Trotter.

- Gandalf and Odo left Bree on Wednesday 28 September, meeting Trotter near Archet, as had been arranged.
- Frodo, Sam, Merry and Folco arrived at Bree on Thursday 29 September, and met Trotter, who gave Frodo Gandalf's letter.
- Trotter was a hobbit; Frodo found him curiously familiar without being able to say why, but there is no hint of who he might really be.
- Gandalf reached Weathertop on Monday 3 October, and left on 5 October.
- Trotter, Frodo and the others reached Weathertop on Thursday 6 October and found Gandalf's note telling that Odo had disappeared.
- They learned from Glorfindel that Gandalf had reached Rivendell, with Odo, coming down from the north by way of 'Dimrilldale'.
- At Rivendell, Gandalf explained that he had been delayed in his return to Hobbiton (having learned that the Ring-wraiths were abroad) through having been held prisoner in Fangorn by Giant Treebeard.
- The Shire hobbits at Rivendell are Frodo, Sam, Merry, Folco, and Odo.

## NOTES

1  After 'I had to make quite sure that you were genuine first, before I handed over the letter. I've heard of shadow-parties picking up messages that weren't meant for them . . .' Trotter now adds: 'Gandalf's letter was worded carefully in case of accidents, but I didn't know that.' Thus Gandalf no longer names Weathertop in the letter, but calls it the 'appointed place'.

2  Barbara Strachey, in *Journeys of Frodo* (Map 11) says:
   At this point I must note what I believe to be a real discrepancy in the text itself. In Bree . . . Aragorn tells Sam that Weathertop is halfway to *Rivendell*. I am sure that this was a slip of the tongue and that he meant halfway to *The Last Bridge*. Everything falls into place on this assumption, since the travellers took 7 days between Bree and Weathertop (involving a detour to the north) and 7 days from Weathertop to the Bridge (with Frodo in a wounded condition and unable to hurry) while there was a *further* stretch of 7 days from the Bridge to Rivendell. Aragorn was well aware of the distance, as he said later (A Knife in the Dark; Bk. I), when they reached Weathertop, that it would then take them 14 days to the Ford of Bruinen although it normally took him only 12.

But it is now seen that Aragorn's words 'about halfway from here (Bree) to Rivendell' in FR go back to Trotter's here; and at this stage the River Hoarwell and the Last Bridge on the East Road did not yet exist (p. 360). I think that Trotter (Aragorn) was merely giving Folco (Sam) a rough but sufficient idea of the distances before them. – The relative distances go back to the original version (see pp. 170–1): about 120 miles from Bree to Weathertop, close on 200 from Weathertop to the Ford.

3   A draft for Gandalf's message has: 'Last night Odo vanished: suspect capture by horsemen.'

The message was changed in pencil to read:

*Wednesday morning Oct. 5. Bad news. We arrived late Monday. Baggins vanished last night. I must go and look for him. Wait for me here for [a day or two >] two days. I shall return if possible. If not go to Rivendell by the Ford on the Road.*

Merry then says: 'Baggins! Does that mean that the Riders have got Odo?'

Gandalf's message that he would return to Weathertop if he could may have been intended as an explanation of why they decided to stay there; see note 4. This pencilled revision preceded the writing of the next chapter; see p. 359.

4   This was changed in pencil to read:

there is nothing we can do but] wait at least until tomorrow, which will be two days since Gandalf wrote the note [see note 3]. After that if he does not turn up we must [make for Rivendell as best we may.

5   The title 'A Knife in the Dark' was pencilled in later, as also on the original chapter, VIII (p. 177).

6   The passage about *cram* was retained in this text, but placed in a footnote.

7   On *Dimrill-dale* see pp. 432–3, notes 3, 13.

8   It may be noted that the name *Asfaloth* of Glorfindel's horse now appears.

9   On the conclusion of this passage see p. 225.

10  The porch still faced west (p. 209), not east as in FR, and the odd statement that the evening light shone on the eastern faces of the hills far above was repeated, though struck out, probably in the act of writing.

# XXII
## NEW UNCERTAINTIES AND
## NEW PROJECTIONS

The first phase or original wave of composition of *The Lord of the Rings* carried the story to Rivendell, and broke off in the middle of the original Chapter IX, at Glóin's account to Bingo Bolger-Baggins of the realm of Dale (p. 213):

> In Dale the grandson of Bard the Bowman ruled, Brand son of Bain son of Bard, and he was become a strong king whose realm included Esgaroth, and much land to the south of the great falls.

This sentence ended a manuscript page; on the reverse side, as noted on p. 213, the text was continued, but in a different script and a different ink, and it begins:

> 'And what has become of Balin and Ori and Óin?' asked Frodo.

Since in the second phase Bingo was still the name of Bilbo's heir, and since 'Bingo' never appears in any narrative writing falling later in the story than the feast at Rivendell, it is certain that there was a significant gap between 'much land to the south of the great falls' and 'And what has become of Balin and Ori and Óin?'

It is therefore very curious that in Chapter XII of the third phase there is a marked change of script at precisely the same point. Though still neatly and carefully written, it is immediately obvious to the eye that '"And what has become of Balin and Ori and Óin?" asked Frodo' and the subsequent text was not continuous with what preceded. Moreover, the latter part of this Chapter XII is not coherent with what precedes, either: for Bilbo says – as my father first wrote out the manuscript – 'I shall have to get that fellow *Aragorn* to help me' (cf. FR p. 243: 'I shall have to get my friend the Dúnadan to help me.')

I do not think that it can possibly be a mere coincidence that both versions halt at precisely the same point; and I conclude that the third phase, in the sense of a fine continuous manuscript series, ended at the same place as the first phase had done – and did so precisely *because* that is where the first phase ended. For this reason I stopped at this point in the previous chapter. I have suggested earlier (p. 309) that when my father said (in February 1939) that by December 1938 *The Lord of the Rings* had reached Chapter XII 'and has been rewritten several times' it was to the third phase that he was referring.

The textual-chronological questions that now arise are of peculiar difficulty, and I doubt whether a solution demonstrably correct at all points could be reached. There is no external evidence for many months after February 1939, and nothing to show what my father achieved during that time; but we get at last an unambiguous date, 'August 1939', written (most unusually) on every page of a collection of rough papers containing plot-outlines, questionings, and portions of text. These show my father at a halt, even at a loss, to the point of a lack of confidence in radical components of the narrative structure that had been built up with such pains. The only external evidence that I know of to cast light on this is a letter, dispirited in tone, which he wrote to Stanley Unwin on 15 September 1939, twelve days after the entry of England into war with Germany, apologising for his 'silence about the state of the proposed sequel to the Hobbit, which you enquired about as long ago as June 21st.' 'I do not suppose,' he said, 'this any longer interests you greatly – though I still hope to finish it eventually. It is only about ¾ written. I have not had much time, quite apart from the gloom of approaching disaster, and have been unwell most of this year . . .' There is nothing in the 'August 1939' papers themselves to show why he should have thought that the existing structure of the story was in need of such radical transformation.

Proposals made at this time for new articulations of the plot were set down in such haste and so elliptically expressed that it is sometimes not easy to understand their bearings (here and there one may suspect a confusion between what had been written in the latest wave of composition and what had been written earlier); and determination of the order in which these notes and outlines were set down is impossible. To take first the most drastic proposals:

(1)   New Plot. *Bilbo* is the hero all through. Merry and Frodo his companions. This helps with Gollum (though Gollum probably gets new ring in Mordor). Or Bilbo just takes a 'holiday' – and never returns, and the surprise party [i.e. the party that ended in a surprise] is Frodo's. In which case Gandalf is *not* present to let off fireworks.

The astonishing suggestion in the first part of this note ignores the problem of 'lived happily ever after', which had bulked so large earlier (see pp. 108–9). For a brief while, at any rate, my father was prepared to envisage the demolition of the entire Bilbo-Frodo structure – the now established and essential idea that Bilbo vanished 'with a bang and a flash' at the end of his hundred-and-eleventh birthday party and that Frodo followed him out of the Shire, more discreetly, seventeen years later. Happily, he did not spend long on this – though he did go so far as to begin a new text, headed:

New version – with Bilbo as hero. Aug. 1939

### The Lord of the Rings

This begins: '"It is all most disturbing and in fact rather alarming," said Bilbo Baggins,' and the matter is the same as in 'Ancient History' – with

Sam's shears audible outside – altered only as was necessary since Gandalf was here speaking to Bilbo, not Frodo; but this text peters out after a couple of sides.

The second part of this note is little less drastic: a return to the story as it was at the end of the first phase of work on this chapter, where Bilbo merely disappeared quietly from the Shire shortly before his 111th birthday, and the party was given by Bingo (Bolger-Baggins); see p. 40. This idea is developed in the following outline:

(2)  Go back to original idea. Make Frodo (or Bingo) a more comic character.

Bilbo is not overcome by Ring – he very seldom used it. He lived long and then said goodbye, put on his old clothes and rode off. He would not say where he was going – except that he was going across the River. He had 2 favourite 'nephews', Peregrin Boffin and Frodo [*written above:* Folco] Baggins. Peregrin was the elder. Peregrin went off and Bilbo was blamed, and after that the young folk were kept away from him – only Folco remained faithful.

Bilbo left all his possessions to Folco (who thus inherited with interest all the dislike of the Sackville-Bagginses).

Bilbo lived long, 111 – he tells Gandalf he is feeling tired, and discusses what to do. He is worried about the Ring. Says he is reluctant to leave it and thinks of taking it. Gandalf looks at him.

In the end he leaves it behind, but puts on Sting and his elf-armour under his old patched green cloak. He also takes his book. Last whimsical saying was 'I think I shall look for a place where there is more peace and quiet, and I can finish my book.'

'Nobody will read it!'

'O, they may – in years to come.'

Ring begins to have an effect on Folco. He gets restless. And plans to go off 'following Bilbo'. His friends are Odo Bolger and Merry Brandybuck.

Conversation with Gandalf as in Tale.

Folco gives the unexpected [*read* long-expected][1] party and vanishes as in original draft of the Tale.[2] But bring in Black Riders.

Cut out whole part of Gandalf being *supposed to come*. Make Gandalf pursue the fugitives since he has found out about Black Riders (the scene at Crickhollow will do – but without Odo complication).

Make Gandalf looking for Folco (in that case Gandalf will *not* be at final party) – and send Trotter.

Find Bilbo at Rivendell. There Bilbo offers to take up burden of the Ring (reluctantly) but Gandalf supports Folco in offering to carry it on.

Trotter turns out to be Peregrin, who had been to Mordor.

Not the least curious feature of these notes is the renewed uncertainty about names: thus we have 'Frodo (or Bingo)', then 'Frodo' changed to 'Folco' (and at one of the occurrences of 'Folco' my father first wrote a 'B'); see also §§5 and 9. For long I assumed that it was at the very time of the writing of these notes that 'Bingo' became 'Frodo', and that they therefore preceded the third phase of the work. Those third phase manuscripts were so orderly and so suggestive of secure purpose that it seemed hard to imagine that such radical uncertainty could have succeeded them: rather they seemed like a confident new start when the doubts had been dissipated. But this cannot possibly be so. This is the first mention of Bilbo's taking his 'elf-armour' (cf. p. 223, §4), and it is only by later revision to the third phase version of 'A Long-expected party' that the story that Bilbo took it with him enters the narrative (see p. 315; in FR, p. 40, he packed it in his bag, the 'bundle wrapped in old cloths' which he took from the strong-box). Similarly, Bilbo's saying that he wanted to find peace in which to finish his book and Gandalf's rejoinder 'Nobody will read it!' only appear in the *revision* of the third phase version of the first chapter (surviving into FR p. 41). Or again, the reference to 'the scene at Crickhollow – but without Odo complication' shows that the third phase was in being (see p. 336). Other evidence elsewhere in these 'August 1939' papers is equally clear. It must therefore be concluded that the temporary confusion and loss of direction from which my father suffered at this time extended even to established names: 'Bingo' might be brought back, or 'Frodo' changed to 'Folco'.

The words 'But bring in Black Riders' are puzzling, since the Black Riders were of course very much present 'in the original draft of the Tale'; but I suspect that my father meant 'But bring in Black Rider' in the singular, i.e. the Rider who came to Hobbiton and spoke to Gaffer Gamgee. The changed story which my father was so elliptically discussing in these notes can presumably be shown in essentials thus:

| | | |
|---|---|---|
| (I) | Fourth version of 'A Long-expected Party', last in the 'first phase'; see p. 40 | Bilbo departs quietly from Hobbiton at the age of 111. |
| | | Bingo gives the party 33 years later and vanishes at the end of it. |
| | | Gandalf leaves Hobbiton after the fireworks at the Party and goes ahead towards Rivendell. |
| (II) | The existing state of the story | Bilbo gives the Party at the age of 111 and vanishes at the end of it. |
| | | Frodo departs quietly from Hobbiton with his friends 17 years later. |
| | | Gandalf fails to come as he promised before Frodo leaves. |
| | | A Black Rider comes to Hobbiton on the last evening. |

Gandalf arrives at Crickhollow after the hobbits have left.

(III)  Projected plot    Bilbo departs quietly from Hobbiton at the age of 111.
*Frodo* ('Folco') gives the Party and vanishes at the end of it.
Gandalf is not present at the Party.
A Black Rider comes to Hobbiton.
Gandalf arrives at Crickhollow after the hobbits have left.

If I am right in my interpretation of 'But bring in Black Riders', the point is that while in a fundamental feature of its structure (III) would return to (I), the coming of the Rider would be retained – so that he would arrive in the aftermath of the Party. And unlike (I), Gandalf would no longer come to the Party (so that, as mentioned in §1, there would be no fireworks, or at least not of the Gandalfian kind), but would follow hard on the hobbits ('the fugitives'), 'since he has found out about the Black Riders'.

Here again, and again happily, my father did not in the event allow himself to be diverted to yet another restructuring (and consequent very tricky rewriting at many points) of the narrative that had been achieved.

Most interesting are the statements that Trotter was Peregrin Boffin, standing in the same sort of relationship to Bilbo as did Frodo, but older than Frodo, and that running off into the wide world he had found his way to Mordor. Earlier (p. 223, §6) my father had noted: 'I thought of making Trotter into Fosco Took (Bilbo's first cousin) who vanished when a lad, owing to Gandalf. He must have had some bitter acquaintance with Ring-wraiths &c.' See further pp. 385–6.

**(3)**  In some points it is still harder to feel sure of the meaning of another outline dated 'August 1939'. This begins with a proposal to 'alter names'.

Frodo > ? Peregrin    Faramond
Odo    >   Fredegar    Hamilcar Bolger

My father subsequently added (but struck out): 'Too many hobbits. Sam, Merry, and Faramond (= Frodo) are quite enough.' He was evidently dissatisfied with the name 'Frodo' for his central character. In §2 he changed 'Frodo' to 'Folco', in §2, §5, and §9 'Bingo' reappears, and here he considers the possibility of 'Faramond'. – This seems to be the first occurrence of either name, Fredegar or Hamilcar.

The text that follows on the same page, seeming quite at variance with these notes on names, reads thus:

*Alterations of Plot*
(1)  Less emphasis on longevity caused by the Ring, until the story has progressed.

(2) *Important*. (a) Neither Bilbo nor Gandalf must know much about the Ring, when Bilbo departs. Bilbo's motive is simply *tiredness*, an unexplained restlessness (and longing to see Rivendell again, but this is not said – finding him at Rivendell must be a surprise).

(b) Gandalf does *not* tell Frodo to leave Shire – only mere hint that Lord may look for Shire. The plan for leaving was entirely Frodo's. Dreams or some other cause [*added:* restlessness] have made him decide to go journeying (to find Cracks of Doom? after seeking counsel of Elrond). Gandalf simply vanishes for years. They are not trying to catch up Gandalf. Gandalf is simply trying to *find* them, and is desperately upset when he discovers Frodo has left Hobbiton. Odo must be cut out or altered (blended with Folco), and go with F[rodo] on his ride. Only Meriadoc goes ahead.

In that case alteration of plot at Bree. Who is Trotter? A Ranger or a Hobbit? Peregrin? If Gandalf is only looking for Frodo, Trotter will have to be an old associate.[3] Thus if a Hobbit, make him one who went off under Gandalf's influence (cf. introduction to *Hobbit*).[4] E.g. –

After Bilbo's little escapade Gandalf was little seen, and only one disappearance was recorded during many years. This was the curious case of Peregrin Boffin –

Since he was a close relation of Bilbo's, Bilbo was blamed for putting notions into the boy's head with his silly fairy-stories; and visits of the young to Bag-End were discouraged by many of the elders in spite of Bilbo's generosity. But he had several faithful young friends. The chief of these was Frodo (Bilbo's cousin).

As regards (1) and (2)(a), these ideas were taken up. In 'A Long-expected Party' as it was at this time (see p. 239: preserved without significant change in the third phase version) the Ring is the only motive that Bilbo refers to in explanation of his decision to leave the Shire; and he clearly associates his longevity with possession of it: 'I really must get rid of It, Gandalf. *Well-preserved*, indeed. Why, I feel all thin – sort of stretched, if you know what I mean.' *Revisions made to the third phase version* brought the text in these respects to the form in FR (pp. 41–3), where it is clear that the Ring is not consciously a motive in Bilbo's mind (however strongly the reader is made aware of the sinister influence it was in fact exerting): he speaks of his need for 'a holiday, a very long holiday' (cf. §1 above: 'Bilbo just takes a "holiday"'), and his wish 'to see the wild country again before I die, and the Mountains.' He still says '*Well-preserved*, indeed! Why I feel all thin, sort of *stretched*, if you know what I mean', but his sense of great age is now not in any way associated with possession of the Ring; and so later, *in revision to the third phase version* of 'Ancient History', Gandalf says to Frodo: 'He certainly did not begin to connect his long life and outward youthfulness with the ring' (cf. FR p. 56: 'But as for his long life, Bilbo never connected it with the ring at all. He took all the credit for that to himself, and was very proud of it.')

The notes under (2) (b) outline a new idea in respect of Gandalf's movements: for many years before Frodo left he had never come back at all to Hobbiton, and Frodo's leaving was entirely independent of the wizard. Learning (we may suppose) that the Ring-wraiths were abroad, Gandalf hastened back at last to the Shire, where he heard to his horror that Frodo had gone. This idea was not taken up, of course (and against it my father wrote: 'But in this case the Sam chapter is spoilt' – he was referring to the end of 'Ancient History', where Sam is discovered by Gandalf eavesdropping outside the window of Bag End).

The words 'They are not trying to catch up Gandalf' are difficult to understand. It seems incredible that my father would be referring now to the first phase version of the story, in which Gandalf had left the Party (given by Bingo) after letting off the fireworks, and was known to be ahead of Frodo and his friends on the journey east; yet in the subsequent versions all that is known of him is that he did not come, as he had promised, to the small farewell party given by Bingo/Frodo before he left Bag End, and was supposed (rightly) to be behind them rather than ahead.

Still more baffling is the passage concerning Odo ('Odo must be cut out or altered (blended with Folco) and go with F[rodo] on his ride. Only Meriadoc goes ahead'). If the meaning of this is that the entire 'Odo-story' of the third phase (his journey with Gandalf from Crickhollow through Bree, the pseudonym of 'Baggins', his disappearance from Weathertop, and his unexplained arrival with Gandalf at Rivendell) was to be abandoned, how (one may ask) can he be 'blended with Folco', since 'Folco' is already a blend of the original 'Frodo and Odo', with the advantage heavily to 'Odo'? It must be remembered that these notes were in no way the logical expression of an ordered programme, but are rather the vestiges of rapidly-changing thoughts. The withdrawal of Odo, in the third phase, from the adventures of the other hobbits had caused Folco (formerly Frodo) Took to take over Odo's part and character in the narrative of those adventures, since that narrative already existed from the earlier phases, and Odo had played a large part in the hobbits' conversation (see pp. 323–4). But the *retention* of Odo in the background, with adventures of his own, would mean that when he re-emerged into the foreground again at Rivendell there would be two 'Odo' characters – the rather ironic result of getting rid of him!

The proposal here is presumably that 'Odo Bolger' and 'Folco Took' should now be definitively joined together as one character, under the latter name. 'Folco' seems indeed now too much 'Odo' for 'blending' to have much meaning; but my father may not have felt this (nor perhaps did he have so clear a picture of the intricate evolutions of his story as can be attained from long study of the manuscripts). In 'go with F[rodo] on his ride', 'ride' is perhaps a mere slip for 'walk': the meaning being that the resultant 'blend' accompanies Frodo and does not 'go ahead' with Merry to Buckland. This is all very fine-spun, but it reflects the extraordinarily intricate nature of my father's changing construction. With 'Who is Trotter? A Ranger or a Hobbit?' cf. pp. 331–2. The story that Trotter was Peregrin Boffin is now definitively present and would be fully developed in revision to the third phase text of 'A Long-expected party' (pp. 384–6).

(4)   The remaining papers in this 'August 1939' collection that are concerned with the opening part of the story perhaps followed the others. These pages of very rough narrative drafting are headed *Conversation of Bilbo and Frodo* – a relationship never otherwise seen at close quarters, before they met long afterwards at Rivendell. The conversation takes place at Bag End before Bilbo's Farewell Party; he speaks to Frodo of the Ring for the first time, only to discover to his genuine amazement and mock indignation, that Frodo knew about it already, and had looked at Bilbo's secret book. This is a different story to that in 'A Long-expected Party', where Frodo had read Bilbo's memoirs with his permission (pp. 240, 315).

### Conversation of Bilbo and Frodo

'Well, my lad, we have got on very well – and I am sorry to leave, in a way. But I am going on a holiday, a very long holiday. In fact I have no intention of coming back. I am tired. I am going to cross the Rivers.⁵ So be prepared for surprises at this party. I may say that I am leaving everything, practically, to you – all except a few oddments.'

★

Mr Bilbo Baggins, of Bag-end, Underhill (Hobbiton) was sitting in his west sitting-room one summer afternoon.

'Well, that's my little plan, Frodo,' said Bilbo Baggins. 'It's a dead secret, mind you! I've kept it from everyone but you and Gandalf. I needed Gandalf's help; and I've told you because I hope you'll enjoy the joke all the better for being in the know – and of course you're closely concerned.'

'I don't like it at all,' said the other hobbit, looking rather puzzled and downcast. 'But I've known you long enough to know that it's no good trying to talk you out of your little plans.'

★

'Well, the time has come to say goodbye, my dear lad,' said Bilbo.

'I suppose so,' said Frodo sadly. 'Though I don't at all understand why. [But I know you too well to think of trying to talk you out of your little plans – especially after they have gone so far.]'

'I can't explain it any clearer,' answered Bilbo, 'because I am not quite clear myself. But I hope this is clear: I am leaving everything (except a few oddments) to you. My bit of money will keep you nicely as it did me in the old days; and besides there is a bit of my treasure left – you know where. Not so much now, but a pretty nest-egg still. And there's one thing more. There's a ring.'

'The magic ring?' asked Frodo incautiously.

'Eh, what?' said Bilbo. 'Who said magic ring?'

'I did,' said Frodo blushing. 'My dear old hobbit, you don't allow for the inquisitiveness of young nephews.'

'I do allow for it,' said Bilbo, 'or I thought I had. And in any case don't call me a dear old hobbit.'

'I have known about the existence of your Ring for years.'

'Have you indeed?' said Bilbo. 'How, I should like to know! Come on, then: you had better make a clean breast of it before I go.'

'Well, it was like this. It was the Sackville-Bagginses that were your undoing.'

'They would be,' grunted Bilbo.

Frodo then tells the story of his observing Bilbo's escape, by becoming invisible, from the Sackville-Bagginses while out walking one day. This, in very brief form, had been used in the fifth version of 'A Long-expected Party' (p. 242), when Bingo told it to Gandalf after the Party – there, merely as an example of how Bilbo had used the Ring for small-scale disappearances to avoid boredom and inconvenience (for of course in the 'received' story Bingo knew about the Ring because Bilbo had told him about it). It was then, in more elaborate form, given to Merry in 'A Conspiracy is Unmasked' (p. 300) as an explanation of how Merry knew of the existence of the Ring (and so was dropped from the sixth version of 'A Long-expected Party', p. 315). Now, in the present text, my father simply lifted the story word for word from 'A Conspiracy (is) Unmasked' and gave it to Frodo, as his explanation to Bilbo of how *he* learnt about the Ring; and Frodo continues here, again almost word for word, with Merry's account of how he got a sight of Bilbo's book:

'That doesn't explain it all,' said Bilbo, with a gleam in his eye. 'Come on, out with it, whatever it is!'

'Well, after that I kept my eyes open,' stammered Frodo. 'I – er – in fact I rather kept a watch on you. But you must admit it was very intriguing – and I was only in my early tweens. So one day I came across your book.'

'My book!' said Bilbo. 'Good heavens above. Is nothing safe!'
'Not too safe,' said Frodo. 'But I only got one rapid glance. You
never left the book about, except just that once: you were called
out of the study, and I came in and found it lying open. I should
like a rather longer look, Bilbo. I suppose you are leaving it to me
now?'

'No I am not!' said Bilbo decisively. 'It isn't finished. Why, one
of my chief reasons for leaving is to go somewhere where I can get
on with it in peace without a parcel of rascally nephews prying
round the place, and a string of confounded visitors hanging on to
the bell.'

'You shouldn't be so kind to everyone,' said Frodo. 'I am sure
you needn't go away.

'Well, I am going,' said Bilbo. 'And about that Ring: I suppose I
needn't describe it now, or how I got it. I thought of giving it to
you.'

At this point my father interrupted the text and wrote across the page:
'This won't do because of the use of the Ring at the party!' – i.e., Bilbo
could not have the intention to give it to Frodo then, before the Party.
But without changing anything that he had written he went on with the
story thus:

He fumbled in his pocket and drew out a small golden ring
attached by another ring to a fine chain. He unfastened it, laid it in
the palm of his hand, and looked long at it.

'Here it is!' he said with sigh.

Frodo held out his hand. But Bilbo put the ring straight back in
his pocket. [A puzzled look >] An odd look came over his face.
'Er, well,' he stammered, 'I'll give it you I expect last thing before
I go – or leave it in my locked drawer or something.'

Frodo looked puzzled and stared at him, but said nothing.

The last lines of the text come after the Party:

Bilbo . . . . goes and dresses as in the older version (but with
*armour* under his cloak)[6] and says goodbye. 'The – er – ring,' he
said, 'is in the drawer' – and vanished into [the] darkness.

I think that this new version is to be associated with the opening notes
under 'Alterations of Plot' in §3 above: it represents a movement away
from the idea that Bilbo was troubled about the Ring, that it was his
prime motive for leaving (rather, his tiredness, his desire for peace, is
mentioned). He has never even spoken to Frodo about it. It seems that
my father's intention had been that Bilbo should simply hand it to Frodo

there and then, without any suggestion of inner struggle; but he only realised, as he wrote, that 'This won't do' – because Bilbo must retain the Ring till the actual moment of his departure. The gift would therefore have to be postponed from the present occasion; and it was only now that he took up the suggestion in 'A Long-expected Party', where Bilbo said to Gandalf: 'I am not going to throw it away. In any case I find it impossible to make myself do that – *I simply put it back in my pocket.*'⁷ The curious result is that the scene actually ends now with a demonstration, in Bilbo's embarrassed and ambiguous behaviour, precisely of the sinister effect that the Ring has in fact had on its owner; and this would be developed into the quarrel with Gandalf in FR, pp. 41–3.

**(5)**  Turning now to those papers dated August 1939 that are concerned with larger projections of the story to come after the sojourn in Rivendell, there is first a suggestion that a Dragon should come to the Shire and that by its coming the hobbits should be led to show that they are made of 'sterner stuff', and that 'Frodo (Bingo)' should 'actually come near the end of his money – now it was *dragon* gold. He is "lured"?' There is here a reference to 'Bilbo remarks on old sheet of notes' – obviously those given on pp. 41–2 (where the same suggestion of a Dragon coming to Hobbiton was made).

**(6)**  Following these notes on the same page is a brief list of narrative elements that might enter much further on:

> Island in sea. Take Frodo there in end.
> Radagast?⁸
> Battle is raging far off between armies of Elves and Men v[ersus the] Lord.
> Adventures . . Stone-Men.

With the first of these cf. the note given on p. 41: 'Elrond tells him [Bilbo] of an island', etc. The reference to the 'battle raging' probably belongs to the end of the story, when the Ring goes into the Crack of Doom.

Most interesting is the last item here. A note by my father found with the LR papers states that he looked though (some, at least, of) the material in 1964; and it was very probably at that time that he scrawled against the words 'Adventures . . Stone-Men':

> Thought of as just an 'adventure'. The whole of the matter of Gondor (Stone-land) grew from this note. (Aragorn, still called Trotter, had no connexion with it then, and was at first conceived as one of the hobbits that had wanderlust.)

**(7)**  This is a convenient place to give a page of pencilled notes which bears no date and in which 'Bingo' appears. At the head of the page stand the words: 'City of Stone and civilized men'. Then follows an extremely abbreviated outline of the end of the story.

At end

When Bingo [*written above:* Frodo] at last reaches Crack and Fiery Mountain *he cannot make himself throw the Ring away.* ? He hears Necromancer's voice offering him great reward – to share power with him, if he will keep it.

At that moment Gollum – who had seemed to reform and had guided them by secret ways through Mordor – comes up and treacherously tries to take Ring. They wrestle and Gollum *takes Ring* and falls into the Crack.

The mountain begins to rumble.

Bingo flies away [i.e. flees away].

Eruption.

Mordor vanishes like a dark cloud. Elves are seen riding like lights rolling away a dark cloud.

The City of Stone is covered in ashes.

Journey back to Rivendell.

What of Shire? Sackville-Baggins . . . . . . . lands. . . . . . . . the four quarters.

Bingo makes peace, and settles down in a little hut on the high green ridge – until one day he goes with the Elves west beyond the towers.

Better – no land was tilled, all the hobbits were busy making swords.

The illegible words might just possibly be interpreted thus: 'Sackville-Baggins [and] his friends hurt [the] lands. There was war between the four quarters.'

Since there is here a reference to 'the City of Stone', while my father said in 1964 that the whole idea of Gondor arose from the reference to 'Stone-Men' in a note dated August 1939, it would have to be concluded on a strict interpretation that this outline comes from that time or later; on the other hand, the hero is still 'Bingo', so that this outline would seem to be the earlier. I think, however, that the contradiction may be only apparent, since in other notes dated August 1939 my father seems still to have been hesitant about the name 'Bingo', and I would therefore ascribe the outline just given to much the same time as the rest of these notes.

It obviously leaves out some things that my father must already have known (more or less): such as how Gollum reappeared. But it is most remarkable to find here – when there is no suggestion of the vast structure still to be built – that the corruption of the Shire, and the crucial presence of Gollum on the Fiery Mountain, were very early elements in the whole.

(8)  On the reverse of the page bearing this outline is the following:

'The ring is destroyed,' said Bilbo, 'and I am feeling sleepy. We must say goodbye, Bingo [*written above:* Frodo] – but it is a good place to say goodbye, in the House of Elrond, where memory is long and kind. I am leaving the book of my small deeds here. And I don't think I shall go to rest till I have written down your tale too.

Elrond will keep it – no doubt after all hobbits have gone their ways into the past. Well, Bingo my lad, you and I were very small creatures, but we've played our part. We've played our part. An odd fate we have shared, to be sure.'

It seems then that at this time my father foresaw that Bilbo died in Rivendell.

(9)    There is one further page dated 'August 1939', and this is of great interest. It is a series of pencilled notes like the others, and is headed 'Plot from XII on'.

> Have to wait till Spring? Or have to go at once.
> They go south along the Mountains. Later or early? Snowstorm in the
>     Red Pass. Journey down the R. Redway.
> Adventure with Giant Tree Beard in Forest.
> Mines of Moria. These again deserted – except for *Goblins*.
> Land of Ond. Siege of the City.
> They draw near the borders of Mordor.
> In dark Gollum comes up. He feigns reform? Or tries to throttle
>     Frodo? – but Gollum has now a magic ring given by Lord and is
>     invisible. Frodo dare not use his own.
> Cavalcade of evil led by seven Black Riders.
> See Dark Tower on the horizon. Horrible feeling of an Eye searching
>     for him.
> Fiery Mountain.
> Eruption of Fiery Mountain causes destruction of Tower.

A pencilled marginal note asks whether 'Bingo' (with 'Frodo' written beside) should be captured by the Dark Lord and questioned, but be saved 'by Sam?'.

Subsequently my father emended these notes in ink. In the first line, against 'Or have to go at once', he wrote 'at once'; he directed that 'Mines of Moria . . .' should precede 'Adventure with Giant Tree Beard in Forest' and come between 'Snowstorm in the Red Pass' and 'Journey down the R. Redway'; and after 'These again deserted – except for *Goblins*' he added 'Loss of Gandalf'.

Some features of this outline have occurred already; the feigned reform of Gollum, his attack on Frodo, and the eruption of the Fiery Mountain, in §7; the acquisition of a ring by Gollum in Mordor in §1. But we meet here for the first time other major ingredients in the later work. The Ring crosses the Misty Mountains by 'the Red Pass', which will survive in the Redhorn Pass, or Redhorn Gate. The Mines of Moria now first reappear from *The Hobbit* – at any rate under that name: the mention in *Queries and Alterations* note 11 (p. 226) of the colony founded by the Dwarves Balin, Ori, and Oin from the Lonely Mountain in 'rich hills of the South' does not show that the identification had been made. The actual link lay no doubt in Elrond's words in *The Hobbit* (Chapter III, 'A Short Rest'): 'I have heard that there are still forgotten treasures to be found in the deserted caverns of the mines of Moria, since the dwarf and goblin war'; and the words here 'These again deserted – except for Goblins', taken with those in *Queries and Alterations* (*ibid.*) 'But after a time no word was heard of them', clearly imply the story in *The Lord of the Rings*. The land of the Stone-Men (see §6) is the 'Land of Ond', and the 'City of Stone' (§7) will be besieged. Here also there is the first hint of the story of the capture of Frodo and his rescue by Sam Gamgee from the tower of Cirith Ungol; and most notable of all, perhaps, the first mention of the Searching Eye in the Dark Tower.

These are references to narrative 'moments' which my father foresaw: they do not constitute an articulated narrative scheme. They may very well not be in the succession that he even then perceived. Thus in this outline Gollum's treachery is brought in long before Frodo reaches the Fiery Mountain, which in view of what is said in §7 can hardly have been his meaning; and the Mines of Moria are named after the passage of the Misty Mountains. This was corrected later in ink, but it may not have been his conception when he wrote these notes: for in none of the (six) mentions of the Mines of Moria in *The Hobbit* is there any suggestion of where they were (cf. his letter to W. H. Auden in 1955: 'The Mines of Moria had been a mere name', *Letters* no. 163).

(10) Something must be said here of 'Giant Treebeard', for he emerged into a scrap of actual narrative at this time (and had been mentioned by Gandalf to Frodo in Rivendell. p. 363: 'I was caught in Fangorn and spent many weary days as a prisoner of the Giant Treebeard'). There exists a single sheet of manuscript, which began as a letter dated 'July 27–29th 1939', but which my father covered on both sides with fine ornamental script (one side of the sheet is reproduced opposite). Among the writings on the page are the words 'July Summer Diversions' and lines from Chaucer's *Reeve's Tale* – for these 'Diversions' were a series of public entertainments held at Oxford in the course of which my father, attired as Chaucer, recited that Tale. But the page is chiefly taken up with a text on which he afterwards pencilled *Tree Beard*.

When Frodo heard the voice he looked up, but he could see nothing through the thick entangled branches. Suddenly he felt a quiver in the gnarled tree-trunk against which he was leaning, and before he could spring away he was pushed, or kicked, forward onto his knees. Picking himself up he looked at the tree, and even as he looked, it took a stride towards him. He scrambled out of the way, and a deep rumbling chuckle came down out of the tree-top.

'Where are you, little beetle?' said the voice. 'If you don't let me know where you are, you can't blame me for treading on you. And please, don't tickle my leg!'

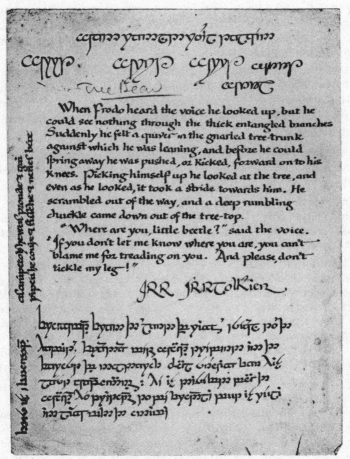

The emergence of Treebeard

'I can't see any leg,' said Frodo. 'And where are you?' 'You must be blind,' said the voice. 'I am here.' 'Who are you?' 'I am Treebeard,' the voice answered. 'If you haven't heard of me before, you ought to have done; and anyway you are in my garden.'

'I can't see any garden,' said Frodo. 'Do you know what a garden looks like?' 'I have one of my own: there are flowers and plants in it, and a fence round it; but there is nothing of the kind here.' 'O yes! there is. Only you have walked through the fence without noticing it; and you can't see the plants, because you are down underneath them by their roots.'

It was only then when Frodo looked closer that he saw that what he had taken for smooth tree-stems were the stalks of gigantic flowers – and what he had thought was the stem of a monstrous oaktree was really a thick gnarled leg with a rootlike foot and many branching toes.

This is the first image of Treebeard: seeming in its air to come rather from the old *Hobbit* than the new. Six lines in Elvish *tengwar* are also written here, which transliterated read:

Fragment from The Lord of the Rings, sequel to The Hobbit.
Frodo meets Giant Treebeard in the Forest of Neldoreth while seeking for his lost companions: he is deceived by the giant who pretends to be friendly, but is really in league with the Enemy.

The forest of Neldoreth, forming the northern part of Doriath, had appeared in the later *Annals of Beleriand* (V.126, 148); the name from the old legends (like that of Glorfindel, see p. 214) was to be re-used.

Six months earlier, in a letter of 2 February 1939, my father had said that 'though there is no dragon (so far) there is going to be a Giant' (*Letters* no. 35, footnote to the text). If my suggested analysis of the chronology is correct (see p. 309) 'Giant Treebeard' had already appeared, as Gandalf's captor, at the end of the third phase (p. 363).

(11)     There remains one further text (extant in two versions) to be given in this chapter; this is the story of Peregrin Boffin (see under §§2, 3 above). One form of it is found as part of a rather roughly written two-page manuscript that begins as a new text of 'A Long-expected Party': very closely related to the sixth or third phase version of that chapter, but certainly following it. I take it up from the point 'At ninety he seemed much the same as ever' (FR p. 29).

At ninety-nine they began to call him *well-preserved*, though *unchanged* would have been nearer the mark. Some were heard to say that it was too much of a good thing, this combination of apparently perpetual youth with seemingly inexhaustible wealth.

'It will have to be paid for,' they said. 'It isn't natural, and trouble will come of it!'

But trouble had not yet come, and Mr Baggins was extremely generous with his money, so most people (and especially the poorer and less important hobbits) pardoned his oddities. In a way the inhabitants of Hobbiton were (secretly) rather proud of him: the wealth that he had brought back from his travels became a local legend, and it was widely believed, whatever the old folk might say, that most of the Hill was full of tunnels stuffed with treasure.

'He may be peculiar, but he does no harm,' said the younger folk. But not all of his more important relatives agreed. They were suspicious of his influence on their children, and especially of their sons meeting Gandalf at his house. Their suspicions were much increased by the unfortunate affair of Peregrin Boffin.

Peregrin was the grandson of Bilbo's mother's second sister Donnamira Took. He was a mere babe, five years old, when Bilbo came back from his journey; but he grew up a dark-haired and (for a hobbit) lanky lad, very much more of a Took than a Boffin. He was always trotting round to Hobbiton, for his father, Paladin Boffin, lived at Northope, only a mile or two behind the Hill. When Peregrin began to talk about mountains and dwarves, and forests and wolves, Paladin became alarmed, and finally forbade his son to go near Bag-end, and shut his door on Bilbo.

Bilbo took this to heart, for he was extremely fond of Peregrin, but he did nothing to encourage him to visit Bag-end secretly. Peregrin then ran away from home and was found wandering about half-starved up on the moors of the Northfarthing. Finally, the day after he came of age (in the spring of Bilbo's eightieth year)[9] he disappeared, and was never found in spite of a search all over the Shire.

In former times Gandalf had always been held responsible for the occasional regrettable accidents of this kind; but now Bilbo got a large share of the blame, and after Peregrin's disappearance most of his younger relations were kept away from him. Though in fact Bilbo was probably more troubled by the loss of Peregrin than all the Boffins put together.

He had, however, other young friends, who for one reason or another were not kept away from him. His favourite soon became Frodo Baggins, grandson of Mirabella the third of the Old Took's remarkable daughters, and son of Drogo (one of Bilbo's second cousins). Just about the time of Peregrin's disappearance Frodo was left an orphan, when only a child of twelve, and so he had no anxious parents to keep him out of bad company. He lived with his uncle Rory Brandybuck, and his mother's hundred and one relatives in the Great Hole of Bucklebury: Brandy Hall.

Here this new opening ends. A slightly shorter version is found as a rider to the manuscript of the third phase version itself: there are some differences of wording but none of substance. Bilbo is here said to have taken the delinquent back to Northope and apologised to Paladin Boffin, when Peregrin 'sneaked round to him secretly'; and Bilbo 'stoutly denied having anything to do with the events.'

The village of *Northope* later became *Overhill*, and was so corrected on the second of these texts.[10] – *Paladin* is already fixed as the name of the father of *Peregrin*: these Boffins are – as names – the origin of Paladin and Peregrin Took in LR. Donnamira Took, second of the Old Took's daughters, appears in the family tree of the Tooks given on p. 317, where she is the wife of Hugo Boffin (as in LR, but there without recorded issue): their son was Jago Boffin, and his son was Fosco, Bilbo's first cousin (once removed), who was 54 at the time of the Party. In the third phase version of 'Ancient History' (p. 319) Jo Button, who saw the 'Tree-men' beyond the North Moors, is said to have worked for Fosco Boffin of Northope, and this is presumably the same person as the Fosco Boffin of the family tree, grandson of Donnamira. In this case Peregrin Boffin (Trotter) – who was 64 at the time of the Party (see note 9), though of course he had then long since disappeared from the Shire – has stepped into Fosco's genealogical place, and his father Paladin into that of Jago. But only into the genealogical place: the Boffin of Northope for whom Jo Button was working has obviously nothing to do with the renegade Peregrin.

It will be seen that in this account Frodo and Trotter were second cousins, and both were first cousins once removed of Bilbo.[11]

## NOTES

1  With 'unexpected party' for 'long-expected party' cf. p. 245, note 1.
2  Actually, the third and fourth drafts of the first phase: by 'original draft of the Tale' my father meant the form of 'A Long-expected Party' as it stood when submitted to Allen and Unwin (see p. 40).
3  I do not understand the force of this sentence.
4  The reference to *The Hobbit* is to Chapter I 'An Unexpected Party', a passage already cited (p. 224).
5  *the Rivers:* the plural form is clear.
6  That Bilbo wore his 'elf-armour' under his cloak when he went is said in §2; see pp. 371–2.
7  This is the wording of the sixth (third phase) version, little changed from that of the fifth (p. 239).

8  Radagast had occurred in *The Hobbit*: in Chapter VII 'Queer Lodgings' Gandalf spoke to Beorn of 'my good cousin Radagast who lives near the Southern borders of Mirkwood.'

9  Peregrin Boffin was five years old when Bilbo returned from his great adventure. The calculation is: 51 to 79 ('the spring of his eithtieth year') = 28, plus 5 = 33 ('coming of age'). According to this story Peregrin/Trotter was 81 years old when Frodo and his companions met him at Bree (Bilbo finally departed when he was 111; Peregrin/Trotter was then 64, and Frodo left the Shire 17 years later). As he said at Bree, 'I'm older now than I look' (pp. 153, 342); Aragorn was 87 when he said the same thing (FR p. 177).

10  *Northope* > *Overhill* also on p. 319. – The name *Northope* appears here on my father's original map of the Shire (p. 107, item I), but it was struck out and replaced, not by Overhill, but by *The Yale*. This is a convenient place to notice the history of this name. Long after, my father wrote in *The Yale* on the Shire map in a copy of the First Edition of FR, placing it south of Whitfurrows in the Eastfarthing, in such a way as to show that he intended a region, like 'The Marish', not a particular place of settlement (the road to Stock runs through it); and at the same time, on the same copy, he expanded the text in FR p. 86, introducing the name: 'the lowlands of the Yale' (for the reason for this change of text, which was published in the Second Edition, see p. 66, note 10). The Shire map in the Second Edition has *The Yale* added here, but in relation to a small black square, as if it were the name of a farm or small hamlet; this must have been a misunderstanding. I cannot explain the meaning of *The Yale*. *Northope* contains a place-name element *hope* that usually means 'a small enclosed valley'.

11  My father's earlier suggestion concerning Trotter (p. 223) also made him Bilbo's first cousin (Fosco Took).

# THE STORY
# CONTINUED

# XXIII

# IN THE HOUSE OF ELROND

In the next stage of the work it is difficult to deduce the chronology of composition, or to relate it to important further revisions made to the 'third phase' of the story as far as Rivendell. Determination of the chronology depends on the form taken by certain key elements, and if these happen to be absent certainty becomes impossible.

At any rate, after 'Bingo' had become 'Frodo' my father continued Frodo's interrupted conversation with Glóin at the feast in the house of Elrond (see p. 369). This continuation is in two forms, the second closely following the first, and already in the first form the latter part of 'Many Meetings' in FR is quite closely approached; but there are certain major differences. I give here the second form (in part).[1]

'And what has become of Balin and Ori and Óin?' asked Frodo.

A shadow passed over Glóin's face. 'Balin took to travelling again,' he answered. 'You may have heard that he visited Bilbo in Hobbiton many years ago:[2] well, not very long after that he went away for two or three years. Then he returned to the Mountain with a great number of dwarves that he discovered wandering masterless in the South and East. He wanted Dáin to go back to Moria – or at least to allow him to found a colony there and reopen the great mines. As you probably know, Moria was the ancestral home of the dwarves of the race of Durin, and the forefathers of Thorin and Dáin dwelt there, until they were driven by the goblin invasions far into the North. Now Balin reported that Moria was again wholly deserted, since the great defeat of the goblins, but the mines were still rich, especially in silver. Dáin was not willing to leave the Mountain and the tomb of Thorin, but he allowed Balin to go, and he took with him many of the folk of the Mountain as well as his own following; and Ori and Óin went with him. For many years things went well, and the colony throve; there was traffic once more between Moria and the Mountain, and many gifts of silver were sent to Dáin. Then fortune changed. Our messengers were attacked and robbed by cruel Men, well-armed. No messengers came from Moria; but rumour reached us that the mines and dwarf-city were again deserted. For long we could not learn what had become of Balin and his people – but now we have news, and it is evil. It is to tell these tidings and to ask for the counsel of – of those that dwell in Rivendell that I have come. But to-night let us speak of merrier things!'

At the head of the page my father wrote the words that stand in this place in FR (p. 241): '"We do not know," he answered. "It is largely on his account that I have come to ask for the counsel of – of those that dwell in Rivendell. But for to-night let us speak of merrier things."' In FR the story of Balin was taken up into 'The Council of Elrond' and greatly enlarged.

Glóin's account of the works of the Dwarves in Dale and under the Lonely Mountain (FR pp. 241–2) is present in the old version.[3] At the end, when Glóin said: 'You were very fond of Bilbo, weren't you?' Frodo replied simply 'Yes', and then 'they went on to talk about the old adventures of Bilbo with the dwarves, in Mirkwood, and among the Wood-elves, and in the caverns of the Mountain.'

The entrance into the Hall of Fire, and the discovery and recognition of Bilbo, are already very close to FR (for early references to Bilbo at Rivendell see pp. 126, 225). The Hall of Fire is said in both texts to be nearly as large as the 'Hall of Feasting' or 'Great Hall'; in the second this hall 'appeared to have no windows'; and in both there were many fires burning: Bilbo sat beside the furthest, with his cup and bread on a low table beside him (in FR there were no tables).

Bilbo says 'I shall have to get that fellow Peregrin to help me' (cf. p. 369) and Elrond replies that he will have *Ethelion*[4] found (in Chapter XI of the 'third phase' Glorfindel calls Trotter *Du-finnion*, p. 361). 'Messengers were sent to find Bilbo's friend. It was said that he had been in the kitchens, for his help was as much esteemed by the cooks as by the poets.' It had been said in the earlier part of the chapter (p. 365) that Frodo could not see Trotter at the feast, and his absence survived into FR (p. 245), but with a very different reason for it.

Whatever Bilbo may have had to say of himself is not reported in the original story. The entire passage (FR pp. 243–4) in which Bilbo tells of his journey to Dale, of his life in Rivendell, and his interest in the Ring – and the distressing incident when he asks to see it – is absent.

They were so deep in the doings of the Shire that they did not notice the arrival of another hobbit. For several minutes he stood by them, looking at them with a smile. Suddenly they looked up. 'Ah, there you are, Peregrin!' said Bilbo. 'Trotter!' said Frodo.

'Both right!' laughed Trotter.

'Well, that is tiresome of Gandalf!' exclaimed Frodo. 'I knew you reminded me of some one, and he laughed at me.[5] Of course, you remind me of yourself, and of Folco, and of all the Tooks. You came once to Buckland when I was very small, but I never quite forgot it, because you talked to Old Rory about lands outside the Shire, and about Bilbo who you were not allowed to see. I have wondered what became of you. But I was puzzled by your shoes. Why do you wear them?'

'I shall not tell you the reason now,' said Trotter quietly.

'No, Frodo, don't ask that yet,' said Bilbo, looking rather unhappy. 'Come on, Perry! I want your help. This song of mine has got to be finished this evening.'

At this point, while in the middle of writing the second text, my father wrote across it: '?? Trotter had better not be a hobbit – but a Ranger, remainder of Western Men, as originally planned.' Of course, looking back over the texts from Trotter's first appearance, there is no possibility that my father had 'originally planned' to make Trotter anything but a hobbit. The first suggestion that he might not be appears in *Queries and Alterations* (p. 223, §6). But by 'originally planned' my father may well have been thinking no further back than to the drafts for the opening of the 'Bree' chapter in the third phase (p. 331), where the idea that the Rangers were Men, 'the last remnant of the kingly people from beyond the Seas', first emerged, though this was not taken up in the chapter as actually written at that time. It may be that he had felt for some time that Trotter should not be a hobbit, but (as he said of the name 'Bingo', p. 221) he was now too used to the idea to change it. Even now, he did not follow up his directive, and Trotter remains Peregrin Boffin.

As in FR, Frodo sits alone and falls asleep during the music; but the song *Eärendil was a mariner* is not present (though the word '?Messenger' written at the top of the page is a hint of it).[6]

He woke to the sound of ringing laughter. There was no longer any music, but on the edge of his waking sense was the echo of a voice that had just stopped singing. He looked, and saw that Bilbo was seated on his stool, set now near to the middle fire, in the centre of a circle of listeners.

'Come now, tell us, Bilbo!' said one of the Elves, 'which is the line which Peregrin put in?'

'No!' laughed Bilbo. 'I leave you to guess – you pride yourselves on your judgement of words.'

'But it is difficult to discriminate between two hobbits,' they laughed.

'Nonsense!' said Bilbo. 'But I won't argue the matter. I'm sleepy, after so much sound and song!' He got up and bowed and came back beside Frodo.

'Well, that's that,' he said. 'It went off better than I expected. As a matter of fact, quite a lot of it was Peregrin's.'

'I am sorry I did not hear it,' said Frodo. 'I heard the Elves laughing as I woke up.'

'Never mind,' said Bilbo. 'You'll hear it again, very likely. Just a lot of nonsense, anyway. But it is difficult to keep awake here, until you get used to it – not that hobbits ever acquire the Elves' appetite for song and poetry and tales of all sorts. They will be going on for a long while yet. . . .

The words of the chant to Elbereth (identical in both texts) are different from the form in FR:

> Elbereth Gilthoniel sir evrin pennar oriel
> dir avos-eithen miriel
> bel daurion sel aurinon
> pennáros evrin ériol.

The sweet syllables fell like clear jewels of mingled word and sound, and he halted for a moment looking back.

'That is the opening of the chant to Elbereth,' said Bilbo. 'They will sing that and other songs of the Blessed Realm many times tonight.'

Bilbo led Frodo back to his upper room. There they sat for some while, looking at the bright stars through the window, and talking softly. They spoke no longer of the small and happy news of the Shire far away, but of the Elves, and of the wide world, and its perils, and of the burden and mystery of the Ring.

When Sam came to the door (at the end of the chapter in FR) Bilbo said:

'Quite right, Sam! Though I never expected to live long enough to be ordered about by Ham Gamgee's boy. Bless me, I am near 150 and old enough to be your great-grandfather.'

'No sir, and I never expected to be doing it.'

'It is Gandalf's fault, said Frodo. 'He chose Sam to be my companion in adventure, and Sam takes his task seriously.'

This was replaced at the time of writing by the ending in FR. Bilbo was in fact 128.

Both texts continue on briefly into what became 'The Council of Elrond' in FR (the title that my father had given to the 'third phase' text Chapter XII, p. 362, afterwards called 'Many Meetings', when he anticipated that it would contain the Council as well as the 'many meetings' that preceded it).

Frodo awoke early next day, feeling refreshed and well. Sam brought him breakfast, and would not allow him to get up till he had eaten it. Then Bilbo and Gandalf came and talked for a while. Suddenly a single bell rang out. [*All the remainder of the text from this point was struck out; see p. 399.*]

'Bless me!' said Gandalf. 'The council is in half an hour. That is the warning. I must be off. Bilbo will bring you to the place, as soon as you are ready. Sam had better come with you.'

The council was held in a high glade among the trees on the valley-side far above the house. A falling stream ran at the side of the meeting place, and with the trickling and bubbling of the water was mingled the sound of many birds. There were twelve seats of carved stone in a wide circle; and behind them many other smaller seats of wood. The ground was strewn with many red and yellow leaves, but the trees above were still clothed with fading green; a clear sky of pale blue hung high above, filled with the light of morning.

When Bilbo, Frodo and Sam arrived Elrond was already seated, and beside him, as at the feast, were Gandalf and Glorfindel. Glóin was there also with [an attendant >] a younger dwarf, whom Frodo later discovered was Burin son of Balin.[7] A strange elf, a messenger from the king of the Wood-elves . . . Eastern Mirkwood was seated beside Burin.[8] Trotter (as Frodo continued to call him instead of Peregrin or the Elvish equivalent Ethelion) was there, and all the rest of the hobbit party, Merry, Folco, and Odo. There were besides three other counsellors attendant on Elrond, one an Elf named Erestor, and two other kinsmen of Elrond, of that half-elvish folk whom the Elves named the children of Lúthien.[9] And seated alone and silent was a Man of noble face, but dark and sad.

'This is Boromir,' said Elrond. 'He arrived only yesterday, in the evening. He comes from far away in the South, and his tidings may be of use to us.'

It would take long to tell of all that was spoken in that council under the fair trees of Rivendell. The sun climbed to noon and was turning westward before all the tidings were recounted. Then Elves brought food and drink for the company. The sun had fallen low and its slanting light was red in the valley before an end was made of the debate and they rose and returned down the long path to the house.

Both texts end at this point. At the end of the second my father wrote: '(The Council must be behind closed doors. Frodo invited to presence of Elrond. Tidings of the world. They decide Ring must be destroyed.)'

While Trotter is Peregrin Boffin, and the long-awaited 'recognition' between Trotter and Frodo takes place, Odo is still present: but in the papers dated August 1939, where the identification of Trotter with Peregrin Boffin first appears, Odo appears to be emphatically abandoned. Once again, Odo seems to have proved unsinkable, even though, as discussed on p. 375, Folco had effectively assumed his character. – Of course, these 'Rivendell' manuscripts may very well belong to the same time, and a step-by-step reconstruction cannot be expected. In any case, the removal of Odo and (much more) the identity of Trotter were questions long revolved, and such notes as 'Trotter had better not be a hobbit' or 'Odo must be cut out' are rather the traces of a long debate than a series of clear-cut, successive decisions.

The text just given was continued in a further manuscript of different form, in which appears the first complete version of the Council of Elrond; but before going on to this, two sides of a single isolated page seem undoubtedly to represent my father's first expressed ideas for the Council. It was written in pencil so faint and rapid that it would be largely illegible had my father not gone over it in ink; and he himself could not be sure in places of what he had written, but had to make guesses at words, marking them with queries. In representing this extraordinarily interesting text I give these guessed words of his in italic within brackets. At the head of the page is an isolated direction that the 'Weathertop business' must be 'simplified'. It would be interesting to know what he had in mind: the only 'complication' that was, in the event, removed was the disappearance of Odo, and it may be that this is what he was referring to. It is clear from the first line of this text that the 'third phase' story of Odo was present.

Ring Wraiths. They will get *(no? new?)* horses *(in time?)*. Odo's capturing explained.

Ring offered to Elrond. He refuses. 'It is a peril to all possessors: more to myself than all others. It is fate that the *hobbits* should rid the world of it.'

'What will then become of the other rings?' 'They will lose their power. But we must sacrifice that power in order to destroy the Lord. As long as anyone in the world holds the Ruling Ring there is a chance for *him* to get it back again. Two things can be done. We can send it West, or we can destroy it. If we had sent it West long ago that would have been well enough. But now the power of the Lord is grown too great, and he is fully awake. It would be too perilous – and his war would come over the Shire and destroy the Havens.'[10] [*In the margin is written* Radagast.]

They decide that the Ring must be taken to the Fiery Mountain. How? – it can hardly be reached except by passing over the borders of the Land of Mordor. Bilbo? No – 'It would kill me now. My years are stretched, and I shall live some time yet. But I have no longer strength for the Ring.'

Frodo volunteers to go.

Who shall go with him? Gandalf. Trotter. Sam. Odo. Folco. Merry. (7)    Glorfindel and Frár [*written beneath:* Burin] son of Balin.

South along mountains. Over the Red Pass down the Redway to the Great River.

'Beware!' said Gandalf   'of the Giant Treebeard, who haunts the Forest between the River and the South Mts.'   Fangorn?

After a time of rest they set out. Bilbo bids farewell; gives him Sting and his armour. The others are armed.

Snow storm.

The reverse of the page, while not continuous with the first side, was certainly written at the same time, and is again in ink over faint pencil:

First he was asked to give as complete an account of the journey as possible. The story of their dealings with Tom Bombadil seemed to interest Elrond and Gandalf most.

Much that was said was now known already to Frodo. Gandalf spoke long, making clear to all the history of the Ring, and the reason why the Dark Lord so greatly desired it. 'For not only does he desire to discover and control the lost rings, those of the Elves and dwarves – but without the Ring he is still shorn of much power. He put into that Ring much of his own power, and without it is weaker than of old [and obliged to lean more on servants].[11] Of old he could guess or half see what were the hidden purposes of the Elflords, but now he is blind as far as they are concerned. He cannot make rings until he has regained the master ring. And also his mind is moved by revenge and hatred of the Elves and Men that (*disputed him?*).

'Now is the time for true speaking. Tell me, Elrond, if the *Three* Rings still are? And tell me, Glóin, if you know it, whether any of the *Seven* remain?'

'Yes, the Three still are,' said Elrond, 'and it would be ill indeed if Sauron should discover where they be, or have power over their rulers; for then perhaps his shadow would stretch even to the Blessed Realm.'

'Yes! Some of the Seven remain,' said Glóin. 'I do not know whether I have the right to reveal this, for Dáin did not give me orders concerning it. But Thráin of old had one that descended from his sires. We do not now know where it is. We think it was taken from him, ere you found him in the dungeons long ago [or maybe it was lost in Moria].[12] Yet of late we have received secret messages from Mordor demanding all such rings as we have or know of. But there are others still in our power. Dáin has one – and on that his fortune is founded: his age, his wealth, and (. . . . . . . ?) future. Yet of late we have received secret messages from Mordor bidding us yield up the rings to the Master, and threatening us and all our allies of Dale with war.[13] It is on this account that I am now come to Rivendell. For the messages have asked often concerning *one Bilbo*, and offered us peace if we would obtain from him (willing or unwilling) his ring. That they said they would accept in lieu of all. I now understand why. But our hearts are troubled, for we guess that King Brand's heart is afraid, and that the Dark Lord will *(move?)* eastern men to some evil. Already there is war upon the *(southern?)* borders. And *(of course that matter whereof?)* I seek counsel, the disappearance of Balin and his people, is now *(revealed?)* as part of the same evil.'

Boromir the *(lord? Land?)* of Ond. These men are besieged by wild men out of the East. They send to the *(F . . . . . ?)* of Balin of Moria. He promised assistance.

Here this text ends. Against the passage beginning '"Yes! Some of the Seven remain," said Glóin' my father wrote: 'No! This won't do – otherwise the dwarves would have been more suspicious of Bilbo.'

In this text, again, there is an apparent contradiction of the 'August 1939' papers: Bilbo gives his mailcoat to Frodo at Rivendell, and had therefore taken it with him when he left Bag End – a story that first appears under the date August 1939 (p. 371, §2), whereas it is also proposed there that the 'Odo-story' be abandoned – a story that is expressly present here. – The Fellowship of the Ring is to consist of five 'Shire hobbits', Frodo, Sam, Merry, Folco, and Odo, with Trotter, Gandalf, Glorfindel, and the dwarf Frár (> Burin).

Whatever the relative age of these texts, and they can scarcely be far apart, there have now appeared the younger Dwarf, Balin's son, who had come with Glóin – precursor of Gimli Glóin's son in LR; the Elf from Mirkwood, precursor of Legolas; Erestor, counsellor of Elrond; two kinsmen of Elrond; and Boromir – so named unhesitatingly from the start[14] – from the Land of Ond far in the South. The Land of Ond is

named in an outline dated August 1939 (p. 381). Treebeard is no longer
placed in 'the Forest of Neldoreth' (p. 384), but in 'the Forest between
the [Great] River and the South Mountains' – the first mention of the
mountains that would afterwards be Ered Nimrais, the White Mountains; and Gandalf warns against him (as well he might, having been his
captive, 'in Fangorn', p. 363).

The passage concerning the Three Rings of the Elves and the Seven
Rings of the Dwarves is to be compared with a passage in the third phase
version of 'Ancient History', p. 320, where Gandalf says that he does not
know what has become of 'the Three Rings of Earth, Sea, and Sky', but
believes that 'they have long been carried far over the Great Sea' – which
is to be associated no doubt with Elrond's words in the present text: 'it
would be ill indeed if Sauron should discover where they be, or have
power over their rulers; for then perhaps his shadow would stretch even
to the Blessed Realm.' In the same passage of 'Ancient History' Gandalf
says that 'the foundation of each of the Seven Hoards of the dwarves of
old was a golden ring', and that it is said that all the Seven Rings perished
in the fire of the dragons: 'Yet that account, maybe, is not wholly true.'

With the menacing messages to King Dáin out of Mordor here cf.
*Queries and Alterations* (p. 226, §11): 'The dwarves might have received
threatening messages from Mordor – for the Lord suspected that the One
Ring was in their hoards.' In the same note it is said that 'after a time no
word was heard of them [Balin and his companions]. Dáin feared the
Dark Lord'; so also Glóin says here that 'the disappearance of Balin and
his people is now revealed as part of the same evil.' At this time the story
was that Sauron demanded the return of the Rings which the Dwarves
still possessed – or Bilbo's Ring 'in lieu of all'; in FR (p. 254) they were
offered the return of three of the ancient Rings of the Dwarves if they
could obtain Bilbo's Ring.

The reference to Thráin, father of Thorin Oakenshield, in the dungeons of the Necromancer, where Gandalf found him, goes back to *The
Hobbit* (Chapter I); but the story emerges here that he possessed one
of the Rings of the Dwarves, and that it was taken from him after
his capture (see FR pp. 281–2, and LR Appendix A (iii), pp. 353–4,
357–8).

The 'Many Meetings' text (extant in two forms) given on pp. 391 ff.
continued into the beginning of an account of the Council of Elrond, held
in the open in a glade above the house; but from the words '"Bless me!"
said Gandalf. "The council is in half an hour"' (p. 395) my father struck
it through, and added the note at the end saying that the Council must be
held 'behind closed doors' (p. 396). A new manuscript now begins,
taking up at '"Bless me!" said Gandalf', and in this is found the first
complete narrative of the deliberations of the Council. This was originally paginated 'XII' with page-numbers consecutive from 'Suddenly a
single bell rang out' (p. 395). As noticed before, my father at this stage

saw all the meetings and discussions at Rivendell as constituting a single chapter, and had given the number and title 'XII. The Council of Elrond' to the third phase chapter which begins with Frodo waking up at Rivendell (p. 362).

The manuscript is partly in ink and partly in pencil, but though very rough is legible throughout. Being in the first stage of composition it is full of alterations, phrases or whole passages constantly rewritten in the act of composition; and many other corrections, made to passages which at the time of writing had been allowed to stand, are probably pretty well contemporary. In general I give the text in its final form, but with more important changes indicated.

'Bless me!' said Gandalf. 'That is the warning bell for the council. We had better make our way there at once.'

Bilbo and Frodo (and Sam [*added:* uninvited]) followed him down many stairs and passages towards the western wing of the house, until they came to the porch where Frodo had found his friends the evening before. But now the light of a clear autumn morning was glowing in the valley. The sky was high and cool above the hill-tops; and in the bright air below a few golden leaves were fluttering from the trees. The noise of bubbling waters came up from the foaming river-bed. Birds were singing and a wholesome peace lay on the land, and to Frodo his dangerous flight and the rumours of the dark shadow growing in the world outside seemed now only like memories of a troubled dream.

But the faces that were turned to meet him were grave.[15] Elrond was there and several others were already seated about him in silence. Frodo saw Glorfindel and Glóin, and Trotter (sitting in a corner).

Elrond welcomed Frodo and drew him to a seat at his knee and presented him to the company, saying: 'Here my friends is the hobbit who by fortune and courage has brought the Ring to Rivendell. This is Frodo son of Drogo.' He then pointed out and named those whom Frodo had not seen before. There was a younger dwarf at Glóin's side, [Burin the son of Balin >] his son Gimli.[16] There were three counsellors of Elrond's own household: Erestor his kinsman (a man of the same half-elvish folk known as the children of Lúthien), [17] and beside him two elflords of Rivendell. There was a strange elf clad in green and brown, Galdor, a messenger from the King of the Wood-elves in Eastern Mirkwood.[18] And seated a little apart was a tall man of noble face, but dark and sad.

'Here,' said Elrond, turning to Gandalf, 'is Boromir from the

Land of Ond, far in the South. He arrived in the night, and brings tidings that must be considered.'

It would take long to tell of all the things that were spoken in that council. Many of them were known already to Frodo. Gandalf spoke long, making clear to those who did not already know the tale in full the ancient history of the Ring, and the reasons why the Dark Lord so greatly desired it. Bilbo then gave an account of the finding of the Ring in the cave of the Misty Mountains, and Trotter described his search for Gollum that he had made with Gandalf's help, and told of his perilous adventures in Mordor. Thus it was that Frodo learned how Trotter had tracked Gollum as he wandered southwards, through Fangorn Forest, and past the Dead Marshes,[19] until he had himself been caught and imprisoned by the Dark Lord. 'Ever since I have worn shoes,' said Trotter with a shudder, and though he said no more Frodo knew that he had been tortured and his feet hurt in some way. But he had been rescued by Gandalf and saved from death.[20]

In this way the tale was brought slowly down to the spring morning when Gandalf had revealed the history of the Ring to Frodo. Then Frodo was summoned to take up the tale, and he gave a full account of all his adventures from the moment of his flight from Hobbiton. Step by step they questioned him, and every detail that he could tell concerning the Black Riders was examined.[21]

Elrond was also deeply interested in the events in the Old Forest and on the Barrow-downs. 'The Barrow-wights I knew of,' he said, 'for they are closely akin to the Riders;[22] and I marvel at your escape from them. But never before have I heard tell of this strange Bombadil. I would like to know more of him. Did you know of him, Gandalf?'

'Yes,' answered the wizard. 'And I sought him out at once, as soon as I found that the hobbits had disappeared from Buckland. When I had chased the Riders from Crickhollow I turned back to visit him. I daresay he would have kept the travellers longer in his home, if he had known that I was near. But I am not sure of it: he is a strange creature, and follows his own counsels, which few can fathom.'[23]

'Could we not even now send messages to him and obtain his help?' asked Erestor. 'It seems that he has a power even over the Ring.'

'That is not quite the way of it,' said Gandalf. 'The Ring has no power over *him* or for him: it can neither harm nor serve him: he is his own master. But he has no power over it, and he cannot alter the Ring itself, not break its power over others. And I think that the mastery of Tom Bombadil is seen only on his own ground – from which he has never stepped within my memory.'[24]

'But on his own ground nothing seems to dismay him,' said Erestor. 'Would he not perhaps take the Ring and keep it there for ever harmless?'

'He would, perhaps, if all the free folk of the world begged him to do so,' said Gandalf. 'But he would not do so willingly. For it would only postpone the evil day. In time the Lord of the Ring would find out its hiding-place, and in the end he would come in person.[25] I doubt whether Tom Bombadil, even on his own ground, could withstand that power; but I am sure that we should not leave him to face it. Besides, he lives too far away and the Ring has come from his land only at great hazard. It would have to pass through greater danger to return. If the Ring is to be hidden – surely it is here in Rivendell that it should be kept: if Elrond has might to withstand the coming of Sauron in all his power?'

'I have not,' said Elrond.

'In that case,' said Erestor,[26] 'there are but two things for us to attempt: we may send the Ring West over the Sea, or we may try to destroy it. If the Ring had gone to the West long ago that would have perhaps been well. But now the power of the Lord is grown great again, and he is awake, and he knows where the Ring is. The journey to the Havens would be fraught with the greatest peril. On the other hand we cannot by our own skill or strength destroy the Ring; and the journey to the Fiery Mountain would seem still more perilous, leading as it does towards the stronghold of the Enemy. Who can read this riddle for us?'

'None here can do so,' said Elrond gravely.[27] 'None can foretell which road leads to safety, if that is what you mean. But I can choose which road it is right to take, as it seems to me – and indeed the choice is clear. The Ring must be sent to the Fire. The peril is greater on the western road; for my heart tells me that is the road which Sauron will expect us to take when he hears what has befallen. And if we take it he will pursue us swiftly and surely, since we must make for the Havens beyond the Towers. Those he would certainly destroy, even if he found us not, and there would be thereafter no way of escape for the Elves from the darkening world.'

'And the Shire too would be destroyed,' said Trotter in a low voice, looking towards Bilbo and Frodo.

'But on the other road,' said Elrond, 'with speed and skill the travellers might go far unmarked. I do not say there is great hope in the quest; but only in this way could any lasting good be achieved. In the Ring is hidden much of the ancient power of Sauron. Even though he does not hold it that power still lives and works for him and towards him. As long as the Ring lives on land or sea he will not be overcome. While the Ring lasts he will grow, and have hope, and the fear lest the Ring come into his hand again will ever weigh on the world. War will never cease while that fear lives, and all Men will be turned to him.'

'I do not understand this,' said Boromir. 'Why should the Elves and their friends not use the Great Ring to defeat Sauron? And I say that all men will *not* join him: the men of Ond will never submit.'

'Never is a long word, O Boromir,' said Elrond. 'The men of Ond are valiant and still faithful amid a host of foes; but valour alone cannot withstand Sauron for ever. Many of his servants are as valiant. But as for the Ruling Ring – it belongs to Sauron and is filled with his spirit. Its might is too great for those of lesser strength, as Bilbo and Frodo have found, and in the end it must lead them captive to him if they keep it. For those who have power of their own, its danger is far greater. With it they might per-chance overthrow the Dark Lord, but they would set themselves in his throne. Then they would become as evil as he, or worse. For nothing is evil in the beginning. Even Sauron was not so. I dare not take the Ring to wield it.'

'Nor I,' said Gandalf.

'But is it not true, as I have heard said, O Elrond,' said Boromir, 'that the Elves keep yet and wield Three Rings, and yet these too came from Sauron in the ancient days? And the dwarves, too, had rings, it is said. Tell me, Glóin, if you know it, whether any of the Seven Rings remain?'

'I do not know,' said Glóin. 'It was said in secret that Thráin (father of Thrór father of Thorin[28] who fell in battle) possessed one that had descended from his sires. Some said it was the last. But where it is no dwarf now knows. We think maybe it was taken from him, ere Gandalf found him in the dungeons of Mordor long ago[29] – or maybe it was lost in Moria. Yet of late we have received secret messages from Mordor offering us rings again. It was partly on this account that I came to Rivendell; for the messages asked

concerning one *Bilbo*, and commanded us to obtain from him
(willing or unwilling) the ring that he possessed. For this ring we
were offered [seven >] three such as our fathers had of old. Even
for news of where he might be found we were offered friendship
for ever and great wealth.[30] Our hearts are troubled, for we
perceive that King Brand in Dale is afraid, and if we do not answer
Sauron will move other men to evil against him. Already there are
threats of war upon the south.'

'It would seem that the Seven Rings are lost or have returned to
their Lord,' said Boromir. 'What of the Three?'

'The Three Rings remain still,' said Elrond. 'They have conferred great power on the Elves, but they have never yet availed
them in their strife with Sauron. For they came from Sauron
himself, and can give no skill or knowledge that he did not already
possess at their making. And to each race the rings of the Lord
bring such powers as each desires and is capable of wielding. The
Elves desired not strength or domination or riches, but subtlety of
craft and lore, and knowledge of the secrets of the world's being.
These things they have gained, yet with sorrow. But they will turn
to evil if Sauron regains the Ruling Ring; for then all that the Elves
have devised or learned with the power of the rings will become
his, as was his purpose.'

Against this passage concerning the Three Rings of the Elves my
father wrote later; '*Elfrings* made by *Elves* for themselves. The 7 and 9
were made by Sauron – to cheat men and dwarves. They originally
accepted them because they believed they were *elfrings*.' And he also
wrote, separately but against the same passage: 'Alter this: make the
Elfrings their own and Sauron's made in answer.' This is the first
appearance of this central idea concerning the origin and nature of the
Rings; but since it does not emerge in actual narrative until considerably
later these notes cannot be contemporary with the text. – In FR it is
Glóin, not Boromir, who raises the question of the Three Rings of the
Elves; but he also, like Boromir in the present text, asserts that they were
made by the Dark Lord. Elrond corrects Glóin's error; yet earlier in the
Council (FR p. 255) Elrond has expressly said that Celebrimbor made
the Three, and that Sauron forged the One in secret to be their master.
Glóin's assertion (FR p. 282) is thus not appropriate, and is probably an
echo of my father's original conception of the Rings. The text continues:

'What then would happen, if the Ruling Ring were destroyed?'
asked Boromir.

'The Elves would not lose what they have already won,'

answered Elrond; 'but the Three Rings would lose all power thereafter.'

'Yet that loss,' said Glorfindel, 'all Elves would gladly suffer, if by it the power of Sauron might be broken.'

'Thus we return again to the point whence we started,' said Erestor. 'The Ring should be destroyed; but we cannot destroy it, save by the perilous journey to the Fire. What strength or cunning have we for that task?'

'In this task it is plain that great power will not avail,' said Elrond. 'It must be attempted by the weak. Such is the way of things. In this great matter fate seems already to have pointed the way for us.'

'Very well, very well, Master Elrond!' said Bilbo suddenly.[31] 'Say no more! It is plain at least what *you* are pointing at. Bilbo the hobbit started this affair, and Bilbo has better finish it, or himself. I was very comfortable here, and getting on with my book. If you want to know, I am just writing an ending for it. I had thought of putting "and he lived happpily ever afterward to the end of his days": which is a good ending, and none the worse for having been used before. Now I shall have to alter that – it does not look like being true, and anyway there will have to be several more chapters, even if I don't write them myself. It is a frightful nuisance! When ought I to start?'

Elrond smiled, and Gandalf laughed loudly. 'Of course,' said the wizard, 'if you had really started the affair, my dear Bilbo, you would be expected to finish it. But *starting* is a strong word. I have often tried to suggest to you that you only came in (accidentally, as you might say) in the *middle* of a long story, that was not made up for your sake only. That is, of course, true enough of all heroes and all adventures, but never mind that now. As for you, if you want my opinion once more, I should say that your part is finished – except as a recorder. Finish your book and leave the ending! But get ready to write a sequel, when they come back.'

Bilbo laughed in his turn. 'I have never known you to give pleasant advice before, Gandalf,' he said, 'or to tell me to do what I really wanted to do. Since all your unpleasant advice has usually been good, I wonder if this is not bad. Yet it is true that my years are stretched and getting thin, and I do not think I have strength for the Ring. But tell me: who do you mean by "they"?'

'The adventurers who are sent with the Ring.'

'Exactly, and who are they to be? That seems to me precisely what this council now has to decide.'

There was a long silence. Frodo glanced round at all the faces, but no one looked at him – except Sam; in whose eyes there was a strange mixture of hope and fear. All the others sat as if in deep thought with their eyes closed or upon the ground. A great dread fell on Frodo, and he felt an overmastering longing to remain at peace by Bilbo's side in Rivendell.

These words stand at the foot of a page. The next page, beginning 'At last with an effort he spoke', continues only a brief way, and was replaced by another beginning with the same words. I give both forms.

At last with an effort he spoke. 'If this task is fated to fall to the weak,' he said, 'I will attempt it. But I shall need the help of the strong and the wise.'

'I think, Frodo,' said Elrond, looking keenly at him, 'that this task is appointed for you. But it is very well that you should offer yourself unbidden. All the help that we can contrive shall be yours.'

'But you won't send him alone, surely, master!' cried Sam.

'No indeed,' said Elrond, turning to him. 'You at least shall go – since you are here although I do not think you were summoned. It seems difficult to separate you from your master Frodo.'

Sam subsided, but whispered to Frodo: 'How far is this Mountain? A nice pickle we have landed ourselves in, Mr. Frodo!'[32]

'Taking care of hobbits is not a task that everyone would like,' said Gandalf, 'but I am used to it. I suggest Frodo and his Sam, Merry, Faramond, and myself. That is five. And Glorfindel, if he will come and lend us the wisdom of the Elves: we shall need it. That is six.'

'And Trotter!' said Peregrin from the corner. 'That is seven, and a fitting number. The Ring-bearer will have good company.'

Here this version of the passage ends. Pencilled beneath is an unfinished sentence: 'The choice is good,' said Elrond. 'Though

Other very rough pencillings read: 'Alter this. Hobbits only, including Trotter. Gandalf as [?guide] in early stages. Gandalf says he will go all way? No Glorfindel.' And below these notes, the single isolated name *Boromir*. – On the back of this page is a remarkable sketch of events to come; for this see p. 410.

The replacement page treats the selection of the Company quite differently:

At last with an effort he spoke. 'I will take the Ring,' he said. 'Though I don't know the way.'

Elrond looked keenly at him. 'If I understand all the tale that I have heard,' he said, 'I think that this task is appointed for you, Frodo, and that if you do not find the way, no other will.'

'But you won't send him off alone surely, master!' cried Sam, unable to contain himself.

'No indeed!' said Elrond, turning towards him with a smile. 'You at least shall go with him, since it is hardly possible to separate you from him – even when he is summoned to a secret council and you are not.'

Sam subsided, but whispered to Frodo: 'How far is this Mountain? A nice pickle we have landed ourselves in, Mr. Frodo!'

'When shall I start?' asked Frodo.

'First you shall rest and recover full strength,' answered Elrond, guessing his mind. 'Rivendell is a fair place, and we will not send you away, until you know it better. And meanwhile we will make plans for your guidance.'

Later in the afternoon of the council Frodo was strolling in the woods with his friends. Merry and Faramond were indignant when they heard that Sam had crept into the council, and been chosen as Frodo's companion. 'Not the only one!' said Merry. 'I have come so far and I am not going to be left behind now. Someone with intelligence ought to be in the party.'

'I don't see that your inclusion will help much in that way,' said Faramond. 'But, of course, you must go, and I must too. We hobbits must stick together. We seem to have become mighty important these days. It would be a bit of an eye-opener for the people back in the Shire!'

'I doubt it!' said Frodo. 'Hardly any of them would believe a word of it. I wish I was one of them, and back in Hobbiton. Anyone who wants can have all my importance.'

'Quite accidental! Quite accidental, as I keep on telling you,' said a voice behind them. They turned to see Gandalf hurrying round a bend in the path. 'Hobbit voices carry a long way,' he said. 'All right in Rivendell (or I hope so); but I should not discuss matters so loud outside the house. Your importance is accidental, Frodo – by which I mean, someone else might have been chosen and done as well – but it is real. No one else can have it now. So be careful – you can't be too careful! As for you two, if I let you come, you'll have to do just what you are told. And I shall make other arrangements for the supply of intelligence.'

'Ah, now we know who really is important,' laughed Merry. 'Gandalf is never in doubt about that, and does not let anyone else doubt it. So you are making all the arrangements already, are you?'

'Of course!' said Gandalf. 'But if you hobbits wish to stick together I shall raise no objection. You two and Sam can go – if you are really willing. Trotter would also be useful[33] – he has journeyed South before. Boromir may well join the company, since your road leads through his own land. That will be about as large a party as will be at all safe.'

'Who is to be the brains of the party?' asked Frodo. 'Trotter, I suppose. Boromir is only one of the Big Folk, and they are not as wise as hobbits.'

'Boromir has more than strength and valour,' answered Gandalf. 'He comes of an ancient race that the people of the Shire have not seen, at least not since days that they have forgotten. And Trotter has learned many things in his wanderings that are not known in the Shire.[34] They both know something of the road: but more than that will be needed. I think *I* shall have to come with you!'

So great was the delight of the hobbits at this announcement that Gandalf took off his hat and bowed. 'I am used to taking care of hobbits,' he said, 'when they wait for me and don't run off on their own. But I only said: I *think* I shall have to come. It may only be for part of the way. We have not made any definite plans yet. Very likely we shan't be able to make any.'

'How soon do you think we shall start?' asked Frodo.

'I don't know. It depends on what news we get. Scouts will have to go out and find out what they can – especially about the Black Riders.'

'I thought they were all destroyed in the flood!' said Merry.

'You cannot destroy the Ringwraiths so easily,' said Gandalf. 'The power of their master is in them, and they stand or fall by him. They were unhorsed, and unmasked, and will be less dangerous for a while; yet it would be well to find out if we can what they are doing. In time they will get new steeds and fresh disguise. But for the present you should put all troubles out of your thoughts, if you can.'

The hobbits did not find this easy to do. They continued to think and talk mainly of the journey and the perils ahead of them. Yet such was the virtue of the land of Elrond that in all their thoughts there came no shadow of fear. Hope and courage grew in their hearts, and strength in their bodies. In every meal, and in every word and song they found delight. The very breathing of the air became a joy no less sweet because the time of their stay was short.

The days slipped by, though autumn was fast waning, and each morning dawned bright and fair. But slowly the golden light grew silver, and the leaves fell from the trees. The winds blew cold from the Misty Mountains in the East. The Hunters' Moon grew round in the evening sky, putting to flight the lesser stars, and glittering in the falls and pools of the River. But low in the South one star shone red. Every night as the moon waned again it shone brighter. Frodo could see it through his window deep in the sky, burning like a wrathful eye watching, and waiting for him to set out.

At the end of the text my father wrote: 'New Moon Oct. 24. Hunters' Moon Full Nov. 8'. See p. 434, note 19.

The manuscript is interrupted here by a heading, 'The Ring Goes South', but without new chapter number, and what follows was written continuously with what precedes.

It will be seen that by far the greater part of the content of the 'The Council of Elrond' in FR is absent; but while the past and present texture of the world is so much thinner in the original form, the discussion of what to do with the Ring is in its essential pattern of argument already present.

Gandalf says that the road to the Fiery Mountain lies through Boromir's land. It may well be that at this stage the geography of the lands south and east of the Misty Mountains was still fairly sketchy, even though Fangorn Forest, the Dead Marshes, the Land of Ond (Gondor), and 'the South Mountains' have appeared in name (pp. 397–8, 401). Further aspects of this question appear in the next chapter.

It is curious that although Elrond says at the outset that Boromir brings tidings that must be considered, we are not told what these tidings were. In the original draft for the Council (p. 398) it is said that the men of Ond 'are besieged by wild men out of the East'; and in the text just given (p. 403) Elrond says that they are 'still faithful amid a host of foes'.

Odo Bolger has at long last disappeared (at least by that name); and Folco has been renamed *Faramond*. That name has appeared in the papers dated August 1939, but there it was proposed for Frodo himself (p. 373). The Fellowship of the Ring now changes again, and not for the last time: as may readily be supposed, the achievement of the final composition of the 'Nine Walkers' caused my father great difficulty. In the first draft for the Council of Elrond (p. 397) there were to be:

Gandalf. Trotter. Frodo. Sam. Merry. Folco. Odo. Glorfindel. Burin son of Balin. (9)

In the rejected page of the text just given (p. 406) the Company becomes:

Gandalf. Trotter. Frodo. Sam. Merry. Faramond. Glorfindel. (7)

A note to this page proposes that the Company consist only of hobbits, with Gandalf at least at first, but without Glorfindel. In the replacement text (p. 408) Gandalf suggests:

Gandalf. Trotter. Frodo. Sam. Merry. Faramond. Boromir. (7) – and this was indeed the composition in the original narrative of the southward journey as far as Moria.

The continuation of the story in the original manuscript ('The Ring Goes South') is given in the next chapter; but before concluding this, there must be given the remarkable outline of future events found on the back of a rejected page of the text of the Council of Elrond (see p. 406). This clearly belongs in time with the manuscript in which it is included. In the outline of the further course of the story dated August 1939 (p. 381, §9) there is no suggestion of the reappearance of Gollum before Mordor is reached; and the reference in this one to Frodo's hearing the patter of Gollum's feet in the Mines shows that it preceded the first draft of the Moria chapter.

*Gollum* must reappear at or after Moria. Frodo hears patter.

*Fangorn Forest.* In some way – hears voice, or sees something off path, or ? alarmed by Gollum – Frodo must get separated from the rest.

Fangorn is an evergreen (oak holly?) forest. Trees of *vast* height. (*Beleghir* [*pencilled above: Anduin*] Great River divides into many channels.) Say 500–1000 feet. It runs right up to the [Blue >] Black Mountains, which are not very high (run NEN – SWW [*i.e. North-east by North – South-west by West*]) but very steep on N. side.

If Treebeard comes in at all – let him be kindly and rather good? About 50 feet high with barky skin. Hair and beard rather like *twigs*. Clothed in dark green like a mail of short shining leaves. He has a castle in the Black Mountains and many thanes and followers They look like young trees [?when] they stand.

Make Frodo be terrified of Gollum after a meeting in which Gollum pretended to make friends, but tried to strangle Frodo in his sleep and steal the Ring. Treebeard finds him lost and carries him up into the Black Mountains. It is only here that Frodo finds he is friendly.

Treebeard brings him on the way to Ond. His scouts report that Ond is besieged, and that Trotter and four [*written above: 3?*] others have been captured. Where is Sam? (Sam is found in the Forest. He had refused to go on without Frodo and had remained looking for him.)

The tree-giants assail the besiegers and rescue Trotter &c. and raise siege.

(If this plot is used it will be better to have no Boromir in party. Substitute Gimli? son of Glóin – who was killed in Moria. But Frodo can bear messages from Boromir to his father the K[ing] of Ond.)

Next stage – they set out for the Fire Mountain. They have to skirt Mordor on its west edge.

In this brief sketch we see the very starting-point, in written expression, of two fundamental 'moments' in the narrative of *The Lord of the Rings*: the separation of Frodo from the Company (subsequently rejoined by Sam), and the assault by the 'tree-giants' of Fangorn on the enemies of Gondor; but such narrative frame as they were given here was entirely ephemeral. We meet also a further early image of Giant Treebeard: still of vast height, as in the text given on pp. 382–4, where his voice came down to Frodo 'out of the tree-top', but no longer hostile, the captor of Gandalf (p. 363), 'pretending to be friendly but really in league with the enemy' (p. 384). Boromir is now said to be the son of the King of Ond; but the death of Gimli in Moria was an idea never further developed. Here is the first appearance of an Elvish name, *Beleghir*, of the Great River, which flowed through Fangorn Forest (see p. 410). The Forest 'runs right up to the [Blue >] Black Mountains'; cf. the outline for the Council of Elrond (p. 397), in which Gandalf says that Giant Treebeard 'haunts the Forest between the River and the South Mountains'. But of Lothlórien and Rohan there is as yet not a hint.

## NOTES

1   The last sheet of the original chapter (see p. 213) had ended with the words 'a strong king whose realm included Esgaroth, and much land to the south of the great falls' at the foot of the page (numbered 'IX.8'), and the reverse was left blank. The first version of the continuation was written out (in a rapid scribble in ink) independently of the old text; the second, also very rough and nearly all in pencil, starts on the unused verso side of 'IX.8', on which however my father wrote in preparation 'IX.9', although at that time he did not use the page. When he returned to it later he did not change the chapter-number but continued the numeration 'IX.10' etc.; this however was mere absentmindedness, since the chapter could not possibly at this time still be numbered 'IX'.

2   The reference is to the end of *The Hobbit*; cf. p. 15 and note 3.

3   In the first version Glóin does not admit to any falling short of the skill of the forefathers: 'He began to speak of new inventions and of the great works at which the folk of the Mountain were now labouring; of armour of surpassing strength and beauty, swords more keen and strong . . .' – The sentence 'You should see the

waterways of Dale, Frodo, and the fountains and the pools!' goes
back to the first draft; in FR (p. 242) the word 'mountains' is an
obvious error which has never been corrected.

4   This name is found only in the first of the two texts, but it appears
later on in the second (p. 395).

5   Cf. pp. 211, 214, 363. – Peregrin disappeared out of the Shire when
he was 33, at which time Frodo was only two years old (see p. 387,
note 9).

6   When my father wrote this passage he evidently had in mind, at least
as one possibility, a comic song, received with the 'ringing laughter'
that wakened Frodo; for at the top of the page he wrote 'Troll Song'
– a passing idea before it was given far more appositely to Sam in the
Trollshaws. But he also wrote 'Let B[ilbo] sing *Tinúviel*', and the
word '?Messenger'. This is a reference to the poem *Errantry*
(published in *The Oxford Magazine* 9 November 1933, and with
many further changes in *The Adventures of Tom Bombadil* (1962)).
Bilbo's song *Eärendil was a mariner* derived (in a sense) from
*Errantry*, and the earliest text of it still begins:

> There was a merry messenger,
> a passenger, a mariner,
> he built a boat and gilded her
> and silver oars he fashioned her . . .

7   In the first text the dwarf with Glóin is named *Frár*; in the margin is
pencilled *Burin son of Balin*. Frár appears also in the outline for the
Council of Elrond on p. 397, again replaced by Burin.

8   The presence of an Elf of Mirkwood was an addition to the second
text.

9   As written, the first text read here: 'two of Elrond's own kinsfolk the
Pereldar or halfelven folk . . .' *Pereldar* was struck out, probably at
once. In the *Quenta Silmarillion* the *Pereldar* or 'Half-eldar' are the
Danas (Green-elves): V.215. The Danas were also called 'the
Lovers of Lúthien' (*ibid.*). In LR (Appendix A I (i)) Elros and
Elrond are called *Peredhil* 'Half-elven'; an earlier name for them was
*Peringol, Peringiul* (V.152).

10  The Grey Havens are first named in the third phase version of
'Ancient History', p. 319.

11  The square brackets are in the original.

12  As note 11.

13  The text stands thus, with two passages both beginning 'Yet of
late we have received secret messages from Mordor', but neither
rejected.

14  The name *Boromir* of the second son of Bor, killed in the Battle of
Unnumbered Tears, had appeared in the later *Annals of Beleriand*
and in the *Quenta Silmarillion* (V.134, 287, 310). For the
etymology of the name see V.352, 372.

15  This sentence is a subsequent correction of 'But the faces of those that were seated in the room were grave.' In a rejected opening of the text Gandalf says: 'We had better make our way to Elrond's chamber at once', and in the western wing of the house he knocks at a door and enters 'a small room, the western side of which opened onto a porch beyond which the ground fell sheer to the foaming river.' In the revised opening as printed the Council of Elrond takes place in the porch (as in FR, p. 252), though it was still described here as a 'room', until this correction was made.

16  This first appearance of Gimli son of Glóin was a pencilled alteration, but not from much later.

17  In the previous account of those present at the Council (p. 395) the three counsellors of Rivendell are Erestor, called 'an Elf', and 'two other kinsmen of Elrond, of that half-elvish folk whom the Elves named the children of Lúthien' – which seems however to imply that Erestor also was Elrond's kinsman.

18  In FR (p. 253) Galdor, here the precursor of Legolas, is the name of the Elf from the Grey Havens who bore the errand of Círdan. *Galdor* had not at this time become the name of the father of Húrin and Huor; in the *Quenta Silmarillion* he was still named *Gumlin*.

19  The first reference to the Dead Marshes.

20  My father bracketed the passage from 'Ever since I have worn shoes' to 'hurt in some way', and wrote in the margin (with a query) that it should be revealed later that Trotter had wooden feet. – This is the first appearance of the story that it was Trotter who found Gollum (in the version of 'Ancient History' in the third phase (p. 320) Gandalf still told Frodo that he had himself found Gollum, in Mirkwood); and Trotter's experience of Mordor, several times mentioned or hinted at (see pp. 223, 371), is explained at the same time.

21  Written in the margin against this paragraph: 'Gandalf's captivity'.

22  See pp. 118–20.

23  An earlier form of this passage makes Gandalf reply to Elrond: 'I knew of him. But I had quite forgotten him. I must go and see him as soon as there is a chance.' This was changed – at the time of writing – to the passage given, in which Gandalf says that he actually visited Tom Bombadil after the attack on Crickhollow – the first appearance of an idea that will be met again, though the meeting of Gandalf and Bombadil never (alas!) reached narrative form. Cf. the isolated passage given on pp. 213–14, where Gandalf says at Rivendell: 'Why did I not think of Bombadil before! If only he was not so far away, I would go straight back now and consult him.' Cf. also p. 345 and note 11. – Gandalf does not mention Odo here, and it becomes clear at the end of this chapter that he had been removed from Rivendell (see pp. 407, 409).

24 In the third phase version of 'At the Sign of the Prancing Pony' it is still apparent that Tom Bombadil was known to visit the inn at Bree (p. 334).

25 In rough drafting of this passage my father wrote: 'and in the end he would come in person; and the Barrow-wights would', striking out these last words as he wrote and changing them to: 'and even on his own ground Tom Bombadil alone could not withstand that onset unscathed.' – 'Lord of the Ring' was first written 'Lord of the Rings', but changed immediately.

26 *Erestor* changed from *Glorfindel*, which was changed from *Elrond*. Cf. p. 396.

27 This reply to Erestor was first given to Gandalf, for Erestor addressed his question to him: 'Can you solve this riddle, Gandalf?' To which Gandalf answered: 'No! I cannot. But I can choose, if you wish me to choose.' The passage was then changed at once to the form given.

28 In *The Hobbit* Thráin was not the father of Thrór, but his son. This is a complex question which will be discussed in Vol. VII.

29 In the dungeons of Dol Guldur in Mirkwood in FR (p. 282).

30 As this passage was first written, Glóin says that the messages from Mordor offered the Dwarves 'a ring'; and that they were offered peace and friendship if they could obtain Bilbo's ring, or even tell where he was to be found. As altered subsequently, his words approach what he tells in FR (p. 254); and the story in the first draft for the Council (p. 398), that the Dwarves still possessed some of their ancient Rings, that Dáin had one, and that Sauron was demanding them back, has already been abandoned.

31 Cf. p. 371, at the end of the outline §2.

32 The chapter 'The Council of Elrond' in FR (II.2) ends here.

33 'Trotter would also be useful' was changed to 'Trotter will also be essential'; and probably at the same time my father wrote in the margin: 'Trotter is connected with the Ring.' This alteration thus comes from somewhat later, when he was reaching the conception of Aragorn and his ancestry. See note 34.

34 Trotter was of course still a hobbit. In the margin my father wrote against this passage: 'Correct this. Only Trotter is of ancient race' (i.e. Trotter is a Númenórean, but Boromir is not).

# XXIV
# THE RING GOES SOUTH

As I have said, this next stage in the story was written continuously on from the first version of 'The Council of Elrond'. After the description of the red star in the South (FR p. 287) there is a heading 'The Ring Goes South', but no new chapter-number, and the pagination is continuous with what precedes.

I give now the text of this earliest version of 'The Ring Goes South' (which extends somewhat into the next chapter in FR, II.4 'A Journey in the Dark'). This is an outstandingly difficult manuscript, and difficult to represent. I think that it was *not* based on any preliminary notes or sketches, except in one passage,[1] that my father wrote it *ab initio* as a full narrative; and this being so it is remarkable how much of its wording survived into the final form, despite the radical differences that Trotter was still the hobbit Peregrin and that neither Dwarf nor Elf was present. The company, as already noticed, consisted of Gandalf, Boromir, and five hobbits – even though one of them, to be sure, was no inexperienced hobbit of the Shire.

My father wrote nearly all of it in ink, but he wrote extremely fast (though with patience – and some aid from the text of FR – all but a few words can be puzzled out), so fast that he often left to stand what he had written but rejected, while racing on to a new phrasing or formulation; and the expression is often rough and unfinished. Subsequently he went over it in pencil, but the great majority of these pencilled alterations belong, I feel sure, to a time very close to the original writing, and some of them demonstrably so. A few are certainly later, and introduce references to Gimli and Legolas that are chronologically and structurally irrelevant. There are also some alterations in red ink, but these only concern certain place-names.

In the text as printed here, I adopt pencilled alterations that seem certainly 'early': few affect the narrative in any important respect, and where they do the original text is given in the notes. The notes are here an integral part of the representation of the manuscript.

## The Ring goes South

When Frodo had been about a fortnight in Rivendell and November was already a week old or more[2] the scouts began to return. Some had been northwards as far as the Dimrill-dales,[3] and some had gone southwards almost as far as the River Redway. A few had passed the mountains both by the High Pass and Goblin Gate (Annerchin), and by the passage at the sources of the Gladden. These were the last to return, for they had descended into Wilderland as far as the Gladden Fields,[4] and that was a great way from Rivendell even for the swiftest Elves. But neither they nor those who had received the aid of the Eagles near Goblin Gate[5] had discovered any news – except that the wild wolves called wargs were gathering again and were hunting once more between the Mountains and Mirkwood. No sign of the Black Riders had been found – except on the rocks below the Ford the bodies of four [*written above:* several] drowned horses, and [?one] long black cloak slashed and tattered.

'One can never tell,' said Gandalf, 'but it does look as if the Riders were dispersed – and have had to make their way as best they could back to Mordor. In that case there will still be a long while before the hunt begins again. And it will have to come back here to pick up the trail – if we are lucky and careful, and they do not get news of us on the way. We had better get off as soon as possible now – and as quietly.'

Elrond agreed, and warned them to journey by dusk and dark as often as might be, and to lie hid when they could in the broad daylight. 'When the news reaches Sauron,' he said, 'of the discomfiture of the Nine Riders, he will be filled with a great anger. When the hunt begins again, it will be far greater and more ravenous.'

'Are there still more Black Riders then?' asked Frodo.

'No! There are but Nine Ringwraiths. But when they come forth again, I fear they will bring a host of evil things in their train, and set their spies wide over the lands. Even of the sky above you must beware as you go your way.'

There came a cold grey day in mid November.[6] The East wind was streaming through the bare branches of the trees, and seething in the firtrees on the hills. The hurrying clouds were low and sunless. As the cheerless shadows of the early evening began to fall, the adventurers made ready to depart. Their farewells had all been said by the fire in the great hall, and they were waiting only for Gandalf, who was still in the house speaking some last words in private with Elrond. Their spare food and clothes and other necessaries were laden on two sure-footed ponies. The travellers themselves were to go on foot; for their course was set through lands where there were few roads and paths were rough and

difficult. Sooner or later they would have to cross the Mountains.
Also they were going to journey for the most part by dusk or dark.[7]
Sam was standing by the two pack-ponies sucking his teeth and
staring moodily at the house – his desire for adventure was at a low
ebb. But in that hour none of the hobbits had any heart for their
journey – a chill was in their hearts, and a cold wind in their faces.
A gleam of firelight came from the open doors; lights were glowing
in many windows, and the world outside seemed empty and cold.
Bilbo huddled in his cloak stood silent on the doorstep beside
Frodo. Trotter sat with his head bowed to his knees.[8]

At last Elrond came out with Gandalf. 'Farewell now!' he said.
'May the blessing of Elves and Men and all free folk go with you.
And may white stars shine on your journey!'

'Good . . . good luck!' said Bilbo, stuttering a little (from the
cold perhaps). 'I don't suppose you will be able to keep a diary,
Frodo my lad, but I shall expect a full account when you get back.
And don't be too long: I have lived longer than I expected already.
Farewell!'

Many others of Elrond's household stood in the shadows and
watched them go, bidding them farewell with soft voices. There
was no laughter, and no songs or music. Silently at last they
turned away, and leading their ponies they faded swiftly into the
gathering dusk.

They crossed the bridge and wound slowly up the long steep
paths out of the cloven vale of Rivendell, and came at length to the
high moors, grey and formless under misty stars. Then with one
last look down at the lights of the Last Homely House below they
strode on, far on into the night.

At the Ford they left the west road that crossed the River; and
turning left went on by narrow paths among the folded lands.
They were going South. Their purpose was to hold this course for
many miles and days on the western side of the Misty Mountains.
The country was much wilder and rougher than in the green valley
of the Great River in Wilderland on the eastern side of the range
and their going would be much slower; but they hoped in this way
to escape the notice of enemies. The spies of Sauron had hitherto
seldom been seen in the western regions; and the paths were little
known except to the people of Rivendell. Gandalf walked in front
and with him went Trotter who knew this country even in the
dark. Boromir as rearguard walked behind.

The first part of their journey was cheerless and grim and Frodo remembered little of it, except the cold wind. It blew icy from the eastern mountains for many sunless days and no garment seemed able to keep out its searching fingers. They had been well furnished with warm clothes in Rivendell, and had jackets and cloaks lined with fur as well as many blankets, but they seldom felt warm either moving or at rest. They slept uneasily during the middle of the day, in some hollow of the land, or hidden under the tangled thorn-bushes that grew in great thickets in those parts. In the late afternoon they were roused, and had their chief meal: usually cold and cheerless and with little talk, for they seldom risked the lighting of a fire. In the evening they went on again, as nearly due south as they could find a way.

At first it seemed to the hobbits that they were creeping like snails and getting nowhere; for each day the land looked much as it had done the day before. Yet all the while the Mountains which south of Rivendell bent westward were drawing nearer. More and more often they found no paths and had to make wide turns to avoid either steep places, or thickets, or sullen treacherous swamps. The land was tumbled in barren hills and deep valleys filled with turbulent waters.

But when they had been about ten days on the road the weather grew better. The wind suddenly veered southward. The swift flowing clouds lifted and melted away, and the sun came out.

There came a dawn at the end of a long stumbling night march. The travellers reached a low ridge crowned with ancient holly trees, whose pale fluted trunks seemed to have been formed out of the very stone of the hills. Their berries shone red in the light of the rising sun. Far away south Frodo saw the dim shapes of mountains, that seemed now to lie across their path. To the left of this distant range a tall peak stood up like a tooth: it was tipped with snow but its bare western shoulder glowed redly in the growing light.

Gandalf stood by Frodo's side and looked out under his hand. 'We have done well,' he said. 'We have reached the borders of the country called Hollin: many Elves lived here once in happier days. Eighty leagues we have come,⁹ if we have come a mile, and we have marched quicker than winter from the North. The land and weather will be milder now – but perhaps all the more dangerous.'

'Danger or not, a real sunrise is mighty welcome,' said Frodo, throwing back his hood and letting the morning light play on his face.

'Mountains ahead!' said Faramond. 'We seemed to have turned eastward.'

'No, it is the mountains that have turned,' said Gandalf.[10] 'Don't you remember Elrond's map in Rivendell?'

'No, I did not look very carefully at it,' said Faramond. 'Frodo has a better head for things of that sort.'

'Well, anyone who did look at the map,' said Gandalf, 'would see that away there stands Taragaer or Ruddyhorn,[11] – that mountain with the red side. The Misty Mountains divide there and between their arms lies the land[12] of Caron-dûn the Red Valley.[13] Our way lies there: over the Red Pass of Cris-caron,[14] under Taragaer's side, and into Caron-dûn and down the River Red-way[15] – to the Great River, and . . .' He stopped.

'Yes, and where then?' asked Merry.

'To the end of the journey – in the end,' said Gandalf. 'But at first the evergreen forest of Fangorn, through the midst of which runs the Great River.[16] But we will not look too far ahead. Let us be glad that the first stage is safely over. I think we will rest here for a whole day. There is a wholesome air about Hollin. Much evil must befall any country before it wholly forgets the Elves, if once they have dwelt there.'

That morning they lit a fire in a deep hollow shrouded by two great holly trees, and their supper was merrier than it had been since they left the house of Elrond. They did not hurry to bed afterwards, for they had all the night to sleep in and did not mean to go on until the evening of next day. Only Trotter was moody and restless. After a while he left the company and wandered about on the ridge, looking out on the lands south and west. He came back and stood looking at them.

'What is the matter?' said Merry. 'Do you miss the east wind?'

'No indeed,' answered Trotter. 'But I miss something. I know Hollin fairly well, and have been here in many seasons. No people dwell here now, but many other things live here, or used to – especially birds. But now it is very silent. I can feel it. There is no sound for miles round, and your voices seem to make the ground echo. I cannot make it out.'

Gandalf looked up quickly. 'But what do you *think* the reason is?' he asked. 'Is there more in it than surprise at seeing a whole party of hobbits (not to mention Boromir and me) where people are so seldom seen?'

'I hope that is it,' said Trotter. 'But I get a feeling of watchfulness and of fear that I have never had here before.'

'Very well! Let us be more careful,' said Gandalf. 'If you bring a Ranger with you, it is best to pay attention to him – especially if the Ranger is Trotter, as I have found before. There are some things that even an experienced wizard does not notice. We had better stop talking now, and rest quietly and set a look-out.'

It was Sam's turn to take the first watch, but Trotter joined him. The others soon fell asleep, one by one. The silence grew till even Sam felt it. The breathing of the sleepers could be plainly heard. The swish of a pony's tail and the occasional movements of his feet became loud noises. Sam seemed to hear his very joints creaking if he stirred or moved. Over all hung a blue sky as the sun rode high and clear. The last clouds melted. But away in the south-east a dark patch grew and divided, flying like smoke to the north and west.

'What's that?' said Sam in a whisper to Trotter. Trotter made no answer, for he was gazing intently at the sky, but before long Sam could see what it was for himself. The clouds were flocks of birds going at great speed – wheeling and circling, and traversing all the land as if they were searching for something.

'Lie flat and still,' hissed Trotter, drawing Sam down into the shade of a holly-bush – for a whole regiment of birds had separated from the western flock and came back flying low right over the ridge where the travellers lay. Sam thought they were some kind of crows of a large size. As they passed overhead one harsh croak was heard.

Not till they had dwindled in the distance would Trotter move. Then he went and wakened Gandalf.

'Regiments of black crows are flying to and fro over Hollin,' he said. 'They are not natives to this place. I do not know what they are after – possibly there is some trouble going on away south: but I think they are spying out the land. I think too that I have seen hawks flying higher in the sky. That would account for the silence.[17] We ought to move again this evening. I am afraid that Hollin is no longer wholesome for us: it is being watched.'

'And in that case so is the Red Pass, and how we can get over it without being seen I don't know,' said Gandalf. 'But we will think about that when we get nearer. About moving on from here tonight: I am afraid you are right.'

'It is as well that we let our fire make little smoke,' said Trotter.

'It was out again (I think) before the birds came over. It must not be lit again.'

'Well, if that is not disappointing!' said Faramond. The news had been broken to him as soon as he woke (in the late afternoon): no fire, and a move again by night. 'I had looked forward to a real good meal tonight, something hot. All because of a pack of crows!'

'Well, you can go on looking forward,' said Gandalf. 'There may be many unexpected feasts ahead of you! Personally I should like a pipe of tobacco in comfort, and warmer feet. However, we are certain of one thing, at any rate: it will get warmer as we go south.'

'Too warm, I shouldn't wonder!' said Sam to Frodo. 'Not but what I would be glad to see that Fiery Mountain, and see the road's end ahead, so to speak. I thought that there Ruddyhorn or whatever its name is might be it, till Mr. Gandalf said not.' Maps conveyed nothing to Sam, and all distances in these strange lands seemed so vast that he was quite out of his reckonings.

The travellers remained hidden all that day. The birds passed over every now and again; but as the westering sun grew red they vanished southwards.[18] Soon afterwards the party set out again; and turned now a little eastward making for the peak of Taragaer which still glowed dully red in the distance. Frodo thought of Elrond's warning to watch even the sky above, but the sky was now clear and empty overhead, and one by one white stars sprang forth as the last gleams of sunset faded.

Guided by Trotter and Gandalf as usual they struck a good path. It looked to Frodo, as far as he could guess in the gathering dark, like the remains of an ancient road that had once run broad and well-planned from now deserted Hollin to the pass beneath Taragaer. A crescent moon rose over the mountains, and cast a pale light which was helpful – but was not welcomed by Trotter or Gandalf. It stayed but a little while and left them to the stars.[19] At midnight they had been going on again for an hour or more from their first halt. Frodo kept looking up at the sky, partly because of its beauty, partly because of Elrond's words. Suddenly he saw or felt a shadow pass over the stars – as if they faded and flashed out again. He shivered.

'Did you see anything?' he said to Gandalf, who was just in front.

'No, but I felt it, whatever it was,' said the wizard. 'It *may* be nothing, just a wisp of thin cloud.' It did not sound as if he thought much of his own explanation.[20]

Nothing more happened that night. The next morning was even brighter than before, but the wind was turning back eastward and the air was chill. For three more nights they marched on, climbing steadily and ever more slowly as their road wound into the hills and the mountains drew nearer and nearer. On the third morning Taragaer towered up before them, a mighty peak tipped with snow like silver, but with sheer naked sides dull red as if stained with blood.

There was a black look in the air, and the sun was wan. The wind was now gone towards the North. Gandalf sniffed and looked back. 'Winter is behind,' he said quietly to Trotter. 'The peaks behind are whiter than they were.'

'And tonight,' said Trotter, 'we shall be high up on our way to the red pass of Cris-caron. What do you think of our course now? If we are not seen in that narrow place – and waylaid by some evil, as would be easy there – the weather may prove as bad an enemy.'[21]

'I think no good of any part of our course, as you know well, Master Peregrin,' snapped Gandalf. 'Still we have to go on. It is no good whatever our trying to cross further south into the land of Rohan. The Horse-kings have long been in the service of Sauron.'[22]

'No, I know that. But there is a way – not *over* Cris-caron, as you are well aware.'

'Of course I am. But I am not going to risk that, until I am quite sure there is no other way. I shall think things out while the others rest and sleep.'[23]

In the late afternoon, before preparations were made for moving, Gandalf spoke to the travellers. 'We have now come to our first serious difficulty and doubt,' he said. 'The pass that we ought to take is up there ahead' – he waved his hand towards Taragaer: its sides were now dark and sullen, for the sun had gone, and its head was in grey cloud. 'It will take us at least two marches to get near the top of the pass. From certain signs we have seen recently I fear it may be watched or guarded; and in any case Trotter and I have doubts of the weather, on this wind. But I am afraid we must go on. We can't go back into the winter; and further south the passes are held. Tonight we must push along as hard as we can.'

The hearts of the travellers sank at his words. But they hurried with their preparations, and started off at as good a pace as they could make. It was heavy going.[24] The winding and twisting road had long been neglected and in places was blocked with fallen stones, over which they had great difficulty in finding any way to lead the pack ponies.[25] The night grew deadly dark under the great clouds; a bitter wind swirled among the rocks. By midnight they had already climbed to the very knees of the great mountains, and were going straight up under a mountain-side, with a deep ravine guessed but unseen on their right. Suddenly Frodo felt soft cold touches on his face. He put out his arm, and saw white snowflakes settle on his sleeve. Before long they were falling fast, swirling from every direction into his eyes, and filling all the air. The dark shapes of Gandalf and Trotter, a few paces in front, could hardly be seen.

'I don't like this,' panted Sam just behind. 'Snow is all right on a fine morning, seen from a window; but I like to be in bed while it's falling.' As a matter of fact snow fell very seldom in most parts of the Shire except the moors of the Northfarthing. There would occasionally, in January or February, be a thin white dusting of it, but [it] soon vanished, and only rarely in cold winters was there a real fall – enough to make snowballs of.

Gandalf halted. Frodo thought as he came up by him that he already looked almost like a snow-man. Snow was white on his hood and bowed shoulders, and it was already getting thick on the ground under foot.

'This is a bad business!' said the wizard. 'I never bargained for this, and left snow out of my plans. It seldom falls as far south as this except on the high peaks; and here we are not halfway up even to the high pass. I wonder if the Enemy has anything to do with it. He has strange powers and many allies.'

'We had better get all the party together,' said Trotter. 'We don't want to lose anyone on a night like this.'

For a while they struggled on. The snow became a blinding blizzard, and soon it was in places almost knee-deep. 'It'll be up over my head before long,' said Merry. Faramond was dragging behind and needed what help Merry and Sam could give him. Frodo felt his own legs like lead at every step.

Suddenly they heard strange sounds: they may have been but tricks of the rising wind in cracks and gullies of the rocks, but it sounded like hoarse cries and howls of harsh laughter. Then stones began to fall whirling like leaves on the wind, and crashing onto the path and the rocks on either hand. Every now and again

they heard in the darkness a dull rumble as a great boulder rolled
down thunderously from hidden heights in the dark above.

The party halted. 'We can't get any further tonight,' said
Trotter. 'You can call it the wind if you like, but I call it voices and
those stones are aimed at us, or at least at the path.'

'I do call it the wind,' said Gandalf; 'but that does not make the
rest untrue. Not all the servants of the Enemy have bodies or arms
and legs.'[26]

'What can we do?' asked Frodo. His heart suddenly failed him,
and he felt alone and lost in dark and driving snow, mocked at by
demons of the mountains.

'Stop here or go back,' answered Gandalf. 'We are protected at
present by the high wall on our left, and a deep gully on the right.
Further up there is a wide shallow valley, and the road runs at the
bottom of two long slopes. We should now hardly get through
there without damage, quite apart from the snow.'[27]

After some debate they retreated to a spot they had passed just
before the snow came on. There the path passed under a low
overhanging cliff. It faced southwards and they hoped it would
give them some protection from the wind. But the eddying blasts
whirled in from either side, and the snow came down thicker than
ever. They huddled together with their backs to the wall. The two
ponies stood dejected but patiently in front of them and served as
some kind of screen, but before long the snow was up to their
bellies and still mounting. The hobbits crouching behind were
nearly buried. A great sleepiness came over Frodo, and he felt
himself fast sinking into a warm and hazy dream. He thought a fire
was warming his toes, and out of the shadows he heard Bilbo's
voice speaking. 'I don't think much of your diary,' he heard him
say. 'Snow(storm) on December 2nd:[28] there was no need to come
back to report that.'

Suddenly he felt himself violently shaken, and came back
painfully to wakefulness. Boromir had lifted him right off the
ground. 'This snow will be the death of the hobbits, Gandalf,' he
said. 'We must do something.'

'Give them this,' said Gandalf, fumbling in his pack that lay
beside him, and drawing out a leather flagon. 'Just a little each –
for all of us. It is very precious: one of Elrond's cordials, and I did
not expect to have to use it so soon.'

As soon as Frodo had swallowed a little of the potent cordial, he
felt new strength of heart, and the heavy sleepiness left his limbs.
The others revived as quickly.

Boromir now endeavoured to clear away the snow and make a free space under the rock-wall. Finding his hands and feet slow tools, and his sword not much better, he took a faggot from the fuel that they carried on one of the ponies, in case they should need fire in places where there was no wood. He bound it tight and thrust a staff in the midst, so that it looked like a large mallet; but he used it as a ram to thrust back the soft snow, till it was packed hard into a wall before them and could not be pushed further away. For the moment things looked better, and in the small cleared space the travellers stood and took short paces, stamping to keep their limbs awake. But the snow continued to fall unrelenting; and it became plain that they were likely enough to be all buried in snow again before the night was out.[29]

'What about a fire?' said Trotter suddenly. 'As for giving ourselves away: personally I think our whereabouts is pretty well known or guessed already – by somebody.'

In desperation they decided to light a fire if they could, even if it meant sacrificing all the fuel that they had with them. It taxed even Gandalf's power to kindle the wet wood in that windy place. Ordinary methods were of no use, though each of the travellers had tinder and flint. They had brought some fir cones and little bundles of dried grass for kindling, but no fire would catch in them, until Gandalf thrust his wand into the midst of them and caused a great spark of blue and green flame to spring out.

'Well, if any enemy is watching,' he said, 'that will give *me* away. Let us hope other eyes are as blinded by the storm as ours. But anyway a fire is a good thing to see.' The wood now burned merrily and kept a clear circle all round it in which the travellers gathered somewhat heartened; but looking round Gandalf saw anxious eyes revealed by the dancing flames. The wood was burning fast, and the snow was not yet lessening.

'Daylight will soon be showing,' said Gandalf as cheerily as he could, but added: 'if any daylight can get through the snow-clouds.'

The fire burned low and the last faggot was thrown on. Trotter stood up and stared into the blackness above. 'I believe it is getting less,' he said. For a long while the others gazed at the flakes coming ..... down out of the darkness, to be revealed for a moment white in the light of the fire; but they could see little difference. After a while, however, it became plain that Trotter was right. The flakes became fewer and fewer. The wind grew less. The daylight began to grow pale grey and diffused. Then the snow ceased altogether.

As the light grew stronger it showed a shapeless world all about them. The high places were hid in clouds (that threatened still more snow), but below them they could see dim white hills and domes and valleys in which the path they had come by seemed altogether lost.

'The sooner we make a move, and get down again, the better,' said Trotter.[30] 'There is more snow still to fall up here!' But much as they all desired to get down again it was easier to speak of it than to manage it. The snow round about was already some feet deep: up to the necks of the hobbits or over their heads in places; and it was still soft. If they had [had] northern sledges or snowshoes [they] would have been of little use. Gandalf could only just manage to get forward with labour, more like swimming (and burrowing) than walking. Boromir was the tallest of the party: being some six feet high and broad-shouldered as well. He went ahead a little way to test the path. The snow was everywhere above even his knees, and in many places he sank up to the waist. The situation looked fairly desperate.

'I will go on down if I can,' he said.[31] 'As far as I can make out our course of last night, the path seems to turn right round a shoulder of rock down there. And if I remember rightly, a furlong or two below the turn we ought to come on to a flat space at the top of a long steep slope – very heavy going it was coming up. From there I may be able to get some view and some idea of how the snow lies further down.' He struggled forward slowly, and after a while disappeared round the turn.

It was nearly an hour before he came back, tired but with some encouraging news. 'There is a deep wind drift just the other side of the turn, and I was nearly buried in it; but beyond that the snow quickly gets less. At the top of the slope it is no more than ankle-deep and it is only sprinkled on the ground from there down: or so it seems.'

'It may be only sprinkled further down,' grunted Gandalf; 'but it is not sprinkled up here. Even the snow seems to have been aimed specially at us.'

'How are *we* to get to the turn?' asked Trotter.

'I don't know!' said Boromir. 'It is a pity Gandalf can't produce flame enough to melt us a pathway.'

'I daresay it is,' snapped Gandalf; 'but even I need a few materials to work upon. I can kindle fire not feed it. What you want is a dragon not a wizard.'

'Indeed I think a tame dragon would actually be more useful at the moment than a wild wizard,' said Boromir – with a laugh that did not in any way appease Gandalf.

'At the moment, at the moment,' he replied. 'Later on we may see. I am old enough to be your great-grandfather's ancestor – but I am not doddery yet. It will serve you right if you meet a wild dragon.'[32]

'Well, well! *When heads are at a loss bodies must serve* they say in my country,' said Boromir. 'We must just try and thrust our way through. Put the little folk on the ponies, two on each. I will carry the smallest; you go behind, Gandalf, and I will go in front.'

At once he set about unloading the ponies of their burdens. 'I will come back for these when we have forced a passage,' he said. Frodo and Sam were mounted on one of the ponies, Merry and Trotter on the other. Then picking up Faramond Boromir strode forward.

Slowly they ploughed their way forward. It took some time to reach the bend, but they did so without mishap. After a short halt they laboured on to the edge of the drift. Suddenly Boromir stumbled on some hidden stone, and fell headlong. Faramond was thrown from his shoulder into deep snow and disappeared. The pony behind reared and then fell also, tumbling both Frodo and Sam into the drift. Trotter however managed to hold back the second pony.

For some moments all was confusion. But Boromir got up, shaking the snow from his face and eyes, and went to the head of the floundering and kicking pony. When he had got it onto its feet again, he went to the rescue of the hobbits who had vanished into deep holes in the yielding snow. Picking up first Faramond and then Frodo he ploughed his way through the remainder of the drift and set them on their feet beyond. He then returned for the pony and Sam. 'Follow now in my track!' he cried to the remaining three. 'The worst is over!'

At last they all came to the head of the long slope. Gandalf bowed to Boromir. 'If I was testy,' he said, 'forgive me. Even the wisest wizard does not like to see his plans go awry. Thank goodness for plain strength and good sense. We are grateful to you, Boromir of Ond.'[33]

They looked out from the high place where they stood over the lands. Daylight was now as full as it would be, unless the heavy clouds were broken. Far below, and over the tumbled country falling away from the foot of the incline, Frodo thought he could see the dell from which they had started to climb the night before.

His legs ached and his head was dizzy as he thought of the long painful march down again. In the distance, below him but still high above the lower hills, he saw many black specks moving in the air. 'The birds again,' he said in a low voice, pointing.

'It can't be helped now, said Gandalf. 'Whether they are good or bad, or nothing to do with us, we must go on down at once.' The wind was blowing stiffly again over the pass hidden in the clouds behind; and already some snowflakes were drifting down.

It was late in the afternoon, and the grey light was already again waning fast when they got back to their camp of the previous night. They were weary and very hungry. The mountains were veiled in a deepening dusk full of snow: even there in the foothills snow was falling gently. The birds had vanished.

They had no fuel for a fire, and made themselves as warm as they could with all their spare furs and blankets. Gandalf spared them each one more mouthful of the cordial. When they had eaten, Gandalf called a council.

'We cannot of course go on again tonight,' he said. 'We all need a good rest, and I think we had better stay here till tomorrow evening.'

'And when we move where are we to go to?' asked Frodo. 'It is no use trying the pass again; but you said yourself last night in this very spot that we could not now cross the passes further north because of winter, nor further south because of enemies.'

'There is no need to remind me,' said Gandalf. 'The choice is now between going on with our journey – by some road or other – or returning to Rivendell.'

The faces of the hobbits revealed plainly enough the pleasure they felt at the mere mention of returning to Rivendell. Sam's face brightened visibly, and he glanced at his master. But Frodo looked troubled.

'I wish I was back in Rivendell,' he acknowledged. 'But would not that be going back also on all that was spoken and decided there?' he asked.

'Yes,' replied Gandalf. 'Our journey was already delayed perhaps too long. After the winter it would be quite vain. If we return it will mean the siege of Rivendell, and likely enough its fall and destruction.'

'Then we must go on,' said Frodo with a sigh, and Sam sank back into gloom. 'We must go on – if there is any road to take.'

'There is, or there may be,' said Gandalf. 'But I have not mentioned it to you before, and have hardly even thought of it while there was hope of the pass of Cris-caron. For it is not a pleasant road.'

'If it is worse than the pass of Cris-caron it must be very nasty indeed,' said Merry. 'But you had better now tell us about it.'

'Have you ever heard of the Mines of Moria or the Black Gulf?'[34] asked Gandalf.

'Yes,' answered Frodo. 'I think so. I seem to remember Bilbo speaking of them long ago, when he told me tales of the dwarves and goblins. But I have no idea where they are.'

'They are not far away,' said the wizard. 'They are in these mountains. They were made by the Dwarves of Durin's clan many hundreds of years ago, when elves dwelt in Hollin, and there was peace between the two races. In those ancient days Durin dwelt in Caron-dûn, and there was traffic on the Great River. But the Goblins – fierce orcs[35] in great number – drove them out after many wars, and most of the dwarves that escaped removed far into the North. They have often tried to regain these mines, but never so far as I know have they succeeded. King Thrór was killed there after he fled from Dale when the dragon came, as you may remember from Bilbo's tales. As Glóin told us, the dwarves of Dale think Balin came here, but no news has come from him.'[36]

'How can the mines [of the] Black Gulf help us?' asked Boromir. 'It sounds a name of ill-omen.'

'It is so, or has become so,' answered Gandalf. 'But one must tread the path need chooses. If there are orcs in the mines, it will prove ill for us. But most of the goblins of the Misty Mountains were destroyed in the Battle of Five Armies at the Lonely Mountain. There is a chance that the mines are still deserted. There is even a chance that dwarves are there, and that Balin lives in secret in some deep hall. If either of these chances prove true, then we may get through. For the mines go right through and under this western arm of the mountains. The tunnels of Moria were of old the most famous in the northern world. There were two secret gates on the western side, though the chief entrance was on the East looking upon Caron-dûn.[37] I passed right through, many years ago, when I was looking for Thrór and Thráin. But I have never been since – I have never wished to repeat the experience.'[38]

'And I don't wish for it even once,' said Merry. 'Nor me,' muttered Sam.

'Of course not,' said Gandalf. 'Who would? But the question is, will you follow me, if I take the risk?'

There was no answer for some time. 'How far are the western gates?' asked Frodo at length.

'About ten[39] miles south of Cris-caron,' said Trotter.

'Then you know of Moria?' said Frodo, looking at him in surprise.

'Yes, I know of the mines,' said Trotter quietly. 'I went there once, and the memory is evil; but if you want to know, I was always in favour of trying that way rather than an open pass.[40] I will follow Gandalf – though I should have followed him more willingly if we could have come to the gate of Moria more secretly.'

'Well, come now,' said Gandalf. 'I would not put such a choice to you, if there were any hope in other roads, or any hope in retreat. Will you try Moria, or go back to Rivendell?'

'We must risk the Mines,' said Frodo.

As I have said, it is remarkable how substantially the structure of the story was achieved at the very beginning, while the differences in the *dramatis personae* are so great. It is indeed very curious, that before my father had even written the first complete draft of 'The Council of Elrond' he had decided that the Company should include an Elf and a Dwarf (p. 397), as seems now so natural and inevitable, and yet in 'The Ring Goes South' we have only Gandalf and Boromir and five hobbits (one of whom, admittedly, is the most unusually far-travelled and widely experienced Trotter).

But as often in the history of *The Lord of the Rings* much of the earliest writing remained, for example in the detail of conversation, and yet such conversation appears later shifted into new contexts, given to different speakers, and acquiring new resonance as the 'world' and its history grew and expanded. A striking example is given in note 8, where in the original text 'Trotter sat with his head bowed to his knees' as they waited to depart from Rivendell, while in FR 'Aragorn sat with his head bowed to his knees; *only Elrond knew fully what this hour meant to him.*' The question presents itself: what is really the relation between Trotter = Peregrin Boffin and Strider = Aragorn?

It would obviously not be true to say merely that there was a rôle to be played in the story, and that at first this rôle was played by a Hobbit but afterwards by a Man. In particular cases, looked at narrowly without the larger context, this might seem a sufficient or nearly sufficient account: the necessary or fixed action was that Sam Gamgee's companion should hiss 'Lie flat and still' and pull him down into the shade of a holly-bush (p. 420, FR p. 298). But this says very little. I would be inclined to think that the original figure (the mysterious person who encounters the hobbits in the inn at Bree) was capable of development in different directions without losing important elements of his 'identity' as a recognisable character – even though the choice of one direction or another would lead to quite different historical and racial 'identities' in Middle-earth. So Trotter was not simply switched from Hobbit to Man – though such a switch could take place in the case of Mr. Butterbur with very little disturbance. Rather, he had been potentially Aragorn for a long time; and when my father decided that Trotter *was* Aragorn and *was not* Peregrin Boffin his stature and his history were totally changed, but a great deal of the 'indivisible' Trotter remained in Aragorn and determined his nature.

It may also be thought that in the story of the attempt on Cris-caron Trotter is diminished from the rôle he had played in the narrative of the journey from Bree to Rivendell, in which, though a hobbit, he is set altogether apart from the others, a wise and resourceful leader of great experience in whom all their hope rests. Now, in these physical circumstances, and beside Boromir, he is one of the helpless 'little folk', as Boromir says, to be set on a pony. Of course, this question cannot be approached without hindsight; if Trotter had in fact remained a hobbit in *The Lord of the Rings* it would not arise. Yet considerations along these lines may have been an element in the decision about him which my father would now shortly take.

## NOTES

1  An isolated page, certainly of this time, does give a preliminary sketch of the passage that begins approximately at 'As the light grew stronger' on p. 426. The writing is at the extreme limit of legibility, in rapid pencil now very faint.

Grey light grew revealing a snow . . . world in which the path by which they had climbed could scarcely be seen. The snow was no longer falling but the sky threatened more to come.

'The sooner we move and begin to get down the better,' said Gandalf. This was easier said than done. Hobbits. One on each journey. [*Struck out:* Boromir carries Frodo (. . precious burden).] Boromir and Gandalf go ahead and feel the way. In places Boromir vanished almost to his neck. They began to despair for the snow was soft. . . . . . . . . With great labour they had gone only ¼ mile down and were all getting exhausted. But suddenly they found the snow less thick – 'even that seems to have been specially aimed at us' said Gandalf. Boromir strode ahead and came back reporting that it was [?soon only white]. At last when daylight was broad they came back to places almost clear of snow.

G. points out the place they had started from the evening before. Council. What is to be done. Moria.

The page continues with some preliminary strokes for the scene outside the West Gate of Moria; see p. 444.

2   Dates were put in marginally against this sentence: 'Nov. 7th?' and
    'Nov. 10–11'; in addition, 'a fortnight' was changed to '3 weeks' and
    'a week old or more' to 'nearly 2 weeks old'.

3   After 'as far as' my father first wrote *Dimbar*, perhaps intending
    'Dimbar in the Dimrill-dales'. The name *Dimbar* had appeared in
    the *Quenta Silmarillion* (V.261), of the empty land between the
    rivers Sirion and Mindeb.
        For this application of *Dimrill-dale(s)* (north of Rivendell) see
    p. 360. When the name *Dimrill-dale* was transferred southwards
    and to the other side of the Misty Mountains it was replaced in the
    north by *Hoardale*, and this name was pencilled later on the text
    here.

4   This is the first occurrence of the names *Gladden* (River) and
    *Gladden* Fields. The river had been shown on the Map of Wilder-
    land in *The Hobbit*, with marshy land at its confluence with the
    Great River, suggesting a region where 'gladdens' would grow.
        At the foot of the page is a note that applies to the names in this
    passage: 'These names are given in Hobbit [fashion >] translation.
    Their real names were *Tum Dincelon*; *Arad Dain (Annerchin)*;
    *Crandir* Redway; and *Palathrin (Palath* = Iris).' *Tum Dincelon* is
    *Dimrill-dale*, in the original application (note 3). I do not under-
    stand the reference of '*Arad Dain (Annerchin)*'. My father first
    wrote *Tar* and struck it out before writing *Arad*. For the names of
    the River Redway see note 15. In the *Etymologies* the Noldorin
    word *palath* = 'surface' (V.380).

5   Cf. the Map of Wilderland in *The Hobbit*; 'Goblin Gate and Eyrie.'

6   According to *The Tale of Years* in LR (Appendix B) the Company
    left Rivendell on 25 December.

7   This passage was rewritten over and over again, and it is impossible
    to interpret the sequence precisely: but it is clear that my father first
    envisaged the Company as mounted, with Boromir's 'great brown
    horse', Gandalf's white horse, and seven ponies, five for the five
    hobbits, and two pack-animals (see note 25). An intermediate stage
    saw Boromir alone on foot: 'There were ponies for all the hobbits to
    ride where the road allowed, and Gandalf of course had his horse;
    but Boromir strode on foot, as he had come. The men of his race did
    not ride horses.' The text printed is certainly the final formulation at
    this stage, and is of course different from that in FR (p. 293), where
    the sole beast of burden was Bill Ferny's pony, whom Sam called
    Bill.

8   Cf. FR p. 293: 'Aragorn sat with his head bowed to his knees; only
    Elrond knew fully what this hour meant to him.' See p. 430.

9   This is the first occurrence of *Hollin*; but the Elvish name *Eregion*
    does not appear. In the *Etymologies* (V.356) the Elvish name of
    Hollin is *Regornion*. – In FR (p. 296) Gandalf says that they have

come 45 leagues, but that was as the crow flies: 'many long miles further our feet have walked.'

10 See the Note on Geography, pp. 440–1.

11 At the first occurrence the name of the 'red horn mountain' was replaced over and over again: first it was *Bliscarn*, then *Carnbeleg or Ruddyhorn*, then *Taragaer (see the Etymologies*, V.391); also written on the margins of the page are *Caradras = Ruddihorn*, and *Rhascaron*. All these names appear on the contemporary map (p. 439). At the next occurrence *Carnbeleg* was replaced by *Taragaer*, and subsequently the name first written was *Caradras* replaced by *Taragaer*, and finally *Taragaer*. I give *Taragaer* throughout, as being apparently the preferred name at this stage. Changes made in red ink at some later stage brought back *Caradras*.

12 On the dividing of the Misty Mountains into an eastern and a western arm see the Note on Geography, p. 438. My father wrote here first 'the great vale', and the replacement word is probably but not certainly 'land'.

13 The name of the vale was first *Carndoom the Red Valley*; above was written *Carondûn* and *Doon-Caron*, but these were struck out. Elsewhere on this page is *Narodûm = Red Vale*; and the name in the text was corrected in red ink to *Dimrill-dale: Nanduhiriath* (in FR *Nanduhirion*). On the former application of *Dimrill-dale* see note 3. At subsequent occurrences the name is *Carndoom, Caron-doom, Caron-dûn, Dûn Caron*, and at the last the name was replaced in red ink by *Glassmere in Dimrilldale* (note 37). Among these forms, all meaning 'Red Valley', I have rather arbitrarily chosen *Caron-dûn* to stand as the consistent form in the text.

14 The name of the pass was first written *Criscarn*, with *Cris-caron* as a rejected alternative; at subsequent occurrences both appear, but with the preference to *Cris-caron* (also *Cris-carron, Cris Caron*), which I adopt. *Dimrill-stair* replaces it twice in red ink, in the present passage thus: 'over the pass that was [*read* is] called Dimrill-stair (*Pendrethdulur*) under the side of Caradras.' The pass was afterwards called the Redhorn Gate, the Dimrill-stair being the descent from the pass on the eastern side; cf. note 21. With *Pendrethdulur* cf. the *Etymologies*, V.380, *pendrath* 'passage up or down a slope, stairway'.

15 The River Redway, the later Silverlode, has been referred to in an outline dated August 1939 (p. 381), and at its occurrence at the beginning of the chapter the Elvish name *Crandir* is given (note 4). Here, above *Redway*, are written the names *Rathgarn* (struck out); *Rathcarn*; *Nenning* (struck out); and *Caradras or Redway*. Written in the margin is also *Narosîr = Redway*. At this time *Nenning* had not yet appeared in *The Silmarillion* and the *Annals of Beleriand* as the name of the river in Beleriand west of Narog, which was

still called *Eglor*. In red ink the name *Celebrin* was substituted
(*Celebrant* in FR). The river is called *Caradras* on the contemporary map (p. 439).

16  It was said in the outline given on p. 410 that Beleghir the Great
River divided into many channels in Fangorn Forest. See the map,
p. 439.

17  While in FR (p. 298) Aragorn says that he has seen hawks flying
high up, he does not say, as Trotter does here, 'That would account
for the silence.'

18  *southwards:* changed in pencil from *northwards*.

19  It was now 28 November (since they walked for three nights after
this and attempted Cris-caron on 2 December, pp. 422, 424). In
notes on phases of the Moon (found on the back of a page in the
previous section of this manuscript) my father gave the following
dates, showing that on the night of the 28th the Moon was in its first
quarter:

| Last Quarter | New Moon | First Quarter | Full Moon |
|---|---|---|---|
| Sept. 18 | Sept. 25 | Oct. 2 | Oct. 10 |
| Oct. 17 | Oct. 24 | Oct. 31 | Nov. 8 |
| Nov. 15 | Nov. 22 | Nov. 29 | Dec. 7 |

20  This incident was retained in FR, but it is not explained. The
Winged Nazgûl had not yet crossed the River (*The Two Towers*
pp. 101, 201).

21  As written in ink, and before changes in pencil produced the passage
given, Gandalf said: 'Winter is behind. There is snow coming. In
fact it has come. The peaks behind are whiter than they were.'
Trotter's reply is the same, but he ends: 'we may get caught in a
blizzard before we get over the pass.' In the margin my father wrote:
'? Cut out prophecy of snow – let it come suddenly.' He struck this
out, but the passage as emended makes the threat of snow seem less
certain.

The words 'on our way to the red pass of Cris-caron' were
emended in red ink to 'on our way up the Dimrill-stair'; see note 14.

22  My father first wrote here (emending it to the text given at the time
of writing): 'But we have to go on, and we have to cross the
mountains here or go back. The passes further south are too far
away, and were all guarded years ago – they lead straight into the
country of the [Beardless Men   Mani Aroman >] Horsemen.' In
the rewritten passage, the reference to the passes further south is
removed, but it reappears a little later: 'further south the passes are
held' (cf. FR p. 300: 'Further south there are no passes, till one
comes to the Gap of Rohan').

Before the name *Rohan* was reached several others were written,
*Thanador, Ulthanador, Borthendor, Orothan*[*ador*]. After *Rohan*
is written: [= *Rochan(dor)* = Horseland]. This is unquestionably

the point at which the name *Rohan* arose. Cf. the *Etymologies*, V.384: Quenya *rokko*, Noldorin *roch*, horse.

A scribble in the margin seems to change 'The Horse-kings have long been in the service of Sauron' to 'Rohan where the Horsekings or Horselords are.' Cf. FR p. 300: 'Who knows which side now the marshals of the Horse-lords serve?'

23 In the original story Trotter favoured the passage of Moria and Gandalf the pass; in FR (p. 300) it was Aragorn who favoured the pass.

24 This passage, from 'Trotter and I have doubts of the weather', is a rewriting in pencil of a much longer passage in which Gandalf introduced at this point the subject of Moria. Gandalf says:

'Trotter thinks we are likely to be caught in a heavy snow-storm before we get across [see note 21]. I think we shall have to attempt it, all the same. But there is another way, or there used to be. I don't know whether you have heard of the Mines of Moria, or the Black [Pit >] Gulf?'

Gandalf then describes Moria; and after this the original text continues:

The hearts of the travellers sank at his words. All of them would have voted at once for the cold and perils of the high pass rather than for the black gulfs of Moria. But Gandalf did not ask for a vote. After a silence he said: 'There is no need to ask you to decide. I know which way you would choose, and I choose the same. We will try the pass.'

The introduction of Moria was postponed until after the Company had been forced back from the pass by the snowstorm; and Gandalf's words about it reappear there in closely similar form (see p. 429 and note 38). The second occurrence of the passage is in ink and an integral part of the chapter.

25 'pack ponies' is a pencilled emendation from 'horses and ponies'; see note 7. But when the travellers halt under the overhanging cliff the reference to 'the two ponies' (p. 424) is in the text as first written.

26 This sentence was marked with a query and enclosed within square brackets at the time of writing. Later my father wrote here: 'Not all evil things are Sauron['s]', and 'The hawks' (referring presumably to the hawks which Trotter saw high up over Hollin, and said 'accounted for the silence', p. 420); and in the margin: 'Gimli says Caradras had an ill name even in days when Sauron was of little account' (see FR p. 303).

27 As first written (but at once rejected) the content of these speeches (from '"This is hopeless," said Gandalf. "You can call it the wind if you like . . ."') was more condensed and was given entirely to Gandalf.

28 In the same passage in FR (p. 303) the date is 12 January; the Company had left Rivendell on 25 December, and so had been in

the wilderness for nineteen nights. But in the original story the journey was shorter: 'when they had been about ten days on the road the weather grew better' (p. 418), whereas FR (p. 295) has 'a fortnight'.

29  This sentence replaced (probably at once): 'But the snow continued to fall unrelenting, and at length Gandalf had to admit that being buried in snow was at the moment the chief danger.' With the words *had to admit* cf. notes 23 and 30.

30  'Trotter' was changed in pencil to 'Gandalf'. In the context of the story at this stage Trotter would be the more likely to say this (see notes 23 and 29), but in the rough preliminary draft given in note 1 it is said by Gandalf.

31  My father pencilled here: 'Boromir knows snow from the Black Mountains. He was born a mountaineer'; but he struck this out. It is said in the outline given on p. 410 that Fangorn Forest extended up to the Black Mountains (changed from Blue Mountains, which are referred to on the contemporary map).

32  Pencilled changes altered the speakers in this passage, but I believe that these are later. The question 'How are *we* to get to the turn?' is taken from Trotter and given to Merry (probably because my father had decided that Trotter was a Man), who goes on 'It is a pity Gandalf can't produce flame enough to melt us a pathway'; and it is Merry, not Boromir, who makes the remark about a tame dragon and a wild wizard. But since subsequently it is to Boromir that Gandalf apologises for his irritability, these changes were casual and not fully integrated into the narrative. Either at this time or later the remark about Gandalf's melting them a path was transferred to Legolas (cf. FR p. 305), and this is obviously a structurally irrelevant addition, like that concerning Gimli in note 26.

33  The descent of the Company through the deep snow was first told quite differently, though the version given replaced the other before it was completed. As first written, Gandalf relented at once towards Boromir (after 'It will serve you right if you meet a wild dragon') and since he appeared already tired gave him a further sip of Elrond's cordial. Boromir was to carry each hobbit down separately (cf. the preliminary sketch given in note 1) and began with Frodo; at the drift he stumbled on a hidden stone and Frodo was thrown into the deep snow and disappeared, but Boromir 'soon recovered him'. Sam was brought down next ('he had disapproved greatly of his master (with the Ring) being left alone and out of reach in any sudden danger'). Boromir was then too tired to repeat the ascent and descent three times more, and this version ends with hasty notes telling that Trotter, Faramond, and Merry were put on the ponies, while Gandalf behind and Boromir ahead, carrying the baggage, 'ploughed their way down dragging and thrusting the ponies forward.'

My father then wrote: 'Or alter all above', and proposed that the whole Company should go down together. In the second version, given in the text, he neglected to mention that Boromir returned once more to bring down the baggage. The story in FR is of course entirely different since Trotter has become Aragorn.

34  *Moria* is translated 'Black Gulf' in the first, rejected occurrence of this passage (note 24). An isolated note earlier in the MS has '*Moria* = Black Gulf', with the etymology *yagō, ia*; here 'Gulf' is a correction of some other word which I cannot interpret. Cf. the *Etymologies*, V.400, stem YAG 'yawn, gape', where *Moria* is translated 'Black Gulf'.

35  This is not the first use of the word *Orcs* in the LR papers: Gandalf refers to 'orcs and goblins' among the servants of the Dark Lord, pp. 211, 364; cf. also pp. 187, 320. But the rarity of the usage at this stage is remarkable. The word *Orc* goes back to the *Lost Tales*, and had been pervasive in all my father's subsequent writings. In the *Lost Tales* the two terms were used as equivalents, though sometimes apparently distinguished (see II.364, entry *Goblins*). A clue may be found in a passage that occurs in both the earlier and the later *Quenta* (IV.82, V.233): 'Goblins they may be called, *but in ancient days they were strong and fell.*' At this stage it seems that 'Orcs' are to be regarded as a more formidable kind of 'Goblin'; so in the preliminary sketch for 'The Mines of Moria' (p. 443) Gandalf says 'there are goblins – of very evil kind, larger than usual, *real orcs*.' – It is incidentally notable that in the first edition of *The Hobbit* the word *Orcs* is used only once (at the end of Chapter VII 'Queer Lodgings'), while in the published LR *goblins* is hardly ever used.

36  Strangely, this is not at all in agreement with what Glóin had said at Rivendell (p. 391): 'For many years things went well, and the colony throve; there was traffic once more between Moria and the Mountain, and many gifts of silver were sent to Dáin.'

37  It is here that the emendation in red ink to *Glassmere in Dimrilldale* is made (note 13). This is the first appearance of the lake in Dimrill Dale; on the contemporary map it is marked and named *Mirrormere*.

38  Gandalf's account of Moria here differs from the earlier form (see note 24) only in that here there is mention of Durin, of the peace between Elves and Dwarves, and of Orcs (see note 35) – the rejected version refers only to goblins. In that version it is said that the Dwarves of Caron-dûn 'sent their goods down the Great River.'

39  'ten' changed in pencil to '20'. In FR (p. 311) Gandalf says: 'There was a door south-west of Caradhras, fifteen miles as the crow flies, and maybe twenty as the wolf runs.'

40  See note 23. In the margin, probably made at the time of writing of the manuscript, is a note: 'Trotter was caught there.' This contrasts with what was said earlier, at the Council of Elrond (p. 401): 'Thus

it was that Frodo learned how Trotter had tracked Gollum as he wandered southwards, through Fangorn Forest, and past the Dead Marshes, until he had himself been caught and imprisoned by the Dark Lord.'

## Note on the Geography and the contemporary Map

The extremely rapid, rough, and now tattered map reproduced on p. 439 can with complete certainty, I think, be ascribed to the time of the original writing of this chapter. It was my father's first representation of Middle-earth south of the Map of Wilderland in *The Hobbit* – which he had before him, as the courses of the rivers show.

Going from North to South on the map, there is *Carrock* at the top; and *Gladden* (River) and *Gl[adden] Fields* (see p. 416 and note 4). *Hollin* is named and roughly marked with a broken line; and the names, struck out, to the right of the mountains are *Taragaer, Caradras* (with the final form *Caradras* beside it in pencil), *Carnbeleg*, and *Rhascarn* (see note 11). The pass is called *Dimrill*, with (probably) *Cris-caron* struck out (note 14); and *Mirrormere* is marked, the first occurrence of the name (see note 37). West of the mere *Moria* is marked; below are two illegible names and below them *Bliscarn* (note 11) and again *Carnbeleg*, all struck out.

The division of the Misty Mountains into two arms here, referred to by Gandalf in the present text (pp. 419, 429) and by Gimli in FR (p. 296), is shown far more markedly on this original map than it is on my father's later ones – where the eastern arm is shown as actually less extensive than it is on mine published in LR. For the names of the valley between the arms of the mountains see note 13.

The vast westward swing of the Great River (marked *great bend*) is already in being, but the placing of *Fangorn Forest* (in which my father's writing of the word *Forest* is a sample of his more rapid script) would later be wholly changed. That the Great River flowed through the midst of Fangorn is stated by Gandalf (p. 419 and note 16). The name *Belfalas* in the North-east of Fangorn is in red ink (the only item that is); afterwards Belfalas was a coastal region of Gondor, and since *falas* ('shore') was one of the most ancient of Elvish words (see I.253) it is hard to see how it could be used to refer to a region of forest far inland. I suspect that my father wrote it on the page after, or before, the making of this extremely rapid map and without any reference to it, so that it has no significance in this context.

For the various proposed names of the river *Redway* in the text see note 15; among them is *Caradras*, which is written on the map (but struck through in pencil).

Across the Misty Mountains further south is written 'Place this pass into *Rohan* further south' (on passes over the Mountains south of Caradras see note 22). At the bottom of the map on the left is written:

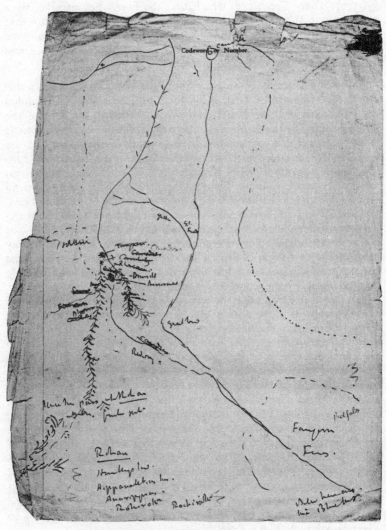

The earliest map of the lands south of the
Map of Wilderland in *The Hobbit*

'*Rohan. Horsekings land Hippanaletians* . . . [possibly *kn* standing for
*kingdom*] *Anaxippians Rohiroth Rochiroth.*' The *Hippanaletians* and
*Anaxippians* ('Horse-lords') are surprising.

At the right-hand corner is: *Below here are the Blue Mts.* Compare
Gandalf's words in the first sketching of 'The Council of Elrond'
(p. 397): 'Giant Treebeard, who haunts the Forest between the River
and *the South Mountains*'; the outline given on p. 410 in which it is said
that Fangorn Forest runs up into the *Blue (> Black) Mountains*; and the
rejected note to the present text in which it was said that Boromir was
'born a mountaineer' in the *Black Mountains* (note 31).

A question arises concerning the line of the Misty Mountains. In this
original text it is said (p. 418), as in FR (p. 295), that south of Rivendell
the mountains bent westward; and this is shown on the Map of the
Wilderland in *The Hobbit*. It will be seen that if the line of the mountains
where it leaves that map, some distance south of the sources of the
Gladden, be continued without further westward curving, a track running south from the Ford of Rivendell will strike the mountain chain
somewhere near Caradhras. This is in fact precisely what is shown on my
father's three maps that exhibit the whole range of the Misty Mountains.
On two of them the mountains run in a straight line from about the
latitude of Rivendell (as also on my map published in LR); on one of
them (the earliest) the line curves very slightly westward from some way
north of Hollin; but on all three a line drawn south from the Ford must
cut the mountains at an acute angle in the region of Hollin, simply
because the line of the mountains is south-south-west.

It is therefore curious that the original sketch-map discussed here does
not really agree with the original text (p. 418). The travellers went south
from the Ford; and on the borders of Hollin 'far away south Frodo saw
the dim shapes of mountains, that seemed now to lie across their path. To
the left of this distant range a tall peak stood up like a tooth': that was
Taragaer, the Redhorn (Caradhras). And when Faramond said that he
thought that they must have turned east, since the mountains were now
in front of them, Gandalf said No, it is the mountains that have turned.
But on the old map, a line drawn south from the Ford would only strike
the mountains far south of Moria and the Red Pass; and this is because
my father bent the mountain-line almost due south in the region of
Hollin, so that the course from the Ford and the mountain-line then
become nearly parallel. This is possibly no more than a consequence of
the speed and roughness with which the map was made – the merest
guide; but it is curious that the dotted line marking the route of the
travellers does actually turn strongly south-east towards the pass – as
Faramond thought that it had!

Barbara Strachey, writing on this question in *Journeys of Frodo* (Map
17), remarks: 'The mountains bent westward as they went; more so, in
my opinion, than appears in the maps of Middle-earth, especially south

of the Redhorn Pass. Frodo said that they seemed to "stand across the path" that the Companions were taking' (FR p. 295). This is arguable; but the point is strengthened by Gandalf's reply to Pippin, who has said that they must have turned east: 'No, but you see further ahead in the clear light. *Beyond those peaks* [i.e. the Mountains of Moria] *the range bends round south-west*' (FR p. 296). On none of my father's maps is there a change in the direction of the main mountain-chain south of Caradhras. But all show some degree of mountainous extension west-wards from the main chain at the point where the Glanduin flows down towards Greyflood: very slight in one (and so represented on my map in LR), more marked on a second, and on the third (the earliest) amounting to a virtual division of the range, with a broad arm of mountains running southwest. On the elaborate map in coloured chalks that I made in 1943 (see p. 200) this is again a strongly marked feature.* It may be that it was to this that Gandalf was referring.

In this connection it may be mentioned that on my map published in LR the mountainous heights shown extending from the main range westwards north of Hollin are badly exaggerated from what my father intended: 'about the feet of the main range there was tumbled an ever wider land of bleak hills, and deep valleys filled with turbulent water' (FR p. 295).

---

*The map referred to here as 'the earliest' (cf. also p. 202) is my father's original elaborate working map of *The Lord of the Rings* (on which my 1943 map was closely based). This map will be studied in Vol. VII.

# XXV

# THE MINES OF MORIA

I have little doubt that the first draft of this chapter was written continuously from the end of 'The Ring Goes South', both from internal evidence and external (the nature of the manuscript). But there is also a very interesting two-page 'Sketch of the Mines of Moria chapter' which, I think, immediately preceded the writing of it. This 'Sketch' is extremely difficult to read, and some words can only be guessed at.

Their adventures must be made different from Lonely Mountain. Tunnels leading in every direction, sloping up and running steeply down. stairs. pits. noise of water in darkness.

Gandalf guided mainly by the general sense of direction. They had brought one bundle of torches in case of need, 2 each. Gandalf won't use them until necessary. Faint spark from his staff. Glamdring does not glow, therefore no goblins near.

How far to go. How long will it take. Gandalf reckons at least 2 days, perhaps more. Thought of a night (or two!) in Moria terrifies them. Frodo feels dread growing. Perhaps his adventures with the Ring have made him sensitive. While others are keeping up spirits with hopeful talk he feels the certainty of evil creeping over him, but says nothing. He constantly fancies he hears patter of feet of [?some creature] behind – [?this] is Gollum as it proves long after.

It was about ten o'clock in the morning when they entered. They had had little rest. They went on (with 2 halts) until too weary to go much further. They came to a dark arch leading to 3 passages all leading in same general direction, but the left down, the right up, the centre (apparently) level. Gandalf unable to choose: he does not remember the place.

They halt for the night in a small chamber (almost like a guard-room watching the entrances) just to [?their] left. A deep pit to right. A loose stone falls in. Several minutes before they hear a noise of it reach bottom. After that some of them fancy a far off echo of small knocks at intervals (like signals?). But nothing further happens that night. Gandalf sleeps little trying to choose the road. [?In end] chooses the right hand upward way. They go for nearly 8 hours exclusive of halts.[1]

Come to a great chamber. Door in [?south] wall. Dim light – a [?high ?huge] chimney like shaft slanting up. Far up a gleam of daylight. The gleam falls on a great square table of stone [*written above:* a tomb].

There is another door in west [*written above:* east] wall. There are lances and swords and [? broken lying] by both doors.

The gleam of light shows carved letters. Here lies Balin son of Burin, Lord of Moria. In the recesses are chests and a few swords and shields. Chests empty except one. Here is a book with some dwarf writing.

Tells how Balin came to Moria. Then hand changes and tells how he died – of [?an] arrow that came unawares. Then how 'enemies' invaded the east gates. We cannot get out of the west gates because of the 'dweller in the water'. Brief account of siege. Last scrawl says 'they are coming'.

I think we had better be going, said Gandalf. At that moment there is a noise like a great boom far underneath. Then a terrible noise like a horn echoed endlessly. Gandalf springs to door. Noise like goblin feet.

Gandalf lets out a blinding flash and cries Who comes there? Ripple of . . . . . laughter – and some deep voices.

Gandalf says there are goblins – of very evil kind, larger than usual, real orcs.[2] Also certainly some kind of troll is leading them.

Plan of defence. They gather at east door. But [?south] door is propped ajar with wedges. Great arm and shoulder appear by the . . . . . door. Gandalf hews it with Glamdring. Frodo stabs foot with Sting. Horrible cry. Arrows whistle in through crack.

Orcs leap in but are killed.

[?Boom] as great rocks hit door.

They rush out through east door – opens outwards – and slam it. [?They fly] up a long wide tunnel. Noise soon shows east door is broken down. Pursuit is after them.

Here follows the loss of Gandalf.

In pencil in the margin against the account of the attack on the chamber is written:

Black-mailed orc leaps in and goes for Frodo with spear – he is saved by the elfmail and strikes down the orc.

This is a very striking example of an important narrative passage in *The Lord of the Rings* at its actual moment of emergence. Here as elsewhere many of the most essential elements were present from the first: the junction of three roads, Gandalf's doubt, the guardroom, the falling stone and the subterranean tapping that followed, the chamber of Balin's tomb, the writing in the book, the troll, and much else. That Gollum should be following them in Moria had been proposed in the outline given on p. 410: 'Gollum must reappear at or after Moria. Frodo hears patter.'

Gandalf's sword *Glamdring* (Foe-hammer), which he took from the trolls' lair and which (so Elrond told him) 'the king of Gondolin once wore', now reappears from *The Hobbit*.

Balin's father (Fundin in *The Hobbit* as in LR) is here surprisingly Burin; this dwarf-name (found in Old Norse) had previously been given to Balin's son, in the first drafts for 'The Council of Elrond' (pp. 395, 397), before he was replaced by Gimli son of Glóin (p. 400).

The story that Bilbo gave Sting and his 'elf-mail' to Frodo before he left Rivendell (FR pp. 290–1) entered in the sketch given on p. 397.

This is not the first reference to the loss of Gandalf; see p. 381, and for the first sketch of the event see p. 462.

This 'Sketch' begins when the Company is already inside Moria. For the story of their approach to the West Gate and the opening of the door there seems to be only the following by way of preparatory outline (though the 'dweller in the water' before the West Gate appears in the 'Sketch', p. 443, in the words of the book found in the chamber of Balin's tomb). It follows and was written at the same time as the sketch of the descent from the Red Pass in the snow (p. 431, note 1).

> Moria's west gates are dwarf-gates (closed like the Lonely Mountain); but openable not at a set time but by a [?special ?speech] spell. Gandalf knows or [?thinks] it must be one of [?three] in ancient tongue – for the Elves of Hollin wrought the spell.
>
> Holly bushes grow before these gates. Then Gandalf knows it is an elf-spell.

I give now the first draft text of the chapter. It was numbered from the outset 'XIV', presumably because my father had decided that 'The Ring Goes South' was a separate chapter and so should be numbered 'XIII', though he never wrote that number on the manuscript. My description of the text of 'The Ring Goes South' (p. 415) can be repeated here still more emphatically. The writing, again in ink not pencil, is even faster and more often indecipherable, the amount of rejected material (often not struck out) even greater; many passages are chaotic. There is also a certain amount of pencilled correction, probably made at different times, and some of it obviously belonging to a later stage. In one case, my father made a quite careful insertion in ink. saying that Gimli was of little help to Gandalf in finding a way through Moria (cf. FR p. 324), though he put in no mention of Gimli anywhere else. The text is thus difficult to interpret and still more difficult to represent.

It will be seen that the entire story of the attack by the Wargs in the night after the Company came down from the pass (FR pp. 310–13) is absent.

## THE MINES OF MORIA

Next day the weather changed again, almost as if it obeyed the orders of some power that had now given up the idea of snow, since they had retreated from Cris-caron. The wind had turned southward in the night. In the morning it was veering west, and rain was beginning to fall. The travellers pitched a tent in a sheltered hollow and remained quiet all the day till the afternoon was drawing towards evening.

All the day they had heard no sound and seen no sign of any living thing. As soon as the light began to fade they started off again. A light rain was still falling, but that did not trouble them much at first. Gandalf and Trotter led them in a detour away from the Mountains, for they planned to come at Moria up the course of a stream that ran out from the feet of the hills not far from the hidden gates. But it seemed that somehow or other they must have gone astray in the dark, for it was a black night under an overcast sky. In any case, they did not strike the stream, and morning found them wandering and floundering in wet and marshy places filled with red pools, for there was much clay in the hollows.[3]

They were somewhat comforted by a change in the weather: the clouds broke and the rain stopped. The sun came out in gleams. But Gandalf was fretted by the delay, and decided to move on again by day, after only a few hours' rest. There were no birds in the sky or other ominous signs. They steered now straight back towards the mountains, but both Gandalf and Trotter were much puzzled by their failure to find the stream.

When they had come back again to the foothills and lower slopes they struck a narrow watercourse in a deep channel; but it was dry, and there was now no water among [the] reddish stones in the bed. There was, however, still something like an open path on the left bank.

'This is where the stream used to run, I feel sure,' said Gandalf. 'Sirannon the Gatestream[4] they used to call it. Anyway our road lies up this course.' The night was now falling, but though they were already tired, especially the hobbits, Gandalf urged them to press on.

'Are you thinking of climbing to the top of the mountains tonight, in time to get an early view of the dawn?' asked Merry.

'I should think of it if there was any chance of doing it!' said Gandalf. 'But no one can scale the mountains here. The gates are not high up, but in a certain place near the foot of a great cliff. I hope I can find it – but things seem oddly changed, since I was last here.'

Before the night was old the moon, now only two days off the full,[5] rose through the clouds that lay on the eastern peaks, and shone fitfully down over the western lands. They trudged on with their weary feet stumbling among the stones, until suddenly they came to a wall of rock some thirty feet high. Over it ran a trickling fall of water, but plainly the fall had once been much stronger. 'Ah! Now I know where we are!' cried Gandalf. 'This is where the Stair-falls were. I wonder what has happened to them. But if I am right there is a stairway cut in the stone at the left: the main path goes further round and up an incline. There is or was a wide and shallow valley above the falls through which the Sirannon flowed.'

Very soon they found the stairway, and followed by Frodo and Trotter Gandalf climbed quickly up. When they got to the top they discovered the reason of the drying up of the stream.

The moon was now sinking westwards. It shone out brightly for a while, and they saw stretched before their feet a dark still lake, glinting in the moonlight. The Gate-stream had been dammed, and had filled all the valley. Only a trickle of water escaped over the old falls, for the main outlet of the lake was now away at the southern end.[6]

Before them, dim and grey across the dark water, stood a cliff. The moonlight lay pale upon it, and it looked cold and forbidding: a final bar to all passage. Frodo could see no sign of any gate or entrance in the frowning stone.

'This way is blocked!' said Gandalf. 'At least it is, as far as can be seen by night. I don't suppose anyone wants to try and swim across by moonlight – or any other light. The pool has an unwholesome look. When it was made or why I do not know, but not for any good purpose, I guess.'

'We must try and find a way round by the main path,' said Trotter. 'Even if there was no lake we could not get our ponies up the narrow stair.'

'And even if we could, they would not be able to go into the Mines,' said Gandalf. 'Our road there under the mountains will take us by paths where they cannot go – even if we can.'

'I wondered if you had thought of that drawback,' said Trotter. 'I supposed you had, though you did not mention it.'

'No need to mention it, until necessary,' answered the wizard. 'We will take them as far as we can. It remains to be seen if the [?other] road is not drowned as well: in which case we may not be able to get at the gates at all.'

'If the gates are still there,' said Trotter.

They had no great difficulty in finding the old path. It turned away from the falls and wound northward for some way, before bending east again, and climbed up a long slope. When they reached the top of this they saw the lake lying on the right. The path skirted its very edge, but was not submerged. For the most part it was just above the water; but in one place, at the northern-most end of the lake, where there was a slimy and stagnant pool, it disappeared for a short distance, before bending south again toward the foot of the great cliff.

When they reached this point Boromir went forward, and found that the path was only just awash. Carefully they threaded their way in single file behind him. The footing was slippery and treacherous; Frodo felt a curious disgust at the very feel of the dark water on his feet.

As Faramond the last of the party stepped onto the dry land, there was a soft sound, a swish followed by a plop, as if a fish had disturbed the still surface of the water. Turning swiftly they saw in the moonlight ripples sharpened [?with] dark shadows: great rings were widening outwards from some point near the middle of the pool.[7] They halted; and at that very moment the light went out, as the moon fell and vanished into low clouds. There was a soft bubbling noise in the lake, and then silence.

It was too dark to seek for the gate in that changed valley, and the rest of the night the travellers spent unhappily, sitting watch-ful between the cliff and the dark water which they could no longer see. None of them slept more than briefly and uneasily.

But with the morning their spirits revived. Slowly the light reached the lake: its dark surface was still and unruffled by any breeze. The sky was clear above, and slowly the sun rose above the mountains at their back, and shone on the western lands before them. They ate a little food, and rested for a while after the cheerless night, until the sun reached the south and its warm rays slanted down, driving away the shadows of the great wall behind. Then Gandalf stood up and said that it was high time to begin to search for the gates. The strip of dry land left by the lake was quite

narrow, and their path took them close under the face of the cliff.
When they had gone for almost a mile southward they came to
some holly-trees. There were stumps and dead logs rotting in the
water – the remains of old thickets, or of a hedge that had once
lined the submerged road across the drowned valley. But close
under the cliff there stood, still living and strong, two tall trees
with great roots that spread from the wall to the water's edge.
From far across under the other side in the fitful moon Frodo had
thought them mere bushes on piles of stone: but now they towered
above his head: stiff, silent, dark except for their clustered berries:
standing like sentinels or pillars at the end of a road.

'Well, here we are at last!' said Gandalf. 'This is where the elf-
way from Hollin ended. The holly-trees were planted by the elves
in the old days to mark the end of their domains – the westgates
were made chiefly for their use in their traffic with the dwarves.
This is the end of our path – and now I am afraid we must say
farewell to our ponies. The good beasts would go almost anywhere
we told them to; but I do not think we could get them to go into the
dark passages of Moria. And in any case there are behind the west
gate many steep stairs, and many difficult and dangerous places
where ponies could not pass, or would be a perilous handicap. If
we are to win through we must travel lighter. Much of the stuff we
have brought against bitter weather will not be wanted inside, nor
when we get to the other side and turn south.'

'But surely you aren't going to leave the poor beasts in this
forsaken place, Mr Gandalf!' protested Sam, who was specially
fond of ponies.

'Don't you worry, Sam! They'll find their way back home in
time. They have wiser noses even than most of their kind, and
these two have returned to Elrond from far away before now. I
expect they'll make off west and then work back northward
through country where they can find grass.'

'I'd be happier if I might lead them back past the wash and
down to the old falls,' said Sam, '– I'd like to sort of say goodbye
and set them on the road as it were.'

'Very well, you can,' said Gandalf. 'But first let us unlade them
and distribute the goods we mean to keep.'

When each member of the party had been given a share according to his size – most of the foodstuffs and the waterskins – the
remainder was secured again on the ponies' backs. In each bundle
Gandalf put a brief message to Elrond written in secret runes,
telling him of the snowstorm and their turning aside to Moria.

Then Sam and Trotter led the horses off.

'Now let us have a look at the gates!' said Gandalf.[8]

'I do not see any gates,' said Merry.

'Dwarf-gates are not made to be seen,' said the wizard. 'Many are quite invisible, and their own masters cannot find them if their secret is lost. But these gates were not made to be wholly[9] secret, and unless things are altogether changed eyes that know what to look for may discover the signs. Let us go and see!'

He strode forward to the cliff-wall. There was a smooth space right in the middle of the shade of the trees, and over this he passed his hands to and fro, muttering words under his breath. Then he stepped back. 'Look!' he said. 'Can you see anything now?' The sun shone across the face of the wall, and as the travellers stared at it, it seemed to them that on the surface where Gandalf's hand had passed faint lines appeared like slender veins of silver running in the stone; at first they seemed like pale threads of gossamer so fine as only to be seen fitfully where the sun caught them; but slowly they broadened and their design could be guessed. At the top, as high as Gandalf could reach, was an arch of interlacing letters in the elvish character; below it seemed (though the drawing was in places blurred and broken) that there was the outline of an anvil and hammer, and above that a crown and a crescent moon. More clearly than all else there shone forth palely three stars with many rays.[10]

'Those are the emblems of Durin and of the Elves,' said Gandalf. 'They are of some silver substance that is seen only when touched by one who knows certain words – at night under the moon they shine most bright.[11] Now you can see that we have certainly found the west gate of Moria.'

'What does the writing say?' asked Frodo, who was trying to puzzle out the inscription. 'I thought I knew the elf-letters, but I cannot read these, they are so tangled.'

'The words are in the elf-tongue, not in ordinary language,' said Gandalf. 'But they do not say anything of much importance to us. Certainly they don't tell the opening-spell, if that is what you are thinking. They merely say: The Doors of Durin Lord of Moria. Speak friends and enter. And underneath very small and now faint is: Narfi made them.[12] Celebrimbor of Hollin drew these signs.'

'What does it mean by "speak friends and enter"?' asked Frodo.

'That is plain enough,' said Gandalf, '– if you are friends speak the password, and then the door will open and you can enter. Some dwarf-gates will open only at special times, or for particular

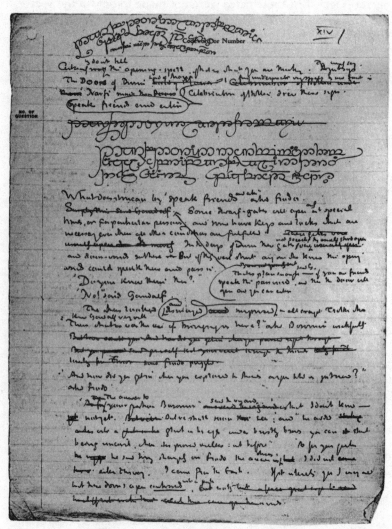

The inscription of the West Gate of Moria

persons; and some have keys and locks which are necessary even when all other conditions are fulfilled. In the days of Durin these gates were not secret: they usually stood open and door-wards sat here. But if they were shut anyone who knew the opening words could speak them and pass in.'

'Do you know them then?'

'No!' said Gandalf.

The others looked surprised and dismayed – all except Trotter, who knew Gandalf very well. 'Then what was the use of bringing us here?' asked Boromir wrathfully.

'And how did you get in when you explored the Mines, as you told us just now?' asked Frodo.

'The answer to your question, Boromir,' said the wizard, 'is that I don't know – not yet. But we shall soon see; and,' he added, with a glint in his eyes under bristling brows, 'you can start being uncivil, when it is proved useless: not before. As for your question,' he said, turning sharply on Frodo, 'the answer is obvious: I did not enter this way. I came from the East. If it interests you I may add that these doors open *outwards* with a push, but nothing can open them inwards. They can swing out, or they can be broken if you have enough force.'

'What are you going to do then?' asked Merry,[13] who was not much disturbed by Gandalf's bristling brows; and in his heart hoped that the doors would prove impossible to open.

'I am going to try and find the opening words. I once knew every formula and spell in any language of elves, dwarves, or goblins that was ever used for such purposes. I can still remember two or three hundreds without racking my brains. But I think only a few trials should be necessary. The opening words were in Elvish, like the written words – I feel certain: from the signs on the doors, from the holly trees, and because of the use for which the road and gates were originally made.' He stepped up to the rock and lightly touched with his wand the silver star that was near the middle of the emblems, just above the crown.

> *Annon porennin diragas·venwed*
> *diragath·telwen porannin nithrad*[14]

he said. The silver letters faded, but the grey blank stone did not stir. Many many times he tried other formulas one after another, but nothing further happened. Then he tried single words spoken in commanding tones, and finally (seeming to lose his temper) he

shouted *Édro, édro!* and followed it with *open!* in every language
he could remember. Then he sat down in silence.

Boromir was smiling broadly behind his back. 'It looks as if we
may be wanting those ponies back,' he said in an undertone. 'It
would have been wiser to have kept them till the gates were
open.'[15] If Gandalf heard he made no sign.

Suddenly in the silence Frodo heard a soft swish and bubble in
the water[16] as on the evening before, only softer. Turning quickly
he saw faint ripples on the surface of the lake – and at the same
time saw that Sam and Trotter in the distance [were] crossing
the wash on their return. The ripples on the water seemed to be
moving in their direction.

'I don't like this place,' said Merry, who had also seen the
ripples. 'I wish we could go back, or that Gandalf would do
something and we could go on – if we must.'

'I have a queer feeling,' said Frodo slowly, '– a dread either of
the gates or of something else. But I don't think Gandalf is
defeated: he is thinking hard, I fancy.'

It appeared that Frodo was right; for the wizard suddenly
sprang to his feet with a laugh. 'I have it!' he cried. 'Of course, of
course! Absurdly simple – when you think of it!' Raising his wand
he stood before the rock and said in a clear voice: *Mellyn!* (or
*Meldir!*)[17]

The three stars shone briefly and went out again. Then silently
a great door was outlined, though not the finest crack or joint had
been visible before. Slowly it began to swing outwards, inch by
inch until it lay right back against the wall.[18] Behind, the foot of a
shadowy stairway could be seen climbing up into the gloom
within. All the party stood and stared in wonder.

'I was wrong after all,' said Gandalf. 'The opening word was
inscribed there all the time. *Speak friends and enter* it said, and
when I spoke the elvish word for *friends*, it opened. Quite simple!
And now we can enter.'

But at that moment Frodo felt something seize his ankle and he
fell. At the same moment Sam and Trotter who had just come
back gave a yell as they ran up. Turning suddenly the others saw
that a long arm, sinuous as a tentacle, was thrust out from the
lake's dark edge. It was pale green-grey and wet: its fingered end
had hold of Frodo's foot and was dragging him towards the water.

Sam dashed up with a drawn knife and slashed at it. The fingers
let go of Frodo and Sam dragged him away; but immediately the
waters of the lake began to heave and boil, and twenty more

writhing arms came rippling out, making for the travellers as if directed by something in the deep pools that could see them all. 'Into the gateway! Quick! Up the stairs!' shouted Gandalf, rousing them from the horror that had held them rooted.

There was just time. Gandalf saw them all inside, and then sprang back upon the heels of Trotter, but he was no more than four steps up when the crawling fingers of the dweller in the pool reached the cliff.[19]

He paused. But if he was pondering how to close the door, or what word would move them from within, there was no need. For the arms seized the door, and with dreadful strength swung it round. With a shattering echo it slammed behind them; and they halted on the stairs in dismay as the sounds of rending and crashing came dully through the stones from outside. Gandalf ran down to the door and thrust up . . . . and spoke the . . . . words;[20] but though the door groaned it did not stir.

'I am afraid the door is blocked behind us now,' he said. 'If I guess right, the trees are thrown down across it, and boulders have been rolled against it. I am sorry for the trees – they were beautiful and old and had . . . . . so long.[21] Well now, we can only go on – there is nothing left to do.'

'I am mighty glad I saw those poor beasts safe first,' said Sam.

'I felt that something evil was near,' said Frodo. 'What was it, Gandalf?'

'I could not say,' said Gandalf, '– there was not time enough to look at the arms. They all belong to one creature, I should say, from the way they moved – but that is all I can say. Something that has . . . . . crept, or been driven out of the dark waters under ground, I guess. There are older and fouler things than goblins in the dark places of the world.' He did not speak aloud his uncomfortable thought that the Dweller in the Pool had not seized on Frodo among all the party by accident.[22]

Gandalf now went ahead and allowed his wand to glow faintly to prevent them from walking into unseen dangers in the dark. But the great stairway was sound and undamaged. There were two hundred steps, broad and shallow; and at the top they found the floor level before them.

'Let us have something to eat here on the landing, since we can't find a dining-room,' said Frodo. He had recovered from the terror of the clutching arm, and was feeling unusually hungry. The idea was welcome to all. After they had eaten Gandalf again gave them a taste of the cordial.

'It won't last much longer,' he said, 'but I think we need it after that business at the gate. And we shall need all that is left before we get through, unless we have luck. Go carefully with the water too! There are streams and wells in the Mines, but they should not be touched. We shan't get a chance of filling our bottles till we come down in Dunruin.'[23]

'How long are we going to take to get through?' asked Frodo.

'I don't know that,' answered Gandalf. 'It all depends. But going straight (without mishaps, or losing our way) we should take at least three or four marches. It cannot be less than forty miles from West-doors to Eastgate in a straight line, and we may not find the most direct passages.'

They rested now only for a short while, as all were eager to get the journey over as quickly as possible, and were willing, tired as they were, to go on still for several hours. They had no fuel or means of making torches, and would be obliged to find the way mostly in the dark.[24] Gandalf went in front holding in his left hand his wand, the pale light of which was sufficient to show the ground before his feet. In his right hand he held the sword Glamdring, which he had kept ever since it was discovered in the trolls' lair.[25] No gleam came from it – which was some comfort; for being a sword of ancient elvish make it shone with a cold light, if goblins were at hand.

He led them forward first along the passage in which they had halted. As the light of his wand dimly lit their dark openings other passages and tunnels could be seen or guessed: sloping up, or running steeply down, or turning suddenly round hidden corners. It was most bewildering. Gandalf was guided mainly by his general sense of direction: and anyone who had been on a journey with him knew that he never lost that by dark or day, underground or above it: being better at steering in a tunnel than a goblin, and less likely to be lost in a wood than a hobbit, and surer of finding the way through night as black as the Pit than the cats of Queen Beruthiel.[26] Had that not been so, it is more than doubtful if the party would have gone a mile without disaster. For there were not only many paths to choose from, there were in many places pits at the sides of the tunnel, and dark wells in which far under the gurgling of water could be heard. Rotting strands of rope dangled above them from broken winches. There were dangerous chasms and fissures in the rock, and sometimes a chasm would open right across their path. One was so wide that Gandalf himself nearly stumbled into it. It was quite ten feet wide, and Sam stumbled in his jump and would have fallen back on the further bank if Frodo had not grabbed his hand and [?jerked] him forward.

Their march was slow, and it began to feel never-ending. They grew very weary; and yet there was no comfort in the thought of halting anywhere. Frodo's spirits had risen for a while after his escape from the water-monster; but now a deep sense of disquiet, growing to dread, crept over him once more. Though he had been healed in Rivendell of the knife stroke, it is probable that that grim adventure had left its mark, and that he was specially sensitive; and in any case he it was that bore the Ring upon its chain against his breast.[27] He felt the certainty of evil ahead, and of evil following. But he said nothing.

The travellers spoke seldom and then only in hurried whispers. There was no sound but the sound of their own feet. If they stopped for a moment they heard nothing at all, unless it were occasionally a faint sound of water trickling or dripping. Only Frodo began to hear or imagine that he heard something else: like the faint fall of soft feet following. It was never loud or near enough for him to feel certain that he heard it; but once it had started it never stopped, unless they did. And it was not an echo, for when they halted (as they did from time to time) it pattered on for some time, and then grew still.

It was about 10 o'clock in the morning when they entered the Mines.[28] They had been going for many hours (with brief halts) when Gandalf came to his first serious doubt. They had come to a wide dark arch opening into three passages: all three led in the same general direction, East, but the left hand passage seemed to plunge down, the right hand to climb up, while the middle way seemed to run level (but was very narrow).

'I have no memory of this place at all!' said Gandalf, standing uncertainly under the arch. He held up his wand in the hope of finding some direction marks or an inscription that might help. But nothing of the kind was to be seen.

'I am too tired to choose,' he said, shaking his head; 'and I expect you are all as weary as I am or wearier. We had better halt here for the night – if you know what I mean. It is all night of course inside, but outside I fancy the night is already come. It is quite ten hours since we left the gate.'[29]

They groped about in the darkness looking for a place where they could rest with some feeling of security. To the left of the great arch was a lower opening, and when they explored it closer they discovered that it was a stone door that was half closed, but swung back easily to a gentle thrust. Beyond there seemed to be a chamber or chambers cut in the rock.

'Steady, steady!' said Gandalf as Merry and Faramond pushed forward, glad to find somewhere where they could rest with some sort of security. 'Steady! You don't know what may be inside. I will go first.'

He went cautiously in followed by the rest. 'There!' he said, pointing with his wand to the middle of the floor. They saw before their feet a round hole like the mouth of a well. Rotting strands of rope lay at the edge and trailed down into the dark pit; fragments of broken stone lay near.

'One of you might have fallen in and still be waiting to hit the bottom,' said the wizard to Merry. 'Look before your feet! this seems to have been a kind of guard-room placed to watch those passages,' he went on. 'The hole I expect is a well, and was doubtless once covered with a stone lid. But that is broken now, and you had better be careful of the fall.'

Sam[30] felt curiously attracted by the well; and while the others were making beds of blankets in dark corners of the room, as far as possible from the well, he crept to the edge and peered over. A chill air seemed to mount up to his face from the invisible depths. Moved by a sudden impulse, he groped for a loose stone, and let it drop.

It seemed almost a whole minute before there was any sound – then far below there was a *plunk*, as if the stone had fallen into deep water in a cavernous place – very distant, but magnified and repeated in the hollow rock.

'What's that?' cried Gandalf. He was relieved when Sam confessed what he had done; but he was angry, and Sam could see his eyes glint in the dark. 'Fool of a fellow!' he growled. 'This is a serious journey, not a hobbit school treat. Throw yourself in next time, and then you'll be no further nuisance. Now be quiet!'

There was nothing to hear for several minutes; but then there came out of the depths faint knocks, that stopped, and were dimly echoed, and then after a short silence were repeated. It sounded strangely like signals of some sort. But after a while the knocks died away altogether and were heard no more.

'It may have nothing to do with that stone,' said Gandalf; 'and in any case it may have nothing to do with us – but of course it may be anything. Don't do anything like that again. Let's hope we get some rest undisturbed. You Sam can go on the first watch. And stay near the door, well away from the well,' he grunted, as he rolled himself in a blanket.

Sam sat miserably by the door in the pitch dark, but kept on turning round, for fear some unknown thing should crawl out of the well. He wished he could cover the hole, if only with a blanket; but he dared not go near, even though Gandalf seemed to be snoring.

Gandalf was actually not asleep, and the snores came from Boromir, who lay next him. The wizard was thinking hard again trying to recall every memory he could of his former journey in the Mines, and trying to make up his mind about the next course to take. After about an hour he got up and came over to Sam.

'Get into a blanket and have a sleep, my lad!' he said in a more kindly tone. 'You could sleep, I guess. I can't, so I may as well do the watching.'

'I know what is the matter with me,' he muttered. 'I need a pipe; and I think I'll risk it.' The last thing Sam saw before sleep took him was a vision of the old wizard squatting on the floor shielding a blazing chip in his gnarled hands between his knees. The flicker for a moment showed his sharp nose and the puffs of smoke.

It was Gandalf who roused them all from sleep. He had watched all alone for about six hours and let the others rest. 'And in the meantime I have made up my mind,' he said. 'I don't like the feel of the middle way, and I don't like the smell of the left hand – there is foul air down there, or I am no guide. I shall take the right hand way – it's time we began to go up again.'

For eight dark hours, not counting two brief halts, they marched on, and met no danger, and heard nothing and saw nothing but the faint gleam of the wizard's light bobbing like a will-o'-the-wisp in front of them. The passage they had chosen wound steadily upwards, going, as far as they could judge, in great curves, and growing steadily wider. On neither side were there now any openings to other galleries or tunnels, and the floor, though rough in many places, was sound and without pits or cracks. They went quicker than the day before, and must have covered some twenty miles or more, perhaps fifteen in a straight line eastwards. As they went upwards Frodo's spirits rose a little; but still he felt oppressed, and still at times he heard or thought he heard away behind and through the patter of their own feet a following footfall that was not an echo.

They had gone nearly as far as the hobbits could endure without rest and sleep, and they were all thinking of a place to halt for the night, when suddenly the walls to right and left vanished. They halted. Gandalf seemed well pleased. 'I think we have reached the habitable parts,' he said, 'and are no great way from the eastern side. I can feel a change in the air, and guess we are in a wide hall. I think I will risk a little light.'[31]

He raised his wand and for a brief moment it blazed out like a flash of lightning. Great shadows leapt up and fled, and for a second or two they saw a vast roof high above their heads. On every side stretched a huge empty hall with straight hewn walls. Four entrances they glimpsed: dark arches in the walls: one at the west by which they had come, one before them in the east, and one on either side. Then the light went out.

'That is all I shall venture on for the present,' said the wizard. 'There used to be great windows on the mountain-side, and shafts leading out to the light and the upper reaches of the mines. I think that is where we are. But it is night now, and we cannot tell till morning. If I am right, tomorrow we may actually see the morning peeping in. But in the meanwhile we had better go no further without exploration. There will still be a good way to go before we are through – the East Gates are on a much lower level than this, and it is a long road down. Let us rest if we can.'

They spent that night in the great empty hall, huddled in a corner to escape the draught – there seemed to be a steady flow of chill air in through the eastern archway. The vastness and immensity of the tunnels and excavations filled the hobbits with bewilderment.[32] 'There must have been a mighty tribe o' dwarves here at one time,' said Sam; 'and every one as busy as a badger for a hundred years to make all this – and most in hard rock too. What did they do it all for? They didn't live in these darksome holes, surely?'

'Not for long,' said Gandalf;[33] 'though the miners often took long spells underground, I believe. They found precious metals, and jewels – very abundantly in the earlier days. But the mines were most renowned for the metal which was only found here in any quantity: Moria-silver, or true-silver as some call it. *Ithil*[34] the Elves call it, and value it still above gold.[35] It is nearly as heavy as lead, and malleable as copper, but the dwarves could by some secret of theirs make it as hard as steel. It surpasses common silver in all save beauty, and even in that it is its equal. In their day the dwarflords of Uruktharbun[36] were more wealthy than any of the Kings of Men.'

'Well, *we* haven't clapped eyes on any kind of silver since we came in,' grunted Sam; 'nor any jewels neither. Nor on any dwarves.'

'I don't think we are likely to until we get further up[37] and nearer to the eastern entrances,' said Gandalf.

'I hope we do find dwarves in the end,' said Frodo. 'I would give a great deal to see old Balin. Bilbo was fond of him and would be delighted to have news of him. He visited him in Hobbiton once long ago, but that was before I went to live there.'

But these words carried his thoughts far away from the darkness; and memories of Bag-end while Bilbo was still there crowded [?thickly] into his mind. He wished with all his heart that he was back there, mowing the lawn, or pottering among the flowers, and that he had never heard of the Ring.[38] It was his turn to watch. As silence fell and one by one the others fell asleep he felt the strange dread assail him again. But though he listened endlessly through the slow hours till he was relieved he heard no sound of any footfall. Only once, far away where he guessed the western archway stood, he fancied he saw two pale points of light – almost like luminous eyes. He started – 'I must have nearly fallen asleep,' he thought; 'I was on the edge of a dream.' He rubbed his eyes and stood up, and remained standing peering into the dark until he was relieved by Merry. He quickly fell asleep, but after a while it seemed to him in his dream that he heard whispers, and saw two pale points of light approaching. He woke – and found that the others were speaking softly near him, and that a dim light was actually falling on his face. High up above the eastern arch, through a shaft near the roof, came a grey gleam. And across the hall through the northern arch light also glimmered faint and distantly.

Frodo sat up. 'Good morning!' said Gandalf. 'For morning it is again at last. I was right, you see. Before today's over we ought to get to the Eastern Gate and see the waters of Helevorn in the Dimrilldale before us.'[39]

All the same the wizard felt some doubt as to their exact position – they might be far to the north or the south of the Gates. The eastern arch was the most likely exit to choose, and the draught that flowed through it seemed to promise a passage leading before long to the outer air; but beyond the opening there was no trace of light. 'If I could only see out of one of these shafts,' he said, 'I should know better what to do. We might wander backwards and forwards endlessly, and just miss the way out. We had better explore a little before we start. And let us go first towards the light.'

Passing under the northern arch they went down a wide

corridor and as they went the glimmer of light grew stronger. Turning a sharp corner they came to a great door on their right. It was half open, and beyond there was a large square chamber. It was only dimly lit, but to their eyes, after so long in the dark, it seemed almost dazzlingly light, and they blinked as they entered. Their feet disturbed deep dust and stumbled amongst things lying on the floor within the doorway whose shapes they could not at first make out.

They saw now that the chamber was lit by a wide shaft high up in the far wall – it slanted upwards and far above a small square patch of sky could be seen where it issued outwards. The light fell directly on a table in the midst of the chamber, a square block some three feet high upon which was laid a great slab of whitened stone.

'It looks like a tomb!' [muttered >] thought Frodo, and went forward to look at it more closely with a curious sense of foreboding. Gandalf came quickly to his side. On the slab was deeply cut in Runes:[40]

### BALIN SON OF BURIN LORD OF MORIA

Gandalf and Frodo looked at one another. 'He is dead then. I feared it somehow,' said Frodo.

Although the outline for the story of the passage of Moria continues well beyond this point (p. 443), this first draft of the narrative stopped here. My father pencilled some barely legible notes on the blank remainder of the page, and years later (when, as I think, the page had become detached from the rest of the chapter: see note 40) he deciphered them as follows.

Balin son of *Burin* was changed to Balin son of *Fundin*, as in *The Hobbit* (see p. 444).

At the end of the narrative in ink is written, as in FR: 'Gimli cast his hood over his face.'

'Runes of ?Dwarves'

'(they) look about and see broken swords and ?axe-heads and cloven shields'

'The ?trodden book is bloodstained & tossed in a corner. Only some can be read. Balin was slain in ?fray in Dimrill dale. They have taken the gates they are coming'

On the back of the page is a first scribbled sketch of a 'Page of Balin's Book' (see note 40).

It may be that my father did not at this time feel that he had reached the end of a chapter, and intended to continue the story; but it is known from his own words in the Foreword to the Second Edition (1966), in which he set down some recollections of the stages in the writing of the book, that he stopped for a long time at precisely this point. He said there that by the end of 1939 'the tale had not yet reached the end of Book I' (and it is clear that he referred to Book I of FR, not to Volume I of *The Lord of the Rings*); and that

> In spite of the darkness of the next five years I found that the story could not now be wholly abandoned, and I plodded on, mostly by night, till I stood by Balin's tomb in Moria. There I halted for a long while. It was almost a year later when I went on and so came to Lothlórien and the Great River late in 1941.

This can only mean that the story was broken off in Moria late in 1940.

It seems impossible to accommodate these dates to such other evidence as exists on the subject. I think it extremely probable, even virtually certain, that these last chapters, taking the story from Rivendell to Moria, belong to the latter part of 1939; and indeed my father himself said, in a letter to Stanley Unwin dated 19 December 1939, that he had 'never quite ceased work' on *The Lord of the Rings*, and that 'it has reached Chapter XVI' (*Letters* no. 37). The chapter-numbers at this stage are unfortunately so erratic that the evidence they provide is very difficult to use; but when it is observed that the number 'XV' was pencilled on the original manuscript of 'The Council of Elrond', and that the chapter which afterwards continued the story from the point where the present text ends – originally called 'The Mines of Moria (ii)' and afterwards 'The Bridge of Khazad-dûm' – is numbered 'XVII', it seems probable that it was to 'The Mines of Moria' that my father referred in the letter of December 1939. In any case 'Chapter XVI' could not by any reckoning be one of the chapters of Book I in FR. I feel sure, therefore, that – more than a quarter of a century later – he erred in his recollection of the year. But it would be out of the question that he should err in his recollection that he 'halted for a long while by Balin's tomb in Moria.' Internal evidence in any case suggests that the 'wave' of composition which had carried the story from the Council of Elrond to the chamber of Balin's tomb came to an end here. All subsequent texts rest on a developed form of the Council and a different composition of the Company of the Ring.

There this history halts also. But before ending there remains another outline scrap, found on the same isolated page as bears the preliminary sketches for the descent from the Red Pass (p. 431, note 1) and the spell that held the West Gate of Moria (p. 444). It is in fact a continuation of the 'Sketch of the Moria chapter' given on pp. 442–3, which ends with the words: 'Pursuit is after them. Here follows the loss of Gandalf.' Written in a faint pencilled scribble it is extremely difficult to read.

They are pursued by goblins and a B[lack] R[ider] [*written above:* a Balrog] after escaping from Balin's Tomb – they come to a bridge of slender stone over a gulf.

Gandalf turns back and holds off [?enemy], they cross the bridge but the B[lack] R[ider] leaps forward and wrestles with Gandalf. The bridge cracks under them and the last they see is Gandalf falling into the pit with the B[lack] R[ider]. There is a flash of fire and blue light up from abyss.

Their grief. Trotter now guides party.

(Of course Gandalf must reappear later – probably fall is not as deep as it seemed. Gandalf thrusts Balrog under him and so . . . . . . . and eventually following the subterranean stream in the gulf he found a way out – but he does not turn up until they have had many adventures: not indeed until they are on [?borders] of Mordor and the King of Ond is being beaten in battle.)

This seems to show clearly that before ever the story of the fall of Gandalf from the Bridge of Khazad-dûm was written, my father fully intended that he should return.

## NOTES

1   To this point the text of this 'Sketch' was struck through, but the remainder was not.

2   See p. 437, note 35; and cf. the corresponding passage in FR (p. 338), where Gandalf says: 'There are Orcs, very many of them. And some are large and evil: black Uruks of Mordor.'

3   In FR (p. 313) the Company moved south towards Moria by day, and they 'wandered and scrambled in a barren country of red stones. Nowhere could they see any gleam of water . . .'

4   My father first wrote here (changing it at once): '*Caradras dilthen* the Little Redway'. For *Caradras* as the name of the river Redway (later Silverlode) on the other side of the Mountains see p. 433, note 15.

5   It was now the night of 5 December, and full moon was on the 7th (see p. 434, note 19).

6   This sentence was enclosed within square brackets, and the concluding words 'from whence they heard the splash of running water' struck out. These changes belong with the writing of the manuscript.

7   Though the word 'pool' is used, the reference is clearly to the lake and not to the 'pool' which they had just walked through. The 'soft bubbling noise' comes from the 'lake'.

8   The whole passage from 'Well, here we are at last' on p. 448 to this
    point is a rider on a slip, replacing the following in the original text:
        'Here is the gate,' said Gandalf. 'This is where the road from
        Hollin ended, and the elves planted these trees in old days; for the
        west-gates were made chiefly for their use in their traffic with the
        dwarves.'
    The replacement certainly belongs with the first writing of the
    chapter, for the dispatch of the ponies by Sam and Trotter is
    subsequently referred to in the text as written.

9   The word 'wholly' is enclosed in square brackets.

10  In FR (p. 318) the hammer and anvil are 'surmounted by a crown
    with seven stars', and 'more clearly than all else there shone forth in
    the middle of the door a single star with many rays.' The original
    draft has no mention of the two trees bearing crescent moons.

11  In FR the inscription on the doors is of *ithildin* which mirrors only
    starlight and moonlight (p. 318). In this original draft, of course,
    the time-scheme is different – the middle of the day, not early night
    (see note 28).

12  This was first written: 'Narfi made the Doors'.

13  Merry replaced Frodo, who replaced Boromir; it was apparently
    said of Boromir that he was not much disturbed by Gandalf's
    bristling brows, and that he secretly wished that the doors might
    stay shut.

14  I cannot interpret this. In FR (p. 320) Gandalf's invocation means:
    'Elvish gate open now for us; doorway of the Dwarf-folk listen to the
    word [*beth*] of my tongue.'

15  The text of this passage, from 'Then he sat down in silence', as first
    written read:
        Only Trotter seemed troubled. Boromir was smiling broadly
        behind his back. Sam ventured to whisper in Frodo's ear: 'I've
        never seen old Gandalf at a loss for words before,' he said. 'It
        looks as if we were not *meant* to pass these gates, somehow.'
        'I have a feeling of dread,' said Frodo slowly, 'either of the gates
        or of something else. But I do not think Gandalf is beaten – he is
        thinking hard, I fancy.'
    Subsequently Sam's whispered speech to Frodo was given to
    Merry, with the addition: 'He ought not to have sent off the ponies
    till he got them open.'

16  Written in pencil here: 'Sound of wolves far off at same time as swish
    in water'. But this would have been added when the time of their
    entry into the Mines had been altered; cf. FR p. 321 and note 28.

17  These words were struck out in pencil and the form *Melin* substi-
    tuted. In the *Etymologies* (V.372), stem MEL, are given Noldorin
    *mellon* and *meldir* 'friend', and also Quenya *melin* 'dear'.

18  In FR there are two doors; and despite the single door described
    here, the inscription bears the words 'The Doors of Durin'; Gandalf

tells them: 'these doors open outwards, but nothing can open them inwards. They can swing out, or they can be broken . . .'

19  As first written (and not struck out) this passage read: 'They had just time; Trotter who came last was not more than four steps up when the arms of the creature in the water came feeling and fingering the wall.'

20  In the first of these lacunas the text seems to read *in it*, or possibly *with* (in which case *his wand* was omitted; cf. FR p. 322, 'he thrust his staff against the doors'). In the second, the word looks like *open* (perhaps for *opening*).

21  The illegible word is just a series of wiggles; certainly not *stood*, the word here in FR. Just possibly, *survived*.

22  The actual reading here is '– not by accident'. The sentence was enclosed in square brackets at the time of writing, but a similar sentence remains in FR.

23  *Dunruin* replaced, apparently at the time of writing, *Carondoom* (see p. 433, note 13). Subsequently *Dimrilldale* was written in in pencil.

24  This sentence was a replacement (to all appearance made at the time of writing; see note 31) of: 'In the confusion of the attack at the Westgate some of the bundles and packages had been left on the ground; but they had still with them one bundle of torches which they had brought with them in case of need, but never yet used.'

25  The words following *Glamdring* are enclosed in square brackets. Glamdring has appeared in the 'Sketch' for the chapter; see pp. 442–4.

26  This sentence was changed in the act of writing, the successive stages not being crossed out: 'than any cat that ever walked', 'than is the cat of Benish Armon', 'than the cats of Queen [?Tamar >] Margoliantë   Beruthiel' – both these names being left to stand.

27  The original passage that follows here was enclosed in square brackets and later struck out in pencil:

While the others were trying to keep up their spirits with hopeful talk, and were asking whispered questions concerning the lands [*struck out:* of Dunruin and Fangorn] beyond the mountains, the vale of Redway, the forest of Fangorn, and beyond, he felt the certainty . . .

This derives from the 'Sketch' for the chapter (see p. 442).

28  In the 'Sketch' (p. 442) it is said, as here, that 'it was about 10 o'clock in the morning' when they entered the Mines. This does not agree with what is said on p. 447, that when 'the sun *reached the south*' Gandalf 'stood up and said that it was high time to begin to search for the gates', and the sun was shining across the face of the cliff when he made the signs appear. This suggests that the door was opened in the early afternoon. The sentence in the text here was altered in pencil to 'five o'clock in the evening', but it is hard to say

to what form of the story this refers. In FR it was fully dark – 'the countless stars were kindled' – when they entered the Mines (pp. 320, 326), and though it was early December it was surely after five o'clock. A few lines below in the present text, however, another change in the time-scheme clearly introduces that of FR; see note 29.

29 The words 'the night is already come' were changed in pencil to 'the night is already old'; and the following sentence, which had been enclosed in square brackets, was struck out. As written, the text agrees with the story that they went into the Mines at about ten in the morning – it would now be about 8 p.m. (see note 28). As changed, it agrees with FR, p. 326 ('outside the late Moon is riding westward and the middle-night has passed').

30 'Sam' replaced 'Merry' at the time of writing, since at the end of this episode it is Sam, not changed from Merry, who takes the first watch as a punishment for casting the stone into the well.

31 This passage was much changed in the course of composition. At first 'Gandalf allowed two torches to be lit to help in exploration. Their light found no roof, but was sufficient to show that they had come (as they had guessed) into a wide space high and broad like a great hall.' It has however been said, by a change apparently made during the initial composition (see note 24), that they had neither torches nor means of making them.

32 The passage in FR p. 329 from 'All about them as they lay hung the darkness . . .' to 'the actual dread and wonder of Moria' was first drafted in the margin of the manuscript here, perhaps quite soon after the writing of the main text.

33 'Gandalf' is an early emendation from 'Trotter', and in the following speech.

34 *Ithil* is an early, perhaps immediate, change from *Erceleb*.

35 This passage was changed in the act of writing from:
     – very abundantly in the earlier days, and especially the silver. Moria-silver was (and still is) renowned; and many held it a precious
This is where the conception of *mithril* first emerged, though not yet the name (see note 34). The reference to *mithril* in *The Hobbit* (Chapter XIII, 'Not at Home') entered in the third edition of 1966: until then the text read: 'It was of silvered-steel, and ornamented with pearls, and with it went a belt of pearls and crystals.' This was changed to: 'It was of silver-steel, which the elves called *mithril*, and with it went a belt of pearls and crystals.'

36 Against *Uruktharbun* is pencilled *Azanulbizâr*, which in FR is the Dwarvish name of Dimrill-dale. If *Uruktharbun* is Moria (and the next revision of this text has 'the dwarflords of Khazad-dûm'), *Azanulbizâr* may have been intended to replace it and to have referred at first to Moria; on the other hand, my father may perhaps

have wished to name the 'dwarflords' as lords in the Dimrill-dale. It may be mentioned that placed in this manuscript, though written on different paper and presumably belonging to a later stage when Gimli had become a member of the Company, is a sheet of primary workings for his song in Moria; and in these occur the lines:

> When Durin came to Azanûl
> and found and named the nameless pool.

In notes written years later (after the publication of *The Lord of the Rings*) my father observed that 'the interpretation of the Dwarf names (owing to scanty knowledge of Khuzdul) is largely uncertain, except that, since this region [i.e. Moria and Dimrill-dale] was originally a Dwarf-home and primarily named by them, the Sindarin and Westron names are probably in origin of similar senses.' He interpreted (hesitantly) *Azanulbizar* as containing zn 'dark, dim', *ûl* 'streams', and *bizar* a dale or valley, the whole thus meaning 'Vale of Dim Streams'.

The name *Khazad-dûm* had already appeared in the *Quenta Silmarillion* (V.274), where it was the name of the Dwarf-city in the Blue Mountains which the Elves called *Nogrod*.

37 The word *up* here is odd (and my father later put a query against it), since the statement that the East Gates were on a much lower level than the great hall where they now were is part of the original composition.

38 This passage survives in FR (pp. 331–2), but there Frodo's thoughts turn to Bilbo and Bag End for a different reason – the mention by Gandalf of Bilbo's corslet of mithril-rings. Moria-silver had only just emerged (note 35), and the connection with Bilbo's mailcoat had not been made.

39 In the previous chapter the name *Dimrilldale* appears as a correction (p. 433, note 13), together with the first mention of the lake in the dale, there called *Glassmere*; *Mirrormere* is named on the map reproduced on p. 439. The Elvish name *Helevorn* (in the *Etymologies*, V.365, translated 'black-glass') given to it here had appeared in the *Quenta Silmarillion* as the name of the lake in Thargelion beside which dwelt Cranthir, son of Fëanor. No other Elvish name for Mirrormere is recorded in published writing, but in the notes referred to in note 36 my father said that the Sindarin name, not given in LR, was in fact *Nen Cenedril* 'Lake Looking-glass'. Translating *Kheled-zâram* as 'probably "glass-pool"', he noted: '*kheled* was certainly a Dwarf word for "glass", and seems to be the origin of Sindarin *heleð* "glass". Cf. Lake *Hele(ð)vorn* near the Dwarf-regions in the north of Dor Caranthir [Thargelion]: it means "black glass", and is probably also a translation of a Dwarf-name (given by the Dwarves: the same is probably the case in the Moria region) such as *Narag-zâram* (that nrg was Khuzdul for ("black" is seen in the Dwarf-name for Mordor: *Nargûn*).'

40   As the manuscript of this chapter was found among my father's
papers it ended at the foot of a page, at the words 'a great slab of
whitened stone' on p. 460. I had assumed that this was where my
father broke off, until, a few days before the typescript of this book
was due to go to the printers, I came most unexpectedly upon a
further page, beginning at the words '"It looks like a tomb!" thought
Frodo', which had evidently been separated from the rest of the
chapter long ago, on account of the inscriptions. It was of course
too late to reproduce these in this book, but an account of the runic
alphabets as my father conceived them at this time and of the writing
on Balin's tomb and in the Book of Mazarbul will, I hope, be
published in Volume VII.

It may be noticed here, however, that it was at this point that my
father decided to abandon the Old English (or 'Hobbit') runes and
to use the real runes of Beleriand, which were already in a developed
form. The inscription on the tomb (*Balin Son of Burin Lord of
Moria*) was first written in the former, and then immediately below
in 'Angerthas', twice, with the same words but in runes that differ in
certain points.

On the back of this newly discovered page, and as I think very
probably dating from the same time, is a very roughly pencilled
design of a 'Page of Balin's Book', in runes representing English
spelt phonetically, which reads thus:

> We drove out the Orcs fro(m) . . . guard
> . . . . (f)irst hall. We slew many under the bright sun
> in the dale. Flói was killed by an arrow . . . . . . . . .
> We did . . . . . . . . . . . . . . . . . . . . . . . . . . . . . . . . . .
> . . . . . . . . . We have occupied the twenty-first hall of
> . . . . . . north end. There there is . . . . . . . . . . . . . .
> . . . . . . . . . . . . . . . shaft is . . . . . . . . . . . . . . .
> (B)alin has set up his chair in the chamber of Mazar
> bul . . . . . . . . . . . . . . . . . . . . . . . . Balin is Lord of
> Moria . . . . . . . . . . . . . . . . . . . . . . . . . . . . . . . . .

And on the right-hand bottom corner of the page, torn off from the
rest, is the name *Kazaddūm*.

# INDEX

This Index is made on the same lines as those of the previous volumes, but the extreme fluidity of names in this case, especially among the hobbits, has proved taxing, as a glance at the entries under *Took* will show. The complexity of the matter to be indexed scarcely allows of a consistent presentation.

Certain names appear constantly throughout the book, and where possible I have reduced the more intimidating blocks of references by using the word *passim* to mean that a name is missing only from a single page here and there in a long series.

Forms are standardized, and no account is taken of the innumerable variants in capitalization, hyphenation, and separation of elements that occur in the texts.

Names appearing in the reproductions of pages from the original manuscripts are not indexed.

*Birthday Party* See *Party.*

*Black Country* Mordor. 131, 216, 218; *Black Land* 129, 131

*Black Gulf* Moria. 429, 435, 437; *Black Pit* 435

*Black Mountains* Range south of the Misty Mountains. 410–11, 436, 440. See *Blue Mountains, South Mountains.*

*Black Riders* (including references to *Riders, (black) horsemen, black men,* &c.) 44, 48, 54–5, 58, 60, 63–4, 66–7, 69–71, 73, 84, 87–91, 95–7, 100, 103–4, 106, 109, 118–20, 126, 129, 131, 151–5, 157–63, 171–6, 178, 185–6, 188–91, 194–9, 207–8, 211–13, 217–18, 221–5, 269, 272, 277–9, 281–2, 285, 287–8, 291–3, 295, 297, 301, 303, 324–6, 328, 336, 339–44, 347–50, 353–68 *passim*, 371–3, 381, 401, 408, 416, 462. See *Ring-wraiths, (the) Nine.*

*Black Tower* 218, 253. See *Dark Tower.*

*Blessed Realm* 182–4, 187, 225, 364, 394, 398–9; *Blessed Realms* 187

*Bliscarn* Early name for Caradhras. 433, 438

*Blue Mountains* (1) Eredlindon. 466. (2) Range south of the Misty Mountains. 410–11, 436, 440. See *Black Mountains, South Mountains.*

*Bob* The ostler at Bree. 135, 164, 174, 345–7; also called *Rob*, 164, 174

*Boffin family* 25, 31; *Boffinses* 13–14, 18, 23, 31; *Boffins* 22, 284, 304, 313, 385; *Boffin-country* 298; *Mr Boffin of Overhill* 254, 284

*Boffin, Fosco* Cousin of Bilbo; son of Jago Boffin. 317, 319, 386

~ *Hugo* Husband of Donnamira Took. 317–18, 386

~ *Jago* Son of Donnamira Took and Hugo Boffin. 317, 386

~ *Paladin* Father of Peregrin Boffin. 385–6

~ *Peregrin* Grandson of Donnamira Took; known in Bree as *Trotter.* 371, 373–4, 376, 384–7, 392–3, 395–6, 406, 412, 415, 422, 430–1; called *Perry* 393

*Bofur* Dwarf, companion of Thorin Oakenshield. 210

*Bolger family, Bolgers* 31, 33, 49, 78, 96, 267, 284, 304

*Bolger, Bingo* Bingo Bolger-Baggins before his adoption by Bilbo. 36–7, 40

~ *Caramella* A relative of Bilbo's (formerly a Took, subsequently a Chubb). 32, 35, 38

~ *Fosco* Bingo's somnolent uncle. 38, 51, 65, 247

~ *Fredegar* Called *Fatty.* 112, 273, 275, 299, 301, 326, 373

~ *Hamilcar* 373. (Replaced by *Fredegar Bolger.*)

~ *Odo* (including all references to Odo both as Took and later as Bolger, see p. 267 note 3). 41–66 *passim*, 69–70, 74, 83, 88–104, 106, 109–10, 112–13, 115, 118, 125, 127–8, 130, 136–9, 141, 148, 155–6, 160–1, 163, 166–9, 171–2, 177, 185, 209, 221–2, 250–1, 267, 273, 275–80, 283–95 *passim*, 299–305, 316–18, 323–8, 330, 336–57 *passim*, 359, 361, 364–8, 371–5, 395–8, 409, 413. Called *Odo Took-Bolger* 316–17, 323; passes as 'Baggins' 339–41, 347, 352, 356, 366, 368, 375

323–4, 326–30, 334, 341, 353–8, 361, 365–8, 370–1, 373–5, 395, 397–8, 406–10, 419, 423, 427, 429, 436, 446, 449, 451–2, 456, 459, 463, 465. (Replaced *Marmaduke Brandybuck*.)

~ *Orlando* 26, 35. (Replaced by *Prospero Brandybuck*.)

~ *Primula* 26, 29, 35, 37–8, 40, 42, 221, 234, 244, 247, 249, 267, 317–18, 386; as Bilbo's wife 29, 40

~ *Prospero* 24, 26, 32, 35. (Replaced *Orlando Brandybuck*, replaced by *Prospero Took*.)

~ *Roderick* = Rory Brandybuck. 317–18

~ *Rorimac* = Rory Brandybuck (in LR). 318

~ *Rory* Grandfather of Meriadoc; often called *Old Rory*. 25, 27, 32, 35, 38, 95, 101, 104, 237, 241, 267, 288, 296, 315, 318, 386, 393

~ *Saradoc 'Scattergold'* Father of Meriadoc (in LR). 106, 267, 301. (Replaced *Caradoc Brandybuck*.)

~ *Theodoric* Son of Gorboduc Brandybuck. 317

*Brandy Hall* 99, 101, 104, 245, 289, 304–5, 313, 386; *Master of the Hall* 301. See *Bucklebury*.

*Brandywine Bridge* 53, 56, 72, 100, 102–8, 132, 170–2, 275, 278, 280, 284, 286, 298, 338, 350

*Brandywine River* (including references to *the River*) 29–30, 35, 37, 42, 52–3, 56, 58, 66, 72, 89, 92, 94, 96–7, 99–100, 103, 105–9, 112, 121, 236, 247, 280, 284, 286, 293, 298, 305, 312, 316, 324, 371, 376

*Bree* 107, 110, 121, 126, 129, 131–5, 138, 140–2, 144, 150, 153–7, 159–62, 164–7, 170–6, 198, 211, 214, 217, 222–3, 235, 269, 329, 331–3, 337–56 *passim*, 359, 367–8, 374–5, 387, 414, 430–1. On the people of Bree see 132–4, 223, 331, and see *Bree-folk*.

*Bree-folk* 132, 154–5, 159, 164, 223, 331, 351; *Bree-dialect* 137

*Bree-hill* 129–34, 165, 174, 223. See *Brill*.

*Bree-land* 133, 332, 342, 354–5; *Breelanders* 132

*Brill* Village in Buckinghamshire ('Bree-hill'). 131

*Britain* 41. *British* (language) 131

*Brockhouse* Hobbit family name. 137, 236, 315

*Brown, Mr.* Assumed name of Frodo Took at Bree. 135–6, 140, 152

*Bruinen* The river of Rivendell (Loudwater). 126, 192, 199–201, 204–5, 210; *Ford of Bruinen* 199, 367. See *Loudwater, River of Rivendell*.

*Buck Hill* The hill in which was Brandy Hall. 298, 304

*Buckland* (village; see 105) 29–30, 35, 37, 40, 46, 53, 55–6, 61, 65, 89, 92, 105–7; (region) 65, 67, 94, 100, 104–5, 107, 109, 160, 175, 244, 273, 275–6, 279–80, 283, 286, 288, 291, 298, 303, 323–4, 326, 366, 375, 392, 401; *Bucklanders* 100.

Road to Buckland 46–7, 50, 66, 72, 89, 92, 97, 105, 107, 288, 291; road within Buckland 104, 106, 286, 298, 304; causeway road 105, 107, 286, 291; *North Gate* 304

*Bucklebury* 92, 97, 100–2, 105, 107, 221–3, 273, 275, 279, 283, 289,

*Necromancer, The*   42, 81, 85, 117, 131, 208, 211–12, 215, 218, 226, 253, 255, 258, 261, 264–5, 268, 270, 272, 311, 321, 363–4, 380, 399; *land of the Necromancer* 77, 85, 255, 269, 319; *Necromancer-rings* 225

*Neldoreth, Forest of*   (1) The northern part of Doriath. 384. (2) Passing name for Fangorn. 384, 399

*Neldorin*   See *Ilverin*.

*Nen Cenedril*   Mirrormere. 466

*Nenning*   (1) River in Beleriand (replacing Eglor). 433. (2) Passing name for the River Redway. 433

*Nine Rings*   See *Rings of Men*. Nine Rings of the Elves, and of the Dwarves, 269

*Nine, The*   270, 364; *the Nine Servants of the Lord of the Ring* 363; *the Nine Riders, Nine Ring-wraiths* 416

*Nine Walkers*   409

*Noakes*   Hobbit family name. Old Noakes (*of Bywater*) 243–4, 249

*Nob*   Servant at *The Prancing Pony*. 135–6, 141, 148, 150–1, 159, 164, 338–9; originally called *Lob* 141

*Nogrod*   Dwarf-city in Eredlindon. 466. See *Khazad-dûm*.

*Noldor*   71–2. See *Gnomes, Wise-elves*.

*Noldorin*   (tongue) 186, 432, 435, 463. See *Gnomish*.

*Nori*   Dwarf, companion of Thorin Oakenshield. 210

*Northfarthing*   298, 313, 385, 423

*North Moor(s)*   54, 66, (71), 72, 84, 254, 278, 319, 324, 386; *moors of the Northfarthing* 385, 423

*Northope*   Village north of Hobbiton Hill. 319, 385–7. (Replaced by *Overhill*.)

*Númenor*   105, 122, 215–16, 295, 320; *the Island* 260, 320, *the Far West Island* 215; *'The Fall of Númenor'* 105, 131, 174–5, 216, 218. See *Avallon, Westernesse*.

*Númenórean*   215–16, 227, 332, 414; Númenórean kingdoms in Middle-earth 189

*Odo*   (including *Odo Took* and *Odo Bolger*) See *Bolger*.

*Ogden*   Hobbit family name. 17

*Oin*   Dwarf, companion of Thorin Oakenshield. 217, 226, 369, 381, 391

*Oldbuck, Gorhendad*   Founder of the Brandybuck clan. 298, 326

*Old English*   35, 86, 131, 141, 145, 173, 205, 304; Runes 467

*Old Forest*   (also often *the Forest*) 29–30, 35, 37, 40, 42–3, 100, 103–5, 109–12, 121, 124–5, 160, 206, 221, 273, 286, 299, 301–3, 326–7, 334, 349–52, 365–6, 401. See *Buckwood*.

*Old Man Willow*   See *Willow-man*.

*Old Norse*   246, 444

*Old Took*   See *Took, Frodo* (1) and *Took, Gerontius*.

*Old Winyards*   Wine of the Southfarthing. 241